W9-BBJ-964

All the Sweet Tomorrows

All the Sweet Tomorrows

Bertrice Small

Ballantine Books
New York

This book is dedicated with much love and great respect to the first hero I ever had, my father, David Roger Williams. You're still my hero, Daddy!

The world has laid low,
and the wind
blows away like ashes
Alexander, Caesar, and all who were
in their trust;

Grass-grown is Tara,
and see Troy now how it is—
And the English themselves,
perhaps they too
will pass!

—Anonymous Irish poem, 17th or 18th century

The Players

THE O'MALLEYS OF INNISFANA ISLAND, IRELAND

SKYE O'MALLEY	known as the O'Malley, chief of her clan
SEAMUS O'MALLEY	her elderly uncle, Bishop of Mid-Connaught
ANNE O'MALLEY	Skye's widowed stepmother
EIBHLIN O'MALLEY	Skye's elder sister, a nun and a doctor
MOIRE, PEIGI, BRIDE, AND SINE	Skye's other sisters, all older
MICHAEL O'MALLEY	Skye's full brother, a priest
BRIAN, SHANE, SHAMUS, AND CONN	Anne's sons, Skye's half-brothers

THE HUSBANDS OF SKYE O'MALLEY

DOM O'FLAHERTY	her first, the Master of Ballyhennessey
KHALID EL BEY *(Diego Indio Goya de Fuentes)*	her second, known as "the Great Whoremaster of Algiers," a Spaniard turned Moslem
LORD GEOFFREY SOUTHWOOD	her third, the Earl of Lynmouth, known as the "Angel Earl"
LORD NIALL BURKE	her fourth, and Skye's first love

THE CHILDREN OF SKYE O'MALLEY

EWAN O'FLAHERTY	born March 28th, 1556
MURROUGH O'FLAHERTY	born January 15th, 1557
WILLOW MARY SMALL	born April 5th, 1560
ROBERT SOUTHWOOD	born September 18th, 1563
JOHN SOUTHWOOD	born December 15th, 1564, died April 15, 1566
DEIRDRE BURKE	born December 12th, 1567
PADRAIC BURKE	born January 30th, 1569

THE STEPCHILDREN OF SKYE O'MALLEY

SUSANNE SOUTHWOOD	betrothed to Lord Trevenyan
GWYNETH AND JOAN SOUTHWOOD	twin sisters, betrothed to Skye's sons, Ewan and Murrough O'Flaherty

SKYE'S FRIENDS

SIR ROBERT SMALL	Skye's business partner
DAME CECILY SMALL	his elder sister, a widow
ADAM DE MARISCO	the Lord of Lundy Island
DAISY	Skye's tiring woman and faithful confidante
SIR RICHARD DE GRENVILLE	Skye's old friend, a sea captain

THE IRISH

THE MACWILLIAM	Niall Burke's father
CAPTAIN SEAN MACGUIRE	the senior captain of the O'Malley fleet
CAPTAIN BRAN KELLY	an O'Malley captain
CLAIRE O'FLAHERTY	Dom O'Flaherty's sister
SISTER MARY PENITENT	the former Darragh O'Neil, Niall's first wife, marriage annulled

THE ENGLISH

ELIZABETH TUDOR — the Queen of England, 1558 to 1603

WILLIAM CECIL, LORD BURGHLEY — the English Secretary of State, and the Queen's greatest confidant

ROBERT DUDLEY, THE EARL OF LEICESTER — the Queen's oldest friend, and favorite

SIR CHRISTOPHER HATTON — another of the Queen's favorites, and Captain of the Gentlemen Pensioners

LETTICE KNOLLYS, COUNTESS OF ESSEX — the Queen's cousin

THE ALGERIANS

OSMAN — a famous astrologer and Skye's old friend

ALIMA — his French wife

Prologue

"*T*his is all your fault, you meddling old man!" Skye O'Malley Burke shouted at her father-in-law, the MacWilliam of Mid-Connaught. Her blue-green eyes flashed fire, and her marvelous long, black hair, unbound and unruly, swirled about her shoulders as she paced furiously about the room. "You've gone and widowed me! Wasn't it enough that your wicked machinations kept Niall and me separated all those years? Now you've widowed me! God curse you for it, old man! I'll never forgive you! *Never!*" Then she burst into tears, collapsing onto the carved oak settle by the fireplace.

The old man's face disintegrated under her fierce attack, and he seemed to shrink in size, as if seeking to escape the terrible, harsh truth of her words. "How could I stop him, Skye lass? Niall is a man long grown," his voice quavered. "He would not listen to me. How could I stop him?"

She looked at him scornfully, and he withered further under her look of contempt. "You knew that Darragh O'Neil was a madwoman for all her religious calling, old man. *You knew!* Still you let my husband ride off to her, and to his own death!" She closed her eyes a moment, and more tears spilled down her cheeks. "Oh, Niall," she whispered brokenly. *Niall! Niall! Niall!* came the mocking echo in her mind.

The old man sniffed piteously as he wiped his nose on his sleeve, then said, "At least we've got the children, Skye lass. We've got Niall's son and daughter."

"*You have nothing,*" she told him coldly. "I will take my children and leave this place. I will go home to Innisfana. I have always hated Burke Castle, but for Niall's sake I lived here. Now my husband is dead, and I will stay no longer!"

Suddenly the MacWilliam grew angry, a bit of his old spirit coursing back through his tired veins. "You'll not take Niall's children from me!" he thundered at her. "They are *my* heirs, the boy in particular. You cannot take them!"

Her fair features darkened with outraged fury, and he could have sworn that sparks shot from her blazing blue eyes. "Do you think that I would let you have *my* babes?" she hissed angrily at him. "I'll see you in Hell first!"

"You've no choice, Skye lass. Padraic is my heir with his father gone, and wee Deirdre after him. I'll not let you take them from me!" For a brief moment he felt sure and strong again.

"Old man, you'll not stop me from whatever I choose to do!" Skye O'Malley declared. Then she rose from the settle and stormed from the room, not seeing his tired shoulders slump forward, defeated by the knowledge that she would leave him if she chose, taking his only grandchildren with her.

He coughed deeply and, turning, spit a clot of black blood into the pewter basin on the table. The blood had been coming up for several weeks now. His instinct told him that he did not have a great deal of time left to live. Until now it had not worried him particularly, for his son had been a strong, wise man, mature for his years. Now, however, Niall was dead, and his only living male heir was six weeks old. The babe was strong, but anything was possible. If the child died before reaching his majority the English would eat up his holdings as they had so many in the past several years. They might anyway.

Where had the time gone? the MacWilliam wondered. It only seemed a short time ago that he had been a young man in his full vigor, ready and eager to bed a hot-blooded wench. Now he was but a broken old man, clutching his faded memories and shattered dreams about him like a tattered cloak; his thin white hair lank upon his bony shoulders.

The MacWilliam sighed sadly. God help Ireland—for surely no one else would. The Irish stood quite alone, England to one side of them, the open sea on the other. In a way it was their own fault, for they had no one ruler to rally them, but rather a thousand petty, bickering chieftains, each jealously guarding his own holding, and each making the alliances best suited to himself, not necessarily to Ireland. It was no wonder that the English with their one strong ruler could overcome the Irish. Irishmen, 'twas true, would not be conquered by war, but rather by their own weaknesses.

Still, and here the MacWilliam smiled a dark, grim smile, his beautiful and willful daughter-in-law was a very powerful woman in her own right. In Ireland Skye was the chieftainess of the wealthy, seagoing O'Malleys of Innisfana. Even though the O'Malley brothers were grown, they showed no great hurry to take the familial responsibilities their late father had bequeathed them, far preferring, as he had, to stay on their ships. Skye was the one with the head for business. In England she was the Dowager Countess of Lynmouth, a fine old English title. Her son from that union was the current earl. True, the golden-haired lad was but six years old, but he was the English Queen's godson, and quite in her favor. Even now he was being raised at court, and was Bess Tudor's pet page. The Queen had a weakness for attractive males, even little ones. Yes, the MacWilliam thought bitterly. Whatever happened, Skye O'Malley would survive. She had more damned lives than a cat!

A solitary tear ran down his worn and wrinkled face. If his son had had her blessed luck he might be alive today. *Darragh O'Neil!* He silently cursed the day he had ever forced his son into marriage with that cold bitch! Niall had originally been betrothed to her older sister, Ceit. That lass had died in an epidemic, but as both the O'Neils and the Burkes were eager for a match between their families, the younger sister had been brought from her convent as a substitute bride. Darragh O'Neil had been within a few hours of taking her final vows, and she was a born nun. She had not wanted Niall Burke. She had not wanted any husband, but after a good thrashing from her father she had done as she was told.

The marriage had, of course, been a disaster. Niall had been wildly in love with Skye O'Malley, then the O'Flaherty of Ballyhennessey's wife; and when she was widowed he was unable any longer to hide that love. His own marriage had been conveniently annulled by Skye's uncle, the Bishop of Connaught, and Darragh had hurried gratefully back to her convent. Niall and Skye were then betrothed, but once more the fates had playfully separated them. Skye was captured by Barbary pirates, lost her memory, and endured much before they were finally reunited. Then, however, she was again another man's wife, and had not even recognized Niall.

He, too, had another wife, the unfortunate Constanza, who mercifully died. As for Skye, she also lost her new husband to death, her English husband whom she had loved deeply. By then her memory of Niall had returned, but she had remained true to her Geoffrey, and the MacWilliam admired her for it. She was a remarkable woman, and he deeply regretted the years she and his son had lost.

At last Skye and Niall had been married. Not, mind you, in any fancy ceremony with gladsome feasting afterward, but by proxy. The bride still mourned her English husband in her English castle, not even aware that her wily uncle, the Bishop of Connaught, had taken advantage of an old law that made him technically head of the family, and used that tenuous authority to marry her off. The MacWilliam chuckled hoarsely, remembering the deception he and Seamus O'Malley had used to wed the reluctant pair. His son had gone off to England expecting a warm welcome. He had not received it. The stubborn wench had led Niall a merry chase, almost driving him to violence.

In the end, however, their love had won out as Niall had accepted that his wife was no longer the unworldly girl he had once adored, but rather an intelligent and passionate woman who had been the beloved of other men. She had been on her own long enough to learn to wield the great responsibility that was hers, and she was not about to give up her power to anyone, even a loved husband. What was hers remained hers. When he had accepted Skye for what she was, the marriage had flourished, and been blessed with two healthy, strong children within thirteen months of each other.

The MacWilliam shook his head sadly. It had all been going so well. The Burkes had pledged their fealty to England's Queen in hopes of gaining a measure of peace, in hopes of surviving. Many of the noble Irish families had done the same in order to save their lands and their people. Most had been betrayed, for the English were not only incredibly savage when they chose to be, but insatiably greedy for the sweet green lands of Ireland. Still, they had so far left the Burkes and their own alone. Baby Padraic's inheritance was intact, and the MacWilliam knew that he could trust his daughter-in-law to keep it that way. Had she not fought so valiantly for her English son's lands and title? She would fight as fiercely for her Irish son also, he knew. The wench knew her duty as well as any man, and often did it better.

Skye O'Malley. She was a beautiful and gallant woman, and he wondered if she would ever be allowed any peace. She seemed destined to find love only to lose it through no fault of her own. Damn Darragh O'Neil! Damn her mad soul to Hell! He began to cough again, and his blood, bright hot crimson, streamed and steamed into the polished pewter basin as his tired heart hammered against his thin chest. His son, his handsome fine boy, was dead, and their immortality rested with a suckling infant not even old enough to lift his head up.

Another bout of coughing wracked his ancient frame, weakening him so that for a moment he did not hear the door to his private chamber reopen. There was a gasp, and then Skye's voice said resignedly, "Old man, will you stop at nothing to force me to remain? Will you even die on me now?"

He grinned wanly up at her. "I've had my way in this life almost as much as you have, Skye lass."

She would have laughed, but the sight of his bright blood in the basin sobered her. Instead, she put an arm about his shoulders. "Ah, Rory," she sighed. She used his Christian name only rarely. "Why did you not tell me of the blood?"

"If I'm meant to die now then I'll die," he said fatalistically.

"I'll send for my sister Eibhlin," she said quietly, and then she helped him to rise and reach his bed. He was hard put not to grin mischievously at her, so apparent was her concern over him. Fate had conspired with him to keep her and the children here. She'd not leave a dying man for all she talked.

Eibhlin O'Malley, a nun at the island convent of St. Bride's of the Cliffs, was famed in Connaught for her midwifery and her healing skills. She was in great demand, and her service among the wealthy had greatly enriched her small convent. Her service among the poor, and there were so many poor, had convinced Eibhlin that if there were a hundred of her it wouldn't be enough. Between her religious devotions and her growing medical practice, she averaged but two to four hours' sleep a night. At home in her convent for a short rest, she still came quickly across a stormy winter sea when called by her younger sister, Skye.

"I'm surprised that he's still alive," she told Skye drily after she had made a careful examination of the old man.

"Can we do nothing?" Skye was troubled. She was still angry at Rory, but she loved him as she had loved her own father.

"You can make him comfortable," Eibhlin said, "and you can promise him not to take the children back to Innisfana."

"Did he tell you I was going to take them?" Skye fenced with her elder sister.

"Well, isn't that what you threatened?" Eibhlin's pretty face peered sharply at her younger sister from between the folds of her starched wimple.

"I cannot bear this castle without Niall. I have never liked it, but without Niall it is impossible!" Skye wailed.

"It is Padraic's inheritance, sister."

"You need not remind me of that, *sister*," Skye retorted sharply. "He will have it! Did I not protect Lynmouth for Robin? Can I do any less for Niall's son?"

"Have you cried yet, Skye?" Eibhlin looked closely at her sister.

Skye's face was a closed and tight mask. "I have cried," she said, "for all the good it did me, which was none. I should be used to it by now, Eibhlin. How many husbands have I buried? Four! No, I take that back. I have only buried three. Niall's body was not found. It is lost at sea, the very sea that has enriched the O'Malleys so." A harsh laugh escaped her. "Our fierce old sea god, Mannanan MacLir, has taken his price from me, but 'tis too dear a price, Eibhlin. 'Tis too dear!" Her voice was trembling.

"Skye!" Eibhlin put a loving arm about her sister, but she felt totally helpless. How could she possibly comfort her sibling for such a loss. Niall Burke had been Skye's first great love, and when they had finally wed everyone expected him to be her last love as well.

"She killed him without mercy, Eibhlin," Skye said. "Darragh O'Neil murdered my husband, and do you know why?"

"No, Skye," Eibhlin replied gently. "I know nothing but that Lord Burke is dead, and tragically at the hands of Sister Mary Penitent."

"*Sister Mary Penitent!*" Skye's voice shook with anger. "*Darragh O'Neil!* 'Twas Darragh O'Neil who murdered my husband! Darragh O'Neil for all her religious calling! She lured him to her side by saying she was dying, and wanted to make her peace with him.

Instead, she stabbed him to death—and condemned her own soul to eternal damnation. She has wantonly widowed me and cruelly orphaned my two children! I'd like to kill her with my own two hands, Eibhlin, but her convent protects her, says she is mad! *I don't believe it!* I don't believe it, but they will not let me in to speak with her. They say that the mention of my name sends her into fits. Fits indeed! The bitch knows full well what she has done! 'Tis naught but a ploy to escape me. God's bones! I'd like to set the English upon that convent!"

"*Skye!*" Eibhlin was shocked. The English in Ireland were at this very time as systematically attempting to wipe out all the religious houses as their late sovereign, Henry VIII, had destroyed those same establishments in his own England. It was not as easy in Ireland, however, as it had been in England. The Irish did not love their English rulers, and this attack on their Church gave them one thing to which they could all rally honestly, peasant and noble alike.

"Oh, I wouldn't, Eibhlin," Skye said contritely. "Uncle Seamus would have my head if I did, but I'd like to do it!"

"I will get Uncle Seamus to aid us," Eibhlin said. "As the Bishop of Connaught he must order an investigation into Lord Burke's death. I will ask him to send me to do the interrogation, Skye."

"Darragh's order is a cloistered one," Skye said. "He'll get nowhere with her Mother Superior. She was Aigneis O'Brien, and she's prouder than all the damned high O'Neils put together. She will say nothing other than Sister Mary Penitent is mad; Sister Mary Penitent is being restrained; that the nuns of St. Mary's will pray daily for Lord Burke's soul."

Eibhlin's pale-gray eyes darkened with anger, and the tone of her voice was more O'Malley warrior than humble nun. "With or without Uncle Seamus's aid I shall get into St. Mary's," she said, "and I will find the truth of it for you, Skye. I do not understand why after all these years Darragh sought to seek out and kill Lord Burke. He did her no harm. Their marriage victimized him as much as it did her, and he helped to restore her to her precious convent. I don't understand why she suddenly felt it necessary to kill him; but I shall find out, Skye. *I shall find out!*"

The two sisters embraced, and suddenly Skye began to weep, a harsh, bitter sound of such intense grief that Eibhlin, holding her and attempting to comfort her, felt her own cheeks wet with silent tears. How long they stood there swaying with their sorrow, clinging to each other, Eibhlin never knew, but suddenly Daisy, Skye's faithful English tiring woman, was running into the room and urgently begging them to follow her.

"'Tis the old man, m' lady! He's dying," Daisy said. "You must hurry, for he wants you!" She quickly turned from them, hastening out of the room.

Skye and Eibhlin swiftly composed themselves and followed Daisy, moving through the icy-cold castle corridors to the warm chamber in which Rory Burke, the MacWilliam, lay eking out his last few moments upon this earth. Already the castle priest knelt by his side administering the last rites to the old man lying in his bed hung with wine-colored velvet. Still the MacWilliam's rheumy eyes lit up at the sight of Skye, and feebly he motioned her to his side, while at the same time impatiently waving the nervous cleric aside.

"You'll not be going home to Innisfana now, Skye lass," he whispered at her with an attempt at humor.

"No, Rory ban, I'll not be going now," she answered him gently. *Please don't die on me, old man,* she silently thought. *You're the last little bit I've left of my Niall. Oh, the boy's his son, but he's a babe, and we have no memories in common. Don't die, old man! Stay with me!*

"The first time I saw you, do you remember the first time I saw you?" he asked.

"Yes," she said. "'Twas the feast of Twelfth Night, and you'd called all your vassals together to celebrate. I was wed but a few months to Dom, and was already carrying his first child. Ah, Rory, when you first saw me you regretted the O'Neil match, you did!" She smiled at the memory of the proud young thing she'd been then.

"I did," he finally admitted to her, "but in the end, Skye lass, you became Niall's wife, and the mother of my only two heirs. Protect them, Skye! Don't let the English take Padraic's heritage! By tomorrow he'll be the MacWilliam, and you must hold his inheritance until he comes of age. Promise me, Skye lass!"

The years were sliding away and she was a young girl again, and her dying father was thrusting the entire responsibility of the O'Malleys of Innisfana upon her slender shoulders. All the ships, her five younger brothers, the goods and the warehouses, and the people—all her personal responsibility. She had it still.

Then, too, there was her second husband Khalid el Bey's vast

fortune to administer, and the monies and estates of her third husband, Geoffrey Southwood, the late Earl of Lynmouth; as well as
the care of her four other children besides Deirdre and Padraic
Burke. Now, suddenly, Niall was torn from her, and his dying father was pressing more responsibility upon her. It was far too
much for one woman alone, and yet she could not refuse him.
How could she? Would there ever come a time when she might be
just a woman? She was so tired of it all, yet she couldn't let him
down.

"I'll do my best, Rory," she said wearily. "I'll do my best."

He smiled up at her, trusting and satisfied. Then, closing his
eyes, he quietly died. Exhausted, she walked from the room as her
sister and the priest, their beads magically in their hands, fell to
their knees and began to say the rosary. Daisy walked a step behind
her, only hurrying ahead of her mistress as they reached Skye's
apartments so she might open the door.

"Get me some wine," Skye said as she sought the relative comfort of a large chair by the fireplace. Sitting down, she watched the
low flames darting among the peatfire, and wondered what she
would do. How long did she have before the English would come
arrogantly to confiscate her infant son's holdings. The old Mac-
William's death would be the perfect excuse for them, for the wily
old man had given them no cause while he lived to abuse him. Not
that the English in Ireland needed excuses to ill treat the Irish. No
one would come to her aid when it happened, and she couldn't
blame them. More than likely, one or more of her Irish neighbors
would try to steal some of the Burke lands, too. Her very gender
gave them the excuse they needed. A woman and child were easy
prey for the cowards they all were. "Well, they'll not have it!" she
said aloud as Daisy put the goblet into her hand.

"What's that, m'lady? Who not have what?" Daisy was puzzled.

"The damned Dublin English, Daisy, and our Irish neighbors,
that's who! They'll not have Burke Castle, or Burke lands! Those
are my Padraic's and I intend that it remain so."

"But what can you do about it, my lady? If we were in England
you might appeal to the Queen, but England is far, and London
farther."

"I'm going to England, Daisy!"

"But you've been forbidden, m'lady! They'll clap you back in the
Tower of London, they will! You can't go!" Daisy's eyes were

round with her genuine concern. She had been with her mistress for seven years, and she loved her dearly. She also knew her well. When Skye made up her mind, little if anything could stop her.

"I've been banished from court, Daisy, but not necessarily from England," Skye said craftily. "I shall go to Lynmouth, and from there I shall appeal to the Queen's Secretary of State, Lord Burghley. If it is Elizabeth Tudor's intention to aid me, I shall be permitted to travel to London. If not, I shall still try to make my appeal from Devon. I cannot sit here, Daisy, and just wait for the English to come and take Padraic's inheritance. When Southwood died I protected his son, and I must protect Niall's son, too. He can have nothing of the O'Malleys, for though I bear the title and the responsibilities of the O'Malley, it all belongs to my brothers and their heirs. If I cannot save Burke Castle and its lands for its rightful heir, then my poor Padraic will be landless and nameless. The ghosts of a hundred generations of Burkes would haunt me into eternity if I let that happen, Daisy."

"When will you go?" Neither Daisy nor her mistress had heard the door open and close, but Eibhlin now stood within the room.

"Now," Skye said. "I cannot lose a minute, sister. The word will be in Dublin quickly enough that Rory Burke is dead. I cannot even stay long enough to bury him, but he most of all would understand my haste."

Eibhlin nodded. "Then I'll be on my way to St. Mary's Convent to learn what I can of Niall's death. Uncle Seamus would approve, I know. Who will you leave in charge here?"

"Connor FitzBurke," Skye replied.

"Niall's bastard brother? Is that wise, Skye?"

"Connor is the most loyal man I know, Eibhlin. He is a simple and good fellow without ambition. It would not occur to Connor to usurp Padraic's inheritance. He will protect the children and their inheritance with his own life. I can't take the children with me. I must travel too quickly."

Listening, Daisy winced, and then wondered why she even bothered. Her bottom had been beaten to leather by now in Mistress Skye's service. One more midnight ride wasn't going to kill her. She never doubted that she would travel with her mistress. After all, no one else could do her lady's hair for court the way she could, and Daisy did not doubt that they'd be back at court. Nor did anyone else know the correct jewelry that went with each magnificent gown. No, she would be riding out with her mistress before the dawn even considered breaking.

"Daisy?"

The tiring woman looked up smiling. "Within the hour, my lady?" she asked, fully knowing the answer.

Skye nodded smiling back. "Aye, Daisy. Just when I thought that our adventures were over, we're off again!"

Daisy couldn't resist a mischievous grin. "I can't say I mind, m'lady. It was getting a bit quiet for me around here."

"God ha' mercy!" Eibhlin cried. "She's surely become one of us!"

"And not a bad thing either," Skye replied as Daisy hurried off. "A tiring woman who can keep up with me on a horse is a valuable asset, sister." Then she sobered. "Will you see to the servants for me, Eibhlin? I will need time to gather my wits before I speak to Connor."

"I'll see to it," was the quick reply, and then Skye found herself alone once more.

She rose and walked over to the windows to look down across the darkened countryside. A waning moon cast its pale, weak light across the soft, shadowed hills. Somehow, she thought, it should have been a wild and stormy night that Rory Burke took his leave of this earth, not this calm and windless time. For all of Ireland's rich mystical heritage, there hadn't been a sign or sound of the ghostly death coach come to take Rory Burke's soul away. Neither had there been the faintest wail of a banshee. She pushed the casement open and heard the frantic scream of a rabbit as a hunting owl found his prey; and then all was silent again. Life went on, she noted. No matter the changes, life went on. Skye O'Malley sighed deeply. There was no more time for mourning.

Part 1

England

Chapter 1

It was the strong sense of family that the O'Malleys possessed that brought Seamus O'Malley to his niece before her hurried departure for England. In his fine stone bishop's house a few miles down the road from Burke Castle, he had awakened suddenly in the middle of the night and known that she needed him. The old man had gotten up from his warm bed, dressed himself, and ridden off up the hill to aid her.

Seamus O'Malley agreed with his niece's assessment of the situation. She had to go to England for the Tudor wench's help. The bishop was a realist. He didn't like the English, but they held the whip hand. He suggested that the news of the MacWilliam's death be kept secret; that he be buried surreptitiously. It was easy enough to do, for the entire castle still slept and the guards on the walls couldn't see what went on inside the building. With the aid of the family priest and Rory Burke's personal servant, the body was placed in the family crypt; the final mass was said in the early dawn after Skye had ridden off under cover of darkness.

Then Seamus took up residence in Burke Castle and, in league with the priest, the servant, and Connor FitzBurke, conspired to keep the rest of Ireland from learning of Rory Burke's death while Skye hurried to gain English aid before little Padraic Burke's inheritance was stolen.

The lady of the castle, said to be keeping a vigil for the ailing MacWilliam, was in truth galloping across Ireland to Waterford harbor, where several of her ships were presently berthed. The need for haste was so imperative that Skye and Daisy rode eighteen hours a day, stopping only to change horses, to eat a hot meal, and to rest a few hours daily. They stayed only with trusted friends, sleeping in the chilly lofts of their barns during the daylight hours to avoid curious eyes, and more curious questions. Even the most loyal servants gossiped.

At Waterford, Skye took passage upon her stepmother's vessel, the *Ban-Righ A'Ceo*, (Queen of the Mist). No sooner had the ship cleared the harbor than she commanded the captain, "Kelly! Set a course for Lundy Island." Then she disappeared into the master's cabin with her tiring woman.

Daisy sighed with relief at feeling the swell of the open sea and the chill late-winter wind that filled the sails. "Every mile we galloped I thought sure the Dublin English would be after us, my lady."

Skye laughed, relieved herself. She always felt vulnerable upon the land, but upon the sea none was her equal. "Daisy, you speak as if you were Irish yourself," she teased her tiring woman. "Have you been with me so long that you're beginning to feel Irish?"

"I'm English all right, m'lady, but I'm Devon English, and that's a whole lot better than being Dublin English. In Devon we're kind people, but those Dublin English are wolves of the worst sort!"

Skye nodded in agreement, and then said, "We've a good strong breeze behind us. With luck we'll make Lundy in two days' time."

"He'll be glad to see you," Daisy remarked quietly, understanding her lady's need. Like most trusted servants, she knew all the intimate details of her mistress's life. They had been together a long time, and if Skye had grown more beautiful with the years, Daisy had changed not a whit. Small and apple-cheeked, her soft brown eyes were loving of Skye and watchful of others. She was no beauty, and never had been, being as freckled as a thrush's egg; but her gap-toothed smile was warm and merry.

"I have to see him," Skye replied. "He is the only friend I have left, Daisy, besides Robert Small, and Robbie is at sea. He is not expected back for at least another month. I must talk with Adam." She curled up on the large master's bed, drawing a down coverlet over her. "God's bones, Daisy, but I'm tired! Take the trundle and get some sleep yourself, girl. We've ridden hard these past three days."

Daisy needed little urging to pull the trundle from beneath the bed, unbind her soft brown hair, lie down, and fall quickly asleep; but her mistress, for all her exhaustion, lay awake and thinking. While Daisy snored, making gentle little blowing noises, Skye thought back over the last few years, and of how she had met Adam de Marisco, the lord of Lundy Island.

Skye's third husband, Geoffrey Southwood, the Earl of Lynmouth, had died in a spring epidemic, along with their younger son. Their older son, Robin, had been put in the custody of the Queen's favorite, Robert Dudley, the Earl of Leicester. Dudley, however, had used his office to rape Skye, and when she had complained to the Queen, Elizabeth had bluntly told her that if she made Dudley happy, then that was that. Outraged, Skye had decided to wage her own private war on Elizabeth Tudor, to pirate the ships and the cargoes that England needed so badly to enrich its coffers. She had enlisted, for a share of the profits, the pirate lord of Lundy Island. Adam de Marisco had fallen in love with her, but believing that she could never fall in love with him, he had settled for being her friend. She had, for a brief time, been his mistress.

When, after her marriage to Niall Burke, she had been arrested by Elizabeth Tudor for piracy, it was Adam de Marisco who had come up with the plan to free her from the Tower. She knew, despite his denials, that he still loved her. Perhaps now it was unfair of her to seek him out. Although she frequently wrote to him, it had been well over a year since they had met, and so much had happened during their separation; but he would understand why she came. She did need him so much! She needed to hear his deep, booming voice calling her "little girl"; to feel his lean hardness against her. If only she might love him the way he had always loved her—but no. It was better that she didn't. She had been widowed four times. She was bad luck to the men who wed her. "I will never marry again," she said drowsily to herself.

She had not realized how tired she actually was. Padraic's birth followed by Niall's murder; the MacWilliam's death; her breakneck race across Ireland to the sea. It had all taken its toll. She fell into a deep sleep; her last thoughts were of Eibhlin and whether she had breached the walls of St. Mary's.

Eibhlin had, and now stood quietly before the Reverend Mother

Aidan, born Aigneis O'Brien. The Reverend Mother was a short, plump woman with a plain, expressionless face. "It is very good of you to see me, Reverend Mother," she said smoothly. She could see that she was not very welcome at St. Mary's.

"We could scarcely refuse our lord bishop," was the icy reply. Reverend Mother Aidan's smooth white hands, adorned with her plain gold wedding band and the more ornate ring of her office, moved restlessly in her lap.

"You know why I am here?"

"I do, but I do not understand it, my sister. Lord Burke's death was admittedly a terrible tragedy, but your investigation cannot bring him back." Her hands clutched at each other in an effort to still themselves. Good, Eibhlin thought, she's nervous. I wonder what it is she hides.

"The bishop wishes to know why Sister Mary Penitent lured Lord Burke to this convent to murder him, Reverend Mother," Eibhlin said provocatively.

"She did not lure him!" came the quick reply. "Dear Heaven, my sister, you make Sister Mary Penitent sound like a loose woman." Reverend Mother Aidan flushed beet red at the boldness of her own words.

"Perhaps lure is not a good word, Reverend Mother. Nonetheless she brought him here under false pretenses." Eibhlin shifted her weight from one foot to the other. She was tired, having traveled all night.

"That has not been proven!" The denial had a hollow ring.

"It has. The bishop has in his possession the message that Sister Mary Penitent sent to Lord Burke. In it she declared that she was dying, that she wished to make her peace with him before she returned to God. Reverend Mother, be sensible," Eibhlin said with far more patience than she was feeling. "Lord Burke had not seen Sister Mary Penitent since the day she left Burke Castle to return here. He wanted their marriage no more than she did. If she was injured by the union then so was he. He held no grudge. Obviously she did, else she would not have killed him. That is not madness. That is revenge."

"She *is* mad, my sister," came the Reverend Mother's shaky voice, "and what is worse, she is cursed. I am not sure that this convent is not cursed as well." The Superior was pale now, and her breath came in shallow pants.

Ah, Eibhlin thought, *here is something new*. "Please explain yourself, Reverend Mother. The bishop is most interested. *And so am I*."

"Sit down, sit down, my sister," the Reverend Mother finally invited Eibhlin; who willingly complied. When both women were settled the convent's Superior began her story. "From girlhood Sister Mary Penitent was always more devout than the others. Her devotion almost bordered on the hysterical. Still, she was obedient and gentle, a perfect daughter of the Church. When she returned to us after her marriage was annulled we received her joyfully; and although more nervous than she had been in the past, she seemed to readjust quickly to our simple convent life.

"There was nothing out of the ordinary here until several months ago when Sister Mary Claire came to us. She seemed to single out Sister Mary Penitent from among us, and was with her at every opportunity. Suddenly the poor girl was jumping at every sound, and weeping at the slightest provocation. We tried to learn what was troubling her, but she claimed it was nothing. After Lord Burke's murder Sister Mary Claire disappeared, and we have not seen or heard of her since. We fear that poor Sister Mary Penitent has . . . has killed her also, though why we do not know, may God have mercy upon both their souls." Reverend Mother Aidan sought the comfort of her beads.

"This Sister Mary Claire, Reverend Mother. Where did she come from? Surely you did not allow a stranger into your house?" Eibhlin's instincts were already alert.

"She claimed to have come from our sister house at Ballycarrick, which was destroyed several months ago by the English. We did not know that any of our sisters there had survived, for it was said they barricaded themselves within their church, and that the English put it to torch, killing them all. Sister Mary Claire claimed that she was in the nearby village nursing an old woman when the English came. She said the people hid her until she could reach us. It was not unlikely, my sister. It has happened a hundred times in Ireland this year."

Eibhlin's heartbeat had increased in tempo as the convent's head spoke. *Sister Mary Claire!* It couldn't be! It couldn't be! Yet it was the sort of foul trick that Dom O'Flaherty's sister Claire would involve herself in for sweet revenge's sake. "Tell me, Reverend

Mother, what did this Sister Mary Claire look like? Can you describe her to me?"

"She had blue eyes, a fair complexion, and blond hair," came the reply.

"Blond hair, Reverend Mother?" Eibhlin was growing more sure.

"She said she had not yet taken her final vows, that she had a year to go before that holy day."

Claire O'Flaherty! It simply had to be Claire O'Flaherty reaching out once more with her evil hand to strike at Skye and Niall. "Reverend Mother, I must now speak with Sister Mary Penitent. I have no other choice!" Eibhlin said urgently.

The Mother Superior sighed resignedly and reached for the small silver bell by her hand. To the nun who answered its call, she said, "Please take Sister Eibhlin, the bishop's representative, to Sister Mary Penitent's cell."

Eibhlin rose and followed the obedient nun from the Reverend Mother's closet and through the halls of the convent. Her guide finally stopped before a simple cell, and said, "In there, my sister."

Eibhlin carefully lifted the dark linen covering that hung across the doorway and moved quietly into the plain tiny room. It was no different than the cells within her own convent; whitewashed walls with no decoration other than a crucifix, and no furniture other than a simple pallet bed set on the floor. Kneeling now before the cross was Darragh O'Neil, deep in prayer. Eibhlin waited politely for a few moments and then spoke softly.

"Sister Mary Penitent, I am Sister Eibhlin, the bishop's representative. I have come to speak with you on the matter of Lord Burke's death."

At first Eibhlin thought that Darragh did not hear her, but then the kneeling woman crossed herself and rose from her prayers. Eibhlin had never seen Darragh O'Neil before. She looked nothing like her aunt, who was the Superior at Eibhlin's island convent of St. Bride's. Ethna O'Neil was a beautiful and serene woman, but her niece's face was pinched and tortured. She was clearly suffering, and putting an arm about her, Eibhlin helped to seat her upon the pallet bed. Joining her there, she looked again upon the woman's face and knew that Darragh was sane for the moment, but how long she would remain sane she could not tell. She did know that she must act quickly if she was to learn the truth.

"Sister Mary Penitent," she repeated softly, "I am Sister Eibhlin, the bishop's representative."

"You're an O'Malley," came the dull, despairing reply, "and His Grace the Bishop is another O'Malley. Have you come to wreak your vengeance upon me?"

Looking at this poor creature so obviously enslaved by her fears, Eibhlin suddenly felt sorry for Darragh O'Neil. "It is not our place to punish you, my sister," she said. "Only God truly knows what is in your heart and soul; but the bishop must know why you have done this terrible deed. Why did you kill Lord Burke, Sister Mary Penitent? Why did you throw his body into the sea?"

Darragh O'Neil lifted her eyes to meet those of Eibhlin O'Malley. The pale-blue eyes were filled with pain and guilt and totally lacking hope. "I did not want to kill him," she said slowly, "but Sister Mary Claire told me that if I did not he would draw me once again into carnal bondage, into his lustful power. I had to kill him! If I had not he would have taken me back! She said it!" Darragh's voice had now risen to a frightened pitch.

"But why would you believe such a thing, my sister?" Eibhlin gently inquired. "You had neither seen nor communicated with Lord Burke since the day you left Burke Castle. For most of your marriage you did not cohabit as a man and wife do. Why did you believe the slanders of this strange woman whom you barely knew?"

"She knew the truth!" Darragh O'Neil declared. "She came from the convent at Ballycarrick. Lord Burke managed those lands for a royal ward, and 'twas known that he was a bold, lustful man unable to keep his hands from any woman who took his fancy. Why, Sister Mary Claire told me that he even raped two novices of her convent! Raped and bewitched them so totally the Mother Superior at Ballycarrick was forced to drive the two poor damned souls from her convent, for Lord Burke had roused their baser instincts so uncontrollably that they did terrible and shameful things to themselves and each other in plain sight of their gentle sisters. It was wicked! As she left the convent, one of the two women shouted that Lord Burke had developed a taste for nuns; that his first wife was a nun; that he had told her he intended reclaiming her and making her his leman! I could not let him do that to me! I could not! Surely you, a woman called to God as I was also called, understand that."

Eibhlin was frankly curious as to what else Claire O'Flaherty had told poor Darragh to rouse her enough to commit murder; and so she asked her.

Darragh's weak blue eyes grew round, and she lowered her voice. "It was not so much the telling," she said. "She showed me. Several times she came to my cell in darkest night, and she showed me what Lord Burke had done to those two novices, what he would do to me. She sucked and bit my poor breasts until they were sore, and she put her long fingers inside of me, pushing them back and forth just like *he* used to put his big weapon within me when I was forced to be his wife. God! How I hated it when he climbed atop me! I couldn't let him do that to me again! *Not again!*" She shuddered her revulsion.

Darragh was trembling now, and Eibhlin, angry as she was, hid her anger for fear of frightening the unfortunate creature any further. "How could you believe her, Sister Mary Penitent?" she asked. "Lord Burke has a beautiful wife, and two fine children. Why would he want other women? In the time in which you lived at Burke Castle did he ever mistreat the servant women or the peasants? He has never been a man to abuse women. What made you believe the woman who called herself Sister Mary Claire?"

"Lord Burke's wife is dead," Darragh said. "Sister Mary Claire told me that Skye O'Malley is dead in childbirth."

"My sister is very much alive," Eibhlin replied.

Darragh shook her head in the negative. "No," she said firmly. "Skye O'Malley is dead, and Lord Burke was a wicked and lustful man. I could not let him force me back into carnal bondage. I could not!"

Darragh O'Neil was quickly sliding away again into her mindless and mad world. "Why did you throw his body into the sea?" Eibhlin asked quickly. "What has happened to Sister Mary Claire? Please tell me."

For a brief moment Darragh's reason returned, pricked by the urgency in Eibhlin's voice. "We lay his body on the beach for the incoming tide. There was so much blood. So much blood. The sea was lapping at his feet the last time I turned to look at him. He'll not come back to get me now, that wicked lustful man!"

"Sister Mary Claire?" persisted Eibhlin.

"Is she not still here?" was the reply. "We returned from the beach together. She was my friend." Darragh's eyes grew vacant again, and she arose from the bed, knelt before the crucifix upon the wall, her rosary clutched tightly in her hands. "I must pray that the Devil will not be too harsh on Lord Burke," she said in a suddenly prim voice. "It is my duty to pray for him despite his many sins."

Eibhlin could see that she had lost the unfortunate woman's attention. She knew now what she needed to know. The half-mad Darragh O'Neil had been used by the vengeful Claire O'Flaherty to murder Niall Burke. It was a pity that Niall hadn't killed the woman himself the last time they had locked horns in London. He had had the Queen's blessing to dispose of her, but instead he had simply driven her from the city and, he had supposed, from his life. It had never occurred to Niall, for he was simply not that kind of man, that Claire would seek to harm him further.

Claire O'Flaherty! Eibhlin arose from the pallet bed where she had been sitting with Darragh O'Neil, and walked from the tiny cell. *Claire O'Flaherty!* Skye's sister-in-law from her first marriage, whose incestuous relationship with her brother, Dom, had driven Skye to leave her husband. *Claire O'Flaherty!* She was the most evil, the most wicked, the most venal woman Eibhlin had ever known. If the Devil had truly fathered a daughter, then Claire O'Flaherty was that daughter.

"M'lady!" Daisy shook Skye's shoulder firmly. "M'lady, you will have to awaken."

Slowly Skye opened her marvelous blue-green eyes and, turning over onto her back, gazed up at her servant. "How long have I slept?"

"Almost a full two days, m'lady, and Captain Kelly says we'll be at Lundy shortly before sunset. I thought you might want to freshen yourself."

Looking down at her travel-stained garments, Skye grimaced. The edges of her doubled-legged skirt and her sturdy woollen hose were filthy. How could her hose be so dirty when she wore boots over them? She shook her head. The boots, she noted, stood cleaned by her bed. She swung her legs over the edge of the bed and stood up. Her silk shirt was stained beneath the arms and her doublet was wrinkled. "Oh, Daisy, I am a disaster," she said, shaking her head.

Daisy chuckled. "A bath will fix you right up, m'lady. They loaded an extra keg of water aboard for you in Waterford, and it's heating in the galley right this minute. Captain Kelly understands your peculiarities. I'll have a man bring the water in, along with a small tub, m'lady."

"Get me something to eat too, Daisy. I'm famished!" Skye's stomach rumbled in confirmation of this statement.

While Daisy saw to her meal and her bath, Skye walked outside and around the deck, greeting her men as she went. The breeze was still brisk and fresh and clean with the first early days of spring. Straining her eyes, she could just begin to make out the far dark rock that was Lundy Island. In less than two hours she would be there; and he would comfort her as he had so many times before. Skye returned to the master's cabin of the ship, where a seaman was just exiting after having delivered the small oak tub and the hot water.

Skye stripped off her grimy garments, handing them to Daisy as she did so. Completely nude, she stepped into the little tub and sat down. "Ahhh," she breathed, pleased, "that is so good, Daisy. I didn't feel my aches until just now." Reaching out, she picked up the small cake of rose-scented soap that Daisy had left on the floor by the tub, and began to lather it between her hands. Daisy moved in behind her mistress, pinning her marvelous dark hair atop her head. Then, taking the soap from Skye, she briskly washed her back and commanded her to stand so she might wash her buttocks and long legs. Quickly she rinsed Skye, commenting. "It's too chilly in this cabin for you to remain for a soak, m'lady. We can't have you getting sick now, can we?" The tiring woman reached for the large rough towel upon the bed, and wrapped it about Skye as she stepped from the tub. Swiftly Daisy rubbed her down, bringing a rosy flush of color to Skye's gardenia skin, and then said, "Get back into that bed, m'lady, until you're good and warm again. I've got nut-brown ale, fresh bread, and some fine cheese for you to feast upon."

Skye settled herself and began hungrily to eat Daisy's simple but filling offerings. "Well, I'm clean, but I'll have to get back into those filthy clothes of mine, worse luck!"

Daisy smiled. "I had a feeling that you'd not reach Devon without a stop at Lundy, I did. The cabin boy is brushing the mud from your skirt and your hose, and I've a clean shirt for you in my saddlebags, along with some fresh undergarments."

Skye flashed her tiring woman and old friend a grateful look. How well the faithful Daisy knew her. When she had finished eating and brushed the crumbs from Captain Kelly's bed, she arose again and began to dress. The clean silk underthings and cream-colored shirt felt good against her skin. Daisy handed her first the finely knit dark green woollen hose and then her matching double-legged skirt. Amazingly, they were clean now and quite restored to respectability. Daisy helped her lady back into her knee-high boots, while Skye fastened a wide leather belt about her tiny waist. The belt's buckle was a greenish bronze oval inlaid with black and gold enamel in a Celtic design. Skye sat again upon the bed while Daisy brushed her long black hair out, freeing it of its sleep tangles. Then she pulled it back and twisted it into one long, plump braid, which she fastened with a bit of dark wool.

A quick knock upon the door followed by Skye's permission to enter brought Captain Kelly into the cabin. He was the youngest of her captains; a man with bright-red hair and warm brown eyes. He was slender and not a great deal taller than Skye; but he had a quick mind, and was a daring seaman. "We're entering Lundy harbor, m'lady. Have you any instructions for me while you're ashore?"

"I want you to go on immediately to Lynmouth," she said. "Daisy will stay with you. Please remain at Lynmouth until I advise you further." Skye turned to Daisy. "See that the castle is made ready for my arrival. I will come the day after tomorrow. Send to Wren Court for Dame Cecily, and my daughter, Willow. I will want to see them both."

"I'll wait till you're safely ashore, m'lady, and I know that you've made contact with Lord de Marisco," Captain Kelly said. "Mac-Guire would keelhaul me from here all the way to the Giant's Causeway if I didn't."

"MacGuire's behaving like an old woman these days," Skye grumbled, but she couldn't help but be pleased that Sean Mac-Guire, the senior captain of her fleet, yet pulled that kind of weight with the other men. MacGuire was her voice on many occasions, and she valued him highly.

"Are you sure you don't want me to go with you?" Daisy asked.

"No, Daisy. I'll be fine. Lundy is no place for a respectable girl such as yourself."

Captain Kelly chuckled. "Nay," he said in a happy voice, "there is not a respectable lass on the island, praise God!"

"Why, Kelly," Skye teased, "I'm surprised at you."

"Well, I'm not!" Daisy snapped. "He has the look of a lecher about him!"

"Mistress Daisy," Kelly protested, quickly contrite. Skye, her glance moving swiftly between the two, suddenly realized that Bran Kelly cared what Daisy thought; and Daisy obviously cared for the handsome young man.

"Now, Daisy," she soothed, "a sailor without a true love is apt to have a roving eye, and so far I've not heard that Captain Kelly's pledged his heart to any lass."

"And none is apt to accept him if he continues so fickle in his affections," Daisy warned ominously.

Skye hid a little smile, and said, "Daisy, take my saddlebags on deck, please. I shall be out shortly."

Daisy bobbed a curtsey to Skye, then tossed her head in a snub toward the captain and hurried from the cabin as Bran Kelly looked longingly after her.

"Seduce her," Skye said warningly, "and you'll answer to me, Kelly. She's no lightskirt, and she is under my protection as well as being very dear to me."

"I'm thinking of settling down," Kelly replied. "I'm past thirty now, and it's time."

"When you make up your mind in the matter I'll give you permission to court her if it pleases her. Until then keep your codpiece tightly fastened, Kelly."

Bran Kelly looked into the serious blue eyes of the O'Malley of Innisfana, his overlord and his mistress, and nodded blushingly. "I'd best go topside," he said, "and see to the landing. Lundy harbor is tricky, as you well know."

She smiled at him. He understood. "I'll come with you, and thanks for the use of your quarters this trip."

Together they went out onto the deck, and while Captain Kelly saw to the lowering of the ship's anchor Skye gazed upon Lundy. It had been over a year since she had seen it, the great granite cliffs rising above the sea, the lighthouse at one end of the island, de Marisco's half-ruined castle before her. She sighed sadly. She had never again expected to see Lundy, or to lean so shamelessly upon Adam de Marisco; but dear God, she needed someone to comfort her, and only Adam would understand that need.

"The boat's ready to lower, m'lady," Kelly advised her. Large ships such as the *Ban-Righ A'Ceo* anchored in Lundy Bay, away from Lundy's dangerous cliffs and rock-strewn shore.

"My thanks, Kelly, for a good trip," she called up to him as she climbed into the small boat.

"Your saddlebag, m'lady," said Daisy, leaning over the rail and proffering it to her mistress.

"I won't be needing it now, Daisy," Skye replied with a quick smile, and then she commanded the lone sailor who would row her, "Let's away!"

The cockle seemed to skim just atop the bobbing waves as it was rowed swiftly into the shore and the long stone quay that served de Marisco as a landing place. The sun, bright scarlet with streamers of gold and purple, was beginning to sink into the dark western sea as they reached their destination. From the grog shop in the bottom of the old castle a giant figure emerged and strode down the quay toward them. Skye scrambled from the boat, and then she began to move quickly forward.

Adam de Marisco, his unruly shock of tousled dark hair blowing in the light breeze, hurried toward her. Though he had spent his youth at both the Tudor and the French courts, he was no elegant gallant, as his thigh-high leather boots, his doeskin jerkin with the horn buttons, and his open-necked silk shirt showed. Despite the chill, he wore no cloak.

"Adam!" she called, running, "Adam!"

"Little girl! Is it really you?" His deep voice boomed across the quiet evening, and then he was sweeping her into his bearlike embrace, burying his face for a long moment into the scented softness of her neck, his blue eyes warm with longing.

"Oh, Adam," she breathed, feeling his familiar bulk and knowing with certainty now that everything would be all right.

"I'm sorry about Niall, little girl."

She pulled away from him and looked up into his handsome face. "You knew? How?"

"A ship put in here several days ago, and its captain told me. They had met with an O'Malley ship, and learned the news from them." He put an arm about her and together they began to walk down the stone quay to his castle. "Was the babe you were carrying a boy?"

"Aye, praise God!" she answered.

"Then at least the old MacWilliam has his heir, Skye." They entered the lower level of the castle and walked through the rather dirty and disreputable tavern there, Skye nodding to those she knew, de Marisco's evil-looking retainers and the ever-present Glynnis, whose ample blowsy charms were well known by the men who passed through Lundy. Together they mounted the stairs to de Marisco's two-room apartment in the one remaining whole tower of the castle. Safely inside the big antechamber with its blazing fireplace, Skye turned to Adam de Marisco, and said, "The MacWilliam is dead. My infant son, Padraic, is now heir to the Burke lands."

He drew a deep breath. "It's not public knowledge yet, is it?"

"Not yet. The Dublin English have had their eyes on the Burke lands for some time now, Adam, but as long as the old man and Niall were alive they knew they had not a chance. We were fortunate in that Elizabeth Tudor needed my O'Malley ships, and dared not to offend me. I intend to send word from Lynmouth to Lord Burghley that I must see him. If I am to protect my Burke son's inheritance from predators, I must have the Queen's blessing. Each day England's fleet grows larger and stronger. If I and my ships are no longer of use to the Queen she will divide the Burke lands among her courtiers without another thought, and Padraic will be landless and nameless. I can't let that happen, Adam. *I can't!*"

He moved over to the oak sideboard and poured them each some rich, sweet wine; the crimson liquid cascading gracefully into heavy, carved silver goblets. Turning, he handed her a goblet, and said, "So, little girl, you're in the same defenseless position you were three years ago when Geoffrey died. Now, however, Elizabeth Tudor has an old score to settle with you, and you are even more vulnerable with two more babes to support."

She nodded, and her sapphire eyes filled with tears which spilled uncontrolled from beneath her black lashes onto her pale cheeks. "Damn," she whispered, "I am prone to weeping these days. I don't know what's the matter with me, Adam."

He snorted impatiently. "Skye, my sweet, sweet Skye! You are human is what is the matter with you. For all your great strength you are human! In the last ten years you have buried four husbands, three of whom you loved dearly. You have borne seven children altogether, one of whom you lost in a terrible epidemic. You have fought the Queen of England, and won, despite your imprisonment in the Tower. All these things cannot help but have taken their toll on you. Now you must once more, unprotected and alone, fight for your children. You wonder why you weep easily, my darling? I don't. I stand in awe of you, little girl. I am amazed you have not gone mad from it all."

She looked up at him, the tears still spilling down her face. "I need you, Adam," she said low. "I have no right to ask it, but I need you so very much!"

"I am here for you, Skye," he said quietly. "I have always been here for you, and I always will be." Tenderly he looked down at her, and then tipped her face upward to his. Bending, he gently brushed her mouth with his. "You're tired and you're worn, little girl. Shall I comfort you as I once did? It seems so long ago, sweet Skye, that we gave of ourselves to each other."

"Oh, Adam, what kind of woman am I?" she whispered low. "My husband is dead but a month—and I loved Niall! Dear Heaven, how I loved him! Still I need you."

He could see that she was trembling with emotion, and with pure exhaustion. She was not really ready to make love with him and, he thought, she might never be ready again. He loved her; he had always loved her, but Adam de Marisco was a realist. Once she had asked him to marry her, but as desperately as he had wanted her he had to refuse, for he knew that he had neither the power nor the great name that he felt Skye O'Malley deserved and needed. Reaching out, he lifted her into his strong arms and carried her into his bedroom. As he carefully deposited her upon his huge bed, he said, "I want you to get some sleep, little girl. Afterward we will discuss our needs, but first you will rest and calm yourself." He drew the fur coverlet over her.

She nodded, strangely grateful to him, but sure she would not sleep. He watched over her as she finally did, wanting her with every ounce of his being. The wine in his goblet grew less, and he rose to refill it, returning quickly to his post. Adam de Marisco was a handsome man, standing six feet six inches tall with a body proportioned to match. His black hair was the color of a raven's wing, and his beard, once full, was now barbered as elegantly and neatly as any court dandy's, the round of his mustache giving his mouth a very sensuous appearance. He had heavy black eyebrows and thick lashes that tangled themselves over his heavy-lidded smoky blue eyes. His aristocratic nose, long and narrow at the nostrils, was a gift from his Norman ancestors.

His wine now finished, he placed the goblet on a nearby table and, fully clothed, lay down next to her. Sometime in the night she whimpered with a bad dream, and he half woke to draw her into the safety of his arms, sliding his big body beneath the coverlet, murmuring comfort in her ear until she quieted and slept peacefully again. Once more he slid into sleep himself, the scent of her damask rose perfume in his nose, clinging to his silk shirt, bringing back a hundred memories that for him were as clear as when they had happened. The knowledge that he was holding her again gave him a wonderful comfort, and he slept heavily, contentedly.

Adam de Marisco dreamed an incredible dream. He dreamed that he was nude, and being attacked by a flock of brightly colored tiny butterflies. Playfully they fluttered over his bare thighs and belly, tangling themselves in the thick mat of black hair on his chest. He could feel an ache of longing in his groin, and with a little moan he opened his eyes. The first thing he saw was Skye's dark head bent over his chest, and he realized that the butterflies were her lips that kissed him lovingly. "Celtic witch," he muttered, yanking her up by her hair so he might see her face.

Her beautiful blue eyes stared half shyly at him, and then she said blushingly, "*I need you, Adam!*"

His breath caught in his throat. She was naked, her pert small breasts as beautiful as he remembered, the dainty pink nipples thrusting forward. She ran a teasing finger down his thigh, and he realized with some shock that he was practically nude himself.

Seeing his look, she chuckled, a distinctively mischievous sound, and said, "You sleep far too heavily, Lord of Lundy. Were I an enemy the castle would now be mine. While you snored and made little happy noises, I removed your pantaloons, drawers, and hose. Your shirt, alas, I could only unfasten."

Moving her aside, he sat up and took off the offending shirt. "You're a shameless and bold wench, Skye O'Malley," he said through gritted teeth, "but I want to fuck you. God's bones, I want to fuck you!"

She reached up, pulling him back down to her, and Adam de Marisco did what he had craved doing all night. He kissed her. His mouth closed fiercely over hers, demanding more of her than he had ever asked. He bruised her soft lips with his own. Her arms slid around his neck and pulled him as close to her as was humanly possible, and her tongue licked at his lips. He could feel the sweet small mounds of her breasts pressing against his furred chest, and he groaned guiltily. He had sworn to himself, when he had realized that Skye could never be his, that he would never again make love to her, but he knew tonight that that was a promise he couldn't keep. She said she needed him, and by God he needed her!

Her softly taunting tongue was almost unbearable in its sweetness. His lips parted, and he allowed that tongue to dart within his mouth, to explore, tease, and caress as it met with his own tongue. Now he took the initiative, chasing her tongue back to her own mouth where he proceeded to harry and badger it with his own until she pulled her head away, moaning as a great shudder raced through her beautiful body and her nipples grew rigid with her desire.

Adam de Marisco smiled as he looked down on her face. She was the most marvelously sensuous woman he had ever known. She gave herself totally and completely to him, trusting him as no other woman had ever trusted. Her eyes opened, and he said softly, "You are so lovely, little girl. When I contemplate all the delights that you offer me, I don't know where to begin." She smiled at him, and lowering his great dark head, he nuzzled at her breast. She sighed and made a soft "Mmmmm" of pleasure.

For a long moment he contemplated those beautiful breasts. He had always thought that she had the loveliest little tits, sweet, and small rounds of honied flesh with their dainty pink nipples. He gently bit at one of them while his big hands kneaded her other breast hungrily. She threaded her fingers through his thick, black hair, one hand moving low to caress the back of his neck. Her touch sent a flash of heat through him, and he shuddered.

Raising his head up he rained kisses on her upturned face, her slender throat, soft shoulders, and palpitating breasts. He swept lower, tonguing her navel, covering her belly with scorching kisses, and she blossomed beneath his loving hands and mouth. "Ohh, Adam," she murmured. "Oh, yes!"

He couldn't resist a chuckle despite his own passion. She was so damned honest even in her desire. "Remember what I once told you, little girl. Love making is a great art. I will not hurry our pleasure, especially as I will not allow this to happen again between us."

"*Adam!*" She tried to sit up, but he gently pushed her back and caught her gaze with his.

"I will not be your lover, Skye O'Malley, and as I once told you I have neither the name nor the power to be your husband. You are dearer to me than any other person on this earth, and I would slay dragons for you, *but I will not be your lover!*"

She did not have to ask him why, for she knew. He loved her, and she loved him, but it was not the abiding love that a woman gives her husband. They both knew it. Along with her business partner, Robert Small, he was the best friend she had in all the world, and she had treated him shabbily by coming to him, and asking, nay, practically begging that he service her as her prize stallion serviced her mares. She flushed with shame at that thought, and said, "Oh, Adam! I beg your pardon. Let me up. I shall go from you now for I had no right to come here at all."

"Nay!" He gently pinioned her beneath him. "Have you become a wanton tease, sweet Skye, that having roused the beast in me you would now leave me?" He laughed softly. "You said you needed me, little girl. Well, now I need you, and I am weary of talk. Talk is for the afterward." His mouth made feathery movements down her body in a swift assault that caught her totally by surprise and left her breathless.

"*Adam!*" she gasped.

"Be silent, my darling!" he answered her, and then his tongue was gently seeking at the honey of her, sending small love darts of pure blazing heat into her very soul. His tongue was wildfire, stroking at the velvet of her greatest secret; rousing her to pleasures both known and unknown. Her beautiful body responded with the hunger of one long denied, and indeed she had had no lovemaking since the fifth month of her last pregnancy. She moaned as the liquid fire bathed her body, as his tongue sought and found, tantalized and pleasured, loved and pained her in both body and soul.

Adam de Marisco took great delight in Skye's response, and when at last she was writhing and creamy with her passion he sat back on his haunches, his great lance thrusting forward. Lifting the almost unconscious woman up, he lowered her carefully onto his weapon as he cradled her in his arms. He was gentle, for she was tight with her abstinence, and as he filled her she cried out her rapture. Together they rocked back and forth until Skye shuddered violently and with a whimper went limp. Satisfied that she had attained her fulfillment, he took his own, laying her back now on his enormous bed to tower over her as he thrust deep and hard and sweet within her throbbing sheath. Then, satisfied, he withdrew from her, and rolled away to catch his breath again before he drew her back into the comfort of his arms.

They slept for several hours, awakening as the early light came through the single window in the tower bedchamber. She knew that he slept no longer by the sound of his breathing, and for a few long minutes she remained silent, unable to speak, not knowing what she might say to him. He solved the problem for her, saying quietly in his deep voice, "How can any mortal woman give such pleasure, little girl? How I wish that I were the man for you, Skye O'Malley."

"I wish you would wed with me, Adam, for you're the strongest man I have ever known. I have always felt safe with you, and you know you've always told me that without a man my wealth and beauty make me vulnerable to those in power. I am ashamed to have used you so, but I did need you. *I did!*"

"Skye, there is no wrong in a woman desiring a man, but 'tis not reason enough for a marriage between us. You know that." He laughed in an effort to lighten the situation. "I cannot help but think that there isn't a man at Elizabeth's court who wouldn't have sold his soul to be in my boots last night." He raised himself up on an elbow and looked down at her. "You do understand however, why, I will not seriously entertain your proposal?"

"I understand, Adam."

"We are friends," he smiled down at her, "and I should hate you to meet a man you could really love and turn him away because of mistaken loyalty to me."

"There will be no one else," she said firmly. "God's bones, Adam! I have outlived four husbands in fifteen years. Dom, of course, was no loss, the pig! Khalid, however, and Geoffrey and Niall are another matter. I loved them, Adam, and I cannot go through the death of another man that I love. I am beginning to believe that I am bad luck for the men that love me. I think I have had enough of husbands! My six children are enough to satisfy any woman. From now on I shall be free! Free to run my own life, and to choose my own companions."

"And your lovers," he said quietly.

"Perhaps," she said slowly, and then she blushed. "I find that I am not a woman to do without a man. Is that so awful, Adam?"

"You could do without a man if you chose, little girl," he said. "Last night was different. You needed to be with a friend, with someone who loves you, with someone who could comfort you."

"Ah, Adam," she teased him. "No one has ever comforted me better than you."

Their eyes met and both remembered their first encounter when he had offered her his help, badly needed, if she would spend one night in his bed. She had been in pain then too, suffering over the loss of Geoffrey, and the loss of their youngest son, Johnny. When she had broken down and wept in his arms he had made passionate love to her. *"Let me comfort you, little girl,"* he had said. Since then it had been a joke between them, and now both laughed with the same memory.

"How long will you be at Lynmouth," he asked her when their laughter had died.

"That will depend on Cecil. First I must send a message to him, and then I must await his decision as to whether I am allowed to go to court so I may petition the Queen for Padraic's lands."

"And if you are not allowed back at court, Skye?"

"Then I petition the Queen from Lynmouth. Robbie will be back soon, and he can speak for me if I am forbidden the Queen's presence."

He nodded. "Where are your children now? Not all together, I hope."

"Nay, Adam, I am too wise for that. My oldest son, Ewan O'Flaherty, is on his lands at Ballyhennessey. My uncle has sent my eldest brother, Michael, to oversee Ewan. He is thirteen now, almost a man. In three years we will celebrate his marriage to Gwyneth Southwood, Geoffrey's daughter by his first wife. Ewan's younger brother, Murrough O'Flaherty, is with the Earl of Lincoln's household. He will need influential contacts, as he is landless. I can give him wealth, but I can't give him lands. Those he must gain himself, Adam.

"Willow is with Dame Cecily Small. My eldest daughter does not like Ireland. I think it must be her father's blood in her that makes her prefer a slightly milder climate. So I allowed her to winter with Dame Cecily as Robbie has been away. They are good company for each other, and Dame Cecily is teaching her all the housewifely arts. Thank God, Robbie and his sister adopted her formally, and gave her their name as well as made her their heiress. Having a Spanish father could harm her socially, and if it were known that Willow's father was once the Great Whoremaster of Algiers!" Skye shuddered. "As much as I loved Khalid, his daughter shall never know *that*." Then she was forced to chuckle. "It would amuse Khalid to know his offspring is a most proper little English girl; but without Robert Small's name to protect her, she would be lost. Most people assume she is actually related to Robbie.

"My little Earl of Lynmouth is page at court. You see, Adam, I am forbidden court, but my Robin is Elizabeth's favorite pet. He grows more like Geoffrey every day, I am told." She smiled softly. "They called Geoffrey the Angel Earl. Our son, Robin, is known at court as the *Cherub*. How proud Geoffrey would be of him," she said. "My Burke children are safe in their castle.

"No, Cecil cannot use my children against me. Only Robin is readily available to him, and as one of England's premier noblemen, he is inviolate. Besides, Cecil is too softhearted to war with children, thank God. A soft heart is the curse of an honorable man, Adam, and Lord Burghley is an honorable man for all he is Elizabeth Tudor's creature."

"You haven't forgiven her, have you, Skye?"

"No, Adam, I will never forgive her for what she did to me. Nor will I forgive her the time she stole from Niall and me, especially now that Niall is . . . is dead."

"Skye, sweet Skye." He took her in his arms and held her against his hard chest. "No more wars with Bess Tudor, little girl. Promise!" He was suddenly afraid for her.

"I promise you, Adam. I am a wiser woman than she who pirated the Queen's ships from right under her nose. The fact that Elizabeth could never prove it was victory enough."

"We were lucky that time, Skye," he admonished her gently.

She chuckled throatily. "I only regret the loss of the emeralds," she said, and he laughed with her. Then she pulled away from him. "Dammit, Adam, I am ravenous! You're a poor host not to feed me."

"I thought you had all you wanted from me, little girl," he teased her, ducking the pillow she threw at him.

"I've not had a decent meal in several days. Does Glynnis cook?"

"'Tis one of her best talents," he remarked, waggling his heavy black eyebrows at her. Skye laughed as de Marisco continued, "I'll have her fetch us something now that you're obviously up and determined to be on your way."

Skye sobered. "Aye, Adam, I have to go. My messenger must be off to Cecil this morning."

Within the hour Glynnis made her way from the taproom below to the tower antechamber, her sturdy legs bowed under the weight of the tray that she carried. "I've brought a bit of everything," she said with a friendly grin. "Ye'll not go hungry this day, m'lady." Glynnis then bobbed a curtsey and left them to contemplate the bounty that she had prepared for them. There were two steaming bowls of oat porridge smothered in stewed pears; a covered silver dish, badly tarnished, of eggs poached in heavy cream, dry Spanish wine, and dill; a platter of pink country ham, sliced thickly; a hot loaf of wheat bread wrapped in a linen napkin to keep it warm; sturdy stoneware crocks of sweet butter and thick honey. A silver pitcher of brown ale completed their repast.

"God's bones," Skye exclaimed, delighted with the meal, "Glynnis can have a job in my kitchens anytime, Adam!" Then she took up a simple wooden trencher and filled it up. The porridge was quickly eaten, the eggs and ham devoured, and Skye, sitting back in her chair wrapped in de Marisco's huge silk shirt, her long legs stretched out, quaffed down half a goblet of brown ale and then reached for the loaf of bread. Carefully she sliced herself a piece, and spreading it first with butter and then with honey, she proceeded to eat it down.

Adam, no mean trencherman himself, watched her with fond amusement and indulgence. He had always admired her fine appetite. Women who picked at their food believing it good manners annoyed him. Skye enjoyed good cooking, and ate as if she did. "I'll sail you to Lynmouth myself," he said, and she nodded, her mouth still full. "Do you want me to stay with you until you hear from Cecil?"

She swallowed. "No. Better Cecil not be reminded of your existence. I may need to run, and Lundy's a safe port for me."

"Always, little girl!" he agreed with a smile that warmed her to her toes.

They left Lundy as the sun was beginning to creep over the horizon, and with a fresh southwest breeze, they were easily and quickly at Lynmouth. He brought his small boat into the little cove beneath the castle's cliffs where a hidden cave had served the Earls of Lynmouth as an escape hatch for several centuries. He would not stay.

"The wind will die by midday, and I'll be becalmed here if I don't go now, sweet Skye. I don't particularly relish rowing home eleven miles." He pulled her roughly into his arms and kissed her quickly, tenderly. "Behave yourself, little girl. If you need me use the old signals. I'll have a boy on watch round the clock." Then while she watched, easy tears pricking at her eyelids, he sailed away from the landing out into the cove, and from there to the beckoning blue sea.

She brushed the wetness from her eyes, and, mounting the worn stone steps within the cave, hurried unseen upward into Lynmouth Castle. Emerging from the narrow passage of the stairway into a corridor in the oldest part of the castle, she gained her own apartments.

"Good morning, m'lady," Daisy chirped cheerfully as she came through the doors. "As luck would have it, I saw Lord de Marisco's little boat as it was sailing into the cove. Shall I get you something to eat?"

"No," Skye replied. "I have already eaten. Is Wat Mason here, Daisy?"

"Aye, m'lady."

"Fetch him at once, Daisy. He's to ride to Whitehall with a message for Lord Burghley."

"Lord Burghley is here in Devon, m'lady, at Sir Richard de Grenville's home."

"He is?" Skye was surprised. "The old spider rarely leaves court. I wonder what has brought him down here."

"The news is of rebellion, m'lady," Daisy said, her voice bright with importance. "Ever since last year when the Queen of Scots fled to England there have been murmurings. There is fear of a rebellion in the north among the marcher lords. They say those who would revolt would bring back the old religion, begging your pardon, m'lady."

"It's all right, Daisy. I was born a Roman Catholic, and I see no reason to change my ways, but I also see no reason to involve myself in a damned rebellion over religion. Religion should be a personal and private thing between a soul and God. The northern lords are fools if they think that they'll dislodge Elizabeth Tudor and replace her with her cousin, Mary Stewart; but then they don't know Harry Tudor's daughter as well as I know her. They'll lose everything, the idiots, and the church won't restore what they've lost! Better to keep one's faith and one's possessions separate. Now go get Wat Mason. He'll have to go to de Grenville's house with my message."

Daisy hurried from the room, and Skye sat down at her small writing table to pen her note to the Queen's Secretary of State and most powerful adherent, William Cecil, Lord Burghley. She had no doubt that the old fox would see her, but whether he would take her part was another thing. Still, Cecil didn't need any more trouble in Ireland, especially with rebellion brewing in England. Thank God for Mary Stewart, Skye thought. I've never laid eyes on her, nor she me, but she has done me a good turn just by being in England for the malcontents to rally about. The note Skye wrote was a brief one, greeting Lord Burghley and saying that the Countess of Lynmouth would like an audience with him before his departure for court. She would either go to him, or be pleased to entertain him at Lynmouth. Would he kindly return his answer with her groom.

Daisy returned with Wat Mason, who knelt in respectful greeting to his mistress. Skye sealed the message with her heavy gold signet ring, the O'Malley sea dragons pressing themselves into the hot green wax. Looking up, she handed the letter to Wat, and said, "Take this to Lord Burghley, the Queen's Secretary of State and Lord Treasurer. He is at Sir Richard de Grenville's home. Deliver it into his hands only, and then wait for his reply. Do you understand me, Wat? You will give my message to no one but William Cecil himself."

"Aye, m'lady, I understands." Wat rose from his knees and hurried from the room.

And now, Skye thought, the game begins. To her surprise, however, she did not have to wait long. Wat was back at Lynmouth by day's end, bringing with him a reply from William Cecil. Eagerly Skye tore the message open and read. Then she smiled with satisfaction and relief. Cecil would come to her. He would arrive at Lynmouth in two days' time, and stay the night before returning to London. She wondered what he would want in return from her. His help would not come cheaply, but Padraic's inheritance and name must be saved.

"M'lady!" Daisy flew into the room. "They're here!"

Skye looked up, startled and for a moment unable to think what Daisy could possibly mean. Then, before she could gather her thoughts, her small daughter, Willow, ran into the room.

"Mama!" Willow threw herself enthusiastically into Skye's arms.

Skye's arms closed about her daughter and she hugged her hungrily. "Ah, my little love, how I have missed you," she said, and suddenly she was weeping happy tears at the sight of Khalid's daughter, so very much like him with his amber-gold eyes fringed in long, thick dark lashes, and her black hair.

"Will you be here for my birthday, Mama?" Willow squirmed from Skye's arms and fixed her with a serious gaze.

"Is it April already?" Skye pretended to consider it.

"Oh, Mama! Of course it is April, and my birthday is in five more days! I shall be nine!"

"So you shall, Willow. I shall soon have to find a husband for you."

"I shall find my own husband, thank you!" Willow replied pertly, and Skye was reminded of herself. Willow might look like her father, but she was her mother's daughter, too.

"You shall only marry the man you love, my darling," Skye promised her oldest daughter.

"You spoil her," a familiar voice snapped, and Skye smiled over Willow's head at Dame Cecily, who was just entering the room.

"So do you," she chuckled.

"I did not expect you in England," Dame Cecily said, settling herself in a comfortable chair by the fireplace.

Skye sat in the chair facing the older woman and, taking Willow onto her lap, replied, "I had to come. I have bad news. The old MacWilliam is dead, and without an adult heir, my wee Padraic's inheritance is in danger. Lord Burghley is at de Grenville's, and will be here in two days' time to speak with me."

Dame Cecily nodded. "Does he know of the old man's death?"

"No one does," Skye said. "We buried him in secret, and my uncle Seamus is now in control of Burke Castle. I've come to present my petition to the Queen if Burghley will allow me back at court. If not, I don't know what I will do. Perhaps Dickon de Grenville will speak for me, and then when Robbie returns next month he can help me also."

Dame Cecily sighed deeply. "Dearest Skye," she said. "I will go to the Queen for you myself, if necessary." Then she reached out and, taking Skye's slender hand in her plump one, said, "I am so very sorry about Niall." Her honest blue eyes filled with sympathetic tears.

Before Skye might answer her, however, Willow spoke up. "Will you get me another father, Mama?" she asked. "I never knew my real papa, but I did so like Geoffrey and Niall."

"I don't think I shall ever marry again, my love," Skye said. "Four husbands are quite enough for your mama, and I think I have all the children I shall ever need. You have not yet seen your new brother, Padraic. He is a fine little boy, just like Niall. Will you come home to Ireland with me this summer, and see him?"

Willow nodded sleepily, for it had been a long day for her. Skye nodded to Daisy, who came forward saying, "Come along, Mistress Willow, and I shall give you a good supper of toasted cheese and sweet Devon cider. Then I shall tuck you into your own bed." Willow climbed from her mother's lap and, taking Daisy's hand, departed the room.

"Have you heard from Robbie?" Skye asked Dame Cecily.

"Aye. His advance ship put into Plymouth just last week. The Portuguese may think that they have a monopoly on the Spice Islands, but Robbie has his friends, too. The holds of his fleet are bulging with cloves, nutmegs, peppercorns, and cinnamon. He also told me to tell you that he has some particularly nice gemstones for you."

"We'll make another small fortune with this trip," Skye remarked. "Even after the Queen's share we will have a fat profit." She smiled almost grimly. "It's all I have left, Dame Cecily. The children, and making a fortune."

"You will love again, my dear."

"Not this time," Skye said. "If I can insinuate myself back into the Queen's good graces I shall not need a man to protect me."

"Remember, Skye, that it was the Queen who caused you to need a husband's protection the last time," Dame Cecily reminded Skye.

"But the Queen knows that should she do to me again what she did last time, I shall revenge myself on her once more as I did before. Even if she couldn't prove that it was me pirating her ships, she knew."

"Make no hasty decisions now, my child," Dame Cecily chided. "Wait until you have spoken with Lord Burghley. He may be the Queen's man, but he is a fair man for all of it."

"Aye," Skye replied. "He is an honorable man."

She kept that thought in her mind as she prepared the castle for Lord Burghley's brief visit. With its young lord away at court, and herself on her estates in Ireland, Lynmouth had been like a sleeping prince. Its mistress back, however, the servants polished and scrubbed, dusted and swept every corner of the castle. Great porcelain bowls of spring flowers began to appear in the main hall, and in the bedrooms herb-scented sheets and comforters appeared on the beds. When William Cecil and Sir Richard de Grenville and their train arrived two afternoons later they rode slowly up the raked gravel drive, admiring the well-manicured green lawns and brightly colored gardens around the castle. The moat round Lynmouth had been filled in in Geoffrey's father's time.

Skye greeted her guests in the Great Hall, noting as she came forward that all the men in the party were most admiring of her. She had chosen to wear a black velvet gown, its very low neckline exposing her creamy chest and the soft swelling of her small breasts. Her neck wisk, a standing, fan-shaped wire collar, was of silver lace, as were the ribbons on her leg-of-mutton sleeves and her underskirt. About her neck was a necklace of silver and Persian blue lapis. Her dark and luxuriant hair was tucked beneath a fetching little silver lace cap.

Curtseying prettily, she said, "Welcome, my lords! Welcome to Lynmouth!"

"Christ's bones, Skye," Sir Richard de Grenville said, "you don't look any older than when we first met, and I hear you've finally given the old MacWilliam his long-awaited heir." He kissed her loudly on both cheeks, and then sobered. "I was sorry to hear about Niall," he finished awkwardly.

"It was a bad end to a good man," William Cecil observed. "Good day to you, madam. I am happy to see you once more in England."

"If I am in England then I cannot be fomenting rebellion in Ireland," Skye chuckled devilishly.

The Queen's man gave a dry bark of a laugh. "As always, Lady Burke, we understand each other," he said. "Now how may I be of service to you?"

"May we speak in private, sir?"

He nodded.

"Dickon," she said to de Grenville. "Will you lead your gentlemen into the hall and avail yourselves of the refreshments my servants have laid out? I know it has been a dusty ride for you all." She turned again to William Cecil. "I have some rare Burgundy in my library, my lord." He followed her from the Great Hall and down a corridor through great double oak doors into a fine booklined room with a beautiful aureole window. The sun pouring through the window at that moment made the room warm and inviting. Skye gestured. "Will you be seated, my lord?"

He sat himself in a large, comfortable chair and gratefully accepted the silver goblet of fragrant wine that she poured him.

After pouring herself one, Skye raised her goblet. "The Queen," she said.

"The Queen!" he answered.

They both drank, and then Skye leaned forward and said, "The old MacWilliam is dead, and my infant son is now the new Lord Burke."

"I had not received *that* information," he answered, admiring the way in which she came right to the point. Most women shilly-shallied about things like this. What was the matter with his Irish spies?

"There is nothing wrong with your intelligence from Ireland, m'lord," Skye said, amused, reading his thoughts. "I had my father-in-law buried in secret, and my uncle now holds the castle and lands for me. Your Dublin English and my fine Irish neighbors believe that Rory Burke lies dying, and even now they wait to steal his lands. That is why it is not public knowledge at this moment, and that is why I have come to you. Without the Queen's blessing and protection, little Padraic Burke will be not only landless, but nameless as well.

"I must appeal to you, my lord. Allow me to return to court so that I may plead my case with Her Majesty. My O'Malley ships harry the Spanish for England, my fleets share their huge profits with the Crown. I ask nothing for myself, m'lord. I only ask for my son, the rightful heir to the Burke lands and titles."

William Cecil stared into his goblet. In the north the marcher lords, Lumley and Arundel, Northumberland and Westmoreland, were already causing difficulties because of Mary Stewart, the Queen of the damned Scots. He knew that because of their religion they were considering pressing her claim to the English throne. God only knew that the Queen had been more than lenient with the Roman Catholic lords. Elizabeth Tudor preferred her own brand of Catholicism to the Pope's, but did not abuse her Catholic subjects provided they were loyal to England before Rome.

Lord Burghley swished the wine about in his goblet, watching as the ruby liquid slid down the polished silver sides of the goblet. There was going to be trouble in England before summer's end. If the Crown did not confirm little Padraic Burke's place he knew that what Skye feared would happen. The Dublin English and her equally greedy Irish neighbors would swarm over Burke lands fighting for the least little scrap of it.

The Irish, of course, would then fight the English. It didn't matter who won; the Anglo-Irish lords would demand monies and men to fight the Burkes and the O'Malleys, and the Queen would have to send those monies and men. Ireland was a bottomless pit for armies and gold, William Cecil decided. The Crown needed no more enemies or trouble in Ireland at this time. Especially enemies who commanded a fleet of ships and were not reluctant to use them against England. Skye's ships patrolled the English Channel and the Bay of Biscay for the Crown, taking Spanish treasure galleons whose cargoes enriched Elizabeth's coffers. They needed O'Malley ships, which meant that they needed Skye's friendship as well.

"Hmm," William Cecil said. He had no intention of giving Lady Burke what she wanted cheaply, and he had suddenly thought of a marvelous use for her. "Madam, I can see to it that your infant son's rights are upheld by the Crown, but in return the Crown would exact a favor from you."

"I have no choice," Skye answered him. "What is it you want of me?"

"There is a small, independent duchy tucked just between Provence and the Languedoc in France. It is called Beaumont de Jaspre. The current duc has recently made overtures of friendship to the Queen. He has offered us trading agreements and hospitality for English trading vessels. We would like to accept his offer, for it will give us a safe port in the Mediterranean and a valuable listening post into France.

"The duc seeks an English wife, for he has only one child; a boy who rumor says is feeble-minded. The Queen has not been able to think of whom we might send to Beaumont de Jaspre. An untried girl would be of little use to us. Her mind would be apt to be filled with thoughts of love and romance. You, madam, will have no such illusions; and will do your duty by England. If you will go as the duc's bride, then I will personally see that your son's rights are fully protected. The boy will grow up as Her Majesty's personal ward."

"*Are you mad?!*" The look on Skye's face was pure shock. "I cannot leave Ireland and England! My life is here. My lands, my wealth, *my children!* Besides I have sworn to never wed again, m'lord. I cannot lose to death another man whom I love. *You cannot ask this of me!*" But she knew that he could, and he did.

"Madam, you have never even met the Duc de Beaumont de Jaspre. Therefore you cannot love him. If he departs this life it should be no matter to you. He is said to be in failing health for all his desire to father children. In all likelihood you will be widowed in a year or two; but in the meantime England will have a listening post in France's bedchamber."

"You are heartless, sir!" Skye cried. "Ask anything else of me and I will gladly comply, but you cannot ask this!"

"I can, madam, and I do! The only way I will support your son's rights is if you will agree to go to Beaumont de Jaspre as the duc's bride." His dark brown eyes looked straight at her.

"I shall appeal directly to the Queen!"

"You are forbidden court. Appear without the Queen's permission, and you'll return to the Tower, where you can do your son no good. Besides, the Queen will accept my advice in this matter. An infant heir is so vulnerable, madam, without strong protection. Who stronger than the Queen? *A grateful Queen*. Think, madam!"

Skye knew that she was beaten. She could refuse William Cecil's infamous proposal and return to Ireland, where she would be forced to fight off the Dublin English and her Irish neighbors for the next fifteen years, until her son was old enough to fight himself; or she could agree to become a stranger's wife. The idea was totally alien to her, but she had no other choices. Still, she would not give in to the Crown without having certain conditions guaranteed her.

"I want the same kind of marriage contract that I had with Southwood and Lord Burke," she said firmly. "What belongs to me remains mine alone. I will not give over my wealth to anyone else. Women are hapless enough creatures as it is in this man's world; but I will not be helpless as well, dependent on someone else for every pennypiece I spend. If the duc will not agree then *nothing*, Lord Burghley, not even your threats, can make me go."

He nodded. "It will not be easy, but if your dowry is sufficiently generous, madam, we should have no difficulties with the duc. It is a simple enough matter to convince him that your estates are entailed to your children. As for your children themselves, they will remain here."

She nodded in answer to him. It would break her heart to leave her children, especially her Burke babies, behind, but it would be safer for them. Padraic and Deirdre must remain on their lands as a symbol to their people. "My uncle, the Bishop of Connaught, must be allowed to govern Burke lands for my son," she said.

"Agreed," William Cecil said. Old Seamus O'Malley might be a papist, but he was an honest one and a popular one. He would give the Crown no difficulties. If they put an Englishman or one of the Anglo-Irish in charge of the infant heir, the regent would eventually appropriate the child's inheritance. Besides, the safety of the

Burke children themselves would be guaranteed in their grand-uncle's care.

"My other children will remain where they are now," Skye said.

"Then you should have no difficulty, madam, in readying yourself fairly quickly. I shall return to the Queen tomorrow. You are to follow in seven days' time. You will advise me of your arrival in London, and I will arrange for you to come to court once more. Where do you intend staying?"

"I will stay at Greenwood," Skye said. "Lynmouth House is too large to open for one person for such a short time."

He smiled his frosty smile at her, pleased as he always was by her sense of economy. Like his mistress, Lady Burke was generous but frugal. She understood that wealth was to be husbanded and increased, not squandered idly. He fully approved her insistence on keeping her wealth in her own hands. She was an excellent manager, far better than most men he knew. "Then madam," he said, "our business is now concluded. I shall look forward to seeing you at court."

She showed him to the apartments where he would spend the night, and then quickly hurried to her own rooms. She could not believe what had just happened. She had vowed never to marry again, and now here she was about to be betrothed to a foreign duke and sent from England and Ireland. This man wanted children, and she was certainly a proven breeder. She shuddered. How could she allow a man she did not know to touch her? To make love to her? The mere thought of it was repellent to her nature. Lord Burghley had said that the duc was not in good health. Perhaps by the time she got there the duc's health would have deteriorated to a point where he could not fulfill his marital duties. One could hope.

Dame Cecily hurried through the door demanding, "Well? Will Cecil support you and arrange for you to go to court to see the Queen?"

"Aye," Skye replied, "but the price is steep. I am to leave here, and journey to a small independent dukedom between Provence and the Languedoc where I will wed with its ruler."

"*What?!*" The older woman's face looked horrified and her hand flew to her heart. "Surely Lord Burghley jests with you, Skye? He cannot ask such a cruel thing of you!"

"But he has, and I must comply with his request, as he knew I must when he suggested it. The duchy has offered England a base on the Mediterranean as well as a listening post into France and, I suspect, the kingdoms of Italy, although Lord Burghley did not say so. The duc is supposed to be in failing health, and Cecil says I shall probably be home in two years or less."

"And afterward will they use the Burke children again in order to gain your aid?" Dame Cecily demanded, outraged. "God's foot! Has Cecil then turned pimp for the Crown?"

"I don't know," Skye said wearily. "I can only hope that Lord Burghley will accept this sacrifice I make as payment in full."

"I ought to give William Cecil a good piece of my mind!" Dame Cecily huffed furiously. "I cannot imagine what he is thinking of to separate you from your children!"

Skye had to laugh. Dearest, dearest Dame Cecily. From the moment Skye had arrived in England several years ago, Robert Small's plump, widowed sister had taken her under her wing; had been a second mother to her; had loved her, and Willow, and all of Skye's children. She was a grandmother to Willow and Robin, but most of all she was a good and loyal friend. "Do not trouble yourself with Lord Burghley," Skye gently admonished the older woman. "It will change nothing. I will not, however, leave England until I have seen Robbie."

"And your Burke children, Skye?"

"If I go back to Ireland now to bid them a farewell I shall not be able to leave them, and I cannot take them with me. It is a long and dangerous trip I make. I do not know anything about this man whom I must marry. Besides, Deirdre and Padraic are both babies. They will not miss me as long as Uncle Seamus sees that they are loved and well cared for. And perhaps if this marriage works out I shall be able to send for them. I must ask you to care for Willow. The O'Flaherty boys are both safe where they are now." A small sob escaped her as she thought of Niall's children, so young and so helpless. How long would it be before she saw them again? Padraic would not even know her. He was just over two months old now. Deirdre, however, was almost sixteen months old. Would she remember her mother? Skye doubted it, and the tears flowed.

Lord Burghley and his party departed Lynmouth the following morning, and for the next few days Skye went about the business of writing her uncle, her stepmother, and the others necessary to the smooth running of her world, of her plans to travel to Beaumont de Jaspre. These letters went off to their destinations by the fastest of the Lynmouth horses, for Skye wanted to hear from her family prior to her departure. She had decided to travel upon an O'Malley ship, and asked that her flagship, *The Seagull*, be awaiting her by month's end in the London Pool. She would insist that she be given a proper naval escort to avoid the danger of pirates, and so she might reach her destination safely. Remembering the evil Capitan Jamil in Algiers, she worried about reaching Beaumont de Jaspre at all; yet she felt she should reach the duchy easier by sea than by having to travel through France during troubled times, and indeed France was in turmoil at the moment.

Just prior to her departure for London Skye received a long letter from her sister, Eibhlin, who wrote of her visit to St. Mary's and of what she had learned regarding the tragic death of Niall Burke. *Darragh is truly mad,* Eibhlin wrote. *As for the evil Claire, she has disappeared as mysteriously as she appeared.*

Skye crushed between her two hands the parchment upon which her sister's letter was written. *Claire O'Flaherty!* "Damn your black soul to Hell!" she whispered fiercely. "I swear by St. Patrick himself that if our paths ever cross, I will kill you with my own hands!" Having said the terrible words, she felt better.

Skye had decided to take Willow to London with her in order to have more time with her eldest daughter, and so Willow might see her beloved half-brother, Robin. She had carefully explained her difficult situation to her daughter, and Willow had understood. She was very much her mother's daughter with regard to finances, and knew that without property and gold a person was helpless; even with them, as her mother was, one was helpless to supreme authority.

"Can I not come with you, Mama?" was her only question.

"Not until I know if this marriage is to work out, my love," Skye said. "I do not even know the duc by reputation, Willow. He may turn out to be a fine gentleman whom I may learn to care for, and who will be good to my children; but he also might turn out to be not quite as nice, in which case I would prefer that my children are safe in England and Ireland. Do you understand?"

"I think so," Willow said quietly. "If he is not a nice man, and I were with you, he might use threats against me to make you do things you would not do otherwise, like Lord Burghley."

"God bless me!" Dame Cecily cried. "She is but nine, and already understands the way of the world!"

"Better she does," Skye said, "and then she will not be disillusioned. You are correct, my love."

"Then it is better I remain here with Dame Cecily," Willow said calmly.

"Much better," her mother agreed. "At least for the present."

Chapter 2

Exactly one week after William Cecil had departed Lynmouth Castle for London, the Countess of Lynmouth followed after him. The great traveling coach with the Southwood family crest emblazoned upon its sides lumbered along the muddy spring roads toward the capital. Inside, however, Skye, Dame Cecily, Willow, and Daisy were quite comfortable. The vehicle itself was well sprung; the red velvet upholstery hid suitably full horsehair and wool padding, which made for comfortable seats; and tucked at their feet were hot bricks wrapped in flannel, which, along with the coach's red fox lap robes, made for luxurious warmth. Skye absently rubbed the soft fur, remembering other and happier times when it had covered her and Geoffrey.

The coachman and his assistant sat upon the box, controlling the four strong horses that pulled the vehicle. Six armed outriders preceded the coach, and six rode behind them. The horses were changed regularly, allowing them to keep up a fairly even rate of speed, and a rider had gone on ahead of them to arrange for overnight and midday accommodations in the best inns.

They arrived in London some four days later and, passing through the bustling city, entered the tiny, quiet village of Chiswick where Skye's house was located upon the Strand on the Green, which bordered the River Thames. It was the last house in a prestigious row that included the great homes of Salisbury, Worcester, and the Bishop of Durham. Next to Skye's home, Greenwood, stood Lynmouth House, which now belonged to her little son, Robin.

Greenwood, a three-storied house of mellow pink brick, stood within its own private grounds. As Skye's coach drove through the open iron gates past the bowing and smiling gatekeeper, and his brightly curtseying wife, she remembered how shabby the house had been on her first visit seven years ago. Now the manicured lawns edged with their private woods stretched out invitingly toward the house. A thought crossed her mind: It's good to be home. She smiled to herself. Greenwood had always been a happy place for her.

"Welcome home, m'lady," the majordomo said as they entered the house. "I have a message from Lord Burghley for you. Where shall I have it brought?"

"The library," she said quickly. "Willow, my love, go along with Daisy and Dame Cecily." Skye hurried to the library, drawing off her pale-blue, scented kid gloves and flinging them on a table as she entered. She unfastened her hooded cloak, pushing back its ermine-edged, dark-blue velvet hood to shrug the garment off. The attending footman quickly caught the cape and hurried out with it as the majordomo hurried in with her message upon a silver salver. Skye took it up, and said, "I wish to be alone." As the door closed shut she quickly opened Cecil's letter.

> *Greeting, madam, and welcome to London. The Queen will receive you at eight o'clock this evening at Whitehall. You are not to wear mourning, as the Duc de Beaumont's nephew will be present, but rather dress to suit your rank and your wealth.*

A sarcastic smile touched her lips. She would have to mourn Niall in her heart, for she was not to be allowed a decent period of grief by the Crown. Oh no! She was to be paraded this very evening before the duc's representative, and had been ordered to dress in her finest feathers. Cecil had never even considered the possibility that she might not show up in London, that she might run for Ireland and barricade herself in Burke Castle! With his customary efficiency he had known that she would arrive today, and had sent his message. She laughed, seeing the dark humor in the situation, and left the library to climb the stairs to her apartments, where she instructed Daisy which dress she would wear that evening.

At a few minutes before eight o'clock Skye's town coach arrived at Whitehall Palace. As her footman helped her down, some half a dozen gallants stopped and stared openmouthed at her. She wore a magnificent gown of deep purple velvet with a very low square neckline. Her breasts, pushed up by a boned undergarment, swelled dangerously over the top of the gown. Its sleeves, full to just below the elbow, were slashed to show their lavender silk inserts, and the turned back cuffs of the sleeves were embroidered, as was the lavender silk underskirt, with gold thread, tiny seed pearls, gold and little glass beads. Beneath her gown Skye's legs were sheathed in purple silk stockings embroidered in twining gold vines. Her slender feet were encased in narrow, pointed high-heeled purple silk shoes.

Her hair, parted in the middle, was arranged in the French fashion that she preferred, a soft chignon at the nape of her neck. There were silk Parma violets and white silk lilies of the valley sewn to a long comb, placed at the top of the chignon. The silk flowers were a delicious extravagance from France.

About her neck Skye wore an incredibly opulent necklace of diamonds and amethysts set in gold, and in her ears were her famous pear-shaped diamonds that fell from baroque pearls. She wore but one ring this night, a heart-shaped pink sapphire on the third finger of her left hand.

She had faintly highlighted her eyes in blue kohl, and reddened her lips, but her cheeks were pink with a combination of excitement, anger, and nerves. Wrapped in a gentle cloud of her damask rose perfume, she moved forward into the palace.

One of the young gallants foolishly stepped into her path, doffing his feathered cap, and bowing low. "Just a word, oh exquisite one, and I shall die happy!" he lisped.

"Stand aside, you silly puppy!" Skye snapped irritably. The reality of why she was here was beginning to sink into her soul.

The gallant almost fell back at the sharp tone in her voice, and she swept on by him, finding her way with quick familiarity as old memories began to assail her. Turning a corner, she bumped into a courtier and, stepping back to apologize, gasped as the courtier caught at her hands, imprisoning them in his own. "*Dudley!*" she hissed at the smugly grinning Earl of Leicester.

"*Sweet Skye,*" he murmured. "I could scarcely believe my good fortune when Bess said you would be returning to us, widowed once more." The implication was plain, and it was all she could do not to shudder with disgust. Robert Dudley slipped an arm about her waist and pulled her close. His mustache tickled her ear as he kissed it, and then he whispered, "You do run through husbands, sweet Skye. Marry me, and I'll never let you wear me out!"

Angrily she pulled away from him, looking at him with distaste. Robert Dudley, the Earl of Leicester, was as handsome and elegant as ever, but she still found his manner offensive and overbearing. "Unhand me this instant, Dudley! I am here because the Queen has special plans for me, and if you should attempt to attack me again I shall make the most outrageous scene this court has ever seen! Lord Burghley will protect me this time, you swine!" She tore his arm from about her waist. "You will crush my gown!"

"And what *special* plans has Bess for you, sweet Skye?" He was completely unperturbed by her anger.

"I am sure that you shall know that shortly, my lord. Now you will excuse me. I am expected in the Queen's chambers."

"I will escort you," he said, taking her arm. She did not deny him that courtesy for she knew that once her betrothal became public knowledge, Dudley would be forced to leave her be. Silently they made their way to Elizabeth Tudor's privy chamber, where the doors were flung wide at their approach by the Queen's own guardsmen. As they entered, Skye recognized only two faces among the women in the Queen's rooms, Lettice Knollys, and Lady Elizabeth Clinton, born a FitzGerald. Lady Clinton was the Countess of Lincoln in whose household Skye's second son, Murrough, was a page.

Suddenly a small blond boy dressed in pale blue velvet and silver lace stepped forward. "Good evening, mother," he said.

"Good evening, Robin," Skye answered, her eyes devouring her son. She wanted to hug him, but knew she could not do so publicly.

"Skye!" Lettice Knollys came forward smiling. "How good to see you again." Her eyes flicked to Dudley.

So that's how it is now, Skye thought amused. "Lettice dear, it is *good* to see you also." She turned slightly. "Beth, how are you?"

Lady Clinton nodded. "I am well, and your Murrough is a delight, Skye. Never have I had such a gracious, well-mannered page in my household. I hope you will let me keep him for a while longer."

"He writes me that he is happy," Skye replied. "I see no reason to remove him from your care, Beth. He is a lucky little boy to be in such a fine house. I hope, however, I may see him while I am here at court. My visit is not to be a long one."

"Send word whenever you want him," Elizabeth Clinton replied graciously.

"*Dearest Skye!*" Every head in the room turned at the sound of Elizabeth Tudor's voice, and Skye swept the Queen a low and graceful curtsey. "We welcome you back to court, dearest Skye," the Queen said.

"I am grateful that you have let me come, Majesty," returned Skye, rising as she spoke, and thinking Bess Tudor had aged little. She was still a handsome and elegant young woman.

"Come into my privy chamber, Skye," Elizabeth said. "The rest of you are to wait here at my pleasure."

The two women entered into the Queen's small private library, and Elizabeth Tudor sat down, motioning Skye into a chair opposite her.

"You know why I am here, Majesty," Skye began.

"Aye, I know. You wish me to confirm little Lord Padraic Burke's rights so that the English in Dublin Pale will not seize Burke lands now that there is no adult male Burke to defend them."

Skye nodded.

"You are willing to aid me in return?" the Queen demanded.

"I have ever been Your Majesty's most loyal servant," was the reply.

"Even when pirating my treasure ships," Elizabeth said drily.

"That was never proven," Skye replied quickly.

"Ha!" the Queen chuckled. "That handsome brute de Marisco saved your pretty neck that time, Skye, but I know it was you! It had a woman's fine hand about it. It was subtle, yet hurtful. Men are more blunt, dearest Skye." She fixed Skye a piercing look. "You are willing to go to Beaumont de Jaspre as the duc's bride?"

"I am not willing, Majesty, but I will go. If you will guarantee my son's rights, I will go."

"You understand that we will also expect you to listen, and pass on to us any interesting and pertinent tidbits you learn with regard to France, Spain, the Papal States, and the Holy Roman Empire?"

"I understand, Majesty."

The Queen nodded. "Then I will confirm your son's rights,

madam. Cecil tells me that you wish your uncle, the old Bishop of Connaught, to be the boy's governor."

"Aye, Majesty. He is a good man, and a wise one as well."

"Very well," the Queen said. "I can find no reason to object. The Duc de Beaumont will be quite surprised to see the beauty that I am sending him. Too many state brides are a disappointment to the grooms."

"Too many grooms are an equal disappointment to the brides," came the pert reply.

The Queen chuckled again. "I remember when poor Anne of Cleves arrived as fourth wife to my father," she reminisced. "Anne was far plumper than her portrait would have had you believe, and nervousness had caused her fair skin to blotch. It was instant dislike on both parts, and my father was furious with his artist, Hans Holbein, who had painted the Princess of Cleves' portrait. Of course my father was no prize either, having grown fat and middle-aged, but he didn't see himself as such. He was plagued with gout in his right foot, and could be very irritable, especially when his foot hurt, which unfortunately it did on her arrival. She graciously gave him a quick divorce." The Queen smiled again at the memory, and then she said, "It is time for us to begin the dancing, dearest Skye. We will introduce you this evening to the duc's nephew, Edmond de Beaumont. He has come to escort you back to Beaumont de Jaspre. You will find him an interesting man."

"I cannot leave London until Sir Robert Small has returned, Majesty. He is due back sometime this month from a most successful voyage. His advance ship is already in Plymouth, and I have had word that the spices he carries will enrich Your Majesty's coffers greatly."

Elizabeth Tudor smiled. "You do not have to leave us until Sir Robert has returned, and you have had time to make your arrangements with him. I know the businesswoman that you are." She took Skye's arm in her own, and together they strolled from the Queen's privy chamber. "Come, ladies! Come, Dudley! My feet itch to dance, and it grows late."

The Queen's party made their way through the corridors of Whitehall Palace to a large room with walls of linenfold paneling and a fine parquet floor. The musicians were already set up in a corner of the room upon a small raised platform. Elizabeth and her party passed through a line of bowing courtiers as they walked to a gilt throne set up at the end of the room. The Queen sat gracefully upon the red velvet cushion set upon the throne, and motioned Skye to one of the low maid-of-honor chairs by her side. The other women quickly found their seats, one being forced to stand behind the Queen's chair; and the courtiers began to come forward to pay their respects to the Queen. Some faces were familiar to Skye, others were not, and she paid little attention to the pageant about her. It bored her. Court usually bored her. Only when most of the courtiers had paid homage to the Queen and the majordomo called out, "Edmond, Petit Sieur de Beaumont," was her interest revived, and she looked up.

Although her Kerry-blue eyes widened slightly, Skye gave no other sign of her surprise and shock, for the man coming toward her was one of the handsomest she had ever seen. He was also a dwarf. He was not misshapen like so many dwarfs, but rather well formed, and he was certainly dressed in the height of fashion. His doublet was made from cloth of gold, sewn all over with tiny golden brilliants and edged in gold lace at the neck and the sleeves. His short, round cloth-of-gold breeches were lined in stiff horsehair in order to puff them out fashionably. His stockings were gold silk, embroidered in gold brilliants and tiny black jet beads, and his flat-soled shoes were of gold leather with black rosettes. His short cape was of black velvet, lined in cloth of gold and trimmed in silver fox. At his waist hung a gold sword, proportioned to his size, and twinkling with rubies and diamonds.

As he reached the foot of Elizabeth Tudor's throne he bowed smartly. "Majesty," he said in a deep voice, a rather large voice for one so small.

"Welcome, Edmond de Beaumont," Elizabeth said. "I hope that you have been enjoying your stay here in England."

"English hospitality is justly famous, Your Majesty," was the reply.

"Lady Burke, come forward," the Queen commanded, and Skye rose from her low seat, and came to stand next to the Queen's chair. "M'sieur de Beaumont, may I present to you Lady Skye Burke, who has agreed to go to Beaumont de Jaspre as your uncle's bride."

Around them there was a hum of surprise.

Skye curtseyed to Edmond de Beaumont, noting with some embarrassment that as she bowed low he was treated to a fine, indeed almost indecent view of her breasts. As she rose he said softly, "My uncle is a *very, very* fortunate man, Your Majesty." Skye blushed to the roots of her raven hair, yet as she raised her eyes to Edmond de Beaumont, she saw that though his face was polite and serious, his violet-colored eyes were laughing.

"I can only hope your uncle is as charming as his nephew, M'sieur de Beaumont," she replied.

"I do not think that charming is a word one would use in connection with Uncle Fabron," was the reply, and again the eyes were laughing at her.

"Oh, dear!" Skye said without thinking, and she bit her lip in obvious worry.

Edmond de Beaumont burst out laughing. "Are you always so honest, Lady Burke?" he asked.

"Our dear Skye is most candid, is she not, Dudley?" remarked the Queen.

"Indeed, Majesty," Dudley replied. "Lady Burke always says what she thinks. A most refreshing, and often stimulating trait, M'sieur de Beaumont."

Skye shot Dudley a look of undisguised venom, which Edmond de Beaumont was quick to note. Now why, he wondered, does the lady so obviously dislike the Earl of Leicester? Did he perhaps rebuff her? No, de Beaumont thought. She did not look like the type of woman who would chase after a popinjay like Lord Dudley.

"You are to go with M'sieur de Beaumont, dearest Skye, for you will have many questions to ask him about your future home, I am sure," the Queen coyly simpered.

Skye stepped from the Queen's side and accepted Edmond de Beaumont's outstretched hand. Together they turned, bowed to the Queen, and, turning again, moved through the crowded room. They made an almost comical sight for the *petit sieur* was only three feet four inches tall, and Skye stood five feet seven inches in her bare feet. No one, however, dared to laugh, for the Queen was a tyrant where good manners were concerned, and this little man was her honored guest.

"And *do* you have many questions to ask me, Lady Burke?"

Skye paused a moment, and then said, "I suppose I shall, m'sieur. I am only now getting used to the idea of marriage with your uncle."

Edmond de Beaumont led her to a quiet alcove with a window

seat. She sat, and he helped himself to two goblets of chilled white wine from a serving man's tray. Handing her one, he sat facing her. "Do you not wish to marry my uncle?"

"I do not have a real choice, m'sieur. I must obey the Queen."

"Is there another gentleman that you prefer to my uncle?"

"No, M'sieur de Beaumont, there is no one else. My husband is dead but two months, and I shall mourn Niall for the rest of my life."

He drank deeply. He was relieved that there was no one else. It was possible that she would learn to love his uncle, and that they would be happy. God only knew that it would save him a great deal of difficulty. His cousin, Garnier de Beaumont, his uncle's only living child, was a half-wit; and so his uncle had made Edmond his heir. But if he became the Duc de Beaumont then he must marry, and what girl would have him? Oh, he was well enough favored, but he was tiny. How often he had been mocked by men and women alike because of his height. His size certainly did not affect his intelligence, but no one ever bothered to find that out about Edmond de Beaumont, because he stood only three feet four inches tall.

This extravagantly beautiful woman, however, did not seem either amused or appalled by his size. She spoke to him plainly, and without guile. He looked up at her again, and said quietly, "I respect your grief, Lady Burke." Then to change the subject he asked, "Do you have children?"

Her smile lit her whole face, and she said, "I have four living sons and two daughters."

"They will like Beaumont de Jaspre," he assured her. "The climate is mild and pleasant most of the year, and your children will enjoy bathing in the sea."

"My children will not be coming with me, m'sieur."

"But why?" He was surprised, and now he understood the reason for the sadness that lurked deep in her fabulous blue-green eyes.

"My eldest son, Ewan, must remain on his lands, m'sieur. His full brother, Murrough, is a page with the Earl of Lincoln's household, and must remain with the court if he is to earn lands and possibly a peerage of his own. My third son is the Earl of Lynmouth. He is the Queen's favorite page, the small boy who now stands on Her Majesty's right. As for my youngest son, Lord

Burke, he is but two and a half months old. He, too, must stay on his lands, and he is much too tender to travel besides. My daughters are to remain here also. Willow is nine, and heiress to my business partner, Sir Robert Small. Deirdre is just sixteen months old, and, like her baby brother, too young to travel."

"I do not understand, Lady Burke, why you agreed to this marriage," Edmond de Beaumont said. "I have been told that you are outrageously wealthy in both monies and lands, and now you say you have children much too young to leave. Surely you are not one of those women who seek a great title?"

"If the choice were truly mine, M'sieur de Beaumont, and your uncle the Holy Roman Emperor himself, I should not wed with him; but the choice is not mine. It is the Queen's will that I do so, and therefore I must."

"Why?" He was distressed for her.

"Because I am Irish, M'sieur de Beaumont, and the English have had a stranglehold on my homeland for several centuries now. I agreed to marry your uncle because if I did not, my infant son's lands would have been parceled out among the Anglo-Irish, those sycophants of the English monarchs.

"I am a realist, M'sieur de Beaumont," Skye continued. "I could not hope to beat the English in a fair fight, for unfortunately the Irish are not a nation able to unite behind one ruler. If we were the English would not be in our homeland. My duty is to my children, and to the memories I have of their fathers. I am responsible for the lands of four families, as well as an enormous commercial interest and a fleet of vessels. Should I beggar myself and my children for an ideal? I think not."

"Madame, I wonder if you are the right woman for my uncle."

"Why?" She smiled at him. "Because I am outspoken, m'sieur?"

"My uncle is used to a more complacent type of female," he smiled back, and she thought that he had a beautiful smile.

"If you complain to the Queen that I am not suitable," she said in a more serious tone, "Elizabeth will wonder what I have done to incur your displeasure, m'sieur. That would endanger my infant son, Lord Burke. I promise you that I shall be exactly the type of wife your uncle seeks. They tell me that he is old, and not in good health. I vow to nurse him most tenderly."

"Who on earth told you that my uncle is elderly, Lady Burke?" Edmond de Beaumont was surprised. "Uncle Fabron is but forty-five, and is in excellent health." He saw the shock upon her face. "My God, they have lied to you in order to gain your cooperation!"

She was very pale, and he placed a surprisingly warm hand over her trembling, clenched ones. "Lord Burghley said that your uncle was an older man in ill health. That I should be home within a year or two at the most. Dear God, my babies! I shall never see my babies again!"

"This is infamous!" Edmond de Beaumont accepted the fact of arranged marriages, but this beautiful woman was being used in a terrible way. "I shall speak to the Queen myself," he said. "You cannot be made to leave your children like this!"

"*No!*" Her blue eyes were huge and frightened. "M'sieur de Beaumont, you must not speak to anyone of this! You will do me no kindness, and I shall lose everything. I have accepted my lot, and so must you." She turned her hand so she might grasp his tiny one. "*Please, m'sieur*," she said.

"Madam, I am already your devoted servant," he answered. "It will be as you wish. I would be your friend."

"You already are, M'sieur de Beaumont, and since you are, I think you should call me Skye." She calmed herself now, assured by his gentleness and air of concern.

"With pleasure, Skye, if you will call me Edmond."

Across the room Robert Dudley sneered to the Queen, "Look how she simpers at the dwarf so sweetly. It sickens me! Is the duc a dwarf also? How amusing that would be, Bess! It would take two of them to equal one Geoffrey Southwood, or Niall Burke!" He laughed nastily.

"Are you jealous, my lord?" Elizabeth Tudor's voice was sharp. "I thought you had gotten over your passion for Lady Burke. Do not try my patience, Robert. I have been most generous with you, and you will repay my kindness."

"I adore you, Bess! You well know it, but you will not marry me. I am only a man, madam!"

"Fie, Rob, lower your voice," the Queen chided. "Others are looking at us, and in answer to your question the Duc de Beaumont is not a dwarf. His nephew showed me his miniature, which was sent for his intended bride. He is a well-favored gentleman. Lady Burke should not be overly unhappy in Beaumont de Jaspre."

"She will be out of the way," Dudley answered. "You do not

fool me, Bess. I know you far too well. Lady Burke is in your subtle mind an enemy. By sending her to Beaumont de Jaspre you rid yourself of that particular enemy."

"I also gain a spy against France, Spain, and the Papal States," the Queen said quietly. "I have no doubt that Lady Burke will hear many interesting things that she can pass on to us."

"By God, Bess," Lord Dudley said admiringly. "You are totally ruthless!"

The Queen smiled archly at the Earl of Leicester. "Dance with me, Rob," she said, "and we shall discuss what to give Lady Burke as a wedding gift."

Skye and Edmond de Beaumont were watching the Queen and Lord Dudley capering merrily to a sprightly tune played by the musicians, when William Cecil came up to sit with them. "So you have made friends with the Petit Sieur de Beaumont, Lady Burke, and you, m'sieur, see the exquisite prize we are sending to your uncle. Do you think that he will be pleased?"

"How could he not be, Lord Burghley?"

"The Queen has decided that you will depart here at the end of April, Lady Burke. M'sieur de Beaumont will travel with you and your party to Beaumont de Jaspre."

"The Queen has promised me that I may remain in England until Sir Robert has returned, my lord. *I will not go until then!* What is all this indecent haste about? I will leave by mid-May. I must first have a trousseau made, for the gowns I have to wear here in England and Ireland will be totally unsuitable in a warmer climate. Would you have me arrive to wed the duc in my shift?"

Edmond de Beaumont chuckled aloud at the look of discomfort upon the face of the Queen's Secretary of State and Lord Treasurer. "There is no great rush, Lord Burghley," he said. "After all, my uncle is in robust health, and the miniature I shall send him tomorrow of Lady Burke should increase his ardor. If we leave in mid-May as Skye suggests, we will be in Beaumont de Jaspre by June, a perfect time for a wedding, especially there."

"Ah . . . yes, yes!" William Cecil began to edge nervously away.

"You have been most kind, my lord," Skye said sweetly, but her eyes were blazing with anger. "How fortunate I am that my husband-to-be is in such fine health."

"Indeed, indeed, madam!" Lord Burghley murmured, and then turned and hurried off into the crowd.

"You are no mean opponent," Edmond de Beaumont laughed.

"What miniature?" Skye demanded.

"Of you? I intended to paint it tonight," he answered her.

"You are an artist?"

"I do competent portraits," he said. "If you would give me but a few minutes I shall do a quick sketch of you for your miniature."

"Would it be easier if I sat for the portrait, Edmond?"

"You would be willing?" He was delighted.

"I would be willing. Besides, your company is far preferable to that of the hangers-on here at court. I am sure that the Queen will excuse us if we ask her."

Elizabeth Tudor was delighted, yet at the same time she felt irritated. She was relieved that Skye was accepting this marriage to the Duc de Beaumont so easily, but she wondered why. What were Skye's thoughts? She had become friendly quickly enough with the duc's charming dwarf nephew. Was she planning some sort of mischief? The Queen smiled brightly at Skye and Edmond de Beaumont.

"Of course you may be excused, M'sieur de Beaumont. You also, dearest Skye. I hope that M'sieur has been able to answer your many questions."

"Indeed, Majesty," Skye replied sweetly. "He is a veritable font of knowledge, and I am now most anxious to reach Beaumont de Jaspre."

The Queen murmured politely and held out her hand for Edmond de Beaumont to kiss. He did so with exquisite grace and elegance, and Elizabeth remarked, "Gracious, sir, your lack of height does not seem to impede your manners. Such delicacy and style!"

"Was it not you, madame, who once remarked that what a person is physically should not deter him in any way."

The Queen laughed heartily. "You are welcome at my court at any time, M'sieur de Beaumont. I like men of beauty and wit, and although your beauty is small, your wit is great!"

Skye curtseyed politely, and then she and Edmond de Beaumont made their way from the hall. When they had exited the overly hot and noisy room Skye asked, "Where are you taking me, m'sieur?"

"I am housed here at Whitehall. My apartments are not far." He moved swiftly along, his short legs seeming to take greater strides than her own long ones. Finally he turned down a corridor and entered the second apartment on the left. Skye recognized the section of the palace as the one in which state visitors were housed.

A swarthy man hurried forward as they entered the antechamber. "Good evening, M'sieur de Beaumont," he said.

"Guy, this is Lady Burke, who is to marry my uncle. I am going to do her miniature tonight and ship it off to the duc tomorrow. Fetch my paints!"

"My felicitations, madame," Guy said. "Your paints, m'sieur. At once!"

"He has been with me since my childhood," Edmond de Beaumont said. "Sit over there, on that tapestried chair, Skye. Damn me, my dear, you are beautiful, aren't you? Your skin! I don't think I have the skill to capture its luminescence. When we get back to Beaumont de Jaspre I want to do a full portrait of you." He rattled on nonstop while Guy brought him his easel, a canvas, his paints and brushes. He was quickly and totally absorbed in what he was doing.

"Would Madame enjoy some chilled wine?" Guy was at her elbow inquiring politely.

"I should, thank you, Guy."

The servant was quickly back with a delicate Venetian crystal goblet of a fruity pale-rose-colored wine. "It is m'sieur's favorite," he explained. "I think you will enjoy it, *Madame la duchesse.*"

Madame la duchesse! God's bones! Skye thought. I am to be Madame la Duchesse! Then she thought of how Cecil had lied to her about the duc's health. Well, there was nothing she could do about that now, but if the duc turned out to be a kind man she was going to try to bring her younger children to Beaumont de Jaspre. Ewan and Murrough were old enough to survive without her. Her poor O'Flaherty sons; they had had so little of her. She sighed. There was no help for it now. The others, however, she *must* have with her. True, Robin and Willow were already away from home for part of the year; but she had always been able to see them. Being sent to live in another country was a totally different thing.

The Lynmouth holdings would be safe from plunder for their little earl was an Englishman. Richard de Grenville and Adam de Marisco would see to it for her. Uncle Seamus would have to oversee the Burke lands, and she would ask Elizabeth FitzGerald Clinton, the Countess of Lincoln, to help him. Beth was an Irish woman, and would understand her plight. It was a chance that would have to be taken, for Skye could not leave her babies. With the Queen's support and her strong family ties, she felt she could protect her children's wealth even from as far as Beaumont de Jaspre.

How heartless of Cecil! He knew that the duc was relatively young, and healthy; and yet he had deliberately misled her into believing otherwise so she would agree to go and aid his mistress, the Queen by her sacrifice. It mattered not a whit to Cecil that Padraic was but newly born, and wee Deirdre yet an infant. He cruelly and selfishly tore her from her children simply in order to advance the Queen's political aims. *I will never trust the English again*, she thought. Yet there was her beloved Geoffrey, who had never hurt her, and Adam de Marisco and Robbie, and Dame Cecily.

"God's nightshirt!" she swore.

"You're frowning," Edmond de Beaumont said. "Don't frown, sweet Skye. Give me that little half-smile you have when you are deep in thought as you have been."

She smiled at him. "Tell me about Beaumont de Jaspre," she said.

"It's a fairyland," he answered. "It is no more than five miles in width, sandwiched in between Provence and the Languedoc. It extends inland a little over ten miles from the Mediterranean. We are fortunate that above our town of Villerose, the land plateaus until it reaches the mountains that are the border of the duchy. The plateau is fertile, and so between our fine crops and the sea we are quite self-sufficient. That is how we have managed to remain independent from the French, although they would like to gobble us up. France's Queen Mother, Catherine de Medici, offered our duc her daughter, Marguérite, to wife."

"And the duc asked the English queen for a wife instead? I find that hard to believe, Edmond. A French princess would have been quite a prize for your duc."

"The offer was not genuine, and Uncle Fabron knew it. The Princesse de Valois is meant for Henri of Navarre."

"What is your uncle like?" she asked.

"He is a serious man, Skye. Bookish and learned. I will be frank with you; I think that he would have been happier as a religious man, rather than having the responsibility of a duchy such as ours. Still, he is a man who accepts his obligations well. You will be his third wife. The first, Marie de Breil, died after many years of still-births and miscarriages. The second, Blanche de Toulon, died giving birth to Garnier, the duc's son. It is a great pity that he, too, did not die, for he is a half-wit. My uncle has been widowed now for five years. Until recently he could not bring himself to wed again. That is why he made me his heir, but I have convinced him that a healthy male child of his own blood would serve the duchy better than the dwarf son of his younger brother."

"You have no brothers?"

"I have four very normal and, to me, very tall sisters." He laughed. "They are all older than I, and after I was born my parents felt they could not take the chance of having another such as myself. Consequently there are no other legitimate male de Beaumonts except my uncle Fabron, Garnier, and myself. My father died when I was twelve. That is why it is so important to me that my uncle remarry and have a son. If I inherit the duchy I must marry, and what woman would have such a fellow as myself? What kind of children would we produce?" He put down his paintbrush and came over to stand by her knee. "Dear, sweet Skye! You are our last hope!"

She shivered. "Do not say that, Edmond! It frightens me to be the hope of survival for a duchy such as Beaumont de Jaspre."

He smiled his incredibly sweet smile at her, and Skye thought what a pity it was that it could not be he whom she was to marry. Edmond might be small in stature, but he was kind and amusing, and obviously quite intelligent.

"What are you thinking?" he asked her.

"Honestly?"

He nodded.

"That I wish it were you I was to wed."

He looked stunned for a moment, and then he said slowly, "Madam, never have I received such a magnificent compliment!" Then, taking both of her hands in his, he kissed them passionately. "I have not regretted my height in many years, Skye, but this night I do."

"Then I have done you a disservice, Edmond, for I would not hurt you for the world."

"You have not hurt me," he answered, his marvelous violet-colored eyes looking warmly into her Kerry-blue ones, and she knew he desired her. Then he quickly changed the subject back to his uncle. "What else would you like to know about the duc, Skye?"

"What he looks like," she said with feminine curiosity.

"He stands about two inches taller than you, his eyes are black, his hair the same."

"He has not your beautiful coloring?" she said, disappointed.

"No. His mother was Florentine, mine Castilian. I inherited her honey-colored hair and violet eyes. Uncle Fabron is more imposing than I am, for his features are regal whereas mine are soft." He turned and went back to his easel. "We have plenty of time to talk, Skye, but let me finish this miniature while we do. You must indulge my curiosity now. Who is this Sir Robert Small you will not leave England without seeing?"

"Robbie?" She smiled broadly. "Robbie is one of the two best friends I have in this whole world! He is my business partner, a marvelous man, and I adore him! He has never married, and his sister, Dame Cecily, is a childless widow. My second husband was a Spaniard, and he died before my eldest daughter, Willow, our only child, was born. Robbie and his sister adopted her and made her their heiress. With all the bad feeling between England and Spain, it is better for my daughter that she have an English surname, be an Englishwoman. Although her parentage is no secret, little is thought of it because she is Willow Mary Small."

"This Sir Robert? He is due back from a voyage shortly?" Edmond de Beaumont asked.

"Aye. His advance ship arrived in Plymouth a short while ago, and Robbie could appear any time between today and the end of the month," she said happily.

To Skye's surprise, Robbie appeared the very next morning, shouting her name as he entered Greenwood's paneled reception hall.

"Skye lass! Dammit, Skye, where are you?" Sir Robert Small, sea captain and owner of Wren Court, an exquisite Devon house, stood with his legs spread wide, his homely, freckled face anticipatory.

Skye's secretary, Jean Morlaix, came hurrying downstairs from the library where he had been working, a smile upon his usually serious features. "Good day to ye, Jean. How is your Marie, and the children?"

"Very well, captain," Jean Morlaix greeted Robbie. "It was a good voyage, I trust?"

"Splendid!" was the enthusiastic reply.

"Robbie!" Skye stood at the top of the staircase's second landing. Her long black hair was tousled from sleep, her feet bare, her pale-blue quilted silk dressing gown open at the neck. With a glad cry she flew down the stairs and into his arms. "Oh, Robbie! You are home safe!"

He hugged her lovingly. She was the daughter he might have had, had he ever taken the time to marry. Then he kissed her on both cheeks, asking as he did so, "Is Niall with you, lass?"

Jean Morlaix stiffened, and Skye's smile faded. "Niall is dead, Robbie. He was murdered this past February by his first wife, the nun. That bitch, Claire O'Flaherty, insinuated herself into St. Mary's Convent, attached herself to poor, mad Darragh like a bloodsucking leech, and then tortured her with the idea that Niall was coming to reclaim her. Claire terrorized Darragh to the point that she was amenable even to murder to save herself. Darragh told the Mother Superior of her convent that she stabbed Niall several times, and there was a great deal of blood. Then she and Claire dragged his body to the beach, and the last thing Darragh remembers of the event is the waves lapping at Niall's body. When the Mother Superior and the other nuns hurried to the beach they found the tide fully in, and Niall's body gone."

"Christ's body!" Robbie swore softly, and then his arms went back around her. For a moment she wept softly, moving her head into his shoulder for refuge, and his weathered, square hand stroked her dark hair comfortingly. "Ah, lass, ah lass, Robbie is here now, and I'll make it all right! See if I don't, Skye lass."

"The MacWilliam is gone also, Robbie," she said, regaining some control." I kept his death a secret, and came to England to gain the Queen's protection for my infant son, Padraic. She will confirm his title and his lands, but only for a price. I am to become the wife of the Duc de Beaumont de Jaspre. I must leave England by mid-May."

"The Devil you say!" he cried. "This is some plot of William Cecil's, I vow. What of your children? Has that old spider thought of your children? Aye! I'll wager he has! He's thought what fine hostages they'll make. Would he separate a mother from her babies? Aye, he would to serve the Queen!"

"Beaumont de Jaspre is at the moment of vital interest to England, Robbie, and the duc requested that the Queen send him a wife. I am the bride they have chosen. I must go," Skye sobbed.

"It's indecent!" Robbie raged. "You've not even had the proper time to mourn Niall decently. I don't like it. I don't like it one bit! What is this duc fellow like, tell me? Does the Queen know the sort of man she's sending you to wed with? She's as quick to send you off to marry as she is to sidestep the issue of marriage herself."

"I met the duc's nephew only last night at Whitehall, Robbie." She slipped from his protective embrace and took him by the hand. "Come upstairs with me, and we will have something to eat. I have not eaten yet, and I'm ravenous."

He followed along next to her. "Aye, I'm famished myself. I came directly from the Pool, I was so anxious to see you. The captain of the *Royal Harry* sent a small sailing vessel out of Plymouth to intercept my *Mermaid*, to tell me to dock here in London, as you were at Greenwood. Aye, I could eat something."

"Beef," she tempted him. "A nice haunch of juicy rare beef?"

Robert Small's kindly blue eyes grew soft with longing. "Do you know how long it's been since I tasted beef?" he said.

"Aye, Robbie, I know. Salted meat and hardtack filled with weevils no matter how carefully it's stored is what you've had to eat these last months."

They had reached her apartments, and Daisy came forward smiling as they entered. "Welcome home, Captain Small," she said.

Sliding an arm about her waist Robbie gave the girl a smack on her rosy cheek. "Daisy, my girl, you're as pretty as ever!"

Daisy giggled. "Thank you, sir," she said, dodging his hand that made to swat at her bottom. "*Sir!*"

Robbie chuckled. "I've missed that too, Skye lass," he said.

Skye laughed, not in the least shocked, for Robbie had a prodigious appetite where women were concerned. It was probably the reason he had never married. No one woman could satisfy him for long. Which was just as well, for big or little; fair or dark, blondes, brunettes, and redheads; Robbie adored them all.

"Captain Small and I would like some breakfast, Daisy. And see that cook roasts a bit of beef for the captain."

"Yes, m'lady." Daisy curtseyed and hurried from the room.

"Come sit by the fire, Robbie," Skye invited, seating herself in a tapestried wing chair. "The mornings still have a chill to them."

"What is the duc's nephew like?" he demanded, not losing sight of the subject as he settled himself in the matching chair opposite her. In the fireplace a good oak blaze crackled warmly, taking the dampness from the riverview room.

"Edmond de Beaumont is a dwarf," she said.

"Is the duc?"

"Nay. Edmond says his uncle is at least a couple inches taller than I am. You will like Edmond, Robbie, when you meet him at dinner this evening. He is an amusing, intelligent man."

"You like him." It was a statement.

"Aye, I like him. He is as outraged as you were that I am forced to leave my babies behind. He offered to speak to the Queen for me."

"You forbade him, I trust?"

"Of course," Skye replied. "He says that his uncle is a serious and bookish man."

"The duc has no children?" Robbie asked.

"One, a boy of five, but the child is a half-wit, and the duc has made Edmond his heir until he has a son of his own."

"So you're being sent to play the brood mare to this duc's stallion in hopes that you'll give him children. I don't like it!"

"Actually, I don't think the Queen cares one way or another whether I give the duc children. She is more interested in the bits and pieces of information I may pick up from France, Spain, and the Papal States to send back to her. I am to be Elizabeth Tudor's ears."

He nodded. "I see now why they are sending you. A young girl would be apt to fall in love with her husband, and become totally engrossed in having and raising a family. No use at all to the Queen and Cecil. You, however, are more mature, and you'll keep your mind on the Queen's business."

"Aye, Robbie," she teased him. "I am to shortly celebrate my twenty-ninth birthday. I am most mature."

He smiled at her, then sobered. "You know what I mean," he said. "You have experienced great love in your life, not just once, but three times. You are barely widowed, and not apt to fall in love easily again. Your duke doesn't sound like the sort of man who will go out of his way to capture your heart. He marries to beget children. You will therefore have the time to serve the Queen, which is exactly what Elizabeth Tudor and William Cecil have in mind. I don't like it, Skye. It could be very dangerous, my lass."

"I have no intention of going out of my way for the Queen, Robbie. This marriage is not to my liking. Once again the Queen has betrayed my loyalty and my friendship. I am cornered like an animal, as she knew I would be when she approved Lord Burghley's plan. But I had no choice but go to her for aid. I am a woman alone. I chose the strongest ally, even if I can't trust her entirely."

Robert Small nodded. Skye had done the best she could in a very difficult situation. He knew that no one, not even a man, could have done better. "I'm coming with you," he said.

"*What?*" Her blue eyes were wide with surprise.

"I'm coming with you," he repeated. "Listen to me, lass. I will make Beaumont de Jaspre my home port on the Mediterranean, for the time being, the way I did in Algiers. There is plenty of trading to be done along the North African coast, in Spain, why, in Istanbul itself! I don't want you cut off from everyone you love; at least not until I know what kind of man this is, and if you'll be happy."

"Robbie, I thank you," Skye said, and her eyes were damp. "I was so afraid, and until now I did not even dare admit it to myself."

"Ye're only human," he muttered gruffly, and she hid a smile.

"I saw Adam de Marisco before I came to London," Skye said.

He noted the brief, sad look that filled her eyes for a moment. "Have you told him of your impending marriage?"

"No."

"Tell him. He may want to see you before you leave England. Be fair, Skye."

"I can't hurt him anymore, Robbie. We cannot see each other that we don't end up in bed. I love him as a friend, and I would be happy to be his wife; but Adam says no. He says it isn't enough for me even if I don't know it. He also told me that he will not be my lover."

"You'll break his heart, Skye, if you don't tell him. Let him make the choice of coming up to London or not; but at least tell him. You can't go off to some Mediterranean duchy for God knows how long without telling him!"

"Very well. I will write him this morning, and send one of the grooms to Lynmouth. They'll see it gets to him from there."

The door to Skye's dayroom opened, and Daisy entered followed by several maidservants laden down with trays of food and pitchers of drink, which were placed on an oaken sideboard. "Set that round table between the chairs," Daisy directed, and when it was done, she spread a fine linen cloth on it herself. Next came the plates, highly polished pewter rounds and matching goblets as well as heavy linen napkins. From a long narrow black leather case Daisy took two twin-pronged gold forks, the newest invention from Florence, and placed one by each plate.

"I've used these before," Robbie noted. "You spear the food with them."

"Aye," Skye answered him. "They're very handy, and help to keep the fingers clean."

"Wine or ale, captain?" Daisy demanded.

"Nut-brown ale?" he asked, and his eyes sparkled.

"Yes, sir!"

"I've not had ale in months, Daisy lass. Pour away!"

Daisy poured the ale into the pewter goblet from a frosty, blue earthenware pitcher, then went to the sideboard for a platter that held a thick slab of rare beef, swimming in its own juices. Taking his fork, she lifted the beef from the platter onto his own plate, then replaced the fork on his plate and handed him a knife. "Cook says you're to eat every morsel of that beef, Captain."

With a quick glance of apology at Skye, Robbie crossed himself in blessing and fell upon the beef, cutting a wedge, popping it in his mouth, chewing it down, a beatific smile lighting his rugged features as he did so.

In the middle of the table Daisy placed stone crocks of sweet butter and honey, and a small cutting board with a fresh, steaming loaf of bread. Next came a bowl of Valencia oranges from Spain. Daisy served her mistress from a small serving dish, spooning onto Skye's plate a fluffy mixture of eggs and tiny bits of ham and green onion.

"Wine, m'lady?"

"The white, please," said Skye, crossing herself. Then she took up a forkful of the eggs.

Their mistress and her guest fed, the servants withdrew. Skye and Robbie ate in silence for the next few minutes. Then as Robbie mopped a piece of bread about his plate, sopping up the beef juices, she said, "Edmond gave me a miniature of the duc. Would you like to see it?"

"Aye," came the reply. "Is he plain or fair?"

"If he smiled perhaps he would be fair. He is certainly not plain." She rose from the table and moved into her bedchamber. Returning, she handed him a small oval edged in gold studded with pearls. Robert Small took the miniature from her and stared down at it. The man pictured was clean-shaven; his skin bronzed by his climate. He had a high forehead and a square jaw. His nose was long and aquiline, the nostrils flaring slightly. His mouth was large, the lips thin. His black eyes were almond-shaped and tipped up just the tiniest bit at the corners. His black hair was cut short, and was curly. He looked at the viewer directly, his face impersonal and cold.

Robert Small did not like what he saw. There was a hint of cruelty in the man's mouth; a touch of overbearing pride in the way he held his head. He would not be an easy man. He did not look to be a man whose heart could be softened by a sweet smile or a gentle hand; and he was certainly not the type of man to be given a beautiful wife. More than likely he would be insanely jealous of any other man who looked upon his bride. Damn Elizabeth Tudor, Robbie thought. She was undoubtedly one of the finest rulers England had ever had for all she was a woman; but she had no heart. That was her greatest failing. She used people, playing with them as a child plays with her toys, moving her subjects this way and that way to suit her own convenience, without thought for their happiness or well-being. It saddened him doubly; once for the Queen herself, for she was basically a good woman, and secondly for Skye, whom he loved with all his heart. She was like his own daughter for all she had been born an O'Malley, and he didn't want to see her hurt.

"Well?" She looked directly at him, and he quickly masked his thoughts.

"You're right," he said. "The duc would be fair if he smiled. As it is, he looks stern, but then perhaps he was nervous posing for his bride. You'll undoubtedly bring a smile to his lips when he meets you."

"There's something about his eyes that frightens me," she said quietly.

"Nonsense," Robbie replied with bluff reassurance. "Don't form any opinions, lass, until you've met the gentleman."

"It makes no difference," she said. "I must wed him, like him or no."

Before they might continue their conversation the door to Skye's apartments opened, and the young Earl of Lynmouth ran into the room. "Mama!" He flung himself into her arms.

"Robin! Oh, my dearest Robin!" Then she began to cry.

"Mama!" Robin Southwood's voice held an amused note that reminded Skye of his late father, Geoffrey, and she wept all the more. "God's bones, Uncle Robbie!" said the boy. "I think I had best leave."

"Don't you dare!" Skye wiped her eyes on her handkerchief, hastily retrieved from her dressing-gown pocket. "It is just that I am so very glad to see you, Robin, and you look and sound more like your father each day." She held him at arm's length. "You have grown taller. Are you happy at court, Robin? I was so proud of you last night. But you are so young to be a page. Are you sure that you wouldn't rather live at Lynmouth, my love? Or perhaps you will come with me to Beaumont de Jaspre."

"Beaumont de Jaspre? Where is that, Mama? Why on earth are you going to a place called Beaumont de Jaspre?" Robin had been out of the room when the Queen had briefly announced Skye's betrothal the previous evening. He had been sent to fetch Her Majesty's pomander.

"I can see that the court gossip has not caught up with you, Robin. The Queen is sending me to Beaumont de Jaspre, which is a small duchy between Provence and the Languedoc. I am to be bride to its duc."

"That is outrageous!" The boy's small face was a mask of stunned anger. "My stepfather is barely cold in his grave, and *she* asks you to marry with another? Surely you have misunderstood her, Mama. The Queen would not do such a thing to you. She wouldn't!"

Skye could not destroy his faith in Elizabeth Tudor. He was an Englishman, and not just any Englishman. Despite his youth, he was one of England's premier noblemen. But his title and all his wealth would amount to nothing if he did not give his complete loyalty to the Crown, and Skye understood that. "Robin," she said quietly as she drew him toward her, "the Queen needs my help very badly. She must have a safe haven for English ships in the Mediterranean, and Beaumont de Jaspre will provide that haven. She must have a listening post into France and Spain, and again Beaumont de Jaspre will provide her with it. All the duc requires of England in return is a wife. It is the Queen's decision that I be that wife, and I am proud that she trusts me to aid her, even though I am Irish," Skye said wryly. "Niall would be proud of me, as would your father, and Willow's, too."

"I had not thought about it that way, Mama," he said, but his lime-green eyes filled with tears, and his small lower lip trembled. "Will I ever see you again, Mama?"

"Oh, Robin!" She hugged him quickly. "I have only to get settled, and then you will come to me. You, and Willow, and Deirdre, and your new baby brother, Padraic. Even Murrough and Ewan, if they want to come also!"

"When do you go, Mama?" His little voice quavered slightly.

"Within the month, Robin." She kissed him soundly, once on each cheek. "Come now, my little love, I've been in Ireland since last autumn, and you didn't miss me at all, I vow! You are having far too much fun with the court, my lord of Lynmouth!"

A small smile touched his lips, and he looked up at her with a look so like his father's that Skye's heart almost broke with the rush of memories. "Perhaps, madam," he allowed, and she laughed.

"You are a villain," she teased him, "and you grow more like Geoffrey every day."

"Robin Southwood!" Willow stood in the dayroom door, her small foot impatiently tapping. "How long have you been in our mother's house and not come to bid me good day?!"

Robin pulled from his mother's embrace and, turning, made his half-sister a most elegant leg, sweeping his small dark green velvet cap with its pheasant's feather from his blond head as he did so. "Your servant, Mistress Small," he said as he bowed low.

Willow curtseyed prettily, spreading the skirts of her rose-pink velvet gown as she did so. "Good day to you, my lord Earl," she said.

Then with a giggle and a whoop the two children were hugging each other as their mother smiled happily at their antics.

"Is there room for me, too?" a slightly deeper voice inquired.

Skye turned to see a tall, dark-haired boy standing in her doorway. "Murrough!"

"Good morning, Mama." He came forward and kissed her. "Lady Clinton has released me from my duties as long as you are in London with the court. I hope that will be all right." He looked anxiously at her. Thank God, she thought guiltily, there was nothing of his father about him.

"Dearest Murrough, I am delighted, and so grateful to Elizabeth Clinton for letting you come!" Skye hugged her second eldest son. "You have grown thin. Are you eating properly? I know how it is with pages. You are always so busy there isn't enough time to eat or to sleep."

He grinned down at her. "Yes, I am eating, but I have grown four inches in the last year, Mama. I guess now that my meals have to go further I need to eat even more if I am to satisfy you. How is Ewan?"

"He's fine," she replied. Then, "You miss him, don't you?"

"Aye, I miss him, and Ireland, too."

"You understand why you must stay here, Murrough?"

"Aye, Mama, I understand. I am landless, and even if you settle monies on me, a man without his own land is nothing."

"There is Joan Southwood to think of too, Murrough. She deserves her own home."

"How is she?" he asked.

"Growing quite lovely, Murrough. Her hair has become a beautiful golden brown, and reaches to her hips; and her eyes have just a hint of Geoffrey's green in them. They are quite a delicious hazel color. She is, of course, as sweet-natured as ever, and works quite diligently on the items of her trousseau she believes you will appreciate. She is half through a large tapestry depicting a knight slaying a dragon. Anne says she is a very accomplished needlewoman. She is going to make you a fine wife."

"I know, Mother, and I thank you for making me such a good match. Joan is a good girl, and will suit me admirably. I'll win her, and the children we will have someday, fair lands in the Queen's service. See if I don't!"

"I know that you will, Murrough." Skye gave him another hug. "You know of my impending marriage?"

"Aye. Is it what you want?"

"No, but I have no choice. I must protect your half-brother's lands, and the Anglo-Irish in the Dublin Pale eye the Burke lands like ravenous wolves. I needed a favor from the Queen, and royalty never gives from the heart."

He nodded in understanding. Murrough O'Flaherty was twelve years old. He had been two when his mother disappeared, and six when he had been reunited with her again. He was nine when his stepfather, Geoffrey Southwood, the Earl of Lynmouth, had died, and ten when he had been sent into service as a page with the Earl and Countess of Lincoln's household. Of necessity he had grown to maturity quickly. He knew that with his mother's money he should never want for the material things in life, but he also knew that if he was to win his own lands, and, he hoped, a title, it must be in the service of England's Queen. He comprehended, perhaps better than any of his brothers and sisters, his mother's difficult position.

"Do you want me with you?" he asked her half hopefully, for he loved her dearly.

Skye's eyes filled with quick tears, which she rapidly blinked away. "Thank you, Murrough," she said. "When I am settled I will want you to visit me, and meet your new stepfather, but I will not spoil the progress you have made here at court." She touched his cheek gently in a maternal gesture of gratitude. "Go and speak with your brother and sister now, my knight errant."

He moved off, and Robbie, who had been sitting opposite her the entire time, sniffed loudly. "They're a fine litter, your children," he muttered.

"Go see Dame Cecily now," she scolded him. "She is probably up and wondering where you are."

"When is Edmond de Beaumont coming?"

"He's been asked for seven. I think I shall have the children, too. There are no other guests. Just you, your sister, and myself."

He nodded. "We'll not be late? I have some business to see to this evening."

Skye laughed. "We'll not be late," she said, knowing that his evening "business" was with a whorehouse.

"The beef was good," he said, rising, and then ambled out of her dayroom, patting the children's heads as he went.

"Who wants to go riding with me?" Skye demanded of her children, and they all noisily assented. "Go and change then," she ordered them. "I shall be ready in fifteen minutes, and anyone who's not won't go!"

The two boys and the girl scattered out the door of her apartments, and Skye called to Daisy.

It was one of those rare, very warm April days in England. There was not a cloud in the flawless blue sky, and the sun shone with a clear yellow light. The flowering trees were all in bloom, the meadows bright green with new growth. Skye and her children rode along the river, enjoying their time together. Afterward they picnicked in the garden behind Greenwood House, watching the river traffic as it passed them by, the children gorging themselves with meat pastries, early wild strawberries, and watered wine. Stuffed and sleepy, they lay upon their backs, talking and blowing at the bumblebees and butterflies who ventured near them. As the afternoon lengthened they all fell asleep in the soft, warm air. It was there Daisy found them; Skye, her arms spread wide and protective about her two sons, Willow sleeping across her mother's lap.

For a moment Skye's faithful tiring woman gazed upon her mistress and the three children. They looked so peaceful that it seemed a shame to awaken them. A tear, and then another slid down Daisy's honest English face as she thought of the exile that she and Skye were facing. It wasn't fair of the Queen to send them away, send her lady who was always such a good mother from her children, but then what would the childless Elizabeth Tudor know of maternal feelings. The tears poured freely down Daisy's face now, and she wept for herself as well. What would happen now between herself and Bran Kelly? He had been close, she knew, to declaring himself. She wondered if she would ever see him again.

"You don't have to come with me to Beaumont de Jaspre, Daisy," said Skye, looking up at her servant, seeing the tears and knowing why Daisy wept.

Daisy plumped herself down in the grass next to her mistress. "And who would take care of you, m'lady, if I stayed behind?"

"It is several weeks before I leave. You could train a clever lass in that time."

"It wouldn't be the same, m'lady."

"No, Daisy, it wouldn't, but I'd not have you unhappy. You have been my friend as well as my servant."

"That's part of it, m'lady. You're going to a strange place, to a strange man, and who knows what you'll find in this Beaumont de Jaspre. You'll need me! I couldn't leave you, m'lady, I couldn't!"

In her heart Skye was relieved. As it was, she was dreading the journey she must make, and knowing that Daisy was going with her made it a lot easier. "Will it help if I tell you that Captain Kelly will be frequently in Beaumont de Jaspre?"

Daisy's face lit up, and she smiled her gap-toothed smile. "Yes, m'lady, it helps a great deal!" she said happily, then added, "Oh, m'lady! I came to tell you it is time for you and the children to return to the house and dress for dinner. M'sieur de Beaumont will be arriving soon."

The sound of the adult voices had awakened the three children, and they stirred, each sitting up and stretching wide. "Come, poppets," Skye said, moving Willow from her lap and standing up. "Our guest will soon be arriving, and we must be dressed and ready to receive him."

Daisy and the three children scrambled up, and together the five gathered up the picnic things, then made their way back through the garden to the house.

"You will all take baths," Skye commanded her children.

"Yes, Mama," Willow replied dutifully, but Murrough and Robin groaned loudly, rolling their eyes at each other in mock horror.

Skye ignored them, and with Daisy moved upstairs to her own apartments, where the two undermaids already had her oaken tub filled with steaming water, fragrant with bath oil of damask rose, her personal fragrance. The tub had been set before the bedroom fireplace, where a cheerful blaze now burned. While their mistress stood quietly the undermaids removed her clothing and riding boots, then hurried off with the garments to clean and freshen them. Daisy helped Skye up the small ladder and into her tub, pinning her mistress's hair up quickly.

"You want a few minutes to soak, I can tell," Daisy said.

Skye nodded. "I'll call," she replied. "Don't let me daydream too long." She sunk deep into the water, seating herself on the little stool placed within the tub, so she might relax in hot water up to her neck. She had dictated a quick note to Adam de Marisco that morning before she went riding with the children, telling him that the Queen had made a political marriage for her and that she would be leaving England very soon. "Tell him," she said to Jean

Morlaix, "tell him that I want to see him, that he *must* come to London." The letter had been off immediately by one of the Lynmouth grooms, and sitting now in her scented tub, Skye wondered whether Adam would come to her. Robbie was right, of course. She couldn't leave England without seeing him a final time.

Dearest Adam! Adam who wouldn't marry her for fear he might ruin her life by taking her from some great new love she was going to find. She almost laughed aloud at the thought. From the looks of the duc he did not fit *that* description. How much better off she would have been if Adam had wed with her, before she had gone to Cecil. At least Adam was her friend and her confidant, her sometime lover, and she enjoyed being with him. She had been vulnerable when she had appealed to Lord Burghley, and he had used that vulnerability against her. It was the very thing Adam had feared. She sighed. The die was cast, and for all intents and purposes she was on her way to Beaumont de Jaspre.

"Daisy!" she called, drawing herself out of her reverie.

"I'm here, m'lady," came the reply as Daisy hurried in to help bathe her mistress. "I've laid out a black velvet gown, m'lady. The one with the black and silver brocade underskirt."

Skye nodded, not particularly interested in her clothing at this moment; she could trust Daisy to see that she looked her best. Dressing was no longer any fun. When she had had Khalid and Geoffrey and Niall to dress for, then she had cared. Her bath finished, she climbed from the tub and stood quietly while Daisy dried and powdered her. Automatically Skye put on her undergarments, her black silk underblouse, and her black silk stockings, which she fastened with elegant silver-ribboned garters. Silently she slipped her feet into plain black silk shoes with silver rosettes. Then came the underskirt and, finally, the dress with its slashed sleeves showing matching brocade.

"Jewelry?" Daisy asked.

"Pearls," her mistress replied. "Pink pearls. That long doublestrand necklace, the matching earrings, and the hair ornaments."

"Very good, m'lady." Daisy hurried to get the jewel case containing these treasures and, coming back with it, she reverently lifted each piece from the red morocco leather case lined in palest blue silk, and handed it to her mistress.

Skye looped the necklace over her head, and the pearls settled down upon her chest coming just above her deep cleavage. Her earbobs, fat pink pearls, hung from her ears on thin gold wires. While Skye saw to her jewelry, Daisy busied herself brushing out her mistress's long blue-black hair and styling it into the soft French chignon that Skye favored. She then affixed to the heavy, silky mane the pink pearl and gold hair ornaments that matched Skye's necklace and earrings.

"Rings?" Daisy held out another open jewel case.

Skye pondered the selection, picking up several rings and discarding them as quickly. She finally settled on a heart-shaped ruby, a black pearl, and a large round diamond. "These will do," she murmured, pushing them onto her slender fingers. Then, reaching for her scent bottle, she daubed her rose fragrance between her breasts, at her wrists, and behind her ears. Had she been dressing for a lover, she would have spent far more time perfuming herself, and Daisy knew it. "There," Skye said, and she stood up. "I am ready, and our guest has not yet arrived. I shall go downstairs to await him, Daisy. Will you see to the children?"

As she descended the stairs, however, Edmond de Beaumont was coming through the door. He was beautifully attired in green velvet. "Madam," he called to her, "you are even fairer today, if such a thing is possible!" he caught her hand up and kissed it.

"Welcome, Edmond!" she returned his greeting, and led him into her reception salon where, to her surprise, Robbie was already waiting. The sea captain turned, his glance closed and thoughtful. "Why, Robbie," Skye said, "I didn't know that you were down already. Edmond de Beaumont, my dearest friend, and my business partner, Sir Robert Small. Robbie, this is the Petit Sieur de Beaumont, Edmond de Beaumont."

The two men greeted each other cautiously, and then Edmond said, "Thank heavens! When you mentioned this man, Skye, I feared that he might be your lover."

"*My lover?*" Her first thought was to be offended—and angry. She didn't need this sort of thing! Her lover, indeed! Then, suddenly, she saw the humor in the situation, and she giggled. The situation was made even funnier to her mind by Robbie, who, having recovered from his initial shock at Edmond de Beaumont's words, began to roar with outrage.

"Christ's bones! That's a filthy French thought if I ever heard one! Has the Queen given you to a froggie then, Skye? I'll not have it! *Her lover!*" His hand went to his sword. "You've been insulted, and so have I!"

"No, Robbie!" Skye cautioned.

Edmond de Beaumont had quickly realized his mistake, but he was a proud young man, and Robert Small's furious tone had begun to offend him. It was up to her to defuse the situation. Reaching out, she touched Robbie's hand in a gesture of conciliation. "Edmond meant no harm, Robbie." Then she turned to the younger man. "I was not aware that you misunderstood the situation, m'sieur." Her tone was cool.

"You said he was your *cher ami*, madame," was the reply.

"I said he was one of the two best friends that I had in this world, Edmond." She bit her lip to keep from laughing. "God only knows what you will think when you meet Adam de Marisco, my other friend."

"I will think him a very lucky man, madame, and I beg that you forgive me. You also, Sir Robert. In Beaumont de Jaspre a woman is not a friend. She is a wife, a mistress, a mother, or a servant. You understand what I am saying?" He looked very anxious.

Robert Small shook his head. "You can't do this, Skye. Even for the Burke lands, you can't marry this duc. You hear his nephew. They have no respect for a woman's intelligence in this place. You will be a thing to this man, an animal to be bred, no more. I can't allow you to destroy yourself in this manner."

"Robbie, I must obey the Queen! I cannot fight off the Anglo-Irish and their English friends. I need a strong ally, and Elizabeth Tudor is that ally. Her price is high, but pay it I must. If I balk now she will destroy me entirely. It will be all right, you will see. The duc and I shall come to a comfortable arrangement between us."

Robert Small looked to Edmond de Beaumont, but now the young man's face was smooth and devoid of emotion. "Well, M'sieur de Beaumont," Robbie demanded, "will Skye be able to come to an agreement with your uncle, or will it be as I have said?"

"My uncle is an old-fashioned man, Sir Robert, but he has a good mind. He is intelligent, and although Lady Burke's independence will come as a bit of a shock to him, he will come to understand that this is the way she is, and I think he will even enjoy it. His first wife was a distant cousin from Florence, and a very timid lady. My uncle's second wife was the daughter of a neighboring nobleman. She was a vapid little thing, really more a child than a woman.

"You, Skye, are far different from either of those ladies. Be patient with Uncle Fabron. It will take you a little time, but I know that you will win him over, and he will appreciate your intelligence as well as your beauty. You are the perfect wife for him. You must not be concerned, for I live at the castle and I will always be there to be your friend."

"I'll be there also," Robbie said. "Be warned, M'sieur de Beaumont, that I will be making my home in Beaumont de Jaspre until I am sure that Skye is safe and happy." He put his arm about her. "This is the daughter I never had, and she is most dear to me and to my sister. Her eldest daughter is my heiress. For all our lack of blood ties, she is my family, and I will not have her hurt!"

Edmond de Beaumont could not help the admiring look that crept into his violet eyes. He had not doubted from the moment he had first seen Skye that she was a woman that men loved, but that she could command such loyalty was indeed impressive. "You may trust me, Sir Robert," he said. "Skye will be happy in Beaumont de Jaspre. I promise it."

The doors to the salon opened, and Dame Cecily and the children entered. Edmond de Beaumont noted the proud, loving look on Skye's face, but remembering her manners, she introduced him to Sir Robert's sister before drawing her children forward to meet him. Dame Cecily, warned to his size, greeted him courteously before turning to her brother, saying, "I heard you roaring like a lion all the way to the second landing, Robert. I hope that you are not giving M'sieur de Beaumont a bad impression of England and the English."

"On the contrary, madam," Edmond de Beaumont quickly interjected. "Your brother has given me the very best possible impression of the English."

"I want you to meet my children, Edmond," Skye now said. "This," she gestured gracefully with her hand to a tall boy who looked so very much like her, "is my son, Murrough O'Flaherty."

The boy, dressed elegantly in black velvet, white silk, and lace, bowed beautifully, a lock of his hair falling across his forehead as he lowered his head. "M'sieur de Beaumont, I am pleased to greet you," he said in a voice that Edmond could hear was but newly changed.

"And I you, sir," Edmond replied courteously.

"My daughter, Willow," Skye said, and Willow, gowned in red velvet, curtseyed prettily.

Edmond de Beaumont bowed in return. "Mademoiselle Willow."

"My son, Robin, the Earl of Lynmouth," Skye said.

"M'sieur de Beaumont."

Edmond looked at the slender boy in sky-blue velvet and exquisitely done lace. His features were incredibly beautiful, if slightly arrogant. The boy had dark blond hair and unusual lime-green eyes. He was obviously his father's son. "My lord Earl," Edmond de Beaumont said politely, and then turned to Skye. "You have fine children, madam, if these three are an example. I only wish my uncle could see them."

"Should our mother's marriage to your uncle prove a felicitous union," Murrough O'Flaherty said, "then your uncle will meet us all, m'sieur. Our duties here in England can spare us for a short time."

Edmond de Beaumont was amused. The older boy was obviously spokesman for his younger brother and sister, despite the disparity in their ranks. The children were obviously disapproving of their mother's marriage, and who could blame them. "I hope you will come to Beaumont de Jaspre soon," he said. "You will like our small country. The weather is like summer most of the year round, and the sea bathing most delightful."

"I have never bathed in the sea," Willow said.

"Ah, mademoiselle," said Edmond de Beaumont, looking up at her, "I shall take you myself when you come. Our sea is the blue of your English sky, and as clear as crystal. The water is warm, and the sea bottom golden sand. Can you swim?"

Willow shook her head.

"Then I shall teach you, mademoiselle! Would you like that?"

"Oh, yes, m'sieur!" Willow's face was pink with pleasure, and Edmond noted to himself that she, too, must favor her father.

"Will you teach me to swim, too?" Robin asked.

"Indeed, my lord, it would be my pleasure," Edmond replied.

"I know how," Murrough said loftily. "My brother and I learned early. We are a seafaring family, m'sieur."

"Can you sail, sir?" Edmond de Beaumont demanded.

"I can."

"Then you, also, will enjoy Beaumont de Jaspre. The sea about us makes for excellent sailing."

"Perhaps, m'sieur, but I doubt that your waters can equal our fine Irish seas."

"Murrough!" Skye was somewhat shocked by her elder son's intractable attitude. "Please tender your apologies to M'sieur de Beaumont."

"For what?" The boy looked surprised. "Our Irish seas are true seas, worthy of our seafaring talents. I have been told that the Mediterranean is naught but a placid Turkish lake."

Edmond de Beaumont laughed heartily. "Indeed the Turks seem to think so, young Murrough O'Flaherty; but would you not enjoy going Turk-hunting in your own ship someday?"

Murrough's face lit up with a smile. "Indeed, m'sieur, I would!"

"Then perhaps you will use Beaumont de Jaspre's fine harbor facilities for your home base. After all, young Murrough, your mother will be our duchesse."

The boy nodded. "It is a good deep-water harbor, m'sieur?"

"It is."

Murrough smiled again. "Then perhaps I shall not find your Beaumont de Jaspre such a dull place after all, m'sieur."

Skye looked in annoyance at her elder son. "I don't know what has gotten into him," she said to Edmond.

"Growing pains, I suspect, plus the fact that he really doesn't like to see you leave England," Edmond remarked.

"He is very protective of me," she said softly. "How funny it is that my son should be so."

Murrough had moved away from them now, settling himself with his younger siblings. Robbie and Dame Cecily were having a cozy chat by the fireplace. Skye sat herself down in a black oak chair with a tapestried seat and back. Edmond de Beaumont sat by her side.

"I do not think it strange that your son is protective of you," he said. "I find it charming and very touching."

"I am going to miss my children, Edmond. This is what makes it hard for me to go willingly to your uncle."

"It will only be for a short while," he reassured her. "You have been separated from them before. My uncle loves children, and will welcome yours. You will give him children of his own, too. You are a healthy, beautiful woman, and he needs you very much. Let me take you to Beaumont de Jaspre, to a man who will love and cherish you. My Uncle Fabron needs you, Skye. He truly needs you!"

She sighed. "We will travel on my own ship," she said, "and the Queen must give us an escort to get us safely past the Barbary pirates."

"And we leave?" He cocked his handsome head to one side.

"Will the beginning of May suit, m'sieur?" There was a small smile upon her beautiful face.

"You will not regret your decision to come to Beaumont de Jaspre, Skye!" he said fervently.

"I hope not, Edmond," she said quietly. "I hope not."

Chapter 3

Adam de Marisco had read Skye's message, and his first thought was to refuse her. Another meeting between them was sure to result in one of their passionate couplings. He had never known a woman who was so sexually attuned to him. To even think about her was to want her unbearably.

"Damn!" he growled softly. He loved her so terribly, but he had always known that he would never have her permanently. His small kingdom, this island of Lundy, was all he had ever really claimed. Oh, he had had his time in the outside world. His lovely mother was a Frenchwoman, and he had spent many years at the elegant French court, but in the end he had returned to this small, lonely rock that was his heritage, and his inheritance.

He had known for many years that his seed was barren, the result of a childhood fever, and so he had never married. He enjoyed women, but until he had met Skye O'Malley there had never been one he wanted to keep; but he wasn't enough for her. Oh, sexually he was more than her equal, and his family tree was as noble as hers, but he was a simple man, an island lord, a man of no power or influence. He might have been. He had the wealth necessary for both power and influence; but he had chosen to avoid such responsibilities. Court intrigues were simply not in his nature; not that they were in hers, but she was a beautiful woman, a woman who had had several husbands of wealth and stature. That was her right. It never occurred to Adam de Marisco that Skye would have been happier living a quiet life. He loved her too deeply to see clearly.

In the end, however, his great love for her won out over his common sense. He traveled to London to bid her farewell. It was very likely that they would never see each other again. He would return to Lundy, and she would travel on to a small Mediterranean duchy where she would undoubtedly live out her life, the wife of a wealthy lordling who would be welcome at both the French and the English courts. His big heart leapt in his chest as he entered Greenwood and she flung herself into his arms in greeting. With a helpless groan he buried his face in her hair, her glorious perfumed hair.

"Adam! Oh, my darling Adam! I *knew* that you would come. I told Robbie that you would!" She snuggled into his arms.

"When do you leave?" he asked her, dreading the answer.

"A few days." She squirmed from his bearlike grasp and looked up at him. "Don't I get a kiss?" she demanded.

"Yes," he said slowly as all his good intentions and his willpower disappeared. "Yes, I think you most certainly do get a kiss," and then his shaggy head dipped downward, his mouth found hers, and he mercilessly took possession of it. Her lips softened beneath his, parting just slightly, enough to pleasure, enough to tempt him onward. "Witch," he muttered against her mouth. "How is it you can wreak this mayhem with me?" His big hand gently caressed her upturned face.

"I'm so glad that you came," she answered him. "I don't think I could have borne to go away and never see you again." Then quick tears came to her eyes. "Oh, Adam! Why are you so stubborn? I have been bartered into a marriage with a stranger! If only you had married me I should not be forced from my homeland and my children!"

"What could I offer you, Skye? Lundy?" He laughed harshly. "I once told you that I was not a star catcher, and you were a bright and brilliant star. How could I pen up a star, Skye? You have always deserved more than I could give you."

"I don't need things, Adam. You could have given me the one thing in this world that I need. You could have given me love, my darling."

"But you could not have given me the same in return, Skye," he said seriously. "We have been over this a hundred times, and it always comes to the same thing. I love you as I have never loved another woman in my life, and you love me. You do not, however, love me as a woman should love a man. You love me as a friend, and that is not enough, little girl! I have my pride too, Skye O'Malley."

"You're too much of a romantic, Adam. You will not have me because I love you as a friend, but you will stand by while I am sent away to marry a virtual stranger who from the looks of him never loved anyone! Somehow your logic escapes me, Adam."

He chuckled. "If this duc of yours turns out to be the great love of your life, Skye, you will thank me."

"I think instead I shall make you regret your foolishness," she said ominously, her slender hands slipping beneath his doublet to rub against his silk-covered chest. "Shall I make you regret your decision, Adam?" He could feel the warmth of her palms through the fabric of his shirt. "Will you be my lover just this once more?" she whispered boldly, standing on her toes so she might kiss him in the sensitive spot just beneath his ear. She could feel his mighty heart pounding beneath her hands.

"You're a betrothed woman," he protested faintly, but his hands were already pulling her closer to him.

She nibbled upon his earlobe. "I may never see you again, my darling," she said low, and then she ran her little pointed tongue around the inner shell of his ear.

"Why are you doing this?" It was his last defense.

"Because in four days I am sailing to a place I don't know, I will marry a man I don't know, and then I will get into bed with him and he will mate with me like some animal, for that is all he wants of me, Adam. Heirs! Heirs for his tiny duchy. And for my body, my healthy and proven fertile body, he will give England a safe harbor on the Mediterranean, and a listening post at France's back door. For my part, I have the Queen of England's word that she will not allow her Anglo-Irish lords—or anyone else, for that matter—to pillage my Burke son's lands. This is not a love match, Adam. It is a business arrangement, and so before I leave all that is familiar and dear to me I want a little loving, a little tenderness, a little caring with someone that I care for, Adam de Marisco."

"Damn you, Skye," he said softly, then enfolded her back into his arms. She sighed with such obvious relief that he laughed gently, and smoothed her dark hair. "I've never known such an honest woman as you are, my darling. Sometimes it can be a little bit frightening."

Edmond de Beaumont, watching all of this from behind the ban-nisters on the second-floor landing of Skye's house, could not quite make out the words said between the two people below. What was obvious was that the giant of a man was deeply in love with Lady Burke, and she cared for him also. As the young Earl of Lynmouth came abreast of him Edmond asked the boy, "Who is that man with your mama, Robin?"

Robin Southwood looked to the main floor of the house, and a smile lit his beautiful features. Ignoring the Petit Sieur de Beau-mont, he ran downstairs, calling, "Uncle Adam! What are you doing in London?" Pure delight was written all over his young face.

Edmond de Beaumont hurried after the boy in time to hear the giant reply in a thunder-deep voice as he swept the lad up into an embrace, "I have come to bid your mother a safe voyage, my lord Earl. Have you come from your duties at court to do the same?"

"We have been here almost a whole month, Uncle Adam. Willow and Murrough and me! We have gone riding with Mother, and we have gone on picnics, and we have shopped and seen the dressmaker. Mother's having all new gowns made, for the climate in Beaumont de Jaspre is warm almost year round. Edmond says so."

"And who is Edmond, my lord Earl?"

"I am Edmond de Beaumont," a voice replied, and Adam de Marisco looked about, puzzled. He could see no one.

"I am down here, m'sieur," the voice came again, and Adam de Marisco looked down. "I am Edmond de Beaumont, Petit Sieur de Beaumont," he repeated.

Adam was astounded. "Is this the man you are to marry?" he demanded, his voice tight.

"No, Adam, this is his nephew, sent to escort me to Beaumont de Jaspre."

"Is the duc as he?" Adam was considering throttling William Cecil.

"I, m'sieur, am an accident of birth," Edmond said. "My uncle is quite as other people, I assure you."

"Edmond, this is Adam de Marisco, the lord of Lundy Island. Remember that I told you I had two best friends in this world? Well, this is the other."

Adam de Marisco looked down at Edmond de Beaumont, and

then he bent and lifted the dwarf up, balancing him so that he sat in the curve of his muscled arm so that they were eye to eye. "This is how two men should speak, m'sieur," he said.

"Agreed, my lord giant! *How tall are you?*"

"I stand six feet, six inches," replied Adam.

"Then you are nearly twice my size, for I stand but three feet four inches."

Skye stood amazed as Adam walked calmly off holding Edmond de Beaumont upon his arm, the two men now talking in earnest.

"What an excellent way for them to speak," Robin observed. "How clever of Uncle Adam to think of it!"

Skye smiled to herself. It was clever of Adam, but then he had always had the knack of putting people at their ease. Elizabeth Tudor's court had really lost a valuable courtier in him, though he preferred his island home to London, and she could not blame him at all.

When Edmond de Beaumont had returned to Whitehall, Robbie gone off prowling the seamier sections of London, and Dame Cecily and the children settled themselves for the night; then and only then did Skye and Adam come together again. She had ordered her cook to prepare a supper for two, choosing the menu herself, for Adam was somewhat of a gourmet due to his days in France. They would begin with mussels in a white wine broth and thin-sliced Dover sole with carved lemon wedges; followed with a second course that was simplicity itself, boned breast of capon upon a bed of watercress with a delicate gravy of champignons and white wine, a salad of new lettuces and radishes, freshly baked bread and newly churned sweet butter; and, lastly, fresh strawberries with thick, clotted Devon cream. It was a plain meal, but one that Skye knew would delight Adam.

Her mode of dress would also delight him, for she was wearing one of her Algerian caftans; a rose-colored silk garment with wide, long sleeves and an open neckline with tiny pearl buttons that moved downward from just below her breasts. Her slippers were delightful confections of matching silk, heel-less with turned-up toes. Her hair was loose, freshly washed, and sun-dried that afternoon. She wore no jewelry.

"I don't know why you didn't marry the lord of Lundy," Daisy remarked to her mistress.

"Because he wouldn't have me," Skye replied.

"Go on with yese, m'lady!" Daisy was astounded. "Ye're funning with me."

"No, I'm not, Daisy. He thinks that I should have a great and powerful lord for a husband, not a simple island chieftain."

"Then he's a fool," Daisy said bluntly as a knock sounded at Skye's bedchamber door.

"Open the door, Daisy," her mistress commanded, "and then you may retire for the evening. The supper is safe on the sideboard, and I'll not need you for anything else tonight."

Daisy curtseyed and opened the door to admit Adam de Marisco. "Good evening, m'lord," she said brightly, curtseying again, and then she was gone, closing the door behind her.

"You're beautiful," he said quietly, his smoky blue eyes devouring her with love.

She smiled back at him. "I've had my cook prepare you a delicious gourmet meal."

"You're the only thing I want tonight, Skye." He reached out for her, but she easily sidestepped him.

"Would you offend my cook?" Her blue eyes were dancing with merriment. "If you leave this marvelous supper untouched you will cause a scandal, for my household will ask why, when I went to the trouble to have a supper prepared for us, we did not eat it."

"One kiss, you Irish witch," he said.

"One kiss and I am lost, you villain! I see I must treat you like my children. You cannot play, Adam, until you have eaten your supper." She attempted to look stern, and he laughed.

"Very well, I shall eat."

Settling himself in one of the two chairs that had been placed on either end of the small rectangular oak table, he waited as Skye served him a plate of steaming mussels and poured him a goblet of pale golden wine. She seated herself, and silently they ate the first course. Clearing the table, she offered the second and he hummed his approval.

"Your cook had a French teacher, Skye lass. I've not tasted this dish since I was last in Paris. The mushrooms are exquisitely fresh, and the wine sauce as delicate as any I've ever tasted. I will tender my compliments in the morning."

She smiled at his pleasure, but ate little. They were going to make love soon, she knew, despite the fact that he had sworn never again to be her lover. As she absently nibbled on a radish, she wondered why it was she did not love him with the passionate and all-consuming love that she had felt for her last three husbands. They too had been her friends. They too had been as skilled and as tender as Adam was at lovemaking. Geoffrey and Niall and Khalid had all been vital, interesting, ambitious men. Adam was certainly vital and interesting. But he was not ambitious. He was content to sit upon his island, and that was not enough for her. For all her desire for a quiet life Skye knew that she was never happier than when she was in the midst of things. Adam, however, wanted peace, and if the price of his peace was to sit upon Lundy growing old, never having a true and abiding love, then he would pay that price. She wondered why he had insulated himself so. It was not the decision of an intelligent man, and Adam de Marisco was an extremely intelligent man.

Suddenly she was aware that he was staring at her, and she raised her eyes to his, a guilty blush coloring her cheeks. His smoky blue eyes were very serious, and for a brief moment she wondered if he could have been reading her thoughts. "I was just thinking," she said lamely.

"About me? About us?"

"Yes."

"And have you decided that perhaps it is not a good idea that we be lovers again, Skye?"

"No, I have decided that there is a mystery about you, Adam. I know now what it is that keeps me from loving you with all my being. You don't love me enough to fight for me, Adam."

He looked stunned. "That's not so, Skye!"

"Yes, Adam, it is. You say you love me, but that you cannot marry me because I deserve a powerful man for a husband, and you are a simple island chieftain. Well, Adam de Marisco, money buys power, and we both have gold enough to spare. You say that you cannot wed with me because one day I might meet the great love of my life, and stay with you out of misguided loyalty, making myself unhappy, which you could not bear. With the exception of my first husband I have loved completely and well all my other husbands. None was ever slow to take me to wife for fear I might meet someone else later on in my life. They wanted me enough to overcome all obstacles. Yet you will not take such a chance.

"In a few short days I will leave England for what Cecil promised me would be a short-lived marriage to an ill man. The Duc de Beaumont de Jaspre is not, however, either elderly or ill. According to his nephew, he is a healthy man in early middle life. I may never see either you or my own Ireland again, and believe me, Adam, this marriage is not a love match." She stood up and, moving to the sideboard, opened a drawer and took out a miniature. "Here," she said, handing him the tiny painting. "Look upon the face of my betrothed, and tell me if that looks like a man who will be a great love to me. It is a cold face, Adam, and his eyes frighten me. His nephew's reassurances are not encouraging, although Edmond seems to have a genuine affection for the duc.

"So I must go to the powerful husband you felt best for me, my darling, but before I go we will have a glorious few days. We deserve it, Adam, and perhaps in that time you will tell me why you have not loved me enough to fight for me, which, my dearest, is why I have never been able to love you completely. You lack ambition, Adam, and I wonder why."

"And do you intend to punish me for it?" he queried her.

"No, Adam. I intend to love you as I have always loved you. Perhaps not enough to satisfy your vanity, but then you have not given completely of yourself, either. One gets out of a relationship what one puts into it."

"Put this thing away," he said sharply, handing her the miniature back.

She took it from him and replaced it in the drawer of the sideboard. A tiny smile touched the corners of her mouth. She had at last reached him. True, it was too late now for them to do anything about being married. That opportunity was gone, and she would keep her word to Elizabeth Tudor; but if she had roused Adam enough then perhaps he might find someone to really love. She hated the thought of his being alone, even though she knew it would take a very special girl to love Adam de Marisco, and to live with him on Lundy.

Coming back to the table, Skye brought with her a basket of early strawberries and bowls of clotted cream and sugar set upon a silver tray. Setting them down, she plucked a large berry from the basket, dipped it in the sugar, swirled it in the thick cream, and popped it into her mouth, neatly detaching the stem and leaves. He grinned at her, relieved. Then, standing up, he said, "Later!"

"Lecher," she purred at him, holding her ground.

His smoky blue eyes narrowed with contemplation, and then, reaching out, he slowly began to unbutton her rose-colored caftan, his big fingers surprisingly nimble with the tiny pearl buttons. Skye started unbuttoning the silver buttons on his padded dark blue velvet doublet. He unbuttoned her to the navel and slid his hands inside the gown to fondle her breasts, delighting in her nipples, which hardened at his gentle touch, thrusting forward like thorns on a rose, to push against his palms. She pushed his doublet off, and loosened his shirt at the neckband. It opened easily beneath her touch, baring him to the waist. Playfully her slender fingers marched up his chest through the dark mat of hair, to clasp themselves about his neck.

His hands slid upward to work her caftan off her shoulders. It fell with a silken hiss to her ankles, leaving her nude. His hands moved to tangle themselves in the heavy, raven mass of her hair, drawing her head to him so he might kiss her. He hesitated just a second, long enough to see her gorgeous eyes close, the thick dark lashes fluttering like dragonflies upon the soft pink of her cheeks. Only then did his sensuous mouth begin a delicate exploration of hers.

He kissed her as if it were the very first time, tenderly tasting her lips, sending delightful shivers of anticipation up and down her spine. He felt her response, and exerted more pressure upon her mouth, gently forcing it open. His tongue plunged into that sweet cavern to dance a mad caper with hers until suddenly they were stroking each other with sensuous abandon. Their passions flamed simultaneously as he tore his mouth away from hers, and began kissing her closed eyes, her cheekbones, the corners of her mouth, her determined chin, the elegant tip of her nose, with hungry ardor while she moved her hands to pull frantically at his shirt, to loosen his breeches.

"Sweet Skye," he murmured softly, "sweet, sweet Skye." She succeeded with his shirt, but before she could entangle him in his half-loosened breeches he swept her up in his arms and carried her to the bed. "Nay, my love, I can do that faster, and a great deal more easily than you can," he gently admonished her.

"Then do it, dammit, Adam. I am not ashamed to admit that I want you, and I want you now!"

He threw his great leonine head back and laughed with pure delight. "God's nightshirt, Skye, you're an incredible woman! You want me, and you tell me so! Well, my blue-eyed Celtic witch, I want you also, and I suddenly find that I want you for all times, not just a few nights! What have I done to us in my pride, Skye?"

She reached up and drew his big body down to hers. "Later," she soothed him, "we will speak on it later, my darling."

He didn't argue. His hands were sliding down her long torso, molding themselves along her waist, filling themselves with her hips, caressing her long legs. She kissed his face ardently, and he groaned with the total pleasure that was beginning to envelope them. She lay upon her back, and he said in a quiet voice, "I don't want you to do anything, sweet Skye, but let me love you. Let me adore the perfection of your beautiful body. For tonight at least, you belong to me!"

He lowered his head, and with his hot tongue began an encirclement of her nipple. Around and around and around until she began to whimper deep within her throat, and he took the entire nipple in his mouth, sucking hard, sending a knife-sharp pulse of rapture through her body. He began again, this time with the other nipple, and when he felt her trembling like a small, wild thing beneath him he ceased the torture, moving his large body down the bed.

Taking one of her slender feet in his hands, he kissed it then began licking it sensuously, his tongue thrusting between the toes, slipping along the outside curve of the arch. His hungry mouth kissed, his tongue lapped tenderly in the hollows of her ankle, and when he reached her knee he began again with the other foot. Pulling himself back up level with her, he licked her chest and quivering breasts; his tongue slid easily over her torso, not missing an inch of skin as he moved along. He turned her over, and she felt the warm wetness against her shoulders, along her spine, the curve of her waist, the mounds of her bottom, the length of her legs, the soles of her feet.

"Dear Jesu, Adam," she gasped, "stop! You will drive me mad!"

He rolled her onto her back again. "Then we shall be mad together, sweet Skye," he said, and lowered his head once more, this time his tongue snaking out to touch her in her most sensitive place.

"Ohh, yes," she breathed as she began to flame wildly beneath his impassioned touch, her beautiful body twisting under his hungry mouth.

He felt as if he would burst with his desire as he tasted and breathed the musky sweetness of her. Finally he could no longer control his own passions, and raising his head, he drew himself up, swinging over her to thrust within her honied sheath. Like some unearthly creature, she wrapped herself about him, moaning wildly, pushing her hips up to meet his frantic rhythm. A soft scream told him that she was near her release and mercilessly he pushed her to the brink only to force her back. She cursed him furiously, and he laughed softly, admonishing her, "You hurry too much."

"I hate you!" she gasped.

"You want me," he countered, "and I want you. I have always tried to teach you patience in pleasure."

"Give me release!" she begged.

In answer he drove deep into her, forcing her body into the mattress with each downward plunge of his hips. She had been grasping him tightly with her hands, but now his subtle torture sent her sharp nails clawing down his back. "Bitch!" he groaned, and then he took her mouth in a savage kiss, forcing her lips apart to catch her tongue, which he proceeded to suck fiercely.

Skye thought she would die in that very minute. Her love juices released themselves in a hot, wild rush, crowning the head of his throbbing manhood, which liberated its own salute to her in the same instant. They shuddered together, lost in a world of white-hot desire that drained them, leaving them weakened and only half-conscious.

He rolled off her, and instinctively she sought for the comfort of his embrace. His strong arms tightened about her as her head fitted itself into the hollow of his shoulder. His breathing was ragged, hers came in soft pants. His big hand began to stroke her, gentle, long touches that soothed them both. He sighed, and then began, "You know that I am unable to have children. As a young boy I suffered a severe fever that burned the life from my seed. Praise God it never destroyed my enjoyment of the fair sex, but I cannot give a woman a child.

"I learned my fate when I was twenty, and had already fallen in love with a girl I sought to marry. I might have said nothing, and let her believe that it was she who could not conceive; but instead I was honest with her and her family. Her father said he would rather she enter a convent than be childless. My *love* said that if I could not be a *real* man she didn't want me." He sighed again. "Her father was a down-at-the-heels French count. She was his eighth child, fifth daughter. Her dowry so small that not even a religious order would have her, as they later found. I loved her back then, Skye. I do not love her now, and yet I can still hear her voice, condemning me for my lack of manhood, for my inability to father a son on her or any other woman.

"I left France then, and returned to Lundy. I had been its lord since I was ten, when my father had died. My mother returned to France with me and my two younger sisters a year after his death. She remarried when I was twelve, and gave her new husband several children. After my betrothal was broken Lundy was my refuge, and no one there knew or cared about my inability.

"I am known as the lusty lord of Lundy for my prodigious appetite for women. Several have even claimed their bastards are mine, and I have paid them off, glad to have my prowess attested to; but I know the truth. Then you came into my life, Skye, and I loved again; but I never admitted it to you. I have never admitted it aloud even to myself, not until now.

"I have always called you a star, a bright and shining star, and so you are, my darling. In wealth we are equal, in lands you far surpass me, but it matters not, for you know I care little for such things. You have given children to each of your husbands, Skye, and perhaps that is what bothered me. If you wed with me you could have no other child. I could not do that to you."

"You were afraid I would scorn you?" she answered him. "Yet on two occasions I have asked you to marry me, Adam, and I have known for some time that your seed was barren."

"Ah," he answered her, "if you had wed me after Geoffrey had died then you would have once again been separated from Niall Burke. You would not have had your little Deirdre and your infant son, Padraic. I will wager, my love, you don't regret those two innocents."

"No, I don't regret them, Adam; but I wonder if the fates ever really meant for me to be wed to Niall. For years everything had conspired to keep us apart. If I had not wed him, then Claire

O'Flaherty would not have revenged herself upon him, for there would have been no need. Now he is dead, and because I must protect those two Burke children I have accepted marriage to a man I don't even know. How much simpler had you wed me, my darling, my dearest, dearest Adam. I could love you; really love you had you cared enough to fight for me. You feared getting hurt again more than you wanted me as your wife."

"And if I suddenly changed my mind, Skye, would you marry me?"

"I would have, Adam, but it is too late now. I cannot break my word to the Queen. We have an agreement for better or worse, and I will keep my part of that agreement as long as Elizabeth Tudor keeps faith with me. Had my marriage to you been a fact, and had I then gone to Cecil, the Burke lands might have been safe by virtue of my strong new husband. I, however, went helpless to the Queen, and she took the opportunity to use me for her own ends. Cecil knows that my word is my bond."

"How I love you," he whispered against her hair, "and what a fool I have been, my sweet Skye."

"We have the next few days, Adam, and when I am gone I want you to find yourself another woman to love. If that French girl had really loved you, your barren seed would not have bothered her. She was not worthy of you Adam, but somewhere there is a girl or a woman who is. Someone who will love you for yourself, not for what you can or cannot give her. Do not be afraid to seek that woman out, my darling!

"When Khalid el Bey died, I told Robbie I should never love again. That loving only led to pain. But without the pain, Adam, how can one know, or enjoy, the sweetness? There may be pain in your search, but when you find your love it will be all the better for the pain."

He hugged her close, and she snuggled deeper into his big shoulder, not seeing the tears in his smoky blue eyes as he turned his head away from her. He knew that she was right and, having unburdened himself to her, he felt better than he had in years. Still, with the unburdening came the terrible knowledge that he loved her deeply; perhaps too deeply to ever love another woman again. Only time would tell the answer, but at least they had the next few days to be together, to love each other, to make memories to carry them through the long years he envisioned ahead.

For two days and two nights they stayed within her rooms, talking, and loving, and even fighting a bit over what she termed his monumentally stubborn nature and he termed her Irish pig-headedness. The children joined them in the afternoons to chatter and play their games, though only young Murrough O'Flaherty understood the relationship between his mother and Adam de Marisco.

"Why didn't you marry him?" he asked his mother in a private moment, when Robin and Willow were totally engrossed in some tale that Adam was telling them.

"Because he didn't ask me in time," she answered.

Murrough nodded. "I don't suppose you could get the Queen to change her mind, Mother? Then you could stay here, and we should not lose you to some strange land, and a man whom we do not know. Could you ask Her Majesty? She admires you very much."

Skye hugged her son lightly. "I wish it were possible, my love, but it is not. The duc has been sent word of my coming as well as my miniature. He would be greatly offended if a substitute bride were sent."

"We could say you died," Murrough suggested hopefully.

"I do not think that M'sieur de Beaumont would lie to his uncle, my love. I am afraid I must go." She patted Murrough. "It will be all right, my son. It will be all right."

They went to court the next day, an unusually hot one for early May, and Skye wore one of her new gowns, a beautiful dress made just for Beaumont de Jaspre. It was a lime-green-colored silk, its underskirt embroidered with gold thread flowers and butterflies; the sleeves sheer and full to just below the elbow, her forearms bare; the neckline extremely low in the French fashion. Several gentlemen of the court gaped quite openly as she glided by them flanked by Adam de Marisco and Sir Robert Small.

"'Tis my emeralds, no doubt, that fascinate them," she teased her escorts, and both men chuckled in spite of themselves.

"Ah, now," Robbie countered, "and I was thinking that it was the roses in your hair."

Garbed in red velvet and cloth of gold, the Queen awaited them. Her long, graceful hands were outstreched in welcome. "Dearest Skye!" Her smile was friendly. "So you come to bid us farewell."

Her gaze swept Skye appraisingly. "I know the duc will appreciate our generosity in sending him one of this nation's most beautiful women to wife."

"Your Majesty is most gracious," Skye answered, her eyes modestly lowered.

"Yes," Elizabeth purred in subtle warning. "I am my father's daughter in many ways." She smiled again. "You will be pleased to know, dear Skye, that I have confirmed your son's rights, and appointed his grand-uncle, the Bishop of Connaught, as his guardian in your absence." She lowered her voice. "You need have no fear, dearest Skye. The English and the Anglo-Irish in the Dublin Pale have been warned that any breach of my sworn word to you will be considered by me as a personal affront. As to your own wild Irish neighbors, your uncle will have to contend with them."

"Thank you, Majesty," she replied. "I am grateful to you, and I will do my part."

"And we all envy the duc," Lord Dudley murmured, "for I can vouch that Lady Burke knows how to please a man well."

"Why is it, Lord Dudley," Skye asked sweetly, "that your bravery only comes to the fore when you are surrounded by others? Since you have certainly never pleased me I cannot know how it is you know that I please a man well."

Robbie and Adam dropped their hands from their swords. They did not need to protect Skye in this instance. She fought Dudley far better with words than they could have with swords. While the Queen and the courtiers about them chuckled at the pompous Earl of Leicester's discomfort, Skye said in honied tones, "Your Majesty knows my two sons, Murrough O'Flaherty and Robin Southwood; but I have brought my daughter, Willow, to greet you."

Elizabeth Tudor turned a kindly glance upon Willow, totally adorable in a burgundy-colored silk gown. Willow curtseyed gracefully, gaining further approval from the Queen. "How old are you, my child?" she demanded.

"I have just had my ninth birthday, Your Majesty," Willow replied.

"And what do you study? You do study?"

"Aye, madam. I study French, Latin, and Greek, as well as mathematics, music, and philosophy. Mama says I must begin Italian and Spanish as well this year; I will one day have a great estate to administer."

The Queen was amused as well as pleased. Had she a daughter of her own she would fully approve such a curriculum. "Can you dance?" she asked Willow.

"Aye, madam. The dancing master comes at eight in the morning four days weekly."

"And the wifely arts, Mistress Willow? Do you learn those also?"

"Aye," replied Willow, "I like them, although I love gardening best."

"You are a good child, I can see," the Queen said. "Perhaps in another year or two your mama will allow you to come to court as one of my maids of honor. Would you like that, Mistress Willow?"

Willow's golden eyes grew round with delight, and she looked to her mother. "Oh, Mother, may I?" she asked.

"In a year or two," Skye answered, "if the Queen still has need of you, Willow, you may certainly come. Now please thank the Queen for her kindness."

"Oh, thank you, madam," Willow said fervently, curtseying again.

"You are fortunate to have such a good little maid for a daughter," Elizabeth remarked.

"I am fortunate in all my children," Skye replied, "even the babes I must leave behind."

The Queen had the good grace to look momentarily uncomfortable, but then she recovered quickly. "You will take the Duc de Beaumont de Jaspre our personal greetings, dear Skye, and you will tell him that England is grateful for the safety of his harbors. As to the rest, I know that I may rely upon you." It was a dismissal, and it was a warning.

Skye curtseyed low, and at least two of the gentlemen standing near the Queen almost fell over in their efforts to gaze at her almost bare breasts.

"Have you really known her, Dudley?" one courtier asked.

"She's as hot and juicy a piece as you could imagine in your wildest fantasies," Dudley replied low. "I had her right after her husband, the Earl of Southwood, died. He'd always kept her well serviced, and she could hardly wait for me to put it in her. Oh, yes, my friend, I know Skye O'Malley well."

"What a shame the Queen is sending her away," the courtier said.

Dudley chuckled. "Bess knows Skye will make the duc a happy

man, and a happy man is a grateful man, grateful to the England who gives him this delicious sugarplum to eat up."

The two men snickered lewdly, but by then Skye and her escort had already left the Queen's reception room.

"When is the next tide?" Skye asked Robbie.

"About six this evening," he replied.

"It doesn't give us much time, does it? Well, let's get back to Greenwood, my loves, so that I may change."

They hurried through the corridors of Whitehall Palace to the Old Palace Stairs, the public landing on the river, and there Skye's barge awaited them. The barge sped down the river to Greenwood, and Skye flew into the house to change her clothing. The undermaids hurriedly packed her beautiful gown away, and the last of the trunks was sent on to the Pool, where Skye's own flagship, the *Seagull*, awaited her arrival. Edmond de Beaumont was already aboard the ship and waiting, having taken his leave of the Queen the night before.

Skye dressed in the clothes she habitually wore aboard ship; a split-legged skirt of light, black wool, natural-colored woollen stockings and dark leather boots, a cream-colored silk shirt, and a wide leather belt with a silver buckle. Her black hair was twisted into one thick braid, a simple hairstyle that would not blow into her eyes. Adam had sat watching her as she dressed, handing her her garments in Daisy's place, as the maid had been sent on ahead.

"Don't come with me to the ship," Skye said to him. "I don't think I can bear to see you receding as the ship sails off."

He nodded, understanding and silently agreeing. Best that their good-byes be said in private. "I'll take Murrough and Robin back to Whitehall, and then tomorrow I'll see Dame Cecily and Willow safely back to Devon," he said.

"Will you keep an eye on the children for me, Adam? Not just here in England, but in Ireland as well. My brother, Michael, is a good man, but he's a priest, and Uncle Seamus is elderly, far too elderly even to take on the responsibilities he has now. My son, Ewan, can use the strong influence of a real man." She flung herself against his broad chest. "My babies!" she wept. "It's so hard to leave the others, but my babies are too young even to know me. Please look out for them, Adam. I can trust you!"

"You will write to me," he said. It was more a statement than a question.

"I will write to you," she answered.

"I will pray for you also," he said quietly, and she looked up at him, startled. He laughed. "I know men don't speak a great deal about God, Skye, but I believe, and I do pray."

Tears moistened her eyes again. "I will pray for you also, my darling. I will pray that you find a woman to love and to keep!"

He smiled down at her, and then his lips met hers in a kiss of incredible sweetness. Their mouths melted into one another until there was no beginning and, seemingly, no end. She wanted the kiss to go on forever, for his touch had transported her beyond the world she knew and into a realm of light and love so pure that she knew nothing would ever be the same again for either of them.

She protested when he reluctantly lifted his head from hers. His arm fell from about her waist, and he touched her cheek lightly with his fingers. "Farewell, Skye O'Malley. Farewell until we meet again." Then Adam de Marisco turned and left her.

For a moment Skye stood rooted to the floor, filled with a feeling of such terrible loss that she thought her heart would surely break. If he had been a fool then she had been a bigger one. She should have insisted that he marry her! Now it was too late.

"Mother?"

She started at the sound of the voice and, looking down, saw her sons standing before her. "Murrough, Robin," she said.

"We came to bid you farewell, Mother," Murrough said. "Lord de Marisco is going to take us back to Whitehall now."

She bent down and hugged her elder son. Then, straightening, she took his face in her hand. "I am proud of you, Murrough O'Flaherty," she said. "You are a good lad, and I love you. Remember what we have spoken of, and act accordingly. Only you can win your lands, my son. I know you will make me proud." Then she kissed him quickly and stepped back, releasing him.

Murrough's eyes were damp, but he manfully forced back his tears. "I will make you proud, Mother, and when you are settled you will let me come to you?"

"You will all come to see me," she promised, and then she turned to her younger son.

Robin flung himself into her arms, and although he was silent, his little shoulders shook. Skye waited until he had composed himself. Robin, like his father, had great dignity. Finally he looked up at her, and his mouth trembled as he said, "My father would not like this, Mother. He would not approve of what the Queen has done, sending you from your children."

"No, Robin," she admitted. "Geoffrey would not like what the Queen has done, but he would accept her decision and abide by it, for your papa was in all things the Queen's most loyal servant. Whatever your feelings in this matter, I expect you to do what your papa would have done. He would have accepted the Queen's choice, and so must you. He would have accepted it with good grace, and you must do the same." She smoothed his wavy, dark blond hair gently. "Will you come to visit me, my lord Earl, once I am settled?"

"If the Queen will allow it, Mother," he answered, and she smiled and kissed him tenderly.

"As I am proud of your brother, so I am also proud of you, Robin. You are the youngest page at court, and the Queen says you are the best of her pages, despite your youth. Continue to add lustre to the Southwood family name, my son."

She took the boys by the hands and walked with them to the door of her antechamber. Then, quickly kissing each of them again, she bade them farewell and thrust them from the room. As the door closed behind them Skye put her back to it and stuffed her fist into her mouth to prevent her cries from being heard by her sons. They had both been so brave and she must not destroy their confidence in themselves, or in her. Inwardly she cursed Elizabeth Tudor for her cruelty in sending her so far away. The woman had no heart. The tears poured down her face in a steady, salty stream, and when Robbie knocked, she did not hear him at first.

"Skye, lass!" His voice cut into her sorrow.

Turning, she fumbled to open the door, and when he pushed into the room she fell against his chest, weeping. "It's too much, Robbie!" she cried. "I don't think I can do it! I don't think I can!"

He held her and made soothing noises, for that was all she really wanted. She would go to Beaumont de Jaspre because she had promised the Queen. Skye O'Malley had never been known to go back on her word, and she wouldn't now for all her sorrow at parting from her children. When he had decided that she had wept enough, he said sharply, "Are you forgetting Willow, Skye lass? Will you go to her your eyes all puffy with evidence of weeping? She's not a babe to gull, you know."

Skye drew in a deep breath, and then she shuddered against him and pulled away. "I'm sorry, Robbie," she said quietly, "but dammit, I love my sons!"

"I know, lass," he said, and taking her by the hand, he led her back into her bedchamber. Pouring some cool water from a silver pitcher into the matching basin, he pointed to it. "Wash your face, lass. Willow and Cecily are waiting to bid us good-bye in the library. God's foot, she's like Khalid! She's always asking about cargo, and the bills of lading for them. She's more your heir than any of the boys, and that's for certain!"

"She's your pet," Skye accused him, and she bent to wash the evidence of tears from her face.

"That she is," Robbie chuckled indulgently, and Skye was forced to laugh, which made her feel better.

She took the linen towel that he handed her, and dried both her face and her hands. "I am ready," she said. "I don't feel so badly about Willow, for she is safe with your sister, but when I thought of my two little boys at court, with no one to protect them . . ." she sighed.

"Adam will protect them. He told me before he left that he will spend his time going between Devon, the court, and Ireland, checking on your children while you are away. He's a good man, and why you didn't marry him is beyond me."

Why was it that everyone always assumed, Adam included, that she wouldn't have him? "He wouldn't have me, dammit!" she swore at Robbie. "It's twice he's turned me down because of some misguided notion. Now he's decided that he does love me, that he does want me, and it's too bloody late!"

He looked at her, astounded. "The Devil you say, Skye lass!"

"Let's go, Robbie," she said. "It isn't polite to keep a duc waiting," and she stamped from the room, gazing quickly about it for one last time. Who knew when she would see her London house again. Right now, all she wanted was to go before the leaving killed her with sorrow.

In the library Dame Cecily and Willow awaited Skye. Willow ran to her mother as she entered the room, hugging her hard, and saying, "I shall miss you, Mama. When will I see you again?"

"Once I am settled I shall ask the duc if you and your brothers can come. Will you like that, my darling?"

"I will be able to come back to England to be a maid of honor to the Queen, won't I, Mama?" Willow looked very anxious, and Skye realized how glamorous and exciting the court must seem to a young girl.

"If you continue to do all the things you should, Willow, then I see no reason why you cannot go to court in a few years' time. I must have good reports from Dame Cecily, though, and you must make me proud when you come to Beaumont de Jaspre."

"Oh, I will, Mama! I promise you I shall be very good, and I shall study my lessons hard! When I go to court someday I shall outshine the Queen herself!"

"It is not very wise to outshine Elizabeth Tudor, Willow. That lesson your Mama has learned." Skye gave Robbie and Dame Cecily a wry smile, and then said, "Come now, Willow, and bid me farewell. It grows late, and we cannot miss the tide." She bent down and enfolded her daughter in her arms. Khalid's daughter. Except this winter and the winter she had been in the Tower, she had never been separated from Khalid's daughter. Suddenly it was like losing him all over again, and she began to feel teary once more. She quickly regained control over her errant emotions, and kissed her daughter twice, once on each cheek. "Adieu, my dearest daughter," she said softly.

"Farewell, Mama. Go in safety with God's blessing." Willow kissed her mother upon the lips, and then quickly turned away before her mother might see her tears. She knew full well how Skye felt about leaving her children, and she understood why she did it. I will never be that vulnerable when I am grown up, Willow thought with the easy confidence of youth.

Dame Cecily and Skye hugged each other, and the older woman did not bother to hide her feelings. Big tears ran down her plump, apple cheeks, and she fumbled irritably for her handkerchief. "I shall miss you, my dear," she sniffled, "but I will take good care of Willow for you, Skye. That I can promise you."

"I know you will look after Willow with love," Skye replied. "What would she or I ever do without you, Dame Cecily? You have been like a mother to me and a grandmother to Willow from the first. I shall miss you also!" She hugged the old lady, comforting her with the promise, "You must come with Willow when Robbie brings her to Beaumont de Jaspre. Edmond tells me it is a lovely country, all flowers and sunshine."

"Well," Dame Cecily said with a small sniffle, "I've never been one to travel, and I've never been outside of England. Lord bless me, I've only been to Plymouth and London in my time; but I might very well come with Willow. I'm not so old yet that I'm to be frightened by something new!"

Skye gave her old friend another hug. "Then come with Willow when she comes!" she said.

"Skye lass, it's growing late now," Robbie admonished.

The two women hugged a final time, and then Skye caught her daughter to her once more. "Be good, my little love," she said, and then releasing Willow, she almost ran out the door.

They hurried through the gardens of Greenwood House down to the private landing where Skye's barge awaited them. The glory of the day had not abated one bit, even now in the late afternoon. The flowering trees scented the air, and already blossoms were beginning to fall, drifting like bits of pink and white silk along the river's green edge. She looked back only once, and then the tears filled her eyes so quickly she couldn't really see. Turning, she climbed into her barge. It was better that way. There were so many memories. Memories of her first trip to London, of Geoffrey, of their falling in love, of Lynmouth House right next to Greenwood, of Niall, and of Robin's birth upon this very river, in this very barge. She had not felt this way since she had fled Algiers. It was as if one door was closing firmly upon her, and although another door loomed open and inviting, through it was the unknown. The unknown had always frightened her.

The river traffic was light at the moment. Business was done for the day, and it was yet too early for the pleasures of the evening to begin. Independent watermen looking for fares to take from one landing of the city to another poled about the river calling out to likely-looking customers along the river banks. They entered the London Pool, and Skye's bargeman steered them skillfully through the many merchantmen and galleons moored or awaiting departure. Her heart quickened as she saw the *Seagull* and the *Mermaid* next to each other.

"The Queen did provide us with a strong escort, didn't she, Robbie?" Skye queried him.

"Aye, lass. We'll be traveling with a total of ten ships. The escort is led and commanded by a young gentleman from Devon named Francis Drake. He's a competent seaman, but God help the Moors if they attack us. He's the fiercest fighter I've ever known. If he doesn't manage to get himself killed he'll one day amount to something, I've not a doubt."

The river barge bobbed and bumped itself against the *Seagull*, and Skye stood up, calling out, "Ahoy, *Seagull!* Where are you, MacGuire? Kelly? I'm coming aboard." She grasped at the rope ladder hanging from the side of the ship, and climbed up to the main deck of the vessel. Clambering over the ship's rail she looked back down into the barge. "Go on to your ship, Robbie. We've no time to visit now, the tide's about to turn."

"Aye, lass. I'll see you later," he said, and then the barge moved off across the space of water separating the two ships.

"So there you are at last, Skye O'Malley." Sean MacGuire stood before her on his sturdy sea legs.

"Good afternoon to you, MacGuire," Skye said. "Thank you for bringing *Seagull* safely to me."

"Ye're so grateful that you've put another captain aboard," he complained to her.

"Bran Kelly is merely an extra man, MacGuire. If you're annoyed, he's just as annoyed. I took him from his own command to sail with me on *Seagull*. I'm going into an unknown situation in Beaumont de Jaspre, MacGuire. I want my own people about me. You understand that."

"Aye," he grudgingly gave in to her. "I don't know why you have to run off and marry some foreigner anyways, Mistress Skye."

"I made a bargain with the Queen, MacGuire."

"She's not our Queen."

Skye snorted her impatience. "Ireland has no queen, MacGuire! It has no king. What it has is a thousand lordlings, a thousand cocks, each on its own dung heap, crowing its own song. Do you know the song those cocks sing, MacGuire? They sing of freedom from England and the English, but not one of those cocks would give up his rights to another man so that Ireland could be united under one Irish king, so we might drive the English from our homeland and be ruled by an Irish king. No, my old friend, they sing, they get drunk, they weep of the grand, great days of yore, but in the end they do nothing except make widows and orphans. Is it a wonder the English abuse us?

"Well, if that's the way it's to be, then I must think of my own first. England rules Ireland, and I'll not lose the Burke lands over a dream. The price of the Queen's protection is that I marry this duc, and I will marry him! I will marry him lest Niall and the old Mac-William rise from their graves to haunt me for losing what the Burkes have fought and died over for a thousand years. Now you nosy old man, that's the last I'll speak on it!"

He grinned wickedly at her, and drawing his pipe from his pocket, he lit it. "You needn't get huffy, Skye O'Malley. I remember you when you were wearing nappies and crawling about the decks of yer father's ship, may God assoil his noble soul."

"Are we sailing on this tide or not?" she demanded, attempting to regain her dignity. It was damned well time MacGuire retired, but she knew he'd die aboard his ship one day, as her father had done.

"If ye weren't so busy talking, lass, you'd see that we've already weighed anchor, and are underway." He chuckled at her chagrin. "You'll find that pretty piece that serves you, as well as the little foreign lord, waiting you in your dayroom."

"Where's Kelly?"

"Sleeping. It's agreed between us that I'll captain the ship during the day and he at night."

She nodded. "A wise decision, considering we've got to avoid the French, the Spanish, *and* the Barbary pirates."

"We'll get there safe and sound, Mistress Skye," he said, puffing comfortably on his pipe.

By evening they had rounded Margate Head and were out into the Strait of Dover. The next morning they were in the English Channel, where a light but steady breeze and a spring rain and fog protected them and their escort from detection by any foreign vessels. Several days later the gray weather left them, and they sailed briskly across the Bay of Biscay under bright blue skies. They were far enough out to sea to avoid coastal vessels. Rounding Cape Finisterre brought them into the Atlantic Ocean. The weather had been magnificent, and Skye was reminded of her first voyage to the Mediterranean. Ten years ago. Had it really been ten years ago? She gazed out over the dark blue sea to the cliffs of Cape St. Vincent rising steep and red-brown above the water. *Khalid. Geoffrey. Niall.* She shook her head. All gone. She seemed fated to be alone. Perhaps the duc would change her luck.

Seagull, Mermaid, and their escort sailed through the Straits of Gibraltar and into the Mediterranean Sea, swinging north once more as they set a course for Beaumont de Jaspre. Several times now they sighted other vessels, but the size of their escort discouraged any unfriendly encounters. As they drew nearer to Beaumont de Jaspre Skye thought that she would even welcome an encounter with Barbary pirates. Anything to stave off the inevitable: her arrival—and her marriage to a total stranger.

"We should be docking in Villerose in less than a half an hour, Mistress Skye," Bran Kelly told her, coming into the dayroom where she was writing a letter to Willow describing the voyage.

"Thank you, Bran," she replied quietly, and then turned to address the man across the room. "Well, Edmond, I have brought you safely home, haven't I?" Her tone was affectionate and amused.

"I admit I do not like sea travel," he said, "but this voyage has been magnificent, Skye! It would have been quicker if we had crossed the English Channel and driven across France, however."

"Quicker if the French allowed Elizabeth Tudor's emissary free access to their roads and inns. Do you think they would have, Edmond?"

He chuckled and hopped down from the window seat in the stern window, where he had been sitting. "Stand up, Skye, and let me have a good look at you."

Finished with the letter, she pushed it aside and stood up. She wore an exquisite gown of delicate lilac-colored silk, styled in the Italian manner. The skirt was full, over several starched petticoats, the underskirt embroidered in silver thread and pink glass beads showing a design of windflowers and dainty, fluttering moths. The sleeves of the gown were full to the midarm, and slashed to show a lilac and silver-striped fabric beneath. The neckline was low and draped with a soft lilac silk-kerchief added for modesty's sake. About her neck Skye had chosen to wear a dainty necklace of small pearls and amethysts set in gold, and from her ears bobbed pearls falling from amethyst studs. Her hair was parted in the center and drawn back over her small ears into a full chignon that had been dressed with purple silk Parma violets and white silk rosebuds.

"You are incredibly beautiful," Edmond de Beaumont said

quietly. "How can my uncle fail to love you, Skye? You are love incarnate!"

"You are extravagant in your praise, Edmond. Remember you have told me that your uncle is a reserved man. Perhaps I shall shock him rather than please him. I have never liked arranged marriages for just this reason. My first marriage was arranged when I was in the cradle, and it was a disaster from the outset. It is better that people get to know one another. Still, I am older than when I was first married, and your uncle has known sorrow also. Perhaps we can console each other, and be happy in the bargain."

"I know it can be so," he said fervently. "Be patient with him, Skye. If anyone can reach him you can."

What a strange remark, she thought, but before she could ask him exactly what he meant, Captain MacGuire was entering the cabin to announce, "Well, we're here, and there's a pretty fancy carriage on the dock, which I suspect is your betrothed's. He'll probably come aboard as soon as we're moored securely."

She panicked. "Where is Robbie? I must speak to Robbie before I leave the ship!"

"Easy, lass," MacGuire soothed her. "I'll have *Mermaid* signaled immediately. You're as fretful as a virgin going to the marriage bed for the first time."

"*MacGuire!*" she shouted at him, outraged.

The old seaman chuckled and, turning about, left the day room.

"You mustn't be fearful, Skye," Edmond de Beaumont said. "My uncle is the kindest man alive. You have nothing to fear from him."

She drew a deep breath, dispelling some of her panic. "I don't know what came over me," she said. "I am behaving like a green girl."

"I shall go ashore," Edmond de Beaumont said, "and greet my uncle. Then I shall bring him back to introduce him to you. It will be far more private if you meet here for the first time, than if you meet on the dock or at the palace." He gave her a quick smile and then hurried out, his short legs pumping eagerly.

She was alone. For how long? she wondered. In a few minutes *he* would walk through the cabin door, and she would no longer be free. She did not delude herself that this would be like any of her other marriages. Lord Burghley had sworn that the duc would sign the marriage contracts that left her her own mistress, but then Lord

Burghley had also sworn that the duc was old and ill, which his nephew had most certainly attested he was not. Edmond had signed the contracts for his uncle in England, but Fabron de Beaumont must ratify them. She would insist he do so before she wed him! It was the only way. She could not after all these years find herself at anyone else's mercy. It was bad enough to be wedding a stranger.

The door to her dayroom opened and Robbie came in. "It looks a fair place, Skye lass," he said.

She nodded.

"MacGuire signaled you wanted to see me."

"You'll not leave me, Robbie?" Her voice was anxious.

"I'll not leave you, Skye. You're my lass. I'll be here whenever you want me." He reached out and took her hands in his. They were cold despite the warmth of the day. "He'll love you, and perhaps you'll love him."

"I don't know why I'm so nervous. I'm a grown woman with four marriages behind me. I've six children!" She whirled, and her gown whirled with her. "God's nightshirt!" she swore, using the Queen's favorite oath. "What is the matter with me?"

"Nothing," he said. "Nothing that won't be solved by your meeting the duc and getting to know him."

"There's no time. We are to be married immediately. Edmond told me that that was the agreement; but Robbie, you must stand behind me. I won't marry the man until he ratifies the marriage contracts agreeing that what is mine remains mine. I won't even get off *Seagull* until that is settled. You'll help me?"

"I will handle it for you, my dear," he said. "Let me do it. These Mediterranean types are not your Englishman."

"Oh, yes, Robbie! Please take care of it for me!"

A knock sounded at the cabin door. Skye froze, but Robbie said in a loud voice, "Enter!"

The door opened, and Edmond de Beaumont entered, followed by another gentleman. Fabron de Beaumont's almond-shaped eyes widened just slightly, but other than that he showed no emotion; his expression remained unsmiling. He was exactly as Edmond had painted him; a serious, aristocratic man of medium height with fierce dark eyes and severely cropped, curly black hair. It worried Skye that she could see no emotion in those eyes, but then perhaps he was as nervous of her as she was of him. If Edmond had been flattering at all to his uncle, it was only in the fact that he had softened the duc's sharp features; the long, narrow nose, the large, thin mouth, the very square jaw. For a long moment there was silence in the room, and then Edmond spoke.

"Lady Burke, may I present to you my uncle, the Duc de Beaumont de Jaspre."

Skye curtseyed gracefully.

"Uncle Fabron, may I present to you Lady Burke, your betrothed."

"Welcome to Beaumont de Jaspre, madame," the duc said. His voice was deep, but musical in tone.

"Thank you, monseigneur," was her reply.

"Uncle, this is Sir Robert Small, Lady Burke's business partner."

Fabron de Beaumont raised an elegant eyebrow. "My nephew tells me that you are a woman of commerce, madame. Is it true?"

"Yes, monseigneur." Skye looked to Robbie.

Clearing his throat, he said, "There is the matter of the ratification of the marriage contracts, M'sieur le Duc."

"I must read them first," was the reply.

"Then I will get them," Robbie said quietly. "The Queen has forbidden Lady Burke to leave her vessel until the contracts have your signature. Until then she must remain on what is technically English soil."

"But the marriage ceremony is set for this evening," the duc protested.

"There is nothing unusual about the contracts, M'sieur le Duc. Lady Burke brings you a very generous dowry, but the contracts permit her to keep her own wealth and to continue to administer her lands and those of her children."

"But that is outrageous!"

"Nonetheless, M'sieur le Duc, that is what the contracts say. Englishwomen are perhaps more independent than other women, but certainly that is why you wanted a wife from Bess Tudor's court." Robbie smiled in a man-to-man fashion at the duc. "Your nephew saw nothing unusual in Lady Burke's request when Lord Burghley explained it to him. He signed believing you would agree with him. Lady Burke's dowry is *very* generous."

"Do you believe yourself capable of administering such wealth, madame?" The duc looked closely at Skye.

"I have been my own mistress in such things, monseigneur, since my father's death. It was he who put me in charge of his fleets and his wealth until my brothers were old enough to manage. At their request I still manage both my family's ships and their monies."

"And what else do you manage, madame?"

"The estates of my young son, the Earl of Lynmouth, and of my eldest son, Ewan O'Flaherty, although Ewan will be old enough in another two years to manage on his own. Then there are the estates of my youngest son, Padraic, in Ireland; and my daughter, Willow's, wealth from her father, my second husband. Then, too, there is my own wealth, monseigneur, from commercial enterprises in which I am engaged with Sir Robert."

"You take a great deal upon such beautiful shoulders, madame," he noted.

"Nonetheless I am capable of it, monseigneur," she countered.

"A woman's first duty is to give her husband heirs and to raise those children."

"You will not find me lacking there, monseigneur. I have given children to all of my husbands—five sons, of whom four are living, and two daughters."

He nodded. "And would you indeed refuse to marry me if I refuse to sign and ratify this marriage contract?"

"Yes, monseigneur, I would," Skye answered, and she lifted her chin slightly as she said the words.

"You are a woman of strong character, I can see," the duc replied, "but that can be a good trait in a woman if you pass it on to our sons. I trust you will do so, madame." There was just the faintest hint of amusement in his voice.

"I will try," she answered him in as serious a tone.

"Then there is nothing for it but I must sign the contracts," he answered, taking them from Robbie. Edmond de Beaumont quickly handed his uncle an inked quill from Skye's desk, and the duc as quickly wrote his signature at the assigned place.

Skye then came forward to place her own signature upon the documents. She had refused to sign them in England, protesting that until the duc himself agreed to her demands her signature was not necessary.

"You sign yourself Skye O'Malley, madame," the duc noted.

"It is simpler, monseigneur, that I use my maiden name. I have had four husbands, and all their names added to my own would make another document." She looked up at him with her marvelous Kerry-blue eyes, and the duc allowed himself a small smile.

"Now that the formalities are over, madame, will you allow me to escort you to your new home?" He held out his hand to her, and after a small hesitation she placed her hand in his. His grasp was firm. "I have planned that we be married immediately," he told her as he led her from the ship and up to his carriage. Nervously she looked about to see that Robbie was coming, too. Noting it, he asked, "Are you afraid of me, madame? Your eyes constantly seek out M'sieur Robert."

"I have never married a stranger before," she said quietly.

He nodded. "A difficult position for you, I can see, but I have never married a woman that I knew. It didn't really matter, madame. They, like you, came to me for but one purpose, to give me heirs. Pastor Lichault says the Bible claims that 'whoso findeth a wife findeth a good thing, and obtaineth favor of the Lord.' King David wrote in his psalms 'Lo, children are a heritage of the Lord: and the fruit of the womb is his reward. As arrows are in the hand of a mighty man; so are the children of the youth. Happy is the man that hath his quiver full of them: they shall not be ashamed.' I, however, am ashamed, madam. I have but one living child, a babbling, drooling idiot who can barely hold his own head up at the age of five. The rest of my children either died in their mothers' wombs or shortly after birth. I want children! I need heirs!"

"You have a fine heir in your nephew, monseigneur," she said.

"Yes, Edmond is a good man, but he will not marry for fear of bearing children like himself, and what normal maiden would allow herself to be possessed by the monster my nephew is?

"If I die without heirs the French will take my duchy, and Beaumont de Jaspre will cease to exist. There have been ducs de Beaumont de Jaspre since the days of the great Charlemagne. That is why I have agreed to remarry. I asked the Queen of England for a noble wife because I felt I needed new blood for my line. Procreation is, after all, the prime motive for marriage."

"So we are taught by Holy Mother Church," Skye replied.

"Are you of the old Church?" he demanded. "I would have

thought that you were of the new faith coming from the Tudor court."

"I am not English, monseigneur, I am Irish. I am of the one true Church. The Queen, however, is tolerant of all faiths. I am sure that I was sent to you because the Queen assumed you, also, would be of the true faith."

"I was born to the old faith," he said.

"Your nephew said nothing to me of your religion," Skye replied.

"When he left Beaumont de Jaspre, madame, I still practiced that ancient faith, although I had become interested in the teachings of Pastor André Lichault. While Edmond was away, however, I became convinced that Pastor Lichault was correct in his teachings, and I converted to his faith. You, too, will convert when you have been taught."

"And have your people converted to the teachings of your Pastor Lichault, monseigneur?"

He frowned. "They persist in clinging to their old faith. It is wrong, though! I have driven their priests out, and I have torn down the painted and gilded idols that they persist in worshiping. Still they resist me, but I will overcome them, for I am their lord and their master!"

The duc's carriage had moved away from the docks, and through the window of the coach Skye could see Edmond and Robbie following them on horses. She breathed a sigh of relief. She was appalled to find that the duc was not only a Huguenot, but a bit of a fanatic as well.

"Is it not better, monseigneur, that a people have a faith than not have a faith? As long as your people are God-fearing and hardworking souls, does it make any difference how they worship God?" she said.

"Yes!" He looked earnestly at her. "You are very beautiful, madame, but you are only a woman. How can you possibly understand?"

"My other husbands have always said that I was an understanding woman, monseigneur. Perhaps I will not comprehend, but how will you know unless you confide in me?" She gave him a small smile to encourage him. She must keep the lines of communication open between them else this marriage be doomed before it even began.

He leaned forward and began to speak. "The Catholic Church has become corrupt, madame. They no longer administer to the needs of their flock. They sell indulgences and absolutions! They own vast tracts of land. They engage in commerce and act as patrons to worthless artists! They are as venal and as lustful as the worst of men! They have lost sight of God!

"Pastor Lichault was once one of them, but in a vision he saw the light. Now he strives to bring that light to others. My people do not listen now, but in the end they will. The only way we will escape the fires of Hell and damnation is to live simply, to pray, to scourge ourselves free of the opulent trappings with which we have surrounded ourselves!"

Skye was astounded by the duc's outburst and his next words sent a chill through her. "You *must* join me in my endeavors, madame. As your husband I command it! Only when we are both free of sin will God reward us with the children that I so desperately want."

This was hardly what she had expected, and she suspected that even the very Protestant Lord Burghley had known nothing about the duc's sudden conversion, either. The man was unstable, and would not make a reliable ally for England. She had been sacrificed to a madman!

"You say nothing, madame."

She chose her words carefully. "I am a daughter of the one true Church, monseigneur. My uncle is a bishop. I have read and studied the teachings of Martin Luther, but I prefer to remain as I have always been although I am more liberal than many of my faith. I have friends who have chosen to follow the new faith, and if they are happy then I am happy for them, but I cannot convert."

"Your gown is much too immodest," he said, ignoring her words. "Are all your gowns so low in the neckline?"

"It is the fashion, monseigneur."

"After today you will not wear such garments. They were made to entice, and to lure a man into lust. I will send the castle seamstress to you tomorrow, and when she has taken your measurements she will make you more suitable garments."

"I choose my own clothes, monseigneur," Skye said sharply. "Whatever the fashion, I am, and always have been, a faithful wife. I do not flaunt my charms before other men."

"You would disobey me, madame?" His look was black.

"No, monseigneur, I would simply overrule you in an area in which you are not competent to judge."

"But the sight of so much beauty is distracting, madame!"

"I do not flaunt my beauty. If you are distracted then the fault is within you, monseigneur. It is not with me."

"You are right," he whispered, and obviously shaken by the truth of her words, he withdrew into himself.

Skye turned to look out the window of the coach at the beautiful little town of Villerose. Her conversation with the duc had disturbed her greatly. He was obviously not a man of strong character if in his nephew's absence he had been led astray by this Pastor Lichault. At least his people resisted this attempt to force them from the true Church. He may think he has driven the priests out, Skye thought, but I will wager that they are still here. I will have to find one. She focused her eyes upon the town.

It was a lovely place, and to her immense delight each building was painted pink and roofed in red tile. The streets were cobbled but not overly narrow, and flowers grew everywhere, in gardens, in windowboxes, hanging from pots and balconies. "Why are the buildings all pink?" she asked the duc.

"It was the favorite color of one of my ancestors. Villerose has been pink for over three hundred years now." He fell silent again, and Skye turned back to the window.

The town seemed filled with small squares, each with its own fountain sending forth a spray of crystal-clear water into the hot afternoon. There were children everywhere, healthy, well-fed boys and girls, running and playing about the houses and fountains. The duchy of Beaumont de Jaspre was obviously a happy and prosperous place, Skye decided as they passed well-filled, busy shops and small open-air markets. It was everything that Edmond had promised her with one exception: the duc. How could she marry this intense, fanatical man? But she knew she must.

The coach wound its way upward through the cobbled streets until it reached the castle, perched upon the crest of a hill above the town, overlooking the blue sea. Like the town, the castle was of pink stone, its tower roofs tiled in red. A wide moat filled with pink and white waterlilies surrounded the building. The carriage drove across the lowered drawbridge into the courtyard, and Skye was further enchanted. In the courtyard's center was a square tiled pool that was edged with a flowerbed filled with brightly colored blooms. At one end of the fountain, a mischievous bronze cupid rode a bronze dolphin from whose open mouth poured a clear stream of water.

"How lovely!" she exclaimed, clapping her hands together.

"I am pleased that you like it," the duc answered. The intensity was gone, and she felt more comfortable with him.

The vehicle stopped and a footman hurried to help them out. Edmond and Robbie were dismounting their horses. They both hurried over to the carriage as Skye exited it.

"Well," Edmond demanded, "what do you think of Beaumont de Jaspre, *chérie*?"

"It's beautiful, Edmond," she said, but Robbie noticed her lack of enthusiasm and drew her away from the duc.

"What is the matter?"

"He's a Huguenot, Robbie. Newly converted by a Pastor Lichault, and quite the fanatic about it. He claims to have driven the priests from his duchy, and he wants to change my wardrobe to something more modest." Speaking about it, Skye didn't know whether to laugh or to cry.

"God's foot!" swore Robbie, who although a member of the Church of England, was a tolerant man.

"Come, madame." The duc was at her side again. "You will want to refresh yourself before we are married. Will a half an hour suit you?"

"So soon? Could we not wait a few days, monseigneur, so that we might get to know one another?"

"Are you able to receive a man now, madame?" he demanded quite bluntly.

Skye blushed at his indelicacy, and whispered, "Yes."

"Then there is no need for us to wait. You know my feelings on the matter, as we have already discussed them in the coach." He took her arm. "Come now. You will see M'sieur Robert Small and Edmond at the ceremony."

There was nothing for it but to follow him, though behind her she heard Robbie growl a low protest. She dared not turn but kept walking, allowing the duc to lead her into the castle. "Your maid should already be here, madame." he said, moving through the main hall of the castle. The walls were hung with many beautiful crimson, azure and gold silk banners, some of which Skye could see were very old. She followed him as he hurried two flights up a wide staircase with magnificently carved bannisters and then down a corridor lit by windows that faced onto the courtyard now bright with the late-afternoon sunlight. He stopped before a pair of doors shaped like upside down U's, and knocked. The door opened to reveal Daisy.

"Welcome, my lady, m'lord," Daisy said.

"Does your maid not speak French?" the duc demanded.

"She is a simple English country girl, monseigneur, but she is a fine tiring woman, and has been with me for many years." Skye turned to Daisy, saying, "Daisy, this is the duc." She then said to the duc, speaking French this time, "Monseigneur, this is my maid, Daisy, whom you would call Marguérite in your tongue."

Daisy bobbed a pretty curtsey, and smiled her gap-toothed smile. The duc barely nodded. "I will come back for you in a few minutes," he said. "You will be a beautiful bride, madame. And because you are so beautiful, and I believe that there is no real malice in you, I will be patient with your rather hoydenish and independent ways." He bowed curtly, and left her standing there surprised.

Daisy pulled her mistress into the room. "Come in, m'lady! Lord bless me, it's lovely here, it is! I ain't never seen such flowers! Isn't the town simply adorable, all pinklike?" Daisy was full of enthusiasm. "Maybe it won't be so bad living here after all."

"Is there some water, Daisy? I must refresh myself before the duc comes back. We are to be married immediately."

"Ohh." Daisy's eyes widened. "He's that anxious, is he?" She giggled with delight. "He's a fine-looking man, m'lady. He might even be called handsome if he'd just smile, but you'll have him smiling soon enough." She hurried off to fetch the water.

Skye looked about her. She was in a square room with pale-gray stone walls. There were fireplaces on either side of the room, their enormous narrow mantels held up by seated golden marble lions with green jasper eyes. The walls were hung with exquisite silk tapestries all depicting tales of knights and maidens and dragons in colorful and bright threads. Each tapestry was beautifully done, and Skye wondered if some past Duchess of Beaumont had lovingly stitched them. She also wondered if that long-dead duchess had loved her husband.

The room had no windows. In its center was a long oak refectory table with a silver bowl filled with peach-colored roses upon it. Their fragrance perfumed the room. The rest of the furnishings consisted of several straight-back, carved chairs with velvet cushions, strategically placed. There was a door opposite her, and another beside one of the fireplaces, through which Daisy had disappeared.

She now reappeared carrying a golden basin. "Oh, m'lady, come just through the other door, please, into your bedchamber."

Skye walked across the room, and opened the door. "I'm sorry, Daisy. I'm daydreaming, it seems."

Daisy hurried into the room behind her mistress. "And why not?" she demanded. "You're about to be married, and this is a beautiful place!"

Skye looked around the bedchamber. It was a tower room and round in shape. There were windows directly before her that extended to the floor, opening onto a small balcony. She could see the sea through them. To her left was a huge carved bed with a linenfold paneled headboard, draped in plain dark green velvet. Opposite the bed was a small fireplace. There was but one candlestand beside the bed, holding a golden candlestick with a fine beeswax taper. There was a low-backed stool with a tapestry cushion at one side of the fireplace.

"It's not very large for the duchess's chambers," she noted.

"The duc's is next door, m'lady. See the little door on the other side of the bed? That goes into his chambers. There's also a dressing room off the antechamber."

Daisy put the basin down on the candlestand, and Skye rinsed her hands and her face quickly. Daisy had scented the water with her mistress's rose fragrance. Skye was very quiet, and Daisy could not help noticing.

"I wouldn't think you'd have bridal nerves after all these years," she remarked.

Skye laughed weakly. "It's all very different this time, Daisy. I don't know the duc, and our conversation in the coach as we came from the port was not reassuring. He is a Huguenot, and a fanatic at that. He wants children desperately, but I do not know if I can give them to him. He frightens me a little."

Daisy looked shrewdly at her mistress. "Ye're taking the potion that yer sister, Eibhlin, gave you, aren't you?"

Skye nodded. "I intend to go on taking it until the duc and I can come to some sort of arrangement. I don't plan to be his brood mare, locked up in this fairy-tale castle forever." She took the creamy linen towel that Daisy handed her, and dried her face and hands. Then, as an afterthought, she pulled the kerchief from her neckline in a gesture of defiance.

They heard the knock on the antechamber door at the same time, and Daisy hurried to open it. Edmond de Beaumont hurried in, his handsome face distressed.

"I did not know," he said. "As the good God is my judge, Skye, I did not know he had become a Huguenot. I didn't even know he was contemplating it. That damned Lichault! He waited until I was gone, and then, like the snake in the Garden of Eden, he wormed his way deep into my uncle's confidence. God, he is an evil creature!"

"Your uncle says he has driven the priests from Beaumont de Jaspre. Is it true?"

"He thinks he has, but Père Henri has already come to see me. He was the family chaplain. He says he understands the difficult position you, the niece of a bishop, must find yourself in, but you are not to fear for your immortal soul. He gives you a dispensation to wed my uncle in this new faith, knowing that eventually you will overcome that man Lichault and bring my uncle back to the true Church."

Skye nodded, but inwardly she was amused. Her religion was a private thing, although she had been baptized a Catholic. Her second husband had wed her in the Moslem faith, her third in the Church of England. That she had loved them both made the difference. But she did not like the duc telling her what she was going to do, and what she was going to be. If this religion of his was really that way, she would cling like a barnacle to her own faith and let the good local priests think she was devout. It couldn't hurt her reputation, and if she could wean the duc from his obviously unpleasant faith, she might be able to learn to care for him in time. Beneath the stern façade she had detected small flashes of humor. She wondered again what he looked like when he smiled.

Another knock sounded upon the door, and this time it was the duc who entered. He carried with him a nosegay of fragrant orange blossoms, white freesias, and tiny white rosebuds, tied with lilac-colored silk ribbons. With an elegant bow he handed the flowers to her. "For you, madame. Pastor Lichault says such things are the Devil's enticements, but I believe that women appreciate such small vanities, especially on their wedding day." He held out his arm to her, and with a return curtsey she took it.

"Will you allow Daisy to see the ceremony, monseigneur? It would mean a great deal to us both."

"Of course!" He was pleased to note that she had deferred to him in this matter.

The duc led the way to the family chapel, where Robbie, Sean MacGuire and Bran Kelly already awaited them. Edmond de Beaumont drew in his breath sharply as they entered.

"What has happened here?" he demanded furiously. "Where are the tapestries, Uncle? Where are the beautiful altar cloths? The candles? The crucifix? The paintings? Where is the tabernacle?"

The chapel was indeed bare and plain with its simple wooden altar. There was no vigil light. The only light was from its windows, magnificent arches of red, blue, gold, and green stained glass.

"Those fripperies were but trappings of the Devil, Edmond. It was my decision to remove them."

"To where? There were pieces in this chapel that go back almost a thousand years! They belong to this family and to the Church!"

"Pastor Lichault would have destroyed them, Edmond, but I had them packed away. I do not want them any longer. Now be silent, nephew, else you spoil my wedding day." The duc nodded to a man who stood by the altar, and immediately the servant ran out through the sacristy to return a moment later with another man.

He has the look of a cadaver, Skye thought. He was very tall, and very thin, and his face was long with narrow lips, a strangely large nose, and eyes that burned with the fervor of a martyr. He was garbed totally in black, and his rather spare, gray hair stuck out from beneath his square black hat at funny angles. As they approached him Skye could see that his fingernails were dirty, and as they came still closer she noted that he smelled terrible and that there was a ring of dirt around his neck.

"Behold the bride!" the stranger said in a voice that was surprisingly masterful and compelling for such an unattractive man. Then he smiled, showing yellowed teeth, some of which were broken.

The duc returned the smile. "Pastor, I would present to you my new duchesse, Skye." It was the first time he had said her name, and she was surprised that he remembered it, since he had kept calling her madame.

Pastor Lichault chortled. "Ah, Fabron, my son, she is not yet your duchesse, not until I have made her so!" He smiled again. This time his eyes fastened upon Skye, and she fought back the urge to shiver as she saw the man mentally undress her, licking his lips as he obviously liked what his imagination showed him. "Well, let us get on with it then," he said briskly. "Will you take this woman to wife, Fabron?"

"I will," the duc said.

"Will you take this man to husband, Skye? Will you accept him as your master?"

"I take him as my husband," Skye said, and the pastor glared at her.

"You are then man and wife," the pastor finally said grudgingly.

If Skye was horrified with this brief display then so were those who witnessed it. Bran Kelly turned to Robbie and said softly, "If that's a marriage ceremony then I'm a Muslim. Do you think it's legal, or is our lady being gulled?"

Robbie shook his head. "I don't know. I suppose if it's all right with the duc then it's legal here."

"It would not be legal in the eyes of the true Church," Edmond de Beaumont said in a low, angry voice, and Sean MacGuire nodded his agreement. "I do not know what has come over my uncle," Edmond finished.

"Come, madame." The duc had taken her hand, and was turning her about. "I have had a light supper set up in the hall to celebrate our nuptials."

"Uncle, you have not given Skye a ring. Where is her wedding ring?"

"There is no need for one, Edmond. We have been united according to God's law in the presence of witnesses. Pastor Lichault believes that wedding rings are a worldly and ostentatious show. I have donated the gold I would have spent on such a ring to him for use among the poor."

"And will you share your happiness with our people as is customary, Uncle? Will there be feasting and dancing for our people this night in Beaumont?"

"Such extravagances are wasteful and unnecessary, Edmond. A marriage is a part of God's law, and there is no cause for undue celebration because one keeps God's law as is expected of him."

"Another of Pastor Lichault's gems?" Edmond de Beaumont remarked sarcastically.

"You will apologize at once, nephew!"

"*Never!* The man is a charlatan!"

"Edmond," Skye pleaded. "For my sake, please." She didn't want this appalling day marred any more than it already had been.

"Very well, *chérie*, for you, but only for you," Edmond replied, smiling sweetly at her. "I regret my hasty words, Pastor."

"Already," the pastor oozed, "our new duchesse exerts a salubrious influence upon this family. It is a good sign," and he smiled his yellow-toothed smile at them all.

The duc led them into the main hall of the castle with its marvelous silk banners and tall windows now red with the sunset. There were two enormous fireplaces in the hall, but neither was lit this night; rather, they had been banked with flowering branches. Daisy had already disappeared, it not being seemly that she eat with her mistress, and so only Skye, the duc, Edmond, Robbie, Sean MacGuire, Bran Kelly, and the pastor sat at the high board. The duc sat to Skye's right, Robbie to her left. The pastor was on the duc's right, and next to him sat Edmond de Beaumont. Bran Kelly was on the other side of Robbie, and on Bran's left was Captain MacGuire.

Immediately the servants in the duc's azure and silver livery began to pour the lovely rose-colored wine that Edmond had told her was a favorite in Beaumont de Jaspre. An enormous mullet complete with its eyes, set upon a bed of greenery and surrounded with whole carved lemons, was presented as the first course. Skye declined the fish. Her stomach was churning nervously at the thought of what awaited her. She had never been to bed with a stranger, a man she had only just met. No! she amended the thought, and a small smile turned up the corners of her mouth. There was Adam!

She remembered back to the first time she had gone to bed with Adam de Marisco. She had come to Lundy to enlist his help, offering him two percent of her profit if he would aid her. He had asked instead for one percent of the profit—and a night with her. She had been horrified, but had agreed, for she needed his help. Without it she could not triumph over Elizabeth Tudor, who had insulted her unforgivably. But with Adam it had been different. He had been teasing and amusing from the beginning, and although she had been hesitant, she had not been afraid.

She glanced almost fearfully at the stern man by her side. He had not kissed her at the conclusion of their brief marriage ceremony, and although he apparently knew her name, he had only called her by it once.

The servants were now offering capon in gingered lemon sauce, baby lamb, artichokes in olive oil and tarragon vinegar, new peas, and fresh bread. Skye nibbled absently.

"Are you ill?" The duc put his hand on hers.

She started, and looked up at him. His eyes were void of any emotion although his voice was kindly. "I am probably tired," she answered. "It has been a long trip."

"Go prepare yourself for bed then, madame," he said quietly. "I will come to you shortly."

She nodded and then, leaning over, said to Robbie, "I am going to retire now."

"I won't leave you, lass. Remember that I promised you. Tomorrow I shall spend the day looking for a house. Send to me when you want me." He leaned over and kissed her cheek.

With a sad little sigh she returned the kiss, and then rose and left the hall as discreetly as possible. How bleak this marriage already was, she thought, thinking of the gaiety of her previous nuptials. She easily found her way back to her apartment, where Daisy had prepared a bath for her.

"You've not had a freshwater bath in several weeks, m'lady," Daisy said, "and I know how you like yer bath."

"I can't tarry tonight," she replied.

"Nay," Daisy said in agreement. "I've laid out the dusky-rose silk gown for you to wear."

"No," Skye said. "The duc is a conservative man. Perhaps it would be better if my nightclothes were more modest until we get to know one another better. Put the rose away and get the pale-blue silk."

Skye allowed Daisy to strip her of her garments, and then while her faithful tiring woman put her gown away and sought the simpler nightrail, she quickly bathed, enjoying the soft warm water scented with damask rose oil and her damask rose soap that lathered so richly. The feel of the satin suds on her skin was almost sensual. She had, thanks to a surprise rainstorm the previous afternoon, been able to wash her long dark hair on the ship before they arrived at Beaumont de Jaspre. Clean hair always made her feel better. Rinsing herself off, she climbed from the tub. Then she took the large bath sheet that Daisy had laid out for her and dried herself off.

Daisy quickly powdered her lady, and then slipped the blue gown over her head. It slid down Skye's lithe body with a hiss. It was a simple gown with long, full sleeves banded at the wrists with silk ribbon. Its neckline was low and scooped, but it was far more modest than the sheer rose-colored silk gown Daisy had originally chosen. That creation would have clung to her lush form as if it had been painted on, not at all like this full gown, which discreetly hid her shape.

At Daisy's sharp command two serving men entered the room and carried the little wooden tub from the bedchamber.

"How on earth did you get them to do that?" asked Skye, knowing full well that her Devon-born servant didn't speak a word of French.

"Well, m'lady, it's not so much the knowing of the words as it is the tone of voice you use, and your hand signals. Don't worry about me. I'll get on just fine. The words ain't so hard to learn. I'll be gabbing away in their own language in no time at all."

"Oh, Daisy!" Skye hugged the girl. "I probably shouldn't have let you come along with me. You and Bran should be married now, and starting your own family."

"Plenty of time for that," Daisy replied tartly. "You're going to need me, m'lady. I can see that."

The little door on the other side of the bed opened, and the duc, in a white nightshirt, entered the room. Daisy bobbed her mistress a quick curtsey and then one to the duc, and hurried from the room.

"You are not in bed," he said. "In Beaumont de Jaspre it is customary for a bride to await her husband in their nuptial bed."

"I wanted a bath," she said. "I have not had a freshwater bath in weeks."

"Pastor Lichault says bathing is a vanity."

"Then surely he must be the most humble of men," Skye replied sharply. "One cannot be in the same room with him without smelling his body odor. It is distasteful. I have never particularly equated dirt with godliness."

"I would be inclined to agree with you, madame," he said.

There it was again, she thought. That faint touch of humor in his voice. He walked around to where she was standing and very gently began removing the pins from her hair, which Daisy had not gotten around to doing. Carefully he placed the pins on the mantel of the small fireplace, which, like those in the Great Hall, was banked in flowers. Her long hair tumbled down, and he ran his hands through it admiringly. Skye stood very still. He worried her yet, for although he was obviously attracted to her, she could see or feel no passion in him or his actions.

"You have beautiful hair," he said quietly. "A woman's hair is her glory." He then turned her so that her back was to him, and to her surprise, he pushed her gown from her shoulders, baring her to the waist. Gently he cupped her small, full breasts briefly caressing them. "And so is her bosom. You have a lovely bosom, madame. I will enjoy seeing our children suckle upon those beautiful breasts, for that is why God gave them to you." Calmly he drew her gown back up again and, taking her by the hand, led her to the bed. "Now, madame, I want you to lie face down upon the bed," he said.

She gasped and turned large frightened eyes to him. Her heart began to pound with certain, terrible memories. "Surely monseigneur, you are not going to make love to me in the Greek fashion?"

"How do you know of such things?" he thundered angrily, grasping her upper arms so hard that she knew she would be bruised come morning. "What kind of a woman has England sent me? No respectable woman should know of such abomination! Answer me, madame!" His black eyes blazed his outraged fury.

"My first husband," she cried, trying to loosen his grasp on her tender flesh. "He loved to humiliate me by doing . . . doing that."

"You did not like it?" His gaze searched her face anxiously.

"It disgusted me," she replied honestly.

He loosed his grip on her. "So it should have, madame, for God forbids such wickedness. You need not fear that I practice such depravity. However, you must trust me when I ask you to lie face down upon the bed, and you must obey me, madame, for I am your lord and master in both God's eyes and man's."

Skye was distressed. He had assured her that he did not practice Dom's particular perversion, yet why did he want her to lie face down upon the bed? The silence hung heavy between them. She wasn't going to find out standing here, and surely he wasn't going to harm her after he had said he wouldn't. With a sigh she lay down upon the bed.

"Move into the center, madame," came the command, and she obeyed him.

He took her left wrist, and she felt him sliding something about it, something soft and yet strong. As she moved her head to look he moved around the bed to grasp her right arm and bind it as well to the carved posts of the bed with a woven silken cord.

She gasped again, this time with shock. "Monseigneur!" she cried, "what are you doing?" Her fear was beginning to rise again. She struggled to control it, trying to draw a calming breath. His actions, however, were not reassuring.

He was now spreading her legs and binding them also to the lower posts of the bed. "I am binding you to the bed, madame. I would have thought that that was obvious to you." He had finished, and moving up by her head, he pulled the pillows from beneath it. Then lifting her with a surprisingly strong hand, he stuffed the pillows beneath her belly so that her hips were well elevated.

"*Why are you doing this?*" Her voice bordered on the hysterical. Dear Heaven, what terrible perversion was he going to practice upon her helpless form? If he killed her what would happen to her children?

"Because," he said, as he carefully raised her silk nightgown up, fully exposing her buttocks and legs, "I am going to beat you."

"*What?!*" Her voice was a shriek. He was a madman!

"I am going to beat you," he repeated calmly.

"But why? What have I done? We do not even know each other! How can I have displeased you so in the short time since I arrived that you would do something so awful as to beat me?!"

Fabron de Beaumont sat by her side, and in a calm voice began to explain. "My beautiful bride," he said in a voice laced with patience, "you are a woman, and women are weak vessels who must be constantly corrected in order to give them true strength. Pastor Lichault advocates the daily beating of a wife until she conforms perfectly, instantly, and without questions to her husband's will. He and I spoke at great length tonight before I came to you. He feels that you are much too independent a woman at present to make me a dutiful wife. Nonetheless we are now wed, and so he felt that I must begin on this our wedding night a program of correction so that I may mold you into the kind of woman that my wife should be. If you are to bear my children you must raise them as I desire, without question, and with instant obedience. Women are inferior to men, and yet you have dared to raise yourself above your humble station, to put yourself on a level with men. You are overproud, Skye, but I am going to save you from yourself. This I promise you."

She was horrified. "How can you judge me so quickly, my lord Fabron?" she asked him pleadingly. "If women are so inferior then why has God chosen a queen for England, a queen who reigns without the aid of a husband? And what of France's Catherine de Medici, a queen mother who has reigned for her minor children with God's blessing?"

"You ask too many questions, Skye," he said. "That is one way I am able to judge you. Women should not ask questions, for Pastor Lichault says they were born to obey without question. As to those two queens you have mentioned, who is to say that it is God who keeps them in power? More likely it is the Devil!"

"Monseigneur, I beg of you, do not beat me!" Skye was becoming extremely frightened. Was her husband a madman? Did he really believe the foolish nonsense that he had been spouting? Pastor Lichault was obviously one of those awful Calvinists who believed that any joy in living was sinful. They were such fools, the Calvinists. She had known some in England, and they were as dangerous as the fanatics among the Catholics. She shuddered with her fright.

"Madame, I do this for your own good. In time, when you have been properly schooled and seen the errors of your past attitude, you will be grateful to me for my perseverance."

"H-how long will you continue to do this?" her voice was shaking. Dear God, she prayed silently, don't let him kill me in his zeal. Let me live to win him over for both our sakes, and the sake of my children.

"When the day comes, my dear, that you admit to your faults, admit that a woman is incapable of running a business—and I suspect that your business partner does it all for you, despite your claim; when the day comes that you admit that you are not suited to running the vast estates that you claim to run, and entrust such things to me, then I will know that you have become the kind of wife I seek, and want. Until that time I will beat you each night before we retire."

He stood up and moved where she could not see him, only to return a moment later. In his hand he now had a birch switch the thickness of her finger. He placed it before her lips and commanded her, "You will kiss the rod of correction, madame. When I am through you will kiss it again and remember to thank me for your punishment."

Skye turned her head aside. In this she would defy him. It mattered not what she did, he was going to hurt her anyway. At least she would not grovel.

His voice grew cold with anger. "I had meant to go easily with you tonight," he said, "but I can see that the pastor is right. You are arrogant beyond reason. You will be given the full measure of your punishment."

She tried a last time. "Monseigneur, I beg you do not do this. If you do I shall complain to my queen who sent me here! She will not be pleased to learn that you are abusing me."

"You will complain to no one, madame. It is my right as your husband to chastise you. Even your corrupt church will not deny me that right! You wished to get to know me better, and I am granting you that privilege. For the next month you will not leave these rooms, and I shall leave them only when necessary. I intend mating with you as often as possible in that time so that you will bear me a child as quickly as possible. *I need an heir!* We will spend the next month mating, and struggling through prayer and punishment to change your behavior." He raised the switch and brought it down sharply upon her bare buttocks.

Skye screamed with surprise. She had not been expecting the

blow so soon, and he gave her no time to recover. His arm rose and fell, rose and fell, rose and fell again in ceaseless motion as he began to beat her in earnest. She cried out again and again with pain as the switch cut sharply and cruelly into her tender bottom.

This was a nightmare! It could not be happening! "Please," she wept, "please, monseigneur, I beg you! Stop! Stop!" Skye felt very ashamed of herself to beg, but she could not stand the awful pain.

His answer was to lash her harder, this time cutting into her legs. She felt the warm trickle of blood as he broke the skin. Skye struggled against her silken bonds, but she could not escape him, and the pillows he had placed beneath her had only served to raise her hips up higher so he might get at them easier. His arm did not seem to tire easily of the punishment; rather, he seemed to be gaining strength from her struggles.

"Bitch!" he hissed at her, and he cut viciously at her writhing bottom. "Admit to your faults! Admit that you are nothing! That man is the master! Admit that you are mindless softness made only for man's pleasure, the cracked vessel for the spilling of his seed! A beast to bear his sons! It is God's law, and you defy that law!"

"No! No!" she sobbed as the switch laid white-hot pain upon white-hot pain. "Women are not beasts! They have minds, too!"

"You are stubborn," he again hissed at her, his arm never flagging in its punishment of her helpless flesh, "but in the end I will prevail, and I will save you from the snares of the Devil, who has so obviously gained possession of your soul!"

She could not stand much more of this torture, and her mind began to drift away into a blessed and quiet darkness. She no longer felt the switch's heat, or heard the duc's voice. *Adam*, she cried out within her mind, and then she felt him loving her as he had so often loved her. She struggled to open her eyes, feeling her desire for him rising, wanting to see his dear face, to feel his caress.

Her black lashes fluttered against her pale cheeks, and she finally managed to raise them to unveil her eyes. To her horror, it was the duc who was upon her, preparing to insert his long, swollen male organ within her helpless body. "*No!*" she shrieked, seeking to force him off her, but though she was now lying upon her back, her buttocks burning like fire beneath her, to her dismay her arms were still bound to the bedposts.

He seemed not to notice her resistance. Instead he moaned with open desire, pushing her nightgown up to her neck and fumbling with her breasts again. "Beautiful, beautiful," he murmured, "such beautiful little tits!" He lowered his head and sucked each one in turn, then rolled the tight nipples between his thumb and his forefinger, pinching them gently again and again until she thought she would scream. His hand roamed over her belly, fondling it, murmuring of the babes she would give him, and then, despite her protests, he was pushing himself into her. He thrust deeply, moving rhythmically as he muttered, "Fuck! You were made to be fucked, Skye! Ah, God! You were born to be fucked!"

She stared at him with horror. She could have been a dead body for all he cared! It made no difference to him whether she was conscious or unconscious as long as he could feel, and touch, and fuck her. What was worse for her was the terrible realization that she felt nothing herself. She, the most passionate and sensuous of women, felt nothing except an awful invasion of her mind and her soul and her body.

The man atop her shuddered with his own release, and then fell over to one side. Within minutes he was snoring and she lay next to him, numb with shock and with shame. Even with Dom, God assoil his black soul, it had never been so dreadful. Dom, for all of his crudity, had loved her in his own fashion, had been proud of her, and jealous of her. This man wanted nothing but to break her, to possess her very soul, to make her a mindless creature fit for nothing more than bearing babies until she finally died of too many children in too few years. She had seen it happen to other women. It might even have happened to her with Dom had she not had her sister, Eibhlin, to help her.

He had not taken the time to unbind her arms before he had fallen asleep, and so she lay uncomfortable and chilled as the night slowly progressed. Her bottom and the tender backs of her thighs ached with the beating that he had given her. She could feel the welts that had been raised on her skin burning like hot embers. Never before had she been subjected to such treatment. Her mind rebeled at the words that he had thrown at her this night. So he believed his warped pastor. He believed that women were nothing but mindless softness. Her bridegroom was in for a shock when he learned that *this* woman was rock-hard!

She wondered if he would eventually untie her, or if he intended to keep her bound to the bed for the entire month. Was Fabron de Beaumont truly mad, or was he simply a crazed fanatic? Had he been like this with his other wives? No. It was not possible. She did not think that Edmond had lied to her, and he had always spoken of his uncle with genuine affection. No. The duc was obviously not a strong man, and had somehow come under the influence of this terrible creature, Pastor Lichault. Perhaps he felt guilt for the deaths of his two previous wives. Or perhaps he had secretly wanted to be a priest, as Edmond had suggested, and he could not because of his family obligations. The Huguenot had seen the duc's weaknesses and wielded his evil influence upon Fabron when he was bereft of all his family. But it could not, *must* not continue! Skye knew she could not stand many more beatings like the one the duc had administered to her this night.

God's foot, but he was a cold man! Her genuine, piteous cries should have wrung his heart, but instead they had only driven him to apply his switch harder. She shuddered, remembering how terribly it had hurt. Then afterward, when she lay barely conscious, to have taken her body, uncaring of how she felt, of whether he gave her pleasure as well as took it! Suddenly a picture of women in war came to her mind, and she realized for all that the duc was her husband, she had been raped. She shuddered again. The man was a monster!

"Are you cold?" His voice, calm now, asked her.

"You have not untied me, monseigneur."

"Forgive me, madame." He was solicitous, and reaching up, he loosened her bonds. Then he drew her into his arms and began stroking her breasts through her nightgown. "I find that I cannot get enough of you." He pushed up her nightgown again and mounted her. Skye stiffened and he noticed. "You do not like it when I fuck you?" he asked.

"No," she answered, honestly not caring if she hurt him. Men were vain about such things.

"Good," he said. "It is not meant that a woman gain pleasure from a man's labor. It is the man's pleasure that is paramount." He thrust into her again and again until he once more spilled his seed. Then the duc slept again.

Thank God, thought Skye, that I have taken Eibhlin's potion. I'll not give this beast children! I am not certain that this family *should* be perpetuated. They produce dwarfs, idiots, and madmen. Better the French come and take the duchy.

I will write to the Queen, she vowed. No, I will write to Lord Burghley! I will explain to him how it is. This marriage is not valid in the eyes of my own Church, and I suspect it is also invalid in the eyes of the Church of England. I must lull the duc into thinking that I am becoming more biddable so that I can speak with Robbie. Bess Tudor has asked many hard things of me, but even she will be shocked to learn of my plight, I know. She will not make me stay here. She cannot!

Skye turned onto her side, away from her new husband who was snoring once again, and gingerly felt the weals he had raised on her skin. She would be revenged for each welt that he had marked on her flesh. That she promised herself. She had no intention of allowing him to further abuse her, even if she had to slit his throat. She could do it, too. Right now he lay helpless next to her, convinced of his own superiority, unbelieving that a woman could wield the power of life and death over any man. She smiled softly in the darkness. Fabron de Beaumont would very shortly learn, much to his distress, what it was like to have Skye O'Malley for an enemy. She didn't think that he was going to like it. Smiling, Skye fell asleep.

Part II

Beaumont
de Jaspre

Chapter 4

Fabron de Beaumont awoke with a start and stared into the blue-green eyes of his bride of less than a day. She was nude and sat comfortably upon his chest, pressing a small but lethal fruit knife against the hollow of his throat. His heart began to pump frantically.

"Do not move, monseigneur," Skye said pleasantly, "else my hand slip; and do not make the mistake of thinking I will not kill you, for if you move I will."

He swallowed hard, and she saw with a certain grim satisfaction the pulse leaping erratically in his throat. "*Why?*" he said.

"You asked the Queen of England for a wife, monseigneur, and she graciously supplied you with one. I must assume that you knew the women of my region are proud and independent ladies. Even the women of France are enlightened in this day and age.

"I am not a creature to be beaten into obedience. I am a woman, monseigneur. I am a woman of intelligence, and wealth, and family. If you should ever raise your hand to me again without just cause I will kill you without hesitation. I will be a good wife to you, and if God wills it I will bear you children. I will not, however, convert to your Huguenot faith. I am not the best of Catholics, but I prefer my faith over others, and I have always granted that others have a right to their own beliefs."

She looked piercingly at him. "Do you understand me, monseigneur? *There will be no more beatings!*"

"And if I refuse to agree, you arrogant bitch, what then?" he demanded, his own dark eyes blazing with outrage and anger.

"I will kill you now where you lie, monseigneur," she said coldly.

"My body is scarred with your marks. I have but to show them to your nephew, and to Père Henri.

"I will claim that as a good daughter of the Church I knew your pastor had no real authority to wed us, and that although I begged and pleaded with you to call back Père Henri to marry us in the only true faith, *you* would not have it." She smiled sweetly down at him. "Then I will claim that I could not live in sin with you, having always been a respectable married woman—and monseigneur, my reputation *has* always been spotless. But you forced yourself upon me, and when I tried to protect my virtue you beat me mercilessly. Having been subjected to a night of your carnal lust and unnatural desires, I did the only thing a good daughter of the Church could have done when you came at me again, threatening my very soul with your wicked perversions. I killed you." She looked down on him dispassionately. "Do you really think that the Church, or your good nephew, will hold me responsible for an act committed in a moment of terror?"

Skye had the upper hand now, and she knew it. She had quickly ascertained the duc was no fool. He would therefore not want a scandal. "The choice as to whether you live or die is up to you, monseigneur. Make it now!" she said, her gaze icy.

"How do you know that you can trust me, madame?" he asked her, unable to keep his eyes from her beautiful breasts. "I could agree, and then when you are off my chest, your knife put away, renege on our agreement. An agreement made under such duress can scarcely be legal."

"You are, so your nephew claims, an honorable man. I must assume that honor extends to a mere woman as well as to your fellow man."

He nodded, rather surprised by her logic. "Very well, madame, I agree. I will not beat you again, but understand that any children you give me will be brought up in my faith, and not yours. I will not allow you to taint my sons with the great harlot Rome."

"I agree," she said without hesitation, knowing that if she decided to bear his children she would be able to teach them love despite Pastor Lichault. She swung lightly off him and lay the fruit knife upon the candlestand. Then, sitting back against the pillows, she drew the finely embroidered linen sheets up to cover her bosom. The simple show of modesty rather intrigued him.

He sat up and looked at her. "You are a formidable woman, madame."

"My name is Skye," she said quietly. "You have said it but once since we first met yesterday. Can you not call me by my name in the privacy of our chambers at least?"

"You have only used my name once also, Skye."

"It is an unusual name, Fabron," she answered him.

"It is peculiar to this region," he said. "It is a family name. From the beginning of time there have always been Fabrons in the de Beaumont family."

There was a long silence between them, and then she asked, "Why do you dislike women so much?"

He thought a moment, then said, "I didn't realize that I did until just now." He sighed. "I suppose I resent the fact that I could not become a priest in my youth, as I wanted to. I was my father's eldest legitimate son. Edmond's father was my only full brother, although my father populated the region with his bastards. One of those bastards was even the son of a young noblewoman. He had few scruples, my father. He was a very carnal man. He was also a very strong-willed one. Eldest sons inherited, and only death was an accepted excuse for shirking one's responsibilities.

"My first wife suffered many years trying to give me a child. Poor Marie. With each miscarriage or stillbirth she became more determined to give me a live son. Such a sweet woman. She died trying, and I believed that God was punishing me for not having followed my conscience. When my second wife, Blanche, finally gave birth to that drooling idiot who is called my son, and then died also, I was certain that God was punishing me.

"When I met Pastor Lichault and confided in him he assured me that the loss of these two women had satisfied God's anger. He says that you are a healthy, vigorous woman who will easily give me children if I can but curb your wicked spirit, which is an affront to God."

"I cannot agree with the pastor," Skye said quietly. "A woman is best handled with love and kindness. Like a flower, she will grow and flourish with a man's love. Unkindness will only make her vengeful and bitter. Besides, if you expect the kind of son who can rule this duchy, it is a strong woman who must bear him for you."

"Did you love the other men you were married to, Skye?" he asked her curiously. "Did they not object to your strong will?"

"I loved three of them," she said. "Each was a different man, and yet each possessed a great capacity to love. Yes, I loved them, and they loved me. None ever objected to my ways." Her face was alight with her memories, and he caught his breath in wonder at how incredibly beautiful she was.

Leaning over and taking her hand, he turned it and kissed the palm. Her eyes regarded him seriously. She felt nothing for him, although she knew he was trying, and so she felt that she must try also. There was no other choice. She withdrew her hand from his and, reaching out, touched his cheek. He looked back at her, his glance equally serious and unsmiling.

"I know that the Bible says it is wrong for a man and a woman to show themselves as God created them, but at this moment I wish for nothing more than to see you naked. Will you grant me that wish, Skye?"

Drawing the covers off, she rose from the bed. "I am sure," she said, "that it is Pastor Lichault who has told you this, Fabron, but I believe he is wrong. The Bible says that we were created in God's image, and if that be so, how can it be wrong to admire what God hath wrought, what God is?" She turned slowly so he might have a full and complete view of her body.

He almost wept at her beauty; the small perfect breasts, the graceful line of her buttocks and legs, the slender grace of her waist, the long line of her back, her shapely arms. Everything was perfection, but for the marks of his rod on her skin. They would fade, but seeing them, he felt guilty. "You cannot be real," he said. "The pastor is right! Women are an invention of the Devil! Cover yourself, madame!"

In answer she flung herself upon the bed next to him. "No, Fabron," she said firmly. She had made up her mind to fight the ignorance and superstition of the Huguenot. She was the duc's wife now, and she was not going to allow Pastor Lichault either to rule or destroy her marriage. "The Bible tells us that woman was created by God from the rib of Adam, the first man."

"How do you know this? Who told it to you?"

"No one told me, Fabron. The Bible has been translated into English, and I have seen it, and read it with my own eyes."

"Your wicked Church forbids that you know what is in the Bible," was his answer.

"The Church forbids many things, Fabron, and I do not always agree with them." She smiled a small smile at him. "I told you that I was not the best of Catholics. The Bible was translated, and I wanted to read what it said. I did."

"Do you always do what you want, madame?" His black eyes were stern, but the little hint of humor was there in his voice again.

"The choice is not always mine, Fabron, but when it is I usually choose to please myself, yes." What a strange man he was, Skye thought. He was tortured and guilt-ridden, and he had been cruel to her, yet she felt sorry for him.

Their eyes met, and then he reached out his hand and smoothed it down the curve of her hip. "It is wrong surely to make love in the daylight," he said low, and she saw he wanted her.

"Has Pastor Lichault said it?" she gently teased, watching him from beneath hooded lids.

"The subject has never come up, Skye. I have never read it was so in the Bible, have you?"

"No, monseigneur, I have not."

His hand moved to fondle her buttock. "Have you ever before made love in the daylight?" he asked.

"Yes," she answered him. She could see how very roused he was by her body, by their conversation, by the picture in his mind that their talk had aroused. With a sob he was pushing her back against the pillows to fumble with her breasts, all the while murmuring, "Surely such pleasure must be wrong! We should not do this thing. We should not!" Yet he was possessing her quickly, before she was even ready for him, moistening his fingers in his mouth and rubbing them against her cleft, pushing eagerly into her to satisfy his own desires.

Skye closed her eyes, and let him have his way as he sobbed and thrust atop her. At least, she thought relieved, he is capable of functioning without cruelty. In time I will teach him to give me pleasure too if I can but free him from his fears. How odd, she thought. For the first time in my life it is I, and not the man, who is in charge of the lovemaking.

Then with a wild cry the duc collapsed, sated with his lust. Although she was not yet ready to forgive him his brutality she felt strangely sympathetic toward him. He was really quite a sad man, a weak man filled with fears and prejudices. He was susceptible, however, to strength in others, and she was strong. Until now there had only been Pastor Lichault to influence him, but she would overcome that unpleasant creature, for if she did not she would find life with her new husband a living hell; and she could certainly not bring her children into such an atmosphere.

For many days Skye and Fabron remained alone together within her chambers. They spoke at length and as she listened she learned much about her new husband. There had never, she decided, been any real love in his life, and he was suffering greatly from its lack. The only person who had ever given him honest affection, it seemed, was Edmond, his nephew. His mother, a distant cousin of France's queen mother, Catherine de Medici, had been a cold and correct woman who, having borne her two children, left them to the casual care of others. His father had been a stern man of high principles and lusty appetites who had never once made an affectionate gesture toward either of his sons, being far too busy running the duchy—and pursuing the ladies, which he did equally well.

The only person who had ever offered Fabron warmth and affection was the castle priest, Père Henri, and perhaps from this had come his desire to join the Church, to emulate the man whom he most admired. His father, of course, would not hear of it, and Fabron de Beaumont had grown bitter. Père Henri had understood both parties, and had tried to mediate between father and son. If it was God's will that Fabron de Beaumont be a priest he would have been born the younger son, Père Henri insisted, hoping to satisfy both men, but this argument wore thin and grew more suspect with each miscarriage of Fabron de Beaumont's wives and their deaths. Then his father died, and there was no escape from his responsibilities. His younger brother was dead, injured in a tournament, and his only legitimate male relation was his dwarf nephew. He was forced to take another wife.

While Fabron awaited his bride Pastor Lichault had begun to work his evil upon the easily susceptible duc. Yes, the cleric had agreed with the guilt-ridden man, the past was indeed God's judgment upon him for not having followed his conscience, but now

God was sending him a new wife. It was time for a fresh start. A new wife, a new faith. The pastor spoke with authority and quoted the Bible with apparent knowledge. Desperate to succeed with this new wife where he had failed with his others, the duc was swayed from the faith of his fathers, and with the zeal of all converts he embraced his new faith with passion.

Now his beautiful new wife had introduced a strong element of doubt into his mind. She was all the things that the pastor had said a woman shouldn't be; she was totally different from any woman he had ever known; and yet after almost three weeks of marriage to Skye he believed that for the first time in his life he might be falling in love. Skye! It was an outrageous name, but he was already used to it and liked it. She had been named after the island from which her mother had come, Skye had told him. Strange, it suited her. She was not a Marie or a Jeanne or a Renée.

She was beautiful, and willful; and gentle and independent; and tender and intelligent. She was, in fact, all the things he had never before even considered in a wife except perhaps beautiful. She had yet to refuse him her body, although his two previous wives had always been seeking excuses to avoid their wifely duties, and then when he had finished with them they had moved quickly away from him. Skye always snuggled next to him, or held him within her own arms. He found he liked that in particular, pillowing his head upon her soft breasts, breathing the marvelous rose fragrance of her. She was cleaner and sweeter than any woman he had ever known.

One night she said to him as he lay sated with pleasure, "Do you know, Fabron, that you have never kissed me?"

He was startled, for he had never been one for *that* kind of closeness. Nonetheless he suddenly wanted to please her, to give back some of the kindness she was bestowing upon him despite their wretched beginning; a beginning he winced at when he remembered it. "Would it please you if I kissed you, Skye?" he asked her anxiously.

"Yes," she said softly, "it would please me greatly, *mon mari*."

Raising himself upon one elbow, he bent his head down and touched his lips gently to hers, drawing away as quickly as though he had been burned. With a soft laugh Skye drew his head back down with her hands, and pressed her mouth to his ardently.

Fabron de Beaumont felt a delicious weakness race through his veins, felt his flaccid manhood tingle and stir to life again.

"*That*, monseigneur," she said as she released her hold on him and drew her mouth from his, "that is a kiss. Not altogether 'an unpleasant thing, is it?"

"Are you mocking me, madame?" he demanded, but his dark eyes belied the sternness of his tone.

"Perhaps a little," she replied. "Laughter goes with love, *mon mari*."

"You lack respect for me, madame," he said, "and I must claim a forfeit for this absence of decorum." Then he was kissing her, sweeping her into his arms, his lips seeking her sweetness with a gentle strength that quite surprised her. For the first time since their marriage a tiny tingle of desire stirred within Skye. Perhaps, she thought, there is hope for us after all.

He held her lightly against him, and she knew that he gained tremendous pleasure from the proximity of her body, the warmth and the silkiness of her smooth perfumed flesh. "Do you like it when I caress you?" he asked her hesitantly.

"Yes," she whispered to him.

"Do you like it when I kiss and caress your lovely breasts?"

"Yes, *mon mari*, I like it very much," was her soft answer.

"I want you to like it," he said in what Skye thought was a shy voice. "I want you to like it when I make love to you."

"Oh, Fabron," Skye said, touched and pleased that she was beginning to get through to him. "When you are gentle and tender with me I, too, find pleasure. Should we both not find pleasure in each other?"

"Pastor Lichault says—"

Her hand stopped his mouth. "What does a priest, a priest of *any* faith, know of passion between a man and his wife, Fabron? I believe that God gave a man his wife not only for companionship and the procreation of his children, but for pleasure as well. I believe that God gave woman her husband for the same reasons. Love me, and I will love you in return. Where is the wrong in that, *mon mari?*"

Kissing her hand, he removed it from his lips, and said, "You make it all seem so simple, Skye."

"It is simple, Fabron. Love me, and I will love you back."

He made love to her then, made love to her as he had not made love to her before. He was tender and considerate. He sought to please her for the first time, and was surprised to find that her pleasure excited him greatly. When she attained the top of the mountain he realized that all the other times she had only pretended in order to please him. It was then he knew that he loved this beautiful woman who, despite his bestial treatment of her that first night, had sought to make their marriage work. *"Je t'aime,* Skye," he murmured in her ear, and she held him close, knowing now that they had a chance to succeed in their marriage.

Their idyll was soon over, however. The next morning they sat at a small table that Daisy set up each day in the window of the bedchamber, eating their simple meal of sweet ripe peaches, fresh bread warm from the oven, salt brie, and watered wine. The long windows stood open, and along the stone balustrade blood-red roses grew over the pink stone. Above them the sky was a cloudless blue, below the sea was a sunlit blue-green. A small black and yellow songbird that had taken to visiting them perched himself amid the roses and sang a song before fluttering to their table to eat crumbs from Skye's hand. Husband and wife smiled at each other.

"How can you do that?" he asked her, intrigued as he always was by her ability to charm the bird.

"The bird knows that it has nothing to fear from me," she said softly. "If you love a wild creature it senses your love."

"More than likely it is witchcraft!" thundered a voice from the center of the room. Startled, the bird fled.

"M'lady, monseigneur, I tried to keep *him* out, but *he* pushed me aside," Daisy said indignantly. It was said in French, but Daisy quickly switched to English. "Beware, m'lady! The old devil's been fuming for days over the duc's neglect of him."

"You presume upon my friendship for you, Pastor, that you would intrude upon the privacy of myself and my duchesse," Fabron de Beaumont said sternly.

Pastor Lichault strode to the table. Skye wrinkled her nose. Did the man never bathe? He smelled as if he slept with the goats. "I come for the good of your immortal soul, Fabron, my son! Since the night I joined you under God's holy law with this woman you have not come to me. You have neglected your spiritual duties, and

God is displeased! He will take his vengence, and this woman will abort your seed as did your other wives. Down upon your knees, both of you! Beg God's forgiveness before it is too late!"

The duc looked suddenly uncertain and frightened; Skye was furious and she leapt to her feet. "You wicked man!" she shouted at the pastor. "It is you who should fall upon your knees and beg God's forgiveness for your distorted, terrible teachings!"

"Whore!" The pastor pointed a bony finger at Skye. "Look at her, Fabron, my son! Look how she flaunts her body like a common harlot of Babylon!" His eyes fastened upon her breasts, and he unconsciously licked his lips. Skye was wearing the sheer, rose-colored silk gown she had refused to wear the night of her wedding to the duc.

"You are looking hard enough," she accused the pastor, "and the thoughts I see lurking behind your evil eyes are hardly those of a holy man!" She was very angry now.

"You have neglected your duties by this woman," the pastor cried. "Her skin is unmarked. You have not beaten her each day as I told you you must, and she is more unbridled than when she came to you. If you will not follow God's will, then I must do it for you, for the sake of your immortal soul!" Reaching out, the pastor grasped at Skye with surprisingly strong fingers, and tearing her gown from her, he began to beat her with his hands about the face and head. Skye screamed and struggled to escape his hold.

With a roar of outrage Fabron de Beaumont leapt at the Huguenot pastor and dragged him off of Skye. Furiously he began to pummel the man with knotted fists as Daisy ran to aid her shaking mistress. "You devil's spawn," the duc snarled at the pastor, who had suddenly become a sniveling, cringing creature. "You lured me from my faith, and almost destroyed my marriage before it even began. Were my new duchesse not a woman of strength and character, I should have destroyed her that first night. God forgive me for the weakling I have been, but am *no more!*"

Then with one sweeping motion Fabron de Beaumont lifted Pastor Lichault bodily into the air and flung him over the balcony. With horror they heard his death scream as he hurtled through the air, then all was silent. Skye and Daisy ran to the balcony and, looking over, saw that he was quite dead upon the rocks below, his neck twisted at a grotesque angle, blood streaming from his nose and mouth.

Turning back to calm her angry husband, Skye saw that Fabron stood, his knees buckling, his eyes bulging from his head, his hands moving frantically from his throat to his head as he struggled to breathe, to speak. Then with a gasping, frantic cry he collapsed onto the floor.

"Get the physician!" Skye commanded Daisy as she knelt by the duc's side. "Get Edmond also—and hurry, Daisy!"

Daisy sped from the room, her legs moving automatically, for she was partially in shock from the events of the last few minutes. Behind her Skye checked to see if Fabron de Beaumont was still alive. He was; his barely noticeable breathing and a faint pulse throbbing in his neck were the only real evidence of his survival. "Oh, Fabron," she said, "I am so sorry! Please don't die, monseigneur. Get well for me, and I shall make you so happy." Skye took his head in her lap, stroking it as she sat quietly waiting. There was nothing else she could do to aid him. He was so still and so white now, and her heart went out to him. She did not know if she would ever love this strange man, but he obviously loved her. Loved her enough to come to her defense against the pastor. She felt no loss over that one's death. He was an evil man who brought only fear and unhappiness to those whose lives he had touched with his withering hand.

"*Chérie!*" Edmond de Beaumont was suddenly there by her side. "What has happened?"

"*Madame la Duchesse.*" It was the physician. "I will take over now." He looked at Daisy. "Help me, girl. We will move him to the bed, where I may examine him more closely." Together the two lifted the limp man over to the bed, still tumbled from the night before.

"What has happened?" Edmond repeated, seating Skye back down in a chair. His eyes lit admiringly on her breasts, the nakedness of which she was totally unaware. Then walking to the bed, he picked up a gossamer knit shawl and draped it over her shoulders.

"Fabron had a terrible argument with the pastor, and became so angry that he threw Pastor Lichault over the balcony. Don't bother to look. He's dead. Then your uncle had some kind of attack." She shivered. "Get Père Henri, Daisy. I'm sure Edmond knows where he has been hiding."

"The room at the top of the old north tower," Edmond said.

Within a few minutes the priest joined them. It was the first time

Skye had seen him, and she liked what she saw. Père Henri was a small man in early old age. Still, he possessed a full head of wavy white hair and kindly warm brown eyes. Although his features were very aristocratic, his speech was that of a less educated and privileged man. He was, she suspected, some lord's by-blow on a peasant girl. With the devotion to duty that had made him loved among the castle folk, he hurried to the duc's side and blessed him. Then, looking to the doctor, he asked, "Well, Mathieu, will he live?"

"Possibly, *mon père*. He has suffered an apoplectic fit. Its severity I cannot tell until he returns to consciousness."

The priest nodded and then moved across the room to Skye and Edmond. "How did this terrible thing happen, Edmond?" he asked.

Quickly Edmond de Beaumont told Père Henri what he knew, and when he had finished the priest put a gentle hand upon Skye's head and blessed her, finishing with the words, "And the Church welcomes you to Beaumont de Jaspre, too, Madame la Duchesse. Now, my daughter, you will tell me the rest of it, from the beginning, from the night when you were joined with Fabron in matrimony."

"You must marry us, *mon père*," Skye whispered. "That creature who called himself a man of God was not fit to do so."

"For the time being, my daughter, you must not worry. The signatures on the betrothal agreement between you and the duc make your marriage legal in the eyes of the laws of this duchy. When the duc is able, we will, however, bestow the Church's approval on your actions." He patted her hand, and repeated as he sat down opposite her, "Now, tell me everything."

She told them of the horrors of her wedding night, of how she had been trying these last three weeks to make a better thing of their marriage. Then she went on to tell them of how the pastor had burst in on them this morning, of the terrible things he had said, of how he had begun beating her—and of how the duc had gone to her defense. The duc had repented his lapse from the true Church, Skye assured Père Henri.

"You are to be commended, my daughter," Père Henri said when she had finished. "Fabron was a disturbed and confused man. You showed true Christian patience in your efforts to win him over and to bring him back to Holy Mother Church. In the end, despite this tragedy those efforts were rewarded, praise God. Will you keep a vigil with me tonight in the chapel for your husband's recovery, my daughter?"

She nodded, and he patted her hand again with approval. She looked at Edmond de Beaumont, whose violet eyes were filled with admiration for her, and asked him, "Will you see that the chapel is restored before tonight, Edmond?" She turned again to the priest. "Will you purify and rebless the sanctity of the chapel, *mon père*, before we begin our prayers?"

Both men looked upon Skye with great approval, and she felt a twinge of guilt. She had not been this religious in years, she thought uncomfortably. She certainly did not want to mislead the two, and yet this was how she felt right now. The duc needed her prayers. Surely God would hear the prayers of even a less-than-perfect Catholic. "I am no saint, gentlemen," she said to salve her guilt. "Please do not attribute to me virtues which I do not possess, lest you later be very disappointed."

Across the room the duc moaned, and Skye hurried to her husband's side. But although he was restless, he was still in an unconscious state. "I am here, Fabron," she said softly, and he quieted.

For the next few days the duc hovered between consciousness and unconsciousness. Skye found herself suddenly in control of the duchy, and the responsibility helped to assuage her worry. With the death of Pastor Lichault the people were able to return freely to their own Catholic faith.

The inhabitants of Beaumont de Jaspre believed that their ancestors had come to Christianity through the efforts of the early disciples who wandered the Mediterranean converting the people. The Beaumontese were devout and simple people who had delighted in their beautiful churches and the many religious festivals they celebrated. Pastor Lichault's stern Calvinistic coldness, his lack of joy, his constant harping upon sin and damnation had angered them as well as frightened them. They welcomed back their priests and the mass joyfully, and did not mourn the pastor despite their clerics' admonitions to forgive.

Then the duc regained consciousness, but he could not move below the waist and he was unable to speak. "In time perhaps," his physician said, but a month passed and there was no improvement. A second month went by, and a representative from the French court arrived. The duc, he said, would obviously not recover. His only child was not fit to rule. Was the duchesse *enceinte?* Skye was forced to admit that she was not. M'sieur Edmond could not possibly inherit because of his disability. There was nothing for it but France take over the duchy. The French King's envoy suddenly found himself imprisoned within his apartments.

"There has to be another way," Skye said as she met with Robbie, Edmond, and Père Henri. "We cannot allow the French to take Beaumont de Jaspre. Is there no other relative who might rule?" She looked to Edmond. "Surely there is *someone*."

"There is Nicolas St. Adrian," Edmond said slowly.

"The duc would not hear of it," Père Henri protested.

"He has no choice. It is either Nicolas or the French, *mon père*."

"Who is Nicolas St. Adrian?" Skye demanded.

"He is the duc's very noble bastard brother," Père Henri replied. "A baron if I remember correctly."

"St. Adrian is not a Beaumontese name," Skye noted.

"It is not, madame," the priest answered. "Many years ago your husband's father fell in love with the only child of an elderly and impoverished noble family in Poitou. Emilie St. Adrian was the love of Giles de Beaumont's life; and the fact that he already had a wife did not prevent him from seducing the innocent girl. When she told him she was with child, expecting him to do the right thing and marry her, he was forced to confess to his deception. She refused ever to see him again, an act that her elderly father fully approved. When she delivered a healthy son, Giles de Beaumont attempted to contribute to the boy's support, but neither of the St. Adrians would hear of it. Everything he sent to the boy was returned unopened. Emilie's old father legally adopted the child, giving him the St. Adrian name, making him his heir, although he was heir to little, God knew.

"Nicolas St. Adrian is some six years younger than your husband. His mother and grandfather somehow arranged to have him educated, the Lord only knows how, and were it not for his lack of money he might have had a brilliant career at court. As it is, he lives alone in his tumble-down castle, helping his peasants to scratch a bare living from his small estate. Both his grandfather and mother are long dead. He has no wife, as he cannot afford one, and he has not the means to go to court and catch himself a wealthy widow who would marry him for his handsome face."

"He must be sent for," Skye said quietly. "There is no other choice. Under the circumstances, I do not understand why Fabron did not make him his heir long ago."

"Madame," the priest said, "the duc is a rigid man. To his way of thinking, his half-brother was a bastard, a creature of no account. The fact that Nicolas St. Adrian lives in Poitou made it easier to enforce that idea within his own mind. I suspect he resented his half-brother. Duc Giles was frequently heard to bemoan Nicolas's loss, for he had frequent reports, through a friend, of the boy's progress, and Nicolas was everything he really wanted in a son. God's justice is often fitting, but how hard it must have been on Fabron to hear that. Duc Giles's attitude did not bother Edmond's father, Gabriel, but it did bother Fabron. He was a sensitive boy, although he hid it well."

"I will speak to my husband," Skye said. "You do see that we have no choice in this, *mon père?* It is either Nicolas St. Adrian or France."

The priest nodded. "Nonetheless the final decision must rest with the duc."

"Very well," Skye said, and together she and Père Henri made their way to the duc's bedchamber.

Fabron de Beaumont lay pale, his dark eyes closed, tucked carefully into his own dark-red-velvet-draped bed. The white linen sheets with their embroidered lace borders were folded neatly back over the light wool coverlet. He was clean and fresh, for Skye had insisted that he be kept that way. Hearing them enter the room, he opened his eyes, and at the sight of Skye they filled with undisguised love. Since his return to consciousness he had shown puppylike devotion to her, and she had been unable to deny him her affection, an affection for which he was obviously and childishly grateful.

She bent and kissed him. "Good afternoon, *mon mari*. Père Henri and I have come to discuss something with you that is of great importance to your family."

He nodded, and gestured with a weak arm that she sit by his side, which Skye did. Père Henri stood by her in the duc's view.

"Fabron, the French want the duchy," Skye said quietly.

His dark eyes flashed, and he made frustrated noises in the back of his throat.

She put a gentling hand on his arm. "I know," she said. "It must not happen, and if it is at all possible we will prevent it, but we need your permission." He nodded, and she continued, "I am not with child, and it is very likely now that you will never be able to give me a child. I need not discuss Garnier with you. His problem is obvious, and poor Edmond is unsuitable. You have only one choice—your half-brother, Nicolas St. Adrian."

Fabron de Beaumont's eyes flashed angrily, and he shook his head vehemently in the negative, but Skye was not deterred.

"You have no alternative, Fabron," she said patiently. "You either turn the duchy over to your half-brother, or you turn it over to the French. In these last days while you have been ill I have spent much time reading the history of your family. It is a proud history, a noble and a very long history. Beaumont de Jaspre has been in existence and ruled by your family since 770. Nicolas St. Adrian is, for all the circumstances of his birth, a de Beaumont. He cannot be blamed for the plain fact that your father, a married man, seduced his young and inexperienced mother. Emilie St. Adrian was of good family, as good as your own.

"I cannot fight the French, Fabron. Despite the fact that Queen Elizabeth sent me to you as a bride, there will be no help from England. You and I both know that I was sent in exchange for your opening your ports to English vessels. It was a marriage of convenience. Had I your child, or the hope of your child, I should fight the French with my last breath, but if you do not name your half-brother your heir, and ask him to come to you immediately, the French will have your lands before the year is out. That is the plain truth, and Père Henri will tell you I do not exaggerate. He was with me and Edmond when we were forced to listen to the arrogant demands of the French envoy. We have detained that envoy until Nicolas St. Adrian can reach us. He is our only hope, Fabron. You must agree!

"If you do not you will put us all at the mercy of France—myself, your unfortunate son, and Edmond. What will happen to me, Fabron, if a French overlord arrives? Who will care for poor little Garnier? Will Edmond be forced to make his own way? As what? Perhaps both he and Garnier can find employment with a traveling fair. My beauty will, of course, guarantee me a protector, and perhaps I can take care of them. Unless, of course, my protector is jealous or not generous enough to support the others."

"*Ma fille!*" chided a shocked Père Henri, "you are too harsh."

"No, *mon père*, I am truthful. You look at me and see a beautiful woman, but you do not know that fate has often dealt harshly with me, and I have survived because I look at life honestly. I have never fooled myself, and I will not fool my husband. We are lost if he cannot overcome his stubborn pride, and agree to make his half-brother his heir." She reached out and gently smoothed the duc's brow. "I am sorry, Fabron," she said, "but you *must* agree, and despite the weakness in your hand you must sign the document making Baron St. Adrian your heir."

He sighed deeply, and she could swear that she saw tears lurking deep within his dark eyes, but then he nodded resignedly.

"You agree?" The priest leaned forward, and said, "You will agree to allow your half-brother, Nicolas St. Adrian, to come to Beaumont de Jaspre as your heir?"

Fabron de Beaumont nodded his head decisively in the affirmative.

"Very well, my son," he said. "I will send for Nicolas St. Adrian as soon as I can have the scribe draw up the papers. It will be immediately!"

Fabron de Beaumont sighed again, and his sad, dark eyes closed wearily. Skye arose, and kissing him gently once more, she stole from the room with Père Henri.

"You must send one of your priests," she said thoughtfully. "I do not think the French will suspect that we send to the bastard line of the family for aid, but it is wise never to underestimate one's enemy. If Edmond should go, his absence would be noted.

"We must send to the Pope also. Catherine de Medici is a devout woman for all she is an ambitious one, and her son will listen to her. The French have too much trouble in the west now to argue with the Pope. If the Holy Father will confirm Nicolas St. Adrian's rights to the duchy of Beaumont de Jaspre then France dare not dispute the claim, and Beaumont de Jaspre is safe. Be sure our messenger to Rome carries rich gifts. I will send him in my own ship with Captain Kelly."

"Madame," Père Henri said, his tone suddenly a very respectful one, "I am astounded at your foresight."

Skye laughed. "I play the game well, *mon père*, do I not?" she said. "You cannot live at a Tudor court and survive without learning to be the perfect courtier. No one ever expects a woman to be responsible, but I have had the responsibility for not only myself and my children, but for vast estates and several great fortunes,

beginning when I was sixteen. It is simply a matter of organiza-
tion."

"No," the priest said quietly. "Not all women could do what you
do, madame."

Skye laughed again. "I am not like all women," she said.

Before nightfall the messenger had been dispatched to the Pope
in Rome, sailing aboard *Seagull* in Captain Kelly's care. He carried
with him a letter from Madame la Duchesse de Beaumont de Jaspre, and one from Père Henri. He would also bring to the prelate
in Rome a pair of magnificent golden candlesticks adorned with
silver gilt vines and leaves and enameled pink and white flowers.
The base of each candlestick was studded with rubies and diamonds. Skye smiled to herself as she personally packed these treasures in red velvet cloth bags, and then into a carved ivory box. The
Dowager Queen of France was in her heart a merchant's daughter,
and known for her parsimony. If Catherine de Medici thought to
present her own case to the Holy Father, she would not send anything to compare with Skye's gift to the papacy.

The following morning the other messenger, this one a young
priest from a wealthy Beaumont family who knew how to ride a
horse well and handle a sword if necessary, left for the castle of
Nicolas St. Adrian in Poitou. They had but to wait.

To Skye's enormous surprise both her messengers returned
within less than a month's time. The one who had gone to Rome
had had an incredible piece of luck. As he and Bran Kelly had
waited at the Pope's court with hundreds of other supplicants who
sought to catch the Holy Father's attention, the Pope had passed
through the room and heard Bran's voice. He had stopped and,
looking at Bran, said, "My son, you have the sound of Ireland in
your voice. I once had a secretary from that land. Am I correct?"

Stunned at being addressed by the Pope himself, Bran could only
nod. The Pope smiled. In a court filled with the world-weary he
was touched by the big Irishman's awe. "Have this young man
brought to me immediately," the Pope said. "I would speak with
him." Bran and his fellow messenger, Père Claude, were hurried
into the Pope's private chambers where the prelate graciously held
out his hand so they might kiss his ring of office. The formalities
over, he sat, and asked, "Now what may I do for you, my Irish
friend?"

In his slow and careful French Bran Kelly explained his mission.

His mistress, Irish like himself, had been but recently wed with Fabron, Duc de Beaumont de Jaspre. Regretfully the duc had suffered an apoplectic fit shortly after the marriage. Now France was demanding that the duchy be turned over to them. The duc, however, chose to bestow his lands and his title upon his noble bastard half-brother, Baron Nicolas St. Adrian, a good and righteous man. He had sent Père Claude and Bran Kelly to ask that the Pope confirm that claim. Here Père Claude proffered the carved ivory box, which was eagerly taken up by one of the Pope's secretaries.

There was a deep and very significant silence when the contents of the box were disclosed. A sensual smile upon his lips, the Pope fingered the workmanship on the candlesticks. He was thinking that Catherine de Medici was far too sure of herself. She believed the Pope to be in her pocket by virtue of their shared nationality. He turned to his chief secretary, and asked in a low voice, "Where is this Beaumont de Jaspre?"

"It is a very small holding on the Mediterranean Sea between the Languedoc and Provence," the secretary said. "The Beaumonts have ruled there since the days of Charlemagne. Although they recognize France as their overlord, they have always been an independent holding."

The Pope nodded. So Catherine de Medici wanted this tiny duchy, and the duc was certainly in a difficult position. Without the Pope's approval of the validity of Nicolas St. Adrian's claim, France would, he knew, take the lands by force. Perhaps it was better for now that France not have the duchy. Perhaps it was better that France's Dowager Queen be reminded that the papacy was not her personal toy, to be used at her convenience.

The Pope smiled at the two kneeling men from Beaumont de Jaspre. "I will confirm the rights of Nicolas St. Adrian's claim to Beaumont de Jaspre, as this is what your duc desires," he said. "Cavelli!" he looked to his chief secretary. "You will draw up the papers; three copies. One for the Duc de Beaumont de Jaspre, one for Queen Catherine of France, and one for us. You will see it is done today. These men must get back to their master. Time is obviously most important here."

"Holy Father, how can we thank you," Père Claude said. "My master and his people will ever be in your debt."

The Pope smiled again, fingering the candlesticks lovingly. It was little enough to do for such munificence.

"We will be happy to take the papal messenger with us as far as Beaumont de Jaspre, Holy Father," Bran Kelly said, "and we will supply him with a fine horse and a purse to continue his journey to France."

The Pope was pleased. This would save him the expense of the man's trip, and the French would have to send him back at their own expense. "Thank you, my son," he said. "Now let me bless you." Bran Kelly lowered his head, hiding a smile as he did so. These Italians were so predictably greedy. By making his offer to pay for the papal messenger he had assured that the man would be dispatched today, and, as the Pope had said, time was important.

They arrived back in Beaumont de Jaspre just three weeks after they had left, and the papal messenger was on his way to Catherine de Medici the following day.

Several days later, Skye's second messenger returned from Poitou bringing with him, to everyone's surprise, Nicolas St. Adrian. They had expected their messenger to bring an answer from the gentleman, but certainly not the man himself.

Skye was caught unawares as Edmond hurried into her chambers, his short little legs pumping in their haste. "He is here, *chérie!* The bastard himself! By God! He did not waste much time, did he? He's come with the messenger—no escort, no retinue. It would appear that the heir is most eager."

"God's foot, Edmond! Could that silly priest have not at least sent a messenger ahead to warn us? Daisy! The sea-green silk gown! Damn, my hair is a disgrace in this heat!" She smiled at Edmond. "Well, my friend, what is he like? Is he a de Beaumont in face and form?"

"*Chérie*, I am not sure Uncle Fabron is going to approve. The bastard is a tall man, and his limbs are well formed and pleasing to the eye. His skin is fair, his eyes . . . his eyes, *chérie*, are green, the green of a forest pond, sometimes dark, sometimes light, depending upon the sunlight. His hair is the rich red-brown of my horse's hide. As to his features, they are strong. The shape of his face is an oval, his forehead is high and his nose is definitely the de Beaumont nose; but his eyes are not ours, and neither are his high cheekbones or narrow chin. It is a very sculpted face of angles and planes. All in all, I would say he is a very handsome man, and he looks like a strong one, too. I do not think that this new blood is going to hurt our family."

"Have you spoken with him?" Daisy was helping her into the bodice of the sea-green gown. Edmond de Beaumont let his eyes roll suggestively as he leered teasingly at her dishabille, and Skye swatted at him with affection.

"I have not spoken with him, *chérie*," he replied to her question. "I felt it was your place to welcome him to Beaumont first. He cannot expect instant greeting, as he has come upon us unannounced." As Daisy finished fastening the bodice, he handed Skye the skirt to her gown. She pulled it over her head and it fell over the several petticoats that she was wearing.

"Hurry, Daisy," Skye instructed her tiring woman. "We should not keep Baron St. Adrian waiting."

"He will think it well worth the wait, *chérie*, when he sees you," Edmond murmured softly, his eyes sweeping her with admiration.

The gown was lovely with its softly flowing full skirts and sleeves that came to just below her elbows, full and fashioned as if they were pushed up slightly, leaving her soft forearms bare. The dress's neckline was very low and scooped and her breasts swelled provocatively with each breath she took. The fitted bodice was embroidered in a swirling pattern of small, sparkling diamantes and pearls. Around her neck Skye fastened several matched strands of creamy pearls to correspond with the pearls in her ears. Daisy then pinned pale-pink camellias to the base of her mistress's chignon, and Skye was ready.

She walked to the door between her room and the duc's and entered her husband's room. "Your half-brother has arrived, Fabron," she said. "I am going to greet him now with Edmond. Will you see him tonight?"

The duc shook his head vigorously in the negative.

"You will see him?" she pressed.

Fabron de Beaumont lay very still, feigning sudden sleep.

Skye was not fooled. "You must eventually see him, monseigneur," she said quietly. Then she bent and kissed him on the forehead. "Good night, Fabron," she said, and then she was gone.

Fabron de Beaumont felt the tears slide down his face quite unchecked. His body had betrayed him, but his mind was still clear and quite active.

Skye and Edmond hurried to the Great Hall of the castle, where they knew Nicolas St. Adrian was awaiting them.

He was a magnificently handsome man with a broad chest that

narrowed V-like into his slim waist. His dress was simple: worn, high leather boots, the short, dark trunk hose showing a shapely thigh above them; a doeskin jerkin over an open-necked white silk shirt. Watching them as they entered the hall, his green eyes never betrayed a thought although his mind was full of them. The dwarf was the nephew. What a pity, for he was certainly well favored despite his height. Nicolas wondered if Edmond de Beaumont resented him, but that he would soon know. They had reached him now, and the duchesse—was she real?!—curtseyed gracefully.

"Welcome to Beaumont de Jaspre, M'sieur le Baron," Skye said in her musical voice. "We are most grateful that you have come."

Reaching out his hand, he raised her up, and their eyes met for the first time. Her blue-green ones widened just slightly, and he knew that she was feeling the same thing that he was. Never in his life had he seen a more beautiful woman than this ravishing creature who now stood before him. In an instant he knew that he wanted her, and knew that she wanted him, too. "Madame," he said, "it is I who am grateful to you, for I understand from Père Michel that it is you who suggested I be made my half-brother's heir, despite my unfortunate lack of the Beaumont name."

"That oversight was hardly your fault, M'sieur le Baron," she answered him. "Now may I present to you your nephew, Edmond, who is known as the Petit Sieur de Beaumont."

Edmond bowed smartly. "If Skye is glad you are here, *Uncle*, then I am twice as glad!"

"You do not wish to be Duc de Beaumont de Jaspre, Edmond?" Nicolas St. Adrian looked closely at the tiny man.

"No, I most certainly do not!" Edmond was most emphatic. "Look at me, Uncle. I am a dwarf, an accident of nature. Even if there were a girl who would wed with me, what guarantee do I have of producing normal children? Never in the history of this family has there been a dwarf, but I have learned that in my Castilian mother's family there were several over the years. I cannot marry, and therefore cannot produce another generation for Beaumont de Jaspre. You, however, can, and from what I see, Uncle, you will have no lack of applicants for your hand!"

Nicolas St. Adrian laughed. He had never found a woman whom he wanted to marry, but perhaps it was his lack of wealth that had prevented him even thinking of such a thing. Now, it occurred to him that he was a very eligible *partie*!

"You must be tired after your long journey, M'sieur le Baron," Skye said. "We were not expecting you so soon, and I fear you will think our hospitality poor, but I must ask you to rest here with some of our good Beaumont wine while I see to your apartments."

"Stay, and serve my new uncle," Edmond said. "I will see to the servants. I know the rooms to prepare."

"Yes, madame," Nicolas St. Adrian said. "I would learn of my half-brother, and this situation with the French. I am, after all, a Frenchman, and I have sworn an oath to serve the king. I can do nothing that would compromise my honor."

Edmond de Beaumont hid a smile as he left Skye and his new uncle. He was some ten years younger than Nicolas St. Adrian, but in many ways he felt older. How innocent M'sieur le Baron was. Edmond did not believe for one moment that Nicolas was going to give up this magnificence, this title and the wealth involved simply because it might offend the French Charles.

Back in the Great Hall, Skye poured Nicolas a silver goblet of Beaumont's fine rose-colored wine, and handing it to him gestured him to a seat. Taking her own goblet, she sat opposite him and raised the silvery vessel: "To you, Nicolas St. Adrian. May you be a good duc for Beaumont de Jaspre."

"I should far rather drink to your marvelous sea-blue eyes, madame," was the disconcerting reply. His own green eyes raked her boldly.

"You wished to know of your half-brother," she answered him coolly, but her pulses were racing and her stomach was fluttering wildly. She had not had this sort of a reaction to a man since she was a maid of fifteen and had met Niall Burke for the first time. She must regain control of herself, for she was a respectable married woman and her poor husband lay ill to death within this very castle.

He could see the turmoil within her, although she sought very hard to conceal it. He caught her gaze with his, daring her without words to play the coward and look away. "Yes," he answered her. "Tell me of my brother's illness, madame."

She blushed charmingly, but to her credit she was brave and did not glance away. "I am your brother's third wife," Skye said. "We were married three months ago, but he suffered an apoplectic fit several weeks afterward, and I was not with child.

"The Dowager Queen Catherine de Medici would like to absorb

Beaumont de Jaspre into France. Without a male heir we could lose our independence. Your half-brother prefers that you inherit. If you agree, you will be invested as Duc de Beaumont de Jaspre in St. Paul's Cathedral next week. Understand that my husband's wealth will remain his while he lives, although you will be given a most generous allowance. You must also agree to care for his son, Garnier, and your nephew, Edmond, after Fabron's death."

"And you, madame? What will happen to you after my brother's death?" His intense gaze caressed her face boldly, causing her to blush again. "Should I not also take care of you?" The words said one thing, his eyes said another.

Skye drew in a deep breath to clear her head, which was whirling. She didn't know how much longer she could sit quietly speaking with this man. He was having the most devastating effect upon her. She could see the steady beat of a pulse at the base of his throat. She wanted to kiss that pulse, to fondle him, to touch his chestnut-colored hair to see if it was actually as silky as it looked. God's bones, she thought, furious with herself, what in Hell is the matter with me? I am behaving like a bitch in heat!

"There is no need to fret for me, M'sieur le Baron," she finally managed to say. How calm her voice sounded, she thought, pleased. "I am a wealthy woman in my own right. When the sad day comes that I am widowed once more, I will return to my own land. My marriage to your brother was a political one. I have left behind small children to whom I long to return, for I miss them greatly."

Sacre bleu! he thought silently. She is exquisite. That skin is totally flawless. Is it as soft as it appears? Mon Dieu, but I want to kiss that adorable mouth! "Perhaps, madame, your Queen will contract another political match for you," he said provocatively.

"God's foot, I hope not!" Skye said with feeling.

He laughed. He couldn't help it, for she was so positive in her feelings. His green eyes had lightened with his amusement, and he asked, "This marriage was not to your liking, madame?"

"For my Queen and your brother it was convenient, M'sieur le Baron. For me it was a necessity, for I am Irish and I needed a favor from Bess Tudor. This marriage was her price, and I willingly paid it."

"What favor did you need, madame? Was it for a lover perhaps?"

"No, M'sieur le Baron, it was not for a lover. It was for my infant son who with the murder of his father became Lord Burke, and the possessor of great land holdings. Without the Queen's protection his holdings would have been gobbled up by others." How dare he presume I would plead for a lover? Skye fumed silently.

"Did you love your late husband?"

"Yes, M'sieur le Baron, I did." Her voice was sharp.

He leaned over, and taking her hand in his kissed it, his eyes all the while never leaving hers. "I apologize, madame," he said, "for my rudeness." He did not let go of her hand.

Dear God, Skye thought, as pure desire coursed through her veins, I want this man, and I don't even know him! She rose to her feet, hoping that her shaking legs would not betray her. "I cannot imagine what is keeping Edmond," she said. "I had best go and see to your quarters myself, M'sieur le Baron."

He rose too, thinking to himself, I must possess her, not just for tonight, but for always! I have found the one woman that I can marry at last, and I shall not let her escape me. "Thank you, madame," he answered her gravely.

He was still holding her hand, and it did not appear as if he intended to let it go.

"M'sieur le Baron," she whispered, tugging to free herself.

"I think, madame, that you will have to call me Nicolas. After all, we are related . . . by marriage." He raised her hand to his mouth once more, his lips lingering slightly longer than was respectable before he finally released her.

Skye thought she was going to faint. She could have sworn he nibbled at her knuckles with his teeth. The sexual tension between her and this man was simply incredible, and she was frankly embarrassed. She hurried from the hall, feeling his eyes on her back as she went. Skye remembered the love that she had felt for Niall Burke when she had first met him all those years ago. She remembered the passion she had first felt for Geoffrey and, when he had won her over, the great love that bloomed between them. What she now felt was akin to both those old feelings, yet it was not like either of them.

With supreme self-control she put it firmly from her, and went directly to her husband's chambers. He had just been fed, and Daisy, who had volunteered to help the duc's serving man when she could, was gently wiping Fabron's hands and lips with a soft cloth that she dipped in rosewater. As she worked she chatted away at the duc, and Skye could see that he was interested and amused in what she had to say. Daisy's French had improved incredibly in the few months that they had been here. She had, it seemed, an ear for languages. Now she was telling the duc of Devon, her home, but the duc's eyes strayed from Daisy as Skye entered the room.

"Good evening, *mon mari*," Skye greeted him. "I have come back to tell you of your half-brother."

Fabron de Beaumont frowned and shook his head in the negative.

Skye laughed gently. "*Non, non!*" she scolded him. "You must listen to me, Fabron. Nicolas St. Adrian is a handsome young man, and even I can see that Beaumont de Jaspre is fortunate to have him to rely on in our hour of need. You will like him, Fabron." She smiled at him encouragingly. "Tomorrow morning I intend to bring him to meet you."

Again he shook his head in the negative, but Skye overruled him sympathetically. "Fabron, if you do not see him people will say you do not approve of him, that you do not want this at all, and then the French will overrun us. You have signed all the documents." She did not tell him of the Pope's support. "Despite the fact that he was born on the far side of the blanket, he is your brother and he is of gentle birth. I see great intelligence in his face."

Fabron de Beaumont sighed deeply and grimaced at her, but then with a slow gesture he reached out and sought her hand. His grip was weak, but she knew it was his only way of saying that he accepted her advice in this matter.

"Thank you, monseigneur," she said. "I understand how difficult this is for you, but it is best for your duchy." Then she smiled. "I must hurry now, for our guest has yet to be fed. He came upon us so unexpectedly. We must not, however, have him think that our hospitality is lacking. This time I really bid you goodnight."

Fabron de Beaumont watched his wife glide gracefully from the room. Trapped in a body that could no longer function, he had never felt more frustrated in his entire life. To be struck down just when he had begun to find happiness with her was unbearable. Nothing had ever prepared him for such misery, and he did not understand it.

Daisy hurried after her mistress. "I only hope those two silly girls I am trying to train to help me have prepared your bath as I instructed them, m'lady."

"Marie and Violette seem willing maids, Daisy. I am sure they will learn under your tutelage."

"Flighty is what they are, m'lady, but then I have no choice. I thought no one could be as foolish as Agnes and Jane back in England, but these two!" Daisy rolled her eyes heavenward, and Skye had to laugh. Although several years younger than her mistress, Daisy had been in service with Skye for over seven years now, and was protective and jealous of her position. "What shall you wear this evening, m'lady?" she asked.

"This dress will be quite suitable, Daisy. I have hardly worn it today. I must bathe, however. The day has been hot. I fear a storm soon. There has been thunder in the hills all afternoon."

As they entered Skye's bedchamber Marie and Violette curtseyed prettily, then hurried to help their duchesse disrobe. Daisy critically checked the bathwater to see that its temperature was just right for her lady, and the bath oil mixed properly. Finding everything in order, Daisy removed the pink camellias from Skye's hair, pulled out the tortoiseshell pins that held the heavy chignon, and brushed the mane free of tangles. Daisy would allow no one to touch Skye's hair but herself. Satisfied that the hair was silky smooth, the tiring woman carefully pinned it atop Skye's head and helped her mistress remove her chemise.

Skye climbed into the oaken tub that she had brought from England, and settled herself in the warm water. It was just the perfect temperature. Skye wrinkled her nose with pleasure at the damask rose scent permeating the room. How she loved that smell! "Let me soak for a bit," she told Daisy, who, knowing her mistress's moods, left the bedchamber shooing the two giggling undermaids ahead of her.

The long windows that opened onto her balcony were open, and she could see the vivid sunset coloring the sea and sky. The colors had the deep intensity of early autumn, and streaked the sea with molten gold. Clinging to the vine outside her windows, a wild canary sang an impassioned song, and Skye's mind, free this last half-hour from thought of her husband's half-brother, was suddenly and inexplicably filled with him again. She was very much disturbed by the way that she had felt toward this man, for he was a stranger. Worse, she sensed that he knew how she felt, and it made her position difficult. What must Nicolas St. Adrian think of her? At least she had done nothing, said nothing, that could be misunderstood. Skye could satisfy herself that she had acted the perfect chatelaine before her husband's half-brother, whatever her confused mind and turbulent feelings.

It was the heat, *and* her wild Celtic imagination, she decided, relieved. It had been a wretchedly hot and still day, and she had not slept well since Fabron's fit. She worried about him as she might worry about one of her children, keeping one ear alert even when she was sleeping. She felt so terribly sorry for her husband. Their marriage had hardly begun under auspicious circumstances, thanks to the evil influence of the now dead Pastor Lichault. Had her life been more sheltered, she might not have been as tolerant and forgiving of him as she was; but she had quickly seen how tortured a man he was, and Skye O'Malley had a generous heart.

The physician had told her that he would not live very long, for his fit had been a severe one and his bodily signs certainly were not good. She could afford to be generous. She would be a good wife to Fabron de Beaumont for as long as he lived. As to Nicolas St. Adrian, her strange reaction to him had been a case of nerves. She had been without a man for longer periods of time before, and she had certainly not played the wanton then. She was not going to do so now!

"Daisy!" she called loudly. "Daisy, come scrub my back!"

Chapter 5

Nicolas St. Adrian had come unexpectedly to the castle of Beaumont de Jaspre. Therefore, his hostess warned him he could not expect an elegant supper. Thinking with amusement that a haunch of venison and a loaf of brown bread was a feast at his castle, he watched with pleasure as the "simple" supper was served. Robbie having gone east on a short trading voyage, there were but three of them at the high board this evening: Nicolas, Edmond, and the exquisite duchesse. The Baron had thought that she might avoid him at the evening meal, but no, to his great elation, she had come, cool and elegant, not quite meeting his eyes. He was certain now that she felt as he did!

The heavy silver wine goblets studded with the duchy's native green Jasperstone were filled with fragrant, dark red wine. There were three dishes offered as a first course: plump steamed mussels in their black shells served with a Dijon mustard sauce, pieces of baby octopus in olive oil seasoned with garlic, parsley, and fennel, and a silver platter of hard-cooked eggs spinkled with the young leaves of summer savory and pungent black peppercorns. The second course consisted of the whole leg of a baby lamb stuck with tiny sprigs of rosemary and roasted with small onions and carrots; a large rabbit pie; tiny larks wrapped in pastry and baked to a delicate golden brown. Each lark had been stuffed with a mixture of chopped oranges and green grapes. There was also a fat capon that had been prepared with a rich brown sauce flavored with tarragon, and salad of young lettuce, radishes, black olives, and artichoke hearts dressed in olive oil and red wine vinegar, and a large bowl of saffroned rice. For desert clary leaves were dipped in cream, fried, and eaten with orange sauce. There was also a large bowl of fresh fruits. Throughout the meal the wine goblets were never empty.

They all ate heartily, Edmond remarking that despite his monster appetite he remained tiny, and teasing Skye by saying that no matter how Madame la Duchesse stuffed her pretty self she remained slender. He then noted that his new uncle was no mean trencherman.

Nicolas smiled, admitting it was the truth. "I am the last of the St. Adrians," he said honestly. "My castle is tumbling down, and not only has my larder been bare, but my purse as well. Your simple meal, madame, is a feast to me. Beaumont de Jaspre is another feast of sorts."

"Then that is why you came to us so quickly," Skye said. "We expected you later, and with a great retinue."

Nicolas chuckled, a rich, warm sound that sent chills up and down her spine. "Alas, madame, I have no retinue, for one must pay retainers, and there was no money. Even my peasants thought me a poor lord. They were forever scolding me about regaining the lost honor of the St. Adrians. I must go to court, they insisted, but how could I explain to them that at court one needs gold, that being Baron St. Adrian is not quite enough. They are such simple, good people. I hope that I will be allowed to siphon some of the bounty of Beaumont de Jaspre back to Poitou to rebuild St. Adrian. It will make a fine inheritance for a second son."

"Then," she said, "you have decided to accept your half-brother's offer?"

"Yes, but under certain conditions of my own, madame. Firstly I will not war with France, to whom I am a sworn vassal."

"You need not," Skye said. "Before we sent to St. Adrian for you, M'sieur le Baron, we also sent to the Pope that he might uphold your claim. Several days before you arrived my messengers returned bringing the Pope's approval of my husband's wishes. Another messenger was sent from the Pope to Paris. On the day of your investiture you will swear an allegiance to France, as have all Ducs de Beaumont de Jaspre before you. You will swear it before Queen Catherine's messenger, whom we have been detaining here since he arrived." Her eyes twinkled at this last.

"Indeed, have you, madame?" His voice was amused. She was quite a woman to so daringly brave the wrath and might of France.

"Indeed, Nicolas, we have." It was the first time she had used his name, and it sent a shiver through him that he well concealed.

"He has been housed most pleasantly," Edmond remarked. "He will have no cause for complaint with his mistress. We have even seen him supplied with the most attractive of maidservants."

"*Edmond, you haven't!*" Skye was shocked. My God, what would Elizabeth Tudor think when she learned that Beaumont pimped for a French envoy!

"*Chérie!* Can you think of a better way to keep an imprisoned man content and good-natured? I certainly can't. Queen Catherine's messenger will have no reason to protest our treatment of him when he returns to Paris."

"I suspect that the hospitality of Beaumont de Jaspre will be most lauded," Nicolas laughed, and his green eyes were damp with his mirth.

"You are both impossible," Skye scolded, but her blue eyes were dancing with merriment, and they both knew that she was not seriously angry.

"Have you any treaties that I should know about, madame?"

Skye looked to Edmond questioningly, and asked, "Other than the treaty made with England, Edmond?" He shook his head.

"What treaty with England, madame?"

"My husband has a treaty with England allowing English ships to stop here to provision and water on their way to and from the Levant and Istanbul." He raised an eyebrow, and she continued, "France and England are not at war with each other, M'sieur le Baron. I believe that even now they court each other."

"So that was why you were sent to my half-brother. Your Queen uses beautiful women in the same way that Queen Catherine does, like chess pieces upon the great board of power; and my pious brother was more than willing to accept England's beautiful pawn." His voice was faintly scornful.

Skye's blue-green eyes grew stormy with outrage, and when she spoke her voice was cutting. "Do you dare to judge me, M'sieur le Baron? What can you possibly know of the games of power, sitting in your tumble-down castle in the midst of the Poitou marshes? How easy it is to be righteous when you have nothing to lose! I, however, have learned that in order to survive one must play the game of life as those in power dictate.

"I have six living children, M'sieur le Baron. I have buried four husbands. I am wealthy in my own right beyond your wildest imaginings! I most certainly did not need your uncle! But wealth, M'sieur le Baron, cannot protect you from royalty. I needed an ally, and Elizabeth Tudor is the strongest ally available in my part of the world. Should I have put my faith in French or Spanish aid? Bah! The French and the Spanish aid the Irish and the Scots only for their nuisance value against the English. Then they depart, leaving us to face Tudor wrath—which usually involves the taking of our lands and our gold.

"*I will not beggar my children for an ideal!* Ideals cannot feed them, or clothe them, or protect them from wicked men. But *I* can, and *I will!* Now, M'sieur le Baron, I will bid you goodnight. It has been a long day for me." Standing, she swept regally from the room, leaving both men somewhat shaken by the passion of her outburst.

Finally Nicolas St. Adrian spoke. "She is magnificent!" he said softly, and his green eyes, still full of her, gleamed thoughtfully.

"She is like no other woman I have ever known," Edmond de Beaumont responded honestly. "She did not want to come to Beaumont de Jaspre. She had to leave her children behind, but her sense of duty, I sometimes think, is greater than a man's. She would not endanger the inheritance of her Burke son, and her Queen's price for protection of the boy's rights was this marriage, and so Skye came."

"She had children by her other husbands?"

"By all of them," Edmond answered. "That is one reason why my uncle was so pleased to have her. She has borne seven children, but lost only one, and him to an epidemic when he was an infant."

"What happened to her husbands?"

"The first died from injuries incurred in a fall," Edmond said. "The second and the last were murdered by women. And the third husband died in the same epidemic that killed their younger son. She did not wish to remarry. She said she felt she was ill luck to the men who loved her, and now she will lose my uncle, too."

"Does she love your uncle?"

Edmond shook his head. "There was no time for love to grow between them, but she is fond of him and will do her duty by him. Skye has been good for this family even in the short while she has been with us."

For a while longer the two men sat in companionable silence, Nicolas absorbing the information Edmond had so freely given him. Finally he spoke. "You need not be afraid that I will not take care of you and little Garnier after your uncle is gone," he said. "I will uphold all the duties of a good Duc de Beaumont de Jaspre."

"I never doubted it," Edmond replied, "but your first duty is to marry, Nicolas."

"*What*?!" Nicolas's voice was mock stern. "Will you instruct your older uncle, little nephew?"

"We need another heir for safety's sake, *Uncle*," the dwarf replied. "I can hardly satisfy that need."

"Why not? Dwarfs are born of normal parents. Why cannot normal children be born of a dwarf parent?"

"No," Edmond said seriously. "I will not pass on that weakness in my seed to another generation. I have watched with fear each time one of my sisters has borne a child. No, the ducs de Beaumont de Jaspre's line of descent must remain pure and untainted, Uncle."

"Do you not enjoy the women?" Nicolas inquired curiously.

Edmond grinned. "Indeed I do, Uncle! In fact," and he hopped down from his seat, "I intend to go into the town tonight to celebrate your arrival. I am much prized by the ladies, for they seem to enjoy sitting me upon their laps and petting me as they would a favored child. Then when they find out that I am as capable a rider as any tall man their delight usually knows no bounds. I am simply careful about spilling my seed where I should not." He winked broadly at Nicolas. "Will you come with me, Uncle? The hospitality of Villerose's taverns is legendary."

"Not tonight, little nephew," Nicolas said with a smile. "I am weary from my long trip. Besides, I should not want to inhibit you," he teased. "With me along you would feel bound to set a good example for your elder, and then you should not have a great deal of fun."

Edmond chuckled. "Not to fear, Uncle. As the good Père Henri will tell you, I am myself no matter—much to his distress, I might add. Very well then, I shall bid you a good evening. Do not wait up for me. Perhaps if it is a very good night I shall not come home at all!" Then he was gone from the hall, and Nicolas sat alone.

He sat sipping at the dregs of his wine for what seemed a long time, but her beautiful face kept appearing in the bottom of his cup. Never in his life had he felt such an intense reaction to any woman. They had just met, he didn't know her, she was his brother's wife, and yet Nicolas St. Adrian knew that he loved Skye. Loved her and wanted her. Out of the corner of his eye he saw a servant yawn, and instantly he felt guilty. Rising from the table, he left the hall so the poor man, his duties finally over, might seek his bed.

Back in his own apartments, he was delighted to find that the servant assigned to him had arranged a bath. A large oak tub had been placed before the fireplace in his antechamber. A small hot fire now burned, for it had begun to rain and the air was damp and chilly. The serving man, a thin, fussy fellow named Paul, worked silently and efficiently, eager to please this new master who was of such importance. Quickly he stripped Nicolas down and, after helping him into the tub, began to gather up his clothes, clucking at their dusty and somewhat threadbare condition.

"With M'sieur le Baron's permission," he said, "I shall have the tailor here tomorrow."

"Alas," Nicolas said, amused, "I have no money, Paul. How will I pay the tailor?"

"Madame la Duchesse will see to it," came the simple reply. "You, M'sieur le Baron, are to be our new duc. Your clothing must not disgrace Beaumont de Jaspre. If you will permit me to observe, M'sieur le Baron, you have an elegant figure. Dressed properly, you will do us proud!"

Nicolas hid his vast amusement as he accepted this compliment of sorts with a gracious nod. Having disposed of his new master's sad garments, Paul returned to begin the task of washing him. With skilled, quick hands he soaped and scrubbed Nicolas from his chestnut-red hair to his feet, observing all the while that it was a sad shame that Madame la Duchesse had not been married to such a fine figure of a young man as M'sieur le Baron. Such a good and beautiful lady deserved better than the Duc Fabron, God pity the poor soul. The duchy was vastly relieved that M'sieur le Baron had come into his inheritance early. Now he must find a wife as lovely as Madame la Duchesse.

"That will not be easy, Paul," replied Nicolas. "Indeed, I believe it will be impossible."

"M'sieur le Baron is right, of course," Paul replied primly.

"There has never been anyone like Madame la Duchesse in Beaumont de Jaspre. She is an angel in her devotion to the Duc Fabron, and it was her sweet and good example that led the duc back to the Church. How sad that she could not have borne the duc a healthy son before the onset of his illness." Paul helped his master from the tub, and began to towel him vigorously.

Nicolas sniffed himself delightedly. "What is that soap you used?" he demanded.

"Madame la Duchesse had it made up, M'sieur le Baron. It is scented with essence of clove. Madame says a man should not smell like a flower in bloom."

Nicolas chuckled richly, and Paul allowed himself a small smile as he began to dry his master's hair, first using a linen towel, then a boar's bristle brush, and lastly a piece of fine silk. Nicolas's hair was soon soft and dry and shining, causing Paul to remark that M'sieur le Baron had a fine head of hair. Nicolas liked this chatty, stuffy servant who had been assigned to him. Paul now brought forth a fine silk nightshirt, but Nicolas refused it, saying:

"I sleep in my skin, unless, of course, it is very cold." He could see that his servant was shocked, though he strove to hide it. Nicolas strode into his bedchamber, and Paul hurried to draw back the coverlet. He then wished M'sieur le Baron a good sleep as he covered his now comfortably bedded master.

The room was quiet as Nicolas stretched himself out, enjoying the sensuous feel of the soft linen sheets scented with lavender. Closing his eyes, he sought sleep, but sleep would not come this night. With a smothered curse he finally climbed from the bed and walked to the long windows that overlooked the sea. Quietly he stepped a small way onto the balcony.

Then in a flash of lightning he saw her standing with her back toward him on the next balcony. She had her face held up toward the mistlike rain that permeated the air. Her long dark hair hung free, and he could see the graceful line of her smooth throat. With a rashness he had never recognized in himself, he knew that he had to have her now!

Stepping back into the room, he saw a small door by his bed and realized that it must lead to her room. Of course the door would be locked, but he put his hand on the knob nonetheless, feeling his heart accelerate as the handle turned. Looking through, he saw a narrow passageway that curved around the spiral of the tower next door. He left his own door open and walked through the passage and around the arc of the wall. Before him was another door, which he was certain would be barred to him. It was not. It swung open with a creak.

Skye heard the squeaky noise, and came in from her balcony to see a barely noticed door in the wall by the small fireplace swing open. Before she could scream, Nicolas St. Adrian stepped into her bedchamber. Her very startled blue eyes swept his tall, nude form, and as her heart began to pound with excitement, she felt an ache of desire begin to swell within and knew why he had come. Suddenly reason returned, buffeting her weakening ethics, and she backed away from him, whispering, "*No!*"

"*Yes!*" he said low. Reaching out he pulled her hard against him. "*Yes*," he said again, and he tipped her face up, his hand tangling into the mass of her soft black hair as he lowered his head to tenderly brush her cool lips with his burning ones. "*Yes!*" he murmured against her mouth, kissing her deeply now, ignoring her palms frantically pushing against his bare chest as his other arm wrapped itself about her waist, pressing her tightly against him.

Skye felt an almost primitive joy taking hold of her as he kissed her. Gentle at first, his lips now coaxed a sweet response from hers, forcing her mouth open to plunge his tongue in to meet her own. They fenced with one another, and as they did the tongues became two spears of pure flame, scorching and blazing with the fires of untamed desire. She shuddered fiercely, and with a supreme effort of will tore her face from his, gasping, "This is wrong, M'sieur le Baron! This is wrong! I beg you to stop. *You must!*"

"Nicolas!" he said harshly, his green eyes blazing with gold lights. "My name is Nicolas! I want to hear you say it! I want to hear my name on your lips! *Say it!*"

"*Nicolas!*" The word as she spoke it was a plea. "Nicolas, I beg you to stop!" Every fiber of her being was tingling, crying out to this stranger. Weakened, she fell back against his arm, her breasts rising and falling rapidly with the passion she sought so desperately to conceal from him. She could not do this thing! *She must not!*

He cradled her tenderly in the curve of a strong arm. Looking down at her with his ardent green eyes, he deliberately held her captive with his intense glance. "*I want you*," he said simply, and then his hand hooked into the neckline of her gossamer nightgown tearing it easily, the two halves opening to reveal her small and perfect breasts, their little rose pink nipples thrusting up with a desire she could not hide. "*Ah, si belle,*" he murmured reverently, his gaze softening, "*si, si belle!*" His free hand reached out to cup a breast, to rub the nipple gently with his thumb.

Skye sobbed helplessly as her conscience warred with her desperate craving to be loved by this stranger. "Nicolas . . . Nicolas, I am a married woman!" Dear God, he must stop caressing her breasts! Every touch of his hand eroded her will, only made her yearn for more and more and more. Never had she betrayed a husband. "*Nicolas!*" Her voice was ragged, and the voice inside her head shrieked a different plea. *Don't stop! Don't stop! Don't stop!* it said.

He didn't seem to hear her. His head dipped, kissing each dainty nipple, sending a tremendous shudder through her, and then he made the decision for them. Sweeping her up, he carried her to the bed, pulled the shredded, peach-colored night rail from her, laid her down, and then, lying next to her, drew her into his arms. "I adore you, Skye," he said in a low and tender voice, "and I believe that you feel the same way, though you strive bravely to deny it out of loyalty to my brother."

Somehow it was easier to speak now that he was not assaulting her senses so wonderfully with his hands and his lips. "I do not know you," she said. "Until this afternoon I never laid eyes upon you. How dare you enter my bedroom and treat me as you might some common trull!? You will leave at once! Again I remind you that I am your brother's wife!" Her words were brave, but Nicolas knew better than to believe her.

"Precious liar," he said, his tone warm and amused. "The moment our eyes met you felt the same passion I did. Why do you fight me, Skye? You do not love my brother."

"He is my husband, Nicolas. If I cannot keep faith with him then I am worth nothing. I have been called many things in my lifetime, but a faithless wife is not one of them."

"Do you love him?"

"No," she said honestly. "Ours was a political alliance."

"Will he recover from this illness, Skye, or will he soon die?"

"He will die," she whispered. "*Nicolas!* Oh, Nicolas, why do you do this to me?"

"Because I would bind you to me, Skye! Bind you so tightly that when Fabron is dead you will not run away back to your England, or Ireland. You have been mine from the moment that our eyes first met. I know it—and you know it!"

Then before she might reply, might protest his possession, he was kissing her again, kissing lips that could not refuse him, murmuring tender endearments against her mouth. *"Je t'aime! Je t'adore! Tu es ma belle amour; ma vie!"* He covered her face with a hundred quick, little kisses, nuzzling in the tiny hollow below her ear, placing slow, hot kisses along the tense muscle of her neck, leaving a trail of long, hungry kisses from the little valley between neck and shoulder down along her arm.

She was paralyzed by the intensity of the passion that he aroused in her. He had attracted her as Niall had first attracted her. *Instantly.* He kindled in her the same fiery hunger that Geoffrey had once kindled in her. In the next room Fabron de Beaumont, her dying husband, lay helpless. Skye's ethics battled with her emotions as Nicolas's lips began to tease the aching nipples of her taut breasts. His warm, moist mouth opened and closed again over one of those little nipples, nursing as strongly upon it as a hungry infant. She arced against him as the desire plunged down her body to center in her woman's core. Ethics lost the battle as she threaded her fingers through his thick, chestnut hair, moaning softly, pressing his head closer to her. *"Nicolas! Nicolas!"* she whispered breathlessly, pleading now for passion rather than against it.

He swung over her, seating himself lightly on her long shapely legs. His hands began a delicate caressing of her body, sweeping up to gently knead her belly, to cup both of her breasts, to smooth over her shoulders and then down again along the curve of her waist and hips. It was like throwing wood on a fire, and her desire flamed for him, yet he did not stop. His hands were warm and loving, his fingers unbelievably sensitive as they sought out her pleasure points. Finally he took her two hands in his and drew them down to his fully aroused manhood. She shyly explored and stroked it, finding him quite long and thick. Her passion-heavy eyes forced themselves halfway open to see him, and she caught her breath at his size.

"I want you to put me within you, Skye," he commanded her softly. "You do it, *mon amour*. Put my hardness within the honeyed sweetness of your luscious body."

Her body languid with his loving, her will mesmerized by his insistent voice, she obeyed his command, a marvelous feeling of relief overcoming her as she slipped his pulsing weapon easily within her. With a groan of pleasure Nicolas pushed himself as deep inside her as he might go, stopping a moment to allow her tight sheath to accept him in comfort. "Ah, *ma doucette*," he murmured in her ear, and then he began a slow, rhythmic thrusting, going deep, drawing his length almost fully out, driving back into her again, and then again and again until she swooned.

He revived her with kisses and soft words, and she cried, "Ah, God, you are still within me!" and shuddered with the hot passion. "You are mine!" he said fiercely. "Whatever has been before is gone, and only we two, now and in this time, exist!" His lean hips ground down upon her again, and Skye found herself lost in a world where only desire existed, desire without end. He pulled her arms above her head controlling her totally while he dominated their pleasure. Beneath him she writhed, panting frantically, her head thrashing from side to side, desperately seeking her rapture; but he sensed every nuance of her mood and held her in firm check until it pleased him to give her release. A disciple of sensuality, Nicolas St. Adrian meant to be master of this beautiful woman. Finally seeing that she could take no more of his teasing, he bent to kiss her lips, thrusting his tongue into her mouth in perfect rhythm with his lower body which thrust into her frantic form.

Her body arced sharply against him, and she sobbed a low cry that she could not contain. She felt as if she could soar like a gull, higher and higher, catching each new spiral of the wind until there was no beginning and no end. The feeling was like nothing she had ever experienced, but then with another cry she would tumble downward as quickly as she had soared up. Her beautiful body shook with each spasm, every tremor more violent than the one before until she felt as if she might be torn apart. She never felt him gain his own heaven, falling into a deep swoon as she found her own.

He too came as close to fainting as he had ever come. Rolling off her, he lay upon his back, his body wet with perspiration, his breath coming in short gasps that finally slowed to normal. When his head had finally cleared, he raised himself up on an elbow and looked down at her. She was still unconscious. Gently he began to stroke her face with the back of his hand, murmuring softly, "*Doucette, doucette! Je t'aime! Je t'aime!*"

She heard his impassioned voice, and knew that he hovered over her. How could she face him? Skye wondered. How could she excuse such wanton behavior on her part? Never had she behaved so with any man, allowing her body to control her mind.

"Open your eyes, *doucette*," he said gently, but she heard the command in his tone.

Ordinarily she would have rebelled at such a tone from anyone, but she felt weakened, drained and helpless before this man. She opened her eyes, and they slowly filled with tears that she was unable to control. Nicolas drew her back into his arms. "Cry!" he ordered her in a firm voice, and in his arms Skye wept out all the sadness that she had been bottling up since Elizabeth Tudor had sent her from England. Her piteous sobs were like a knife to his heart, and he tightened his arms about her, rubbing his face against her silken hair, murmuring soft, unintelligible sounds of comfort to her.

Skye cried so much she thought she could cry no more, and then she cried further, until her eyes were swollen with the salt of her tears. She was so very aware of him; his heart beneath her ear beating quietly and steadily, the smooth firm skin of his chest, and the warm male scent of him. Finally her weeping eased, then ceased altogether. She nestled very still against him, not wanting to raise her eyes to him, not wanting to face him, and he understood.

"You must not be ashamed, *doucette*," he said in a quiet voice. "When I first set eyes upon you I knew that this was to be the way of it between us."

His certainty irritated her, but before she might reply, Daisy was knocking frantically at her door, and calling to her, "M'lady! M'lady!"

Nicolas St. Adrian was quickly off the bed and gone, pulling the small door opposite her closed as he went. Not a moment too soon, Skye thought guiltily as she yanked the bedclothes smooth. The door between her bedchamber and her antechamber opened, and Daisy stuck her head in calling, "M'lady! Are you awake?"

"Hmmm? What?" Skye murmured sleepily, keeping herself well hidden beneath the bedclothes, and praying Daisy wouldn't come far enough into the room to discover her mistress's torn night rail on the floor and her mistress quite naked beneath the coverlet.

"'Tis the duc, m'lady! He's taken a turn for the worse."

"Go and waken M'sieur le Baron," Skye commanded, "and then find Edmond as well."

"Yes, m'lady." Daisy's head disappeared around the door, which was then pulled shut.

Skye leapt from the bed and ran to the trunk at its foot, to draw forth another night garment, kicking the shredded ruins beneath her bed as she did so. She then found her light, quilted velvet dressing gown amid the rumple of the bedclothes, and put it on, too. Hurrying to her dressing table she ran the brush through her tangled hair so that it had some measure of order to it. Barefoot, she opened the door next to the head of her bed and hurried through into her husband's bedchamber.

Père Henri was already there, as was the physician, Mathieu Dupont. She saw the priest administering the last rites to Fabron, and with huge eyes she looked at the doctor. "Docteur Dupont? What has happened to my husband?"

"Alas, madame, I feared this. It is another fit, this one fatal. I was amazed that the first one did not kill him, and he has been having small ones ever since. This, however, is his death blow. There is no doubt."

Skye moved to the side of her husband's bed. "I am here, *mon mari*," she said so he might hear.

Fabron de Beaumont's dark eyes opened, and his mouth twitched in a soft smile. With great effort he reached out to take her hand, and his, shrunken and feather-light, was chill with impending death. Skye fought back the urge to pull away. Suddenly to everyone's great surprise, the duc spoke haltingly, "Nicolas . . ."

"Where is M'sieur le Baron?" Skye demanded. "Fetch M'sieur le Baron!"

"I am here," Nicolas came forward from the shadows, a dark green velvet dressing gown wrapped about him.

For a long moment Fabron de Beaumont looked at his half-brother, and then he said, "It is good."

Quick tears sprang to Skye's eyes, and her husband, glancing at her, spoke a final time. Fixing Nicolas with a pleading glance, he said, "Take care . . . the boy . . . my wife . . . Edmond."

"I will care for them as tenderly as you would yourself, my brother," Nicolas vowed. "This I swear to you on the Blessed Virgin's love of her own family."

Fabron de Beaumont smiled weakly a final time, and then his eyes closed as he slipped once more into unconsciousness. As the early sun crept over the duchy of Beaumont de Jaspre, Fabron, its forty-fifth duc, died peacefully in his bed, surrounded by his wife, his half-brother and heir, his nephew, who had been found in the arms of a plump barmaid, his priest, and his physician.

Mathieu Dupont pronounced the Duc Fabron dead, and Père Henri fell to his knees in prayer. The rest joined him, and when he was through Skye spoke with quiet authority.

"You must anoint M'sieur le Baron immediately, *mon père*. There is no time to lose. Beaumont de Jaspre must not be without a duc for even a day. Though there can be no celebration while we mourn my husband."

The priest rose from his knees. "Madame la Duchesse is correct," he said. "It is not as if M'sieur le Baron were la Duc Fabron's son or nephew."

"Or legitimate brother," Nicolas finished quietly.

"Or legitimate brother," the priest echoed. "That is a fact, M'sieur le Baron, but you have His Holiness's blessing in this. No one will gainsay you your rights. Nonetheless I agree with Madame le Duchesse. I will anoint you as soon as you can dress." He smiled warmly at Nicolas. "There is no need to tempt the French needlessly, my son."

Nicolas turned to Skye, his eyes suddenly soft. "You will come?" he said.

"Of course, M'sieur le Baron," she answered. "Edmond and I will both come as your witnesses. In fact I think, *mon père*, that we should send for representatives of Beaumont's best families, even under these sad circumstances. It is not that I would make a festive occasion, but—"

"Yes," the priest nodded. "The more witnesses the better."

"I will see to it immediately," Edmond said. "They will be in the castle chapel within the hour." He hurried from the room.

"We must have a mass," Skye said. "Will you come to my apartments, *mon père*? I would make my confession."

"Of course," Père Henri agreed, and then he turned to Nicolas. "Shall I also hear your confession, my son?"

Again Nicolas looked at Skye, this time his glance unreadable. "Yes, *mon père*, I will also make my confession," he said after a long moment.

It was the hardest thing she had ever done, for the memory of the previous night burned into her consciousness like a brand. She felt terribly guilty, and yet she did not feel one whit guilty. She could not deny that she had wanted Nicolas, but had he not sought her out she certainly could have controlled her turbulent emotions. All this she honestly told the priest, slow tears trickling down her face. "This is what comes of marrying for expediency's sake instead of true love, *mon père*, but what could I do? I had to protect my children!"

The priest was silent for a few minutes while he thought over her confession. He had lived many years, and as a priest he had heard far worse than what she had just told him. He sighed and then said quietly, "You have indeed sinned, my daughter. There is no way around it. I can easily understand your weakness of the flesh in this particular incident, but you have broken one of God's laws, and so although I will give you absolution, I will also impose a penance upon you. For the next three nights you will keep a prayerful vigil with me in the chapel for the repose of your late husband's tortured soul."

Skye raised her head and gazed into the priest's face. "*Merci, mon père! Merci vraiment!*" She was relieved, if not repentant.

Her marvelous blue-green eyes shone like rain-washed jewels. As he blessed her Père Henri could not help thinking that if Beaumont de Jaspre's handsome young duc was anything like his late father—and judging from his quick seduction of Skye, he was—there could be a serious problem with these two living under the same roof. Blessed Virgin! There could even be a scandal! She was the most beautiful woman Père Henri had ever seen. What normal man could resist wanting her—indeed, taking her? He sighed, dreading the days ahead.

Leaving Skye to dress for the hasty ceremony, he moved on to the chambers of Nicolas St. Adrian. Nicolas was already dressed in black velvet, Paul fussing about him. The serving man was shooed out, and Nicolas knelt to make his confession. He readily admitted his seduction of Skye, and in a voice that led the priest to believe he was not one bit sorry. "Do you not feel guilty, my son," Père Henri demanded, "for leading this virtuous woman into sin?"

"I do not consider loving a woman to be a sin, *mon père*," came the disconcerting reply.

"She was your brother's wife. You have committed adultery!" was the stern answer.

"She was meant to belong to me," Nicolas returned stubbornly. "We will mourn the brother I did not know for one year's time, as is proper, and then, *mon père*, I intend to wed Skye."

"*You cannot!*" The priest was thunderstruck. "She was your brother's wife! The Church forbids such things!"

"Fabron de Beaumont was my half-brother, *mon père*. We never knew each other. A common father was our sole link, a link only acknowledged as a last resort. The Pope has upheld my tenuous claim to this duchy. I will ask him for a dispensation to wed my brother's widow. It is not an unusual request, and you know it."

The priest sighed. What could he say? At least the new duc intended to make an honest woman of Skye. If God counted good intentions then perhaps it would be all right. "My son," he said, "I will grant you absolution, but I will also impose a penance upon you. In three days' time the Duc Fabron will be interred with his ancestors. For three nights following his burial you will keep a vigil with me in the chapel."

"Agreed!" was the quick answer.

Père Henri blessed Nicolas, and left to prepare for the mass and the anointing of the new duc. He smiled to himself as he went, thinking it was a fine penance he had imposed upon the lovers, particularly Nicolas. He knew human nature well enough to know that he was not going to keep them apart; but, and here he chuckled, he would give a new cathedral to see the look on Nicolas's face when he discovered that he could not bed Skye for the next six days.

Madame la Duchesse de Beaumont de Jaspre shone like the sun at the simple anointing of the new duc. She wore a cream-colored satin dress in the manner of the English court. The underskirt of the gown was embroidered in gold thread with bumblebees, and the slashed sleeves of the dress shone with cloth of gold. Upon her head she wore for the first time the Beaumont ducal crown, a dainty gold headpiece set with diamonds and green jasperstone. About her neck was a simple gold cross. Despite her husband's death, she could not wear mourning. Mourning worn for the old duc would be considered ill fortune for the new duc.

As each quickly invited guest arrived Skye explained the Duc

Fabron's death early this morning. She then went on to say that Baron St. Adrian, Duc Fabron's half-brother, had both her late husband's and the Holy Father's blessing to inherit Beaumont de Jaspre. "We must anoint him immediately lest our more powerful neighbors seek to annex us," she explained.

The half-dozen important families of Beaumont de Jaspre agreed with Madame la Duchesse. Nicolas St. Adrian must be installed officially, and quickly, before word of Fabron de Beaumont's death was bruited about. Nicolas St. Adrian, standing by Skye's side, was introduced to each family group, and the Beaumontese liked what they saw. He was young and healthy, and new stock; new blood for the duchy. They could go on another five hundred years with his descendants, which meant that theirs would also be safe.

The sun poured through the long, narrow stained-glass windows of the chapel while upon the altar the beeswax candles flickered a delicate golden light. The reflections from the windows splashed blue and red, rose, azure, and green over the worshipers in the chapel. Nicolas St. Adrian was declared the rightful heir to the duchy by Père Henri, the Pope's approval to his claim being read to the assembled. Then the priest anointed with holy oil Nicolas's head, lips, and hands. The kneeling man was then crowned by his nephew, who firmly placed the golden ducal coronet upon his uncle's head, mischievously whispering as he did so, "Better you than me, *mon brave!*" Skye placed the ducal scepter with its ball of polished green jasperstone in Nicolas's hands, and the new duc arose and turned to face his subjects.

"*Vive, le Duc Nicolas!*" Edmond and Skye said in unison.

"*Vive le Duc Nicolas!*" replied the others in the chapel. "*Vive le Duc! Vive le Duc!*"

A short, solemn mass was then offered for the repose of Fabron de Beaumont's soul. Afterward Skye invited all the guests into the Great Hall, where a toast was drunk to the new duc's health and long reign. Then the invited dispersed and returned to their own homes, and the mounted criers, dressed in the azure and silver livery of the de Beaumont family, made their way down into the town and to the four corners of the small duchy to announce the death of Fabron de Beaumont and the anointing of his half-brother, Baron St. Adrian, as the new duc.

An official Beaumont de Jaspre messenger was sent in the company of France's newly released messenger to the Queen Mother, Catherine de Medici, and her son, King Charles. The royal messenger had been witness to Nicolas's investiture and afterward to his swearing fealty to France as Beaumont de Jaspre's duc. The duchy's messenger carried the written account of Fabron de Beaumont's death and his half-brother's constant loyalty to his overlord, Charles IXth.

Nicolas St. Adrian's day was busy. By the time all the messengers had been dispatched, and he had arranged for his half-brother's body to lie in state in the tiny cathedral of St. Paul's beginning the following day, the afternoon had gone. "Where is Skye?" he asked Edmond as they sat eating the evening meal in the Great Hall.

"I saw her just a while ago," Edmond said. "She wants to keep to her chambers for the moment. She said she would have Daisy bring her something to eat. She looks tired, and she told me that she must keep vigil for the next three nights in the chapel."

Nicolas cursed softly under his breath as he realized the real punishment in Père Henri's penance. Then he chuckled to himself. It had been a long time since anyone had gainsayed him what he wanted. His gentle mother and his crusty old grandfather had spoiled him terribly in an effort to make up for his lack of a father and the social stigma attached to his birth. Well, she was worth the wait, but he would at least see her before she imprisoned herself in the chapel for the night.

Anticipating such a move, however, Skye had already left for the family chapel when Nicolas arrived in her chambers. How could she concentrate on serious prayer and true meditation if all she could think of was his kisses? What had happened between them last night was wrong, was immoral, had indeed been a sin against God's laws. She was too much of a realist to say it would never happen again, that she would never lay in his arms weak with his loving; but for the next three nights she intended to put all her energy into relieving her guilt for having betrayed her dying husband. It mattered not that he had never known, would never know. If she could not keep faith with herself, then how could she keep faith with anyone else?

Nicolas instinctively understood her mood, and kept from her, but when she emerged exhausted after the third long night of her vigil he was waiting outside the chapel. Wordlessly they looked at each other, and then he picked her up just as her trembling legs were about to give out, and carried her to her own rooms. She was already asleep when they got there, her head nestling on his shoulder, her breath coming as softly as a child's.

With a little cry Daisy hurried forward as he entered the room. Marie and Violette gaped openmouthed, but were quickly brought back to their senses by Daisy's sharp command. "Hurry and open the mistress's bed, you useless things!" The two quickly obeyed, only to be shooed out when they had completed their task. Daisy looked at the new duc and sighed. She had been with Skye long enough to know the look of a man in love with her mistress, and Duc Nicolas was clearly a man in love.

"I'll care for her now," Daisy said, but Nicolas said in a firm, not-to-be-argued-with voice, "No, Daisy, I will take care of her. She'll sleep for a while, so send away those two silly creatures who help you. However, I would like you to busy yourself about the apartment until I need you."

"She'll rest more comfortably, my lord, with her gown off," Daisy said helpfully.

"I'll do it," he answered, and Daisy retreated.

Skye had worn very simple clothes to keep her vigil. Now Nicolas undid her black silk skirt and drew it off her. Turning her over, he undid the bodice and, turning her over, pulled it away also. Two white silk petticoats followed, along with her underblouse. Gently he removed the dainty jeweled garters that she wore to hold up her silk stockings, and then rolled the stockings down off her legs and feet. Daisy had already removed the shoes.

Quickly he removed his own clothes and, getting into bed with her, drew the covers over them, to fall asleep holding her in his arms.

He awoke several hours later to find her already awake and staring at him with huge distressed eyes. "How do you feel?" he asked her.

"Still tired," she answered honestly.

"Go back to sleep then," he said, drawing her down into the curve of his arm so that her head might rest on his shoulder. She lay her dark head upon him, but she did not sleep, and he knew it. "What is the matter, *doucette?*"

Skye sighed. "I thought I had prayed it all away, but alas, I have not!" She was obviously very distressed.

"What?" he asked.

"My desire for you, Nicolas."

"You will never stop wanting me, *doucette*, as I will never stop wanting you. Go back to sleep now, my angel. This afternoon we bury my half-brother and tonight I must begin my three nights of penance."

"Père Henri has ordered you to pray three nights also?" He heard the laughter in her voice as she realized what the priest had done. He was glad, for it meant she still had a sense of humor. To be able to laugh was a good thing.

When Skye awoke he was gone, and Daisy was bringing her a goblet of freshly squeezed fruit juice. "You'll have to hurry, m'lady," Daisy said, "for the old duc's funeral procession is to begin soon."

Skye arose and was dressed in the appropriate black. Descending to the courtyard, she found herself amid a small uproar. Little Garnier de Beaumont had been brought forth by his nurse to take his place in the procession. Skye had never seen her unfortunate stepson in the few months she had lived in Beaumont de Jaspre, but now she understood Fabron's desperate need and desire for an heir. The child was fat, and not totally in control of his limbs. His head was enlarged and his eyes were slanted in an odd fashion. The head lolled, as if it were too heavy for his neck. He did not talk, but rather made little animal noises that his old nurse pretended to understand completely.

Now the old woman stood adamant, defending *her* baby's rights while both Nicolas and Edmond argued furiously with her. Skye listened a minute, and then, brushing the two men aside, said gently, "You cannot send the boy to his father's funeral, old nurse. Poor child, he does not understand, and all this anger is frightening him." She stroked the boy's cheek, smiling and speaking softly to him. "There, *mon petit*, everything is all right." She turned again to the nurse. "You know that he is not a normal child, nurse. He cannot, therefore, be expected to behave in a normal manner in this situation. Duc Nicolas has promised that he will care for this child as tenderly as if he were one of his own. Now take Garnier back to his own rooms, nurse." Skye then bent and kissed the child in a loving gesture.

The old nurse nodded, satisfied. "Madame la Duchesse is kind, and she understands." Then the old woman took her charge by the hand and led him away.

"Now, gentlemen, may we go?" Skye walked to her white palfrey and was helped up into the saddle by a groom.

The funeral procession wound its way down the hill from the castle to the little Cathedral of St. Paul, Skye leading the way as Fabron de Beaumont's widow. When the service had concluded, and Fabron had been interred in his tomb beneath the marble main altar in the family's crypt, the packed cathedral emptied out and Nicolas St. Adrian, the new duc, led the procession back up the hill. One era had ended and another was beginning. The people of Beaumont de Jaspre were getting their first good look at their new duc, and they liked what they saw. As they made their way through the narrow winding streets of the town, languid, ripe-mouthed beauties with melting invitations in their dark sloe eyes leaned from their balconies to pelt their new lord with flowers. But he saw none of them. He was far too engrossed in the woman who rode at his side. He could not take his eyes from her.

At one point she whispered over the roar of the crowds, "Do not look at me so, Nicolas. You will shame me."

Seeing them together, Edmond de Beaumont wondered why he had not noticed it before. His new uncle was obviously hopelessly and completely in love. Now he understood all those questions about the English treaty, and knew why he himself was being sent back to England almost immediately with Captain Kelly. Nicolas St. Adrian wanted his brother's widow to be his wife. For the briefest moment Edmond was overcome by a feeling of terrible hopelessness. If he had only been born normal then perhaps Skye would have been his. Then he shrugged. What was, was. Besides, if she had *that* kind of love for him his height wouldn't matter. He looked at her now and saw the soft rose blush staining her cheeks as she gently scolded Nicolas. They were two of a kind, Edmond thought. Proud, passionate people who would do very well together. He considered himself fortunate to have her friendship, for never had he known anyone like Skye O'Malley. She was unique.

There would be no festivities honoring Nicolas's possession of the duchy. The celebrations would come later when he married, and now the speculation began as to when and whom Nicolas would marry. Several important families had marriageable daughters, and in neighboring Provence and the Languedoc there were several noble families whose nubile offspring might make Nicolas St. Adrian an eligible *partie*. The new duc, however, appeared in no hurry to choose a wife.

Edmond de Beaumont departed for England aboard Skye's own ship, *Seagull*, several days after the funeral. When she had asked him why he returned to the Tudor court he replied that she must ask Nicolas. She had wanted to leave with him, but knew that she must stay at least until the spring to officially mourn poor Fabron. It was the least she owed him.

As *Seagull* sailed from Beaumont de Jaspre's main harbor Skye watched from her bedchamber balcony. For the first time since she had left England she was actually alone except for the faithful Daisy. Robbie, certain that she was settled, unaware of Fabron's death, wandered the eastern Mediterranean in his leisurely voyage to Istanbul. Now Bran was gone back to England, taking Edmond once more to Elizabeth Tudor's court.

Nicolas came up behind her, slipping an arm about her waist, and drawing her back against him. "Do you wish you were with Edmond?" he asked.

"Yes," she answered honestly.

"Do you have a lover you miss back in England, Skye?" She could hear the jealous note in his voice.

"My children are there, and in Ireland," she said, sidestepping his query and realizing that she hadn't thought about Adam de Marisco in weeks. "When I was forced to leave him my youngest son was just over two months old. His little sister isn't even two years old, Nicolas. I have four other children as well. I miss them. Yes, I wish I were aboard *Seagull* on my way home."

"I will never let you go," he said quietly.

"Nicolas, you must." There was a note of quiet desperation in her tone.

"Do you know why I have sent Edmond to England, Skye?"

"No, he would not tell me. He said that I must ask you."

"I sent him to your Queen to ask that you be given to me as my wife. I offer England the same terms my brother did, the ports of Beaumont de Jaspre."

Skye shook her head and laughed ruefully. "I sent a letter to William Cecil asking to be allowed to come home now that Fabron is dead."

"Which request do you think that your Queen will favor, *doucette?*"

"Do not be cruel, Nicolas. We both know that your ports are of value to England."

"*You* are of value to me!" His arm tightened, and he put his face in her hair near her ear. "Skye, sweet Skye! I love you! From the moment of our first meeting I have loved you. I want you for my wife. I want you for the mother of my sons and daughters. You feel much more for me than you did for my brother. I will teach you to love me, *doucette!* I need you so much!"

"Do not seek to marry me, Nicolas," she begged. "When my beloved Niall was murdered I realized that I was ill luck to the men who have loved me, and wed me. Everyone dies in time, Nicolas, but these were young men! None were safe, even your half-brother Fabron, whom I did not love. It is as if I am not meant to have a husband. I would not want my ill luck to endanger you. Seek some young girl of good family to make your wife."

"No. I want you." He turned her about, taking her face in his two hands, looking down into her blue-green eyes. "*Doucette*, I warn you I will not be denied. I could take you for my mistress and marry some other, but I do not want you for my mistress. I want you for my wife. I have made the decision, and you must abide by it." He kissed her upturned nose. "You will be my wife."

Skye was outraged. I have made the decision, he had said. She took a deep breath. "Nicolas," she said calmly, "it is I who must make the decision as to whether or not to marry you. You will not control me! No man ever has. I am my own mistress. I have always been, and I will always be! If you can understand that then perhaps you will have come a little way toward understanding me. If you learn to understand me then perhaps we shall be friends. I am not so foolish as to deny that we are attracted to one another, but lovers should be friends."

Nicolas chuckled indulgently, and sweeping her up into his strong arms, he walked across the room to dump her on the bed.

Then he stood, legs spread, above her. "*Doucette*," he said, "how can one so wise be so innocent? No woman is her own mistress, even your own Queen. There is always someone to answer to, else Elizabeth of England would have married her horsemaster. You must answer to England's Queen, and she will give you to me without a second thought. Therefore you must answer to me." His green eyes twinkled. "I will expect a proper and obedient wife, Skye."

She sat up, a look of outrage on her beautiful face. "A proper and obedient wife?!" She scrambled off the bed on its other side. "Why, you pompous, arrogant ass of a Frenchman! Answer to you? I'd sooner answer to the Devil himself! Elizabeth Tudor may give me to you as a wife, but you may live to regret it, Nicolas St. Adrian!"

He grinned engagingly at her across the bed, and then flopped down upon the mattress. "Come to bed, *doucette*," he said in a deceptively bland voice.

"Ohhhhhh!" she shrieked with frustration. "I do not believe that you have heard a word that I have said, Nicolas! You are totally and utterly impossible. *I will not marry you!*" Skye stamped her foot angrily to punctuate the point.

Reaching up, he grasped her arm in an iron grip and yanked her down onto the bed atop him. "You, you stubborn jade, have not heard a word that I have said! I mean to make you my wife. My God, woman, you behave as if I had made you an indecent proposal!"

"I have had enough of husbands!" she shouted at him. "It matters not if I fall in love or not, I always lose them too quickly to death, and it's worse when I love them."

"Then you love me!" he shouted back at her, his face alight with pleasure.

"I hate you! You are arrogant, stubborn, impossible, and totally devoid of understanding!"

"*You love me!*" His face was just inches from hers.

"No!" She squirmed to escape his grip.

"*You love me!*" He rolled her over, and she was pinned quite helplessly beneath him.

"*Never!*" Damn the man, Skye thought.

"*You love me*," he said softly, and then his mouth was covering hers in a deep and passionate kiss.

She struggled a moment beneath him, and then, realizing the futility of her position, she lay still. She would give him nothing. She had to convince him of her disinterest. She had to convince herself. She liked him. God's foot, it was more than like, but she couldn't, nay she must not give in to her own desires! She was bad luck for husbands, and then there were her children to get back to in England and Ireland.

"Doucette, doucette," he whispered against her lips, and she shivered. *"Aimes-moi, doucette. Aimes-moi!"*

Skye turned her head away from him, feeling quick tears starting to prick her eyelids. "Oh, you are a bad man, a wicked man," she said low. "How can you do this to me, Nicolas? You claim to love me yet you subject me to this terrible torture."

"I only seek to make you listen to your own heart, Skye," he answered her, and his hands began to move on her breasts, stroking softly, subtly.

She felt her breasts beginning to swell and grow taut with the sweet desire that he was able to rouse in her. Her nipples were tingling and sensitive, so sensitive that the silk of her night rail felt irritable against them. "I do not deny you arouse lust in me," she said in a desperate voice, "but that is not love!"

"It is a beginning, *doucette.*" His fingers were carefully undoing the tiny pearl buttons, and when he had bared her to the navel he pushed the fabric of her gown aside and bent to kiss her breasts.

"Don't!" Her voice was ragged. Dear God, she would explode with the wanting.

"Hush, my love," he said patiently. "Hush." Then he was kissing her again, warm and demanding kisses that left her weak and helpless to deny him any longer. She kissed him back with sweet, slow kisses, feeling his firm lips parting, the soft rush of breath from his mouth to hers, the velvet tip of his tongue exploring delicately within that delicious amorous cavern.

His head moved back to her breasts, nuzzling at them, rubbing his rough cheek against their silken skin. He ran his tongue in the valley between the twin perfections and then moved on to teasingly encircle and softly lick at each nipple. A flutter of pleasure rippled through Skye, and she murmured low. Her arm extended to allow her to gently caress the back of his neck. Now it was his turn to murmur as her skillful fingers sent delighted shivers through his big frame.

Skye moved both her hands to his chest and pulled his white silk shirt open, sliding her palms over his smooth skin up to his broad shoulders and down his long arms, pushing the shirt ahead of her. Then she wrapped her arms about his neck and pulled him down to her. As his chest descended upon her breasts and he felt the marvelous soft fullness of her, he groaned. "Ah, *doucette*, this is what you were made to do; to love a man, and in turn be loved by one."

"You talk much about making love, Nicolas," she teased him, and he chuckled.

"I will make you pay for that insult," he threatened.

"Will you?" she goaded him. "What will you do to avenge yourself?"

"Love you until you beg for mercy," he threatened.

"I never beg for mercy, Nicolas," she said softly. "I am used to winning all my battles."

He laughed at what he believed was her audacity. "*Doucette*, you are a woman, and women have no battles. Women are tender creatures, to be delicately nurtured. Women should be protected, loved, and adored. It is the way of the world."

Skye pushed him away, and unprepared, he rolled onto his back. She sat up and, looking at him, said, "I think, Nicolas, that you have been too long in your Poitou marsh. Where on earth did you ever get such foolish ideas about women? Your ideas are a hundred, nay two hundred years out of date. In England a queen reigns in her own right. In France a queen mother is the power behind the throne, in fact the real power in France. Women are not mindless ninnies. If I were one, you would not be half as interested in me as you are.

"You know nothing about me, Nicolas St. Adrian, and I know that unless you can accept the kind of woman that I am we shall be very unhappy together. You should not have been so quick to send to England for Elizabeth Tudor's permission to wed me. You may find that you do not like the woman I am, and I shall not change."

He suddenly looked very confused, and Skye felt her heart go out to him. "Listen to me, Nicolas, and I shall tell you the sort of woman you have been lusting after." Then Skye proceeded to tell him of her marriages, her children, her personal wealth, her lands, her children's lands and wealth. She finished by telling him, "If my Queen commands me to wed with you, you are right, I must do so; but understand that though I give you a dowry, and Elizabeth will surely beggar me wedding me twice in a year, I retain and control my own wealth. Can you live with that, Nicolas? I will not marry you simply to play the docile mare to your randy stallion!"

"My ideas of women come from my mother," he said slowly. "She was a gentle and trusting creature who needed looking after. My father broke her heart, and she never married. I think that my grandfather lived as long as he did simply because she needed caring for, and without a husband, who would do it? Had she not had a strong man in her life she would have been prey to others, as she was to my father. I was seventeen when she died. My grandfather died shortly afterward. I was a man, and could care for myself, and he believed his duty done."

"Did you never go to court?" she asked him.

"There was no money for such things. Manners, my letters, how to read, riding, how to fight, these things my mother, my grandfather, and my grandfather's old squire taught me."

"What about young women? Surely, even though you were poor, you met the daughters of the neighboring nobility?"

"When I was a child I played with the peasant children. When I grew old enough for social occasions I was not invited to the homes of our neighbors. First there was the stigma of my birth, and then there was the stigma of my poverty. My birth might have been overlooked, but my poverty, never! Many a noble bastard has gone on to great things, but none without wealth or the hope of it."

She nodded, understanding his predicament. "Your grandfather taught you that women were sweet and mindless creatures meant for cherishing, and giving a man pleasure; but nothing more. Your gentle mother certainly did not give lie to his interpretation. I will wager she always had a very protective serving woman about her to fend off anything that your grandfather couldn't."

"Berthe was with her until she died," he answered.

"Nicolas, you know nothing about women," Skye said.

"I know how to love them," he answered her. "Is that not enough? Perhaps I do not know women of my own class, but there are just as many kinds of women among peasants as among the nobility, and I have met and dealt with them all. Are noblewomen really so different, *doucette*?"

"Noblewomen are taught to be freer than peasant women, *mon brave*. Now I will admit that not all of them take advantage of their opportunities as I have done, but many do. If you desire a docile and obedient wife who will never question you or your commands, then I must beg that you wed with a young and innocent girl, and certainly not with me. I am too set in my ways to change."

"But I am not, *doucette*, for you see that I have far more to lose by not changing than you do." He reached up and wove his big hand into her long, black hair. "I love you, *chérie*," he said, softly drawing her halfway down to him.

"Oh, Nicolas," she whispered, totally disarmed. Had he really listened to her, or was he simply blinded by his desire?

"Help me to learn about you, Skye," he begged. "I cannot be happy without you, and I will not lose you." Pulling her all the way down for a moment, he gently kissed her lips. "*Aimes-moi, doucette!*"

"I keep my own wealth, and I want my children here, at least those of them that can come to me. Especially my babies in Ireland, for my uncle and my brothers can hold the Burke lands now, but I cannot let my babies grow up not knowing their own mother. My eldest and his brothers can visit us, but their lives are in England and in Ireland. Willow must come! How she will love Beaumont, Nicolas!"

Her face was radiant with the thought of her children, and he thought she must be a good mother to care as much as she did. "I will love your children," he promised her, "and we will also have our own."

"And my wealth?" She would not let him escape.

"It remains yours, *doucette*. I want you happy, and besides, I have never had much wealth. What would I do with it?"

"You will learn these things, Nicolas," Skye told him. "The Beaumont coffers are full. Edmond will teach you, for he has a clever head with figures, and oversaw Fabron's wealth as well as the public funds. You must learn lest others less honest take advantage of you."

"I will learn it all if it will please you," he said.

"No, no," she fussed at him. "You must learn because you want to, because you want to be a good duc! It is important to Beaumont de Jaspre." She sighed. His own small holding in Poitou had been a poor one, and there had been no need for him to learn the many and varied things that overseeing a vast estate entailed. "Wealth is a great responsibility, Nicolas. The truly great lords understand that, and so must you. Do not be one of the foolish ones who think that wealth is only for personal gratification. First comes your family, but there will be times when the duchy must come before it for the good of everyone, including your family."

"*Doucette*, you have convinced me that I have a great deal to learn, and I promise you that I shall learn it, but I do not wish to begin those lessons now. Now I wish to make love to you." His heavy-lidded green eyes were laughing down at her.

"You would then give me lessons," she said teasingly, surprising him. "If you would do so, Nicolas, then you had best rise from my bed and take off your clothes. I have always found it damnably hard to make love in one's clothes." So saying, Skye swung herself off the bed and slipped off the demure pink night rail that he had already unbuttoned. When she turned back to face him he caught his breath with wonder and delight as her lush body was illumined by the moonlight streaming through the long windows and the firelight from the small hearth.

No peasant girl of his acquaintance had had as magnificent a form as Skye. Her small breasts were set high on her chest and thrust impudently forward. Her slender waist curved enticingly, tempting a man to encircle it with his hands. Below it, her hips flared in womanly fashion and flowed into long, shapely legs and feet. He knew the feel of her incredibly soft skin and long thick hair. She was a most sensuous feast for a man, and he groaned low, his desire beginning to swell and pulse beneath his garments. Rising, he tore off his clothes, and then looking across the bed at her, he held out his hand.

Skye let her blue eyes sweep over him as his had so boldly swept over her. Tall and fair-skinned, he was really quite handsome with his sleepy green eyes and his wavy red-brown hair, a recalcitrant lock falling boyishly over his forehead. Without his clothes she could see how long his legs were, and how surprisingly shapely for a man. She could also see how aroused he was, and she smiled mischievously as she stared directly at his open desire. Then she reached out, touched his hand, and climbed back into the bed.

Stretching out her fingers, she teasingly caressed and fondled him as he stood by the side of the bed. He throbbed beneath her touch, and she laughed low; a provocative sound that sent a fierce stab of desire through him. He wanted nothing more than to bury himself within her, to make her beg, to make her cry aloud with her passion; but for the life of him he couldn't move. Her touch was mesmerizing him, sending waves of pure pleasure racing through him, forcing him to stand very still lest she stop. Skye trailed her long fingers up over his belly, and then down between his thighs and around his hips to squeeze his hard buttocks in her small, skillful hands. "Bitch!" he whispered.

"Come to me, Nicolas," she said low. "It is you who began this fever in me. Do you now regret it, or do bold women frighten you?"

It was an audacious challenge, and one that released him from her power. He flung himself atop her, pinioning her firmly beneath him. His hard thighs pressed down against her soft ones, his belly and chest flattened themselves on her as his mouth took hers in a ruthless kiss. Skye gasped, but quickly recovered and returned the kiss, her little tongue daring his to do battle. To her surprise and intense delight, he responded by giving her a sensuous tongue bath, his flicking spear moving like wildfire down her throat, across her breasts, down her navel, thighs, calves. Turning her over, he licked slowly up her legs, across her buttocks, up her backbone, and over her shoulders. Gently he nipped at the back of her neck, pushing her long black hair aside to nuzzle it.

By the time he turned her again onto her back she was gasping with hot desire. It felt wonderful, and she wanted to give him some of the same pleasure she felt in return. "Let me love you, Nicolas," she begged him, attempting to sit up.

"No, *doucette*," he whispered back. "You may be very good at the facts of business, my love, but I am even better at the facts of love. Tonight you will be loved, and loved, and loved again by me. Another time I will let you love me in return, but not tonight." His hands moved up to fondle her breasts, to tease at the little pink nipples, to kiss them, and nip gently at them, to lick them into hard little knobs of pleasure-pain.

She let him have his way, her will to fight or argue totally lost beneath his skillful hands. She cared not what he did to her as long as he didn't stop the pure bliss that was invading her veins, replacing her blood. She felt him spread her legs, and then his kisses were sending gentle tremors through her as they touched the soft flesh on the inside of her thighs. Then he raised his head slightly and kissed the smooth woman's mont of her. Skye stuffed her fist in her mouth but it still did not entirely prevent the sound of her cries from coming to his ears as his tongue sought out and found the hidden sweetness of her. With wicked skill he ran his tongue down the moist rose-pink flesh, thrusting within the very entry to her. His tongue moved back upward and flicked teasingly at the tiny sensitive jewel of her womanhood.

A starburst of delight exploded in Skye's brain and body. Reaching up, he pulled her fist from her mouth and heard her moans of rapture. Lowering his head again, he once more began the delicious torture, not stopping until her frantic little mewling sounds told him that he had driven her far enough. Swinging over her, he thrust himself deep inside her, pushing her once again to passion's brink, loving the feel of her nails as they dug sharply into his muscled shoulders. He was a master at lovemaking, and he knew it, but this time it was impossible for him to be patient. He wanted his release, and he knew that she did, too. With a shout of exultation he poured himself into her quivering, vibrating warmth.

It was too much for her, and Skye, to his astonishment, began to weep. Nicolas gathered her into his arms, loving her all the more for the passion that could set her to weeping in the midst of their fulfillment. "*Doucette, doucette,*" he murmured, pressing small kisses on her wet face, "*doucette, mon amour, je t'aime! Je t'aime!* Don't cry, my love! Ah, *doucette*, you will break my heart!" He held her hard and close, rocking her back and forth like a child.

"I am so afraid," she sobbed. "I am so afraid, Nicolas! I don't want anything to happen to you, but if we wed it will! *I just know it will*. It does every time I love, and I cannot bear any more! I cannot!"

"You do love me!" he breathed happily.

"Yes—no—I don't know! All I know is that I don't want anything to happen to you!"

They had to deal with her fear, and he was wise enough to know it. "We cannot marry for at least a year, *doucette*," he said. "To mourn my brother any less time would be disrespectful. We cannot even announce our intentions before then. If nothing happens to me in that time, Skye, will you believe that nothing will? Surely there must have been some man in your life whom you cared for and who was not hurt by this phenomenon you believe in?"

Skye stopped crying. There was Adam. Adam had never been really harmed for loving her, but then Adam had never been married to her. Some instinct warned her not to mention Adam, for she had seen that Nicolas could be jealous. "There is no one," she said softly.

"Then I shall have the honor of being the man to destroy your dragon, *doucette!*" he said gaily. "Do not fear, *ma chérie!* I am a lucky man. I always have been. I was conceived a bastard, and my father might have disowned me, but my mother and my grand-father did not. They loved me and nurtured me. My grandfather even legitimatized me, allowing me to inherit his title, such as it was. My half-brother made me his heir, the Pope confirmed it, and now I am a duc. A wealthy duc! I shall be lucky in love, too! In a year's time I shall marry you, and we shall make beautiful children together, and we shall live happily ever after as they do in all the children's tales." He tipped her face up and looked down into her blue-green eyes. "Do you believe me, my beautiful *doucette?* Will you trust me to make everything all right?"

She looked into his eyes, eyes that were filled with love for her, eyes that honestly believed the words he spoke. He was so sure of himself. He was so sure of his ability to make everything all right. She wanted to believe that he could, and why not, she thought. "I will trust you, Nicolas," she answered him. "Oh, my darling, I will trust you! Perhaps this time it will be all right."

In the days that followed it seemed that she had made the right decision. Nicolas St. Adrian was a perfect lover, and he was also a man of his word. He worked very hard to understand the sort of woman that Skye was, and as he came to understand her he found he liked an independent woman. He began to admit to himself that as sweet as his mother had been, he had sometimes found her help-lessness irritating and cloying. It had been an effort for her to choose between venison and rabbit pastry for her supper, and he wondered why his father had been attracted to her in the first place. He could only suppose that it was his pretty mother's innocence that had been so enticing. Skye, however, had no such difficulty reaching decisions. She was a woman who seemed to know exactly what she wanted, and how to get it. She was a woman who knew power and had dealt with it, and she quite fascinated him.

To her immense delight, Skye found that as well as being a magnificent lover, Nicolas had an excellent mind. That he had never had the opportunity to learn the things she knew had not been his fault; and under her tutelage he began to acquire an excellent knowledge of finance, and trading, politics and government, courtly behavior and maneuvering that would stand him in good stead in the years to come. Skye enjoyed teaching so apt a pupil, and the days slipped by, turning into weeks, and gradually into months.

In Beaumont de Jaspre Skye found herself living a life far different from any she had ever lived. Away from the mainstream of a powerful court and a powerful country, their lives were quiet and calm. The de Beaumonts had never had an important court like some of the larger city-states, but now with an elegant and gay young duc the livelier members of the little duchy's nobility began to congregate about the castle. It was quickly apparent to the young women among this group that Nicolas St. Adrian had chosen his duchesse. They accepted this with as good a grace as they could under the circumstances, but it did not prevent some of the bolder among them from flirting outrageously with the duc. Nicolas was flattered by their attention, but he had made his decision within the first hour of his arrival in Beaumont, and his heart remained true to Skye.

As Christmas approached she began to grow sad once more. A year ago she had been pregnant with Padraic, and Niall had been alive. With their baby daughter, Deirdre, and the MacWilliam they had celebrated in the Great Hall at Burke Castle. Huge oak Yule logs were dragged into the hall to be burned in the enormous fireplaces. The hall itself was decked in garlands of pine and holly. There were great haunches of venison to eat, and casks of frozen cider into which red-hot pokers were plunged, the sweet liquor being drawn off a little at a time into the silver goblets. There was a minstrel who could sing all the stories of old, of the time when Ireland was free from England, and the land was peopled with giants and fairies, and great heroes and brave, beautiful women; of a time when grand and noble deeds were done, and love was always undying.

Nicolas could see the sudden, drastic change in her mood, and intuitively sensed that she was thinking of another and happier time in her life. He half hoped that she was pregnant, so he might have an excuse to marry her now; but Skye had told him quite gravely when he had once mentioned it that they would not have children until after they were married. The positive way in which she spoke led him to believe that she practiced some forbidden sort of contraception, but he would not press her on it. She was not yet his wife, and he realized that she needed time; a time to grieve that had been denied her before and that he would not deny her now.

Nicolas had a wonderful surprise for Skye, something that he knew would make her gay and happy once more. Each day he scanned the mouth of Villerose's harbor for the return of Bran Kelly's ship, which, he hoped, would bring Edmond, the Queen of England's blessing on his union with Skye, and the surprise. Three days before Christmas the *Seagull* sailed back to Beaumont de Jaspre's main harbor.

Nicolas and Skye rode down the hill from the castle and through the town, a small coterie of guards escorting them. It was a perfect Mediterranean day, and she looked so very beautiful in the deep-blue silk riding dress, its sleeves lavishly trimmed in cream-colored lace, which dripped gracefully from just below her elbows, her lower arms being bare. Upon her hands she wore cream doeskin gloves embroidered in tiny freshwater pearls and gold thread. Although the sun was quite bright and it was a warm day, Skye had chosen not to wear any headdress. Instead, her long black hair was bound back only by an embroidered ribbon. She rode a white palfrey with a red leather saddle and a bridle that was hung with tinkling silver bells.

The road wound down from the castle through the pink town with its balconies filled with their profusion of brightly colored blossoms, the millefloral scent perfuming the air around them. Upon some of the balconies hung cages of songbirds trilling happy tunes. It was all so beautiful that Skye wanted to cry. It would be so wonderful to have her children with her. How they would enjoy the days of golden sunshine and warm weather. She sighed, determined not to be sad and spoil Nicolas's mood. He was trying so hard to make her happy, and it was not his fault that he was unable to supply her with the one thing that she needed to complete her happiness. As they passed through the main square of the town the market-day crowds took up the delighted cry, *"Vive le Duc! Vive Madame la Duchesse!"* It was impossible not to smile, and wave a hand at these friendly people who were obviously so eager to love them.

Ahead, the street opened into the harbor area. The docks of Beaumont de Jaspre were alive with ships unloading their goods from all over the Mediterranean and northern Europe. She could smell the fragrance of spices, the strong scent of uncured hides and fish all mingling into a smell particular to docks the world over. The vessels were flying flags from virtually every nation: England, Norway, France, Spain, the Ottoman Empire, Sweden, Algiers, Morocco, Portugal, Scotland. There were so many languages being spoken that when she tried to concentrate on one, her head began to spin.

They were able to ride directly to Skye's ship, which had been given a preferred dockage near the open-air harbor market. She could see the O'Malley flag fluttering in the soft afternoon breeze around the ship's mast. On the open main deck she could see some of the crew moving about. They came to a stop before the gangway, and dismounting, Nicolas helped her from her saddle. Bran Kelly appeared from the main cabin, and calling out to him Skye waved. He flashed her a delighted grin and waved back. Skye hurried aboard.

"Have you brought Edmond back?" she demanded.

"Indeed, m'lady, I have, and a surprise from your duc that I hope will please you." Bran turned to Nicolas. "Now, sir?"

Nicholas smiled. "Now," he said.

"If you will come into the main cabin with me, m'lady," Bran said politely, and Skye, puzzled, followed as he opened the door and stepped back to allow her through first.

Walking over the threshold, Skye suddenly stopped, and stared hard. Then without warning she burst into tears. Instantly she was surrounded by her children all laughing, shouting, and crying themselves. A small dark-haired little tot peered wide-eyed around Edmond de Beaumont's legs at her, and another, a fat blue-eyed baby boy, gazed seriously at her from his nurse's arms.

"Are you not glad to see us, Mama?" the practical Willow demanded.

Skye O'Malley stared at five of her six children, quite overcome with pure and total joy. *She had everything!* Speechless for a brief moment, she held out her arms to the children and the three older ones rushed to her, all talking at once. She hugged Murrough. God's nightshirt! He was taller than she was now. How had that happened in only seven months? She kissed Willow, her beautiful and treasured little daughter. Willow's cheeks were damp, but she smiled a blindingly radiant smile at her mother, and words were not necessary between the two. "Robin!" She finally found her voice, and gathering Geoffrey Southwood's son into her arms, she hugged him hard. Robin, usually very conscious of his position in life, did not complain, but kissed his mother's cheek enthusiastically.

Skye stepped back and viewed her offspring delightedly. Then, turning, she looked at Nicolas. "Thank you," she said quietly. He smiled back at her, but said nothing. Words were unnecessary.

"*Chérie,*" Edmond de Beaumont said, "here is a little child who would greet you." Gently he drew Deirdre from her hiding place behind him.

Kneeling, Skye held out her arms to the small girl, a soft smile touching the edges of her lips. Niall's daughter looked so very much like her. Deirdre Burke was indeed her mother in miniature, with her camellia-fair skin, a tumble of dark curls, and her blue-green eyes. Thumb in her rosebud mouth, she eyed Skye suspiciously.

"Silly one!" Willow scolded her baby sister. "This is our mama."

Deirdre looked at Skye, then at Willow who nodded her head vigorously, then at Skye again. She took a hesitant step forward, then another, and, reaching out, Skye pulled her youngest daughter into her arms to kiss her on her fat cheeks. The little girl snuggled into her mother's embrace happily, and Skye almost wept. Deirdre was just two, and in the several months in which she had been separated from her mother, she had forgotten her entirely. She would never remember Niall, her father, and this fact did cause Skye to shed a few sad tears, especially when she looked up and saw her youngest child, Padraic, who was as much his father's image as Deirdre was her own.

"You are happy now, *doucette?*" He was standing by her side.

Skye stood up holding Deirdre in her arms. "I am very happy, Nicolas. How can I thank you?"

Deirdre looked at Nicolas. "Papa," she said in a definite voice. A huge grin spread over Nicolas's face. "Indeed I shall be," he said happily, "if the Queen of England has granted my request. Nephew Edmond? Am I to be a happy bridegroom?"

"Indeed, my enthusiastic uncle, you are. You have England's blessing upon your union."

"I thought you were already married, Mother." Murrough stepped protectively to his mother's side.

Deirdre squirmed in her mother's arms, holding out her fat baby hands to Nicolas, who delightedly took her. Deirdre snuggled down into his arms, and coyly repeated, "Papa." Her look was one of supreme self-satisfaction, and if her older siblings were slightly embarrassed by her behavior she was not one bit concerned.

Skye hid a smile at the older ones' discomfort. "The duc whom I wed seven months ago, Murrough, died shortly afterward. This gentleman is Nicolas St. Adrian, his heir, and Beaumont's new duc. He will be your stepfather come the spring, when my year of mourning is over."

Murrough nodded, and then, turning to meet Nicolas's gaze, bowed politely. "How do you do, my lord?" he said.

"I do very well—Murrough, is it?"

"Yes, my lord. I am Murrough O'Flaherty."

Skye reached out to draw her other two older children forward. "Nicolas, this is my son, Robin, the young Earl of Lynmouth, and my oldest daughter, Willow Small."

"Welcome to Beaumont de Jaspre, children," Nicolas said.

Willow curtseyed prettily, and Robin bowed gravely.

"Are these all of your children, *doucette?*" Nicolas asked admiringly.

"No, my eldest is not here. Why did Ewan not come?" she asked Murrough.

"He did not feel it wise to leave Ballyhennessey at this time, Mother."

"Has there been difficulty?" Skye looked worried, wondering about her oldest child, who would in three months' time be celebrating his fourteenth birthday.

"Not really. The English are most respectful of the Earl of Lynmouth's older brother." Murrough chuckled and added, "Although it does infuriate Ewan to have to hide behind Robin's title. Still, Uncle Michael insists he do it. The problem has been with Ewan's neighbors, old Black Hugh Kenneally of Gillydown to be specific. He thought that because Ewan was barely weaned from his mother's teats, as he put it, he might take some of the lands of Ballyhennessey for himself."

"What did Ewan do?" Skye's voice was tense.

"Burned Black Hugh's fine house down about his ears, put his fields to the torch, and drove off his sheep. They were arguing about the sheep when I last heard. Ewan felt Black Hugh owed him some sort of fine for the inconvenience to which he'd been put. Black Hugh wanted his sheep back, feeling that having his house and fields burned was fair enough. I'll wager that Ewan keeps at least half of the sheep!"

"So he should," Skye said. "I am glad that your brother did not hesitate to exact revenge upon Black Hugh. He must be strong else his other neighbors think him easy prey. As for hiding behind Robin's name, 'tis only his pride that makes him angry. What is important is that he retain his lands and his power. There is no shame in Ewan having the right family ties."

"Even if they be English?" Murrough teased his mother.

"If more Irish had learned to put the English to use," Skye said wryly, "we would not have half the troubles we have between us."

Nicolas stood, amazed at the conversation between Skye and Murrough. He had been even more amazed to hear Skye's approval of her oldest son, Ewan's, actions. This tough and fierce side of her was not something that he had seen before. He had not even suspected she had such a side. Then he laughed at himself for a romantic fool. She had been telling him of her lands, of her wealth, of the lands and wealth she administered for others. She had to be strong to hold such power!

"Are you still sure you would wed such an independent woman as myself, Nicolas," she gently teased him, and then put a soft hand on his arm.

"The first moment I laid eyes on you, *doucette*, I knew that there was but one woman for me," he said quietly, "and you are she."

Skye looked about the cabin of the ship at her children. "Let us go home, Nicolas," she said. "I seem to have everything that I need to be a happy woman now." Reaching out, she took her infant son from his red-cheeked Irish nurse and, turning, she walked through the door onto the deck and into the bright sunshine of the December afternoon, her children, Edmond, and Nicolas trailing in her wake.

Chapter 6

*T*he winter was a mild, sunny one, the rainy season coming only in February, and then giving way to a beautiful warm March when the hillsides filled with softly blowing red and blue windflowers. It had been a wonderful winter, and for the first time in many months Skye O'Malley and her children felt loved and safe. Beaumont de Jaspre was a happy place. The menace of France had subsided with the Pope's message to Queen Catherine, and Nicolas's unquestioned loyalty. There was no Elizabeth Tudor and her court to overshadow their happiness.

It was the first time since Geoffrey's death and the early days of her reunion with Niall that they had all been together. She saw her two older sons gradually become boys again, dropping away the sophisticated courtier's veneer that they had worn on their arrival as easily as a snake sheds his skin. Nicolas took them hunting in the small range of mountains that served as one of Beaumont's borders. He took all the children swimming on a deserted beach below the castle. The boys were like young dolphins, splashing and diving. Willow, however, was content to paddle around the shore with her baby sister, Deirdre; and tiny Padraic crowed with delight when Nicolas took him by his little hands and floated him in the gentle sea. The baby wriggled with pleasure in the warm waters, his plump little arms and legs moving busily. Her children quite obviously approved of Nicolas St. Adrian, Elizabeth Tudor certainly approved of him, and Skye began to believe that she might even dare to love him.

He assuredly adored her, and he seemed to genuinely care for her offspring. She could see that he was a man who loved children easily, and would do well with them. If only she were not plagued by that tiny nagging doubt that would not leave her in peace. She yet worried that if she married Nicolas he would be touched by the bad luck that seemed to strike at all of her husbands. Still, she had no choice. The wedding was set for the day after her one-year period of mourning was over. When he had told her that, she had blushingly protested his lack of decency, but Nicolas had laughed, saying that no one who had seen her would lack for understanding of his unseemly haste.

Robin and Murrough intended to stay with their mother until midsummer, then return to court. The other three children would remain with Skye and Nicolas. Bran had sailed in early spring for Bideford to fetch Dame Cecily back for the wedding. Bran and Daisy were planning to marry shortly after Skye and Nicolas. Robbie had returned in midwinter from his voyage to Istanbul. He was very surprised by the turn of events that had made Skye a widow, and was now making her a bride again. Nonetheless he fully approved of Nicolas, and the two had become very good friends. He had never really warmed to Fabron de Beaumont, but liked his half-brother.

It was too perfect, and she had known it. The messenger came a month before the scheduled wedding. They tried to protect her from him, Nicolas and Robbie both. Nicolas did not like the look of the dark man. To the young duc he was an infidel to be wary of, but Robbie knew better. The dark man came from Algiers.

"Give me the message," the Devon sea captain demanded of the messenger in flawless Arabic. "I will see that she gets it."

"I cannot do that, sir," was the polite reply.

"Who has sent you?" was Robbie's next question.

"I will only speak to Skye Muna el Khalid," was the answer, and then the thin man in the long white robes stood silent.

"I'll have him thrown in the dungeons beneath the castle," Nicolas said impatiently as Robbie translated the conversation.

"It will do you no good," Robbie remarked. "You could pull his fingernails off with burning pincers and he would not say another word. The only way we will learn anything further is to get Skye so she may hear his message."

Nicolas sighed. Some instinct warned him that this strange man was about to destroy his happiness. Nonetheless he had no choice. He sent a servant for Skye.

Coming into the Great Hall, her eye instantly found the man in white, and she stopped, growing pale. She, too, had recognized the garments of Algiers, garments she had never again thought to see. "Who is this man?" she begged of Robbie.

"We don't know, lass. He arrived here asking for you. He will say nothing of who he is, or who has sent him. He seems to speak only Arabic. Do you remember the language?"

She nodded and then, drawing a deep breath, walked over to the man. "You wish to see me?"

"You are Skye Muna el Khalid?"

"I am she."

The man in white bowed low and respectfully. "I am Haroun, the servant of Osman the astrologer," he said. "I bring you a message from my master."

"Have you been offered refreshment, Haroun?" Skye asked. "You have traveled far if you come from Osman." Skye turned to one of the castle servants. "Bring cakes and fresh fruit juice," she commanded.

"You are kind, lady," Haroun said. "Let me do my duty, and then I will gladly partake of your hospitality."

"Speak then, Haroun, the servant of Osman."

"The message my master sends to you is this. Your husband is not dead. He whom Osman once told you was your true mate lives. You must come to Algiers immediately so that my master may tell you the truth of this matter."

He who is your true mate. The words rang frighteningly in her head as she collapsed in a dead faint. Nicolas's hand went to his dagger, but Robbie, who had understood Haroun's words, cried out, "No, lad! I don't think the messenger's news is bad. Here," and he bent to cradle Skye, "help me to revive her." He looked to a stunned servant. "You! Get wine!"

"I did not mean to harm the lady," Haroun said worriedly to Robbie.

"You've just shocked her, man," was the reply. "Did your master say to tell it that way?"

"Yes, sir. I have but repeated the words given me by my master, Osman."

"Osman is growing dotty," Robbie muttered as Nicolas took Skye from him and, lifting her into his arms, carried her to a nearby settle.

Carefully he propped her up, rubbing her wrists, calling her name softly, almost frantically. A serving man ran up with a small goblet of wine, and gently Nicolas began to force some of the potent liquid down her throat. Skye coughed and then her eyes flew open.

"*He is alive!*" she cried.

"Who, *ma doucette?* Let me send the infidel away."

"No!" She turned her face to the messenger, Haroun. "Is there any more message?" she almost begged him.

"I have said it all, lady," he answered her, sorry to see the wonderful light go from her beautiful blue eyes.

"How can I be sure you are who you say?" Skye demanded.

"That's the first intelligent thing you've said," snapped Robbie, relieved. "What the hell is he talking about?"

"Osman sends word that Niall is alive."

"What? Are ye daft, lass?! Niall Burke was murdered by a crazy nun, and dumped in the sea. How the hell can he be alive, and how do you know that's what he means anyway? He who is your true mate? What kind of gobbledygook is that?"

"When Khalid was murdered by Yasmin and Jamil, and I grieved for him, Osman told me that my future was with the man I had first loved, the man of my own homeland, Niall Burke." She turned to Haroun again. "Where is the proof you are who you say?" she demanded.

"My master said if you asked for such proof I was to tell you what he once told you. Follow your instincts. They will never fail you," Haroun replied. "Play out your part as Allah has foretold."

Skye grew pale again. "He is from Osman," she said with finality.

"What kind of proof is that?" Robbie yelled.

"They are Osman's words to me before I left Algiers. Since he spoke them to me when I was alone, I must accept them as proof of Haroun's honesty. He could only have learned them from his master."

Robbie snorted irritably. "You, Haroun, how did you know where to find Skye Muna el Khalid?"

"A vessel belonging to this lady stopped in Algiers several weeks ago. I brought its captain to see my master, and my master asked this captain, an old man with a strange and unpronounceable name."

"MacGuire?"

"Aye, lady!" Haroun's dark face cracked in a small smile. "My master asked this man to take a message to you, but the old man said that you were not in your homeland, but rather in this place. I was therefore dispatched to fetch you to my master. He says that you must waste no time in coming to him, for the man who is your true mate is in danger."

"Can we sail tonight?" Skye demanded of Robbie.

"Aye, but I think you're crazy, lass. Let me go to Osman, and see what it is he has to say, if indeed it is really him. Have you forgotten Jamil? God, what Jamil would not give to wreak his revenge upon you, Skye. Algiers is too dangerous for you, lass."

"No! I will go, Robbie! *I must go!*"

Robbie looked at Haroun. "Is Captain Jamil still alive, man?"

"He lives, sir, but at this time he is gone from the city to Istanbul to seek a cure for his illness. It will be safe for the lady. My master would not call her were it not safe."

"We sail tonight!" Skye said in a voice that brooked no argument.

Nicolas St. Adrian had stood by, looking from one to the other while they had spoken back and forth and to the dark Haroun. The quick language that they had used was not familiar to him, and he had not understood a word that they had said. He had known instinctively, however, that he was somehow about to lose Skye, and all his emotions gathered themselves to fight this. He could not, would not, let her go from him. "Tell me, *doucette*," he begged her. "Tell me what this man has said, and why I feel you are about to go from me?"

She had forgotten him! She had forgotten this gentle and tender man who loved her so deeply, who intended to make her his bride in a month's time. For the last few minutes it had been as if he had not existed, for the truth was that only Niall Burke existed for her. Her hands flew to her face in distress, and her beautiful sapphire eyes, dark in their sorrow, looked into his face. "I cannot marry you," she said softly. "My husband is alive. Haroun has brought me word from an old friend in Algiers that Niall is alive. Osman would not lie to me. I must go to Algiers, Nicolas. I must find Niall."

"Do not leave me," he begged her.

"I have no choice, Nicolas," she said low. "Niall is alive. I cannot wed another while my lawful husband lives."

"Let Robert go," he said. "Let Robert go to find out if what this man says is true. Stay with me until he returns."

"Aye!" Robbie chimed in. "That's what I told her too, Nicolas, but she will not listen. As always she is stubborn!"

"*Niall is alive!* Osman says he is in danger," she shouted at them. "*I must go to him!* I must, and I will. To send Robbie is to waste precious time. Wasted time could cost my Niall his life! If that happens I shall never forgive either of you. *Never!*"

"Go then," he shouted back at her. "Go, but if this turns out to be a fantasy, promise me that you will return to me, *doucette!* At least give me that hope."

"Osman would not lie to me," she said softly.

"Promise me!"

She looked into his face and saw that there were tears in his green eyes. "Oh, Nicolas, what have I done to you! You see! Did I not warn you, my darling? I destroy in one way or another the men who love me. It has ever been thus, and I do not know why it should be." She leaned over and kissed his cheek. "I promise that if this is a wild and futile chase I will return to you, my dear Nicolas, for surely no woman has ever been so fortunate in love as she is unlucky."

"Let the children stay with me," he said. "You will return to me, I know it."

"If I am not back by midsummer, or you have no word of me, you must send them *all* home, Nicolas. Padraic must be on his lands, and Murrough and Robin have their places at court. Then, too, you must choose another wife."

"*No!*" His handsome face was anguished. "No," he repeated softly.

"Yes," came the voice of Edmond de Beaumont, and the dwarf hopped down from the large chair where he had been sitting quite hidden. He had heard all, and now he spoke urgently to his uncle. "Have you forgotten why you were made Fabron de Beaumont's heir, Nicolas? Of all the eligible men in this family only you are whole, normal, able to father the next generation. For that, my Uncle, you will need a wife."

"I have Skye," came the stubborn reply.

"No longer, I think," Edmond de Beaumont said sadly. "It pains me also, Nicolas. Never in my lifetime has this castle been as happy as it has been since she came into it bringing her laughter and joy for life and love. We should, however, do Skye's memory a great disservice if we allow ourselves to fall back into the old and gloomy ways." His violet eyes brimmed with sympathy for his uncle. Of them all, he understood her loss best, for Edmond de Beaumont loved Skye, too. Looking at her now, he said, "Must you go, *chérie?*"

"Yes, Edmond, I must go. If Osman says that Niall is alive, then Niall *is* alive. How, or where, or why I do not know, and I will not know until I see Osman."

He nodded. "Then you must go, and you will go with our prayers."

"The children," Skye said, "I must tell the children." Without a further glance at either of them she turned and hurried from the hall.

They stood watching her go, each man lost in his own thoughts. Robbie wondered if what she was about to do was foolhardy. How could Niall be alive? And if he was, how in Hell did Osman know about it? Still, and here he grimaced, he remembered Osman. He was an honorable man, and had been a true friend to Khalid el Bey.

Seeing Skye go from the hall, Nicolas thought his heart would surely break. How could he lose her now, just before their wedding? Surely this was not happening! It was a bad dream from which he would shortly awaken. A sound, something like a sob, escaped his lips. It was no dream. It was a real and waking nightmare. He was about to lose to a dead man the only woman he had ever loved.

In his agile mind Edmond de Beaumont cursed the twist of fate that had wrought this terrible situation. His uncle was shattered, grief-stricken at the loss of Skye. It was going to be difficult, if not impossible, to find a bride who would suit Nicolas St. Adrian now; but a bride would have to be found quickly else the menace of France arise again. The knowledge of Skye's affair with Nicolas prior to their marriage had kept the French at bay, for Skye might have been with child, a child who would have been the next heir to Beaumont de Jaspre. Now, however, Skye would be gone, and without a wife Nicolas would be prime target for a French assassination. If he were to die then Beaumont de Jaspre would fall like a ripe fruit into the lap of Queen Catherine.

While the men behind her thought their thoughts Skye practically ran from the hall to find her children. By chance they were all gathered in the garden, and the older three, instantly seeing her distraught look, hurried toward her. Skye collapsed upon a marble bench, her white skin unusually pale. Reaching his mother first, Murrough sat next to her, putting an arm about her.

"What is it, Mother?" he begged her, and then Robin and Willow were squeezing in on the other side of her.

"Do you remember my speaking of my old friend, Osman the astrologer, in Algiers?" They all nodded, and Skye continued. "I have had a message from Osman, a strange and frightening, yet wonderful message. Osman begs me to come to Algiers, for he says that Niall is alive!"

"It is possible," Murrough said thoughtfully, "although the odds are quite incredible, Mother."

She was stunned by his words. "How is it possible, Murrough?" He was the first person who had not said she was mad to go, and she wondered why.

"Remember the mad nun's words, Mother. She left Niall's body upon the beach for the sea to claim. Later, when the others went back to the beach, the tide had already come in, and they assumed the sea had taken Niall's lifeless body. We know that she stabbed him, but was he really dead? Did his lifeless body indeed wash out to sea? Mannanan MacLir usually returns the dead shells of those whose souls he has taken. Niall's body was never found, Mother. Therefore it is possible that he was not dead, but badly injured; and it is equally possible that he is alive today, and your friend, Osman, knows his whereabouts," Murrough concluded triumphantly.

"God's bones!" Skye said, totally surprised by her son's reasoning. "You are a scholar, Murrough! You have a mind that reasons!" For a moment she forgot her own problems. "Is that what you want, my son? To be a scholar?"

"I do for now," he said with a smile, thinking that he was only applying common sense to the situation and that this was a strange time for them to be having this little talk; but then if his mother was rushing off to Algiers to find Niall Burke, Heaven only knew when he would see her again.

"Where would you study?" she demanded of him.

"Merton College at Oxford," he answered her promptly.

"Your father studied in Paris," she said in one of her few references to Dom O'Flaherty, "for all the good it did him." Then she smiled at him. "When I return from Algiers I will see to it that you go to Oxford, Murrough. Of course it will mean that you and Joan must wait to wed. Will you mind that?"

"Arrange it now," he said quietly. "You do not know how long it will take you to find Niall, and I cannot bear another year playing the popinjay of a page in the Earl of Lincoln's household. For Robin the court is a joy, as he is, for all his age, one of England's premier noblemen. I, however, am a different matter, Mother. Both of my parents are Irish, and there are some English who cannot abide anyone Irish."

"Who has dared to mistreat you," she demanded angrily, but Murrough soothed his mother quickly.

"No one would dare to mistreat me, Mother. I am the son of the Countess of Lynmouth, and brother to Lynmouth's earl. I am generous with my allowance, which always assures friends, and the Countess of Lincoln is Irish herself. No one short of a fool would mistreat Elizabeth FitzGerald's personal page. Still, there are tiny insults and sly innuendos that I must constantly face with good cheer, for if I lost my temper and fought I should be called a brawling Irishman. I do not like the court, Mother. I know that you have told me that I must make my way there in order to win my own lands for Joan; but Joan is like me, Mother. She is shy and gentle. She wishes no more than to be my wife someday, and to raise our children in a peaceful place.

"I wish to study at Merton College. Then—and I think you will be amazed at my decision—I want to go to sea. Someday I hope to captain one of your ships, Mother. You have said that I will never lack for money, and that money will allow me to buy a fine house with a pretty garden where I can live with my family between voyages. Joan is almost three years younger than I am, and she is really yet a little girl. There is no hurry for us to wed, and we had hoped to wait until she was sixteen. That will give me six years in which to make my way in this world."

Quiet Murrough, she thought. She had never seen this side of him before. He was really still a boy, and yet he seemed this minute like a young man. Skye was not sure she was ready to have a young man for a son. "Why have you not spoken to me before?" she asked him.

"There was never any time," he said honestly, and she knew that to be true.

"I will write to Lord Burghley tonight before I leave for Algiers," she said to him. "I will also write to the Countess of Lincoln, and to my secretary, Jean Morlaix. If it can be arranged you will be at Oxford in time for the Michaelmas term."

"Thank you, Mother," Murrough said, hugging her hard.

"What about the rest of us?" Willow demanded. "If you go rushing off to Algiers what is to become of the rest of us?"

"You will all remain here until midsummer," Skye said. "By that time I hope to know the many answers in the Niall puzzle. If he is alive, as Osman claims, then you will all leave for England and Ireland at that time. If, however, it turns out that Osman was mistaken, and I have been chasing after naught but a ghost, then only Murrough and Robin will return to England. You, Deirdre, and Padraic will remain here, and I shall return to marry with Nicolas, as we had planned."

Willow nodded. "Poor Dame Cecily is certainly going to be mightily surprised when she finally arrives, Mother. She hates to travel, but she hates to travel upon the sea most of all."

"You may go back through France," Skye promised. "You shall see Paris, and then you will have nought but a quick trip across the channel."

"Paris!" Willow breathed. "Oh, Mama, you must give me my entire allowance for next year if I am to go to Paris!"

"What?" teased Skye. "So you may spend it all?"

"Every pennypiece!" Willow said almost reverently. "I shall buy laces, and embroidered laced gloves, and a silk dress."

"And where will you wear them?" Robin mocked, a little unkindly. "Will you display your finery before the pigs and peasants of Devon?"

Skye was about to scold her little son quite severely, but Willow was quite able to take care of herself. "The Queen has asked me to be one of her maids of honor, my noble brat of a brother!" she said smugly.

"She hasn't!"

"She has," Willow said, a small, satisfied smile spreading over her face. "After all, Robin, if I am to find a noble husband I must go to court."

"You have no great name," Robin protested. "To win a great man you must have a great name."

"I have something better," Willow replied.

"What?" He looked at her disbelievingly.

"I have gold," Willow said wisely. "I am a great heiress, and I possess a great deal of gold. I will have no lack of suitors for my hand once I am at court."

Shocked, Skye could only gape at her daughter, but she quickly recovered and said, "I hope that you will marry for love as well as a great name, Willow."

"Love," Willow replied with the certainty that only a ten-year-old could possess, "can be extremely hurtful. I should prefer a far more businesslike arrangement."

"You had best seek love, my daughter," Skye remarked. "Once you marry your great wealth will belong to your husband, and if he does not love you but another, you will find you have made a very bad bargain. You could easily end up with nothing."

"I shall retain my own wealth as you have, Mother," was the cool reply.

"That is not usually the way of things in marriage, Willow. Had the men I married not loved me they would have never agreed to my demands. Best you seek love among the great names, my daughter." Then she laughed lightly. "At ten you are much too young to be discussing marriage. At least wait until I return to wed, Willow."

"She must not come to court this year, Mother," Robin said worriedly. "The Queen's maids of honor are always fair game for the lechers. She is much too young!"

"Look who speaks of youth," Willow scoffed. "Her Majesty's youngest page; he who is three years younger than I am; he whom they call the Cherub!"

"He who has been at court two years, and knows more than you do, Mistress Ignorance!" came back the quick reply.

"Enough!" Skye ordered her quarreling offspring.

"Robin is right," Murrough put in, and Willow sent her older brother a furious look.

"I know he is," Skye said. "Willow is not going to court until she is at least thirteen."

"*Mother!*" Willow protested.

"*If* I allow her to go at all," Skye continued with a warning look at her daughter. Willow fell silent.

"You will leave tonight?" Murrough asked.

"Yes," Skye answered him. "Osman says that time is most important, and to linger here would only hurt poor Nicolas more. He is, as you may imagine, quite heartbroken."

"You do not believe you will be returning to Beaumont de Jaspre, do you, Mother."

"No, Murrough, I do not. I keep saying *if* Osman is correct, *if* he is right; but I know that he would not have sent for me if he were not certain." A sad little smile flitted across her beautiful face for just a brief moment. "I shall, of course, be staying in his house in Algiers." She looked at Willow. "It was your father's house once, my dearest, and I never thought to see it again. Dear God, the memories it will bring back to me! I do not know if I can bear it. Algiers! Never did I expect to be in Algiers again!"

"What of the wicked Turk who sought to make you his wife?" Willow asked a bit fearfully. She had heard the story of Skye's flight many times, and until now it had been a romantic fairy tale in which her beautiful mother was the enchanted princess. This, however, was reality, and Willow was afraid for Skye.

"He is in Istanbul, my love," Skye reassured her. "He cannot hurt me. Poor Jamil was never my match." Skye stood up from the bench. "Come, my loves. It is already late, and I must make other arrangements before I leave." She looked at her two Burke children, who lay sleeping in the grass with their nurse. "Be sure the bairns are well cared for," she implored her elder children, and they nodded their promise.

When she arrived at her apartments Daisy was already packing for her. "You'll not be needing all these fancy clothes you've got," said the ever-practical Daisy. "I've the thought you won't want to stick out like a red silk banner, m'lady, and so I am packing only those outlandish garments you brought with you from Algiers years back. I hope that there's enough, for most of them are in England at Lynmouth."

"If my stay is lengthy," Skye said, "I can have more made, but I expect that these few will do."

"Is it really true that Lord Burke is alive, m'lady?" Daisy's eyes were wide.

"So Osman's messenger has said."

"Can you really trust this Osman?" Daisy was suspicious.

Skye laughed. "Yes, he is trustworthy, Daisy."

"What does a tiring woman wear in Algiers, m'lady? I have to know what to take for myself."

"You cannot come, Daisy," Skye said.

"Not come?" Daisy was scandalized. "Who will take care of you, I should like to know, if I don't come with you?!"

"It is far too dangerous, Daisy. If I have to leave Algiers in a hurry the way I did last time, I should prefer not to have to worry about anyone else. It is easier if I am alone. Besides, I want you to remain and wait for Dame Cecily. She will be returning with Bran Kelly any day now. When they arrive you are to marry Captain Kelly, as you have planned. Père Henri tells me that you have completed your instruction, and are ready to become a good Catholic wife. I will not have you and Bran wait any longer on my account.

"If I am not back by midsummer you and Dame Cecily will have to return with the children to England. You will go overland, and I am going to ask Bran Kelly to accompany you. The Burke children are to go on to Ireland. Robin will go back to court, Murrough to Oxford, and Willow home to Devon. You are also to go with the Smalls. I shall station Bran Kelly with you in Bideford until I return. God's bones, I've much to do before we sail!"

While Daisy finished the packing Skye went to the small writing table in her anteroom and quickly began to write several letters. One went to Lord Burghley explaining the entire situation. She could not, she wrote, remain in Beaumont de Jaspre under such dubious circumstances. She was leaving immediately for Algiers to seek the truth of the matter. Their original bargain, she reminded Cecil, involved her marriage to Fabron de Beaumont. She had kept her part of the bargain, and she expected Elizabeth Tudor to keep her part. If Lord Burke was indeed alive, they would be returning to England before they went on to Ireland, and they would come to court to tell the Queen their adventures. If, on the other hand, Lord Burke was indeed dead and this but a flight of fancy, she would return to Beaumont de Jaspre to wed with Nicolas St. Adrian, and thus continue to serve the Crown. In view of her continued loyalty, Skye wrote, would Lord Burghley kindly arrange for her second son, Murrough O'Flaherty, to enter Merton College at Oxford in the Michaelmas term? It was his desire to study at this time, and not return as a page with the Countess of Lincoln's household. She closed assuring the Crown of her constant devotion, and tendering her good wishes for the Queen's upcoming birthday in September.

Skye's second letter was sent to her uncle, the old Bishop of

Connaught. In it she outlined all that had happened, her own plans, and her plans for the children. She begged him to watch over all of her offspring in the event she did not return. She then outlined what she wanted done with the O'Malley shipping interests, and how she wanted her children's wealth disbursed, and the children raised. She knew how much this letter was going to pain Seamus O'Malley, but she also knew the dangers involved in her trip to Algiers, and she wanted those she loved cared for in the event she should not return. This letter she closed by asking for her uncle's prayers.

A letter was also sent to her stepmother, Anne, and one to her brother, Michael, the guardian of her eldest son, Ewan; a final missive went to the Countess of Lincoln, thanking her for her care of Murrough these last few years, and explaining his desire to go on to Oxford rather than remain with the court. At last she was finished, and as she arose from the writing table she felt as if a chapter in her life were closing. She wondered what the next chapter would bring her.

Back in her bedchamber, Skye saw through the windows that the day was almost gone. Upon the bed were laid out her seagoing clothes, the double-legged skirt, the silk shirt, the hose and the undergarments. By the bed stood her high boots. Daisy, however, was nowhere in sight. With a sad sigh Skye began to pull off her own garments, not even bothering to pick them up as they fell to the floor. She stood only in her chemise when the door between her room and Nicolas's opened, and he entered her chamber.

She wanted to weep at the pain she saw etched in his handsome face. Why was it that she was always giving such agony to those good men who did naught but love her. Why should her love bring such pain? Instinctively she held out her arms to him, wanting to comfort him somehow. "Oh, Nicolas," she murmured against his reddish hair. "Dear, dear Nicolas! I am so sorry, my love. I am so sorry!" Her arms closed about him, and she held him as she would hold a hurt child.

He shuddered against her. "I don't want you to go," he said softly.

"You know I have no choice. If Niall Burke is alive how can I stay with you, Nicolas? We could not marry. Our children would have no right to inherit Beaumont de Jaspre."

"Do you love Niall Burke?" His voice was ragged.

"I have loved him since I was fifteen," she cried.

"Do you love me?"

"You are asking me to choose, Nicolas, and the choice is not mine to make."

"Do you love me?" he repeated.

"I had begun to, Nicolas. Yes! I had begun to love you."

"This is madness," he said to her. "How can your husband be alive after all this time? You go but to chase a dream, *doucette!*"

"Perhaps," she allowed. "But if Osman has said he is alive, then he is alive. I do not know how, but if I did not go to find out the answer to this puzzle, Nicolas, I should always wonder. If Niall is indeed alive I cannot in good conscience marry you, for I should be committing a mortal sin."

"You will come back to me," he said firmly, and he pulled back from her, looking with love into her face.

Now it was Skye who wanted to cry. "Seek elsewhere for a bride, my love," she said softly. "It is unlikely that I will ever come back, Nicolas. I cannot ask you to wait for me. Every day that you remain unmarried you endanger your duchy, and you are the last hope of Beaumont de Jaspre. How your people love you! Since you came from your home in Poitou there has never been such gladness here. Find some sweet young girl to make your wife, the mother of the next generation."

"*No!*" He was suddenly angry; frustrated that what he wanted so desperately was being torn from him. "I will only marry you, Skye. If I cannot have you then I want no woman. I shall go back to my holding in Poitou, and to Hell with Beaumont de Jaspre!"

Skye became equally angry, and her hand flashed out to make very hard contact with his cheek. Stunned, he fell back, for she had put all her strength into the blow. "Coward!" she said furiously. "Is this how you keep your promise to Fabron de Beaumont who so generously bestowed his realm and his wealth upon you? You gave your half-brother a death-bed promise that you would rule this duchy and keep it safe from the French. You gave him your promise to care for Edmond and Garnier. Do you think a French overlord will care for them? They will be thrown into the streets to fend for themselves, if they are not driven from Beaumont entirely!"

Her hand had left a bright red mark on his cheek, and rubbing that mark, Nicolas tried to explain. "I have never loved anyone before you," he said in a low voice. "How can I live without you?"

"You think only of yourself, Nicolas," she said scornfully. "I told you once that wealth and power are a great responsibility, to be wielded carefully. I have been wielding both since I was scarcely more than a girl. There have been times when it has been hard for me not to yield to my own desires, but I have not, and you cannot! If you love me you will let me go, Nicolas, because you cannot keep me now. All the devils in Hell could not keep me here by your side now that I know my Niall is alive!"

For a moment he closed his eyes, and she knew that he was fighting back the tears, as she struggled to contain her own sorrow. She must be strong, and she must instill in him some of that same strength. But she had not lied to him when she had said that she was beginning to love him. How could she not when he adored her so, and was so good both to her and the children? She had felt so safe with him.

"I will never forget you, *doucette*," he said.

"Nor I you, Nicolas," she answered him.

"You are sure?" For the briefest moment his green eyes held a flicker of hope.

"I must go," was her simple reply, and for an equally brief moment Skye wondered if she was totally mad. Then, regaining control of herself, she said brightly, "You will have a wonderful time, Nicolas. You are now a most eligible man of considerable wealth. Think of all the lovely girls available to you, but choose quickly lest the French be tempted to a rash act."

He sighed deeply, and she almost screamed with the sadness in the sound. "What kind of a girl should I choose, *doucette*? After you, *mon amour*, how will I be content with anyone?"

"I think, perhaps, a very young girl, Nicolas, but choose one with spirit, intelligence, and a sense of humor. Do not look for one who reminds you of me. Trust Edmond's judgment, for he is a very wise man and he loves you dearly. He will want you to be happy."

Nicolas reached out for her, but Skye quickly sidestepped him. "Will you not kiss me good-bye, *doucette*?" he said softly.

She glanced down at the gossamer of her chemise, and then shook her head. "Not as I am now, Nicolas." A small smile lit her eyes. "You are very wicked, *mon brave*, even to suggest it. Go now, and let me dress, for I shall be late if I do not hurry."

With another deep sigh he turned and left her to dress. She knew how difficult the interview had been when her hands began to shake as she buttoned her shirt and fastened her skirt. He was such a good man, and she knew how deeply he was hurting, for in a strange way she was hurting, too.

"It's almost time, m'lady." When had Daisy entered the room?

"Where are the children?"

"Waiting in the anteroom to say good-bye, m'lady." Daisy's honest eyes grew misty. "Are you sure I can't go with you, m'lady?"

Skye hugged her tiring woman affectionately. "I am going to miss you terribly, Daisy," she said, "but it is much too dangerous for you to come with me. Besides, I shall need you to watch over the children until Dame Cecily arrives and you begin your return journey home."

"I'll worry about you the whole time you're away, m'lady."

"You concentrate on marrying Bran and making him a happy man," Skye counseled, and then before Daisy could become overly emotional Skye gave her a quick kiss on the cheek and hurried from the bedchamber into the anteroom where her children awaited her.

"I wish I could go with you," Murrough said enthusiastically. "Algiers sounds so exciting, Mother."

"Algiers is dangerous," Skye replied.

"I should like to fight the infidel!" Robin said bravely.

"The infidel would be enchanted by your blond hair and your light eyes, my darling. He would geld you like a horse, and if you survived the operation you would become the plaything of some wealthy man with a taste for boys. Not exactly the fate for an Earl of Lynmouth. Stay home, my sons, so that I do not have to fret over you."

"I far prefer to go home to England," Willow said primly.

Skye smiled, faintly amused. "I am relieved, Willow, that you do not choose to seek adventure as your brothers do. You will be safer back in your own homes, my darlings. Murrough, I have written to both Lord Burghley and the Countess of Lincoln regarding Merton College. I am sure they will comply with my wishes."

"Thank you, Mother!" His blue eyes shone with delight and gratitude, and Skye felt great satisfaction to have pleased this second son of hers by such a small act. Murrough stepped forward and bent to kiss her. "Take care, Mother," he said. "This time I feel no sadness because I know that you but go to return to us."

She hugged him hard. "Dearest Murrough," she murmured. "I do love you, my son."

Murrough stepped back, rosy with a mixture of pleasure caused by her words and embarrassment at her public affection. "God speed," he said as he pulled away from her.

"Murrough is right," Robin said. "I don't feel sad either, Mother. Find Niall, and then both of you come safely home to us." Robin put his arms about her neck and kissed her lovingly.

"Are you sure I can't go to court while you're away, Mama?" Willow wheedled.

Skye laughed. "No court," she said. "You will return to Devon with Dame Cecily, and continue with your lessons. You are not accomplished enough to go to court yet."

Willow sighed dramatically. "I don't know why you persist in treating me like a child, Mama," she complained.

"I would think the answer to that is obvious every time you look in the mirror," Murrough teased.

"She spends *all day* before the mirror," Robin said wickedly.

"Boys!" Willow huffed, and then she hugged her mother in farewell. "Don't be long, Mama. I miss you so when you're away from me."

"I will return as fast as I can, my darling," Skye promised her daughter, then kissed her.

The little Burke children slept with their nurse in the next room, and Skye slipped into their nursery to say a silent good-bye. They were far too young to understand her going or what it was she sought, but someday, she vowed, they would comprehend and, she hoped, bless her for what she was about to do. Her own eyes misted as she looked at them in sleep; Deirdre, so much like her, and Padraic, who grew more like his father with each passing day. She wanted him to know his father! It was for them as well as herself that she went off on what many would call a mad mission.

"They are both beautiful and peaceful as they sleep so sweetly in their innocence," Edmond said quietly in the dimness of the room. "I would to God that you had been able to give the de Beaumonts such fine children."

"The fates have willed it otherwise, dear friend," she answered him.

He took her hand, and with a final glance at her babies they walked from the room. "You will let us know your position before another bride is chosen? If you can come back to us . . ." he trailed off.

"I will get a message to you immediately," she said rather than argue with him.

"You won't be back, will you?" he said.

"I keep examining the messenger's words over and over again, Edmond," she replied, "but they are true. Osman would not lie."

"Satisfy my curiosity, *chérie*. Just who is this Osman in whom you have so much faith? Can you really trust him? Was he that good a friend?"

Skye paused a moment, wondering whether to tell him the truth. Why not? she thought. Perhaps it would help convince him. She drew a deep breath. "Edmond," she said, "Niall Burke and I were to be married after the death and mourning of my first husband. Before our nuptials could be celebrated, however, it was necessary for me to make a trip to Algiers. My trading company wished to do business with the Dey, and when he heard that the head of the O'Malleys was a woman he insisted upon seeing me. He had given us a pendant to put atop our mast that would guarantee us safe conduct through Barbary waters, but the pendant was lost in a storm and we found ourselves in a fight with pirates. We won, but I was taken from my flagship and Niall was shot as he attempted to rescue me. I believed him dead, and lost my memory as a consequence. Khalid el Bey, known as the Great Whoremaster of Algiers, bought me as a slave. He intended to train me for his finest brothel, the House of Felicity. Instead, he fell in love with me and married me.

"When Khalid was murdered in a plot concocted by his evil friend, Capitan Jamil of the Casbah fortress, I was forced to flee Algiers. Jamil coveted me, and had decided to have both me and my lord Khalid's wealth. I was pregnant with Willow at the time, but it didn't slow me down, Edmond. With the help of Osman, who had been my husband's dearest friend, I converted Khalid's holdings into gold and fled Algiers with my personal servants via Robbie's ship several days before my period of mourning was to end.

"Now do you understand why I trust Osman? If he calls me then I must go, Edmond. If he says that Niall is alive then he is, and I will find him! I must do this not only for myself, but for Deirdre and Padraic as well. They have a right to their father, and I have a right to my husband."

"My God!" Edmond ejaculated. "You are amazing! You are more than amazing! *You are formidable!*" He stopped and, moving in front of her, took her two hands in his tiny ones. "What you have told me, *chérie*, will remain between us. I see now why you trust this Osman, and . . ." he sighed sadly, "I understand now that you will not be back."

"Find Nicolas someone quickly, Edmond. Do not let him mourn me until I become so idealized in his memory that no other woman could possibly satisfy him. Find him someone who will understand and be patient with his pain. Someone who will see what a fine man he is, and be willing to wait for him to heal. My instinct tells me it should be a young girl, not necessarily an heiress, or even an eldest daughter, but a girl who would be pleased for such a plum as the Duc de Beaumont de Jaspre to fall into her lap. Find him someone who will love him, Edmond."

"Yes," was the resigned reply, "I will find someone who will love him, and eventually with God's good luck he will love her, too. Poor girl, I do not envy her her lot, for it will be a difficult one. Nicolas will not be easy to placate."

They continued down into the lovely courtyard of the castle. Skye had decided to leave at twilight when Villerose's streets would be fairly empty. No announcement had been made of Skye's departure, and would not be until she was long gone. It would be most difficult to explain to the people, but explain they would have to eventually. Skye suggested to Edmond as they entered the courtyard that they wait as long as possible in order to protect Beaumont de Jaspre from the French, and give him an opportunity to look over the possible candidates for Nicolas's hand.

"With my children here it is unlikely that anyone will notice me gone for a good week. The servants, of course, must be told to keep silent."

Daisy was waiting with her mistress's cloak, and she wrapped it around Skye, pulling the hood up to disguise her lady from prying eyes. With trembling fingers Daisy fastened the heavy gold frog fasteners, and then stepped back. Her eyes were teary, and Skye gave her a quick hug, chiding, "None of that, Daisy. I'll be back before you know it!"

"God s-speed, m'lady!" came the quavering reply, and then Daisy turned and fled back into the castle.

Skye watched her go, and then said, "Poor Daisy. We have never been parted since she came into my service. She even went into the Tower with me. Watch over her, Edmond, and see that she and the children get safely off at the proper time."

He nodded, and then Skye saw Robbie and Nicolas coming toward her. The young duc had dressed himself in his finest clothes, and the dark green velvet was very flattering to his rich chestnut hair and his forest green eyes. About his neck was the heavy gold chain of Beaumont, its lion pendant lying on his chest.

"How handsome you are," she said sincerely as he stopped in front of her.

"How beautiful you are," he answered, looking down into her face, and Skye's heart contracted painfully. His hand gently pushed back her hood so he might have a last look at her, and then he bent his head and briefly and tenderly brushed her half-parted lips with his own. For a long, heart-stopping moment their eyes met, and then he gently drew the hood back up over her head. "*Au revoir, mon coeur*," he said, and then turned and walked from the courtyard into the castle, never once looking back at her.

"Go with him!" Skye begged Edmond.

"Aye," Edmond said, and catching her hand up kissed it fervently. "God speed, *chérie*," he murmured, and then he too was gone after his young uncle.

A silent servant helped Skye to mount her white palfrey while another aided Robbie. Then together they trotted their horses from the flowered courtyard and across the drawbridge. As they went Skye said in a sad, resigned voice, "I have been here just over one year, Robbie. How macabre! Where will I be a year from now, do you think? Will Niall and I be safely home in Ireland?"

"Lord bless me, lass, who knows?!" He wasn't going to let her feel sorry for herself, and he could see the terrible emotional toll her farewell from Nicolas had taken. "One thing I can promise you, Skye. Wherever you are a year from now it will not have been a dull year, for you've never been a dull woman. By God! I do enjoy trying to keep up with you, my lass! 'Twill be one of two things for me: either I'll never grow old following after you, Skye O'Malley; or I'll be old before my time!" He chuckled. "I can just see Cecily's face when she gets here and finds us gone. She's always said I make a fuss over nothing when it comes to your constant adventures, Skye lass. Now she'll see," he chortled wickedly. "Now she'll see!"

Part III

North Africa

Chapter 7

Algiers shimmered in the mid-day heat. The sun glared off the deep-blue waters of the harbor and reflected back onto the white, white buildings of the city. Skye's ship, *Seagull*, was anchored a short distance out in the harbor. Robbie had no intention of allowing Skye ashore until he had made absolutely certain that Jamil was not in the city.

"You're an old woman," she teased him as he climbed down the side of the ship into the small dinghy that would take him into the docks.

"Ye're damned right, I am!" he shot back, not one bit intimidated. "Do you want to spend the rest of your days in slavery to Jamil, lass?"

"I'd sooner be dead!"

"Then I'll just be on my way to find Osman," Robbie said with a chuckle. "Besides, ye're getting too old to be running around in diaphanous trousers and beaded tops."

"*Too old*?!" She looked outraged. "I'm not yet—"

"Yes, you are!" he laughed. "Not that you look it, Skye lass. Be patient, and I'll not be long."

She watched the small boat skitter across the waves and into the docks. Robbie would have no hard time finding Osman, for the famous astrologer had bought Khalid el Bey's house from Skye when she had fled Algiers over ten years ago. Robbie, who had been Khalid's business partner, was most familiar with the house. She could see it from here. Slowly she raised her eyes up to gaze on the house in which she had been so supremely happy. It stood elegant and proud atop a high hill overlooking the entire city. She wondered if the gardens were still as lovely. She would soon know.

When Bran Kelly had returned to Devon for Dame Cecily, Robbie had allowed the young captain to take his own ship, the *Mermaid*, for he wanted the cargo he had traded for in Ottoman Turkey brought back to England. Consequently, it was *Seagull* that had brought them to Algiers, and old Sean MacGuire who had captained her. Now the senior captain of the O'Malley fleet kept his mistress company as she paced anxiously up and down the deck of her ship.

"If he's to be found, ye'll find him," MacGuire said comfortingly. She nodded, but said nothing.

After a while MacGuire, taking out his old pipe and putting it between his teeth, spoke again. "Niall Burke's a tough one, and that's for sure. I remember the cosh we gave him on the head to make him more manageable the morning after yer first marriage. If he had a headache he never said so."

"If he's here," Skye said slowly, "I keep wondering how he got from a deserted beach on Ireland's west coast to North Africa."

"Yer friend Osman is sure to know, m'lady Skye."

"Yes, Osman . . ." She stared off again across the harbor to the white building upon the hill.

Time. Time moved so slowly here in Algiers, she recalled. She hoped that Robbie would remember to hurry. The voyage from Beaumont de Jaspre had not been a long one, only a few days, but with each hour that had passed the last year had faded and her memories of Niall Burke become stronger. The how and why began to haunt her, and she grew more and more anxious to reach Algiers, to speak with Osman. Was it a hoax perpetrated by Jamil, or had Osman really sent for her?

"You'd better change out of those clothes if you intend to be ready when he gets back," MacGuire said after what seemed a very long while.

"There's time," she said, not even stopping her pacing.

"Nay, m'lady, there's no time. Look!" He pointed out toward the docks. "There's Sir Robert's boat now making its return trip."

"Holy Mother!" Skye ran to her cabin and, once inside, began with suddenly clumsy fingers to get out of her sea garb. If she really wanted to cause a stir all she needed to do was appear in the streets of Algiers unveiled and dressed as a sea captain. Opening the tiny trunk of clothes that Daisy had so carefully packed for her, she drew out an exquisite caftan of pale-mauve silk. The neckline was modestly high and embroidered in tiny purple glass beads that extended down from the round of the neck in a band two inches wide and six inches long. Such a band also ringed each of the wide sleeves. Sliding the caftan on, she then undid her long hair from the confining single braid in which she always dressed it when at sea. She brushed the dark mass free and fixed a band of mauve silk with the identical purple beading on her head to contain the hair and keep it from falling into her eyes.

Makeup! Skye scrambled through the trunk, and there it was: a small ebony box containing little ivory pots of color, each set carefully in its own niche, and several sable brushes. The inside lid of the box was mirrored so she might see what she was doing no matter where she was. Skillfully she outlined her eyes with blue kohl and darkened her lashes. Neither her lips nor her cheeks needed the addition of color, for Skye had always been a healthy woman.

Finished, she gazed into the mirror and her eyes widened in surprise, for staring back at her was a woman she thought she had left behind some ten years ago when she had escaped Algiers and the unwelcome advances of Capitan Jamil. It was uncanny, and not a little frightening, for the woman in the mirror did not look a day older than the nineteen-year-old girl she had been. True, her eyes were wiser, and her cheekbones etched more finely now, but other than that there was no change. Skye shivered, and then shaking off the feeling of déjà vu, she closed the makeup case with a snap, stood, replaced the ebony box in her trunk, and walked from the cabin.

Robbie's small boat had already reached the *Seagull*, and he had just climbed to the deck when she exited her cabin. Stunned, he stood looking at her for a long minute. Then he shook his head in wonder. "How is it possible?" he said, the rest of his thought unspoken.

"I had the same reaction," she answered him, and then, "You've seen Osman?"

"Aye, and his palanquin is awaiting you. We've permission to bring *Seagull* into the docks. She's been given a preferred berth. It seems that old Osman's reputation has grown mightily in these past years. Half of Algiers doesn't make a move without him, and the rumor is that the Dey doesn't get off his couch without Osman's advice."

"What did he tell you?" she begged anxiously.

"Nothing, Skye lass. It's you he wants to see."

It took a very short time to bring *Seagull* into her berth on the busy waterfront of Algiers. Here there were ships and goods from every part of the known world. The air was fragrant and the noise was incredible, with many voices speaking many languages in an unending cacophony. By the time Skye's vessel had been made secure she had added a black silk yashmak to her costume. This long black cloak covered her from her head to toe, and her identity was further hidden by the mauve silk veil that was attached to the hood of the yashmak, and drawn across her face. She was the proper Muslim woman, garbed for the street and for travel.

They were docked next to an Ottoman galley, and as the light wind blew Skye's veil aside to reveal her face for a moment there were whistles and ribald shouts from the men chained to the top tier of oars. Some of the words she understood, others she did not, but their meaning was clear. Her eyes clouded with distress, and she said with strong aversion in her voice, "God's nightshirt, I hate those damned galleys! To chain men to an oar rather than use the wind and the water by your own skill is disgusting. Find out if there are any English or Irishmen among them, MacGuire. They can sail home with us."

"What about Scots or Welsh?"

"Buy them," she said tersely. "I don't care from what part of our islands they come, I'll not stand by and see them die in some sea battle, unable to escape because of their chains!"

Sean MacGuire nodded. "How long will you be gone?" he demanded.

"I don't know, but Robbie will be back to the ship as soon as we know anything. Give the men liberty in shifts, and tell them I want no trouble, nor do I want it known that I am in Algiers."

"There's not a man aboard who'd betray you, m'lady," Sean MacGuire said feelingly.

"Nonetheless you will remind them once again, MacGuire," Skye said sternly.

"Aye, O'Malley," he said quietly, and she knew he had gotten her point.

She nodded at him, her expression unreadable beneath her veil.

Then she turned to debark. At the foot of the gangway a palanquin awaited, and as Skye stepped into it she felt as if she were stepping back in time, into a life that had ceased to exist for her with the death of her second husband, the fascinating Khalid el Bey. The vehicle was carved and gilded, and hung with silk curtains of azure blue, while inside it was upholstered in silken stripes of red and green and purple and gold, with pillows done in cloth of gold. She settled herself comfortably, and the draperies were drawn to hide the palanquin's occupant. Robbie was given a finely caparisoned horse to ride.

The palanquin was carried by eight slaves, all coal-black and dressed in baggy scarlet pantaloons. Their feet, the soles of which were toughened by their work, were bare as were their chests. They were not, however, oiled, as was fashionable for blacks, nor did they wear jeweled collars about their necks to advertise their owner's wealth.

As the procession left the docks and began to wend its way through the city, Skye was assailed by a thousand memories triggered by the sights she could just see through the gauzy draperies; by the sounds of the busy city; by the smells of the vendors' stalls. For a moment she lay back, and of all her experiences of this city the one she suddenly remembered was her return to Algiers from her wedding trip with Khalid. They had both been dressed all in white, and their sleek black hunting panthers, leashed but still impressive, had loped elegantly along by their sides. He had ridden his great white stallion, she a dainty golden mare with a long, white-blond mane and tail that he had given her. She sighed. How simple her life as his wife had been; but still she could not regret all the times since. Osman would have said that it was her fate.

Osman. She visualized in her mind this man who had turned her world so topsy-turvy with a simple message. He had not, as she remembered, been a tall man; rather, he had been of medium height and build; really quite unimpressive a person until you looked into his eyes, for Osman's eyes saw what other people did not see. They saw beyond the everyday and into the heart and soul. They saw beyond today, and even, she had always suspected, past tomorrow. They were strange and yet wonderful golden-brown eyes that had always shone kindly upon her. Looking at Osman's bald head and bland moon-round face, few realized the power behind those eyes. Khalid had seen it, and had always been the astrologer's friend.

When she and Khalid had been married he had given each of the six men he had invited as wedding guests a slave girl. She remembered how she and Khalid had chosen each of the six girls to suit the personality of a guest. She had chosen for Osman a lovely dark-blond girl of French extraction named Alima. The astrologer had shortly afterward made Alima his wife, and she knew that they now had several children. It pleased her to think that Osman and Alima were happy, and they must be, for he had taken no other wives, and had no harem of concubines.

Suddenly the palanquin was set down, the draperies drawn aside, and a hand extended to aid her in getting out; and as the hand drew her up she looked into the smiling face of Osman the astrologer.

"Welcome, my daughter," he said, and looking into his eyes at that moment, she knew that her quest was not a vain one.

"Osman," she began, but he put his hand up to stop her.

"I know you are anxious, Skye, my daughter, but first I would settle you. A few more minutes will not matter now that you are here." He turned to Robbie, who had dismounted his horse. "Welcome again, Captain. It does my heart good to see you here." Then Osman led them both into his house, the house in which she had lived with Khalid.

Skye let her eyes dart about the square entry hall, and it all looked the same as the night she had left it. For a brief second she expected to see Khalid come through from the gardens, his white robes swirling about his tall figure. She walked through the entry into the beautiful gardens beyond, and stood looking, feeling the tears fill her blue eyes, dimming her vision momentarily before spilling down her cheeks. The orange and lemon trees were larger, fuller; the pines taller. The T-shaped pool with its spraying fountains and border of roses was as lovely as ever. On one of the white marble benches near the house a woman sat surrounded by several children. Seeing Skye, she rose and came toward her.

"My lady Skye? Is it truly you?" Alima, the wife of Osman, stood before her. Seeing Skye's tears, Alima put her arms about her mentor. "It has been as happy a house for Osman and me as it was for you and the lord Khalid. It is a good place, and I gladly welcome you back to it."

The sudden sadness passed, and Skye drew away from Alima, saying, "When I learned I must return to Algiers I knew the first moments would be hard. It is over now, Alima, and I thank you for your gracious welcome."

"Let me show you to the rooms I have set aside for you. They overlook this garden, for I know how much you loved it." With quiet assurance Alima led Skye back into the house and upstairs to two lovely airy rooms in a different wing of the house than she had lived in with Khalid. Already two silent slave girls were unpacking her small trunk. A third hurried forward bearing a silver basin filled with rosewater for the lady to wash away the dust of her travel. When Skye had done so Alima led her back downstairs into Osman's library, where the astrologer and Robbie waited for her. Having brought Skye to her husband, Alima quietly departed.

Skye knew that Osman expected her to remain calm, and so she seated herself upon the floor cushions and patiently accepted a tiny cup of boiling Turkish coffee before looking expectantly toward him.

The astrologer looked back calmly, his powerful gaze instilling in her a strange sense of peace. Then he began to speak. "In the city of Fez I have two nephews, the sons of my late sister, Lilitu, who was the wife of a vastly wealthy merchant. The elder of my nephews is named Kedar, and he inherited his father's wealth and business when my brother-in-law, Omar, died. Kedar was a man grown when my sister bore her younger son. His name is Hamal, and my sister died giving birth to the boy. Omar had recently been killed when a spirited new horse had thrown him and broken his neck. He had not, however, changed his will. He was awaiting the birth of his second child to do that, for had Hamal been a female, arrangements would have been different than if he were a male.

"Kedar has always taken care of his little brother, but he has never offered to share their father's wealth. My elder nephew is a man of strong will and strong opinions. Three years ago, when Hamal was fifteen, Princess Turkhan, a daughter of Sultan Selim II, saw my young nephew. The royal princess is a most unusual woman. She came to Fez twelve years ago as wife to its wealthiest man. When he died she inherited everything, and because she is an Ottoman princess she is a law unto herself. Her father is obviously delighted to have her off his hands, and no one has control of her.

"In Fez she is respected for her good words and her generosity to the poor. She is powerful by virtue of her family, and by virtue of her wealth. As you know, my daughter, this is an unusual thing in the Muslim world; but no one dares criticize her way of living, though it is most shocking. Princess Turkhan keeps a harem of mèn for her pleasure, as a man might keep a harem of women. Fez is a holy city, and the mullahs are appalled, but they can do nothing, for she is too important and too powerful. When she saw Hamal she wanted him, and after finding out who he was, she went to my elder nephew.

"Kedar was within his rights, of course, but to this day I am shocked at what he did. He sold his younger brother to the princess—for a very fancy price, I might add. When he told me I was very angry, but, as he explained it to me, the boy is handsome and charming, though not particularly bright. Kedar did not believe that Hamal could ever take his place in the family business, and so he did what he believed was the best thing for him. As much as I disapproved of the act, I am forced to admit it was the wisest course for the boy. Princess Turkhan has adored him, cossetted him, and spoiled him from the beginning.

"Then several months ago the princess acquired a new male slave, a man who has resisted her from the moment she laid eyes upon him, and can only be kept under control by means of opiates. The princess is fascinated and intrigued by this man who will not have her. She will do anything to possess his body and soul, but to date she has been unsuccessful. Oh, she can force him, but it is not the same as his surrender to her love would be. My nephew, Hamal, says that she is making herself quite sick over the new slave.

"I was interested by his story, and so out of curiosity I asked him to find out more about the man. At first the slave was loath to speak frankly with Hamal, who is Turkhan's favorite pet. Gradually, however, my nephew's honest sweetness won him over, and he confided that his name is Niall Burke."

Skye gasped and grew white, but Osman held up a warning hand. He was not yet finished with his tale. With a shudder Skye fought to regain control of her turbulent emotions, while the words, *He is alive,* sang in her veins.

"Niall Burke told Hamal that he was a nobleman in his own country, a place called Ireland. He told Hamal that he had a beautiful wife called Skye, and children. When I heard that, my daughter, I knew it was you. It could only be you, for who else would have so outrageous a name as Skye? I was going to send to Ireland for word of you, but then Haroun learned that you were but across the sea in Beaumont de Jaspre. That you had married its duc. Why did you marry another man when your husband was still alive?"

"My husband was believed dead," Skye replied, grateful now to be allowed to speak. "He was thought murdered by a mad religious woman and his body thrown into the sea. I was sent by Queen Elizabeth to Beaumont as part of a political alliance."

Osman nodded his bald head. "Niall Burke could only remember bits and pieces of what happened to him, my daughter. He remembered being attacked, but then his next memory is of being aboard a ship where he was nursed back to health before being put in the galleys to row. He manned an oar aboard a Barbary pirate ship for several months before he was seen here in Algiers by an enterprising slave merchant from Fez who thought the princess might be interested in him. He bought Niall Burke from the pirate ship and transported him back to Fez. The slave merchant's judgment was correct, for when Princess Turkhan saw your husband she bought him, and at the price the slaver wanted. Niall Burke has not proved the most tractable man, however. Princess Turkhan has tried everything to win him over, but he has resisted her. Now Hamal tells me his mistress has decided that she must have a child by Niall Burke. She has not ever allowed herself to become pregnant before. Her unwilling slave is resisting her more than ever, though, and the more he resists the more determined Turkhan becomes."

"Did he not tell the princess who he was?" Skye asked. "Did he not tell her that he could pay a fabulous ransom to her?"

"My daughter, you know that this is the East. When Khalid bought you do you think that he would have accepted ransom for you even had you known who you were? The princess bought your husband because she wanted *him*, not because she sought to make money. She is already incredibly wealthy. Even if you communicated with her, telling her the truth and offering to pay well for Niall Burke's return, she would refuse you, and she is legally within her rights.

"No, you will have to go to Fez yourself, but my nephew, Hamal, will aid you. Hamal wants your husband out of the princess's life before this obsession she has drives her mad. But we have a complication. As I have said, my daughter, Lord Burke has persisted in defying Princess Turkhan. He simply will not yield, which only intrigues her further. Now, however, Hamal tells me he has begun to grow despondent. Because of my deep fondness for you, Skye, I have sent for you, for if Lord Burke is to escape Princess Turkhan he needs his hope renewed. There is only one way that that can be achieved, I believe."

All of Skye's old instincts had begun to resurface as she listened to Osman speak. She was no longer Skye O'Malley, but rather she was Skye Muna el Khalid, one of the most famous women in Algiers. "If Hamal loves his princess so, Osman, why does he not simply rid himself of Niall? There is poison, a sharp knife in a dark garden, a pillow held over the face. There are any number of ways to rid oneself of a rival in the harem. Why has he not used one of them?" She was frankly suspicious.

"Hamal is a gentle boy," Osman replied, "and he knows that Niall's death could destroy the princess, especially if it were proved he had a part in it. Turkhan would then lose both the men for whom she truly cares. Besides, my nephew honestly loves his princess. If, however, Niall were to escape, the princess would be enraged and her love would turn to hate for Niall. A woman scorned is a terrible thing, my daughter."

Skye nodded. She certainly knew the truth of that statement. "Can you arrange for me to get to Fez?" she said. "I will, of course, take my own people with me. I do not need many, but if a rescue plan is to succeed I must have my own people about me."

"There is only one way you can get to Fez, my daughter," Osman said. "Fez is a holy city, and foreigners, women in particular, are allowed nowhere near the city. Only you alone can travel there."

Skye looked puzzled. "You say foreigners, especially women, are not allowed into Fez. How then in Heaven's name can *I* enter it?"

"You can only enter Fez if you are a member of a household whose master is a native of the city. You will enter Fez with my other nephew, Kedar."

"He will do this for you? How generous a man he must be!"

"You misunderstand me, Skye, my daughter. Kedar is a religious man. He will not break the taboo of Fez, his native city, even for a family tie."

"Then how?" she demanded.

"You must be very brave, Skye, my daughter. What I am about to propose to you will not be to your liking; but it is the only way,

I swear to you." Osman's wise face was troubled, and Skye felt an awful foreboding.

"How?" she repeated.

Osman sighed. "In two days' time my nephew Kedar arrives here in Algiers. He comes once a year to visit me, and to seek my advice on organizing his life for the following year. I must tell you, Skye, that he is a very sensual man; a connoisseur of beautiful women; a devotee of all that is voluptuous and erotic. When he arrives I would present him with a beautiful slave girl who I shall tell him is called Muna, which as you know means *desire* in our tongue."

Robbie, who had been quietly listening, now burst out, "How in the name of the seven djinns is that supposed to help Skye get into Fez?" He looked first at Osman and then to Skye.

Skye was very pale, and for a moment Robbie wasn't sure she was even breathing. Finally she said, "Do you know what it is you are asking me to do? Surely, Osman, there is a better way! You cannot ask this of me!"

"I have told you the facts of the situation, my daughter. If there is another way then enlighten me, I beg you. I am appalled at what I must ask of you, but it is the *only* way. The knowledge that you are near can rally Lord Burke's flagging spirits and give him new courage. It is almost too late now."

"What is it you two are talking about?" Robbie asked. "I can't understand a word of it!"

"Fez is a holy city closed to foreigners, Robbie. Osman says the only way I can get into it to rescue Niall is to pretend I am a slave girl. He would present me to his nephew as such."

"*What?!*"

Skye almost laughed at the honest outrage on Robbie's very weathered English face. "I must pretend to be a slave," she repeated.

"I heard you the first time!" Robbie roared. "It's out of the question! Do you know what you'll have to do if you're this Kedar's slave woman? Ye're not the type of woman a man buys to scrub his floors or cook his food! Are ye daft, Skye lass? Besides, so far all we have is someone's word that this man is Niall Burke. What if he isn't? What if this is someone who knows that Niall is dead, and is using his name?"

"To what end, Robbie? Why would someone use Niall's name?"

"To gain the opportunity of ransom, lass!"

"It is rare a captive can be ransomed, Captain Small," Osman said quietly.

"Perhaps he didn't know that," Robbie said, grasping for any reasonable explanation.

"I considered the possibility that you might need proof of some sort," Osman said, "and so I asked Hamal to obtain it for me. The man who calls himself Niall Burke stands several inches over six feet in height. He has dark hair and silver eyes. He is lean and hard of body, according to Hamal, obviously a man who has kept himself in shape; and he bears the scars of a severe wound in the region of his belly."

"It is Niall!" Skye cried, and her face was suffused with pure joy. "He is alive, Robbie! *He is alive!*"

"All right," Robbie muttered, defeated. "I would have said it could be anyone until Osman mentioned the wound. It's Niall, all right, but he'll not be overly happy to find out that you've put yourself into the harem of some lusty Arab in order to reach Fez. And what happens when you do reach Fez? How in hell are you going to rescue a man penned in a harem when you're penned in a harem, too? Answer me that, Skye lass!"

Skye looked to Osman. "Does your plan go beyond getting me to Fez, my old friend?"

"The key is Hamal," Osman said. "Although he is the property of Princess Turkhan, she is so fond of him that he is allowed his freedom as if he were not a slave. As her favorite, he is not without influence. He comes and he goes as he pleases. He has the run of her home—*and* the run of his brother's home. This will allow him to help you, my daughter."

"What is the quickest escape route, Osman?" Skye asked.

"The river that runs through Fez empties into the Atlantic Ocean, my daughter, but it is not a navigable river. You will have to return the way you came, back here to Algiers. Hamal believes he knows a way, but it all depends on you making yourself indispensable to Kedar."

"How do you and Hamal communicate, Osman?" Skye was curious, for she knew it was close to six hundred miles between Fez and Algiers.

"The pigeons, my daughter," was the smiling reply. "The birds are our messengers, and we use a code that I taught Hamal when he was a little boy. It amused him then, and it now amuses us that we may communicate without anyone knowing what we speak of, Skye. I was in Fez several months ago to teach briefly at the university. Hamal and I discussed much of this then, but I could not seek you until I had returned to Algiers. Had Jamil not departed for Istanbul, I should have come to you myself in Beaumont de Jaspre."

"Did you arrange for Jamil's departure?" Skye looked closely at her old friend.

Osman chuckled, and his dark eyes twinkled with glee. "It is strange," he said, admitting nothing, "that word of a cure for Jamil's impotence should come at this time."

Skye grew serious once more.

"Did you ever see Niall, Osman?" she asked.

"No," he answered, sorry to disappoint her. "The princess does not know me, and it would not have been possible under the circumstances for me to enter her house. Hamal visited me at his brother's home, or at my quarters at the university."

"You're determined to do this?" Robbie said, and Skye could hear the worried concern in his voice. "'Tis total madness, y'know."

"Niall is alive," Skye answered him. "My husband, the father of my babies, is alive! Oh, Robbie, you of all people know what we have both been through over the years. I love him! I have always loved him and he has always loved me! When I learned that Darragh had killed him I was sick with anger and outrage that after all we had endured he should be taken from me again. I must free him from this bondage he is enmeshed in, just as he would free me. I will not be beaten, Robbie! *Not in this!*"

Robert Small bowed his head in a private agony. He had no argument to offer, and as difficult as the situation was he knew that she was right. If they attempted to go through official channels it could take forever. More than likely the spoiled and determined Princess Turkhan would hide Niall, and they would be forced to accept defeat in the end. The Moroccan sultan was not about to offend the wealthy and powerful daughter of his overlord, the Ottoman sultan in Istanbul. They would not jeopardize themselves over an infidel nobleman. "I'll support you in any way that I can, Skye lass," Robbie said quietly, and he hugged her where she sat, tears running down his face.

Skye's own beautiful blue eyes were wet with tears as she said huskily, "Thank you, Robbie! Thank you!"

"It is decided, then?" Osman asked.

"Yes," came the reply. "When your nephew arrives you will present him with a new slave girl named Muna. I wonder though, Osman. Am I not too old for this? I am not the girl I was ten years ago."

"You look it," Osman said. "Does she not yet look a girl, Captain Small? Your face is youthful, and I suspect that, despite all your children, your body remains youthful also."

Skye chuckled. "I have had four children since we last met, my old friend Osman. Although I am in better condition than many women my age, I am still not a girl of nineteen."

"Fear not, my daughter. We will tell Kedar that you have had children. It will only serve to increase your value in his eyes. A Fasi is very much a family man."

"What in the name of all that is holy is a Fasi?" Robbie demanded.

"A Fasi is a native-born citizen of Fez, my friend. I am a Fasi although I have lived here in Algiers for more years than I ever lived in Fez."

"How old do you intend to tell your nephew I am?" Skye asked.

"How old are you now, my daughter?"

"I am twenty-nine," she answered.

"Ye're thirty," Robbie contradicted her bluntly.

"Robbie!" Her face wore an outraged look. "A woman is always permitted to lie about her age."

"Not when she's dealing with Osman, and taking her life in her hands," he snapped. "If I know my old friend he'll be wanting to plot your own chart now that you remember your past life."

Osman's face broadened in a smile. "You are correct, Captain. When Skye was with us those ten years ago, and without her memory, I could only plot her chart to a certain degree, and by using my *other* powers. It was never totally accurate. Now I can do a complete horoscope, and I shall if she will but give me her birthdate."

"I was born December 5th, 1540," Skye said, "and I shall not be thirty officially until December, Robbie!" She smiled smugly at him.

Osman frowned. "I believed you born under the sign of the

Ram," he said, and then his face relaxed. "Of course! Now I see it! You were conceived beneath the sign of the Ram! You are born under the sign of the Archer. Both are fire signs, my daughter. You are powerfully protected. Do you know the hour of your birth?"

"I was born at nine minutes after nine o'clock in the evening," Skye answered.

"I will work on your chart tonight," Osman said. "I must have all the knowledge I need before I send you forth to Fez." He turned to Robbie. "I will ask you to say your good-byes now, Captain. If Skye is to prepare for her role she will need time, and there is little time before Kedar arrives."

"How will I know when to expect Skye and Niall?" Robbie asked.

"Hamal will get a message to you. Remember that it will be almost two months before Skye reaches Fez. Then she will need time to make contact with Hamal, which will not be easy. It will be between three and four months, possibly more, before they can act, and return to Algiers. You will need to cultivate great patience, my friend."

"Go back to Beaumont de Jaspre," Skye said. "Tell Nicolas that I will not be returning. Then see that the children are sent home immediately. There is no need to torture my poor Nicolas any further, and if all evidence of my residence in Villerose is wiped away, then perhaps he will seriously consider choosing a new bride. The children will go overland to the channel coast, for I have promised them a visit to Paris. Bran is to take them from France to England. I had intended that my Burke children be sent directly to Ireland, but I think that it is better that Bran meet with you when he has gotten them all safely to England. In case anything should happen to one of you, better I have the both of you as guardians. The Burke infants can stay with your sister at Wren Court, Robbie. They will be no trouble, as they have their own staff, and I will wager that Dame Cecily adores having them."

"Let me stay at least until you leave for Fez," Robbie begged.

"No," she answered. "If I am to convince Kedar that I am nothing more than a captive slave girl I must be totally cut off from my real life. It is going to be hard enough to be subservient, Robbie!" Her blue-green eyes were laughing at him now, and he guffawed loudly.

"Aye," he said, "I suppose it is best I leave you alone to prepare for your role. It wouldn't do to have you telling this great merchant of Fez how to run his business. I don't think that that is quite what he's going to expect of you." Then he grew serious. "You'll take care of yourself, lass? You'll not take chances?"

"I am taking a chance when I travel to Fez as Kedar's slave," she said softly. "There is no escaping the danger, Robbie, but I am mindful of it. I am not afraid." She leaned over and kissed him.

No, she wasn't afraid, he could see it. Her belief that she could find Niall and escape back to safety shone like a silvery aura about her. Robert Small prayed silently that that faith be justified. She had so very much to lose.

He rose slowly to his feet and drew her up. "All right, then," he said, "I'll be on my way. Walk me to the door, and we'll say our farewells there." He turned. "Osman, my friend, will you come also?"

"No, Captain. I will bid you farewell here. We will meet again, I know; and believe me that all will go well, my friend. May Allah watch over you."

Robbie nodded. "I've never known you to be wrong, Osman," he said. "I know that I can trust you."

Together Skye and Robbie walked to the main entry of Osman's house. There was really nothing left for them to discuss, so she simply hugged him, and said, "Take care, my dearest friend."

"It is you who should take care," he muttered, and then he held her close against him in a fatherly embrace. "I wish to Heaven you wouldn't do this thing," he said, "but I know that you must. God's bones, lass, come home safely!" Then he quickly released her, and was gone out the door. She was certain she had seen tears in his kindly eyes.

With a sigh Skye turned from the door and walked back to Osman's study, where the astrologer awaited her. Wordlessly he handed her a tiny porcelain cup of newly made coffee. Slowly she sipped the burning, bitter liquid until at last she felt calm again. Sensing her recovery, Osman spoke.

"There is no one among my slaves who knows who you are. We will therefore begin the charade now. You are Muna, a slave girl whom I have bought to give my nephew, the lord Kedar of Fez. You are a captive, but for beautiful captives like yourself there is no ransom. You were widowed a year ago, and were being sent by your family to marry a wealthy Florentine merchant. You have two babies, but your husband-to-be did not want you to bring your children to this new marriage.

"Just as it entered the Mediterranean, your ship was captured by pirates who brought you to Algiers, where you were placed in a private bagnos. I bought you. You arrived today at the same time my old friend, Captain Small, arrived. I have returned your trunk, by the way, to your ship. I will see that you are clothed properly to entice my nephew." He thought a moment. "Have I forgotten anything, Muna?"

"No, my lord Osman," she answered meekly.

He smiled. "Very good, my daughter! Now, for the next two days you must immerse yourself in the character of Muna. Does my history of your past satisfy you?"

"It is fine, my lord, but I would ask one question. You have still not told me how old I am to be."

"Aiii!" Osman clapped his plump hand to his smooth forehead. Then he nodded at her with a small smile. "You can easily pass for twenty, my daughter. Your skin is so marvelously translucent it makes you seem much younger than your years. One other thing. You must have a potion that will prevent your conceiving a child by my nephew. Such a thing is unthinkable!"

"I have my own potion, Osman, but you have sent it back to the ship along with my trunk," she laughed.

"It works?"

"I have never conceived a child while I took it," she answered him.

"I will have it fetched immediately, then," he said. "There is no use switching potions if yours works. Return to your quarters now, my daughter, and I will send the seamstress to you. She will outfit you completely within the next two days. When Kedar arrives you will be ready for him."

Skye rose from the silken cushions, bowed low to Osman, and left him. The next two days proved busy ones as the seamstress and her assistants sewed a lavish wardrobe for the beautiful slave girl Muna. In Osman's household only his wife, Alima, knew the truth about Muna. The two women spent most of their waking hours together in the garden, surrounded by Alima and Osman's children. Altogether there were seven of them: five mischievous little boys ranging in age from nine to two; and two little girls, one seven, and one an infant who had been born around the same time as Skye's son, Padraic. Alima refreshed Skye's memory on Eastern customs; any other gaps of knowledge would be put down to her status as a slave.

"What is Kedar like?" she asked Alima.

"I know little about him," came the reply. "Osman is a very jealous man, and does not allow even his male relatives into the women's part of the house. I have seen him, of course; Kedar is an attractive man, Muna. He stands a few inches taller than you, and is very powerfully built although he is not fat. He is as fair of skin as you are, for when he lifted his arms once and his robe fell open, I could see where the sun had not reached the whiteness of his skin. The first time I met him I was quite curious, and boldly lifted my eyes to his for just a second. He has eyes as powerful as his uncle, my husband. They are hazel in color, and his hair is a dark brown. His features are pleasant, the eyes well spaced, his face narrow, his nose very aquiline, his lips quite sensuous, as they are a bit wide."

Skye nodded, satisfied. At least the man wasn't ugly. "Is he intelligent?" she said, wondering if Alima would know what she really meant.

With her shrewd peasant soul, however, Alima understood. "Yes, he is intelligent and very clever. I also suspect he has some of his uncle's powers, although Osman has said nothing about it. He is very possessive of what is *his*, Muna, so if he decides you please him—and you *must* please him if you are to get to Fez—he will want to own you totally. Beware of him, for I believe he is a dangerous man."

Again Skye nodded, and then she asked a final question. "What if he decides to sell me, Alima?"

"Do not fear, Muna. Osman intends to ask him to resell you to him for my sake if Kedar should grow tired of you. Kedar cannot refuse that request."

Alima's words reassured Skye considerably, particularly when late that very afternoon Kedar arrived. The two women watched from behind the latticed windows of an upper story as Osman greeted his nephew in the gardens of the house. Kedar moved with a sleek grace that reminded Skye of the panthers she and Khalid el Bey had kept for hunting. Kedar held his head high, and his step was at once light and very assured. The two men embraced, and then Osman, knowing that the two women watched, pushed back the hood of his nephew's white traveling robes.

"Let me look at you, son of my beloved dead sister," he said, and Skye could see that the face in profile was arrogant, hawklike, and Arab.

"It is good to see you again, my Uncle," Kedar replied, and Skye was struck by the very deep timbre of the man's voice. It was a voice used to giving orders, used to being obeyed.

"Have you seen enough, Muna?" Alima whispered.

"Yes."

"Let us go then, for Osman will shortly send for you, and I would be certain your garb is perfection."

Below them, Osman led Kedar into the cool interior of the house to a small salon. The two men settled themselves comfortably upon low, cushioned red velvet divans, and immediately a slave appeared with a silver basin filled with warmed rosewater and a soft linen towel. Kedar washed the dust of his travels from his face and his hands, and dried them carefully. His were the hands of an aristocrat, long and slender with well-tapered nails. When he had finished, and the slave had hurried off with the used towel and the basin, two other slaves entered the room. One carried a plate of gazelle horns, curved pastries made of flour, ground nuts, and honey. The other was the coffeemaker, who immediately set to work grinding beans and then brewing a dark and rich coffee. When he and his nephew had been served Osman waved them from the room, and sat chatting companionably with his nephew. At last, the courtesies all observed and the traveler made comfortable, Osman said, "You know that each year when you visit me I have a gift for you. This year it is something very, very special. Knowing how proud you are of your harem, my nephew, I have purchased an exquisite slave girl for you. It was not at all what I had in mind, Kedar, but I saw the woman by chance, and knew that she was perfect for your collection of rare and unusual beauties. I know that your good manners will force you to take my gift, but should, Allah forfend, the girl displease you, then allow me to buy her from you when you return to Fez."

"If you like her so well, my Uncle, then why give her to me?"

"You misunderstand, Kedar. I do not want her for myself, but she and my wife have become good companions in the short time she has been in my house. I would do it for Alima. I do not think, however, that you will want to sell her to me. She is one of the most beautiful women I have ever seen."

"Is she European?"

"Yes. English."

"A blonde?" Kedar sounded interested.

"No, a brunette. But what a brunette! Her skin is like a gardenia petal! Would you like to see her?"

"Why not, and I thank you for such a delightful surprise, Uncle. As you know, I do not travel with any of my women, and I have been a month in coming from Fez."

Osman clapped his hands, and instantly a slave appeared. "Fetch the slave girl Muna," he ordered, and the slave, nodding, bowed himself out of the room.

"Muna," Kedar smiled. "You have named her Muna? She is *that* beautiful?"

"I do not believe that a man can see her and not desire her," was Osman's reply.

Kedar smiled, faintly amused. He had never known his uncle to be a particular connoisseur of female flesh. He could only assume that his aunt by marriage was a pretty woman, for he had never been allowed to see her unveiled; but he had seen her children and they were certainly attractive. Kedar believed that Alima was a Frenchwoman, but he had never asked, for it would have been considered too personal a question and extremely bad manners. He sipped at the dregs of his coffee and nodded at his uncle. "The woman must be memorable if she has impressed you," he remarked drily.

Osman smiled an almost mischievous smile, and said, "You have but a moment to wait, nephew."

The sound of his words had barely died when the door to the salon opened and Skye entered. Her head was lowered, and she had barely entered the room when she was on her knees, her head touching the floor in perfect obeisance. In that position Kedar could see little more of her than a rather charmingly rounded section of hip. Osman noted the easy frustration of his nephew, and said, "Rise, Muna." She stood quickly, silently, her head still lowered. "Raise your head up," Osman commanded, and Skye slowly, almost shyly lifted her head. Kedar caught his breath audibly as he gazed into a pair of magnificent blue-green eyes, and Osman smiled softly to himself. His nephew was hooked as easily as any foolish fish offered a delectable bit of bait. Truly his weakness was women. "This is your new master, Muna, the lord Kedar."

"My lord," she whispered, and he was forced to lean closer to hear her. In doing so smelled the delicious fragrance of her rose perfume, which he instinctively knew suited her admirably. She was indeed a perfect rose.

"Remove your garments," Osman commanded sharply, and Skye turned startled eyes to him, a slow blush suffusing her cheeks.

"No, Uncle, it will not be necessary," Kedar said. His hand reached out to touch Skye's arm, his fingers caressing the satiny round of her shoulder. "The woman is shy, and I would not force her. Later she will display to me her obviously bounteous charms. Is that not right, my beautiful Muna?" His fingers continued their caressing.

"Yes, my lord," Skye said low, and then she trembled, unable to control the tiny ripple of fear that rolled over her. This was no fat and lazy merchant prince who could be easily led through his own lust by a beautiful woman. His hazel eyes were too much like Osman's eyes; knowing and seeking. Why had she ever agreed to this insane plan in the first place? It wasn't going to work; she was going to be caught like a bird in a net if she went to Fez as this man's slave! Then in her mind's eye Skye saw Niall, her beloved Niall; and taking a deep breath, she calmed this flight of nerves that had possessed her.

"Send her to my quarters, Uncle," Kedar said, then added in a lower, more intimate voice to Skye, "I will not keep you waiting long, my beautiful Muna. Very soon you will be cured of your charming shyness toward me."

"Go, Muna," came Osman's voice. She turned, and with a low bow toward each of them left the room.

"She is exquisite," Kedar said quietly as the door closed behind Skye. "I suspect, my Uncle, that words alone will not adequately express my gratitude. Tell me, though, how it is she speaks our language if she is a recent captive?"

"The owner of the bagnos in which I saw her brought her from the ship that had taken her captive. Because she was so filthy and disreputable-looking she escaped being chosen by the Dey's chief eunuch. The fool could not see her beauty beneath all the dirt and rebellion, but the bagnos owner could. She remained full of fight, however, and it took several months to calm her and train her in the simple rudiments of being a slave. I am afraid she is not greatly accomplished, but she was so beautiful I could not resist. The bagnos owner told me that she appears to be intelligent. He was only forced to discipline her twice, and he did go lightly with her. She has not been marked in any way at all, and she was quick to learn that unruly behavior would only bring on severe chastisement. It was while she was in the bagnos that she learned our language. I have discovered that she speaks several other European languages. She was obviously educated by her family, though why they bothered I do not know. She is only a woman."

"True," Kedar replied, "but an intelligent woman, I have found, is usually far more intriguing than the women who can only spread their legs and prattle on about nothing. Her active mind will make her far more interesting, Uncle."

"I bought her for her beautiful face and body," Osman said, sounding somewhat aggrieved.

"Those I intend enjoying as soon as possible, my Uncle, but first I would bathe the dust of that long road between Fez and Algiers from my body."

"Will you eat with me afterward, my nephew?"

"Not tonight, Uncle. Tonight I intend to put to use the magnificent gift you have given me. I have been a full month without a woman. The whores in the roadside caravanserais are not even fit for camel drivers, and besides, they are all diseased. I never touch them."

"You know your way to the baths, nephew. Alima has seen that the slaves are ready and awaiting your arrival. Enjoy! I shall speak with you tomorrow."

"As always, Uncle, your hospitality is munificent," Kedar said, and then withdrew, hurrying down the hallway from the salon to the spacious baths that Osman had added on to the house soon after he had bought it. As his uncle had said, the slave girls who attended the bath were awaiting him, and they quickly had his clothes off. They were pretty black girls, and he knew them all. Merrily they joked back and forth with him as they soaped and scrubbed him down. Their hands were everywhere on his body, caressing and rubbing with practiced and seemingly detached skill. After all, it was their job to wash the master and his family, and anyone else they might be asked to wash. Still, knowing he was a passionate man, and that his forced abstinence had rendered him as randy as a stallion in a herd of mares in season, they teased him gently as his male organ responded to their tender touches. The lord Kedar had been known in the past to ease his hunger upon the humble bath girls, and they were hopeful.

Today, however, they were doomed to disappointment. He grinned regretfully at them, and shook his head.

"Ah," said the eldest of them, a full-figured girl named Nigera, "the lord Kedar would save his strength for the new slave girl, Muna. It is she who will feel the sting of his mighty lance this night."

The others giggled behind their hands at Kedar's enthusiastic nod. "What do you know of the woman?" he asked, curious.

"She arrived a little time ago," Nigera said. "She and the lady Alima became friends. Muna is a sweet woman and a courteous one, from what I have observed here in the bath. She comes with the mistress and her children."

"She is very good with the children," observed another of the bath attendants. "They say she had children in her old life. Sometimes I would catch her sighing over the lady Alima's youngest daughter, and there would be a sad look upon her face."

The bath attendants had finished washing Kedar, and now they rinsed him off. Next they shaved several days' growth of beard from his face, for he preferred to be smooth-shaven, and then they scrubbed his wavy dark brown head clean. Finally they led him to the hot tub, where he would soak for a while relaxing his travel-weary muscles. He pondered their chatter. Muna was not a virgin, praise Allah, for he was in no mood to deflower a maiden tonight. He wanted a woman who knew what passion was all about. She might be reluctant, but coaxed firmly and gently, she would quickly succumb. His smile was rather predatory as he contemplated this delightful gift of his uncle's choosing.

She had been dressed exquisitely but simply when she had come to the salon. Her full pantaloons had been a gossamer-sheer blush-colored silk shot through with silver threads. The ankle bands and the sewn-in hip band had been embroidered in pink glass beads and silver thread. The pantaloons had ridden just over the bottom of her hip bones, and she had been nude above, save a sleeveless, open bolero of blush-colored silk edged in silver trim which just barely clung to the soft swelling of her lovely bosom. He had very much wanted to see that bosom, but her charmingly modest blush when his uncle had ordered her to disrobe had frankly disarmed him. She had worn no jewelry, of course, having had no previous master to deck her with delicate baubles. She would, he suspected, cost him a fortune in jewelry, and he smiled to himself anticipating her delight and pleasure at the wonderful gifts he would give her. Her dark hair had been caught back with a pearl-embroidered pink ribbon, and he was looking forward to loosening it, and running his fingers through it.

An ache in his groin told him that he was becoming aroused again. Cursing softly, he forced his mind away from his beautiful new slave, and silently began to recite verses from the Koran. It was an excellent discipline. No man should allow a woman to insinuate herself so deeply into his soul that he couldn't do without her. Several minutes later Nigera tapped him, saying, "It is time, my lord," and he rose from the pleasantly heated marble tub. He walked across the tiled floor of the bath and entered another bright and airy room, where he seated himself. Silently two slave girls pared the nails on both his hands and his feet. Then they trimmed his now dry hair. He walked to a massage bench and lay down, to give himself up to the ministrations of Nigera's supple fingers for the next hour. When she had finished massaging him thoroughly she helped him sit up and handed him a cup of boiling, sweet Turkish coffee. Gingerly he sipped the hot drink from the tiny eggshell cup. He felt refreshed and revived, and quite ready for a long evening of pleasurable sport with Muna.

Standing, Kedar held out his arms as a comfortable loose caftan was wrapped about him. He slid his feet into the soft slippers that were offered him, and with a smile of thanks to the bath attendants he left the room and walked toward his own apartments. As he reached them the eunuch guarding the door flung it open at precisely the right moment, and Kedar walked through into a large room.

It was a simple but elegant room with walls that were covered in black, red, and white tiles in a geometric pattern a quarter of the way up and whitewashed above. To the left of the door were three casement windows, the wall above the windows decorated in a fan-shaped pattern of designed plaster. The floor was cool red tile, but over a good portion of it was a fine, thick red, blue, and gold rug. On either side of the room were low, armless divans of red brocade with plump white pillows embroidered in gold thread. In the center was a footed brass brazier, and from the dark beamed ceiling hung a brass lamp with amber glass. Near the divans there were

polished low, round ebony tables, upon which rested smaller decorated brass lamps with their amusingly curved mouths spouting
wicks.

Opposite the salon door was a large double couch curtained in
red velvet and cloth of gold. Over the couch was a brocaded cloth
of gold awning with wide red velvet stripes, and the walls around
the high couch were hung in embroidered red velvet. The couch
was covered in a matching brocaded velvet fabric with a busy geometric design upon it. Enormous feather and down cushions in
multi-colored silks and velvets were piled upon it in the corners and
along the back. A long red velvet cushion with silk tassels at each
corner had been set upon the tiled step to the couch.

She should have been awaiting him there, but she was not. Instead, she was sleeping upon the couch, within the curtained alcove. Tonight Kedar thought he would be indulgent, but he would
teach her her proper place in his life. He was not an Ottoman to be
ruled by his women. For a long moment he stood looking down at
her, and then kneeling upon the cushions, he studied her at close
range. His uncle had been right. She was indeed a beauty. He
didn't need to touch her hair to know that it was soft. And her
skin! Allah! Had there ever been such skin? Reaching out, he lifted
back one side of her ridiculous little bolero, exposing her breast.
For a long time he studied the flawless contours of that breast
without even touching it. It had the most pleasing roundness to it,
and yet the impudent way in which the small pink nipple tilted
upward enchanted him. Here again there was no hurry to touch,
for he could see with his sharp, knowledgeable eye that the skin
was soft, smooth, and firm.

It was then that Skye opened her eyes and caught him in her cool
blue-green gaze for a brief moment before lowering her long black
lashes in feigned modesty. A tiny smile played at the corners of
Kedar's mouth. For a small second she had made him feel like a
little boy discovered just as he was about to be naughty. The fact
that she could do that on such short acquaintance delighted him.
"You cannot blame me for contemplating your beauty, my fair
Muna," he said in his deep voice. "You have already ravished me
with your face and form."

"It is not for me to say, my lord Kedar," she answered. "I am but
your humble slave."

"You recite the words perfectly," was his answer, "yet I do not think for one moment that you believe them."

"I was not raised to be a slave, my lord Kedar."

"Nonetheless you are an exquisite one, and I give thanks to the beneficent Allah who has given you to me, my fair Muna." He was pleased to see that captivity had not broken her spirit. Skye smiled inwardly to herself at his words. She had decided not to be overly meek with this man. It would quickly bore him. His next words caused her to start. "Disrobe for me now, Muna. I would see your beauty entirely rather than through the taunting diaphanous silk of your charming costume."

Skye could not help the shiver that raced through her. This was the moment she had dreaded, for now there was no going back. Once again she wondered if she were mad in what she was attempting to do. Despite what Osman said, there were no guarantees that she would find Niall. What if he was dead by the time she arrived in Fez? Nothing was more fierce than a woman rejected by a man she desires, and Princess Turkhan was a powerful woman. A slave had no rights. He could be killed by his master simply because it amused his master to kill him. For a single second she contemplated racing from the room and begging Osman to stop this charade immediately, before it was too late. Then came the horrifying realization: It was already too late.

Silently she slipped from the soft couch, turning to keep her back to him. With a motion so fluidly graceful that he wasn't even certain how she had accomplished it, Skye slipped the little bolero off and dropped it to the floor. Seated upon the couch now, Kedar admired the long line of her back. There was not a mark on her skin. It was as pristine as an unwritten parchment. Skye carefully loosened her pantaloons, and they puddled around her ankles before she stepped out of them. As she turned he had just a quick glimpse of her breasts and belly before she was kneeling before him, her dark head pressing into the wool carpet. "As my lord commands," she murmured at him.

Ravish. The word entwined itself about his brain. He wanted to ravish her; to leap from his position upon the couch, press her back into the rug, and ravish her! Instead, he took several deep breaths to calm himself. He did not believe in hurrying a woman along passion's pathway, but he had to admit to himself that he had never before desired a woman as greatly as he did this one. Perhaps it was his abstinence on his journey; but Kedar knew it was not. He was not a man to neglect his harem, often sending for two or three women in a single night; but neither was he one of those weak fools who could not survive a day without shoving himself into a warm and willing woman. No. This one was different, and he was fascinated. "Stand up," he commanded her, and watched with pleasure as she gracefully rose from her obeisance.

She, in turn, watched him from beneath lowered lashes as he stood and came down from the couch on the dais toward her. He stopped and then studied her in a slow and leisurely fashion, giving an occasional command which she obeyed silently. "Turn, Muna," and she could feel his eyes moving from her shoulders down to her buttocks, down her legs to her feet. "Turn again." His hazel eyes moved from her feet, up her legs, to her beautifully plump, pearl-smooth Venus mont. He could see that her cleft was fine, long, and deep, an indication, according to harem tradition, of a passionate woman. His eyes continued their inspection to her pleasingly rounded belly, to her lean, flat, and long torso, to her breasts. "Raise your arms," he commanded her. "Put them behind your head."

This had the effect of raising her breasts upward so he might have a complete view of them. Skye had never felt more debased in her entire life as his glance fastened hungrily upon her round breasts. She wondered almost bitterly if he would ask her to open her mouth so he might inspect and count her teeth. She had never until now understood the awful and terrifying degradation of being a slave. Oh, she had legally been the slave of Khalid el Bey until he freed her before their marriage; but Khalid had never treated her like one. He had from the beginning been a man in love. Kedar was not a man in love. He was a man in lust; a man delighted with his new possession, as his careful inspection of her person indicated.

Kedar, however, was not entirely insensitive to his slave. He saw the flush of embarrassment that stained her cheeks as she was silently forced to comply with his wishes. He saw the quickening of her heartbeat in the visible fluttering in her chest, a pounding pulse at the base of her slender throat. He noted that she was trembling ever so slightly, although she forced herself to stand grimly still. Yes, her spirit was still there, and he was glad! He would not break it, only tame it, but then a truly wild thing was never really completely tame. The pleasure at that particular thought washed over him like a soothing balm.

Reaching out, he touched her for the first time. He touched her as he would touch one of his thoroughbred Arab mares to gentle it. His hand smoothed down from her shoulder to her buttock in a slow and easy motion. "Don't be afraid, my fair Muna," he said in his deep, velvet voice; but Skye couldn't restrain the fierce shudder that rolled over her, for the purr in his voice was that of a well-fed and powerful cat. One arm came strongly about her waist, and drawing her close to him he touched her lips gently with his. Then, to her surprise, he loosened her, and holding her lightly, cupped a breast firmly in his other hand. She raised her arm instinctively to fend him off, but he chided her in a mock-stern voice. "No, Muna, it is my right. You belong to me now. I will be patient, fair one, but you are no virgin to fear me." He pulled the silk band from her head, and her long black hair swirled loose.

"I do not know you," she whispered. To her surprise, Skye found that she really was afraid of this man, and what was worse she did not know why.

"It is no matter," he answered. "You are mine, you are beautiful, and I desire you." His thumb rubbed insistently against her hardened nipple, and Skye had to bite her lower lip to keep from screaming aloud. "You have marvelous breasts," he continued. "See how perfectly you fit my hand just to overflowing, Muna? I believe that you have the most perfect breasts I have ever seen." He smiled down at her. "The bath girls say you are no maid, and they believe that you had children. Were you married, my fair one?"

"Yes, my lord. I am a widow. I have two children, little boys who will now be orphaned, and left to the mercy of my late husband's family." Her head drooped sadly.

"Did you nurse your sons, Muna?"

"Only a little while, my lord. Then came the wet nurse, for women of my class are expected to attend court with their husbands. I could not do that and nurse my babies."

So she was of that high a rank! Kedar was impressed, and very pleased. He quickly decided to have children by this exquisite slave woman, but already his passion for her was so great that he did not want her to waste her time nursing children when she might nurse him. His mother had nursed him until he was six, and he had developed a taste for breast milk that even today was not lost. The idea of being within Muna's fair body while he drank of her milk excited him tremendously, and without meaning to he crushed her tender breast in his hand. Skye cried out with pain, and Kedar, instantly remorseful, caressed her tenderly. "Forgive me, my fair Muna. I was quite lost in contemplation of your charms." He soothed her breasts, clucking worriedly, wondering aloud if he had bruised her soft skin.

My God, Skye thought, I am naught to him except a possession! He feels nothing for me but the need to own me, to sate his bodily lusts.

Kedar returned to a closer exploration of her body, moving his hand downward to rub across her fluttering belly. His touch was like fire against her skin, stroking seductively, sending tiny darts of fear through her. She wondered if Osman had known the kind of man his nephew really was when he had turned her over to Kedar. This was not a man to be satisfied with the mere taking of her body. He wanted far more than that. He wanted *her*. He wanted her soul and her mind as well as her body. Could she resist him? Already her treacherous body was beginning to stir under his touch.

His fingers moved downward again, this time coming to rest atop her cleft. Gently he moved his hand back and forth, touching her ever so lightly but insistently. She couldn't let him do this to her, she thought frantically, but her legs seemed made of jelly; and then he demanded, "Tell me about the first time, Muna? Was he gentle? Did you like it?"

"My lord . . ." she stuttered her shyness at such an intimate question, and then she almost wept to remember Niall, to remember how it had been with him that first time.

"*Tell me!*" he murmured against her ear, his tongue licking it softly, his fingers slipping deeper into her cleft to coax the honey down from the hidden recesses of her fevered body.

"H-he was gentle," she whispered, "and yes, I liked it."

"Was he a good lover, my fair Muna?"

"My lord, I was a maid when I went to my husband. I have known but one man in my lifetime. How can I know the answer to such a question?" Her answer was certainly in keeping with the story Osman had concocted about her, and she must remember that story else Niall be lost.

Kedar smiled, satisfied. It was what he had wanted to hear, as it meant that she had not played the wanton as so many of these married European women did. He was glad that her husband had been a kind and gentle lover, her only lover. It meant that she was not afraid of the act, and that was good. No matter if her husband had been a proficient lover, he, Kedar, was a better one. By dawn the beautiful Muna would have a strong comparison, and he knew that her late lord would suffer by that comparison.

She was almost fainting against his strong arm, and so he lifted her up into his embrace. Walking to the velvet-draped couch in the alcove, he carefully placed her upon it. Her blue-green eyes heavy, she watched as he swiftly removed his white robe. Through thick lashes she peeped at him, quickly assessing his assets as he had assessed hers. He stood probably no more than three inches taller than she did, but he was powerfully built with a barrel chest, narrow waist, and sturdy legs. His body was pale and totally devoid of hair. His manhood, however, was totally out of proportion for a man under six feet. In its already half-roused state it was quite long, and she noted with trepidation that it was thick. The circumcised ruby knob of it reminded her of the head of a battering ram.

He caught her look of fear, and coming down beside her upon the couch, he murmured again in her ear, "Do not fear, Muna. Your sweet sheath will accept all of me and weep for more, I promise you!" Then he was kissing her, his lips raining a hundred little kisses on her face, scorching at her temples, her closed eyelids, her sculpted cheekbones, her stubborn chin, and the corners of her trembling mouth. His two hands pinioned her lightly against the soft velvet-covered mattress. He was strong, and she knew he could break her should he decide that was what he wanted. He was kissing her now upon her lips, testing the texture of her mouth. The kisses demanded an answer that she knew she would have to give, and the only way she could do that was to abandon herself to total passion. Niall! her tortured heart cried out. Forgive me, my darling, but I must do this if I am to save you and bring you back to me, to our babes!

Then she kissed Kedar, hesitantly at first, the kiss deepening with the increasing pressure of his lips. "Muna, Muna!" he spoke low against her mouth, and she shivered with the dark intensity of his voice. Gasping, she opened her lips to him as he ran his tongue quickly across them. Her breath came in little pants as his tongue licked the side of her face, then along her slender neck. Finding the palpitating hollow of her throat, he buried his lips there, growling, and she was again reminded of a sleek and savage cat. He terrified her. He was like an animal, possessive and totally sure of himself and his prowess. He reeked of his own masculinity. Then suddenly his tongue was entering her mouth, seeking delicately, probing gently.

Skye moaned, trying to escape the building fury of his fierce passion, but he held her firmly now, refusing to accept any rejection on her part. It would be an endless battle between them, and the knowledge of that was an incredible aphrodisiac to Kedar. Her tongue struggled to escape his, but he caught at it and sucked upon that delectable morsel. His fingers now sought her cleft once more, and pushing two of them gently within her he moved his hand slowly back and forth until with a soft cry she had her first tiny orgasm. With a smile he drew his fingers out and, pressing one of them against her lips, said, "Taste, my fair Muna. Taste your own sweet honey." She obeyed him, sucking the salty sweetness from his finger, and then watching almost mesmerized as he sucked the second finger once she had finished. He then drew the two wet fingers between the valley of her breasts in a slow and seductive motion, his hazel eyes holding her blue-green ones with a forceful magnetism.

"Tell me what pleases you," he demanded.

Skye pretended confusion. "My lord," she said low, "I have been taught by the women in the bagnos that it is not what pleases me that matters, but rather, what pleases you. I have been told that it is the woman's duty to please her master, to ride him to pleasure. Is it not so?"

"For some, perhaps," he answered, smiling, "but I believe a man is better served when he may conquer the woman beneath him. There will be times when it pleases me to let you ride me, fair Muna, but that is my decision. I will lead you in our lovemaking. You need not fear, my beautiful one, that you will displease me." His fingers then trailed back up between her breasts. "Tonight," he said, "I want to learn about you. I want to know what gives you pleasure, what excites you, how your luscious body responds to sensuousness. Tell me what your last lord did when you made love together."

"We . . . we made love," she replied helplessly, deciding that lack of sophistication in this area was what would make him happiest.

"He touched your body?"

"Yes."

"Your breasts? He rode you?"

"Y-yes."

"What else?" Kedar demanded.

"What else is there, my lord?" Skye's blue-green eyes were guileless, but inside she was trembling again as she wondered where this line of questioning was leading. Was he a gentle man, or was he one of those who gained pleasure through pain?

A slow, satisfied smile lit Kedar's features. "There is much, much more, my fair slave, than the little that you have described to me. I can open a whole new world to you, and I intend to!"

In a corner of the divan rested a woven gold basket, square in shape and without a handle. Within the basket were several bottles carved from different-colored marbles and alabaster. Without even looking closely, Kedar reached out and drew forth a narrow-necked vessel with a silver and cork stopper. He opened it, and a strong fragrance, vaguely familiar, wafted out.

"Musk rose," he said, seeing her curiosity. "It is a special lotion for the body. Turn onto your back and let me rub some on you."

Skye rolled over and lay waiting tensely for his touch. When it came it was gentle yet strong. He had warmed the lotion in his hands so as not to shock her delicate skin, and his sure, long strokes swept up her back from her buttocks, kneading the muscles with a firm motion. His touch was strangely soothing, and she began to relax. What an odd man he was, she thought. Seeing his open lust, she had thought he would be quick to mount her and sate that desire. Instead, here he was massaging her with tender hands and making no effort to hurry her. Perhaps it would not be so dreadful to pretend to be his slave for the next few weeks until she found Niall, and with young Hamal formulated a plan for their escape from Fez.

"Do you like this, Muna?" he whispered into her ear. Then he very gently nipped at the back of her neck, pushing her long hair aside first.

"Yes, my lord, it is most pleasurable," she answered him.

He laughed softly and resumed his massage, working now on each of her long legs, the firm thighs and calves, her slim feet. "I once had a slave girl from Cathay," he said, "who taught me that there is a particularly sensitive spot on the foot." His fingers dug into her foot, and suddenly Skye felt a stab of desire race through her. She gasped, surprised, and Kedar laughed again. "Yes, my fair Muna, right there." He moved on to her other leg and worked it as he had the first. "Turn over now, beautiful one," he ordered, and she obeyed.

"What happened to your slave girl from Cathay?" Skye asked.

"She died under my lash," he said casually.

"*Why?*" Skye was horrified.

"I caught her betraying me with one of my guard. He was forced to watch while I beat her. Just before she lost consciousness for good, my head eunuch decapitated him. I then finished her punishment. No one takes what is mine!"

"You killed her," Skye whispered. "Dear God!"

He tipped the alabaster flask of pale-pink lotion into his hands, and then put aside the bottle to massage her breasts and her belly. "It should not concern you, beautiful Muna. I am normally a kind master, but you must understand that I could not allow one of my women to escape severe punishment for such unconscionable behavior."

"Could you not have sold her off?"

"To whom? Who would want a faithless woman? Besides, I would not be shamed by the public knowledge that one to whom I had given the title of *favorite* had openly cuckolded me." He sat astride her hips, his supple hands smoothing the silky pink liquid over her soft belly, across her quivering breasts. His eyes, hazel green with small flickering gold pinpoints of light, bore into her blue-green ones. "Tell me what you are feeling now, Muna?"

Skye forced her thoughts from the unfortunate woman whom Kedar had so easily killed. She realized that without warning her body was beginning to feel restless and strangely hot beneath his hands. She shifted nervously. "I feel strange," she whispered. "Hot. A little . . ." she hesitated to give him any advantage. "A little frightened," she finished, unable to think of another word.

"I don't want you to feel frightened," he said soothingly. "I want you only to feel pleasure." He leaned forward across her, and reached into the gold basket. Drawing out a small crystal flask from the container, he uncorked it. "Open your mouth," he commanded, and when she did he poured a small amount of clear, apricot-flavored liquid into it.

Skye swallowed, and then asked softly, "What is it, my lord?"

"Nothing to be afraid of, Muna. It will calm your fears and relax your body," he soothed, and then he dipped a long finger into the flask, rubbed the liquid upon one of her nipples, and, lowering his dark head, began to suck upon it.

The shudder that ripped through her almost tore her apart. Her whole body was suddenly aflame, burning with the need to love and be loved. She moaned, arcing her body against his mouth, her hands sliding across his shoulders and back, her nails raking ever so lightly. His growl of laughter sent another shudder through her, and then he was releasing her nipple and drizzling some of the clear apricot fluid over her navel. Bending his dark head again, he lapped at the liquid with his tongue, following the wet line down her belly and pearly Venus mont into her cleft, which had opened like a pretty pink shell to his questing tongue. Like Cupid's arrow, his tongue darted quickly here and there, touching and teasing everything sensitive until Skye was writhing with the need to be possessed by him.

There was another growl of laughter as he lifted his head once more. "Now," he said, "you must do the same to me, my beautiful slave." Lying back, he poured some of the liquid onto his own belly. "Come, Muna, and pleasure your master," was his command.

Skye rolled slowly over onto her belly. Her entire body felt relaxed yet incredibly desperate for total sexual fulfillment. She shifted herself until her head was over his belly, and then she began to lick at him, moving lower and lower until she encountered his fast-stiffening manhood. She stopped for a brief moment, but his hand pushed her head forward and he said in a tense voice, "Take me in your mouth, fair Muna!" She obeyed, part of her mind amazed at her easy compliance with his order, while the other part of her brain craved with a strange intensity to do the act. In the few seconds of clarity she had before tumbling into the sensual abyss Skye realized that both the lotion he had massaged her with and the apricot-flavored liquid were aphrodisiacs. Then without another thought for what she was doing, her only desire being for pleasure, she began to run her tongue around the ruby head of his great lance, to lick the length of him with slow and sweet strokes, to take him into the warm cavity of her mouth to nurse upon until she tasted the first salty drops of his juices. Then he wrapped his hand into her dark hair and, pulling her away, groaned, "Enough, houri! You will surely unman me if I allow you to continue."

Skye whimpered a protest, but Kedar was now ready to couple with her, and he had no intention of being denied what he instinctively knew was going to be an incredible pleasure. Later he would teach her refinements to increase his pleasure; later he would allow her to suck him dry; but not this time. Rolling her onto her back, he mounted her and with one swift motion drove himself into her wet and waiting sheath. Her small cry of pleasure-pain only increased his desire. She was very tight, and he knew that his first assault had hurt her a little, but that would shortly change. With an easy and rhythmic motion he moved himself back and forth, watching through blazing, half-closed eyes her every reaction and listening with a fine-tuned ear to her little mewing cries. Skilled, he knew just how far he might drive her.

Dear God, how full he fills me! she thought. At first Kedar's great weapon had hurt her, and for a small moment she had wanted to escape him. Then the initial tension flowed from her, and she opened herself to him. She could feel him touching the very walls of her passage, and her womb, and the fire he was fanning within her helpless body was threatening to consume her. "Yesss, yesss!" she urged him on in a husky voice. "Oh, don't stop, my lord! Please don't stop!" She was going to die, but she didn't care. She wanted to die! Then she felt herself shattering into a million tiny starbursts, and all was black.

Kedar leaned back to watch the woman beneath him. She had reached her first peak, and had fainted away. He, however, was not yet ready to succumb to passion. He could wait. He was an unusual man, and he knew it, having the ability to sustain an erection for long periods of time. He took several deep, long breaths to clear his head while he enjoyed the soft throbbing of her body which enveloped his huge manhood. His hands reached out to fondle her round breasts, taking delight in the silkiness of her skin. Cruelly he pinched her pink nipples, and she moaned, but remained lost to him. He knew the pleasure that pain could occasionally bring, and wondered if she did, but he doubted it. She was delightfully innocent for a nonvirgin, and it was a marvelous combination that stimulated him. Pleasure through pain was another little refinement that they would eventually explore together, he thought with a small smile. Then her breathing told him that she was once again with him.

"Open your beautiful eyes, Muna."

Skye, still under the influence of the drugs he had given her, docilely obeyed his voice. Her will was sapped, but her awareness was intensely acute. "You are still within me, my lord," she whispered.

"We have only begun, fair one," he said as he began again the very voluptuous movement that had driven her mad before. Her eyes began to slide shut, but his sharp voice snapped them open. "*No!*" he said. "This time you will look into my eyes while I take you, Muna."

"I can't," she whispered.

"*You will!*" came the unrelenting answer. Then he moved swiftly until she knew that she didn't want him to stop, but when her eyes began to close, he ceased the pleasure.

"No," she whimpered, "don't stop, my lord!"

"Open your eyes, Muna! I won't stop if you keep your lovely sea-blue eyes open."

It was a terrible effort, but Skye managed to force her eyes to open, disclosing to him the desire within herself, and Kedar gave a soft, triumphant laugh. "Please," she begged as the sexual stimulants that he had fed her rendered her helpless to him, and to her own lust.

Slowly he initiated the erotic motion she craved, and obedient to him, her eyes never left his. She felt as if she were drowning in his fiery gaze, knew that her soul was not even her own at this minute. Suddenly he ceased his movements, and she pleaded once more, "No, don't stop, my lord Kedar! *Don't!*"

"In a moment, in a moment," he soothed her, "but first if I am to continue to give you this pleasure you must do something for me, fair Muna."

"Anything!" she sobbed rashly, and he smiled cruelly down at her.

"You will repeat after me," he said softly, "I am my lord Kedar's slave."

"I am my lord Kedar's slave," she said quickly, looking eagerly to him for approval.

He smiled again. "I exist solely for his pleasure."

"*No!*" she whimpered, the part of her that was still herself rebelling at his words.

"Say it! Say, *I exist solely for his pleasure*, or I shall withdraw from you." He thrust softly into her several times to entice her, and she moaned. "*Say it!*"

"I . . . I exist . . . solely for his . . . pleasure."

"Very good, my beautiful slave," he approved in his deep, purring voice, and then he gave her the pleasure she so desperately desired from him; his lean hips driving deeply against her until her senses exploded once more into fiery fragments of helpless passion. Then, to his surprise, his own love juices burst forth to flood the raging fire within her womb. With a gasp that was half from irritation he rolled from her, amazed to have lost his perfect control. She had beaten him without even realizing it, and he chuckled to himself. It had been a long time since he had enjoyed a woman so very much. By Allah, his uncle had chosen well! With a sigh of total contentment Kedar used the last of his strength to roll her inert body from the divan onto the cushion below where a proper houri belonged. He then stretched himself out, thoroughly satisfied, and quickly fell asleep.

Chapter 8

"*Muna!*"

Through the haziness of her barely conscious mind Skye heard the sharp command in Kedar's voice. She struggled to wake herself, but she was totally exhausted by the previous night's mental and physical battle with him. Still, she tried, for she dare not anger him or displease him before she had gotten to Fez. Shaking herself, she managed to keep her eyes open until they finally began to focus. Only then did she raise her head to him. "My lord?"

He lay on the couch above her, stretched out on his side. His hazel eyes glittered though but half open, and again Skye was reminded of a sleek feline. "I desire you," he said. "Pleasure me!" He rolled onto his back, and his manhood thrust straight into the cool, early-morning air.

God's bones! thought Skye irritably. Is the man never sated? She knew, however, what was expected of her. Hiding her annoyance, she pulled herself onto the couch by his feet. Her slender hands caressed his length as she moved herself up his hard body. His legs fell apart as her touch ignited his already inflamed passions, and Skye rose to swing herself over him, her fingers teasing at his nipples. With a groan his hands caught at her hips, and forced her down upon him. His quick penetration was almost painful, and she couldn't help the soft cry that escaped her lips.

He didn't notice, or if he did it didn't matter to him. What mattered was his own gratification. "Ride me, beautiful Muna," he murmured huskily at her, his eyes closed with enjoyment. "I know that you European women ride upon horses, my exquisite one. Have you ever ridden astride?"

"Yes, my lord," she answered him.

"Ahhh," he almost purred, "then think of me as your horse, my beautiful slave. I am the stallion that you ride to the hunt! Ride me well lest I throw you!"

Skye knew that her performance with him now would be the difference between going and staying. She had to please him, and please him so greatly that she became like a drug to him, a drug that he could not do without. "In my own land, my lord, I was a horsewoman without peer," she whispered back at him provocatively, and then she gripped him tightly between her silken thighs. Balancing herself with her hands on either side of his head she leaned forward, brushing her breasts across his lips while her hips began the love rhythm. She moved on him slowly, teasingly, with tantalizing motion, and Kedar suddenly felt he was not totally in control of the situation.

"Lean back, Muna," he commanded her tensely.

"As my lord wills," she answered softly, but there was a mocking tone to her voice that he did not fail to catch.

The little bitch! he thought angrily. She dares to seek to best me in this battle. Reaching up, he grasped her two beautiful breasts in his hands and gently crushed her soft flesh over and over again, until she began to squirm and moan, losing the rhythm.

Skye was furious at him. She sought to intrigue him, to rouse his passions, and he took it as an affront to his masculinity. She attempted to regain control of the situation by running her hands over his chest, but Kedar growled at her. "No, Muna! Domination is my right, not yours." He lifted her off him, and set her next to him.

"I but sought to please you, my lord," she protested.

"I forgive you," he said smoothly, and Skye seethed as he continued: "You are as my uncle has said, unschooled. I will enjoy teaching you how to be an obedient slave, my fair Muna. Lay on your belly now. I would relieve my lust for you." He pushed her gently over and, mounting her, effected a quick rear entry before she could even protest. He filled her sheath totally, moving smoothly to sate his own desires. He held her down with his hands on her hips, but other than that did not touch her. When his desire had burst within her he withdrew, leaving her aching with her lack of satisfaction.

Skye shuddered with actual physical pain. Her own desire was high, and she did not know how to satisfy it. She knew that Kedar had done this to her deliberately, to teach her that he was the master and she the slave. With a frustrated sob she began to weep softly, unable to contain herself. Her cries brought her mercy, for his ego was instantly gratified by her tears.

He rolled her onto her back again, and gently caressed her belly, but rather than ease her sexual tension the seductive motion only increased it. With a wicked smile he leaned across her to the gold basket and drew forth an object. "Here," he said, "this will ease your suffering, my beautiful Muna," and he pressed it into her hands.

Skye opened her eyes, and then gasped with shock. "What is it?" she demanded of him, thrusting the *thing* from her.

Kedar picked it up and looked upon it with a critical eye. "It has been made to exact specification," he said. "It is very prized by the women in my harem. I cannot, you will understand, pleasure them all at the same time." He let his eye move over the object again, and then said, "It is quite accurate in both size and shape, Muna. It is called a dildo. Take it in your hands, my beautiful slave, and use it. It will ease your distress."

Skye looked upon the dildo as if it were a viper. As Kedar had said, it was shaped and sized as he was. It was carved of ivory, and complete in every detail from the circumcised head of the penis to the veins all the way down its length. At the base of the dildo had been inserted a polished wooden stick by which the user could grip it.

"Take the ivory," he commanded her softly.

"*No!*" She was horrified.

"Take the ivory, Muna," he repeated, and she heard the menace in his voice.

"*Please,*" she pleaded, hoping that he would relent; but she realized that if he didn't she was going to have to obey him. She could not displease him. She had to get to Fez! She had to free Niall!

He saw the weakening in her defiance. "Take the ivory," he said. "I want to watch you while you use it." His hand moved over her belly again, fanning the fires within her.

Skye shuddered, and then she picked up the dildo with shaking fingers. She was terribly embarrassed. "I have never seen such a thing, let alone used one," she said. "I don't know where to begin, my lord."

Kedar sat up facing her, his back to the velvet-covered wall, his legs crossed tailor-fashion. Leaning forward, he pushed a pillow beneath her hips. "Open your legs," he commanded her, and when she had complied he began to stroke and rub at the very core of her femininity. "You're very beautiful there," he murmured softly, his hazel eyes watching the movement of his hand on her moist sensitivity. "I possess many beautiful women in my harem, but I have never seen any woman as fair as you in so many ways. I would have all of you, my fair Muna."

Skye shuddered again as his clever fingers stoked her fires. Her instinct was to flee from this man, this terrible man who indeed wanted all of her, even that which she had never given to any man. It was a dangerous game she had elected to play, and now there was no going back. His fingers were having the desired effect, and she moaned low in her passion. "Please, my lord, please take me," she begged him, knowing that he would refuse, would impress his iron will on her.

"Use the ivory!" came the excited command. "Use the ivory!"

"Please, my lord! Not that! You take me!" There was a frantic sound to her voice, and Kedar smiled to himself.

"Use the ivory, Muna! I am the ivory, and I command it!" Allah! he thought. The sight of her sweet sex aroused and honied and eager inflamed him more than he had anticipated. Still, he would force her to his will lest she believe she could control and wheedle him at her desire.

Drawing a deep breath, Skye thrust the ivory into her body, gasping as the smooth, cold length of it slid into her. Through her half-closed eyes she could see Kedar watching her with obvious enjoyment, his hazel eyes darting from her face to her hands as they worked the dildo. The ivory did nothing to ease her discomfort, but still she moaned and thrashed her head about, knowing he expected a good show. Kedar, however, was not entirely fooled. He could see that the dildo was not having the effect that he had hoped for, and so he leaned forward once again to tease the pink pearl of her womanhood. It was as if he had touched her with fire. Her hands fell from the ivory as she moaned in earnest this time, and Kedar took up where she had left off, one hand playing with her tiny jewel, the other working the ivory dildo. She quickly cried out her release, and he immediately withdrew the dildo from her.

"There, beautiful Muna, that was not so terrible," he purred at her, fondling her quivering breasts. "Now I shall reward you, my exquisite, blue-eyed slave. You have been very good, beautiful Muna; very, very good." Kedar slid his hard body over Skye, and drove into her. "There, my pet, is that not better? I should not spoil you, but I cannot resist you at this moment."

She had barely descended from the mountain only to have him once more force her back up it. She whimpered a small protest that made him laugh softly, and then his mouth was closing over hers in a searing kiss. Again the panic gripped her as she felt herself out of control, but Kedar was not aware of her fear. He parted her lips and sucked upon her tongue while his lean hips thrust again and again until they both reached perfection.

He had swept her along with his own passion, and now she lay panting and drained. The fear had left her when he had released her. He lay next to her now, equally spent, his breathing ragged. Finally he said hoarsely, "Dear Allah, how you have destroyed me, Muna! Go now and leave me, exquisite slave. I would rest."

Skye could barely drag herself from the couch, but she knew that she had to get out of the room. She needed to be by herself in order to recover her own strength. On shaking legs she slowly exited, having first gathered up her pantaloons and bolero and quickly dressed. Stumblingly she made her way back to the women's quarters in another wing of the house, and finding her own rooms, she fell across her bed, instantly asleep from the strain and shock. Sleep was the best medicine for her, thought Osman, who had been visiting his wife, and had seen Skye as she passed by Alima's rooms.

The famous astrologer went to his library and, seating himself comfortably, began to contemplate the entire situation. He knew the kind of man that his nephew was, but he also knew that Skye was strong enough to survive Kedar's carnality. In the two days since Skye had arrived back in Algiers he had completely done her natal chart, as well as that of Niall Burke. Lord Burke's had been quite straightforward, but Skye's chart was amazing; according to his calculations, she had barely begun to live. It would not, however, be all to her liking; but then she had a strong and old soul. Skye O'Malley would survive, whatever the odds.

Osman had also studied his nephew's natal chart quite carefully, for Kedar figured so importantly in this matter. Kedar was strong, and his stars were equally strong, but the influences controlling

Skye's chart were far more powerful, and Osman knew that she would be able to control her own destiny even in his nephew's hands. A small smile played about the astrologer's mouth and crinkled the corners of his eyes. He imagined that right now the exhausted Skye was yet in shock after a night with Kedar. Osman had to admit that his nephew was the most sexual man he had ever known, and his capacity for women was legendary even in Fez. Still, once Skye recovered from her initial trauma and her survival instincts surfaced, she would be formidable. Osman felt almost sorry for Kedar. He knew that his nephew had never been in love, and he hoped that Skye would not arouse that emotion in him. He did not want to hurt him. It was difficult being torn between such a good friend as Skye and his family.

Osman emptied his mind now of all thought, and relaxing his body, he began to meditate. Alima found him that way some time later in the morning. Gently she shook her husband, understanding what it was he did. The life came slowly back into the astrologer's eyes, and smiling up at his lovely wife, he said, "Kedar is awake, and wishes to know if I will eat the midday meal with him."

Alima laughed and shook her head at him. "I don't know why I even bothered to come and get you," she said. "Couldn't you at least humor me by pretending that you don't know what I have to say before I even speak?"

"You are too easy," he teased her back. "Your mind is like crystal to me. I know all where you are concerned, my love."

"*All?*" Alima smiled provocatively at her husband.

"Woman, your thoughts are much too immodest!" Osman pretended displeasure, but Alima was not one bit fooled.

"It will be a long, hot afternoon, my husband, and I will wager that your nephew will not waste it idly."

Osman chuckled, and then he asked, "How is Muna?"

"At this moment her thoughts of you are not entirely kindly, my lord. She is in the baths. She would speak with you, she says, before Kedar calls her to him again."

Osman nodded. "I can enter the women's quarters without any question since this is my house. When she is safely back in her own chamber, Alima, then send for me. We three will speak together. It is better you be with us, as there is no true privacy for us and your presence, my wife, will divert suspicion."

Alima nodded. "I will arrange everything, my lord," she said, and then left him.

Osman rose from the cushions and went to find Kedar. He was curious as to what his nephew had to say about the new slave girl, Muna. Kedar had bathed earlier, and now lay stretched out upon his couch while his personal body slave, a giant black named Dagan, massaged him. Seeing his uncle, he waved the slave away and pulled a length of cloth about his loins. Osman noted Kedar's powerful chest and muscled arms. He was in excellent physical condition, which, considering his appetites, Osman thought, was amazing. Youth, he decided, was obviously the key.

"Uncle!" Kedar's greeting was enthusiastic. "How do I thank you for Muna? She is incredible, magnificent! I have not enjoyed a woman so in years!"

"I am pleased to have given you such pleasure with so small a trifle as a slave girl, my nephew."

Kedar grinned. "You were right, of course. She is quite unschooled, but she is intelligent, I can see, and will be easily trained despite the streak of stubbornness I find in her. Firmness is the key to managing a woman. Firmness and discipline. One should never be afraid to punish even a beautiful creature like Muna."

"You did not punish her?" Osman tried to keep the nervousness from his voice. "The girl cost me a pretty penny, Kedar."

"Allah, no!" Kedar laughed. "I'm afraid I grow weak with age, Uncle. I could not destroy that gorgeous skin she possesses. If Muna should ever become recalcitrant I shall have to think of a way to punish her without using the lash. No, but she sought to defy me a little last night, and I was forced to be quite firm. She responded well, and became quite pliant afterward."

"Yes," Osman answered, "I suspect that reason will always overcome any outbursts on Muna's part. Tell me, nephew, how long will you be with me this trip? We had so little time to speak last night, so eager were you to have the slave girl. I understood, of course. Your trip from Fez was a long and lonely one."

"I am no longer lonely," Kedar smiled. "I shall probably stay with you a good month or more, Uncle. I have a great deal of business to conduct while I am here in Algiers, and now that you have made me so comfortable I am in no hurry to depart."

The two men chuckled companionably and, after a few more minutes of idle conversation, ate a light repast. Then Osman excused himself and hurried to the women's quarters. He found both his wife and Skye awaiting him in Skye's bedchamber. "Good day, my daughter," he said calmly.

Skye glowered at Osman, and then a small smile touched her lips. "I cannot say that you did not warn me that he was a lustful man, Osman," she said, "but you did not tell me that he was built like a bull, and totally insatiable. I am exhausted, having been at his tender mercy this past night. Still, I know that it is the only way for me to reach Fez, to free my husband. Now, however, we must speak seriously."

Osman nodded. "You have doubts, I know."

"You are certain that your younger nephew, Hamal, will aid me in rescuing Niall? If the boy truly loves his princess perhaps he will have had second thoughts by now."

"I am in constant touch with Hamal, Muna." He looked closely at her. "But if Hamal should change his mind, my daughter, what would you do? You would not, I know, leave your husband to languish in the princess's harem."

"No, Osman, I would not. I should find a way."

"I know," came the answer. "It is your fate to travel to Fez."

"Is it my fate to return, Osman?" Skye's glance was a candid one.

"You will see your green land again, my daughter," was his reply. "Now tell me what else it is that troubles you."

"It is your nephew, Osman. He is a frighteningly possessive man. Will he allow me any measure of freedom or will I find myself walled up in his harem?"

"I will speak to him, Muna. He has told me that he intends to stay a month here in Algiers. I will convince him of the need to allow you to move about the city, properly attired, of course."

"He plans to stay a month? Osman, can you not convince him to spend less time here? You yourself said that every minute counts!"

"He is just arrived yesterday, my daughter. I can hardly send him back today. I do not know what his business is, but I shall soon learn it. Perhaps then I may speed his affairs along, and you will return to Fez at an earlier date. Be patient, my daughter. You have yet to learn that everything will take place in its own time, and not a moment before."

A knock sounded upon the door, and a slave girl put her head into the room. "The lord Kedar has sent his slave, Dagan, to bring Muna to him."

Skye nodded. "I will come," she said, and the girl departed the room. Skye rose. "It is barely two hours after noon," she said, making a small moue with her mouth. "I did manage to get six hours' sleep. Heaven only knows how long it will have to last me!"

"He will probably leave you this evening to have dinner with friends and conduct some business," Osman said reassuringly.

"He will return though, old friend, and he will expect me to be eagerly awaiting him."

"And you will," Osman said quietly.

"Yes," Skye replied. "I will." Then she was gone from the room, and Alima looked to her husband with troubled eyes.

"Will she be all right, my husband? We should ill repay the kindness of the late Khalid el Bey should we put her in any danger."

"You are a gentle flower, my Alima," Osman said, "but for all her delicate looks Skye is tempered of as fine a steel as the Toledo blade. She cannot be broken or bent. She will survive, never fear."

While Osman reassured his wife, Skye was following the huge Dagan through the house back to Kedar's chambers. The few hours' sleep and the steam of the bath had combined to give her a radiant glow. Her cheeks were flushed rose, and her eyes sparkled like a fine Ceylon sapphire. She wore a simple gauze caftan of turquoise blue, and her black hair had been braided into one thick plait and dressed with tiny freshwater pearls and silver lamé ribbons.

Kedar's eyes lit up at the sight of her. He reminded her of a panther contemplating its meal, and Skye suppressed a small shiver as she slipped to her knees, bent forward, and touched her forehead to his slipper. "Rise, Muna," he said, pulling her eagerly up to him. "Dear Allah, how is it possible that you are so radiant?" His mouth descended quickly upon hers, and Skye slid her arms about him, pressing her lush form against him. Kedar shuddered, and pulled away in surprise. "No woman has ever done *that* to me," he said, looking at her curiously.

"I did not mean to displease you, my lord," she said meekly.

"I know that, beautiful one. I am simply surprised at myself. I thought having sated myself upon your beautiful body just several hours ago I would be replete. No woman has ever touched me as you have, and I find, however, that I am not."

"You have but to command me, my lord Kedar."

A slow smile lit his features, and he turned to the black slave who stood awaiting his master's commands. "Well, Dagan, did my uncle not present me with a perfect jewel?"

"Yes, master. The lord Osman was most generous."

Kedar turned to Skye. "And you, my fair Muna. What do you think of Dagan? He has been with me for ten years now, and I trust him with my life."

"I did not speak to the man, my lord, not knowing if it was permitted."

Kedar laughed. "Dagan is not a man, my beautiful slave. He is a eunuch. I should not allow him near you were he not gelded." He turned to the slave. "Stay, Dagan. I want to give Muna the lesson I give all the women I take into my harem."

The black man smiled broadly. "Yes, master!"

Kedar gently began to unbutton the little pearl buttons that held together the halves of Skye's caftan. When they were all undone he pushed the gown off her shoulders, and it silently slid to the floor. She stood very still while his hands wandered casually over her breasts. "Each woman, my fair Muna, should have something to fear. Most of the women in my harem fear the lash should they displease me, but your skin is so incredibly lovely that I would never mark it. It was therefore necessary to devise a punishment that you would fear, and I have decided on the bastinado. Have you ever suffered this form of chastisement?"

"No, my lord." She knew of the bastinado, of course, but never had Khalid used such cruelty.

"Then you cannot be fearful of that which you do not know. I intend to give you a lesson in the bastinado now, my fair Muna. You will then understand and be afraid. You will also comprehend that if you should at any time displease me, you will be put to this discipline." Kedar turned to Dagan. "I will hold her," he said, and then he instructed Skye in a quiet voice. "I want you to lay upon your back on the floor and elevate your legs upon these pillows."

Skye was terrified. "My lord," she pleaded with him, "please do not do this!"

For a moment he was tender, gathering her into his arms and crooning to her. "There, my jewel, of course you are frightened, but I will not excuse you this lesson. Only when you have felt the pain can you be truly afraid. Only then will I have a deterrent to unruly behavior. Come, Muna, it will only be five strokes. Were I really punishing you it would be twenty or more, depending upon your offense." He drew her down to the rug, kneeling with her, positioning her with great care. Then he sat across her hips and, leaning forward, held her slender legs in a firm grasp. "Begin, Dagan," he commanded the black.

The sharpness of the first blow caused her to cry out. Over Kedar's bowed head Dagan grinned cruelly down at her as he administered the second fierce blow. This time Skye shrieked in earnest. "Please, my lord Kedar! Please, no more! No more!" Kedar was, however, a man of his word, and the third, fourth, and fifth blows fell upon the tender, now burning soles of her feet, the pain so intense that Skye fainted, taking the only escape open to her.

She was unconscious but a few moments, awakening to Kedar's purring voice. "There, my jewel, now you know the price of offending me, do you not?"

"Yes, my lord," she managed to whisper.

"Repeat the words I taught you last night, fair Muna."

Skye shivered. She knew exactly what he wanted her to say, and every fiber of her being rebelled against saying *those* words. Still, she was now quite terrified of the bastinado, and realized that should she really displease him, he would not hesitate for a moment to use it again. She rolled onto her stomach, and from there into a kneeling position, her dark head touching the rug. "I am my lord Kedar's slave," she said low. "I exist solely for his pleasure."

Above her, Kedar smiled, satisfied, and raised her up to face him. "You learn quickly, my jewel," he said approvingly. "I believe you will eventually become my favorite." Tenderly he brushed a tear from her cheek. "There now, fair Muna, there is naught to cry about. You please me mightily." He smiled down on her, and then drew her over to the awninged couch. She was shivering with shock, and he pulled her gently down upon the couch with him, wrapping his arms around her. "Dagan, fetch refreshments," he commanded his slave.

Skye was suddenly very aware of her nudity. "Please, my lord, may I have my garment?"

"Do not be embarrassed before Dagan, my jewel. It means nothing to him, and I prefer you like this for now." He kissed her lightly, absently caressing her breasts. "You are so beautiful," he murmured. "Your skin is so flawless, so perfect."

They were words she was to hear over and over again during the next few weeks. She fascinated and consumed him with her beauty.

He cared for nothing else. He rarely spoke to her on any subject of importance; his words being those of her master, her lover. Her days took on a pattern of sameness. She slept the morning away, went to him in early afternoon after visiting the baths, left in late afternoon, slept again, bathed, ate supper alone or with Alima, and sometimes Osman, then awaited Kedar's return from his business and social rounds late in the evening. She then spent the entire night with him, departing in early morning for her own rooms. As a lover, he was insatiable, and totally unlike any man she had ever known. He cared only for his own pleasure, and took her with great gusto at least three times each night, and very often as many as six. He never seemed to tire of exploring, caressing, and kissing her.

Skye was frankly frightened of Kedar. He was a man of mercurial temperament, and she feared offending him. The threat of the bastinado was a real and terrifying one to her. Still, she sought ways in which to intrigue him, for she did not want him to grow bored with her. She found that quick changes of mood on her part interested him greatly; and so she was shy one moment, daring the next. She knew he particularly enjoyed her reactions to his lovemaking, and so even when he moved too quickly to arouse her she pretended great passion. It stroked his ego, and he rumbled his contentment like the great cat she pictured him. "You are perfection," he would murmur against her ear. "Sweet, honeyed perfection!" More often than not she would shiver at his words.

The day before they left Algiers for Fez, Osman came to Skye's chambers in the women's quarters. He felt some guilt for the faint purple circles under her eyes, but there was a new air of determination about her that he had never seen before. "I have had word from Hamal, my daughter. He says you are to come ahead. Your Niall still lives."

"Thank God!" Skye breathed fervently.

"Skye," it was the first time he had called her by her own name in weeks. "I am quite frankly worried about your effect upon Kedar. If you had set out to enchant him—and I know you have not—you could not have done a better job of it. He can speak of nothing but you and your beauty when he is with me. If I did not know better I should say he is falling in love with you, and that, my daughter, must not happen! I knew his reputation, of course, but frankly, until now I was not fully aware of his appetites. I wonder if I have not set you too hard a task."

"You have said it yourself, Osman. There is no other choice. Niall is alive, and I will not rest until I have freed him. How could I, knowing what I know, return to my former life? There is only one way to Fez for me, and I am already on that road. Why do you fret so? Have my stars changed suddenly, Osman?"

"No, they have not changed. You will always attain your heart's desire, Skye, though the road to it be roughly paved, though you yourself may not even know what it is you want. In the end you will gain your goals. In this have you been singularly blessed."

"Then tomorrow I leave for Fez," Skye said quietly.

"Does he abuse you?" Osman flushed at the boldness of his own words to her, but he was truly distressed at the situation in which he had placed her. He had never seen his nephew so consumed by anything, let alone a woman. Then, too, Alima had mentioned that Skye had an occasional bruise, and marks on her body that might possibly indicate that Kedar was mistreating her.

"Your nephew is enthusiastic in his wooing of me," Skye said wryly. "No, he has not actually hurt me, although he has threatened me with the bastinado should I misbehave. He illustrated that threat with a sample of that particular punishment. He does not, you see, want to mark my skin with a lash. His small lesson was a warning that my behavior should always be decorous. I will admit, Osman, that he frightens me."

"Allah curse him! I shall speak to him this day, my daughter." Osman was angry, and his eyes blazed as Skye had never seen them blaze, for he had always been a gentle man toward her.

"Osman!" Her voice was tight with warning. "You cannot tell him how to treat his possession, and you know it. You presented me to him as a gift, and you know that the only justice for a slave is that which the master gives. Right now Kedar, for all his fierceness, adores me, but he is not stupid. Interfere and he will wonder why. He might even grow jealous, and I dare not have that."

Osman sighed, resigned. "You are correct, my daughter. I have allowed my paternal feelings for you to cloud my own judgment. Do not fear, Skye. Whatever happens I will get you out of Fez when you choose to leave. I will not permit you to languish in my nephew's harem. That is most certainly not your fate!"

Skye gave him a mischievous smile that touched his heart. He had not seen her smile in some days now. "I should hope not, my old friend, although, quite frankly, I will welcome reaching Kedar's harem. Perhaps when he has all his women available to him again he will not use me so frequently. I never thought to grow tired of lovemaking, Osman, but, dear Heaven, I have! Your nephew's prowess is surely unequaled for he can make love the entire night without ceasing, and seems not to suffer from the lack of sleep as I certainly do!"

Osman shook his head sympathetically. "It is said that he had his first woman at the age of ten. My late sister was shocked, but her husband thought it a marvelous thing to have sired so randy an heir, especially since Kedar was his only child at the time."

"Does Kedar have any children?" Skye asked. "He never speaks of his women, but then he rarely speaks with me at all except to command me to his will."

"Although he has no wives, he does have several offspring, but unlike most Fasi men, he seems to care little for them. I don't even think that he could tell you their names, ages, or sex. He does not care for children, I believe." Osman decided it would be wise to say nothing of the fact that Kedar had confided in his uncle that he wished to have children by Muna. Skye had enough to worry about, and as long as she had her special potion she would not conceive. "You do have your special potion?" he asked her worriedly. "Do you have enough to last you several months, my daughter?"

"I have just made a fresh batch. Kedar allowed me to go with Alima to the marketplace, and I was able to obtain the ingredients that I need. It looks and smells like a fragrance, and will be thought to be such, Osman.

"It amused Kedar to let me visit the market. He loved the idea that I might wander at will and no one would know what a 'delicious morsel' I am, to quote him. No one can tell who I am when I am dressed in my yashmak and veiled. Kedar tells me the marketplaces in Fez are legendary."

"You will enjoy them, my daughter. The merchant in you will delight at the variety of goods available. Remember to buy with an open hand. You are the favorite of the lord Kedar, and he will be generous with you. Buy gifts for the other women and children in the harem often, and you will quickly make friends."

"I am not going to Fez to make friends, Osman."

"Nonetheless you do not want to make enemies of any of Kedar's other women. Women can be vicious when jealous, my daughter. Have you so quickly forgotten Yasmin? Be charming and friendly, and above all be generous. You do not know when you will need a friend, even in Kedar's harem."

"None of his women would dare to betray him, Osman. He is a man quick to punish an offense real or imagined. And no one will risk his lash for me, be I generous or not. He beat one of his favorites to death, you know. Still, I will take your advice and be friendly."

"I will rest easier knowing that, Skye," was Osman's reply. He rose up from the divan as she did, and taking her hands in his said, "Go with Allah's blessing, my daughter. He will not fail to hear your prayers, for your mission is a just one. One bit of advice, and one only I give to you. Consider carefully before you act. Do not allow fear or enthusiasm to drive you to any rashness. You will survive!"

She looked into his wonderful and mysterious eyes, and for a brief moment she felt swept away. She knew as she gazed into their depths that she would indeed survive, and something akin to exultation poured over her. She would succeed in her rescue of Niall! They would return home to Ireland, and happily raise their children as they grew old together! Skye found her voice. "Thank you, Osman, my old friend. Thank you!" Putting her arms about his neck, she kissed him on the cheek.

The astrologer actually blushed, but nonetheless he hugged her back. Then without another word he left her. "Farewell, my friend," she called after him, and Osman turned. The look in his eyes was a tender one. "Farewell, my daughter," he answered softly. As she watched him go Skye wondered if she should ever see him again after she departed Algiers tomorrow.

Despite the fact that they were to leave for Fez in the very early morning, Kedar did not change his habits at all that night. If anything, his excitement over leaving Algiers increased his appetite for Skye. He loved to lie nude, propped up by the multicolored pillows, his legs spread, while she knelt between his limbs, her buttocks on her heels, her arms out for balance, her long dark hair loose about her. His hands would hold his penis up while she would administer to him with her mouth, her tongue, her little teeth. Soon he would have no need to brace his manhood, and she would obediently roll onto her back to receive him.

When he had taken her three times that night she dared to beg him, "No more, my lord, else I cannot rise to leave for Fez."

A growl of laughter was his answer, but he left her alone to sleep on the pillow below his couch until just before the dawn, when his foot prodded her awake. In a surprisingly thoughtful gesture, he said, "If you wish to bathe, Muna, go now and do so. There will be little chance for a civilized bath for the next month. Occasionally we may camp by a spring, but unless I can guarantee you total privacy you will not be able to avail yourself of it."

Skye scrambled to her feet. "Thank you, my lord," she said, catching up her caftan and putting it about her as she hurried from the room lest he change his mind and his lust get the better of him.

"Wait!"

She turned, thinking, Dear God, not again.

"I have a small gift for you," he said. "When you have bathed be sure to put it on." He held out an object.

"Thank you, my lord," she said softly as she took it. "A bracelet. How lovely!"

"No, an anklet. I had it specially made for you. Once you put it on it cannot be removed except it be cut off. Go now!"

Skye left the room fingering the anklet as she went. It was a slender circle of pure gold, engraved with several Arabic letters and a delicate geometric pattern. Here and there amid the pattern was a tiny sapphire imbedded in the gold. It was really quite beautiful.

Hurrying to her room, she awoke her own slave woman, Zada, and sent her off to instruct the bath woman Nigera and her helpers. Zada had been her first gift from Kedar. He had escorted her, properly garbed so that only the merest slit of her eyes showed, to the slave market to purchase a servant for her. He had thought to buy her a European woman so she would not be lonely. It had been a very kind gesture on his part, but Skye had insisted she preferred a young Arab girl. Had he insisted upon the European, she would have felt guilty leaving the woman in Fez when she and Niall escaped. The Arab girl, however, would be reassigned a new mistress and no harm would be done.

"They await you in the baths, mistress." Zada had returned.

Skye nodded, and went off to bathe. When she returned Zada had laid out the garments in which she would travel. Silently she put on the long, cream-colored silk chemise, a pale-beige djellabah embroidered in brown silk thread and tiny topaz, and soft, brown kidskin slippers. The djellabah was hooded, and had long sleeves. Before Zada raised the hood and fastened the gold gauze veil across Skye's face, she brushed her mistress's long dark hair and dressed it with narrow gold ribbons in the single braid that Skye favored. "Go to my lord Kedar," Skye said, "and say that I beg his permission because of the heat of the day to put aside my yashmak."

Zada obediently followed her mistress's instructions, and returned several minutes later to say, "The master says you must wear the yashmak as far as the cart. You may remove it before you enter the vehicle, but not until then."

"Very well," Skye answered. "Fetch the lady Alima to me now, Zada. I would say my good-byes."

Zada once more hurried out, returning several minutes later with Alima. Skye then dismissed the slave girl, telling her to see to her own last-minute preparations. "I think she spies for Dagan, who reports everything I do to Kedar," Skye said, amused.

"He is so frighteningly possessive of you," Alima returned. "Must you go, my lady Skye?" Alima spoke French so that anyone listening would not understand her words.

"There is no other way for me, Alima. If Osman were in the same position as my husband is, would you not try to aid him? How can I return to my home knowing that Niall is alive. How can I face our children with such knowledge on my conscience. Better they lose both of us than I return to them leaving their father behind in bondage."

"You love him very much, don't you?"

"Yes, Alima. I love Niall with every fiber of my being! I will not rest until we are safely together again."

"Be careful, my lady Skye," Alima begged her. "Make no move unless you are absolutely certain that Kedar will not catch you. He is a very cruel man, as you already have learned."

"Yes," Skye said, shuddering as she remembered the bastinado. "He is very cruel. Yet, Alima, he can also be kind. See the anklet that he had made for me? It is quite lovely." Skye handed the narrow golden circle to Alima. "You read Arabic. What has he written on it?"

Alima took the anklet and studied it carefully. As her eyes moved across the Arabic script her face darkened. "He is a beast!" she muttered. "He makes a charming gesture, and then ruins it with his ego!"

"What does it say?" Skye demanded.

Alima looked up at Skye, and said quietly, "It says *Muna, Property of Kedar*."

"I will not wear it!" Skye stormed.

"You have no choice, my lady," Alima said sadly. "It is the bracelet of a privileged slave. Once you fasten the clasp about your ankle the only way you will be able to remove it is if a goldsmith saws it off." She handed Skye back the anklet.

Skye's eyes were dark with anger, and she longed to throw the offending gold circle onto the nearest trash heap. She knew, however, that she dare not. Bending down, she fastened the bracelet about her right ankle. She knew the punishment for offending Kedar, and she had no wish to ever taste the bastinado again.

As she rose up again her eyes met the sympathetic ones of Alima. "You are far braver than I could ever be," Osman's wife said.

Skye shrugged. "As you have said, I have no choice."

"Mistress, it is time to go." Zada had materialized from wherever she had been.

"Get the yashmak then, Zada. Hurry! We must not keep the master waiting." She looked at Alima, and there was mischief in her blue-green eyes again. "You don't think she speaks French, do you?"

Alima laughed. "Never. She's just a little Berber girl, one of too many daughters in her family. They sold her off. That's what she told Nigera." Then Alima's face grew serious and, stepping forward, she hugged Skye hard. "Be careful, my lady, and Allah go with you!"

Skye hugged Osman's wife back. "I shall endeavor to be careful, Alima. Thank you for all your hospitality, and don't stop your prayers, I beg you. I shall need them!"

Then Zada was bustling about her, importantly pulling up the hood of the djellabah, fastening the veil about her face, helping her into a black silk yashmak whose hood fell to just below her eyebrows, and adding a second black silk veil.

"You will smother me," Skye protested.

"Dagan says the master insists you be properly veiled," was the prim reply.

Skye gritted her teeth and grew silent. There was no arguing, for although she was Kedar's favorite concubine, she was as much a slave as Zada and Dagan. There was no appeal of the *master's* word. She stood quietly while the slave girl went about the job of thoroughly muffling her, and when Zada had finished Skye looked to Alima, merriment suddenly filling her eyes at the silliness of the situation. "I don't know who he thinks will see me between here and your courtyard that I must be so encased," Skye said in French.

"It is simply another instance of his impressing his will upon you, my lady Skye," was the answer.

"We must not keep the master waiting," Zada said.

Skye and Alima embraced a final time, and then Skye followed her slave girl from the bedchamber, through the house that had once been hers, and into the main courtyard, where Kedar's vast caravan was nearly assembled. The Fasi merchant had brought a rich cargo to Algiers from the interior, and now he was returning with an equally lavish one. There were numerous pack animals, donkeys, and camels, all laden down with the goods. The train was to be escorted by a large group of armed and mounted mercenaries who had come from Fez with Kedar, and would now return with him.

The caravan would travel at a brisk pace during the day, but at night they would stop and set up their tents in order to eat and rest the animals. They would travel approximately twenty miles each day, following the caravan track that led through a narrow piece of land that was bordered by the Atlas Mountains. It was dangerous by virtue of the bandits who preyed upon poorly guarded caravans. Kedar had never lost so much as a camel in all his years of traveling the route, for he was willing to spend the monies necessary to hire enough guards to protect him and his goods. It was a poor economy, Kedar believed, to stint on protection only to lose a valuable cargo.

Skye traveled in a covered cart drawn by two sturdy donkeys. The inside of the vehicle had been quilted in red silk and fitted with two dark blue pallets. Dagan drove while Skye was forced to remain within the cart with Zada. Her only escape from total boredom was the opportunity to look out through the gauze drapery veiling over the back of the cart. When she became tired of sight-seeing she could sleep. She had little in common with Zada, whose only concern in life seemed to be beautifying her mistress in order to retain Kedar's devotion so they both might get ahead in the harem. Zada often sat up front with Dagan, chatting for hours with him about Kedar's house in Fez.

Dagan believed he saw the handwriting on the wall. Never in his ten years with his master had he seen Kedar so obsessed with anything, let alone a woman. This one, Dagan decided, could end up being Kedar's first and only wife. Consequently he took the time to make friends with the ambitious Zada. Best to have a friend in the future mistress's camp. Even Kedar might be softened and influenced by a wife.

The trip gave Skye some respite from Kedar's possessive passion, for she only saw him for a short time each night. During the day he rode at the head of his caravan, his sharp hazel-colored eyes watching the hills around them and the trail ahead, never missing anything. He ate the midday meal with his men, although sometimes he would come by her cart afterward to see that all was well with his beautiful slave. He ate his evening meal alone, or with one of the senior men among his mercenaries. When the camp was quiet for the night, the fires burning in lonely splendor and the pickets alert and watchful, then would Kedar take his own pleasure.

In a curtained-off portion of Kedar's tent they slept upon soft down and feather mattresses covered in scarlet velvet. Having eaten alone herself, and then washed in a small wooden tub as best she might, Skye was expected to await her master within the alcove. When he came he would take her twice, and then fall immediately into a deep sleep. For Skye it was a relief, for Kedar's only interest was in satisfying his natural and normal lust with these brief encounters. She might have been anyone, and his attitude gave her hope that his desire for her was now waning as they grew nearer Fez, and his large harem.

When they were a week from their destination they met with another party of heavily guarded merchants coming from Fez and going to the coast. Most of the men were known to Kedar, and it was decided that they would eat together that night. Already several young kids had been butchered, and were roasting over the cookfires. They had met up with the other group in late afternoon, and so had stopped early, setting up their tents in an open place by a cold mountain stream. Skye was allowed to bathe in the stream, and she delightedly washed her long hair which, despite Zada's care and brushing, was filled with trail dust. Even the prissy Zada was pleased, and afterward brushed attar of roses into Skye's damp tresses.

They returned the few feet to the tent to find Kedar awaiting them. His eyes swept over her, lighting with pleasure at the cloud-soft billow of her fragrant hair. "I want you to dance for my guests tonight," he said. "Do you know the Dance of the Veils?"

"Yes, my lord." Skye was extremely surprised. He was always so strict about shielding her from other men's eyes, and yet he was now asking her to dance before his friends.

"You will dance it then, my jewel, and wear your hair loose like it is now."

"My lord, do you think it wise to display me before others?"

"Are you questioning me, Muna?" His voice was suddenly menacing.

"My lord, I only thought . . ." she began.

"*You thought?* Slaves do not think, Muna. They obey, and although I have given you an order, you are attempting to defy me."

"No, no, my lord! I would not disobey you, I swear it!" Skye was becoming frightened now, and she desperately attempted to placate him. He was in one of those moods where the least thing set him off.

"I think, my jewel, that you need a lesson in deportment." Reaching out, he trailed his fingers in leisurely fashion down her cheek, but his eyes were cold with anger. "You have displeased me, Muna."

Skye shuddered at his touch, and beside her she heard Zada suck in her breath. "Please, my lord!" she whispered, tears filling her eyes.

"Dagan! Get the rods." His voice was toneless.

Skye's heart began to hammer wildly, and she slid to her knees, reaching out to wrap herself about his legs. "Please, my lord, not the bastinado! I am my lord Kedar's slave. I exist solely for his pleasure! *Please*, my lord!" Her voice was frantic with pleading, but in her heart Skye hated Kedar with every fiber of her being. She wanted to take a knife and plunge it into his heart! That he could torture her so cruelly both mentally and physically was appalling to her. *Niall!* She silently cried out to him. *Niall!*

Kedar shook himself loose of her clinging arms. She was pulled roughly to her feet, and her caftan ripped off, exposing her nudity beneath. Then she was once more slammed down on her back upon the floor of the tent. Two slaves were called to hold her shoulders and arms down, and a round ottoman piled with pillows was shoved against her to force her long legs upward. Two additional slaves were called to hold her legs steady, and Zada was ordered to sit across her mistress's hips to hold her down. Skye was already sobbing with terror, and being so successfully immobilized frightened her even more. "Pl-please, m-my lord!" she begged him once more.

"Dagan, begin the punishment," came Kedar's cold voice.

"Twenty strokes, my lord?" Dagan asked.

Kedar debated for a moment with himself, and then he said, "Fifteen. I am of a mind to be merciful, and it is her first offense."

"Please, no, my lord!" Skye was growing frantic now.

Kedar nodded to Dagan and the rod descended. A piteous shriek sounded throughout the camp, followed by several others in fairly quick succession. When she fainted to elude the pain she was almost brutally revived, the bastinadoing stopped until she was fully conscious once more. Then it began again, and Skye felt the pain sweep from the burning soles of her tortured feet up her legs almost to her hips. Pinioned down, she still fought them, begging and pleading with Kedar for the mercy she knew he was not going to give her. Yet she continued to cry out to him in the vain hope that she could touch some cord within him. She struggled to stay conscious lest she offend him further and prolong her punishment.

Sitting astride her hips, Zada whispered to her the number of strokes. "Eleven. Twelve. Courage, mistress! Fourteen. Fifteen!"

It was over. The hold on her arms, shoulders, and legs was released, and Zada arose. With a sob Skye curled herself into a tight ball upon the rug, and wept desperately. Suddenly with frightening awareness she realized that all about her was quiet. Slowly she raised her head. Dagan, Zada, and the other slaves were gone. Only Kedar remained, and the light in his eyes was unmistakable. Dear God, she thought horrified, he couldn't!

"Do you know how much I want you, Muna," he whispered

hoarsely. "Dear Allah, how I want you now!" He knelt by her side, fumbling eagerly for her lush breasts, and she knew that she dare not refuse him. Kedar pushed Skye onto her back again and, pulling his robes up, thrust quickly into her. He pounded against her all the while telling her how she excited him, how watching her being beaten had made his passion rise to the point where he could not deny himself her body. Then without warning he poured himself into her, and fell upon her breasts panting. They lay that way together for several long minutes, and then Kedar recovered himself. Standing up, he looked down at her and said, "You will dance for my guests tonight, Muna. See that you are ready when I call you to me."

She nodded at him, her beautiful blue eyes still wet with her pain and her shame as he strode from the tent. Skye pulled herself up, crying out softly at the pain she felt in her feet, and then Zada was there to help her.

"I have something that will take the pain away, mistress. Dagan brought it to me. He begs your forgiveness."

"He enjoyed it, the brute!" Skye accused.

"No, no, mistress! Dagan would be your friend," Zada assured her as she helped Skye into the privacy of the sleeping alcove.

Skye glowered at the girl. Naturally Dagan would be her friend if he thought that Skye had Kedar's ear. Well, at least his eagerness to be friendly proved to Skye that her position with Kedar was a strong one.

"How lord Kedar loves you!" Zada enthused.

"In my country we do not beat the women we love," Skye muttered irritably.

"Here, we do!" Zada grinned broadly at her. "And then to mate with you afterward! What a man he is! How I wish a man like that had carried me off before my family sold me, but then I am not beautiful like you, mistress. Lie back now and let me put the salve Dagan gave me on your poor feet."

"Will it ease the pain? The lord Kedar commands that I dance this evening."

"You will dance. Never fear, mistress. The master has given orders that you rest, and be fed the choicest part of the kid and other delicacies."

"The veils, Zada. You will have to seek among my things for them."

"The colors, mistress?"

"Black. All black, the better to show off my skin; the black ones with the bits of gold thread shot through them, Zada."

Zada nodded and then knelt to gently smooth the ointment that Dagan had told her to use over Skye's poor red feet. When she had finished, she covered Skye with a light wool coverlet and hurried off to find the veils. Suddenly exhausted, Skye quickly slipped into sleep.

She rested for just over an hour, and then Zada was gently shaking her awake. The slave girl had brought her a plate filled with succulent pieces of roasted kid, small grilled onions and pieces of green pepper, freshly baked flat bread, and a goblet of icy mountain water flavored with orange syrup. Sitting up, Skye found she felt better. She was hungry, and the burning pain in her feet was greatly eased. She finished everything on the plate, and then Zada brought her a small dish of sweetmeats.

"Dagan prepared these especially for you, mistress," she said.

Skye looked at the plump, moist apricots filled with a mixture of chopped and honied nuts, and the colorful jellies that smelled of vanilla, cinnamon, and almond. They were beautiful, and looked absolutely delicious. Skye reached out and took a red jelly, which she popped into her mouth. "This is marvelous," she said, quite pleased. "Tell Dagan I thank him for such delicacies." She ate a second jelly, and then one of the apricots.

"I will go and prepare your bath," Zada said.

Skye lay back munching contentedly upon another apricot and several more jellies. How kind of Dagan to go to such trouble for her, for how, out here along this ancient camel track, he had managed to prepare such delights she couldn't imagine. Perhaps he was not the villain she had branded him. She was beginning to feel quite relaxed and filled with goodwill by the time that Zada returned.

"I have prepared your bath, mistress," Zada said, "and afterward the master has ordered that Dagan massage your body."

"If I get any more relaxed," Skye remarked, "I shall fall asleep."

"It is the jellies, mistress."

"What is in them?" Suddenly Skye wondered if this was some other nasty plot of Kedar's.

"They are made with hashish, mistress. It comes from a plant, at least the tops of a plant. It won't hurt you. Our people have used it for many years, and it's only to make you feel good."

"Eat one!" Skye commanded.

"Oh, may I?" Zada's brown eyes were round with delight, and she quickly popped a green jelly into her mouth before Skye might change her mind. "Thank you, mistress!"

Skye rose to her feet feeling somewhat dizzy, but her mind, though fuzzy, said, If Zada eats them they aren't poison.

"No more now, my lady," Zada chided her. "Save them until just before you must dance. They will inspire you."

Zada helped Skye into the small wooden tub, and Skye noted that tonight the water smelled of roses and musk. She sat quietly as the slave girl pinned up her long hair and gently washed her. Zada worked quickly, and then as quickly dried her mistress. Leading her back to the velvet mattress, she instructed Skye, "Lie upon your belly so Dagan may begin the massage."

I don't want Dagan to massage me, Skye thought in the fuzzy recesses of her benumbed brain, but she couldn't seem to say it aloud. Then she felt the black's supple fingers upon her body, and she didn't care any longer.

Dagan dug his long fingers into her soft flesh with a practiced skill. His clever hands smoothed over her skin with a firm but gentle touch. Up and down her back, her legs and buttocks, her shoulders and arms, her feet. Together he and Zada rolled Skye onto her back, and then Dagan massaged her belly and her breasts, the fronts of her legs and her feet, and shoulders, and arms. Through her foggy consciousness Skye protested, but the black seemed to consider touching her a job, perhaps even a boring job, and nothing more.

When he had finished they let her rest a few minutes, and she floated deliciously through them. She had never felt more relaxed, more sensual. Her head finally cleared just as Zada said, "It is time to dress you, mistress," and helped Skye to her feet. The slave woman clasped a delicate gold chain made of tiny, flat, filigreed links just below Skye's hips. To it she attached three sheer silk veils on each side of Skye, a larger veil in back over her buttocks, and one the same size that hung to her ankles in front. Then, while Skye stood silently, Zada outlined her eyes in blue kohl and painted her nipples in carmine. Her whole body was tingling, and reeked of roses and musk. As Zada brushed her hair with a brush dipped in musk, she said, "Would you like another of the jellies, mistress? Best to have them now, for you will soon dance."

Skye popped several more of the sweetmeats into her mouth, licking her fingers to remove the sticky residue. The euphoria began to return, and Skye suddenly realized that whatever it was that they had put into the confections—hashish, Zada had called it—was most definitely responsible. Every movement she made now seemed exaggerated and sweeping. Zada fastened a small chain about Skye's neck, and to it she attached a veil that fell over her breasts and down past her waist. Another veil covered her shoulders and back, and an even longer one was placed across her face. Zada's lithe hands moved suggestively over Skye's body, fluffing and positioning the veils so they would float correctly.

"You are so beautiful, mistress," she murmured. "You are like a goddess belonging to the old ones. Every man who sees you dance will want you. That is what the master desires, to be the envy of his friends. You must dance your best so that they all lust for you." Zada caressed Skye's breasts and belly and buttocks, her hands moving swiftly, and her words and her movements began to communicate themselves to Skye's blurred and confused mind.

She felt a tingling between her legs, and her beautiful breasts began to almost ache with their tightness. Outside in the main portion of the tent she began to hear music, and with a sly smile Zada fitted her fingers with the four shiny brass tals. "Go," she whispered in Skye's ear. "Go, and drive them wild with your beauty and sensuality. Our lord Kedar will be pleased." Skye stepped out from behind the curtained alcove and walked across the tent to prostrate herself before Kedar.

"Rise, Muna," he commanded her, his hazel eyes quickly taking in the black veils with their tiny golden stars. It was a perfect costume for her, her white limbs glowing mysteriously through the dark silk. "This, my friends, is the magnificent gift that my uncle, the famous Osman, presented to me on my arrival in Algiers. She has easily become my favorite, even though there is a tiny streak of willfulness in her that needs curbing."

"A little spice never hurt a tasty dish, Kedar," remarked a black-bearded man, and the other guests chuckled.

"In that case, Hamid, it is fortunate I am fond of spicy food," Kedar replied, and the chuckles became guffaws of laughter.

Skye let her misty eyes wander about the group that sat eating about a low table. There were seven or eight men, but she could not seem to concentrate upon them or upon much of anything else for that matter. She could still feel Zada's hands lightly brushing her, and rather than repel her the way a woman's touch always had, Skye felt sexually aroused and her passion seemed to be growing instead of fading.

"Dance, Muna!" She heard the command in the murky recesses of her cloudy mind. "Dance for us, my jewel!"

The three musicians began to play, and almost instantly the throb of the drum and the whine of the reed pipes began to communicate themselves to her. Skye began to dance slowly, her body weaving sensuously in time to the music. For some minutes she wove and bobbed across the floor in front of them, and then as the music began to increase in tempo she started to remove her veils.

Kedar and his guests had been watching with mild interest, but now they eagerly leaned forward, fascinated. The six side veils were quickly disposed of, as was the long head veil, and her long hair swung out and floated free with her erotic motions. The music grew more intense as the back and breast veils were tossed aside. Only three veils remained, the two covering her lower limbs and her face veil. Arms outstretched, Skye danced, first thrusting her lush breasts forward, and then pushing out her hips in an obvious and suggestive movement. Around and around she twirled as the tempo of the music grew faster and faster. Kedar chuckled softly to himself as Skye removed the last three veils, for he noted that several of his guests had slipped their hands beneath their robes to discreetly ease their longings.

Now Skye, totally nude, moved closer to Kedar and his guests. Teasingly she clanged the brass tals beneath their noses as she dipped and swooped, almost brushing several of them with her full, red-nippled breasts. She was lost in a hazy world of her own, and only the insistent beat of the drum, the nasal shriek of the reeds, and the erotic movement of her own hungry body held any meaning for her. The men who sat watching were filled with fierce lust for her, the ripe rose musk scent of her voluptuous body, the dance itself; but obedient to the tempo, Skye was aware of nothing but herself. As the music reached a wild crescendo Skye twirled in the final amorous and sexually impassioned movements of the dance before falling to the floor before Kedar, her beautiful body posed in a gesture of total submission to the master.

Kedar's guests roared their approval, clapping and shouting, tossing gold coins and small jewels at her. With eyes wide Skye looked up at Kedar, who was beaming with approval at her. "Take the tributes, my jewel. You have earned them this night."

"They are not half worthy of her, Kedar," said the man named Hamid. "I do not expect you want to sell her, but should you ever grow tired of her I will pay you whatever you desire. She is indeed exquisite."

Skye did not stay to hear any more, but quickly gathered up the tribute showered upon her by Kedar's friends, for to leave it would have been terribly insulting. Then she fled back across the tent floor to the alcove. Suddenly she felt depressed, as if she might cry. Dagan and Zada were awaiting her, the former grinning broadly, the latter chattering delightedly. She gave them each a gold coin, but as she did so Zada noted her sad face and looked quickly to Dagan.

"The master will come soon to pleasure himself, and he will not be pleased to find her weeping," she hissed at the black eunuch.

"Come, mistress," Dagan murmured soothingly, and drew her down upon the velvet mattress again. "Let me rub away the tension you have built up during your dance." He knelt and began to massage her feet, which had begun to ache once more. "Give her the sweetmeats, little fool!" he snapped at Zada. "We have not much time, and she must be eager and ready for the lord Kedar."

"Here, dearest lady Muna," Zada said sweetly, "eat, and all will be well again, I promise you. Oh, how marvelous you were when you danced! We could both see how pleased the master is with you." Zada gently forced several small jellies into Skye's mouth, and then began to caress her breasts. As quickly as the depression had come upon her it began to slide away beneath the tender ministrations of the two slaves. Zada's hand brushed across Skye's belly, and Skye felt her own desires beginning to stir again. Beyond the curtained alcove Zada and Dagan could hear Kedar bidding his guests a jovial goodnight, and they hurried to prepare Skye for him.

Zada leaned over and began to whisper softly and suggestively into Skye's ear. She knew that the hashish in the sugary confections Dagan had prepared had already loosened Skye's inhibitions once this evening. Now just a little bit of suggestion, and she would eagerly welcome the master. "Only a moment more, my lady

Muna," she murmured, "and the lord Kedar will come to you." Zada fondled Skye's breasts gently. "Soon the master will fill you full with his fine big manhood. The pleasure will be magnificent, won't it? Allah, how I wish I might lie beneath him while he pumped himself into me! How fortunate you are, my lady Muna."

"Yes," Skye breathed, "oh, yes! Quickly, Zada, remove the stain from my nipples. My lord Kedar loves to nurse upon my breasts, and I would not poison him." Skye was beginning to feel hot with her longing to be possessed by Kedar. God, how she wanted his bigness inside her, and she wanted it now! He was like a mighty stallion, his stamina being so great. With a smug smile of satisfaction Zada wiped Skye's nipples free of red stain. Skye was already writhing with anticipation. None of them heard Kedar enter the alcove.

For a long moment he stood watching as his favorite black massaged and soothed Skye's feet; as Zada erased the last traces of red from Skye's lush breasts; as Skye herself moved upon the velvet mattress in love's rhythm. He could see that they had drugged her, and he smiled, amused. He liked it that his slaves were so eager to please him, but now he wanted them gone. He was already hard and aching beneath his robes. "Disrobe me!" he snapped, and both Zada and Dagan leapt to their feet to remove his few garments. "Find your own beds," he commanded them, and without even waiting to see them gone, he lay down next to Skye.

"My lord," Skye said softly, turning to face him.

He pulled her into his arms to kiss her, and she obediently opened her mouth to receive his tongue, sucking upon it in a most ardent and suggestive fashion. Her hips glued themself against him, and as he was unwilling to wait any longer to satisfy himself, he rolled her over and thrust into her. To his delight, she gave a soft shriek and climaxed immediately.

"What a hot and wanton bitch you are, my jewel," he purred at her. "Did you enjoy displaying your bounteous charms tonight to my friends?"

"There was no one for me but you, my lord Kedar," she panted beneath him. *"No one!"*

"Ahh," he rumbled, "if I thought that you were lying to me, my fair Muna, I should kill you now, but I know that you are not." His big body moved hungrily and insistently upon her until she was moaning and pleading once more for release, a release it did not yet suit him to give her. For some time he used her, turning her body this way and that in order to enter her from different angles, offering pleasure one moment, pain the next. It was the pain that finally began to clear away the cobwebs of the drug, and Skye realized with shock and self-loathing that she had been encouraging Kedar in a most salacious and lascivious manner. She dared not cease at this point, for she was frankly terrified of offending him. She never again wanted to suffer the tortures of the bastinado as she had this afternoon, and so she continued to behave in a lewd and eager manner until with a grunt he released his seed into her. Then he rolled over and began to snore.

Skye gave a soft sigh of relief. She was furious at herself for not having realized that she was being drugged. Now her mouth felt dry, but at least her heart rate was beginning to slow down from its fevered pitch of a few minutes ago. She rose from their bed, and went across the alcove to pour herself some freshly squeezed fruit juice. As she drank it thirstily, she vowed she would never be given hashish again. She would flatter Kedar into believing that it was an insult to him to feed her the stuff; she did not need such things to increase her ardor and natural passion for him. With a small giggle Skye drank another goblet of the fruit juice. Then, suddenly beginning to feel very relaxed, she returned to the mattress, where she quickly fell asleep.

In the early morning as they sat eating sticky sweet figs, and drinking boiling, bitter coffee, Skye said slyly, "I am glad that you are not angry with Dagan and Zada, my lord. They only did it in their efforts to please you."

"Did what, my jewel?" Kedar was instantly alert.

"Fed me the hashish in an effort to stimulate my senses." She laughed a tinkling, light laugh. "As if I needed any other stimulation than your look, or touch, my lord; but then they did not mean to be offensive to your manhood. They only meant to please you." She licked her fingers delicately. "I will go and dress, my lord, so I do not keep the caravan waiting." With a sweet smile to him, Skye arose and began to pull on her clothing.

"Dagan!" Kedar's voice was sharp, and Skye hid a smile. Her barb had obviously found its mark.

"My lord?" Dagan appeared from the other side of the tent.

"Did you feed Muna hashish last night?"

"Yes, my lord. I made her the jellied confections so dearly loved by the ladies of your harem. Since she had earlier defied my master I hoped to make her more willing to dance. I would not allow her to disgrace you, my lord."

"Your motives were good," Kedar said, "but never feed Muna any of your little potions again, Dagan. Giving her the drug implies that I am not man enough to inspire her. You did not mean that now, *did you*?" Kedar's voice had grown menacing.

"No, no, my lord!" Dagan had felt Kedar's lash too often to court his anger now. He fell to his knees. "Pardon, my lord! I only sought to please you!"

"Only the fact that we cannot tarry in this place saves both you and that busybody Zada from a beating. Be grateful for my mercy, and do not rouse my displeasure again."

"Thank you, master, thank you!" Dagan babbled, backing from the alcove.

Kedar turned to Skye. Her expression was bland and totally disinterested. Demurely she raised up the pale-blue hood of her djellabah. Walking over to her, he tipped her face up to him. "There, my jewel," he said quietly, "Dagan will not feed you any of his little tasties again, but if you had simply asked me, my fair Muna, I would have happily seen to it. It was not necessary to suggest any lack of masculinity on my part. You are beautiful, and I am discovering you are clever, but you cannot hope ever to deceive me." He lightly slapped her cheek with his riding glove, holding her sapphire eyes prisoner with his strange hazel ones. "You will remember that, my jewel, won't you?"

"Yes, my lord," she said, refusing to flinch or lower her eyes to him.

Kedar smiled. "Good!" he said. "Now put on your yashmak and get to the cart."

"Yes, my lord."

He watched her go, a half-smile on his face. She was quite a puzzle, his fair Muna. Woman incarnate, she could drive him to heights he had never before attained with any other, and yet he knew that he had seen only a part of her. She had been wonderfully uninhibited last night, but that had only been the drug. He had instantly sensed when she had become aware of herself again and withdrawn from him, although she had worked very hard to conceal it. There was far more to her than she had revealed to him, and as much as he had enjoyed her lack of inhibitions last night he wanted her to have those same feelings for him within her heart and soul.

Kedar had inherited a little of his uncle's second sight, though he had never sought to develop it. Such development would have taken too much self-discipline, and he did not have the time to devote to it. Still, now and then he could accurately sense certain things or feelings in people or events. There was something special about Muna, his hidden senses told him, and he longed to know her secret. Then he laughed at himself for a fool. Muna was a totally exquisite creature whose sole reason for being was to give him pleasure. Allah had created her to be a houri on earth, and he, Kedar, was the fortunate man gifted with her. There was no more.

Outside he could hear the activity of the camp almost ready to depart. He strode from the tent so they might strike it. Immediately several men swarmed in to dismantle the shelter while both Dagan and Zada hurried out with the tent's scant furnishings packed in small trunks. Walking over to the cart where Muna had already settled herself, Kedar climbed into the vehicle.

Her eyes widened in surprise. "My lord?" she questioned him.

Settling himself next to her, Kedar reached up and loosened one side of her veil, exposing her face. His hand then reached up to cup her head and draw her toward him. He saw the pulse in her slender throat leap, and then his mouth descended upon hers. His kiss was a searing one that demanded her surrender, and her lips softened beneath his. She was breathless when he released her.

"See that your performance tonight outshines the one you offered me last night, my jewel," he said softly as he refastened her veil. Then he vaulted from the wagon, the gauze draperies fluttering lightly with his passage.

Chapter 9

Before them the city of Fez nestled and clung to a cuplike valley, descending from Fez Eldjid, the newer town on the heights of the hills, to the crowded rabbit warrens that made up the most ancient part of the city at the bottom of the valley along the river. At first approach Skye could see only a long line of tall towers and walls surrounding the city, which was seemingly invisible behind the ramparts. She shivered, wondering if once she was behind that seemingly impenetrable barrier she would be able to escape.

As they passed through a huge horseshoe gate into Fez Skye saw that, unlike the cities along the coast, Fez was a dour place. Its buildings were a dirty white with green tile roofs, and from the street the plainness of their walls was broken only by doors. There were no windows visible anywhere, and the facelessness of the structures was rather frightening. Throughout the city stands of trees—cypress, ilex, date palms, and various fruit trees—were welcome green islands dotting the hillsides that tumbled downward into the old city.

Skye would quickly discover that though none of Fez's homes had windows on the street side, the beauty and luxury of their interiors were astounding. She would also find that the wealthy now built their homes in Fez Eldjid escaping the overcrowding of the old city where the magnificent Qarawiyin Mosque, the university where Osman had taught, and all the main bazaars and markets including the famous Quaisarya, the silk market, were also located. For now, however, all that mattered was the fact that she was in Fez, and somewhere in the city Niall Burke was held. She wondered how long it would be before Kedar's young brother, Hamal, would contact her.

Kedar's home was a marvel of several connecting structures built around flowering and fountained courtyards and lush gardens. From the street it was as anonymous as all the other buildings around it, but once inside she found herself in a paradise of incredible beauty. The floors were all laid with small black and white tiles in a geometric pattern. Some of the floors were covered with thick, lush rugs in reds, blues, and golds, or blues, golds, and dark green. The walls were partially tiled in yellow, white, and black, and whitewashed above the tile except in the public rooms where the walls above the tiles had designs carved into their stone. The ceilings in all the rooms were painted magnificently in various colors, in incredible geometric patterns and designs.

Dagan had escorted Skye and Zada to the women's quarters of the house, a separate wing consisting of baths, kitchens, gardens and terraces, salons, dormitorylike bedchambers, and private bedchambers.

"How many women are there in the master's harem, Dagan?" Skye asked as they had hurried along behind him.

"I am not certain of the correct number, my lady Muna, but it is over forty, I know."

Two coal-black eunuchs pulled open a gilded wrought-iron double gate, allowing them entry into the harem area. Dagan brought them to the main salon, where at this time of day most of the women were settled chattering, sewing, playing musical instruments, or reading. At their entrance there was immediate silence and hostile eyes swung toward Skye, assessing her beauty and her worth to Kedar, and instantly classing her an enemy.

Dagan grinned delightedly to discomfit them. "The master sends you all his greetings upon his return, ladies. This lovely creature by my side is the lady Muna, a gift to our lord Kedar from his uncle in Algiers. She is in his favor."

"Perhaps along the trail, where the only other choices were diseased nomad wenches, sheep, and camels," said a voluptuous blonde with almond-shaped black eyes. She looked insolently at Skye, and popped a small apricot into her mouth.

"How do you keep your hair *that* color, my dear?" Skye asked in flawless Arabic. "In my own country I had a brace of hunting dogs with fur that same hue." Her look was bold and it dared the other woman to retaliate. In a harem of this size Skye knew that only the very strong survived.

The blonde gasped and scrambled to her feet. "How dare you!" she shrieked as she leapt the small distance between Skye and herself, her fists upraised.

Skye didn't wait. Hooking her fingers into the blonde's hair she grasped hard, and flung her opponent across the room. "How dare you!" she replied. "In my own land I am a great lady. Here I have found favor with my lord Kedar. We need not be friends, but you will treat me with the respect due my station. I am not, like you, some peasant wench thrust into a better situation. You will remember that in the future."

The blonde sprawled among a pile of pillows, arms and legs akimbo, her mouth open in complete surprise. The room was deathly still, and then there was a throaty, amused laugh as a tall, very elegant woman stepped forward from among a group of women. "Welcome to Fez," she said. "I am the lady Talitha, now only occasionally in our lord Kedar's favor, praise be to Allah." Talitha's skin was the color of molten gold, her black hair cut short so that it clung caplike to her skull in kinky curls. Her eyes were a wonderful shade of light green. With a smile she turned to Dagan. "Is she to have a private chamber?"

"Yes, lady, and you will see that none of the others mark her. He is adoring of her flawless skin."

"I shouldn't wonder," Talitha said. "Don't worry, Dagan, I will care for her as if she were my own child." She then turned her gaze upon the other women in the room. "You heard," she said in a suddenly hard voice. "Anyone who touches Muna will answer first to me and then to our lord Kedar. Frankly I don't believe any of you soft, overripe bitches are capable of taking on this one, but be warned nonetheless."

"You will be safe now," Dagan said, and then he left Skye and Zada.

"Come with me," Talitha said, and they followed her from the salon. "There is a lovely room available overlooking the mares' meadow and the mountains beyond the city walls."

"Are you in charge of the harem?" Skye asked.

"I have the honor and the burden of being Kedar's harem mistress," Talitha replied drily. "I was the first woman he ever bought.

I have two daughters by him, but as his appetite has grown his need for me is less."

"Do you love him?"

"No, but I am grateful to him. I was born in a brothel in Rabat. My mother was a whore of Berber and Negro origin. My father was her French lover. I know that for certain because my mother did not enter the brothel until after my father left her, and she was already pregnant with me. She was a beautiful woman, and so she went to the finest brothel in Rabat and offered to sell herself to them if they would wait until she had borne her child. They gave her the gold on which to live comfortably until I was born, and then she joined them. I was raised there, and Kedar bought me from the brothel owner who felt that, at twenty, I was a bit too long in the tooth to satisfy his customers. I am therefore grateful to the master. I have a good home. My children are safe, and I am respected. Ah, here we are." She flung open a beautifully paneled wooden door, and they entered into a lovely bright room. "What about you, Muna?"

"I am a captive," she said. "The lord Osman bought me to give to the lord Kedar."

"For a captive you speak our language quite well," Talitha remarked.

"I was in the bagnos for several months, and I fortunately have an ear for other tongues."

"Were you ill that you were kept in the bagnos, or," here she cocked her head, "were you, as I suspect, loath to accept your portion."

Skye laughed. "I needed convincing," she admitted. "You must understand, Talitha, that I am an Englishwoman, a respectable widow with children. The thought that I should never see my babies again, never return to my own land, was not only frightening but heartbreaking to me."

"But now you accept your fate?" Talitha looked a little disbelieving.

"What choice do I have?" Skye asked.

"And our lord Kedar?"

"He is different from any man I have ever known," Skye said slowly, not quite sure what it was Talitha wanted her to say.

Talitha laughed. "He is a hard man, Muna, but believe me, there are worse masters. All Kedar demands is perfect obedience in his bed. The rest will be easy if you are not a gossip, for he hates those whose tongues wag incessantly.

"You'll probably be spared his company for a while, however, as you have had him all to yourself these last two months. Kedar needs variety and, like a large honeybee, he will now begin to go from flower to flower until he is sated once more." She smiled mischievously at Skye. "I imagine you can use the rest, Muna. Our lord and master can be quite exhausting, and I don't believe I have ever known anyone who spent two solid months catering to him. It is indeed possible you are the first woman to be that long with him."

"I will do whatever my lord commands me," Skye said sweetly.

Talitha laughed once more. "You *must* be in Kedar's favor," she said, amused. "Well, we shall see! I will leave you and your servant now to rest," she ended and, turning, left the room.

The door had no sooner closed behind her than Zada began to chatter busily. "What a fine room! Look at the view, my lady Muna. These carpets are very good, aren't they? Ohh, the couch is large, isn't it? I imagine the lord Kedar will visit you here, for you are in his favor. How fortunate we are to have such a rich master! We can be very happy here, but of course it would be wise for you to become pregnant as quickly as possible. Dagan says that the lord Kedar will probably marry you, and never before has he taken a wife. What an honor for you!"

"Be silent, chatterbox!" Skye said. "Don't you realize that harem walls have ears! The lord Kedar is undoubtedly quite tired of me by now and, as the lady Talitha has said, will seek solace among the variety of his other women. You must expect nothing, Zada."

"If he were bored, mistress, you would not have been given this fine chamber with its beautiful, thick rugs, silk hangings upon the wall, and a couch large enough for two people."

Skye ignored her servant's babble and, changing the subject, said, "Find out where the baths are, and if I may bathe at any time I choose. It has been over a month since we left Algiers, and in all that time I have not had a decent wash. I want a bath as quickly as possible."

"Of course, you must be perfection when our lord Kedar comes to you tonight."

Her mistress ignored her remark, and Zada hurried from the

room, full of importance and certainty. Skye frankly hoped that Talitha's assessment of the situation was the correct one, and that she would not be troubled by Kedar for several days at the very least. She looked about the room. The walls were tiled halfway up, as was the rest of the house, in lovely turquoise blue and pure white. Above them the wall was painted white, and the wooden moldings were stained a dark brown. The white ceiling had large, dark beams, and between each beam was painted a design of turquoise blue and black swirls and dots. The dark-stained wooden floor had a large thick carpet in shades of gold and white with a knotted white fringe. There were several small square carpets in turquoise and white beneath the windows, and two that were oval-shaped, one on either side of the large couch.

The couch itself was a square set upon a gilded dais. It had a large feather and down mattress, and was covered in turquoise-and-gold-striped silk. There were wonderful large pillows, both plain and embroidered in several shades of rose, upon the couch. The room also had some nicely designed carved chairs, and two brass tray tables, one large, one small, as well as both hanging and portable lamps in ruby glass, brass, and copper.

As Zada returned she was preceded by several eunuchs who brought in Skye's beautifully fitted trunks and, at Zada's instructions, set them about the room.

All the eunuchs but one departed, and Zada introduced the one. "This is Min'da, your personal eunuch, my lady Muna. You see, I told you that you were important to our lord Kedar," she finished smugly.

Skye lightly slapped Zada's cheek. "You are overproud, Zada. I am blessed by Allah to have our lord Kedar's attention. May I always be able to please him. But if Allah should will it otherwise, then may I accept my portion as gracefully as I now accept what he has given me."

The eunuch, a light-skinned Negro, half smiled. "You are indeed wise, my lady Muna. Dagan says that you will go far, and it may be that he is correct."

Skye's eyes met those of the eunuch. He was his master's man, of that she was certain; and Zada would also be loyal to Kedar. She was truly alone. What if Hamal had decided at the last minute not to help her? What if Niall had finally pushed the princess beyond her endurance, and been killed during the month in which she had been traveling from Algiers to Fez? How could she get word to Osman, and even if she did how could he help her now? Skye was tired, dirty, and under emotional strain. Helpless tears filled her eyes and threatened to spill down her cheeks.

"You, Zada!" Min'da snapped. "Help me to get your mistress to the baths. She is exhausted, and needs to be bathed and then allowed to rest." He put a strong arm about Skye. "Come now, my lady Muna, and let me help you."

Skye sagged against the eunuch, relieved for the moment to have an excuse to put her worries from her mind. She did need a bath, and she did need to rest. From the first day she had met Kedar, over two months back, there had not been a night she hadn't been forced to cater to his whims, except for the few days when her link with the moon was broken and she was considered unclean. She let herself be led off, and within minutes was soaking and steaming all her worries and troubles away.

Min'da was obviously well respected among the bath women, for they did not seem to resent either his presence or his quick orders regarding her comfort. "What is your fragrance?" he asked her quietly.

"Damask rose," she said softly, and he nodded, his eyes approving.

"It is the perfect fragrance for you. Few can wear its blend of sophistication and innocence well."

The bath women exclaimed with delight over Skye's fair skin, fairer than that of any of the other harem women, they said. The Fasi aristocracy prized fair skin, in both men and women alike. They also were lavish in their praise of her hip-length black hair, which they washed gently, lathering a wonderful rose-scented soap into thick suds that gently removed the trail dust from her beautiful tresses. Twice they washed her hair, afterward rinsing it thoroughly, the final rinse a mixture of herbal vinegar and water for shine, the bath mistress said.

Skye was beginning to feel relaxed. She had been washed, pumiced, and denuded of the little body hair they could find on her. Now, while two young slave girls dried and brushed her hair, she lay on her stomach and enjoyed an expert massage. A most soothing rose lotion was smoothed over her skin and rubbed into her body with long, firm strokes. She didn't even protest when they massaged her breasts and belly.

Skye was but half awake when they stood her up, slipping a white gauze chamber robe over her now clean body. Min'da lifted her in his arms and carried her back from the baths to her room, setting her gently upon her large couch. "That was wonderful," she murmured at him, and he smiled down at her.

"Are the tears gone now, lady Muna?"

"Yes," she said and, closing her eyes, appeared to sleep. With a satisfied nod the eunuch left the room, giving instructions to Zada as he went.

"Let her sleep for exactly six hours. I will be ready then with a meal for her, and the master will join her at the eleventh hour tonight. Do you understand?"

"The lord Kedar will visit her tonight? *Really?*" Zada's eyes were round with satisfaction, and her smile was a trifle smug.

"I have said it, woman," the eunuch snapped. "I do not say what I do not know or mean. Remember that in future. If we are to work together for lady Muna's eventual triumph over the rest of the women then you must obey my instructions and not question me, Zada. I have been in lord Kedar's harem for seven years now, and I know all there is to know, and more."

"If you are so important, Min'da," Zada retorted, "then tell me why it is you have not succeeded with one of your charges before?"

"I almost did two years ago," was the reply, "but the ungrateful wretch escaped my vigilance, and was caught cuckolding my lord Kedar with one of his guard. The little fool almost destroyed me and had it not been for Dagan's intervention, I, too, might have died. Dagan, however, convinced my lord Kedar that I was not to blame, and he spared me. I have been used on general duty in the harem ever since, but today Dagan once more gave me my own charge, the lady Muna. I will succeed with her, and if you follow my lead, Zada, you will also find yourself in a place of honor, as personal maid to our lord Kedar's only wife. You would like that, wouldn't you?"

Zada nodded, now more respectful, but also still curious. "Why is Dagan so good to you?" she asked. "Why should he care if you succeed or not?"

"Dagan is my brother," Min'da said, and then he haughtily stalked from the room.

Skye had heard it all, and with Min'da's final words to Zada she again felt depressed. Min'da had obviously been the personal eunuch to the unfortunate girl from Cathay whom Kedar had beaten to death. Now given a second chance, he would be virtually impossible to elude, and if she could not evade his watchfulness how could she aid her beloved Niall? With a little sob Skye turned her face into one of the pillows and wept softly. *Niall!* she cried in her heart. *My darling husband, where are you? Niall!* Without even realizing it, she fell into a troubled sleep, a sleep made restless by faceless and frightening images that arose from the depths to haunt her; and while she fought against her tortured dreams Niall Burke fought against a nightmare of another kind.

Skye would have been shocked by his appearance had she seen her husband now. Eight inches taller than his wife, his months in the galleys had hardened his elegant frame, giving him strong muscles where once there had only been their suggestion. Still, he was far too thin.

His big nude body was spread wide upon a large couch, his long arms and legs manacled to prevent his escape. His midnight-colored hair was longer, and his silvery eyes were now the lackluster gray of dirty pewter. The elderly crone who served as his female eunuch had already fed him with the spiced drink that was always ordered for him before these sessions with Turkhan. At first he had refused to drink it, and spit it out when they forced it down his throat. There had been no admonishments on his behavior, but the next time a tube of sheep intestine was jammed down his throat into his stomach, and the liquid poured through it. The third time the cup was again handed to him, but the female eunuchs stood by ready to use the tubing should he prove difficult. Niall Burke had drunk down the potent liquid then, having no doubt in his mind that they would use force again if they had to.

He was already beginning to feel the peculiar euphoria that began shortly after the liquid entered his body, and to his disgust his anxieties were once more melting away as his breathing began to grow slower and more shallow. He seemed to lose control of himself every time they pressed the goblet on him and induced him to drink, and he didn't understand it; but then as his inhibitions slid away he demanded petulantly of the eunuch, "Rabi, where are my sweets?"

The old one cackled merrily. "So eager, so eager," she said. "You are always so eager for the comfits, Ashur. Open your mouth then, and I shall pop them in. You will like them tonight, for they are your favorite—vanilla."

Obediently Niall opened his mouth, and Rabi fed him the candies. The jellied squares with their bright jewel colors fascinated him. They tasted so good, sweet, and strongly vanilla-flavored. They had never had anything like them at home in Ireland. *Ireland!* Dear God, would he ever survive to get back there again? He had to survive! That was why he so docilely accepted the spiced drink and the sweets they fed him each time Princess Turkhan wanted him in her bed.

In the beginning he had fought her like a madman, and they had chained him like an animal in her garden until he had regained some measure of sanity. He had welcomed his release from the Turkish galley where he had been incarcerated since his recovery from Darragh's attack. He had almost lost track of the time, for that was how it was when one's life was confined to a rower's bench. When, however, he had learned that he had been purchased to serve as a stud animal to an Eastern princess, he had gone wild. He had tried explaining to Turkhan, who spoke fluent French, their one common language, that he was an aristocrat in his own land; that he was willing to pay whatever ransom she desired; that he had a beautiful wife and two children he longed to return to in Ireland; that he was Lord Niall Burke.

"I shall call you Ashur," had been her answer. "Do you know what Ashur means, my tall one? It means *warlike one*, and I can tell," here she ran her tiny hand slowly over his bulging biceps, "that you are indeed a fierce warrior."

Nothing he had said had penetrated her brain, he decided, and so he began to explain again. Turkhan had waved her hand impatiently, saying, "I heard you the first time, Ashur, now you will hear me. I am not interested in purchasing captives for ransom. I am a wealthy woman, a connoisseur, a collector of beautiful things; and you are a beautiful thing. Never have I seen such blue eyes, my tall one. I suspect that you are a good lover, and I shall teach you to be an even better one, I promise you."

"*Never!*" he spat angrily at her.

Turkhan had laughed, a deep velvet sound, the sound of a woman used to getting her own way. "Do you know to whom you say never, Ashur? I think you do not or you would not be so bold.

I will therefore forgive you your mistake, and tell you who I am. I am the daughter of Sultan Selim II of the Ottoman Empire, defender of the true faith and overlord of this city."

"I don't give a damn who your father is," Niall had shouted at her. "I won't be your stud, woman! I'm an Irishman, not a prize stallion!"

Her eyes had narrowed with annoyance. "Whoever you *were*, my beautiful Ashur, you *are* no longer. Whatever was is no longer. Your only reality is what you are now, and that is Ashur, a slave in the harem of Princess Turkhan. Your goal is to please me, your mistress; and Ashur, you *will* please me, I can promise you. *You will please me*."

It gave Niall Burke small satisfaction to know that so far he had not really pleased her. She was beautiful, he had to admit. By any culture's standards she would have been considered beautiful. She was not a tall woman, standing barely over five feet in height; but she appeared taller, for she had a regal bearing along with long and slender arms and legs. She held her beautiful head high, her flame-colored hair cut straight across her forehead, hanging turned under just below her shoulders. She had an oval face with an aristocratic nose, a lush red mouth, and almond-shaped eyes fringed in thick black lashes that were the amber gold of a lioness. Her body was slim and lithe like a boy's, except for large, marvelous breasts that thrust proudly from her chest.

He had learned in the year he had been imprisoned in her palace that she was a well-educated and an intelligent woman; but she was proud and stubborn, too. Despite his constant refusals, despite the fact that every time they made love she had to force him to do it, in spite of his atrocious behavior, she had made him her favorite along with the boy, Hamal, who had been in her harem some three years, and was genuinely in love with her.

That was an interesting situation, Niall thought as he lay awaiting Turkhan. Hamal had told him that he had been born a free man also, but that his older brother, a wealthy merchant, had sold him to the princess. Hamal didn't seem to mind at all, as he cared for his mistress and she obviously cared for him. Niall smiled to himself. Whether Turkhan realized it or not, the boy manipulated her to suit himself; but unfortunately, he had not been able to help Niall. The princess had determined that Niall was to father a child on her; but he was equally determined that she would not have his child. No son of his was going to be mothered and raised by *her*. Niall had rarely resorted to prayer in his entire lifetime, but he prayed now that the flame-haired bitch who held him captive would not conceive his child. So far his prayers had beeen heard.

Only Skye had ever given him children, his darling little daughter, Deirdre, and his only son, Padraic. Dear God, the lad had barely been born when he had last ridden off from Burke Castle. What did the boy look like now, Niall wondered, and Deirdre, too. Had Skye mourned him long? Was she still mourning him? Had she remarried? She had never been a woman to be without a man for a long time. He wondered whose wife his wife was now? The thought of her with any other man maddened him beyond reason.

Dear God, Claire O'Flaherty had had her revenge on them all! If he ever got free of Fez, he was going to search the she-witch out himself, and kill her once and for all. He could yet remember awakening aboard a rocking ship to find her standing over him, gloating. He hadn't understood why she was there, or even how she had gotten there, but he knew he was not dreaming. Before he had even had a chance to question her, he had slipped back into an unconscious state.

"You look so fierce, my beautiful Ashur," Turkhan murmured as she slid onto the bed next to him. Her little white hands began to slide across his body, caressing and seeking the sensitive places that would arouse him. "What is it you think of, my beautiful one?"

"I think of deceit, and of revenge, my Princess," he answered her.

Turkhan shivered at the dark depths in his eyes. "I command you to think of passion instead," she said.

Niall's harsh laughter rebounded off the walls. "It shall, of course, be as you command, my Princess," he answered her mockingly.

"Oh, Ashur," Turkhan whispered, allowing her vulnerability to show for just a brief moment, "is it really so difficult to love me?" She lay her sleek head on his chest, and it occurred to Niall that he had been going about this thing all wrong.

For months he had been fighting her, and it had gained him nothing. What a fool he had been! If he had appeared to give in to her demands from the start he might have gained her trust, and escaped months ago. Instead he had behaved like a violated virgin. What an idiot he was! Skye had always accused him of not seeing the overall picture, of being impulsive and heedless of the havoc his quick actions wrought.

His mind snapped back to the present. Turkhan, having stimulated his manhood to erection, was preparing to mount him as she always did. "Unchain me, my Princess," he said quietly. "I think it is time I showed you how an Irishman makes love to his woman."

She looked suspiciously at him. "What game is this you play with me, Ashur?"

"Are you afraid, my Princess?" was his slightly mocking reply.

Her pale skin flushed with the open challenge, and she licked her lips. For months she had been forced to compel his participation, and although he claimed to be the father of children, she could not conceive. She had filled him with opiates and hashish and other well-known aphrodisiacs to insure his potency. Perhaps the secret lay in his being willing.

"Don't you want to feel my arms about you, Turkhan?" he murmured gently. "Unchain me, lass."

The tone of his voice made her shiver openly, and Niall knew that he had won. Slowly Turkhan arose from the wide couch, walked across the room, and opened a small carved ebony box. Removing the key from the box, she returned to the couch and unlocked the four manacles that had held him prisoner. While she returned the key to its hiding place, Niall Burke sat up, rubbed his wrists, and swung his long legs over the bed. Every movement he made felt exaggerated to him. It was always so after they fed him with the jellies, and the goblet. Still, he realized that he suddenly felt very good. His big body was burning with desire, his erection was yet quite firm, and now as his blue eyes swept over the beautiful and petite creature standing before him he had but one thought: to couple with her. It was what she wanted, and right now it was what he wanted as well.

Reaching out, he pulled her against him and bent low to find her lush mouth. "What an incredibly beautiful little bitch you are," he said against her lips as he pressed teasing kisses against them; and Turkhan shivered again, her mind half fearful, half thrilled that he was at last yielding himself to her. Niall lifted her tiny frame up in his arms, and set her gently on the soft feather and down mattress, then joined her.

"Oh, love me, my beautiful Ashur!" she whispered frantically.

"I will love you, my Princess, but there is no great hurry. I promised you that I would show you how the men of my land love their women." He leaned over her, his fingers brushing back her soft hair. "Do you want me, Turkhan?" he asked her.

His gentle touch was destroying her, Turkhan thought, but she could not help herself from gasping, "Yes, Ashur! Allah, yes, I want you!" His satisfied growl of laughter frankly frightened her, but she dared not move lest she break the spell and he revert to the sullen and angry man that he had been until just a few minutes earlier.

While she lay so still, her golden eyes lowered modestly, Niall took the opportunity to examine her closely. Her skin had the same texture and color of the milk-white roses that grew in her garden. He slid his hand across her flat belly, enjoying the softness, and heard her catch her breath. Niall smiled to himself. She was a hot little piece. He moved a hand up to fondle one of her big, cone-shaped breasts, rolling the large coral nipple between his thumb and his forefinger. Turkhan moaned, and catching his head in her two tiny hands, she drew it down to her breasts. He laughed at her impatience, but nonetheless took the offered nipple in his mouth to suck upon it, worrying it faintly with his teeth, and sending tiny darts of delight through her entire body.

Turkhan couldn't believe the pleasure that Niall was giving her. She had never allowed any man to take the lead when making love with her, and yet she suddenly realized that she didn't want him any other way. Let Hamal, her little lamb, love her gently with tender touches and wailing Persian love songs. But Ashur! Allowed his own way, he was loving her with a fierceness she had never known, and she adored it!

He had now transferred his attentions to her other breast, and when he had finished with it he began kissing, nipping, and licking at her skin. Turkhan almost screamed with rapture, especially when his head dipped to the V between her legs and he began nuzzling at the secret of her womanhood. No man had ever kissed her *there*, or loved with his mouth the tiny pearl of her femininity. She wasn't even sure that it was right, but she was now past caring and she didn't want him to stop. Something strange and frightening and yet wonderful was happening to her. She felt a sudden tightness, then a swelling, and then an incredible burst of pleasure unlike anything she had ever felt before—and it was only the beginning of the delight. She was suddenly beneath him and he was filling her full with his great and pulsing manhood. Turkhan almost swooned with bliss, for never had she lain beneath a man. She had been told that a woman mounted the man, as that was the only way he might obtain pleasure. It was an incredible and magnificent experience. He was driving deep and fast inside her, and she began to moan, her flame-colored tresses whipping around her thrashing head as she lost control and her world dissolved about her. Turkhan arced her body upward to meet his thrusts. Her long nails raked his back, leaving bloody weals across it as a primitive scream exploded from her throat only to be stifled by his brutal kiss, which was the last thing she remembered before plummeting down into the raging darkness.

Regaining consciousness, she began to laugh softly with the irony. She had once told him pridefully that she should make a better lover of him than he was, but now Turkhan knew better. He had taken her where no man had ever taken her, and now she knew that all these years she had been only half a woman, that before Ashur they had all cheated her. She rubbed her kiss-bruised lips gingerly and, opening her eyes, looked directly at him.

"Why didn't you tell me?" he demanded of her.

"Because until just a little while ago, my beautiful Ashur, I did not know myself," she answered him candidly.

He didn't believe her. "You grew up in a harem," he snorted scornfully, "surrounded by women, and you never knew the pleasure that can be between a man and a woman? They never told you?"

"I was sent from my father's house when I was ten years old," she said quietly. "My mother was a Circassian dancer in my father's harem who just happened to catch his eye one time. That one time was enough to get her pregnant, but my mother was obviously not interesting enough to retain my father's favor. He never called her to his couch again, and she died giving birth to me. I was given to one of the other women to nurse, but once it was no longer necessary that I have milk to survive I was left to myself. I was nobody's child, Ashur. My grandmother, Khurrem, took an interest in me for a while, but as I grew they tell me I began to resemble Cyra Hafise, my father's grandmother who had been my grandmother's mortal enemy.

"When I was almost ten years old my father needed monies for his fleet, and word was sent to all the great cities of his empire. Fez responded so generously that my father's curiosity was aroused. He was told that the largest contribution, indeed three quarters of what had come from the city, had been given by one Ali ibn Achmet. Further investigation revealed that Ali ibn Achmet was the city's wealthiest merchant, an old man who had never married, but was very devout and extremely loyal. At my grandmother's urging, my father decided to reward Ali ibn Achmet's generosity and loyalty by presenting him with an Ottoman princess for a wife.

"The choice was left up to my grandmother, and she chose me, saying, 'Although you look like the cursed Cyra Hafise, you are *my* granddaughter, and more like me in your actions than any of the others. This is your chance, little Turkhan, and I shall give you the best piece of advice I can. Be soft-spoken, appear meek, but never let *anyone* own you. This includes your husband, my child. Let no man truly own you. Amass all the wealth you can, and when the old man we send you to dies, be sure he has named you his only heir. Do whatever you must to insure that inheritance, but gain it, for wealth is your guarantee of power, little Turkhan. Wealth, and your inviolate position as an Ottoman princess.'

"That, my Ashur, is the only thing I learned in my father's harem. I learned nothing of love, or of women's ways; but I consider what my grandmother, Khurrem, taught me the most valuable lesson I have ever learned in life.

"I never knew until tonight the real pleasure that can be between a man and a woman. This you have taught me, and if it never happens again at least I shall be content having known it once."

My God, Niall thought, *what a complex and sad woman she is*. "It can happen again, Turkhan, and it will," he promised. "Shall I make it happen for you again, my Princess?" Leaning over her, he brushed her lips with his own, but all the while he was thinking that he had at last found a sure way to control her. A few nights of unending delights, and she would be *his* slave. Reaching out, he crushed one of her breasts in his hand while he murmured with hot breath in her small ear, "Answer me, Turkhan! Do you want the pleasure again?"

"Yes!" she whispered urgently. "Yes, my Ashur! I want it!"

Niall marveled afterward that he had not thought to cooperate with his captor before. For all her position and wealth and power, Turkhan was like any other woman in love. Niall knew that he would have to move very carefully else he arouse suspicion. Already young Hamal questioned his motives.

"I do not understand this sudden turnabout," Hamal said. "For months you have battled with Turkhan to regain your freedom."

"While you, our lovely mistress, and everyone else here has told me that regaining my freedom is an impossibility. I am a thick-headed Irishman, Hamal, but I now believe you all. If my life is to be here then I am better off cooperating, aren't I? Besides Turkhan is an exquisite woman, and I am a healthy man. I could resist her no longer."

"What of your wife?" Hamal demanded. "Do you no longer think of her, Ashur?"

He shrugged fatalistically. "Skye undoubtedly believes me dead, and has probably remarried. It has been almost two years now, and she would need a strong husband to protect Burke lands and my small son's inheritance. My father is an old man, and could not aid her." He lost heart once more, for his spoken thoughts could very well be the truth. She probably had remarried, and he was never going to return to her or to Ireland. Yet deep in his heart he still believed that Skye belonged to him, and to him alone!

"You belong to me, and me alone," Kedar murmured against her mouth as she lay half conscious beneath him. He thrust his enormous lance hard into her quivering sheath, and she shuddered with shamed pleasure.

Skye had hoped for a respite from Kedar's lust once they had reached Fez, but his ardor had only seemed to increase. She was the object of much speculation within his harem. Many were jealous of her, and more were fearful of her influence over their master. Skye would have laughed if the situation were not so absurd, and she would have been terribly lonely had it not been for Talitha. The beautiful harem mistress sensed that Muna did not enjoy being the exclusive object of the master's affection. Skye was also nervous because Hamal had yet to contact her, though surely he must know that she had arrived.

"Open your eyes, my jewel, and ravish me with a look," Kedar commanded her, his passion spent.

Skye slid back into the here and now, looking at him with her cool gaze. "You are a magnificent lover, my lord," she said honestly, and that was something else that was beginning to bother her. He was an incredible lover, and of late she had been genuinely responding to his lovemaking. She simply couldn't help it. Skye had experienced enough at thirty to know the difference between love and lust, but still it distressed her to give this man anything of her real self. She was prostituting herself in order to help Niall, but to enjoy it seemed wrong. She sighed deeply, and he mistook her motives as he usually did.

"We will make love again this night, my fair Muna," he said in an amused and indulgent tone. "It pleases me that you are losing some of your shyness, and are becoming as insatiable for me as I am for you."

She laughed lightly. "It is impossible not to want you, my lord," and she boldly caressed his cheek with a teasing hand.

He caught her hand and, turning it palm up, placed a moist and burning kiss upon it. "You delight me, my jewel, and I would reward your behavior. Tell me what you would like?"

Skye paused a moment as if in thought, and then said, "Would you allow Talitha and me to visit the bazaars in the old part of town, my lord? I have not spent my pin money since I arrived. The vendors who come to the harem do not bring with them a great variety of goods, and there has been nothing that I desired."

What a delight she was, Kedar thought tolerantly, once more amused by the simplicity of her request. He was also feeling somewhat pleased with himself for his firm handling of this beautiful slave of his. She was responding perfectly these days, and had been worth every moment he had spent on her. He chuckled aloud. How feminine she was, wanting to shop the bazaars, and how intelligent not to waste her precious dinars on the cheap baubles and bangles the vendors brought into the harem to sell. More and more he considered the possibility of making her his wife. If only she would conceive a child. He turned his hazel eyes upon her.

"So you would visit the bazaars, Muna? Very well, my jewel, but you and Talitha must be well veiled, and well guarded. I will have no one making free with either of you. You may go tomorrow."

"Oh, thank you, my lord!" Skye wound herself around him, her beautiful arms entwining themselves about his neck, her breasts pressing suggestively against his smooth chest. Her pouting red lips invited his kiss, and while he tasted her mouth she reached down and fondled his manhood with clever hands until he was hard and eager again. Never interrupting their embrace, she moved herself over him, guiding his length into her warmth. Kedar pulled his mouth from hers and groaned with pleasure as she moved on him with a fierce rhythm. His big hands tangled themselves in her dark hair, and he muttered almost incoherently against her mouth. Skye slipped her arms about his middle, and lifted her legs to wrap them about him. Kedar gave a growl, shifted his weight, and pushed Skye back onto the pillows, taking control of their lovemaking once more as the pleasure began to build for them both.

She tried to fight it back, but her body would not obey, and instead she soared upward. The feeling built and built until Skye believed she was going to burst with the burning bliss that raced through her veins. He was commanding her to tell him how much she wanted their passion, and terrified that he might stop, she said the words that she knew he wanted to hear, then felt more shamed than ever. Like boiling wine, the perfection poured over her, and somewhere in the timelessness she could hear his howl of victory. Her last thought then was that she must find Niall before it was too late; she must escape from this terrible man before he destroyed her completely.

Afterward, as they lay together in the quiet, he said, "Never has any woman given of herself as you give to me, my jewel, and yet I cannot have enough of you. You are as much an aphrodisiac to me as the hashish and the opiates. I have never felt for another woman that which I feel for you."

"You honor me, my lord," Skye replied softly, but her mind was wild with panic at the thought that he was falling in love with her, that he might attempt to make her his wife. He could do it even without her consent, for in Islam a wedding was held with just the consent of the bride's father or guardian. In the case of a slave, a master need only arrange it with the local iman. She tried to calm herself with the thought that Osman would have foreseen such a thing, and not put her in such a position. What a disaster it would be if Kedar married her, especially with her husband still living! No, Osman would have foreseen it, Skye reassured herself as Kedar pulled her into his arms and fell asleep.

When she awoke the following morning she was alone, the imprint of his head on the pillow the only evidence that he had been there at all. She was no longer required to sleep on a cushion below him, and that, Talitha had told her, was quite an honor. No other woman in the harem save Muna and Talitha was accorded that honor. Skye stretched lazily, but her mind was already active with a hundred different thoughts. Today they would visit the old town with its bazaars, and hopefully she would have an opportunity to find out where the residence of Princess Turkhan was located.

The door to her room swung open. "So," Talitha said with a merry chuckle, "you have wheedled a trip to the bazaars for us, my clever Muna. You must have indeed pleased Kedar last night. He came early to my chamber, smiling and purring like a well-fed panther, to tell me that I would accompany you. Tell me, Muna, what is your secret with him? In all the years I have known Kedar he has never been so expansive and so generous." She hefted a well-filled purse in her palm. "Gold dinars, Muna! A purse full of gold dinars from our lord and master to be used by us for our heart's delight. *What do you do to him?*"

Skye sat up, her cheeks pink with her blushes as Talitha's frank gaze took in her nude beauty. Reaching for a cobweb-thin pink wool shawl, Skye said, "I am only his obedient slave, Talitha."

Talitha's mouth quirked with amusement as Skye modestly pulled the shawl about her. "You are a strange one, Muna. There is an air of mystery about you. Perhaps it is that which fascinates Kedar so very much. At any rate, thank you for including me in your little adventure. We shall be the envy of the entire harem. Hurry and dress! I don't want to waste a minute of this day. It has been a long time since I last left this house, and I am eager to go."

As Talitha hurried out, Zada came hurrying in with a tray of food. "Allah only knows when you'll eat again," she fussed at her mistress.

"I am ravenous," Skye admitted.

"I am not surprised," was the reply. "The women of the harem say that the lord Kedar never stops his lovemaking during the entire night. I wonder that you can lift your head from the pillow this morning. Ohh, they are all so jealous of you, my lady Muna! He is going to make you his wife. They all say it is so. I knew that you would be successful with him!" She placed the tray upon the little table by the couch.

Skye didn't bother to answer Zada, for she knew that anything she said would be repeated and embellished upon until her words were totally unrecognizable. Instead, she concentrated upon the meal that her slave woman had brought her. There was a lovely polychrome ceramic Fezware bowl in white, blue, and orange that was filled with peeled green figs. A matching plate held flat bread, hot and fresh from the oven, and there was a second bowl with a honeycomb in it. A silver goblet studded with lapis was filled with limewater. Skye ate hungrily, and when she had finished she rose, allowing Zada to wrap her in a gauze robe so she might walk to the baths. The slave woman followed carrying her mistress's special soaps and scents.

Zada's black eyes darted back and forth as they moved through the harem. Fully aware of the envious gazes thrown at Skye, she puffed out her chest with pride as they moved quickly along, feeling enormously pleased with herself for having such an important and beautiful mistress. Already the servants of the other favored ones were beginning to come to her with little gifts and gossip. When the lady Muna became the lord Kedar's wife, *his only wife*, Zada would be the most influential serving woman in Kedar's harem. She smiled smugly to herself as they entered the bath, considering how fortunate she was.

The baths were empty this early in the morning except for the bath attendants, who had been alerted that the lady Muna would be bathing and tumbled over themselves in their efforts to serve her lest the master's favorite be displeased. Skye silently allowed them to do their job, and when they had finished with her she thanked them each with a smile, then returned to her quarters with Zada to dress.

"Do not deck me out like an idol," she snapped at Zada, who wanted to run bracelets up and down her arms, bering each of her slender fingers, and place a fillet dripping with small jewels on her head and forehead.

"You are the chosen of the lord Kedar," Zada protested.

"I am only my lord Kedar's humble slave," Skye insisted. "If you deck me out in every jewel he has given me you will draw attention to me, which would displease my master. A show of wealth will also encourage the merchants to charge me double, Zada. I would look like all the faceless women in a plain black yashmak."

Zada sighed disappointedly, but allowed that the lady Muna was probably right, and dressed her as she desired. When she had finished Skye was as anonymous as every other black-garbed figure in the streets of Fez would be. The top of the yashmak fell just below her eyebrows, and her outdoor veil was securely pinned to it. Only the barest slit for her eyes was allowed. She could have been twenty, or eighty; the fairest woman alive, or the ugliest; but no one in the streets of the city would know it.

"Are you ready, Muna?" Talitha's voice emerged from an equally well-swathed figure.

Kedar had arranged for them to travel in a curtained litter, for it was unthinkable that his women walk to the bazaars. Skye couldn't resist peeping at the city from behind a corner of the curtains as they moved from Kedar's house at the top of the ravine, down the twisting, winding streets to the bottom where the markets of old Fez were located. She was enchanted by the one-arched bridges that spanned the river, a contribution of the Moors who had settled in Fez when driven from Spain. Skye noticed how crowded together the houses were as they descended lower and lower into the most ancient part of the city. It was also darker here, for it seemed almost impossible for the sun to find a place to slip between so it might shine. Finally Skye let the curtains fall back into place, and following Talitha's lead loosened her face veil.

"What made you want to visit the bazaars?" Talitha asked.

"I don't like being penned up," Skye said. "In my land women move about freely. I even ride horses. I cannot stay in that house all the time else I go mad. When our lord Kedar asked me last night what he might gift me with I begged him for a day at the bazaars. It means more to me than jewels could."

"No wonder you fascinate him, Muna. You are so unusual for a woman."

"There are other European women in our lord's harem," Skye said.

"Yes," Talitha admitted. "We have girls from Provence, the Languedoc, Castile, Naples, and Genoa, but not one of them was from a noble family as you are. Two are merchant's daughters, but the rest are peasants, and all are used to obedience to higher authority, as are the women of the East. You, however, belonged to the higher authority, Muna."

"I answered to my Queen," Skye said.

"Not your king?"

"England has no king. Our Queen is a virgin without spouse who rules in her own right."

"Incredible!" Talitha exclaimed. "Such a thing would never be allowed here. A woman needs a man to answer to else she be unnatural."

Skye almost laughed at Talitha's outrage. There were many who thought Elizabeth Tudor odd and unnatural. Before she might comment though, the litter was set down with a tiny bump and the curtains drawn aside. Quickly they refastened their veils as Min'da carefully helped them out. "I will escort you, and the litter will follow us," he said.

Together Skye and Talitha began walking through the busy and noisy bazaars, starting first with the Quaisarya, the magnificent silk market. It was an incredible place, and Skye was at a loss as to where to look next. The stalls were filled to overflowing with a profusion of marvelous silks in a rainbow of jewel-bright colors. There were plain colors such as scarlet and emerald, topaz and sapphire and amethyst; and prints, deep purple with gold dots, crimson with silver, black and cream; and gauzes shot through with silver and gold; and silks in all colors sewn with freshwater pearls and jewel chips. It took a while for her to overcome the shock of so much beauty before she could intelligently choose and make her purchases. Finally she picked a rose-colored silk gauze shot through with silver, and a lovely blue-green that matched her eyes. These she would have the harem seamstresses sew into garments for her.

Leaving the Quaisarya, they moved on down a narrow street, visiting the various shops inhabited by gold- and silversmiths. As they stood admiring bracelets in one of these, a handsome young man entered. He was as slender as a willow, of medium height with fair skin, dark, curly hair, and meltingly soft brown eyes.

"My lord Hamal," the shopkeeper said, hurrying forward. "I have the earrings that you ordered ready for you."

"Good day, Hamal," Talitha said.

Skye's heart was hammering wildly. There could hardly be two Hamals of Talitha's acquaintance, and therefore this had to be Kedar's younger brother. She wanted to scream that she was Niall's wife, to ask if her husband were alive, but she dared not.

"My lady Talitha, what do you here? I did not realize that my brother was in the habit of allowing his women to visit the bazaars, or has his harem finally revolted and strangled him?"

Talitha laughed. "You grow more wicked each day, Hamal! Tell me that you are not truly happy with the princess."

Hamal grinned boyishly. "I am happy, Talitha, although I doubt that when Kedar sold me to her he meant it to be so. Who is this shy creature hiding behind you?"

"This is Muna, your brother's new favorite, and rumored to become his wife soon. We would not be here but that she pleases him so he allows her to visit the bazaars."

Hamal's eyes flicked casually over Skye. "So Kedar finally thinks to take himself a wife. I cannot imagine my brother caught by that most tender of passions, yet if you say it then I must believe it. What is your secret, lady Muna? How did you capture my brother's cold heart?"

"Pay no heed to Talitha, my lord," Skye said softly, "she but teases you with harem gossip. I am naught but my lord Kedar's humble slave. Nothing more."

"Where do you come from, my lady? Your speech is that of my friend, Ashur, who is a favorite of my princess."

"There are no men named Ashur in my land, my lord."

Hamal smiled pleasantly. "Ashur is the name that my princess has given him. It means strong and warlike one. The name he bore in his own land was Niall Burke."

"Then we are indeed from the same land, my lord Hamal. The name I bore in our homeland was Skye."

"Excuse me, my lord," the goldsmith interrupted, "but are the earrings satisfactory?"

"As always, Yusef," Hamal said graciously as he examined them. "Your work borders on genius. The earrings are perfect, and Princess Turkhan will love them." Reaching into his robes, he drew out his purse and paid for his purchase. Then he turned back to the two women. "We will meet again soon, my ladies," he said, and bowing, he went from the shop.

It was all Skye could do not to run after him and beg for news of Niall. Obviously he was still alive, from what Hamal had said. At least she had that, and Hamal's promise that he would see her soon.

"He is quite different from our lord Kedar," Skye remarked to Talitha.

"Yes," Talitha said. "It is strange to think that they come from the same mother, and yet they do. If Kedar is fierce and strong, then Hamal is gentle and tender. Still, they are brothers."

"Is lord Hamal married to a princess?" Skye asked innocently.

Talitha laughed. "No. Kedar sold his brother to the princess when the boy was fifteen. It is an odd situation, Muna. The princess is the daughter of the Sultan in Istanbul, and as men keep a harem of women, she keeps one of men."

Skye pretended to be shocked. "Why, Talitha, that is as outrageous to me as my Queen is to you!" she said.

Talitha laughed again. "I suppose it is all in the eye of the beholder," she said good-naturedly. "Do you see anything that you like here?"

"Yes," Skye said, and she bought a beautiful gold aigret holder with three perfect white feathers, the gold studded in small sapphires. "For my lord Kedar to thank him for this day," she said sweetly.

They moved on to the street of the cobblers and spent a good deal of time trying on slippers of various styles, finally settling on several pairs each. When the voice of the muzzin sounded from the topmost pinnacle of the Qarawiyin Mosque they knew it was midday and, like everyone else in Fez, they fell to their knees facing east for the prayer period. Upon rising, both Skye and Talitha admitted to hunger, and Min'da purchased small hot lamb kebobs from a street vendor for them. They ate the kebobs greedily, licking the last bit of tasty grease from their fingers while Min'da bought water from another vendor for them to drink; and sweet dough balls deep fried and then dipped in honey and chopped almonds for a treat.

For another hour or so they wandered happily through the open markets, and Skye was fascinated by everything she saw. Beneath gaily striped awnings sat the street merchants, their merchandise spread out before them for all to see. Farmers from the surrounding countryside came with their produce, the various fruits and vegetables piled high. Others had cages and pens of live animals and poultry for sale. There were rug merchants, copper and brass smiths with trays and bowls and lamps, leather goods from the tanners, and cloth merchants with their silks, cottons, velvets, wools, and gauzes blowing in the afternoon breeze. There were horse traders and slave merchants. Skye watched frightened and sad as a fair-skinned girl with long blond hair was sold to a fat man with the tiny eyes of a boar who pinched and prodded her mercilessly before finally making his purchase. Tears rolling down her face, the girl was led away.

"Let us go back," Skye said quietly, her joy in this short day of freedom totally spoiled.

"It is the way here," Talitha said. "Let that scene remind you how fortunate you are. We are among the privileged slaves. That poor girl was just bought by a local brothelkeeper."

"How can you know that?" Skye was saddened even further for the blond girl.

"I do not for sure, of course, but I recognize the breed from my younger days."

"I can bear no more," Skye said, and turning, she climbed back into the litter.

"So that is your weakness," Talitha remarked as she joined her and pulled the curtains shut. "Do not let the others in the harem see that you are so softhearted, Muna. They will use it against you. Nothing would please them more than to destroy you."

"You do not want to destroy me, Talitha."

"I do not seek to catch the lord Kedar's attention. I have had enough of that in my youth. I am content to rule his harem for him, and enjoy my daughters."

As they returned to Kedar's home high above the old city, Skye took the opportunity to find out where the princess lived. Turkhan, it seemed, was no different from all the other wealthy people in Fez, having a large pink palace in the newer part of the city, but some distance from Kedar. They arrived back safely, and Min'da escorted them to the enclosure of the harem, which was surprisingly quiet and empty but for serving women and the children.

"Ha!" Talitha said with wisdom born of long experience. "I will wager he is in the mares' meadow, Muna. Quickly, let us go to your room, and we shall see."

Puzzled, Skye followed Talitha to her chamber, where they found Zada peering eagerly through the latticework. "What is it? What are you watching?" Skye demanded of her servant.

Zada turned, her brown eyes large. "In the meadow below," she said low. "The master and his women."

"You could have gone," Talitha said, amused. "It is not forbidden for pretty servants to join in the sport held in the mares' meadow, Zada."

"I would not go unless I had my mistress's permission, lady Talitha."

"What a loyal child she is," Talitha remarked, further amused. "Come, Muna, and see what games our lord Kedar plays today."

They moved to the lattice-covered windows and looked down. Skye caught her breath in shock. Below her, the mares' meadow, a well-clipped green lawn dotted with trees, was filled with the women of Kedar's harem. All were naked and posed upon all fours. Their hair had been bound up, and to each woman's head was attached a curved polished brass headpiece from which flowed a horse's mane. A narrow gilt belt encircled each woman just below the belly, and at the base of their spines thrust forth a polished brass holder from which sprang a matching and stiffly arched horse's tail. Kedar was garbed in the same outlandish equipment, but as the women stood still as if mares browsing, he in his role of stallion moved among them, mounting them from the rear and thrusting into them. The women giggled as, finishing with one, he snorted and whinnied triumphantly as would a great stud stallion. He then moved on to another of his "mares," his erection still plainly eager.

Skye turned away, embarrassed by the tableau below her.

Talitha laughed softly. "You do not like his games, Muna? The eunuchs bet among themselves as to which woman will cause him to spill his seed."

Before Skye might reply Dagan entered her room, saying, "I was given orders by my lord Kedar that you and the lady Talitha were to join him in the mares' meadow if you returned in time. I have brought your things." He placed two sets of manes and tails on a table.

"Go and fetch a third for Zada," Talitha commanded, and with a grin Dagan left the room.

"I can't," Skye protested.

"If you refuse him it will be the bastinado, and afterward he will think up some particularly bestial delight to shame you with before the other women, Muna. Do not think because he considers making you his wife that he will be one bit more lenient with you. Kedar will not be disobeyed, and you know it."

"He will use me before them all," Skye said low, and she began to tremble.

"Yes," Talitha said, refusing to coddle her. "He will take you before them all, and if you cry and shake you will give the other women a weapon that they will delight in using against you. Like all men skilled in the sensual, Kedar enjoys occasional perversions. Show distaste for his little game in the mares' meadow, and those few women he owns who keep his interest only by their skill at perversion will think up delights that will have you screaming in your dreams for months to come."

Skye drew a deep breath in, and said, "I will go, and I will somehow manage not to show my revulsion at the situation."

"Good," Talitha encouraged her. "Remember you have what all those bitches wish they had. He cares for you. I even believe that if Kedar were capable of love, he would love you. Make him proud, and show them that you are his true mate!"

His true mate. The words reminded her of Osman, that he had once believed that Niall was her true mate. Was Niall forced to submit to such degradation as Princess Turkhan's favorite as she was forced to here in Kedar's harem? Skye pushed the troubled thoughts from her mind. She had at last met Hamal, and she was confident that he would shortly contact her and arrange their—her and Niall's—escape from Fez. In the meantime she must concentrate on getting through the rest of the afternoon. Quickly she removed her clothing.

Skye stood silent and still as Zada did up her hair, and Talitha's and helped them with the headpieces. She watched the other woman as she affixed the belt with the horse's tail, and then copied her by putting on her own. The mane and tail were a silky ebony black, and shone quite effectively against her gardenia-white skin.

Mischievously Talitha tossed her golden mane, which complimented her own golden beauty. "Any eunuch who bets against you will lose his dinars," she remarked, "yet I wonder if Kedar can contain his lust until he is in you."

"Hush!" Skye scolded her. Suddenly seeing the humorous side of the situation, she began to giggle.

Talitha chuckled back at her. "I know just what you are thinking, Muna. You are aware that men can be fools, are you not?"

"Yes," came the reply, "now be silent lest I disgrace myself with a fit of laughter down there, which I can assure you will be far worse than if I trembled and wept."

Dagan returned with a headpiece and tail for Zada, who had torn off her clothing in her eagerness. They waited the few minutes it took the slave girl to prepare, and then followed Dagan downstairs and outside to the mares' meadow.

"Go into the center of the meadow, and I will tell the master that you have come," Dagan whispered.

The three women picked their way through the others, and reaching the center of the green lawn, they knelt down on all fours. Talitha had a rather bored look upon her face. She had done this Allah only knew how many times before, and it all seemed rather silly to her. Kedar visited her couch often enough to keep her from being totally frustrated, for she had been his first woman and he still found her rather attractive and exciting. She had never fawned over him like the others, and he found her elusiveness intriguing.

Zada, on the other hand, was trembling with excitement at the thought that the master might honor her. She was not a virgin but it had been some time since she had had a man, although Dagan liked to fondle her, and push his supple fingers into her until she whimpered with pleasure. It wasn't the same, however, as having a real man's weapon shoved up inside you, Zada thought, and prayed that she would be fortunate.

Skye simply knelt, resigned to the fact that Kedar meant to have her else they would not have been called to the meadow. At least the grass felt cool beneath her hands and knees.

She heard a horse whinny near her, and then Zada gasped. Turning her head just slightly for a moment, Skye saw Kedar mounted upon her servant, pounding hard into her. Zada's face was a study in pure bliss, and Skye turned away, ashamed that women could be driven to welcome such degradation. With a moan that could only be described as rapturous Zada collapsed into the lawn, and Kedar moved on to enjoy Talitha. A small boy eunuch hurried along with the master, wiping the spendings from his encounter away with a soft cloth moistened in rosewater, finishing just as they reached Talitha. Kedar circled the kneeling woman, snorting and pawing. Talitha responded by pretending to shy away with a nervous little nicker. With a grin Kedar pounced upon her, thrusting quickly back and forth until she too collapsed with a little shriek. The little eunuch swiftly refreshed his master, and then Kedar's eyes swept to Skye.

She braced herself discreetly for his assault. As with Talitha, he first circled her, and unable to help herself, Skye shifted nervously on the grass. Kedar snorted an equine warning and moved closer, nuzzling at her bottom, causing her to start warily. His big hands now closed over her hips, and she felt his hardness beginning to prod at her. She tensed, remembering her first husband, who had punished her when it pleased him by forcing her in the Greek fashion, but Kedar was not interested in loving her as he might a boy. With unerring skill he found her woman's passage, and drove deeply into her. Slowly he began to move back and forth within her, growing more excited as the moments passed. She knew she could not remain passive and please him, and so she began to tighten her vaginal muscles about him, teasingly nipping at him with the devil's bite. With a growl he pushed her down upon the grass, and bit at her neck. "Vixen," he murmured, and then his passion burst within her.

They lay sandwiched together for some moments, and then he whispered in her ear, "I waited all afternoon for you to return so I might have you, my jewel. You have spoiled me for the others, you beautiful bitch. I am only satisfied by you."

Her heart was still hammering wildly, but she knew that she was expected to respond to such ardor. "What a wonderful day you have given me, my lord. First the bazaars, and now your loving. I am the most fortunate of women!"

"You do not mind that I have taken you before the others?"

"I prefer that our love be between us alone, my lord, but I am not ashamed to show it before the others. You will, however, make them even more envious of me than they already are."

He rolled off of her and, standing up, pulled her up with him. His arm was wrapped tightly about her waist, her breasts pushing against his side. She looked up at him, her sapphire eyes never wavering, and Kedar wanted to ravish her once more where they stood, she excited him so. "The day is not yet ended, my jewel," he murmured, and bent to kiss her slowly and tenderly. "I adore you, my fair Muna," he said low, and then, releasing her, called to the others, "The games are ended, my pets. Return to the harem, all of you but Talitha and Muna."

The women began trooping back into the house while the young eunuch sponged down his master with rosewater, and Dagan and Min'da removed the trappings of the games from Talitha and Muna. They then loosed the women's hair, and after brushing it out, took a small portion of it from the center of their heads and braided it with a strand of small pearls. Kedar put an arm around both of his favorites, and they began to walk slowly back to his quarters. It seemed not to bother him that they were all nude.

"You have both pleased me greatly of late," he said expansively, "and so I have a special treat for you. Today while you shopped in the bazaars I had a visit from my brother, Hamal. He brought with him an invitation to dinner at Princess Turkhan's palace. The princess, it seems, has become interested in expanding her own trading empire. Right now she sends her goods to the coast via the services of others, but Hamal has convinced her that she should save a great deal of money if she had her own caravans. I would not have thought that my brother had a head for business, but it seems that he may. He has told her that if she would send her own people to the coast to buy and sell then I am the best man to speak with about it.

"Two days from now I am invited, and of course if I go for the evening meal then I am also invited to remain the night, for it would be too dangerous to travel the streets after dark. The invitation allows that I may bring two of my favorites with me to make my night a pleasant and happy one. I have chosen you two, Talitha and Muna."

"My lord Kedar," Talitha quickly spoke up. "How generous you are!"

Skye's heart was pounding wildly, but she controlled herself so she might speak her gratitude also. "My lord Kedar, we are unworthy of such pleasure. How can we thank you?"

He stopped and, smiling down into her upturned face, said, "By giving me a preview tonight of the pleasures you will give me two nights from now. You and Talitha are perfectly matched with your white and gold skins. It would give me great pleasure to see you make love to each other before I take you both."

For a moment Skye thought she had not heard him right, and then realizing that she had, the world began to crumble about her. She was tumbling back through the years to a time when she had surprised her first husband in an incestuous act with his sister Claire; and they had seen her; caught her and raped her. She had had a horror of any intimacy with a woman since then. It had been months in fact before she could even let her maid touch her. Now she was being faced with the thing in the world she feared most.

Talitha saw her turn her white face, and sensed instantly that something was very wrong. "My lord Kedar," she said, "you know that I would not spoil your pleasure for the world, but I do not believe that Muna has ever made love with another woman. She is apt to be clumsy at first, unless, of course, you will excuse us for the next two days so I may school her to please you. It will be well worth the wait, I promise you," she tempted him, and then bent and bit at his shoulder in a provocative manner looking up teasingly at him from beneath her thick lashes. "Did the girl you took before you delighted me this afternoon please you? She is Muna's maidservant, and really quite mad for you, my lord. She would keep you amused this night, I vow."

Kedar licked his lips in anticipation. He was disappointed, but he knew that Talitha was right. It would be better if Muna had some knowledge of what would be required of her, and the little Berber savage had been a hot piece. She might prove an enjoyable one-night diversion. "Very well," he growled, "but see you teach her well, Talitha." He gave them each an affectionate pat on their bare bottoms. "Go to your own quarters, and send the Berber girl to me."

"Of course, my lord, immediately," Talitha murmured soothingly, and grasping Skye's hand firmly, she hurried her off before Kedar could change his mind.

"I can't do it," Skye protested as they re-entered the harem. "I simply cannot do it!"

"You do not have a choice, Muna. I saw how horrified you were, and so I rescued you before you did something foolish like refuse Kedar. I know it still chafes at you, having once been a free woman, but you are no longer free. Kedar has the power of life and death over you, and you know that he is not an easy man. If he desires that we make love together for his amusement, then you have no choice but to obey him. Do not worry. I will show you what to do, and it will not be so terrible, I promise you."

"No," Skye said. "I would rather die."

They had reached Skye's chamber, and Talitha pulled her into the room, commanding Zada as she did so, "The master desires your company, fortunate one. Hurry lest you keep him waiting and displease him." With a little cry of delight Zada ran from the room, and Talitha turned back to Skye. "Have you gone mad?" she snapped at her. "If it pleased Kedar to kill you he would do it so painfully that your last hours would seem like years. Are your childish scruples worth that, Muna?"

"Once," Skye said in a small, tight voice, "once long ago, a woman forced me, and I wanted to die for the shame."

Talitha sighed. So that was it. Muna had been raped by a woman at one time in her life. "It won't be rape between us, Muna. It will be two friends seeking to give each other gentle pleasures, and nothing more. We are friends, aren't we?"

"I cannot do it," Skye whispered.

"You have to," was the equally adamant reply. "Come." Talitha put an arm about Skye, who instantly stiffened with alarm. "You will have to overcome your fears, at least to Kedar's eye. What we do means nothing, Muna. Please try."

"What will it be?" Skye asked.

"No more than a little kissing and caressing, Muna. Not really so awful. Let us sit down, and I will show you what is expected of us." She drew Skye over to a low divan, and together they sat down amid the brightly colored cushions. Gently Talitha began to caress Skye, and it was all Skye could do not to scream with her revulsion. It was not that she disliked Talitha, but the memory of Claire O'Flaherty's bestial abuse of her kept leaping to mind. She began to weep soundlessly, and seeing her tears, Talitha kissed them tenderly away. "There, my lovely friend, don't weep. It is not so awful, is it? Women are far more considerate lovers than men, Muna." She continued to speak gently to Skye for some minutes, all the while kissing and caressing her. Skye steeled herself against her embarrassment and distaste, finally admitting to herself that there simply was no other way. If she was to survive, if she and Niall were to escape safely from Fez, she must accept even this.

Talitha now began to instruct her as to what she must do, and without further protest Skye obeyed her friend. Only when they lay stretched out together on the cushions and Talitha lowered her head to kiss Skye's Venus mont did Skye resist once more. "Oh, no, Talitha! Please not there!" Talitha pushed Skye's hands away, and with a sigh Skye ceased her outcry, forcing her mind to think only of Niall Burke.

Finally Talitha said, "There! Now that was not so awful, and you were fine, Muna. Tomorrow we will practice a little more, and you must participate fully then."

"Talitha, I can force myself to stay still when you kiss and touch me intimately; but I will not be aggressive with you. I cannot; it is not my nature. I think women loving women is an unnatural thing."

"For some women it is the preferred way, Muna."

"Not for me," Skye replied. "Not ever!"

"You prefer Kedar?"

"I prefer a man's touch."

Talitha laughed at the way Skye had avoided her question, but held her peace. "Let us eat the evening meal together after we visit the baths," she said. "From the look in Kedar's eye your Zada will not be back until morning, and I will wager he shortly sends for others, too. You would think that his little games in the mares' meadow would exhaust him, but such things seem to increase his appetite rather than diminish it."

It was a relief to Skye that after their initial session of lovemaking Talitha returned to her normal self. Uncomfortable as she was, she believed that now she had met and identified herself to young Hamal her stay in Fez would soon be at an end. Then she and Niall would be free, and returning to Ireland, to their children and a normal life. She wondered if she would see Niall when she visited Princess Turkhan's palace in two days. More than likely, he would remain incarcerated behind the harem walls, and she would be kept locked with Talitha in a guest apartment. They would be so close, and yet separated. "But not for long," Skye whispered to herself. "Not for long, my love."

"What is it you say, Muna?" Talitha inquired of her.

"What?" Skye was drawn sharply from her reverie.

"You said something just now," Talitha repeated.

"I did?" Skye shook her head. "I cannot remember," she said, "and so obviously it was not important. Not important at all."

Chapter 10

*H*amal led Niall Burke into the large gardens that were a part of Princess Turkhan's estate in Fez. The gardens were the only place where the two men might speak without being overheard. No one followed them to listen, for Hamal was the most trusted of the princess's slaves, and of late his companion had been far easier to manage. They strolled along a path of carefully raked marble chips, lined by tall, fragrant cedar trees. Ahead of them was a rose garden filled with brightly colored flowers. The sight of it reminded Niall of Skye, a thought he pushed from his mind. He could not afford to weaken now.

"Did your wife ever speak of her friend in Algiers, Osman the astrologer?" Hamal asked him suddenly, and Niall stopped in mid-stride.

"Yes," he said hesitantly. "Why do you ask me?"

"Osman is my uncle, Ashur. Last year he came to Fez, which is his native city, in order to teach for a few months at the university. We spoke of you, and my uncle recognized who you were immediately. We decided then that you must be helped to escape. Do not cry out, my friend, but your wife is here in Fez. She is a brave woman, and from the moment she learned that you lived nothing would do but that she free you."

"*Where is she?*" Niall's pulses were racing madly.

"In the house of my brother, Kedar," Hamal said.

"She has brought a ransom large enough to tempt the princess?"

"Have you heard nothing we have told you these past months, Ashur? *There is no ransom.*"

"I do not understand then," Niall replied.

"Your wife has come to Fez in order to encourage you in your escape from the princess. She could only enter the city as the member of a Fasi household so she and my uncle Osman devised a plan wherein she would pretend to be a slave girl and he would present her to my brother Kedar when he made his yearly visit to Algiers. This was done, and your wife came to Fez as a slave named Muna, in the harem of my brother Kedar."

"Christ's bloody bones!" The oath exploded from Niall's mouth without warning, and Hamal looked nervously about him.

"Be silent, Ashur!" he begged the big man. "Do you not realize the danger we are all in because of this plot? If Turkhan learns what I have done we will both die, never matter that she loves us. Think of your wife, too."

"'Tis precisely what I am thinking of, Hamal, for I am no fool to believe that a man who would sell his own brother into slavery would bring my wife to Fez out of the goodness of his heart. Kedar is not in on this little game, is he?"

"No," Hamal replied low. "He believes her a slave, and has used her as such. She has, in fact, become his favorite, and there is talk that he will make her his only wife. I had planned to wait a little while longer in hopes that he would grow bored with her, but he grows more enamored of her with every day that passes. We no longer have the luxury of time."

"The little fool," he muttered low. "'Tis just the sort of thing that Skye would do to come after me." He smiled softly. "Wait until you see her, Hamal. She is the most beautiful woman ever created, and of even greater import is her spirit. Her spirit is unconquerable! She is a great and gallant lady, my Skye!"

"She would have to have a strong spirit to survive with my brother. Kedar is not an easy man," Hamal replied. "I spoke with your Skye two days ago in the shop of Yusef the goldsmith. How beautiful she is, though, I could not tell. She was properly muffled in a black yashmak. We will see her and my brother tonight, Ashur."

"*What?!*" Niall was surprised.

"Turkhan has decided to expand her trading empire, has asked my brother, Kedar, to come for the evening meal. He is allowed to bring with him two women, and I expect that your wife will be one of those women. They will stay the night, and then in the morning Kedar and the princess will discuss business."

324 · *All the Sweet Tomorrows*

"Is there any chance that I can speak with her?" Niall's voice was hopeful.

"No, Ashur, my friend, there is no hope that you may speak with one another. Turkhan would be furious should any lovely woman speak to you, and Kedar is a fiercely jealous man." He put a friendly hand upon Niall's arm. "You will have to be very brave, my friend. It will not be easy to sit calmly paying court to Turkhan while Kedar is cared for by your wife."

"How can I possibly behave normally seeing my wife in the hands of your brother, Hamal?"

"You have children, do you not, my friend? Think of them if you will not think of yourself and your wife. Would you orphan the babes who cannot remember you? Would you deny them both their parents? Your wife must bear you a great love to have dared this deception. How often have you told me of the insurmountable obstacles that you and your Skye overcame in order to be together? Before you destroy the small chance you have of being together once again think of what she has gone through for you, and do not let her sacrifice be a vain one, Ashur."

Niall sighed. "Why are you helping me, Hamal? Is it merely so you may have Turkhan to yourself again?"

Hamal smiled at the question. "You are the first serious rival I have had for Turkhan's affections, Ashur. None of the others mean anything to her. They are passing fancies, toys, simple amusements. You, however, are a different animal. I am not afraid of you, for I know that your heart is elsewhere and always will be, even if you are forced to spend the rest of your life among us. Were I certain that I might have rid myself of you by the usual harem means, I would have; but had any harm befallen you, I would have been under immediate suspicion. Though you know it not, I have twice saved your life. Turkhan's pretty pets are a jealous lot, my friend.

"I love Turkhan, and I always have. Although Kedar does not know it, I went out of my way to bring myself to Turkhan's attention three years ago. In the beginning I saw becoming her favorite as a means to gain my own place in this world. Kedar would never have shared our father's wealth with me, and had I allowed him to see how really intelligent I am, he would have kept me beneath his thumb for all my days. I would have never been really free.

"When I came to the princess I intended to work my way into her favor, and eventually gain control of her wealth for myself. I am, in truth, the product of my brother's upbringing. But I had had very little experience with women other than stolen kisses and fondlings of the slave girls in Kedar's house. I was a virgin when I arrived in Turkhan's bed; a fifteen-year-old boy who, despite his outward face of confidence, was in actuality quite terrified. What if I failed her, and she sent me from her forever?

"She was nineteen then, and very experienced. Experienced enough to know that I was untutored. She was gentle and kind, Ashur. She taught me to make love as the Turks make love, and I began to gain skill and faith in myself. I also fell genuinely in love with Turkhan.

"I still mean to have her wealth, and to run her trading empire. My time is almost near, Ashur, for when you leave her she will be devastated and turn to me for comfort. Then I will act, and become a free man once more, rid Turkhan of her harem, and make her my wife. That is how it should be. I will never take other women into my life, for she is all the woman I ever want, but I must be all the man she wants."

Niall looked at Hamal with new respect. Until this moment he had believed him just a soft and kindhearted boy. Now he knew better, and it frankly surprised him. "How will you help us to escape?" he said, coming directly to the point.

Hamal spoke in a controlled voice. "It will take a few more weeks to complete my arrangements, but I plan that Turkhan shall insist that Kedar escort her personally from here to Algiers through the Taza Corridor, so the princess may see the route herself and visit the port city. That is when you and your wife shall both escape, for I am certain neither the princess nor my brother will travel without their favorites."

Niall could feel himself trembling with excitement. Hamal made it sound so simple, so easy. How could he wait a few more weeks? His heart beat erratically, and he drew several deep breaths to calm himself. "I think that I need some of Rabi's special brew," he said to Hamal. "I am as eager as a virgin for her bridegroom."

"Yes," Hamal answered. "You must not betray us, Ashur, by any undue show of enthusiasm. Let us return to the palace now, and seek out Rabi and her sherbets. They will soothe you, and take the edge from your excitement. We will speak again, and I will fill in all the details that you must know."

Back within his own chambers, Niall eagerly downed the special

fruit sherbet that old Rabi had made for him, his hands trembling
as they clutched at the cup. *Skye!* Tonight he would see Skye! She
knew that he lived, and she had, brave and bonny lass that she was,
come to aid him. God's bones, how he loved her!

Rabi noted his mood, and commented, "How excitable you are
today, Ashur. What has made you so?"

"Hamal tells me that his brother will be visiting the princess
tonight, and that we are going to be allowed to have the evening
meal with them. I am excited that my lady Turkhan trusts me
enough to allow me such an honor. I am also curious to see the
brother of my friend."

Rabi cackled and, standing above him, stroked his dark hair in a
motherly fashion. "Indeed, my handsome charge, you are being
allowed a very special privilege. Not only will Hamal's brother be
there, but his two beautiful favorites as well."

"They cannot possibly rival my princess for beauty," Niall said
quickly.

Rabi cackled again, this time with delight. "You are falling in
love with her, Ashur! It is good! It is good!" The old woman
lowered her voice, and spoke confidentially. "Please her, and you
will soon control her. Give her a child, and you will be master of
this harem! Your fortune will be made, Ashur, and not even the
gentle Hamal will surpass you in power!" She patted his arm, nodding wisely. "Rest now, my big one, and I will call you in time."

He didn't argue, sleeping easily for several hours before Rabi
woke him and hurried him off to the baths. There, he allowed the
elderly women who served as bath attendants to wash him, all the
while enduring the hostile stares of the other young men in the
harem. Turkhan kept about twenty males in addition to Hamal and
himself. Most were of Mid-eastern extraction, but the princess did
have a red-haired Venetian, two Greeks, a blond and over-muscled
young Swedish boy who, like Niall, had been taken from a galley, a
surly Russian, and two slender blacks from the forests to the far
south. That they were jealous of him was very apparent. Since Niall
had arrived the princess had spent much time with him, at their
expense. They refrained from any open action now because they
had already tried once to teach this upstart his place, only to have
been badly mauled by the infuriated Niall. They had also been
whipped by their furious mistress, and threatened with being sold
off. More subtle means had been blocked by Hamal who, after

their second attempt at poisoning Niall, had threatened to tell Turkhan if it happened again. That would mean an excruciatingly painful death, and none was willing to risk that. So the men of the princess's harem vented their frustration on Niall through verbal means.

"How does an Irishman fuck?" one of the Greeks said.

"Like a pig," the other answered.

"No, my friend. Pork is forbidden a true believer, and our fair princess is a true believer."

"Then he must fuck like the dog he is," a dark-eyed Egyptian said.

Niall smiled pleasantly at the group of men. "I thought that only Greeks fucked each other like the dogs they are," he said. "As for the rest of you," and he looked mockingly at them, "you've nothing left to fuck with, impotent eunuchs that you are. No wonder that Turkhan prefers only Hamal and myself. Hell, my infant son had a bigger pizzle than any of you have."

"If it weren't for the potion that old witch gives you, Ashur, you wouldn't even be able to get it up," the Venetian snarled.

"Rabi's potion but gives me extra strength to please my princess with, Ibrahim. Pity you'll never again have the chance." Then with another smile he walked out of the baths, leaving the others behind to fume with a rage they couldn't exhibit lest they anger their mistress. Staring after Niall admiringly, the old bath women chuckled with glee at the exchange.

Rabi was awaiting him, and carefully rubbed musk oil into his sun-bronzed skin until it gleamed and shone with a rich color. Niall enjoyed sunning himself in the gardens, and the dark tan he had now achieved only made his marvelous silver-gray eyes more silvery. He walked and swam regularly, which had kept him from growing fat like several of the harem men who were content to loll about; but his big slender body was of late growing a trifle too lean, for his appetite had fallen off. Still, his bronze skin, dark hair, and silvery eyes combined with his basically sound body to insure his good looks.

Rabi handed him balloon-legged white silk pantaloons, the ankles embroidered with three-inch bands of gold threads, small pearls, and rubies. About his waist was fitted a belt of gilt leather, six inches wide, its rectangular buckle studded with rubies. Niall's feet were shod in gold leather slippers with turned-up toes, and about his neck was hung a heavy gold chain with a heart-shaped pendant carved from a large dark red ruby that lay upon his bare chest. Upon both of his upper arms the old woman clasped wide gold arm bands. Niall felt somewhat ridiculous outfitted as he was, but he knew that it was the fashion here in Fez as much as horsehair padding was in the clothing of European men at the courts of England, Spain, and France. Sipping at the sweet grape sherbet that Rabi had given him, he wondered if Skye would laugh when she saw him, but then he considered what she would be wearing, and felt his anger rise for a moment only to slide away. There was nothing that he could do about it. *Soon.* Soon they would be together again, and all would be as it once had been.

"You are the handsomest man I have ever seen," Rabi said admiringly as she brushed musk into Niall's dark, wavy hair.

"They are a handsome pair," remarked Selwa, the female eunuch who attended to Hamal. "Look to my little lamb, Rabi. Is he not magnificent tonight?"

Hamal grinned sheepishly as he burlesqued a twirl. He was as exquisitely garbed as Niall, but his pantaloons were of midnight blue silk, the ankle bands embroidered in silver and studded with tiny diamonds and sapphires. About his neck hung a silver chain with an incredibly opulent pendant, a quarter moon carved from a single enormous diamond with a long sapphire star hanging above it. His belt and his slippers were of silvered leather, both studded with sapphires and diamonds. Hamal was as fair of skin as Niall was bronzed with the sun, for Fasi men of the upper classes abhorred sun on their skins, thinking it a mark of the peasants.

"Come, Ashur," Hamal said. "We cannot be late, as Kedar is always on time." He grinned mischievously at the two old women as they departed the chamber. "Have a delightful evening torturing the other women as to the failure of their charges," he teased Selwa and Rabi, and they chortled gleefully, indicating that was exactly what they intended to do.

"Is she here?" Niall asked Hamal nervously.

"Yes," was the short reply, "but you must remember, Ashur, that you can show no recognition of your wife. Whatever happens you must show nothing except devotion to Turkhan. My brother is very, very possessive of his Muna. Let him catch you in so much as a glance, and he will destroy you himself. If either of you betrays the other I can do nothing to help you, nor will I even attempt to aid you. If you will not think of yourself you must think of her."

Niall nodded. "I understand, my friend, but you must promise not to be jealous of me tonight. I shall dedicate myself to the princess, and make her the happiest of women."

"Do not hurt her, Ashur." Hamal's soft brown eyes were filled with concern.

"How can I avoid hurting her, Hamal? If I am to succeed in our plan I must appear to be totally enamored of her. She must be completely certain of me, Hamal. Do not fret, my young friend. It has been my experience that women's hearts may be bruised, but they are seldom broken. She will appreciate you far more, having been betrayed by me."

Hamal sighed with regret, but he knew that his companion spoke the truth. Better Ashur love Turkhan well before he made good his escape. Turkhan would be furious that something she desired did not after all desire her, but the time had come for him to make his move; his princess must begin to behave like the woman she was instead of a spoiled tyrant. She might be an Ottoman princess and have more freedom than any other woman save the Sultan's mother, but she was still a woman. Sultan Selim II was at fault for allowing Turkhan to remain unmarried. Hamal smiled to himself. He would soon change all of that.

They had reached the dining chamber, a lovely rectangular room with half-tiled walls of sky blue and white, above which rose rough white-plaster walls. The dark ceiling beams were intricately carved, and the wide-beamed floors were covered in thick wool rugs woven in a medallion design of gold and deep blue on a dark red background. They entered the room by walking down two steps. Two low, polished ebony tables had been set directly opposite the entry, behind which lay a number of brightly colored cushions in silk, wool, and cotton. The room was lit by large wall torches that had been fitted into carved golden holders. In each corner of the room stood tall gold censers burning pungent incense, and in the center of each table was a low crystal vase filled with fragrant pink lilies.

Turkhan had reached the room only a moment before the two men, and turning, she cried out with delight at their costumes. "You are magnificent, both of you!" she purred with approval.

"And you, my Princess," Niall murmured almost reverently, "fill my eyes with such incredible and flawless beauty that I am struck blind by the sight."

Turkhan colored in surprise. "Why, Ashur," she said softly, "you are beginning to speak like a Persian poet."

Hamal shifted uncomfortably. He thought that Turkhan was behaving like a young girl. She was almost simpering. Then he realized that he was jealous. Ashur's very flattering remark had pleased her before he might even comment. He suddenly realized that Ashur had been not jesting when he warned him not to be jealous of him this evening.

Turkhan did not notice her young favorite's quiet mood. "Let us seat ourselves before my guest and his women arrive," she said. Garbed in a cloth of silver djellabah whose deep V neckline and wide sleeves were embroidered with small black pearls and pink sapphires, she was looking quite beautiful this night. Her red-gold hair was dressed in two long narrow braids that were looped up on either side of her face, and a long cape of hair that had been dusted with diamond dust streamed down her back. From her dainty ears hung pink sapphires set in silver.

"Are my brother's women to join us?" Hamal inquired curiously.

"It did not seem fair that I deny him their company as I have yours, my lamb," Turkhan said.

"Have you seen them?"

Turkhan laughed. "How well you know me, Hamal. Yes, I watched them through the peephole in their quarters. Both are quite lovely. Tonight if you are very good, my darlings, we shall watch the unsuspecting Kedar as he makes love to his women. I am told that he is considered a highly skilled lover. Perhaps you will both learn something from him that will please me," she teased them.

Niall felt a chill sweep over him. "You have a secret peephole in the guest quarters?" he asked.

Turkhan laughed. "Of course I do. My grandmother Khurrem said that such things were invaluable when you wish to know more about a guest than they wish to reveal."

Suddenly the princess's eunuch majordomo announced, "The lord Kedar, my Princess."

Turkhan looked lazily up from beneath her thick black lashes as Kedar and his women entered the room. "You are welcome to my house, Kedar ibn Omar," she said. "Pray be seated so the meal may begin."

"I am honored by your invitation, Highness. I hope that I may be of assistance to you." Kedar seated himself, and impatiently waved Skye and Talitha to their seats, one on either side of him.

With a swift look Skye saw Niall on one side of the princess. Her heart leapt almost painfully within her chest, for he did not look well. Quickly she lowered her eyes lest anyone see her anger at the proprietary way in which Turkhan openly caressed Niall.

"You would not be here in my house, Kedar, were I not sure that you could be of assistance to me," Turkhan said sharply. "Your brother has assured me that your knowledge of trading routes to the coast exceeds that of anyone else in Fez. Hamal has always been trustworthy."

Kedar felt a surge of impotent anger sweep over him at her bold words. That a mere woman could speak to him in such a tone infuriated him. Ottoman princess or no, if he had her in his power for even a single night he would have her tamed and begging for mercy. Instead, he was forced to give a pleasant reply, but both Hamal and Turkhan had seen the quick anger that had flashed for a moment in his eyes. "I am pleased that my young brother is such a source of joy to you, Highness. I raised him myself."

Turkhan smiled sweetly, but there was a triumphant look in her eyes that Kedar did not miss, and he ground his teeth in frustration. Seeing that her master was incensed, Talitha leaned forward, took the cup that had been placed before him, and held it to his lips. "Drink, my lord," she said, and then in a lower tone: "You cannot offend the princess, my lord. Calm yourself, I beg of you."

Kedar turned to look at Talitha, and he nodded his agreement. He took the cup and drank a long draught of the icy and tart lemon water. "You are wise, Talitha," he said, "with a wisdom that matches your beauty." His hazel eyes scanned her, and the anger drained away. She was most beautiful this evening, and her costume extremely flattering, and pleasing to his eye. She was garbed all in sheer pale-gold silk. Her pantaloons were edged at the ankles in tiny sparkling topaz which matched the topaz sewn to her cloth-of-gold hip sash and her satin bolero. She wore a long-sleeved blouse with a soft open neckline that matched her see-through pantaloons. A headdress of gold chains and twinkling topaz formed a fitted cap over her short-cropped curls. She was everything that a woman should be, and Kedar was delighted with her, for he felt she brought honor upon him.

A leg of baby lamb was brought out and offered to them. Next followed saffron rice, artichokes in olive oil and tarragon vinegar, haunch of young gazelle in raisin sauce, pigeon pie, capon with lemon, and new peas with small onions. A platter of sizzling keb-obs made of kid, green peppers, and small onions was passed; and blue and white Fezware bowls of yogurt and purple and green olives were set upon each table.

"You will forgive the simplicity of the meal," Turkhan said.

"A well-cooked meal is never simple," Kedar replied, "and your cook prepares well." He opened his mouth to take the piece of lamb that Muna was feeding him. He was feeling expansive now and with the constant attentions of his women, at less of a disadvantage. He beamed benevolently at Muna. Her garb—or lack of it—was as pleasing to him as was the elegance of Talitha. Muna wore diaphanous blush-pink pantaloons with pearl ankle bands. Her hip sash was of pink and silver stripes, and above the waist she was nude. Her small, perfect breasts, their nipples stained with carmine, thrust forward proudly. Her waist-length hair was loose, held only with a narrow silver band at her forehead. For a moment Kedar's eyes lingered on Muna's breasts, and he thought of the pleasure she had given him over these last few months, of the pleasure she would give him this night.

Skye's eyes again stole across the room to feast for a brief moment upon Niall. She knew that he must be feeling foolish in his Eastern dress, and she wished she could tell him how magnificent he appeared with his tanned chest. He looked thinner, and she wondered if he was getting enough to eat, then chided herself for a fool. If only he would look at her instead of paying such outrageous attention to the red-haired princess. Skye thought if her husband touched Turkhan with another intimate touch, or gave her one more secret smile, that she was going to throw herself across the room and strangle the smug bitch! Kedar's voice snapped her back to her role.

"The princess sets a satisfactory table, but I should far rather feast upon your flesh, my jewel." His voice was husky with desire.

She raised her sapphire eyes to him, and smiled a slow and seductive smile. "Would you shame me before *that* woman, my lord?" she murmured low. "I am for your pleasure only, and not the eyes of prying voyeurs, my lord." Her red mouth pouted adorably, and Kedar wanted her desperately. Her pure female fragrance wafted up at him, and he grew dizzy thinking of what it felt like to be deep inside of her.

Niall Burke stared for a second at his wife, and ground his teeth silently as Kedar fondled her with a familiar hand. In his mind he had accepted what Skye had done in order to reach him, but accepting the fact was far different from watching the reality. Hamal's brother was an attractive man, and obviously a potent one. He openly handled Skye with the pleasure of a man who is fond of his favorite possession; and she seemed to enjoy it. She smiled seductively at him, and murmured in a low musical voice words that could not be distinguished. Niall wanted to leap the distance between himself and Kedar so he might stick a knife into the bastard's gullet.

"You are deep in thought, Ashur," Turkhan's voice brought him back.

"I dream of tonight, if I dare, my princess." He touched her face with the back of his hand, smoothing it over her soft skin.

"Tonight," she whispered conspiratorially, "we shall spy upon our guest, the three of us, and then we shall all play together, my glorious one. I shall exceed your dreams, Ashur, my beloved."

Boldly Niall leaned forward and kissed her upturned mouth quickly. "Your pardon, my Princess, but I could not resist."

Turkhan laughed shakily, and tapped his cheek with a long sharp nail in mock chastisement. Then she turned to Kedar. "Which of these women is the one Hamal tells me your uncle in Algiers gave you?" she asked him.

"You may present yourself to the princess," Kedar said to Skye.

She arose gracefully, walked across the floor, and fell to her knees in total obedience. "Highness, I am Muna," she said, her head bowed to the floor, her body bent.

"Stand up so I may see you, girl! You are reputed to be most fair, but how can I tell when you are in that position?"

Skye stood up, and posed tall and proud before Princess Turkhan. Her chin was high, her silken hair flowing about her like a dark cape. Her beautiful eyes, however, were lowered lest she offend her hostess.

Turkhan let her glance slide critically over the woman who stood before her. That she was extravagantly beautiful was irritatingly obvious. Her well-shaped limbs were quite visible through the gossamer of her pantaloons, and Turkhan could see that she was finely made. "Where did your uncle obtain such a prize?" she demanded of Kedar.

"She was a captive in Algiers, Highness," he answered. "It was by chance he saw her, and knew that she would please me, which she well does."

"You have trained her that quickly?"

"She is of noble birth in her own land, and really quite intelligent," Kedar replied. They spoke about Skye as if she were not even in the room, or worse, were an inanimate object; and as they blithely continued to discuss her fine points, Skye let her eyes stray to Niall once more.

Her heart struggled within her as he stared directly back at her, his silvery eyes bright with his longing. She felt tears pricking behind her eyes, and she fought furiously to keep them from showing. *Niall!* She cried his name silently.

Dear God, he thought, how can she be so very beautiful despite everything? *Oh, sweetheart, I want you so much!* If only they might make good their escape this very minute. Instead, he would be forced to watch while another man made love to his wife. If that didn't drive him mad then nothing ever would. *I love you, Skye,* he said in his heart.

Kedar was holding forth. "Each one of my women has a weakness, Highness. It is always useful to discover what form of pain terrifies. I would never whip Muna, even with a carefully plied lash, for just look at her skin. Turn, my jewel, and let the princess see." Skye moved obediently, dragging her eyes reluctantly away from Niall. "You see, Highness, the skin is flawless. It would be a crime against Allah himself to destroy such beauty wantonly, and yet still a deterrent is needed. In Muna's case it is the bastinado. She does not like the bastinado—do you, my jewel?"

"No, my lord," Skye whispered.

"You have used it on her?" Turkhan was interested.

"Have you ever known a willing captive?" Kedar remarked. "In Muna's case I must admit that she was a trifle reluctant, but of course that is no longer so—is it, my jewel?"

"Thou sayest, my lord," Skye replied.

"I prefer the use of opiates and hashish myself," Turkhan said.

"To use physical force upon a slave is an admission of having lost control." She looked at Skye casually. "You may return to your master, girl. Now my beautiful Ashur was not easy at all—were you, my handsome one? Until recently he fought me at every turn, but then he finally accepted his fate. He has been my joy ever since."

"A man that powerful could be dangerous, Highness," Kedar said. "Better he were in the mines, or sat upon an oarsman's bench in a galley. I wonder that you keep such a creature about."

"Ashur illustrates my point perfectly, Kedar. I have never physically mistreated him. I have not had to, for my sherbet and special comfits keep him totally under control. If you do not believe me then ask your brother."

"Why even bother to argue the point further," Hamal said. "You both have your methods, and they work for you. You are content with Muna, my brother, and you with Ashur, my Princess." He smiled his sweet smile at both of them. "Kedar," he continued, "will you speak a little to my Princess of the trading routes that you use when going to the coast?"

The servants began to clear away the remnants of the meal from the low tables, and to replace the main course with bowls of fresh fruits. There were bunches of fat, green grapes, perfect little pink-gold apricots, big dark figs, and sticky-sweet dates. There were plates of ram's horn pastries, and bowls of pistachio nuts and sugared almonds. A wizened old man squatted in a corner making coffee, which was soon served in tiny porcelain cups. The coffee was incredibly hot, and very bitter.

"You must drink at least two cups," Talitha said as she heavily sugared both their cups. "Kedar will expect a full performance from us tonight. It would not do to disappoint him, Muna."

Skye drank the coffee with the air of one condemned. She had practiced making love with Talitha for two days now, but she could still not reconcile herself to the act of intimacy with another woman. She knew that there were women in this world who much preferred women lovers, but Skye O'Malley was simply not one of them. She dreaded what was to come, and had thought hard as to how she might escape the onerous task without offending Kedar. She had not, however, been able to find an excuse that he would consider acceptable.

The princess had not arranged for entertainment, and so after they had finished the meal they sat but a brief time talking before Turkhan arose, putting an end to the evening. "Tomorrow, Kedar ibn Omar, we will speak more fully. Your brother will bring you to me. Good night." She left the room trailed by her two favorites.

Kedar might have been irritated at having been dismissed so perfunctorily; but the good meal and his two women had mellowed him. He was feeling very relaxed, and was now ready to begin a round of sensual adventures. Followed by Talitha and Muna, he hurried from the dining room and back to his own chambers. As they entered the room Zada and Dagan rushed forward to serve their master and his concubines.

"Bathe quickly," Kedar commanded them. "You also, Zada."

When they were safely in the women's bath Talitha remarked, "He is in rare form tonight if he wants all three of us. We shall be lucky to satisfy him by dawn. Most men grow less passionate with the advance of the years, but Kedar grows more so. Imagine what he will be like at sixty, although I don't expect we shall be here to see it!" Then she and Zada laughed, but Skye didn't think it very funny.

"Be silent," she said to them. "The lord Kedar is with Dagan just on the other side of this wall, being bathed himself. What if he should hear you, and be offended?"

"You are correct," Talitha said, and the three grew silent as they washed themselves. When they had finished they cleaned their teeth with ground pumice, chewed several mint leaves to sweeten their breaths, and brushed their hair free with brushes moistened in musk and attar of roses. Then, not bothering to dress, they returned to the bedchamber where Kedar, similarly refreshed by Dagan, awaited them comfortably seated upon his couch smoking hashish through a water pipe. The gray-blue smoke perfumed the room and curled gracefully up about his head. He, too, was unclothed.

Kedar's pulse was racing, and as his glance flicked over the three women he felt his excitement rising fast. His original intention was to have Talitha and Muna make love while he amused himself with the Berber girl, Zada; but as he took in the nude beauty of the three women it suddenly dawned on him how much the tall, slender Talitha with her short-cropped black curls resembled a young boy, and how ultrafeminine the full-bosomed and full-hipped Zada was. Let them make love, he thought, while he amused himself with his delicious Muna.

"I have changed my mind, Talitha. You will couple with Zada. Muna, my jewel, sit by my side, and let us watch." He patted the cushions next to him, and feeling the relief wash over her, Skye sat down gratefully. Kedar slipped an arm about Skye's waist, and nibbled a moment upon her ear. "I am too jealous to allow anyone else, even my faithful Talitha, to touch you," he whispered to her, and then looking at the other two, he snapped, "Begin! Talitha will play the boy, and Zada the maiden."

"As my lord commands," Talitha murmured, smiling, and then she embraced Zada, kissing her soundly upon the mouth. Zada responded quite avidly, wrapping her arms about Talitha's neck and pressing her lush form against her partner's elegant one. As the two women began to fondle each other Kedar began to stroke Skye's breasts, and she was able to look away from her two companions in order to concentrate upon Kedar. He, however, kept his eyes glued to the two women and did not notice Skye's distaste.

In the few days since Kedar had taken Zada, the maidservant had become quite impossible. Kedar's attentions had convinced her that she was in his favor as much as Talitha or Muna. She would, Skye knew, do anything to retain his attentions, and although Skye was repelled by the two women now writhing upon the rug before them she could not blame Zada for her actions. This was Zada's world, and the only chance she had in it was to please her master; perhaps even to bear him a son. If in order to enthrall Kedar she must do certain things, Skye knew that Zada would do them willingly.

"Look! Look!" Kedar noticed that she was not watching the two women, and forcibly turned her head.

They had, Skye thought, done just about everything possible for two women to do. They had kissed, and caressed, and licked and tickled, and sucked and rubbed each other for several long minutes; but to Skye's surprise, Talitha was now rising, and Dagan hurried forward to strap about her hips a red leather harness from which protruded an ivory dildo identical to the one Kedar occasionally made her use. The device fastened securely, Talitha knelt down over the panting Zada, spreading her short, shapely legs wide. Playing her role of the boy to the fullest, she thrust forward, pushing the dildo into her victim. Zada shrieked, a sound of both pain and delight, as Talitha moved back and forth upon her, and Kedar's excited breathing rasped sharply as he leaned forward to get a closer view. Glancing down, Skye saw that his own masculine weapon was poised firmly forward.

"My lord, you are hurting me," she whispered as his hands cruelly crushed her soft breasts.

His grip loosened, but he did not for several moments turn his head from the two women performing before him upon the thick rugs. When finally Talitha collapsed upon Zada, Kedar let out a long sigh of obvious satisfaction, and once more turned his attention to his companion. He tsked to himself over the red welts his rough fingers had imprinted upon Skye's tender, creamy flesh. Pushing her back amid the cushions on the couch, he fastened his mouth over her nipple, and sucked forcefully while his hand vigorously teased her other one. Automatically her hand entwined in his dark hair, and smoothed down to caress the back of his neck, which she knew he liked. She could feel him against her leg, hard and demanding, but she knew that he would not take her quickly. The two other women had built his excitement high, but it had not yet peaked, and Kedar enjoyed the foreplay almost as much as the act itself.

His head lifted and moved to her other breast, which he bit at softly but sharply. She gave a small cry of protest, and in answer he rolled them off the couch onto the carpeted floor. Skye lay flat on her back as Kedar slowly rubbed his swollen maleness over her face, pausing suggestively at her mouth. She kissed the throbbing length of him with what he believed to be great fervor, and Kedar growled to the other two women. "Open her legs, and hold them wide." Skye felt her legs being grasped, and pulled up and apart, while Kedar continued to rub himself against her breasts, torso, and belly as he knelt by her side. Her arms were stretched above her head, and for the moment she felt absolutely nothing. Half her brain was with Niall, although the other half kept track of what was happening to her, and she occasionally moaned with convincing passion.

Kedar now moved himself around and between her legs. Resting on his elbows he spread her nether lips with his fingers and then his hot mouth found her and began to feast upon her sensitive woman's flesh.

"Allah!" Turkhan whispered as she peered at the tableau before her. "Your brother is most inventive, my little Hamal."

"Wait, my Princess," Hamal said, "Kedar is but warming to his beautiful subject."

"You think *she* is beautiful?" Turkhan queried him sharply.

"Yes, I do," Hamal answered. "She is nothing like you, my magnificent mistress, but she is fair in her own foreign way. To compare you would be like making a comparison between a rose and an exotic lily. Impossible!"

Turkhan was well pleased by Hamal's little speech, and reaching out, she caressed his cheek, although her eyes never left the scene being played in the guest apartment. The slave girl was writhing and moaning in earnest now, her shapely hips pushing upward to meet her master's eager mouth. Kedar sucked aggressively upon Skye's little jewel, and his tongue then licked at her with sure strokes until she opened for him and he was able to push his tongue into her with a lingering, agonizing slowness. For several long minutes he moved his tongue back and forth within her—an exquisite torture. Finally he was no longer able to hold back his own lust, and pulling himself up, he drove into her well-prepared body.

"Allah!" Turkhan exclaimed again. "He is a bull!"

"Perhaps," Hamal teased, "Kedar should have sold himself to you and left me in charge of our father's business."

Turkhan laughed softly at his jest, but her eyes remained glued to the tiny peephole. "You are very silent, Ashur," she noted. "Are you not impressed by the lord Kedar's incredible performance with his slave girls?"

"He is too obvious, and far too heavy-handed a lover for my taste, my Princess," was Niall's tight reply, but he, too, could not take his eyes from his peephole. His anger was so great that his entire body felt icy. Strange, he thought, I should at this minute be strangling that devil who so possessively rides my wife, yet I am numb. I can barely even feel my heart, and I am so cold. So damned cold! He focused again upon Skye. Her head with its marvelous wealth of dark hair was thrown back; she was moaning audibly as she approached her peak; he could even see the distended delicate blue veins in her slender white neck. Did she enjoy Kedar's lusty attentions? Were women like men in that the fulfillment came even if the love was not there?

"This becomes tedious now," Turkhan said. "Let us go and play our own little games, my darlings. I have heard that men when they have no women to amuse themselves often put their own lances into each other. Tonight you and Hamal will amuse me thusly before I allow you to take me. Come! There can be nothing else Kedar can do after he has satisfied his passions upon his slave girl Muna."

Hamal hid a knowing smile. For all her power, Turkhan was incredibly ignorant in matters of lovemaking. Kedar was only beginning, but for Ashur's sake his younger brother did not bother to tell his mistress that. He could not really imagine how Ashur felt, but he knew what they had just witnessed was not to his friend's liking. European men had very strange ideas about their women.

In the meantime he and Ashur would have to convince the princess not to force them to the particular perversion she was so innocently suggesting. Hamal was quite sure that Ashur would be in total agreement with him, although he knew that several of the young men in Turkhan's harem often amused themselves thusly, particularly as their mistress was so engrossed these days with Ashur.

Kedar was equally engrossed with Skye at that moment. His lust was running quite high this night, its fires stoked by the delicious performance Zada and Talitha had given for him. Once, twice, three times he brought Muna to a wailing peak; but Kedar was barely satisfied. Now, he noted with some slight annoyance that she lay unconscious. He rolled away from her and lay on his back. Instantly Zada was there, flinging herself upon him with great enthusiasm. Braced upon her hands, her head thrown back, she rode him like a fury while Talitha squatted over his head and presented herself for his loving attentions. Eventually the two women exchanged places, and finally Kedar was replete with their bodies and released his first burst of passion into Talitha.

For several minutes the three lay panting with exhaustion upon the soft rugs. Zada was the first to rise, and with Dagan's aid she bathed with cool rosewater first her own sex, and then those of Talitha, Kedar, and the still unconscious Muna. When she had rejoined her master and the others Kedar said, "Help Talitha to rouse Muna from her swoon, my spicy little Berber." Zada felt a glow of pleasure at the endearment. She would do whatever he wanted, for she loved him. When Talitha began to suckle on one of Muna's breasts, Zada moved to Muna's other side and imitated the older woman. Clawing her way up from the dark depths and finding her two companions thus engaged, Skye wondered if she would survive this orgy. She had never seen Kedar so aroused, and she was more frightened now than she had ever been in her months with him. She had to survive! *She had to!* She was so close to success!

The night became a blur of sensuality where one body blended into another; and one sexual act followed another so closely that she soon became confused as to who did what to whom. She was spared the worst of it, however, for Kedar was truly jealous of anyone else, even another woman, touching her. Eventually, Skye never remembered when, they all fell into a deep sleep, the bodies tangled together. When she finally woke the sun was streaming into the room, and as Skye stretched gingerly her gaze met the very amused one of Talitha.

"So, sleepyhead, you are finally awake," the older woman greeted her.

Skye nodded. "Where is the lord Kedar?"

"Meeting with the princess. It is at least two hours past the noon hour."

"The last thing I remember is the dawn," Skye replied.

"We were up in time to see that our lord Kedar was fed and bathed properly," Zada said smugly. "You could not be roused."

"Are you so in our master's favor, Zada," Skye said sharply, "that you dare to offend me?"

"The master *is* pleased with me," Zada retorted pertly. "*He is!*"

"That is not what I asked you! Now, unless you have been relieved of your duties by the lord Kedar, you will fetch me something to eat and to drink. My mouth feels like cotton, and I am ravenous."

Zada hesitated a moment, looking to Talitha for support, but Talitha took that moment to assiduously study her long nails. Defeated, the servant girl hurried out to do Skye's bidding.

"You are stronger than you pretend to be," Talitha remarked calmly.

"You know that I am of the nobility in my own land," Skye replied. "I am used to commanding servants."

"Yet I have never seen you act so authoritatively," Talitha said. "Is it true, then, that Kedar will make you his wife?"

"I know not," Skye answered truthfully, then added to confuse Talitha, "but it will be as he, and he alone, desires. He is the master." Talitha might think what she would, but she would never be able to say that Muna *said* she was to be Kedar's wife. Skye stood up. "I am going to bathe."

"I'll come with you," Talitha replied. "So far there has been little time for indulging anything other than Kedar's various appetites."

Skye laughed. "Does Kedar know how sharp your tongue is?" she asked, genuinely amused.

"No more than he knows how strong you are, Muna, my friend. Hurry now lest that little upstart Zada try to join us. I can bear no more of her chatter today. Is she never quiet?"

"No," was the short reply, and the two women departed quickly for the guest bath.

They bathed in leisurely fashion, and then returned to the apartment and ate what Zada had brought them. Kedar was still with the princess, and Talitha and Zada lay down to sleep while they could; but Skye took the opportunity to walk in the gardens that opened off of the guest quarters. The day was warm but not uncomfortable, and she enjoyed the peace and the solitude of her own company. Slowly she strolled along the carefully raked gravel paths. About her a multitude of bright flowers bloomed in exotic and riotous fashion, their many scents almost overpowering in the still air.

"My lady Muna." She heard Hamal's voice, but looking about did not see him. "I am on the other side of the hedge," came the explanation. "It is better that we not be seen talking. Just walk along. I will keep pace with you."

"Which way?" Skye asked.

"Toward the fountains at the end of the hedgerow."

"Have you some news for me, Hamal?"

"I have managed to convince both my brother and the princess of the advisability of journeying to Algiers. As I have explained to Turkhan, she cannot entrust her goods to her own caravan people until she knows the risks and variables of the trail. Since Kedar, having never over the years lost a shipment, is really the expert in this, I suggested that he go with her to aid her. Also the Dey of Algiers is an old friend of the princess's father, Sultan Selim II. He will aid her in her dealings in Algiers, and Kedar will benefit by meeting the Dey through Turkhan. Everyone will profit all around."

"What of Niall, Hamal? What of my husband?"

"The princess will take both myself and Ashur, your husband, with her."

"But how are we to escape?" Skye's voice had a nervous edge to it.

"Kedar has confided in me that he is so enamored of you that if you could not go along he would not go."

"Oh, God!" Skye whispered. "I will never escape him!"

"Courage, Muna! You must only put up with my brother for a few more months. I have already dispatched a pigeon to my Uncle Osman. Your ships will be awaiting you in Algiers. Do not fear! Has my uncle not said it was not your fate to remain in this part of the world?"

"We cannot compromise Osman," Skye said firmly.

"Do you think I am so foolish as to endanger him?" Hamal's voice sounded hurt.

"I do not like returning to Algiers," Skye fretted. "There is danger in that city for me."

"What danger?" Hamal was curious.

"My second husband was Khalid el Bey, the Great Whoremaster of Algiers. He was murdered by his best friend, Capitan Jamil, the Sultan's commandant of the Casbah fortress, in order that Jamil might possess both me and my beloved Khalid's fortune. Your uncle helped me to escape, Hamal. When Osman sent for me a few months ago, Jamil was in Istanbul. By now, however, he will have returned. If he suspects for one moment that I am there, he will attempt to exact revenge on me for spurning him."

"Even if this Jamil is there he can do you no harm," Hamal soothed her. "Kedar is not apt to let you run loose in the city, and it is unlikely that Jamil will ever meet my brother and discover that they both covet the same woman. Besides, all this happened long ago," Hamal said with the certainty and assurance of his youth. "Surely Capitan Jamil has forgotten you by now." Then he quickly amended, "Not that you are a forgettable woman."

Skye was forced to laugh. "Stop!" she begged him. "I am but thirty, and you make me feel like an old woman."

"You are *thirty?*" He sounded amazed, and Skye was overcome with a fresh fit of giggles.

Suddenly she felt more certain than she had in days. She had been frankly worried about escaping with Niall from Fez, and making their way alone through unfamiliar and hostile territory to the coast. She had almost been beaten down by Kedar's overpowering sensuality, but now she suddenly felt lighthearted again. She wished she might share that good feeling with Niall.

"When do you think we will be leaving, Hamal?"

"It will be at least two months before we can depart from Fez. It will take that long to prepare a caravan large enough to hold the goods of both the princess and my brother. The trip itself is at least a month. Three months at the earliest, between three and four months more likely."

"It will be necessary to create a diversion in Algiers in order that Niall and I can escape." Skye said. "Then we will need to travel in a large convoy in order to circumvent the Dey's corsairs. The Mediterranean is virtually an Ottoman lake. Have Osman alert my men as to our arrival."

"My uncle is right," Hamal said admiringly. "You are really an amazing woman. You know so very much about the world. In a sense I envy you your knowledge. I have lived here in Fez my entire life. I have never been more than a few miles from the city. I have never even seen the sea."

"Ask Niall to tell you about our homeland, and about England and its Queen and her court, Hamal. Now you must tell me how my husband fares. I have spoken with you on everything but that which is dearest to my heart." Skye had reached a large, azure-blue tiled fountain. The fountain was round, and filled with bright golden fish darting to and fro. In its center a crystal spray bubbled forth, shooting at least nine or ten feet into the air. Hamal was still nowhere to be seen, but Skye knew that he had not left her.

Knowing you are here heartens him, as he is distressed by seeing you with my brother."

"I was distressed at seeing him with the princess," Skye answered tartly. "He seemed to be paying her most ardent court. I had been told he was resisting her fiercely; he did not look last evening as if he were resisting her at all."

A chuckle sounded behind her. Her obvious jealousy in the face of her seeming passion for Kedar amused Hamal. "Ashur decided a small while ago that to fight Turkhan was not the proper tactic. So instead, he began to court her, and believe me, Muna, when he escapes her, Turkhan's fury will know no bounds. I imagine Kedar will feel the same way at your flight."

Skye walked slowly around the fountain, pausing a moment to dip her hand in the cool water. "Out of respect for your uncle, my dear friend Osman, I will say nothing to you of your brother but that I will be glad to escape his clutches, Hamal."

Again came the rich chuckle from the green shadows of the hedgerow. "If Kedar knew you, Muna, really knew how strong and disciplined a woman you are, he would be very frightened. If you could but be yourself, how easily you would vanquish him. I almost wish I might see it, for it would destroy him."

Skye hid a small smile as the truth dawned upon her. "You hate him, don't you, Hamal? Despite your gentle manner and soft appearance, you are as ruthless as he is; and, I think, far more clever."

"By right half of our father's wealth was mine, and yet my brother robbed me by selling me to the princess."

"Still you love Turkhan, your uncle tells me."

"Yes, Muna, I love her, but that does not wipe out Kedar's crime. As long as I am a slave I can inherit nothing. I strive for the day that Turkhan will free me. I will marry her then, claim my father's wealth from Kedar, and with Turkhan's wealth I shall be far more powerful than Kedar. He will regret having attempted to disinherit me."

"Are you not afraid I shall expose you, Hamal?"

"To whom, Muna? Not Kedar, for you care nothing for my brother. To my uncle? He would understand, I assure you. Do not fear, lady, I shall aid you and Ashur in your escape once we reach Algiers. Now I must return to the palace. Do not be frightened if I do not attempt to speak with you until we arrive in Algiers. There is no need."

"Hamal!" Skye called softly. "Tell Niall that I love him."

"I will," came the reply.

She was alone again. She walked once more around the fountain, watching the fish flashing golden amid the crystal bubbles. Escape from Algiers was assured in Skye's mind. As much as she disliked, no, detested, spending further time with the salacious Kedar, it was a small price to pay for what in the long run was going to be a better situation for both herself and Niall. Completing her second circle of the fountain, she began to retrace her steps back along the tall green hedgerows toward the palace.

"Where have you been?!" Kedar's fingers dug into the soft flesh of her upper arm.

For a moment anger flashed in Skye's eyes, and then a warning glance from Talitha reminded her of her situation. "I was but walking in the princess's garden, my lord. Is it not allowed? Have I breached the code of good manners?" Her voice sounded distressed and anxious.

Kedar's grip loosened somewhat. "It would have been better if you had taken Talitha or Zada with you, my jewel. I do not like you walking alone."

"Perhaps she was meeting a lover," Zada said spitefully.

With a roar Kedar rounded on her, releasing Skye as he attacked the now terrified Zada, beating her viciously about the head and shoulders.

"My lord, my lord!" Skye protested. "'Twas but the ill-considered jest of a jealous woman!"

Even Talitha, who normally would not involve herself, added her voice to Skye's in an attempt to stop Kedar. "My lord, if you kill her you will have lost a valuable slave. How often have you admonished us not to waste?"

"Owwww! Oh! Oh! Arrrrgh! Mercy, master! Mercy!" the unfortunate Zada wailed.

"Bitch! Little savage animal!" Kedar snarled. "How dare you suggest such perfidy against your mistress, your better? Do you think that because I have relieved my lust into your worthless body you are as good as she?" He cuffed her a blow on the side of the head. "You will receive twenty lashes when we return, worthless one!" So saying, Kedar shoved Zada away from him angrily.

Ignoring the fallen woman, Talitha and Skye quickly set about calming the furious Kedar. While Talitha hurried to bring him a cool and refreshing drink, Skye wiped his brow with a cloth wrung out in rosewater. "You must not be angry with Zada, my lord," she implored him. "She is but an ignorant Berber, and the honor you have done her has gone to her head."

Talitha held a goblet of lemoned sherbet to his lips, saying, "Has this sort of thing not happened before, my lord? And it will continue to happen if you will not confine yourself to your harem."

"The women of my household are there to please me," Kedar grumbled. "*All of them!*"

"That may be your right, my lord," Talitha persisted, "but if there is no distinction between mistress and servant then the servants will believe that they are as good as their mistresses, and this sort of thing will happen again and again."

Kedar snatched the goblet from Talitha and drained it. "You have been with me many years, Talitha, and I have never known you not to act in my best interests. I will think on what you have said."

Skye could not help but raise an eyebrow. Such a reasonable concession on Kedar's part was surprising. Talitha merely smiled, and said quietly, "You will decide what is best, my lord."

Skye did not see Niall again. They left the princess's palace in the afternoon to return to Kedar's house. In the corner of their litter Zada sat sniveling, and, finally annoyed, Talitha rebuked her sharply. "Be silent, girl! You have brought this misery upon yourself."

"Muna *was* meeting a lover," Zada insisted. "I saw a man in the garden walk the same way that she did."

Skye quickly debated with herself whether she should admit to meeting Hamal, and finally said, "The lord Kedar's young brother, Hamal, was on the other side of the hedgerow from me, Talitha. He but bid me good day, and returned to the palace lest he compromise me. Should I say something to our master?"

Talitha laughed. "Of course not, Muna. More likely, Hamal feared that you would compromise him with Princess Turkhan, especially now that she has shown such favor toward that handsome brute, Ashur." She turned stern eyes on the complaining Zada. "Say a word to Kedar, and I will have you poisoned, foolish one."

Zada nodded. She had no doubt that that old bitch meant every word of it. "Will I really be given twenty lashes?" she quavered.

"Probably," Talitha said drily.

"Speak to Kedar, Talitha," Skye intervened. "Zada has already been sufficiently punished.

"No," Talitha said. "She deserves to be beaten. I will try, however, to see that her sentence is cut from twenty to ten lashes."

The next few weeks passed quickly in a haze of sameness for Skye.

Almost every evening, except during the period when she was considered unclean, she joined Kedar in an orgy of dark sensuality. During the day she slept heavily and long in order to counteract the debilitating effects of the previous night, and to prepare for the night to come. How Kedar kept up such a strenuous pace she did not understand. He seemed to gain his strength from the sexual encounters he had with his women. With less than five hours' sleep he was up early each morning, busily preparing for the journey back to Algiers. He had not said yet that he would take Skye, and she fretted with uncertainty as he had always left his women behind when he led a caravan before.

Finally a week before the trek was due to begin she could bear it no longer. Kedar was feeling benevolent and relaxed that evening. Before him danced half a dozen attractive and supple girls, their sheer, rainbow-colored skirts whirling prettily as they swayed and dipped in time to the reed and drum. He was alone but for his favorite, Muna, who popped small, very sweet dates stuffed with almonds into his open mouth. She pressed her breasts suggestively against his arm, and spoke breathily into his ear.

"How I shall miss you, my lord, when you are gone to Algiers. I am not sure I can bear to be without you. Surely I shall have pined away before you return." She ran her tongue around the inside of his ear and blew softly into it.

Kedar turned his head and gazed into her gorgeous sapphire eyes, which appeared to him to be liquid in their desire for him. Her mouth was but inches away from his, and he was unable to resist kissing her. Her lips seemed to part eagerly, and her soft tongue taunted his by playing hide and seek with him, slipping out to swiftly brush against his before sliding away. Kedar felt his lust begin to build. He had not intended to take her, but as she flamed beneath his touch he suddenly realized he did not wish to be, nay, could not be without her for three to four long months. She had a hypnotic, almost druglike effect upon him. She had infected his blood much as the opium infected those who overindulged. He would take her with him! He would marry her in Algiers in his uncle's house, where he had first seen her. He knew that Osman, romantic fool he was, would enjoy that very much.

Releasing her from the kiss, he allowed her to cling possessively to him. "Did I not tell you, my jewel, that you are to go with me?

The princess takes her two favorites, and I certainly cannot be without you."

Relief poured through Skye's veins, rendering her almost weak to the point of swooning. Seeing it, Kedar was pleased, and found that he was also extremely flattered. Her concern at being parted from him was obviously quite genuine, and he thought that perhaps she was falling in love with him, but she dared not say the words for fear of giving offense. Many masters of such luscious creatures sought only the willing bodies of their women, and wanted nothing more. Indeed, he knew many men who sold off the women who fell in love with them, for they did not want clinging females who grew possessive with their love. Kedar knew that his women gossiped among themselves, and undoubtedly Muna had heard such stories. Beguiled by her attitude, Kedar considered that Muna was the first woman to ever really love him, and he was further gratified. He had been wise to wait all these years. She was going to be the perfect wife. She was discreet, obedient, and incredibly sensual. What more could a man ask for? he asked himself. Whatever else it might be, the slaves could supply.

Freed of her anxiety, Skye knew she must say something. "I am so happy you will not leave me behind, my lord," she murmured, her voice soft with actual elation.

Kedar smiled into her perfumed hair. "I should not admit this to you, my jewel, but I would be bereft without your sweet company. Were I only to be gone a month though, I should not expose you to the rigors of the caravan trail. What if you are with child?"

"I am not, my lord."

"My only displeasure with you," he replied, a small frown creasing his brow.

"What does it matter?" she cajoled him. "You have several sons and daughters by your many concubines, my lord. If I grew round with child then I should not be able to grace your couch as I do now. I do not wish some other to take my place," she pouted at him.

"No one," he vowed fervently, "no one, my fair Muna, my adorable precious jewel, could possibly take your place with me!"

Skye smiled at him, and Kedar was so blinded by his growing approval of her that he did not see the cruelty in the smile. God's bones, she thought to herself, how I despise you! No. It is more than despise. I hate you, Kedar! When I flee from you with my beloved Niall I hope you suffer the tortures of the truly damned, for that is what I have suffered at your hands. Not once have you touched me with love, only with lust. You are the most depraved man I know, and I wonder if I shall ever be clean again, or really free of your touch. Still, if I may aid my dearest Niall to safely reach home, perhaps we may together free ourselves of the terrible memories this wicked land has given us, and build our lives with our children once more.

Kedar had begun to make love to her now, and Skye was still so engrossed in her own thoughts that she responded automatically. He, however, was so totally fascinated with her by now that he did not even notice. Pride of ownership surged through him, and he almost howled his triumph of possession as he quickly emptied his lust into her womb. When he fell on her breasts, panting with exhaustion, she finally noticed, and her lip curled with disgust as she wondered if she would ever get the stink of him and his unbridled passion off her skin, out of her nostrils. She shuddered, and again Kedar misinterpreted her feelings, assuming the shiver was one of satisfaction.

"We are so perfectly suited, my jewel," he said.

"Indeed, my lord," Skye replied. "Indeed."

Chapter 11

lgiers! Skye had wondered when she left Algiers those many months ago whether she would see the city again. Nor had she ever really thought to see Osman ever again, yet here he was hugging her, his eyes wet with unshed tears.

"Allah be praised, my daughter, you are safe!" He stepped back and viewed her critically. "You are thinner."

She nodded. "It has not been easy. You have seen Hamal, my friend?"

Osman nodded. "As you know, he rode in ahead of the caravan three days ago so that we might be warned of your imminent arrival. The old Dey is in quite a dither over the prospect of entertaining the Sultan's daughter. He was even prepared to invite Kedar to stay at the palace, but Hamal discouraged it, saying that Kedar was only a business acquaintance of Turkhan's, and besides, he was my nephew, and would want to stay with me. Getting your husband Niall out of the palace will be hard enough, but we should never have gotten you out."

"Are my ships here, Osman?"

"Some in port, some lying just off the coast over the horizon." Osman paused, and then said quietly, "Skye, my daughter, Jamil is back in the city."

She sucked her breath in sharply. "*I knew it!* I somehow sensed he would be here should I return."

"It is said that his potency is restored."

"Find me an assassin, Osman!"

"Would you have his death on your conscience, my daughter?" Osman was shocked.

"Khalid must be revenged! How his murder has haunted me all these years, Osman. I want Jamil dead! He deserves to die!"

"Perhaps," Osman agreed, "but I shall not let you make this grave error, Skye, my daughter. It was Khalid's fate to die else you would not have returned to your own land, to your own destiny. I warned Khalid the morning he told me that he was going to wed with you, but he would not listen. When he made that decision his fate was sealed; but remember, Skye, it was his right to decide his own fate. His choices were clear, and so are yours. In Allah's good time Jamil will be punished, but it is not up to you to wield the sword of justice over his head." Osman put a comforting arm about her. "How strong your passions are, Skye. You are so consumed with your thoughts of revenge it does not even occur to you that you might be in danger yourself."

"It is only logic, Osman. I am in no danger, and I know it. The memory of Skye Muna el Khalid is long gone from Algiers, and of the few who know Muna, the slave of the lord Kedar, who would connect the two? I am simply an anonymous woman, as are all respectable women in this city. If Jamil came into this house tonight, he would still not know I was here, for he would certainly not be allowed the run of your women's quarters.

"I am more concerned as to when I may see Robbie," she said.

"Not until you escape, Skye," Osman cautioned. "It is too dangerous for him to appear in my house, and I cannot take the chance that he be seen in your presence."

"Who would speak, Osman? I managed to avoid bringing anyone here from your nephew's house by pretending that I was deeply desirous of serving him personally, and could take care of myself. As a reward for my devotion, he promised to buy me half a dozen maidens to serve me here in Algiers. Talitha was eminently relieved to be left behind, and much to Kedar's annoyance, that chatterbox, Zada, found herself with child and had to be left behind."

"The little Berber Kedar bought to serve you is with child? Who is the father?"

"Kedar!" Skye laughed. "Has he ever been averse to dipping his spoon into a handy honey pot?"

Osman sighed deeply. "Kedar has never learned to be select in his lusts," he remarked.

"Robbie," Skye reminded Osman.

"Yes, my daughter, yes! Do not be impatient. Hamal and I have spoken, and we have already formulated part of the plan for your escape. Tomorrow the fast of Ramadan begins. For the next thirty days no true believer will eat or drink between dawn and sunset. Immediately after the sun has set, the feasting begins, and by the second hour after midnight all are asleep, filled with food and drink, to sleep until the noon hour of the following day. Business is conducted in those few hours until sunset. Hamal and I think the best time for you to make your escape would be in the early hours just before the dawn. It will be easy to slip some potent sleeping drug into Kedar's cup in order to allow you to slip away."

"And Niall, Osman? What of my husband?"

"Hamal and I believe he should not escape at the same time as you do. The coincidence would be far too great, and my family is far too involved now with Princess Turkhan to become the objects of her vengeance. You will be safe at sea upon your ship, where Kedar will not even consider seeking you."

"Get Niall out first, Osman," Skye said. "I wouldn't be able to rest easy if I had to leave him behind. He didn't look well to me in Fez, and the few times I managed to catch a glimpse of him on the caravan trail he looked ill. Frankly," and here Skye's brow furrowed with concern, "I am fearful for him, Osman. His ordeal, it seems, has been far worse than any I have suffered here in Algiers or Fez."

"If you wish it, my daughter," Osman promised. "Give me your husband's birthdate now so I may plot his natal chart, as I have yours." Guilelessly Skye did so, unaware that Osman was fearful for her. He had sought her own charts and updated them. He saw within Skye's current stars great pain and personal tragedy; a tragedy that might well scar her emotionally for the rest of her days. Yet in the midst of the darkness was one great light, a dominant Leo, who might save her from herself. Knowing that Lord Burke had been born under the sign of the Scorpion Osman now knew that he was not that man. With a sad shake of his head and a deep sigh, Osman set about to again plot Niall Burke's stars, knowing even as he did so what the end result had to be.

The fast of Ramadan began, and was strictly kept throughout the city of Algiers by rich and poor alike. The town was fairly quiet during the day, but once the sun had set the scent of delicious foods could be smelled all over the city, and it was said that the starving grew fat on the smells alone.

In the depths of Algiers a tailor sewed upon a costume that his color-blind and tired old eyes could only half make out. Still, his stitches and seams were neat with years of practice, and when he had finished he was paid a generous although not munificent sum. Too many dinars would have caused questions to be asked. The costume, that of a Janissary captain, was smuggled into the Dey's palace and hidden carefully by Hamal. Niall's escape was set for the ninth night of Ramadan.

Returning from the Dey's magnificent and rich feast, Turkhan demanded the immediate attendance of both of her favorites. Although they had traveled with her to Algiers and the Dey knew of their presence in his palace, Turkhan had wisely chosen not to flaunt her harem boys before her father's representative. Now they appeared nude before her, as she preferred, but before she might direct their play into sexual channels Hamal was pressing a cooling goblet of lemonade upon her and Niall was stretching her out upon the floor pillows to massage her lush body with strong hands.

Turkhan drank deeply, and then purred, "I shall fall asleep, Ashur."

"If you do," he murmured low, with hot breath against her ear, "I will not let you sleep long, my Princess. Only long enough to gain the strength you'll need for a long night of my loving. Send Hamal away, my beautiful one."

Turkhan shivered with anticipatory delight. She pretended to consider Niall's request while she drained the cup. Then she said, "My little lamb, seek your bed now."

Hamal knelt down, tenderly kissed Turkhan's mouth, rose up, and left them. Niall returned to his ministrations of Turkhan's voluptuous form, and was soon rewarded by her even breathing. Still he kept on, and then she began to snore lightly. "My Princess," he whispered, and then his voice grew normal. "My Princess? Are you awake?" Turkhan slept on, and satisfied that his massage and the opiate in the lemonade had done their work, Niall rose and left the room.

He encountered no one along the short route to his own quarters. Hamal was awaiting him with the Janissary captain's costume. Niall dressed quickly, and as he slipped the clothing on he felt sure and strong for the first time in months. As Hamal adjusted the sash about his waist and fixed the hat upon his head, Niall nervously popped jellies into his mouth. It was going to work! He knew it was going to work. His spirits soared! In a few minutes he would be outside the Dey's palace in the city of Algiers, and Robbie would be awaiting him.

"Now remember, Ashur," Hamal cautioned, "if you are stopped you must reply in Turkish. You could not have reached a captain's rank unless you spoke Turkish.

"Go back to Turkhan's chambers, and leaving through her bedchamber, cut across the Dey's garden to the western wall. You will find a door hidden beneath the vines halfway down the wall. It is open, and the hinges have been oiled so it should swing silently. Keep to the shadows. You should have very little trouble, for the garden is not brightly lit, but be cautious. Someone could be wandering. The old Dey, it is said, does not sleep well; or perhaps one of his women. One of your own people will be waiting for you on the other side of the wall."

"Hamal!" Niall grasped the younger man's hands in his. "How can I thank you?"

"Ashur, my friend, if I did not think that you were wrong for my Turkhan, I should not do this. She is in love with you, and your defection will cause her pain. I will, of course, be here to ease that pain. I understand your feelings for your beautiful wife, and I have ever been a fool for happy endings. We will both be happy—you with your lady, I with mine. Go now while all sleep!" He pressed a small flat gilt box in Niall's hand. "A small token. Those damned jellies that you like so well made just as old Rabi prepares them for you."

Niall grinned almost boyishly. "Farewell, my young friend Hamal, and thank you." Then he was quickly gone from the room.

Hamal heaved a soft sigh of relief. In just a few short minutes Ashur would be gone from their lives, and Turkhan would be his alone! She would be angry and heartbroken by turns. She would demand that the Dey find her favorite, but within the hour Niall would be safely at sea. Turkhan would have no choice but to turn to him for her solace. Faithful Hamal. A small smile played about his lips. Faithful Hamal, who would soon be a free man again, a man who could legally claim half of his brother's wealth, as well as all of his princess wife's. He chuckled. Kedar would be quite surprised to discover his adversary was as ruthless as he himself was. And why not? Had he not learned at his brother's knee before Kedar had so cruelly sold him into slavery? Hamal slipped silently back into his own small chamber next to Ashur's, and, lying down, fell into a guiltless and satisfied sleep.

In the meantime Niall had quietly re-entered Turkhan's chamber. For a moment he stood over her, staring down at this bold woman who had demanded everything from him, expecting no less. Then without a backward glance he walked into the warm, black night of the Dey's garden. Briefly he stood listening in the shadows, and then hearing no sound other than the night insects, he began his stealthy walk across the garden to the west wall. He moved quickly and silently, pausing every few minutes to listen, to look about him. High above him on the walls of the palace the Dey's own men paced their watch, but not quite as alertly as usual, being full with food and fermented fruit juices. Only a direct attack by the infidel would have roused them now.

Ahead of him was a small fountain that he was forced to circumvent. He paused for a moment, confused as to his direction, and for a brief second panic set in. But breathing deeply to calm his fears, Niall pressed onward, finally gaining the western wall. Carefully he felt his way along it, the thorny vines catching at his clothing. He smothered a curse as his hands grew badly scratched and pricked, but at last he felt the smooth surface of the little door beneath his bleeding palms. Sliding his hands downward, he found the latch. Slowly, cautiously he pressed down on the handle, and the door swung silently open. For a surprised moment he stared out into the street, then almost leapt through onto the cobbles, banging his forehead in the process. This elicited another curse. Then, remembering his danger, Niall Burke pulled the little garden door closed behind him, and hurried off down the street.

At the bottom of the street a shadow joined him from a doorway, and he almost wept to hear a soft Devon voice say, "Let's go, m'lord! Wouldn't do to have the Turks catch us now, would it?"

"Robbie? Is it you?" His heart was hammering joyously, and even the damned English tongue sounded good to his ears after so many months of first French, and then Arabic and Turkish.

"Aye, m'lord, 'tis me, and glad it is I am to see you. We've not far to go, but 'twould be best if we were silent now lest we cause suspicion by our speech. Follow me!"

The ease of his escape after so many months of torturous captivity amazed Niall. Robbie was dressed like a corsair Reis, and the few people they passed thought nothing of the two men, one a Reis, the other a Janissary captain walking together toward the harbor. They reached it fairly quickly, for the Dey's palace was quite nearby. Niall followed Robbie through the maze of docks until they arrived at a vessel he recognized as Skye's flagship. With suddenly shaking legs he somehow managed to mount the gangway, expecting at any minute to hear a commanding voice from behind shout at him to stop. There was no voice, and he gained the deck to again follow Robbie into the main cabin.

"Sit down, m'lord." Robbie moved quickly to the sideboard and poured Niall a generous dollop of smoky Irish whiskey. He didn't like the look of the man's color at all. Handing it to the seated man, he said, "Drink it, m'lord. I've got to go topside and get us underway."

"Where is Skye, Robbie?"

"The plan was that we get you out first. Lady Burke will be coming along in a few more nights."

"No! I'll not leave without her, Robbie!" Niall had risen in protest.

"M'lord," Robbie said patiently, although his blood was beginning to boil angrily, "I have not the time to explain it to you, for we are yet in danger. But I promise I will come back once we have cleared the harbor. If you are considering acting foolishly, remember all the lives involved in getting you out, especially Lady Burke's." He then turned on his heel and slammed out of the cabin.

Defeated, Niall sat heavily and pondered the amber liquid in his glass. He didn't understand, and he was frightened for Skye. Was she even alive? He had caught glimpses of her as they had traveled from Fez to Algiers, although it hadn't been easy. She had been forced to ride in a heavily guarded, silk-draped wagon. At least he and Hamal had been given horses to ride, although they were expected to pace their mounts on either side of Turkhan's palanquin. He had not even managed a small sight of her in the last week before they reached Algiers, and then he had been housed in the Dey's palace while she had gone with Kedar to Osman's home. Surely if she were dead, or injured, or ill, they would have told him, wouldn't they? Reaching into his robes, he drew out the gilt box Hamal had given him. He opened it and devoured three jellies. For some reason they always seemed to help him when he grew edgy.

He frowned irritably. He was a man. He had never been given to fears and qualms before he had come to Algiers. Granted, his had been a rather harrowing experience, but surely the shock would wear off now that he was safe among his own people again. When he could hold Skye in his arms once again it would be all right. He needed his wife. He needed Skye! Absently he reached for another jelly, and then he rose and refilled his goblet, savoring the whiskey as outside on the deck he heard the noise and the activity of the sailors beginning to get the ship underway. He heard the gentle creak of the vessel as it eased away from its dock and began to make its way out of the harbor. Looking out of the great window at the stern of the cabin, he saw the dark outline of the city, of the palace itself where Turkhan lay soundly asleep, unsuspecting that he had at last escaped her web. Dawn would not break for several hours yet, and by then they would be safely at sea. He didn't know how long he sat silently watching as the city grew more and more distant, but suddenly he felt the full swell of the sea as the ship passed out of the sheltered harbor.

The door to the cabin opened and Robert Small entered the room again. "There now, m'lord. We're safely away."

"Skye? Why isn't she aboard?" Niall demanded anxiously.

Robbie poured himself a whiskey and seated himself next to Lord Burke. "It was thought if you both escaped at the same time a link between you might be established which would in time lead back to Osman and his family. "'Twould be a poor way to repay Osman, for 'twas he who told us you were yet alive, and arranged for Lady Burke to get to Fez to verify your existence."

"When will she come, Robbie? When?" Niall stuffed another jelly into his mouth, which, despite the whiskey, seemed dry and scratchy.

"A few days at the most, m'lord. We'll just sit quietly off the coast waiting for her. Bran Kelly and his crew will be there to take her out."

Niall nodded. "He's a good man, Bran. Did he ever marry Skye's little Daisy?"

"Last year, m'lord, and within nine months of the wedding she gave him a red-faced and squalling son. They're waiting in Devon for you both."

"No England," Niall said. "I want to see Ireland again! I want to go home."

"The children, most of them, are at Wren Court with Cecily."

"My bairns?" Niall was surprised. "Why?"

"Mistress Skye felt them safer with Cecily in Devon."

"Safer than with my father at Burke Castle?" Again Niall was surprised by Skye's seemingly strange actions.

Robbie hesitated a moment, and then he began to speak. He was going to have to tell Lord Burke everything, for the man was full of questions, having been out of touch almost three years.

When his friend had finished, Niall nodded. Now he understood. Skye had done well despite the odds, but then she had always been competent in a man's world. The fact that she had survived without him he found unreasonably irritating, even though he knew that she had done it before. She was an unusual woman, but he loved her.

"Then we wait," he said to Robbie, and the little man heaved a great sigh of relief. Niall laughed. "What, Robbie? Did you think I was going to order an immediate attack upon the city of Algiers in order to rescue my wife?" He was beginning to feel better, almost elated with the sure knowledge that he would soon see her.

"You've been known in the past to act rashly, m'lord," was the honest reply.

"True, Robbie. 'Tis a fault Skye's often accused me of, but I think my time in captivity has taught me patience." He grinned mischievously. "Although I will not guarantee it, for once I am back in my own land I may very easily revert to my old ways."

Robbie chuckled. "I'll not question yer behavior in Ireland, m'lord, only here while we have yet to regain Mistress Skye. Ye'll find the cabin comfortable, and if you need anything you've but to ask. As you've said, we wait."

In the early afternoon Skye met Alima in the baths, who whispered once they were out of earshot of the bath attendants, "Your husband escaped this morning, and is safely at sea, dearest lady."

"Thank God!" Skye breathed, and Alima squeezed her hand comfortingly.

"Osman says that the princess is hysterical and furious by turns. The Dey is embarrassed that a prized slave could walk with ease from his well-guarded palace, and no one claims to have seen him go. He has not been seen in the town, and it is a great mystery. The city guards have, of course, been doubled. It will be difficult for the next few days for you to leave. My husband advises patience."

Skye laughed ruefully. "From the moment I was introduced to Kedar I have been patient, but the next days will be the worst, Alima. Still, knowing that my Niall is safe lifts the burden from my heart!"

Again Alima squeezed Skye's hand and smiled warmly at her. "Let us walk in the gardens after we have bathed," she suggested, "and perhaps you will tell me again of life in your Queen's fabulous court."

"Of course!" Skye agreed generously. She knew how very much Alima enjoyed hearing of Elizabeth Tudor's court, and French-born as she was, of the beautiful clothing worn by the men and women alike. Skye had many times explained in detail the quantity of beautiful gowns in her own possession, and as the two women wandered hand in hand in the garden she wondered if her clothes would now be all out of style. It was a thought she shared with Alima, who clapped her hands excitedly and exclaimed, "Oh, I hope so, lady Skye! Then you can have all new gowns made! How wonderful!"

Skye laughed, and it was the merry sound of her laughter that attracted the notice of the blond woman who had been pacing restlessly in Osman's library. The woman peered through the latticework that covered the windows down into the garden. She stared hard, and her breath quickened with excitement. "Who are those women in your garden, lord Osman?" she demanded sharply.

Osman arose from the rather disquieting chart he had been silently reading, and peered down. "It is my wife, and my nephew's favorite, Muna, who is her dearest friend. Why do you ask, lady Nilak?"

"The dark-haired one reminds me of someone I once knew." She turned from the window with reluctance, and then asked, "Well, lord Osman? You are reputed to be the most famous astrologer in all of Algiers, in fact one of the best in the known world. What does my chart tell you?"

"It tells me you have done much evil, lady Nilak. It tells me that you are not one bit repentant for your wicked ways. You are as much the director of your own fate as are the stars."

She laughed harshly. "I am not interested in the past, lord Osman. Tell me of the present! Will the lord Jamil marry me? Tell me of the future! Will the Sultan make him the new Dey? Will we rule Algiers together? These are the things that interest me, nothing more! Jamil has recommended you highly. Tell me what you see?"

"I see death in your chart," he said flatly.

Horrified, the woman stepped back, her hand going to her throat. "*You lie!*" she hissed at him. "You are nothing but a fraud! A faker! You know nothing! *Nothing!*"

"I see your death," Osman repeated, "and before dying you will cause the death of at least two people."

With a small shriek of anger and horror Nilak turned and fled the room. Osman did not bother to follow her. He was far too excited by what he had learned. Quickly he drew both Skye and Kedar's charts from their places on the shelves. Reaching up, he drew down yet another rolled parchment, this one belonging to Jamil, once the capitan commander of the Casbah fortress, now retired with the rank of full commander, or agha. Spreading the three charts upon the large library table next to the one he had just done for the lady Nilak, he studied them carefully with growing interest. There was no mistake. The four people represented were fated to meet, and their conjunction would end in death for three of them. Osman closed his eyes briefly. Most of the time he enjoyed his *gift* of sight, but there were times, times like this, when he saw things that gave him pain. Then he did not enjoy his special ability. Perhaps, just perhaps, he might be able to prevent a tragedy, for every soul was offered two paths by which to travel. Wearily he sat down and tried to think what he might do.

While Osman pondered on what he had seen, Nilak hurried downstairs and climbed back into her silk-draped palanquin. Sharply she ordered her slaves to quickly return her to her house. The girl in the garden had been Skye O'Malley's twin, and Jamil had been enamored of Skye when she was in Algiers. If she, Nilak, could bring the girl to Jamil's attention, and if she could buy the wench from Osman's nephew, would not Jamil be grateful to her? Would he not see that she loved him, and was looking out for his interests? She did not care if Jamil fucked the girl a dozen times a day, as long as she, Claire O'Flaherty, now known as the lady Nilak, was Jamil Agha's wife.

She smiled contentedly. She was going to make Jamil so very happy, and then too, she would be happy as wife to the Sultan's new Dey. Surely Jamil would gain the appointment to govern Algiers once the old man who now ruled for Sultan Selim II retired, which, according to rumor, would be any day now.

Claire had gone to Istanbul with Jamil, and while the physicians had worked to successfully cure his disability, she had made friends with the Sultan's favorite, Nur-Banu, a Venetian noblewoman by birth. When Claire had told her that she, too, was a Western noblewoman by birth, the two had struck up a small friendship which Claire carefully cultivated. It had been Nur-Banu who had compared Claire's blue eyes to the lilacs that grew in the Sultan's gardens. Thus Claire became Nilak, the Persian for bluish lilac flower. Even Jamil had been pleased and delighted that the Sultan's favorite had so honored the woman he considered making his wife.

Claire smiled again thinking how her luck had changed since the day that Niall Burke had driven her out of London, naked and stripped of all her wealth. For a moment her face darkened as she remembered the taunts of the onlookers, the jeers of the goodwives, the garbage that had been thrown at her, fouling her hair, clogging her nostrils. Sometimes she could clearly feel the sharp sting of his dog whip upon her shoulders and back, and when she did, she hated Lord Niall Burke with such a fierce hatred that she would not be able to sleep at night with the remembering.

When London had been left behind, Niall had slashed furiously at her helpless body with a final few strokes, and then had tossed her a long shapeless sack. "It's better than you deserve, bitch!" he had snarled at her. "Don't ever let me see your damnable face again, madam. The next time I will kill you!"

Claire laughed with the memory. The next time they had met she had come close to killing *him!* Killing, however, was not what she had had in mind. A quick death would have been too easy, and she had wanted Niall Burke to suffer, for having spoiled her successful venture as Claro, the most corrupt and famous madam in all of Bess Tudor's London. God's cock, how she hated Niall Burke.

The Devil, however, had smiled on his own. Claire had grimly begun walking. She slept that first night in a hedge by the side of the road, where she had been found the following morning by an elderly merchant traveling down from London. He, good soul, knew nothing of Claro and the scandal she had caused in the Tudor court.

Adney Darton was a godly and gentle man who had neither chick nor child, and he accepted Claire's story of being an orphaned noblewoman fallen upon hard times. Generously he took her home with him. Claire kept his house and attempted to cook his meals, seeking to insinuate herself into his life. He was therefore devastated when she announced that she would have to leave his home. What would people think of an unmarried maiden of poor, but good background, living in the house of an unmarried man. She could stay no longer, she said.

Adney Darton was old enough to be Claire's grandfather, but he proposed marriage, as she had expected he would.

Claire demurred.

Adney Darton fell to his knees and begged Claire to accept his suit.

"Yes," she whispered finally, inwardly unable to believe her good luck. The old man couldn't be long for this world, and within a short time she would be a rich widow!

The banns were quickly posted, and within the month Claire became Mistress Darton. It was then that she learned her husband had one living relative. Isham Darton arrived too late to prevent the wedding, but in time for the funeral of Adney Darton, who had perished in the act of consummating his marriage. Isham Darton was furious, for his cousin had thoughtfully rewritten his will prior to his marriage, and the marriage was quite legal. Claire Darton was now a wealthy woman, and Isham Darton had lost his inheritance.

Isham Darton, considerably younger than Adney, had coveted the elder's wealth. It was clear that he lusted after Claire, and Claire succumbed to his blandishments. Isham Darton was a vigorous lover, almost as venal and lustful as Claire, who set about to lure the man into marriage.

Isham Darton suggested that Claire come with him to Algiers, where he was going to set up a trading company. Boldly Claire told him she would only go as his wife, and to her delight he agreed without hesitation. Isham Darton had already decided that Claire would be easy to dispose of in Algiers, and as her husband he would inherit her fortune. Isham and Claire planned their marriage for the day after her year's mourning was over.

In the meantime Claire proposed that she travel to her former home in Ireland to visit a final time the graves of her dear, departed father and brother. He need not accompany her. Claire had sailed to Ireland upon one of her late husband's two ships to work her evil; paying its captain a rather large sum to take the wounded Niall Burke aboard, and sell him into the galleys.

Returning to England, she was married to Isham Darton, and together they set sail for Algiers. As they crossed the Bay of Biscay, Isham Darton was swept overboard in a severe storm. The widow kept to her destination. Claire settled herself in Algiers. As a single, seemingly respectable, and very wealthy European widow living in a Turkish city, she had quickly come to the attention of Capitan Jamil of the Casbah fortress.

Claire knew that she must remain a proper matron, or she would not be able to associate with the right people. She also intended to add to her wealth by continuing trading. If the damnable Skye O'Malley could do it, then so could she! She soon had a thriving business going, and there wasn't a man in Algiers who drove a harder or tighter bargain than Claire Darton. She remained very circumspect in her behavior, and that in itself was most taunting and provocative to the men of Algiers. They very much wanted to meet with the beautiful blond woman with the lilac-blue eyes. How, though, was the big question.

Capitan Jamil succeeded where all others had failed. Soon he would retire, and the rich wife he had picked for himself those long years ago, the magnificent Skye Muna el Khalid, had eluded him. He had arranged her husband's murder, but somehow she had discovered he was responsible, and fled him, transferring all of Khalid's riches out of Algiers. Then, through her maidservant Skye had sent him a plate of sweetmeats containing a potent drug which had rendered him unable to function as a man. For five long years he had been totally impotent, and then his manhood had begun to revive, but only slightly. Another four years had passed, and then he had heard of a physician in Istanbul who could cure him.

He had not the gold he would need to pay the physician, but he knew that the rich infidel widow did. Jamil waited a few weeks until the days grew shorter with the approach of the winter season and the evenings came early. He arranged for the lady Claire's palanquin to be set upon as it passed through a particularly dark, deserted area. Then he and a small troupe of mounted Janissaries arrived to beat off the attackers. When the tumult had died down, he presented his compliments to the lady and personally escorted her to her house, begging permission to call again. Claire had said that she would think on it, but by the time his gift, a carved lavender jade bracelet wrapped in a handkerchief of cloth of gold, arrived the next afternoon Claire had ascertained who her rescuer had been, and whether he could be of use to her. He could, and consequently Capitan Jamil was invited to take coffee with her.

The relationship had quickly blossomed. Jamil was genuinely intrigued by Claire's blond beauty as well as her vast wealth; and Claire for the first time since her brother, Dom, had died, loved another human being. Strangely, he had been able to consummate their relationship the first time he attempted to do so, but he had been quite honest with regard to his situation. Eventually he had told her of the doctor in Istanbul who could cure him. Her revenge against the Burkes had been successful, and she was in love. She begged her lover to let her foot the expenses to the capital for them both so he might be cured. Jamil refused. Claire persisted. He refused again, but now she would not be denied, and finally he gracefully gave in to her pleas.

It was while they were in Istanbul that she learned of his previous involvement with Skye O'Malley. Jamil did not know then that Skye Muna el Khalid was Skye O'Malley; but Claire knew. How strange, she thought, that she was so passionately in love with the very man whom her bitterest enemy had scorned, and almost destroyed by turning him into a partial eunuch. She would settle with Skye O'Malley once she and Jamil were married. She would destroy Skye's own shipping interests by using the corsair Reises who would be under her husband's command once the Sultan appointed Jamil the new Dey. For now, however, she was delighted that the famous physician who treated Jamil had been successful. Her lover had regained his full potency, and was a veritable bull in their bedchamber.

Before they departed Istanbul for their return to Algiers, he proposed marriage, as she had known he would. She blushingly accepted, despite the fact that he warned her he would want, nay, he would keep a harem. Claire, now the lady Nilak, cared nothing for the others he might bed as long as he loved her, and she was his wife with the power a dey's wife had. Jamil smiled at her honest admission thinking that they were really quite suited, and agreed that their marriage would take place in the month of Shawwal following the fast month of Ramadan.

Ramadan was now half over, and Claire was feeling quite pleased with herself at having discovered a Skye look-alike. How happy Jamil would be, and she, Claire, would insist on paying Osman's nephew whatever he wanted for the slave girl. It would be one of her bridal gifts to her beloved Jamil.

Arriving at her home, she hurried to find Jamil. He was being vigorously massaged by two young black girls, but as she entered the room he sat up smiling at her, his arms outstretched. Claire flew into them, and was rewarded with a kiss; a kiss that flamed into quick desire for both of them. "Get out!" Claire hissed at the two slaves, and they fled. Jamil didn't even wait for the door to close behind them before he was pulling her clothing off and drawing her down onto the couch with him. Being already hard, he wasted no time on the preliminaries and, parting her thighs, thrust into her with one smooth motion.

"Ahhh, Nilak, my love," he murmured, moving quickly on her, and Claire sighed with delight.

Afterward, as they lay together, he nibbling on her shoulder, she said excitedly, "I have just come from the house of Osman the astrologer, my darling, and what do you think I saw? A slave girl walking in the garden, the favorite of his nephew. She is a twin to Skye O'Malley! The same gardenia skin, the same marvelous black hair, and although I was not close enough to tell, I will wager the same blue eyes! I want to buy her from Osman's nephew for you."

"No," he said. "You must be mistaken. There could not be two women in the entire world who look like Skye Muna el Khalid."

"But she does, I tell you!" Claire insisted. "I know her as well as you do, Jamil. After all, she was married to my brother. This slave girl could be her twin!"

Jamil Agha sat up. "You are certain?" he said sharply.

"I am certain."

"Perhaps it is she, the beauteous Skye herself," he half whispered to himself. "Dear Allah, to have her in my power!"

"It cannot be Skye, Jamil. She grieves in Ireland for her dead husband, and besides, Osman knew her, too. How could Skye become the favorite of his nephew without him knowing it? This wench looks very like her, but she's much younger."

"Let us go to Osman's house now!" Jamil said eagerly. "It is almost sunset, and he is a hospitable man. I am sure I can get a look at the girl if the family is at the evening meal, and if she is all you say she is, then we will buy her then and there." He scrambled to his feet. "Help me to dress, Nilak, and then see that the slaves ready my horse."

As she aided her lover Claire began to grow uneasy. Perhaps she had made a mistake in mentioning the favorite of Osman's nephew, and her startling resemblance to Skye O'Malley. Jamil was far too eager, and what if this little upstart of a slave were to supplant her in her beloved's affections? Never! she reassured herself. Let Jamil sate his lusts on the girl. She, Nilak, would be his legal wife in just a short while, and then if the girl grew difficult she would simply disappear. Besides, Jamil would soon grow tired of her as he did of all women but Claire. She smiled to herself, and went to order Jamil's horse and her palanquin.

It was a simple but filling meal that was served in the house of Osman that night. A whole red-eyed mullet had been poached and was presented upon a bed of greens surrounded by lemons carved to represent seashells. A well-roasted capon stuffed with dried peaches, apricots, and plums sat on its platter of blue Fezware surrounded by matching bowls of saffroned rice and steamed artichokes. One enormous bowl of couscous had been placed midtable, and the marvelous scent of the wheat grains, the lamb chunks, and the many vegetables assaulted the senses of the four diners. An individual loaf of flat bread, warm from the ovens, was placed at each setting as were small kebobs of kid, green and red peppers, and small onions hot from the grill. There was a small bowl of yogurt at each place for dipping, and a large glass dish filled with green and black olives.

When the diners had done justice to the meal, and their profuse compliments had been sent to the cook who waited anxiously in the kitchen, the table was cleared of the main meal, and the fruits, large Seville oranges, dark purple grapes, golden pears, and fat green figs, were brought out, along with delicate gazelle horn pastries and bowls of pistachio nuts. A slave was handing around the delicate porcelain cups of black coffee when Jamil Agha boldly entered the room.

Osman almost swallowed whole the grape he had just popped into his mouth, and Alima gasped audibly. Jamil did not notice. His eyes were glued upon Skye, who was wondering what bad fairy had pushed Jamil back into her life on the very night she had planned her escape from Algiers. Skye knew that her only hope was in being Muna, the slave girl of the lord Kedar, and no one else. Then her eyes moved to the woman who mincingly accompanied Jamil, and she felt her anger well. Claire O'Flaherty! *The cursed Claire!*

Crossing the room in large, quick strides, Jamil reached Skye and pulled her roughly up. "By the soul of the prophet," he murmured excitedly, "you are truly a twin to Skye Muna el Khalid! *I must have you, and I will!*" His hateful hand was cupping her chin.

Angrily Skye yanked her head away from his grasp as Kedar, recovering from his shock, leapt to his feet with a roar of pure outrage and his hand went to his dagger. "You are a dead man!" he hissed. "No one touches what is mine without my permission! You have offended me, whoever you are, and I will have satisfaction!"

Jamil, with another burning look at Skye, reluctantly turned to Osman. "Is this loud fool your nephew, Osman?"

Osman nodded, feeling strangely calm. "My nephew, Kedar ibn Omar, my lord Jamil Agha."

"For your sake I will forgive him. Tell the fool who I am."

"Kedar, this is Jamil Agha, retired commandant of the Sultan's Casbah fortress and, it is rumored, soon to be the new Dey of Algiers."

"His rank does not give him the right to touch my property without my express permission, and where Muna is concerned you know my feelings, Uncle." Kedar turned to Jamil. "My lord," he said, "this woman is my betrothed wife. You have rendered me a fierce insult by your actions. If, however, you will offer me an apology, for the sake of my uncle, who obviously knows you well, I will consider the matter closed. I would be reluctant to come between my uncle and a friend."

"I want to buy the woman," Jamil answered.

"*What?!*" Kedar was astounded.

"I want to buy your slave woman," Jamil repeated. "Look at her,

Osman! Is she not the twin to Khalid el Bey's wife, Skye? *I must have her!*"

"She has dark hair and blue eyes like the lady Skye, I will grant you, Jamil Agha, but other than that I see no great resemblance."

"*You must!* She is a mirror image of the lady Skye. Nilak, come forward, my love! You know my betrothed wife, the lady Nilak, Osman. She knew the lady Skye in her own land. Is this woman not exactly like her, Nilak, my pet?"

"Exactly, my lord," Claire answered slowly, aware that the Kedar's slave girl was fixing her with a murderous gaze. "In fact if I did not know that Skye O'Malley was in Ireland or England at this time I would swear it was she."

"I fail to see a true resemblance," Osman said stubbornly.

"*I want her!*" Jamil said urgently. "Name your price, nephew of Osman! Whatever you desire I will pay, for I must have her!"

"She is not for sale," Kedar repeated icily. "She is to become my wife shortly." He stared angrily at Jamil Agha.

"Name your price, Kedar ibn Omar. Everything in this world has a price."

"She is not for sale, Jamil Agha. Can you not understand me? I am to marry this woman when the fast month is over. She is the one I have chosen to bear my heirs. *She is not for sale!*" Kedar's mouth was set in a grim line, and his eyes were snapping angrily. Some instinct told him that this Jamil Agha was a great danger to him, and all his senses were poised and alert.

"I must have her," Jamil repeated almost hypnotically, and seemingly to himself. "*I must!*" He looked directly at Kedar. "If you will not sell her to me then I must take her. I am a Janissary, and by the Sultan's own law what I desire is mine. I would not cheat you, Kedar ibn Omar, so I ask you a final time to name your price. If you do not then I shall simply confiscate this slave for myself."

Kedar felt anger, an incredible raging, burning anger, overcome him in a quick sweep. The blood pounded in his ears and in his head. Then, suddenly, he saw floating in a red mist before his bulging eyes the smug, satisfied face of Jamil Agha. He could almost hear his enemy's unspoken words. You are helpless. The woman is now mine. There is nothing you can do to prevent me taking her! In his mind's eye Kedar saw the flawless nudity of Muna writhing beneath the other man, gaining pleasure from him, giving pleasure to him. His control snapped, and with an animal bellow of undiluted rage he swiftly brought his hand up, threw himself at Jamil, and drove his dagger deep into the other man's throat.

Jamil died in an instant, his eyes wide with surprise as he crumpled to the floor, his dark red blood pumping out to stain both his robes and Kedar's. Osman stared both shocked and surprised, while Alima and Skye clung to each other, horrified, all three watching as Nilak added to the tragedy by stabbing Kedar in a screaming fury at almost the same moment as Jamil hit the floor. She drove her own dagger into Kedar's chest, following him down onto the floor to rage and cry as her bloodied weapon descended again and again and yet again until finally Osman pulled her off the already dead body of his nephew and disarmed her.

"Have the servants call the guard," Osman commanded his shaking wife, and Alima fled the death chamber.

Nilak was silent now, but slowly she raised her eyes and fixed them upon Skye. "*It is you, isn't it?*" she said despairingly.

Skye turned away, uncertain as to whether to answer her old enemy.

"Skye O'Malley!" Claire hissed the name. "It is you! I know it! At least tell me I am not mad."

Skye whirled about. "You have always been touched with madness, Claire, and you destroy everything you come in contact with. You were responsible for the destruction of your brother, and poor Constanza Burke, my husband's former wife, and now both Jamil Agha and Kedar."

"You don't mention your beloved husband, Niall Burke," Claire taunted nastily. "Perhaps you don't know that I was responsible—"

"I know what you were responsible for, Claire! I know that you drove poor Sister Mary Penitent to attempt murder. I know that you saw that my husband was sold into the galleys, but he is free now, Claire! He is safely on board one of my ships, and I join him tonight! In that, Claire, you have failed!"

"*I hate you!*" Claire snarled venomously. "I have always hated you!"

At that moment the doors to the dining room opened to admit a Janissary Capitan and several of his men. Osman quickly stepped forward, and Skye with incredible instinct moved back into the shadows, slipping behind a tapestry.

"My lord Osman, what has happened here?"

"Praise Allah, Capitan Amhet! There has been a terrible tragedy here. My nephew and Jamil Agha fought over this woman, and when Kedar killed Jamil, she killed Kedar."

"That is not so!" screamed Claire. "He lies! He lies! There was another woman that my beloved lord Jamil wished to purchase, and this Kedar took offense; and drew his dagger and murdered Jamil Agha!"

Osman shook his head. "As you can see," he said quietly, "there are but four places at my table. My nephew, myself, this woman, and Jamil Agha ate here tonight. The lady Nilak was betrothed to Jamil Agha, and yet she flirted outrageously with my nephew, who is, as you well know, a connoisseur of beautiful women. He was intrigued and beguiled by her charms, by her immodest and un-veiled face and blond fairness. She is the cause of all of this!" Osman's voice began to rise hysterically. "She is a wicked infidel woman who has caused the deaths of my old friend and my be-loved nephew! I demand the Dey's justice! I demand it now!" Then he broke into harsh sobs that he tried hard to contain, obviously embarrassed to show such a weakness before other men.

The Janissaries looked away in order that Osman might have a moment to collect himself, then Capitan Amhet said, "We will take the woman before the Dey now, my lord Osman. Will you come with us to tell him your tale?"

"He lies!" Claire screamed once more, but she was silenced by a brutal blow to her head from the capitan.

"Silence, infidel bitch! How dare you dispute the word of the famous lord Osman. His honesty is legend." The Capitan pushed her back into the arms of two of his men. "Hold her and keep her silent," he commanded.

"It is late," said Osman, seemingly beginning to recover from his bout with grief. "The Dey is old, and I would hesitate to awaken him at so late an hour. Take the infidel woman with you, and keep her the night. After first prayers at dawn I will appear before the Dey to demand justice."

Capitan Ahmet let his dark eyes slide over Claire's full bosom. "My men could use a treat before they must return to the fast in the morning," he said meaningfully. "I will take your suggestion, my lord Osman. I will see you at the palace directly after first light." Capitan Ahmet then signaled his men with a wave of his hand, and they half-dragged, half-carried Claire from the chamber.

"Rest well, Capitan," Osman said softly, and the capitan turned in the doorway and laughed. Osman waited until he heard the main door to his home close and the tramp of the patrol move off down the silent street before he said quietly, "You may come out now, Skye, my daughter."

"They may kill her with their attentions," Skye said as she came back into the light of the room. "Then again they may not. Claire was once a famous whore in London."

"Better she die under the Janissaries' attentions this night, my daughter, for if she lives, she will not survive the hooks."

Skye shivered. She knew all about the infamous hooks that were imbedded in the city walls, which served as places of execution for those unfortunate enough to be condemned to them. Claire, having actually murdered one man, and having been accused of being responsible for the murder of another, would most certainly be sentenced to the hooks. Her death would be a most painful one, for the city executioners knew just how to toss a body onto the hooks so that the condemned victim lived in screaming agony for some time—a warning to those tempted to mayhem, an amusement to others. "God have mercy on her," Skye whispered.

"You pray for such an enemy, my daughter?"

"It is a horrible way to die, Osman, even for Claire."

He placed a fatherly arm about her. "You must rest now, my daughter. I will send a message to your ship that you will be delayed until morning."

"No, I would go now," she said.

"In the morning, my daughter," he repeated gently. "Trust me, Skye. Have I ever disappointed you?"

"No," she responded, suddenly feeling totally exhausted as the shock of what had happened began to set in.

Osman led her from the room and put her into the capable hands of his wife. Together the two women moved automatically toward the women's quarters, where the slaves, not even daring to speak, helped the lady Alima to put Skye to bed.

"I shall not sleep," Skye insisted, although her eyes were heavy.

"Drink this," Alima insisted, pushing a small cup of sweetened pomegranate juice on her friend. "There is in it a tiny drop of opium, which will take you quickly to the land of pleasant dreams, dearest friend. Think happy thoughts as you drift away, my lady Skye. You are free of Kedar! Your beloved husband awaits you, and soon you will be reunited. Soon you will be home in your own land with your children." Her pleasant voice droned into Skye's consciousness, and Skye soon found herself asleep.

When she awoke she felt just the tiniest bit groggy, but a trip with Alima to the household baths quickly made her mind sharp and quick again. "Where is Osman?" she asked as they returned to Skye's chamber.

"He has gone to the Dey's palace to testify against the lady Nilak," Alima responded.

"If she lived through the night," Skye remarked.

"She must have, else my husband would be back already. He will be here to escort you safely to your ship, my lady Skye. Do not fear."

Osman returned close to the noon hour, a grim smile of satisfaction upon his face. The two women hurried to his library, both full of curiosity. "She has been executed upon the hooks," he told them, "although she will probably live on for several hours. Her goods and wealth have been divided between the Dey's treasury and Capitan Ahmet. It is over, Skye, my daughter. A door is closed, and another is opening for you once again. Are you ready to depart?"

"I am ready," Skye said quietly.

Her good-byes to Alima were said swiftly and privately within the library, and then, escorted by Osman, Skye entered the large palanquin with him. This time she felt no sadness in departing the house that had once belonged to Khalid, for it was now so clearly Osman's house. The bearers lifted the palanquin and began to move easily down the hill with their burden. Skye quickly noticed that they were taking the most direct route to the harbor, where her own flagship waited. As they exited the harbor gate nearest to the Dey's palace Osman commanded her, "Look back and up a moment, my daughter."

Skye turned, and the sight greeting her eyes caused her to gasp with horror and pity. She swallowed hard, forcing the bile back down her throat. Above her on the wall, Claire O'Flaherty, also known in her lifetime as Claro and Nilak, writhed weakly and helplessly, one of the vicious hooks securely jabbed through her midsection, another through a shoulder.

"Never again will her evil trouble you, Skye, my daughter. She has met her just end, and you are at last free of her wickedness," Osman's voice said quietly. "She will die shortly, and her body will rot there upon the hooks, scavenged by the carrion birds and whipped by the elements until it is no more. A fitting finish for a consummate villainess. Turn away now, Skye, my daughter. It is over."

"It is a picture I will remember always, Osman," Skye said feelingly, and she was unable to stop the tears that spilled down her pale cheeks.

"You will forget," he answered her with certainty. "I did not show you such a sight to distress you, but rather to assure you of your adversary's end. She will never harm you or yours again, Skye, and I wanted you to be certain of that fact." He reached out and touched one crystalline tear with a fingertip. "What a magnificent soul is housed in that beautiful body of yours, my daughter! It touches me beyond all that you can weep for so cruel an enemy. She would not have wept for you."

"Perhaps not, Osman, but her last hours have certainly made up for the evil she created. It saddens me even now that we were so assuredly fated to be enemies."

He shrugged fatalistically. "It was Allah's will, Skye, my daughter. One should never question God."

The palanquin suddenly stopped, and was set down carefully. Osman parted the draperies and stepped out, turning to assist Skye from the vehicle. They were directly before the gangway of her ship. Without a word she walked swiftly aboard, the astrologer following behind. Within the safety of the master cabin she pulled her veil aside. Eyes shining with unshed tears, she caught his hands and raised them up to kiss them fervently.

"Thank you, my dear friend," she said in a voice filled with emotion. "Thank you for everything. Just over the horizon my dearest husband awaits me, and I should not have gotten him back had it not been for you, Osman, and your family. We are ever in your debt! My children and I will remember you in our prayers each night as long as we live, for you have returned to us the thing most precious to us, a husband and a father."

Osman hugged her paternally, half in affection, half in concern. It was better that she not see his face at this moment. "Remember, Skye, my daughter, that all that happens is Allah's will, and with regard to each of us, our chosen destiny. Will you try not to rail against your fate, whatever it may be? Will you trust in the Creator to care for you no matter what? Though sometimes the storm seems dark, and without end, the light will eventually overcome it. That much I can promise you."

She drew away and smiled up at him. It was the first relaxed and genuine smile he had seen on her face in a very long time. "I am learning, Osman. Slowly, I will grant you, but I am learning. I will try to accept, and to trust, no matter what. For now, however, I see nothing but happiness ahead for me. Niall and I will return to Ireland, and I think I shall never roam again."

Osman smiled back at her. "Be happy, Skye, my daughter. Allah only knows that no one deserves it more than you do."

"Will we meet again, Osman?" she asked, her curiosity getting the better of her.

"Perhaps," he answered, and then raising his hand in a gesture of farewell, Osman the astrologer turned and without another word left the ship.

Finally the gangway was pulled aboard, and the O'Malley sailors loosened the lines that bound them to the dock, tossing them back to the quai. As the ship began to move Skye closed the cabin door and slowly began to remove her clothing. Thoughtfully she gazed at each piece of the silken gauze garments, smoothing them carefully as the memories crowded in on her. Then with a sigh and a shake of her head she folded the clothes resolutely and began to draw on her own things, the split-legged skirt, the silk shirt, her hose, her boots, her belt with its Celtic buckle of bright enamel. For a long moment she felt very odd in such garments, for she had grown used to her silken draperies. With a laugh she began to brush her hair, then braided it firmly into one single plait. A quick glimpse in the cabin's pier glass told her that Skye O'Malley had returned, and with a grin she whirled away from it, opened the door, and walked out upon the deck.

"Welcome back, m'lady," Bran Kelly said.

"Thank you, Bran. How is Daisy?"

"Well, and our first bairn, a lad, also."

"Bran! Congratulations! I see I shall have to train another girl to be my tiring woman now, but I don't mind as long as you and Daisy are happy."

"I doubt Daisy will let you, m'lady, but time enough to argue with her when we get home," Bran chuckled.

"How soon until we reach Lord Burke's ship, Bran?"

"A few hours if this breeze will hold, m'lady. No more, I promise."

Skye walked to the bow of the ship and stood there quietly, her face into the wind, never once looking back at the city. Yes, Algiers had seemed a different place this time, quite unlike the city she remembered adoring so in her days as Khalid el Bey's wife. Then it had seemed a magical, colorful, wonderful place filled with love. This time she had seen its harshness and its cruelty. The memory of Claire O'Flaherty twisting in agony would live with her for a long, long time. Skye breathed deeply of the soft and warm sea air to clear her head of the memories. Looking back was not the answer. She wanted to look forward now. Just over the horizon was her husband, and she could hardly wait to reach him. Indeed, had she believed that she could swim faster than her ship could sail, she would have gone over the side and into the sea.

Niall! Niall! She cried to him with her heart.

"Skye! Skye!" Niall Burke twisted frantically upon the bed of the master cabin. "Robbie? Robbie, are you there?"

"I'm here, lad." Robbie placed a calming hand on Niall Burke's feverish forehead, and his face puckered with worry.

"Where is Skye, Robbie? Where is my wife?" Niall begged plaintively.

"She's coming, laddie," Robbie soothed the ill man. "She's on her way this very minute."

"I'm thirsty, Robbie. So thirsty." Niall moved restlessly once more.

"Here, laddie." Robert Small held a goblet of wine to Lord Burke's lips. "Drink this."

Niall gulped at the goblet eagerly, but seconds later he was vomiting the liquid back into a basin. "Where are my jellies, Robbie? The comfits help when I feel poorly."

"They're gone, m'lord. You ate the last of them several days ago. If you only knew what was in them we might make you some."

"I don't know, Robbie. I've told you I don't know! Old Rabi made them for me, and Hamal gave me a box just before I escaped; but I have no idea what was in them." Niall's voice was reproachful and irritable at the same time. Then suddenly he slipped into a light slumber.

Robbie sighed. It was clear to him that Lord Burke had been poisoned with some potion. Why else would he be in such a state? Perhaps when Skye came aboard her presence would encourage her husband to make a swift and full recovery. Robert Small got up and moved to the cabin door. "Keep an eye on his lordship," he commanded the ship's boy. "If you need me I'll be topside waiting for Lady Burke."

"Aye, sir!" came the obedient reply.

Robbie stamped out on deck, glad to be free of the stifling cabin. With relief he drew in great lungfuls of clean sea air. "Any sign of her?" he asked MacGuire as he came abreast of the old captain.

"Crow's nest spotted a sail out of Algiers harbor making for us just a minute or two ago. It's just visible now on the horizon. How's his lordship?"

"Not good. I think he's dying, Sean, and I don't know what in hell is killing him!"

"Fash, man! Niall Burke's stronger than that. I've known him since he was a brash young boy. He can't be dying!"

"He is, I'm telling you," Robbie argued worriedly. "He's constantly thirsty, yet he can't hold anything either liquid or solid on his stomach, and for two days his bowels have suffered with the bloody flux. What sleep he can manage is disturbed by nightmares of horrendous proportions, his eyes are red, his skin and mouth so dry that both his lips and his elbows are peeling. I've never seen anything like it, man!"

"Maybe we should cup him," MacGuire suggested halfheartedly.

"Cup him? Jesu, man! You'll kill him for sure! God's bones, I hope this wind holds! Maybe the sight of her will revive him."

"If he dies it'll kill her," MacGuire said ominously. "To lose him once was bad, but to lose him a second time after what she's been through . . ." He crossed himself nervously.

Robert Small stared grimly out to sea. The very same thought had crossed his mind, but he had anticipated a possible bad end to this whole venture, and had come prepared for it. He wasn't going to let her die, and neither was Adam de Marisco. De Marisco had been frantic when Robbie had returned to England and told him what Skye had done. The island lord had come off his lonely rock ready to mount an expedition to rescue Skye. Now, Adam de Marisco was waiting patiently in Robbie's own cabin to give her aid and comfort should she need it.

Robert Small watched with a sense of foreboding as Bran Kelly's ship drew closer and closer to his own.

"Captain Small! Lord Burke is awake and calling for you." The cabin boy looked anxiously up at him, tugging him back into the present.

"Tell Lord Burke that his wife's ship is almost upon us, and that I will stay on deck to greet her. We will both be with him as soon as she is aboard."

"Aye, sir." The boy hurried back to the master cabin.

Bran Kelly maneuvered his vessel carefully in the rolling sea until the two ships were bobbing next to one another. A plank was put between them, and Skye swiftly crossed the small space, flinging herself into Robbie's arms. With a relieved groan he hugged her, enjoying the lovely fragrance of damask rose that always surrounded her. "God, Skye lass, thank heaven we have you back safely!"

She was taller than he, but she still managed to press her face into his leather jerkin, inhaling his tobacco scent. "Robbie," she murmured almost incoherently. "Dearest Robbie!"

For a long moment they stood locked in a close and mutually loving embrace, and then Skye pulled away. "Where is Niall, Robbie? Where is my husband?"

He looked up at her. "Niall is in the master cabin, Skye lass, but he's not been well for several days now."

"Not been well?" she repeated.

"I don't know what it is, lass. He's had the bloody flux, and he vomits. I'm not a doctor," he finished helplessly.

She whirled from him, and ran directly across the deck to the owner's cabin. She burst through the door, stopping short as she saw Niall Burke struggle to rise up from the bed to meet her only to fail and fall weakly back upon the coverlet. "*Niall!*" She was at his side in an instant, her eyes huge in her white face, taking in his appearance and knowing that it was not good. "Niall!" she repeated. He had gotten so gaunt! She had not seen him in a month, and he had gotten so thin, and so wasted. Kneeling, she took his hand in hers.

Niall Burke opened his silvery eyes, and his glance was sad, but filled with love. With trembling hand he reached up to touch her cheek, and then he sighed. "I had forgotten how soft your skin is, Skye, my love," he said low.

"Oh, Niall," she whispered, "my dearest, dearest love. It will be all right now, I promise you. We are on our way home again. In just a few weeks' time we shall see Ireland again, and the children are waiting." Skye had no idea that she was crying, the hot tears pouring down her face unchecked. "God's bones, Niall! The children won't know either of us. You went away just after Padraic's birth, and Deirdre was still a babe then. He'll be three and a half now, and she's almost five, my darling. High time we got back to our bairns, Niall! High time we gave them more brothers and sisters!"

"I'm dying," he said.

"*Nooooooo!*" She sobbed the word, but even as she did so she felt her heart constrict painfully, as if a hand were squeezing it hard.

"I don't want to," he whispered plaintively, "but I am. I don't know why, but I am."

She couldn't breathe. For a moment panic threatened to envelope her, but then her chest heaved and air filled her lungs. "You are very ill, Niall, my love," she said in a firm voice. A voice that belied her pounding heart; "but it doesn't mean you are going to die. I won't let you die! The ship is well provisioned with fresh foods and water, and I shall cook for you myself. Remember you told me how ill you were those years ago when Constanza took care of you? It's just a recurrence of your old illness. You'll see," she finished brightly. "I shall make you well again."

He sighed sadly. "Skye, I am dying. When Constanza cared for me I was suffering from the effects of a nasty wound, and shock. I don't know what this is, but I cannot last much longer." He fell back on the bed again, barely conscious with the effort of trying to make her understand.

"Don't die, Niall," she pleaded piteously with him as if he had personal control over the situation. "You can't die! Not after what I have been through to help free you! *You can't die!*"

His silvery gaze enveloped her again. "I know what you have been through, my love, I know. You are so brave, Skye, my darling. You have the heart of a lion, my love, and the soul of an angel. I shall miss you, but I am grateful that Darragh's blade did not kill me. I rejoice that Claire's plot did not prevent us from saying our good-byes. Now I know that there is a God in Heaven, Skye, for he has heard my most fervent prayers. He had granted me a final glimpse of you, my dearest heart."

She focused on him through the grayish blur of her tears, and saw that he spoke a greater truth than she was willing to recognize. "Don't leave me, Niall," she said quietly. "I cannot bear it if you leave me now. *Not now!*"

"The choice is not mine to make, Skye. Now kiss me, my darling wife. One kiss before I must leave you. A final memory for me to take with me on my journey." His glance was steadfast, almost sympathetic of her plight, for he knew it would be far harder on her than it would be on him.

Skye wanted to flee this nightmare. In her brain pounded the one thought! *Had it all been for this?*

"Skye!" His voice was urgent. His hand pulled loose of hers.

Slowly she bent her head, her eyes closing as her lips met with his. For a brief moment she felt incredible joy at the touch of his mouth on hers, but then the pressure of his kiss slackened and, lifting her head, Skye saw that his silver eyes were suddenly dull and sightless; Niall Burke was dead. She sat frozen by his side for some time, feeling nothing; neither heat nor cold, certainly not the beat of her heart. She was numb to her very soul. Finally Skye slowly rose and, reaching up, gently drew his eyelids shut. "Farewell, my first love, my final love. You're home safe in Ireland now, Niall Burke. You're safe at long, long last!"

She turned as the door to the cabin opened, and Robert Small entered the room. "He's dead, Robbie," she said in a calm, detached voice.

"Skye . . ." He moved toward her to comfort her.

"Set a course for Beaumont de Jaspre, Robbie. I will not give my husband's body up to the sea. I will ask permission of Nicolas to bury Niall in the cathedral at Villerose. In a few years when the flesh has rotted from his bones we will bring his remains home to Ireland. He would want it that way. As would the old Mac-William."

"Skye, 'tis madness you speak. Let us bury him now."

"If you give him to the sea, Robbie, then I will follow him into the sea. Do you understand me?" Her voice was flinty hard, its tone unlike anything he had ever heard from her before.

Robert Small knew instinctively that he must not argue with her, or anger her. She was poised on the very brink of madness, and the merest, faintest touch would send her hurtling into its dark depths.

"All right, lass," he said quietly. "We'll do it your way. Do you want the body removed from the cabin now, or shall we leave it?"

"The cargo hold is empty but for ballast?"

"Aye."

"Then put him there, Robbie, but not in the dark. Let there be candles about him, and a velvet cloth on his bier. I want a watch about him the entire time, and I shall pray by his side until we reach port."

"Let me have the boy bring you something to eat before you begin your vigil," Robbie suggested gently.

"Some wine," she answered. "Nothing more. I could not eat now."

"Some wine," he repeated, and backed from the cabin.

She stood where he had left her, silent and stonelike. The door opened again, and she heard a small voice say, "M'lady, the wine you asked for is here." Looking down, Skye encountered the curious glance of a flame-haired boy about nine. "The wine, m'lady." He held out a small tray upon which rested a goblet.

"What is your name, boy?"

"Michael, m'lady."

"Michael what?"

"Don't know, m'lady. Captain Small found me in an alley with me head all bloodied. I don't remember nothing except I'm called Michael."

"I have a brother named Michael, Michael. He is a priest. Would you like to be a priest?"

"No, m'lady! I wants to be like Captain Small!"

Skye looked down at the boy and, touching his hair with a gentle gesture, said, "Perhaps you will be like him one day, Michael. He's a good man to follow."

"Yes, m'lady," the boy said, and then hurried from the room.

The doorway was instantly filled by Adam de Marisco's huge bulk. "Skye." He stood looking anxiously in at her.

"Come in, Adam," she said.

"You're not surprised to see me, little girl," he stated flatly.

"Have you not always been there when I needed you, Adam?"

He stepped across the threshold and closed the door behind him. "I should never have let you go from me, Skye."

"The choice was neither yours nor mine, Adam. We are both

Elizabeth Tudor's loyal servants. Besides, once my friend, Osman, knew where Niall was, he would have found me wherever I was. Have I not given you enough pain, Adam, that you seek me out to suffer further?"

"I only suffer because you suffer, Skye." His arms went about her, and he held her tightly against his chest. Then without a word Adam picked her up, carried her across the cabin, and sat down with her in the stern window seat. He cradled her tenderly as he would have cradled a child, and sighing, she pressed her face for a moment against his silk-covered chest. The smell of him was familiar and reassuring. "Can you not cry, little girl?" he asked her.

She shook her head in the negative. "I seem to have no tears left in me, Adam. I have wept so often for Niall Burke that now in the hour of his death there is nothing inside of me but a vast and cold emptiness."

He understood. Of all the people she knew in the world he understood the best. "I am here, Skye," he said quietly. "I will not leave you."

"I know, Adam," was her answer, and then they settled into silent sorrow.

It didn't surprise him that she fell asleep in his protective embrace. He watched her slip from the painful reality of consciousness into a deep slumber, not moving as several seamen led by Robbie entered the cabin and quietly removed Lord Burke's body. Then the boy, Michael, returned to change the sheets and coverlet upon the bed, and when he had departed Adam de Marisco placed Skye into it, carefully removing her boots, her hose, her belt, and her double-legged skirt. Having tucked her snugly beneath the down coverlet, he slipped from the cabin knowing that she would sleep for many hours, for Robbie had put a sleeping draught into her wine. Sleep, Adam knew, was the best healer of all.

Skye slept for almost two days, her vigil forgotten, and by the time she awoke they were arriving in Beaumont de Jaspre. Her long rest had wiped the dark smudges from beneath her beautiful sea-blue eyes, but she was as calm and emotionless as when she had fallen asleep. She sat propped up by several large pillows, giving orders from her bed. On the small table by her was a plate with the remains of an egg that had been poached in marsala to tempt her appetite. Skye had eaten it, but it had had no taste. She ate to survive, nothing more.

"Will you go to Edmond de Beaumont, Robbie, and request a place in the cathedral for Niall's body? Tell him I will meet all expenses involved, and of course there will be a generous donation to the bishop for his kindness. Then go to the coffinmaker. I want the finest."

"What of the young duc, Skye lass?"

"What about him?" She looked puzzled.

"He loved you," Robbie said helplessly.

"He has, I am sure, by this time found a bride. Besides, I am not interested in taking another husband, Robbie, and I am most certainly not interested in Nicolas St. Adrian. He was a most charming and loving man, but that moment is past. One should always know when a moment is past, when it is time to walk quietly away."

"What if they want to see you?"

"Then they are most certainly welcome to visit me on board this ship, but please make it most clear, Robbie, that I will not set foot in the castle."

Robbie bowed formally. "As you wish, Lady Burke," he said shortly, and backed from the room.

"What will you do once Niall is buried, Skye?" Adam de Marisco asked.

"I don't know, Adam. Sail home, but then where is my home? Is it at Burke Castle? I think not. I have never liked Burke Castle, but I lived there because it was Niall's home. Innisfana is the home of the O'Malleys, but it really belongs to my stepmother Anne and her sons. Ballyhennessey is Ewan's holding, and Lynmouth is Robin's. Only Greenwood, my London house, is truly mine, and for now I am not of a mind to live in London. I don't know where I belong, Adam." She smiled a small, rueful smile. "Skye O'Malley, the wealthy and all-powerful," she gently mocked herself, "is without a place to lay her head."

"Come with me," he said to her.

"Where?"

"I am of a mind to visit my mother," he said slowly, a smile lighting his big features.

"And where does your mother live?" she demanded, a small smile surfacing on her own lips.

"In the valley of the Loire. I told you that my mother remarried when I was twelve. My stepfather is the Comte de Cher, and the owner of Archambault, a château located on the River Cher a small ways from Blois. Archambault cannot rival Chambord, or Amboise, or Blois, or even Chenonceaux; but it is a charming and warm place. I would like you to see it, Skye. I would like you to meet my family."

"How strange," she remarked seriously. "I have never thought of you having a family, Adam."

"Yet I do. Though I left France twenty years ago to return permanently to Lundy, I have occasionally made visits to see my mother and her family; but this time I have not been back in seven years. Did you know that I have two full sisters, a half-sister, and two half-brothers, Skye? They are all grown and married, but I have family, sweet Skye. I have a family almost as large as your own. Come with me to them!"

"Why not," she answered flatly. "There is nothing else for me to do now."

"You will have to go home eventually, Skye. You have your children, but for now I think it best you come with me and purge your grief for Niall Burke."

"Adam, my children do not need me. With the exception of the last two they are virtually grown, and the little ones have done without me for two years. If I never came back it would not matter to them. I have no husband, and I am not needed by anyone. The O'Malleys have obviously managed quite well in my absence, so what is to keep me from joining you at Archambault?" she said dully.

He had never heard her sound like this, so spiritless, so lacking in enthusiasm for everything, life in particular. He would have rather she had screamed and raged at the heavens for Niall's death. He would have far preferred she sobbed and wept at her loss. This cool detachment was a little frightening. Adam prayed it would pass with time.

She was wrong, he thought. Her children did need her, and more important from his point of view, he, Adam de Marisco needed her. Once he had lost her; once he had deliberately let her go. Now he had no intention of ever letting her go again. She didn't know it yet, but he was never going to let Elizabeth Tudor use Skye again. He would never again let her be helpless in the face of the Queen's demands. Skye would not return across the channel until she was his wife. Once she had accused him of not loving her enough to fight for her. This time he would fight any and all who tried to take her away from him. Skye was his for now, and for all time!

Part IV

France

Chapter 12

$\mathcal{E}$dmond de Beaumont sighed sympathetically. "Of course Skye may bury her husband in the cathedral, M'sieur Robert. *Pauvre belle!* How is she?"

Robbie shrugged. "She grieves, but shows it not. Her mien is strange and distant, but I have known her for so long that I know she is in shock over the suddenness of Lord Burke's death."

Edmond nodded. "Will she see me?"

"Of course," Robbie said, "but she did say that you must tell the duc she'll not set foot in this castle."

Edmond nodded. "I understand, but I doubt he will."

"He has a wife?" Robbie prayed the answer would be yes.

"But of course!" Edmond said. "We could not take the chance of the French claiming Beaumont de Jaspre. Three months after Skye left him Nicolas was married to Madelaine di Monaco. Their first child is due within the next few weeks."

"Good!" Robbie said. "She's poised on the edge of insanity, Edmond, and she'd not be able to cope with the young duc spouting a lot of passionate nonsense at her. I'm glad that Nicolas is happy."

Edmond nodded again, but said nothing. It was better that Robert Small not know that Nicolas still hungered for Skye. He had done his duty to the duchy by marrying a young daughter of Monaco's Prince Honoré. The Duchesse Madelaine was a lovely child of sixteen with pale-gold hair and soft, brown eyes. Where Skye had been tall and slender, Madelaine was petite and round. The two women were alike only in their sensitivity and intelligence. Edmond had chosen his uncle's bride carefully, seeking someone who would understand Nicolas's disappointment, and be willing to wait for it to ease. He had found the perfect candidate in Madelaine di Monaco, who adored the young duc from the first, but sensing his pain sought to soothe it.

"I hope for your sakes the babe is a boy," Robbie said pleasantly.

"Yes, we all pray for it," Edmond answered. "Still, both Nicolas and Madelaine are young and healthy. They should quickly fill the nursery of the castle."

The door to Edmond's library opened, and a lovely blond girl entered the room. "*Petit ami*, I heard that we had a visitor."

"Yes, Madelaine. This is an English lord, my friend Robert Small. Robert, may I present to you Madelaine, the Duchesse de Beaumont de Jaspre."

Robbie, his court manners elegant, bowed low over the little duchesse's hand. "Madame," he said. "I am honored."

"*Merci*, M'sieur Robert. I hope your stay in Beaumont will be a happy one."

"Alas, Madame la Duchesse, my mission is a sad one, but it need not concern one so fair."

"Robert has asked our permission to bury one of his passengers, an Irish nobleman who died aboard his ship. The gentleman's widow asked he be buried here rather than at sea," Edmond explained.

"The poor lady!" Madelaine exclaimed. "Is there something that I might do for her? Something that would give her pleasure even in her grief?"

"*Merci*, Madame la Duchesse," Robbie said, genuinely touched by the young girl. "Lady Burke needs nothing at the moment but a bit of peace. This incident has been very hard on her, as you can well imagine."

"I will go with Robert now, Madelaine," Edmond said, hopping down from his chair. "Where is Nicolas?"

"It is his day to sit in the Cours des Aides, Edmond. It should soon be over, though. I peeked earlier, and there were not many cases to be heard or judgments to be rendered today."

"Will you ask him to come to me when he is finished, Madelaine?"

She nodded, and then turned her sweet smile on Robbie. "Will you stay and dine with us, M'sieur Robert?"

"Alas, Madame la Duchesse, I cannot. My thanks, however." He made her a polite leg, and the young duchesse nodded toward him before departing the room. "She's lovely," he said to Edmond. "He ought to be damned happy with her!"

"She loves him," was the simple reply.

"Does she know about Skye?"

"Only that there was another woman, and that the woman and Nicolas could not marry," Edmond said. "No one in Beaumont de Jaspre would take it upon themselves to tell her about Duc Fabron's wife, for they would not hurt Madelaine."

"Good! Then with luck she need never know who Skye is."

"Unless Nicolas makes a fool of himself, Robert. He is not entirely over losing Skye."

"Surely he wouldn't risk hurting the lass, especially since she is soon to give him a child?"

"No, no, of course you are right," Edmond said, and prayed that Nicolas would behave sensibly. He walked to the table, stood on his toes to reach a decanter, and poured them each a small goblet of Beaumont rosé. Then Edmond handed Robbie his glass, regained his chair, and, lifting his goblet, said, "To better days, *mon ami!*"

"Aye," Robbie agreed, and together they downed the wine.

As the cool, sweet liquid slid down their throats the door to Edmond de Beaumont's library swung open again, and Nicolas St. Adrian, Duc de Beaumont, strode into the room. "*Where is she?*" he demanded, his green eyes flashing with impatience.

"Sit down, *mon oncle*," Edmond warned the duc. "Sit down, and you will be told what you need to know."

Nicolas flung himself into a chair, and with a gesture of frustration ran his hand through his auburn hair. "Please," he said to Robert Small, "where is she? Is she all right?"

"Lady Burke is aboard her ship, which is anchored at quaiside in your harbor, monseigneur," Robbie said. "She has returned to Beaumont de Jaspre to ask that you allow her to bury her late husband, Lord Niall Burke, in a niche in the cathedral. She intends in several years, when the flesh has left his bones, to return those bones to his own home in Ireland. In the meantime she must inter him where she can retrieve him when the time comes. M'sieur Edmond has graciously agreed to allow Lord Burke burial space."

"*Ma pauvre doucette*," Nicolas said softly. "I must go to her!" He stood up, and was gone from the room before the tiny Edmond could prevent his leaving.

"Nicolas!" the dwarf's voice followed his uncle.

"Don't fret yourself, Edmond," Robbie said, an amused smile creasing his face. "Do you remember Lord de Marisco?"

"The black-haired giant? Indeed I do!" Edmond replied.

"He is with her aboard her ship, and he will not allow Nicolas either to hurt her or to make a fool of himself. It is better this way, my friend. The young duchesse will not be party to any of what transpires between those three, and Nicolas will understand once and for all that Skye is not for him."

Edmond relaxed back into his seat. "You are right, Robert! It is better this way. More wine?"

And together the two sat companionably quaffing the Beaumont rosé while Nicolas St. Adrian called for his horse and then hurried from the castle down through his tiny capital to the harbor. It wasn't hard to find her vessel, for the pennant flying from its mast, the gold sea dragon upon a field of sea blue, was as clear a signal as a beacon on a black night. As he stamped up the gangplank he was met by Bran Kelly.

"M'sieur le duc," Bran said, bowing politely. "It is good to see you again."

"And you, Captain Kelly. Your good Daisy is well, I trust."

"Yes, monseigneur."

"Announce me to your mistress, Captain."

"As you will, monseigneur. Please to follow me." Bran led him across the deck to Skye's quarters, knocked at the door, and, entering, said, "Duc Nicolas to see you, m'lady."

"He may enter," came her voice, but Nicolas was already pushing past Bran into the cabin.

"*Doucette!*"

"Monseigneur." Her voice was impersonal, her gaze equally so.

Nicolas St. Adrian felt some of the confidence drain out of him. The pale, beautiful woman garbed in black who stood before him was somewhat forbidding. His remembrance was of a passionate creature whose every movement, every gesture, every word was filled with life and love. The lady before him was, however, quite distant and cool. He recognized the face, and the exquisite form, but as for the rest . . . "I welcome your return to Beaumont de Jaspre, madame," he said feebly.

For a second her manner softened. "Thank you, Nicolas. I am so sorry to inflict this pain upon you, but there was nowhere else I might go. You do understand?"

He nodded slowly, and then he said quickly, "I have never stopped loving you, *doucette!* Never!" and his arms were about her, drawing her close to him.

"I, however, stopped loving you the moment I knew that my beloved Niall was alive!" she said harshly, pushing him away, freeing herself from his unwanted embrace. "For shame, Nicolas! Do you think that because my husband is dead I shall come running to you? What of your bride? What of the child she carries?"

"They mean nothing to me, *doucette!*" he exclaimed rashly. "*You!* Only you mean anything to me! I have prayed! Dear God, I have gotten down on my knees and prayed for your return to me! I have not prayed like that since I was a child!"

"You are still a child, Nicolas! A selfish little boy! Do you hear what you are saying? You are saying that you will abandon your wife and your heir for me. Where is your sense of responsibility, Nicolas? Did I teach you nothing?! Your duty is to Beaumont de Jaspre, and then to your people. You also now owe a duty to your wife, and the child that will soon be born. I do not want you. I want no man ever again. All I ask of you is that you allow me to bury my husband here. If you are not of a mind to grant me that request, then tell me now, and I will be on my way."

"*Doucette*, I implore you," he said, and she felt a certain pity for him.

"Nicolas," Skye said in a sad, yet patient voice, "I implore *you*. I implore you to give up this fantasy you seem to have about me. I loved you. I will not deny that fact, but now I question the quality of that love. I felt no reluctance in leaving you, Nicolas. I was only sad to go because I disliked hurting you.

"I would have never returned to Beaumont de Jaspre were it not for Niall. Even if I had not found him, Nicolas, I would have gone home to Ireland, or perhaps back to Elizabeth Tudor's court; but I would not have come back to you. Instinctively you must have sensed that, and you did what you should have done. You married and begat an heir." She reached out and touched his face gently. "I left the *Gull* this afternoon, and walked about the market by the harbor, a hood about my head so I might not be recognized. The talk is all of the little Duchesse Madelaine and her coming child, Nicolas. They say she is a madonna; and that God blessed them greatly when Duc Fabron made you his heir and you took Madelaine di Monaco to wife.

"You have done the right thing, Nicolas. Why can you not see it? Why do you seek to destroy that which has brought you the most happiness? Can you tell me truthfully that you do not love your wife?"

"Of course I love her!" he exclaimed. "One cannot know Madelaine and not love her. She is sweetness itself, but with you it was different. She is honey, but you are fire, *doucette!* How I crave your warmth!"

Skye allowed herself a little smile. Nicolas would ever be the romantic Frenchman. He was irrepressible. "Fire, *mon brave*, can destroy you," she said. "Hear me well, Nicolas. When Niall Burke died, I died. Oh, I realize that my mind and my body still function, but believe me when I tell you that I am a dead woman. There is naught left inside me but a wasteland. Go home to your wife, Nicolas, and leave me be."

He stood staring dumbly at her, and Skye would have sworn that there were tears in his forest-green eyes. Then, suddenly, from the corner of the cabin a shadow arose, and Nicolas was stunned to see a giant of a man with raven-black hair and smoky blue eyes come forth. "You have heard Lady Burke, lad. Go now."

Pure unreasoning anger swept over Nicolas, and blindly he drew his sword. "Who is this man?" he shouted at Skye. "He is your lover! I know he is your lover!" He lunged murderously at Adam.

Adam de Marisco stepped easily aside, and with a quick movement disarmed the younger man. "I am Adam de Marisco, the lord of Lundy Island, M'sieur le Duc. My own holding is larger than this tiny bit of land you call a duchy. I have known Skye for many years. I intend to marry Skye when she is over her grief. It is an honest offer which I can make her, but you cannot, monseigneur. Now you may leave this ship under your own power, as Lady Burke has asked, or I shall toss you from the upper deck if you so choose, M'sieur le Duc." He smiled affably down into Nicolas's surprised face.

"Adam!" Skye gently admonished him. Then she turned to Nicolas. "Please go, Nicolas. What was once between us is but a memory."

"Yet a sweet memory, *doucette*, and one I will remember all of my life." The anger had drained from him as Adam's sensible speech penetrated his brain. Gallantly he took her hand and raised it to his lips to kiss it ardently. "You are welcome in Beaumont de

Jaspre as long as you choose to stay, and I shall not disturb your mourning again, Skye. Forgive the impetuosity of my behavior, *doucette*. I have really tried to be as you advised me to be, and I believed I was succeeding until I learned of your arrival."

Skye gently disengaged her hand from his. "You are strong of will, Nicolas. You will not backslide again. Now go home to your wife. After Niall's funeral, I do not want to see you again."

He nodded and, sending a warning look at Adam, said, "I will know if you are not good to her, Monseigneur de Marisco." Then he turned, and was quickly gone from the cabin.

"If you laugh I shall never forgive you!" Skye snapped at Adam, whose whole face was collapsing with mirth.

"I cannot help but wonder what revenge your little French cock would take on me were I to mistreat you."

"You had no right to tell him that I will marry you," she said with more spirit than he had seen her show in the last few hours.

"But you are going to marry me, Skye. I have no intention of allowing you to be used by anyone ever again."

"Even you, Adam?" she asked cruelly.

"Even me, little girl," he said affably, and Skye found herself totally nonplussed by his attitude.

Niall, Lord Burke, was placed in a wooden coffin, and the coffin put into a marble vault in the chapel of St. Anne in the duchy's cathedral. Père Henri, now Bishop of Beaumont de Jaspre, blessed the tomb and then said a mass over the remains. He had hoped to comfort Skye, and so that he might not be hurt she told him that he had; but the truth was that she felt empty. Niall was dead, and she was haunted by the thought that it had all been for nothing.

She bid Robbie and Bran Kelly a hasty farewell. "I can't go back," she told Robert Small. "Not yet. I am not ready to face either my family or my children or the Queen. Especially not the Queen, and Lord Burghley. God only knows what plan they have for me this time, Robbie, and I am not strong enough to deal with them."

"Where will you be?" he questioned her.

"With Adam. He will make no demands on me, Robbie. He is taking me to visit his mother at Archambault in the Loire Valley."

Robert Small nodded. He had never seen her so low. She would be safe with Adam de Marisco, and for now that was all that mattered. "Shall I tell the Queen if she asks where you are?"

"Can you deny Elizabeth Tudor, Robbie?"

"Yes," he said without hesitation, "I can for you, Skye lass. If asked, I shall say you are in France, but I know not where."

"Thank you, Robbie," she replied, hugging him hard.

Nicolas St. Adrian had insisted on outfitting them for their journey. "You are, whether you remember it or not, the dowager duchesse of this little kingdom of mine," he told her firmly. "I would be remiss in my duties to my late brother if I did not see that you had a coach, outriders, and your own saddle horses."

She thanked him there in the cathedral, where she had been making her good-byes. "You are generous, Nicolas."

"You will also find all your clothes packed and stored in the coach, *doucette*. Your Daisy would not bring them back with her to England, saying that you would have no use there for 'French feathers,' as she so tartly put it. Those feathers, however, will stand you in good stead now as you travel across France."

"You once more have my thanks," she told him.

He nodded briefly. "Go with God, *doucette*," he said, lifting her hand to his lips and placing a tender kiss upon it.

"Thank you, Nicolas," she said softly, "and I hope that it is a healthy son your petite duchesse carries." Then Skye turned away from the young duc and, slipping her arm through Adam's, left the cathedral.

At the foot of the steps was a fine, dark blue traveling coach with the coat of arms of Beaumont de Jaspre emblazoned on its sides. Upon the box sat a coachman and his assistant. There were a dozen armed outriders, four of whom would ride before the coach, four behind, and two on either side. There were two mounted grooms, each leading a pedigreed horse. The coachman's assistant was quickly down to open the door of the vehicle and help Skye into it. The interior was as elegant and as luxurious as the exterior, the walls padded in fine, soft, cream-colored leather, the seats done in pale-blue velvet. The windows, which could be raised or lowered, were Venetian glass edged in bright brass. On each side of the coach were delicate crystal vases filled with fragrant arrangements of dried lavender and lemon thyme, and small, carefully mounted crystal lamps, their gold holders fitted with pure beeswax tapers.

"You will find that the back of the seat facing you pulls down, madame," the coachman's assistant said. "Should you need it, there is a lap robe, as well as a basket with fruit, cheese, bread, and wine."

She nodded her thanks, and the assistant withdrew to climb back onto the box while Adam pulled himself up into the coach. The door securely shut, the vehicle rumbled slowly off across the cathedral square, through the narrow streets, and finally onto the north road that led to France and into the Loire Valley. Skye never looked back. She had done what her instinct had told her to do with Niall's body. He had not been lost to the sea, and in this she had cheated Mannanan MacLir. One day Niall Burke would come home to Ireland and be buried in Irish soil next to his father, where he belonged. She could almost feel the old MacWilliam's approval of her deed.

They rode in silence the entire day, and when evening came the coach stopped at a comfortable-looking inn. Despite the elegance of their equipage, only one room could be given them, for the inn was crowded. Adam offered to sleep in the stables with the outriders, but Skye would not hear of it.

"I think that we can share a bed platonically," she said, and he nodded.

"I think you only agree to let me in your room so you will have someone to maid you," he teased her gently. Skye had refused to take a girl from Beaumont to be her servant. She was not so helpless, she had declared, that she could not care for herself the relatively short time of their journey. Once they were at Archambault, Adam's mother would see she had someone to care for her.

They ate a simple country meal of roasted duck, artichokes with olive oil and tarragon vinegar, new bread, a soft cheese, and a bowl of early cherries. The innkeeper served them a smooth, rich Burgundy wine with their meal. Afterward they watched as a troupe of gypsies played and danced in the courtyard for the guests' coins.

When the gypsies had finally disappeared back to their encampment, Adam and Skye climbed the stairs to the inn's second floor where their room was situated. It was a cheerful, airy chamber overlooking the moonlit fields. There was a fireplace in which a small fire burned to ward off the evening's chill, a chair, and a big, comfortable bed with blue and white linen hangings. The bed had been opened by a maid, and beckoned them enticingly. Their coachman had brought Skye a small trunk that he told her contained the things she would need on her journey. "The Duchesse Madelaine packed them herself for you, madame."

"You know the duchesse?" Skye queried him, curious.

"Ah, yes, madame. My wife is her tiring woman. We came with her from Monaco."

"Your mistress knew that I was the last Duchesse of Beaumont?"

"Yes, madame."

"You will thank her for me when you return to Beaumont de Jaspre. Her kindness is appreciated."

Skye thought about Nicolas's young wife as she opened the tiny trunk and lifted out a simple white silk nightgown. She was far wiser and more mature than Nicolas suspected. Skye smiled. Nicolas, although he didn't know it, was in very good hands, and Beaumont de Jaspre was going to prosper.

"What are you smiling about, little girl?"

She looked up at him. "Nothing, Adam. Just a woman's thoughts. Will you unhook my gown?" She felt his big hands gently undoing the fastenings.

"There," he said when he had finally undone the last of them. Adam hadn't realized the effort it would take on his part not to touch her. Am I a ravening beast, he questioned himself, that I cannot undo her gown for her without wanting to make love to her? Dear God, he loved her so very much! He wanted to take her in his arms and comfort her. He wanted to drive away all the bad times in her life, and make her remember only the good. Slowly he turned away and began to undress himself, pulling from his saddlebags a white silk nightshirt that he rarely wore. Tonight, however, it would be best to have as much as he could put between himself and Skye. When he turned back to her she was seated on the edge of the bed brushing her long black hair with a gold brush. "Would you rather I slept on the floor, little girl?" he asked in what he hoped passed for an impersonal voice. "I could easily wrap myself in the coverlet, and with a pillow for my head I should be quite comfortable."

"The floor is damp," she said, looking up at him with a smile. Then her eyes widened, and Skye giggled.

Adam looked puzzled. "What is it?" he asked.

"You're wearing a nightshirt!" she exclaimed, amused.

"You're wearing a nightgown," he countered.

"I've never seen you in a nightshirt," she answered.

"I never felt the need to wear one with you, Skye," he said solemnly.

She thought a moment, and then said, "Oh," in a small voice, and her teeth caught at her bottom lip.

"I'll sleep on the floor," he said.

"No, Adam, you'll catch your death if you do. Look! The bed is large, and comfortable." She paused a moment, then added, "And if I am not ready, or able to . . . to . . . you know what it is I say; we are two grown people who surely can control our passions. I know I am being unfair, Adam, but I need you near me! Do you understand what it is I am saying?"

"Get into bed, Skye. The night has grown chill. You need your sleep, and we have an early start."

Obediently she climbed into the big bed and snuggled down beneath the warm coverlet. Bending, Adam blew out the single candle, and only the low firelight lit the room as he slipped in next to her. For some minutes they lay in silence upon their backs, each stretched out long and stiff, and then Adam quietly reached out and took her hand in his large paw. "You say nothing, and yet I can hear you screaming with your pain, little girl. Tell me now! Tell me what is in your mind and heart. Tell me before it grows so big that there is no controlling it, and you destroy yourself."

"It was all for nothing," she said, the anguish plain in her trembling voice. "It was all for nothing, Adam." She sighed, and a shudder rippled through her slender frame. "Niall is dead. He is as dead now as he was to me two years ago; but two years ago I had learned to live with it. Do you know what I have done, Adam? I have whored. I am no better than those women who inhabit the waterfront brothels in every port. I used my body, and I have been used. I did not think when I agreed to Osman's proposal that it would be so hard, and perhaps if my husband had survived it might not have been; but Niall is dead now, and I cannot reconcile myself to the fact that it has all been for nothing."

"You got him out of Morocco, Skye. He died a free man."

It was as if she did not hear him, or if she did the facts were not enough to soothe her. "Kedar," she said. "God's blood, Adam, how I hate the very sound of his name! He was Osman's nephew, and the man whose slave I was. Look at my ankle, Adam." She stuck her foot out from beneath the coverlet, and in the dim light from the fire he could see something glittering on her ankle. "Do you know what is written on the medallion of the anklet? It says, *Muna, Property of Kedar*. I have not yet had the time to have a smith remove it. *Property of Kedar*, Adam, and I was most assuredly that. My very life depended upon his goodwill. He possessed me with a ferocity I have never known, Adam. He took everything I was forced to offer, and much I did not. I spent those months in his possession, terrified that he would devour me both body and soul with his passion, with his terrible need to consume me. He did things to me, Adam, things that I did not imagine a man could do to a woman, and it was never enough! Oh, God! I shall never be free of him! The memories of him will haunt me all my life, and the memories of my beloved Niall will haunt me, too. I see now that it would have been better if I had left him to meet his end in Morocco rather than to betray the vows we made before God when we were wed. Oh, Adam! I am so lost!"

With a low growl of anger Adam climbed from the bed and flung the covers back. Gently he lifted her ankle in one hand while with the other he snapped the gold band from her leg as if it were a ribbon. Striding to the window, he threw back the shutters and flung the offensive anklet as far as he could. Then he closed the shutters again, and calmly climbed back into the bed.

Skye turned and, pressing her head into his shoulder, began to weep. Stunned, Adam wrapped his arms about her and let her cry. Tears, he knew, were a catharsis. There was nothing else he could do, for he could never completely wipe away the terrible memories she would retain of her time with Kedar. Gradually her sobs died, and her breathing evened out and she slept nestled against him. Adam also slept then, only to be awakened by piteous cries as Skye, caught in the middle of a dream, relived some of her Moroccan adventure. *He did things to me, Adam, things that I did not imagine a man could do to a woman*, she had said. He was both horrified and shamed by what a member of his sex had done to her. Skye was a woman to be cherished and adored. She was a good companion and a brave comrade. She had been made to be loved, and she was the best friend he had ever had. It both pained and angered him that she had suffered so.

It took them eight days to reach Archambault from Beaumont, and during those eight days Adam learned in detail Skye's adventures in

Morocco. After that first night he had insisted that she tell him everything, and as more and more of her agony came to the surface, the less violent her nightmares became. As he listened he realized how very much he loved her. This time she was not going to get away from him, and the afternoon they neared his mother and stepfather's château through the exquisitely rolling green countryside of the Loire River Valley he told her so.

"You are going to marry me, Skye."

"I will never marry again, Adam. I have had all I can of belonging to a man. I will be my own mistress until I die. Please try to understand that, my darling."

"I understand that you have had a terrible experience, Skye, but I am determined that you will be my wife. Being married to me will not make you my property. You will always be your own woman; but you will be my wife as well. I love you, little girl. I have for so very long a time. My greatest treasures are my good name and my honor. I would bestow my name upon you."

"How cruel you make me feel to refuse such a magnificent gift, Adam, but no. I must be free! Please try to understand."

He sighed. "You need time, Skye, and I am willing to give you all the time you need."

"You are impossible!" she scolded him.

"I am a man in love," he countered. "You are the first woman I have asked to marry me in twenty-two years, Skye."

"Oh no, Adam de Marisco," she cried, outraged. "You shall not make me feel guilty because the daughter of some obscure count once refused your suit! You know better where I am concerned."

"You will marry me!" he laughed, pulling her into his arms and nuzzling her neck with his lips. "Dammit, little girl, I love the smell of you!"

She pushed half-heartedly against his chest. "I won't!" she said stubbornly. Yet Skye felt lighter of heart than she had in months. Adam de Marisco was so very good for her, and she knew it.

Suddenly he was serious again, and he gently tipped her face up to his, his thumb and forefinger on her chin. His smoky blue eyes seemed to envelope her, and she thought for a startled moment that she might faint, but she didn't. Instead her heart raced madly, and a faint flush touched her skin as he murmured in his deep voice, "I adore you, you sapphire-eyed Celtic witch!" And then his mouth was closing over hers in a tender and melting kiss that left her both breathless and near to tears. "You see," he teased her when he had lifted his lips from hers, "you are yet alive, and still very much a woman, little girl."

She was surprised. When Niall had died she had thought that she could never again stomach a man's touch. Not after Kedar and his excesses. Still, this was Adam, her dearest and most beloved of friends; but deep in her heart Skye knew that was not the whole truth. She had always loved Adam in her fashion, and she strongly suspected that love was now deepening in a far different way. *I will not give up my freedom,* she thought furiously to herself. *I won't!*

Adam's mouth was smiling knowingly at her, and she hit him upon the chest with her fist. "I will be my own woman, you ass! I will never again belong to anyone but myself! Stop smiling, Adam! Oh, I hate you when you are smug!"

He began to laugh, and his laughter warmed her, much to her outrage. "In the end, little girl, you will marry me," he said in a voice deep and tender with his love for her. "You may take your time, Skye; whatever time you need to admit to what you know in your own heart. God only knows I have proved a patient man where you are concerned."

"Hah!" she snapped at him. "How many times did you turn me away, Adam de Marisco? Twice, as I recall, and now suddenly it is I who would turn you away, but you will be patient. I swear to you I will not marry again! I will learn to use men as they use women. I wonder how patient you will feel when you see me flirting with another man, Adam."

He grinned infuriatingly at her. "Get it out of your system, little girl, and when you are ready to be sensible again I will be waiting patiently for you, as I always have."

"Ohhh!" God's bones, he was making her so angry. He was treating her as if she were a child instead of a woman of thirty-one who had just come through a terrible experience. Skye drew in a deep breath to scold him further, but he forestalled her, saying:

"Look, there is Archambault!"

Unable to resist, Skye looked through the coach window. There on a gentle hill that rose above the River Cher, she saw a charming small château with its steep red-tiled roof, its four rounded corner towers, and very French dormer windows. Below it along the river were the vineyards of Archambault, and behind them a generous estate of fields and woodlands. It was a perfect summer's day with a cloudless, deep-blue sky and bright golden sun. The river ran cheerfully by the green vines and ripening fields of maize and wheat. The forest was in full leaf. There were cattle grazing in the fields, and sheep, too. It was altogether the most peaceful scene Skye had ever seen. She had not believed that there was any place on this earth *that* peaceful.

The coach rumbled onward up the hill to the château, drawing to a stop before a tier of steps crowned with carved and gilded double doors of weathered oak. As the vehicle stopped, the doors to the château were swung open by a liveried servant, and several footmen came running down the steps followed by a rather beautiful woman in a taffeta gown the color of purple primroses, its low-necked bodice embroidered in silver and crystal beads. The woman's hair was coiffed as Skye wore hers, parted in the middle, drawn back and gathered into an elegant chignon. There were pearls in her hair.

"Adam!"

"*Maman!*" He sprang from the coach, and caught her up in a bear hug of an embrace, squeezing her until she shrieked, and kissing her soundly upon both cheeks.

"Put me down, you great oaf!" she scolded him laughingly. "You are destroying my coiffure, and what will your lovely Skye think of me if you do!"

"She will think what I think. She will think you are the most beautiful, the most marvelous mother in the whole world!" He set her gently on her feet.

Gabrielle de Saville's glance softened with the fondness a mother harbors for her firstborn, then quickly she demanded, "Well, where is she, my son? Where is this paragon you have written me about?"

Skye felt her cheeks coloring as she heard Adam's mother's words. As she stepped down from the coach, her small hand in Adam's big one, she had no idea of how lovely she looked. She was wearing a simple light silk traveling dress of leaf green with a soft scooped neck and comfortable hanging sleeves, which were cool for coach travel. She had only a simple strand of pearls about her neck and matching earbobs in her ears. She looked fresh and very beautiful.

"Maman, may I present to you Skye, Lady Burke, better known as Skye O'Malley. Skye, my mother, the Comtesse de Cher."

"You will call me Gaby, my dear," Adam's mother said graciously, "and I shall call you Skye. You are every bit as fair as Adam has written. Welcome to Archambault! I hope you will stay with us for a long visit."

Skye blinked back her sudden tears. "Madame . . . Gaby . . . your welcome is most kind. I am so grateful for your hospitality."

Gaby de Saville put a motherly arm about Skye. "There, my dear, you are safe now. Here at Archambault nothing will hurt you. Adam has written to me a little bit about your bravery and how you sought to rescue your poor husband from Morocco. I am so sorry about his death."

Skye bowed her head.

"Come," said the comtesse, "we must not stand here. The family is gathered inside waiting to meet you."

As they walked up the steps and into the château Skye looked admiringly at Adam's mother. She had borne her eldest son when she was fifteen. She was now fifty-seven, yet her thick, dark blond hair was still full of warm golden lights, and her eyes, the same smoky blue as her son's, were bright and knowing. She was nearly as tall as Skye herself, and she was as slender as a girl, with fine, full breasts. Adam, Skye decided, did not look like his mother except for the color of his eyes and his nose, for Gaby de Saville had given her son her aristocratic, elegant French nose. The comtesse's face was that of a little cat, though, with a pointed chin, and a provocative rosebud of a mouth. As they followed her into a lovely salon with long windows looking out onto a colorful garden of brightly colored flowers Skye thought that she was going to have a friend in this charming Frenchwoman.

The salon was filled with chattering people who all stopped in mid-sentence and stared as they entered the room. In the moment of heavy silence that followed a scholarly looking man detached himself from the group and hurried forward to place an arm about the comtesse.

"Skye, my dear, this is my husband, Antoine de Saville, Comte de Cher."

"M'sieur le Comte, you are so kind to offer me your hospitality," Skye said, holding out her hand to be kissed. She liked the look of this balding, somewhat paunchy man whose brown eyes twinkled appreciatively at her.

"Madame, how could I refuse such beauty," the comte said, kissing Skye's hand fervently.

His greeting seemed a signal for the room to erupt. "Adam!" three of the women shrieked, flinging themselves at him. With a delighted roar Adam de Marisco managed to envelope them all in a crushing embrace.

"*Mes enfants! Mes enfants!*" Gaby cried. "You must wait to greet your brother until after I have introduced our guest.

"Pardon, maman," the three said with one voice as they stepped away from Adam.

"Skye, my dear, these three ill-mannered creatures are my daughters. This is Isabeau, and Clarice, and Musette."

The three women curtseyed, as did Skye in return. She knew that Isabeau Rochouart, and Clarice St. Justine were Adam's full sisters, children, like him, of Gaby's first marriage to John de Marisco. The two sisters looked like their mother, but their hair was dark, as was their brother's. Musette de Saville Sancerre was Adam's half-sister, and she, a miniature of her mother, was just twenty-five, the youngest of Gaby's children.

Now the others came forward to be introduced. Alexandre de Saville, the oldest child of the comtesse's second marriage, a widower with three young children. Yves de Saville and his wife, Marie-Jeanne, with their children. Robert Sancerre, Musette's husband, and their three children. Then there was Isabeau's husband, Louis, and their daughter, Matilde, who was sixteen. The last to be introduced was Henri St. Justine. He and Clarice were the parents of four children ranging in age from nineteen to eleven, and they had all come to see their Uncle Adam.

Skye was both delighted and astounded by the size of Adam de Marisco's family. This was certainly a side of him that she had never known or even suspected existed. For her, he had always been the rather lonely island lord whose mother had remarried and lived in France. He had mentioned his sisters, Isabeau and Clarice, in passing, but she had never realized that his mother had had a second family, and that Adam was so obviously beloved by them all, even his two younger half-brothers. She stood now almost shyly as they clustered about him, kissing and hugging him, and chattering all their news.

Then she felt a hand on her arm, and she was led off to a comfortable settle. "They will all talk at him for the next ten minutes until they realize he is really here, and intends to stay for a time," said the Comte Antoine de Saville, smiling at her.

"I did not realize that his family was so large," Skye said.

"He does not talk about them?"

"No," she answered slowly, "but now I suspect he kept this knowledge to himself lest he grow lonely for you while living by himself on Lundy. He would not neglect his small holding."

"Perhaps now," the comte said, "that will change, madame."

"Of course it will, darling," Gaby said, seating herself next to them. "Adam tells me that he plans to wed with our lovely Skye."

"*No!*" The word burst harshly forth from between her lips as Skye reddened with embarrassment.

"Oh dear," Gaby murmured, looking equally chagrined.

"You don't understand, Gaby," Skye said in an effort to explain. "I love Adam, but I will not marry again. Each of my husbands has suffered death. I am a jinx! Besides, I want to be my own woman now, not someone's possession. Has Adam told you that I spent close to a year in the harem of a wealthy Moroccan in my effort to rescue my husband? For the Arabs a woman is a possession like a sword, or a hawk, or a garment; and I was treated exactly like that. I have had all I can take of that sort of treatment at a man's hands, and I have been most frank with Adam about it. Still he persists!"

"You say you love him, my dear," Gaby said.

"I do! It is a strange love, for it has grown during the time I have been happily married to others, yet love Adam I do. I want his happiness, Gaby, but I am not that happiness. He must understand that!"

"Of course, my dear, of course," Adam's mother soothed. "Men can be so obstinate when it comes to women. They simply do not understand us." She smiled at Skye, thinking what a lovely daughter-in-law she would be. The Irishwoman was everything Adam had written of her. She was beautiful, intelligent, and warm. That she did not know her own mind right now was most apparent to Gaby de Saville. When the shock of her experiences in Morocco and the death of her husband had worn off, then she would see clearly that Adam de Marisco was the only man for her. "We are going up to Paris in a few weeks," she said brightly to Skye. "King Henri of Navarre is marrying with our own Princesse Marguérite de Valois on the eighteenth of August. You will naturally come with us."

"I should love it!" Skye exclaimed. "I have never been to Paris."

"Then that is settled," Gaby replied. She stood up. "Come, my dear, I will show you to your apartments now. You must be exhausted after eight days on the road."

"I am," Skye admitted. "We passed through some lovely cities—Avignon, Lyons, Nevers, Bourges—but we didn't stop. Adam very much wanted to get to Archambault to see you all."

Gaby de Saville led her guest from the salon, where Adam was still surrounded by his family. Catching Skye's eye as she passed him, he grinned and shrugged helplessly, and she was forced to smile back at him. He blew her a kiss with his fingertips. "He is a good son," the comtesse was saying as they moved up the main staircase of the château to the bedroom floors. "You have no idea how hurt and ashamed he was when that wretched Athenais Boussac spurned him, and then, not satisfied with merely refusing my son, made his bad luck a public thing. He has, of course, told you of her?"

"I have heard the story," Skye replied. "He never mentioned her name to me."

"How like my Adam! A gentleman even in regard to *that* one!"

"She was a fool, Gaby! The fact that he cannot sire a child has had nothing to do with his abilities as a man." Skye stopped a moment as they reached the carved door of what was to be her apartment while at Archambault. "You know that we have been lovers, Adam and I."

"But of course, my dear!" the comtesse laughed.

"It does not shock you?"

"You are both free of any spouses, and of an age, my dear Skye, if you will forgive my mentioning it, that should allow you both to choose your own course in life. You and my son are good for each other, and despite what you say, I suspect that one day I shall welcome you as my *belle-fille*. No!" Gaby put two fingers on Skye's lips to stifle her protest. "Do not argue with me, my dear. Leave me some hope!"

Skye had to laugh. Gaby's attitude was so very much like Adam's. "Now," she said, "I know where Adam gets his stubbornness."

Gaby chuckled back as she opened the door to the chamber and ushered Skye into the small salon. "His father was equally pigheaded," she said. "Oh, the fights John and I used to have! They fairly made the old walls of Lundy Castle ring. He's been dead over thirty years now, my dear, and I still miss him! Without my dearest and kindly Antoine I don't know what I would have done."

"Then Lundy was still whole when Adam was young?" Skye looked about the little salon. It was a most charming room with its linenfold paneling and a wall of diamond-paned windows that overlooked the river and the fields. There was a small fireplace flanked by stone greyhounds with a fire already laid and ready to light.

"Yes," the comtesse replied. "John de Marisco unfortunately got into an argument with Henry Tudor over the favors of a rather amply charmed lady of the court. She was more than willing to take on both King and courtier. The King, however, was not of a mind to share even a temporary mistress. In a temper King Harry sent one of his ships out of Bideford, and they blew the castle almost to bits. Both my husband and the lady in question happened to be in residence at the time. They were killed."

"How terrible for you!" Skye sympathized.

"The loss of the castle, or the loss of my husband?" was the reply.

"Both," Skye said.

Gaby de Saville laughed. "Yes," she answered, "it was terrible. John occasionally strayed, and I knew it, but then I am a Frenchwoman, and we are taught to ignore such things. Still, this particular piece of foolishness cost my children their home, and Adam his full birthright. The King was furious, and could not bear the sight of us, having transferred his anger to all the de Mariscos now that John was dead. When Adam, then but eleven, accused the King of murdering his father, our fate in England was sealed. We were banned from court, and having no other place to go, I brought my children home to France. We were welcomed at King François's court, as my father had been one of his most trusted advisors in his younger days. The King gave us a small pension, took Adam on as a page for Queen Eleanor, and the next thing I knew he arranged a marriage for me with my dear Antoine." She smiled. "Sometimes things work out for the best, even when it doesn't seem they will."

"Sometimes," Skye agreed, "and then again sometimes not."

The comtesse, ignoring the last part of Skye's remark, said pleasantly, "I hope you will be comfortable here, my dear. Your bedchamber is to the right, and Adam's to the left. I see that you have not traveled with a servant, and so I shall choose a competent woman for you, if I may."

"Please, Gaby, do. I did not take my Daisy to Morocco with me, as the dangers involved were far too great. She is now back in England, and I did not like to bring a girl from Beaumont de Jaspre only to have to send her back." A mischievous smile turned up the corners of her lovely mouth. "Adam has been a most helpful maid to me these last few days."

Gaby laughed. "A role in which I do not see my son as successful, but I shall take your word for it, Skye. Is there anything I might get you now?"

"Oh, if I might only have a bath! It was impossible along the road, and my hair and the very pores of my skin are filled with dust."

The comtesse nodded with understanding. "I shall see to it immediately, my dear. Now, I shall leave you to yourself. A servant will attend you presently." Then with a quick smile Gaby turned and was gone, closing the door behind her.

Skye looked more closely at the salon. The wide floorboards of the room were clean and polished, and the windows were hung with natural-colored linen drapes with a rose and green design. On one wall was a long dark oak table flanked by chairs on either side, and on either side of the fireplace were tall wooden chairs, their high backs and seat cushions embroidered in rose and cream tapestry. Before the fireplace was a fine oak settle with a dark green tapestried seat cushion. Built-in bookcases filled with leather-bound volumes lined another wall of the salon. Skye smiled to herself. She was not of a mind to read right now, but she would eventually see what reading matter the de Savilles had furnished this guest apartment with.

There was a door on the bookcase wall, and opening it, Skye peered into a tiny, windowless chamber furnished with a narrow cot and a small trunk. This would be a servant's room. Walking to the end of the room, she opened the door to what Gaby had said would be Adam's room. It was a medium-sized chamber with a small fireplace, a bed, and a small candlestand. Next to the fireplace was another door, and Skye walked through it to find herself in her own bedchamber. This room was furnished with a much larger bed, two candlestands, and a comfortable chair by its fireplace. It had two other doors, one leading back into the salon, and one opening into a fair-sized garderobe. Skye looked with pleasure at the bedchamber's dusky rose velvet drapes and bed hangings. High-breasted stone maidens flanked the small fireplace, and upon the mantel was centered a little bowl of pink roses that perfumed the room. The windows looked out over the gardens with woodlands beyond. There was a warmth about the room that appealed to Skye, and she knew that she was going to be happy here.

"*Bonjour!*" The voice came from the salon, and Skye hurried back into the main room of the apartment to confront a tiny, black-eyed woman of middle years dressed neatly in the clothing of an upper servant.

"Good day," she said.

"*Bonjour*, madame. I am Mignon," the woman smiled. "Madame la Comtesse has sent me to take care of you." She turned quickly as she heard the door opening behind her. "Ahh! The footmen with your bath, madame. Into the bedchamber, *mes amis! Vite! Vite!*" She hurried ahead of them, leaving Skye standing rather amused.

The footmen who struggled with the bulky oak tub were followed by a brisk procession of their fellows, each lugging two buckets of steaming water until, finally, the tub was filled. Mignon stood in the bedchamber door, and said, "Come, madame. I am ready to begin." Skye nodded, and walked into her bedchamber. Mignon had flung the windows wide, and the soft warm summer air was easily dispelling the dampness of the room and mingling the fragrance of the cut roses in the bowl with the many flowers blooming in the gardens below.

Mignon quickly undressed her new mistress, saying as she did so, "I have prepared a basin of warm water, madame, and I will first wash your hair. *Mon Dieu!* Never have I seen so much dust! Did you roll in it, like a naughty puppy?"

Skye laughed. "I might as well have," she said ruefully. "It was eight days of travel, and no rain to hold the dust down on the roads."

"We do not need the rains now," Mignon replied. "The more sun, the sweeter the grapes, the better the wines this harvest." Gently she pushed Skye over so that her long dark hair was in the porcelain basin. Then with quick, deft movements she began washing Skye's hair.

Skye sniffed disbelievingly. "Damask roses!" she exclaimed.

"*Mais oui*," came the calm reply. "Is it not your scent?"

"Yes, but how did you know?"

"Madame la Comtesse told me." Mignon rinsed, and began a second washing.

How much had Adam told his mother about her? Skye wondered. Obviously he had written quite a bit to Gaby. Skye was touched. He really did love her, she thought, and realized that when he had turned her away saying that she needed a greater, more powerful husband than he could be, he had done so because of that love. Khalid, Geoffrey, Niall—all had loved her deeply; but had they loved her as much as Adam de Marisco obviously did? Comparison was unfair in this instance, Skye knew, yet she was touched by his devotion to her, and sad that she could not accept his proposal. Adam deserved to be happy, but could she bring herself to marry again? Not now. Perhaps, and the thought slipped into her mind unbidden, much to her annoyance, perhaps later. He had said he would wait, but would he? Suddenly Adam de Marisco was of a mind to marry, and he might grow tired of a woman who could not make up her mind. Well, if he did, Skye thought mutinously, then so be it! She had had all she could bear of being owned.

Mignon was now wringing out Skye's long black hair, having emptied a final bucket of rinse water over her head. Vigorously she toweled her mistress's waist-length hair, then politely said, "If you will sit for a few moments, madame, here on the window seat with your hair spread out in the sun, I shall prepare your bath for you."

Skye stretched herself so she might lie straight out, the back of her head resting upon the windowsill while her flowing hair fell over it and blew in the gentle breeze. Having clean hair felt wonderful, and Skye closed her eyes for a moment in the bright sunlight, humming lazily to herself as Mignon poured the bath oil into the waiting tub and mixed it with a wooden paddle. It was several long minutes before the scent suited the tiny Frenchwoman, and by that time Skye's mane was almost completely dry.

"Sit up, madame," Mignon said with a cluck of satisfaction. Swiftly she pinned the hair atop her mistress's head. "You will find your tub perfection," she said as she helped Skye up a pair of steps and down into the water.

"Ohh, yes," Skye murmured as the hot, fragrant water soaked into her skin and tired muscles.

Mignon chuckled. "Eight days in a jouncing coach is exhausting," she said sympathetically.

"Could I soak for a few minutes?" Skye begged, and Mignon smiled.

"Of course, madame! I will begin to unpack your things, which the footmen have brought up to the garderobe. I am going to find you a comfortable *robe de chambre* so you may rest for a few hours until the evening meal. I have ordered up some fruit, cheese, bread, and wine for you, as I suspect that you are hungry." Then she was off to the garderobe as Skye's thanks rang out.

What a jewel, Skye thought, and how fortunate she was that Mignon was available to serve her. Skye sighed, and snuggled down deep into the warmth. She could feel the very pores in her skin welcoming the heat and the silken bath oil. How foolish those poor women were who thought bathing was injurious to health, and covered their body odors in layers of perfume. Bathing was truly heaven-sent, and nothing cleaned a body like soap and water.

"Do you want company?"

Skye didn't even bother to open her eyes. "Not now, Adam," she pleaded prettily. "I don't know the last time I so enjoyed a bath."

His deep laughter rumbled about the room. Her refusal did not, he knew, stem from prudishness, or a cold nature. She simply did not wish to share her tub this time. Her enjoyment was plainly written upon her face. "I've already instructed old Guillaume to have a tub prepared for me, but I stopped on the chance you might be willing to share, little girl. I will be back when I have bathed."

When she opened her eyes briefly he was already gone. Why was he coming back? Then the truth dawned on her. For almost two weeks she had slept in the same bed with him, and other than hold her close in the night he had made no move to touch her. Adam was a man, however, and he had his needs as she had hers. He wanted her; she had not needed to see his face or the look in his eyes to know that. She had heard the longing in his voice. Adam was the one man she would never use, Skye thought seriously. If he wanted to make love to her, then they should make love. She smiled to herself, and then a tiny frown creased her brow as she remembered that no man had made love to her since Kedar.

"Are you ready to be washed, madame?"

Skye jumped at the sound of Mignon's voice. "Y-yes," she managed to answer as her eyes flew open.

"I am sorry, madame," Mignon apologized. "I did not mean to startle you."

"It's all right," Skye assured the tiring woman. "I was merely thinking."

"About M'sieur Adam?" Mignon inquired slyly. "I have known him since he was a boy. He is, how you say it, *formidable! Magnifique! Un grand homme passionné!* He is your lover?"

"She is to be my wife, you nosy creature," Adam chuckled from the door that connected their two rooms. "She is in mourning now for her last husband, but we have known each other a long while, Mignon, and Skye will marry me sometime next year."

"M'sieur Adam!" Mignon dropped the sea sponge with which she had been washing Skye's back, and clapped her hands together with delight. Then she ran to him, took his face in her two hands, and kissed him on both cheeks. "*Bon chance*, M'sieur Adam!" she exclaimed. "I am so happy for you! Did I not tell you those long years ago when that wretched Mam'selle Athenais spurned you that somewhere there was a wife for you. Madame Skye is far more beautiful than that other one!"

"She has a good heart too, Mignon," Adam said seriously.

"You are impossible!" Skye fussed at him. "Go and bathe, you great fool. You stink of half the roads of France! Mignon, this water grows cold!"

With another chuckle Adam disappeared back through the connecting door into his own room. Mignon, realizing the truth of Skye's complaint about the bath water, clucked and fussed as she swiftly washed her new mistress, then assisted her from the tub to dry her. "Madame la Comtesse tells me we are to go to Paris for the royal wedding," she chatted. "I did not think to be included in that journey. What a tale to tell my grandchildren!"

"You are married?" Skye was surprised.

"To Guillaume, who valets M'sieur Adam. He is much older than I, of course, but we have been married many years. I had my two babies before I came to be a tiring woman. When Comtesse Gabrielle married with M'sieur Antoine and brought her children to the château, Guillaume was assigned to be M'sieur Adam's valet. Now my husband is retired, but when he learned that M'sieur Adam would be visiting nothing would do but that he serve his old master. We have several grandchildren, madame, and they will enjoy the tales we will bring back of the royal wedding in Paris."

Skye smiled, remembering how very much Daisy enjoyed the galas and entertainments at court. "A wedding is a wedding," she said. "I expect this one will be far more lavish, nothing more. Still, perhaps we can find some special treat to bring back to the little ones."

"Madame! You are too kind!"

"I have children too, Mignon, and I know that even the smallest of gifts delights them."

Mignon fairly hummed with approval of her new mistress as she helped Skye into a pale-rose silk caftan with tiny pearl buttons. Seating her, Mignon unpinned Skye's hair and began to brush it out. Only faintly damp, it shone with soft blue lights and was sweet with the scent of roses. At last the tiring woman was satisfied. "There, madame, it is done. Now where shall I serve you? In the salon?"

"No," Skye said. "I am weary. Bring me a small piece of bread with a bit of cheese and a little wine. I will eat it here by the window, and then rest."

Mignon hurried to do as she was bid, and when she had placed the plate and goblet by Skye's side, she said, "Your gowns are frightfully wrinkled from all that travel. While you rest I shall see if I can get one in decent condition for you to wear tonight."

"*Merci*, Mignon," Skye replied as the woman departed the room.

She chewed slowly, savoring the fresh, crisp bread with its covering of soft, ripe cheese. The golden wine was sweet and very mellow to her taste. Her gaze moved out through the windows into the gardens below, where several children were playing under the careful supervision of three nursemaids. For a moment Skye wondered how her own children were faring. Then she shook her head irritably. They were all safe, and well fed, and warm, and clothed. They survived quite well without her. Quick tears sprang forth from her beautiful eyes. She was being unfair to her children. They survived without her because they had to, but she knew that they didn't like being apart from their mother any more than she liked being apart from them. Still, she was not quite ready to return to England: not yet ready to be a mother again, to pit her wits against those of Elizabeth Tudor. The last two years had been very harsh, and she needed time to regain her strength. She brushed the remaining crumbs from her lap, drained the goblet of the last sip of wine, and, standing up, walked over to the bed and lay down.

God's bones, she was tired, and her head had barely hit the down pillows when she was asleep. She had no idea how long she slept, but she awoke to find the shadows long in the room, and Adam snoring lightly by her side. She gazed down on him for a moment, and then smiled. He was such a big man. He made her feel small, which she most certainly was not. There were the faintest flecks of silver in his shaggy black hair now, and she wondered how many of them she had given him. Strange, she thought, she had never noticed how beautifully sculpted the planes of his face were. The skin stretched over his high cheekbones was smooth, although tanned with the sun of the outdoor life he preferred living. She liked the way he wore his beard now, clipped close and coming down from the round of his mustache, which enhanced his sensuous mouth. He was such a handsome man.

"Do you intend to eat me, or just paint me, little girl?" he inquired humorously as he opened his eyes and looked up at her.

"I was just deciding what a handsome man you are," she said frankly.

"You mean you never noticed until now?" he demanded in a slightly aggrieved tone.

"No," she giggled, "but gazing at you in sleep, I looked closer than I ever have. I've always thought you were handsome, but on more acute inspection I have decided you are *very* handsome."

She was resting on an elbow looking down at him as she spoke, and now his arm came up to draw her down to him. "Come here to me, little girl," he said in a low, deep voice, and then his mouth was finding hers, tenderly kissing it, gently seeking a response that he knew existed, despite her protests. For a moment Skye was startled, even surprised, although she had been expecting him to ask to make love to her. Then she realized that it was because for the first time in well over a year she was being kissed with love, not just lust. This was not Kedar with his voracious appetites for her body, with his insane passion to possess her totally. This was Adam—Adam, her gentle giant who had loved her for so long. She felt her tears flow unbidden as a mixture of joy and relief flooded her. He lifted his head slowly, and tenderly began to lick the tears away. Skye shivered at the pure sensuousness of his simple action, knowing at the same moment that she wanted him not just for now, but for all time.

She wanted to laugh at how foolish she had been in her grief over Niall's death. Adam had understood, bless him. He had understood the pain, and the disappointment, and the anger that had welled up in her, and he had loved her nonetheless, and said he could be patient. Men were born to die, and if she had lost previous husbands it had only been in the fabric of life. Do not fight your fate so hard, Osman had always warned her. With a sudden burst of clarity Skye knew that Adam de Marisco was her fate.

"Oh, Adam," she whispered almost brokenly, "I love you!"

He lifted his great head, and with a mischievous grin he replied, "I know that, little girl. Why do you think I was so damned willing to be patient? You simply needed time to come to yourself again."

She hit at him weakly with her fist. "How could you know when I didn't?" she demanded.

"You knew too, Skye O'Malley, you knew that you loved me. You were just not willing to admit to it. I was sure, being the sensible creature you are, that eventually you would." With a smooth action he turned her so that she now lay upon her back, and he hovered over her. "I love you, my Celtic witch. I have loved you from the first, but you were not ready then to love me. In my foolishness I thought that you should be married to a more powerful, more important man, but I was wrong, little girl. I am the only man for you, Skye!" He bent his leonine head down and brushed her mouth with his very lightly, sending a pleasant tingle through her. "Yes, I am the only man for you, my darling, and you are the only woman for me!"

"I am still not sure that I want to marry again," she said softly.

"That feeling will pass," he said with such certainty that she had to laugh.

"Adam!"

"Well, it will! Besides, we should wait a year."

"A whole year?" she teased him.

"Well," he reconsidered, "perhaps not a whole year. After all, little girl, Niall was presumed dead over three years ago, and the Queen gave you no time to mourn then."

"That is why I need a little time now, Adam," was her reply. "I was hustled into marriage with the Duc de Beaumont de Jaspre three months after Niall's alleged murder. It was indecent of Elizabeth Tudor, but I needed her help, and she needed a bride to send to the duc. Give me time now, my darling. We will go up to Paris with your family, and enjoy all the festivities that go with the marriage of a royal princess and an heir to France's throne. We do not need to be married to have a good time, my darling Adam!" Her eyes twinkled humorously at him. "We have never needed to be wed to have a good time, my lord of Lundy!"

"You are a minx," he said, and his own eyes twinkled back at her. Then his hand moved to the little pearl buttons on her rose-colored caftan. "Do you remember the last time that you wore this for me?" he asked. Skye shook her head in the negative. "When I came to London just before you departed for Beaumont de Jaspre. You told me that you were being sold into marriage, a loveless marriage, and that before you went we would spend our time together loving each other so we might have sweet memories. Do you remember now, Skye?" He bared a soft, round breast and, bending, kissed it tenderly.

"Yes," she whispered. "I remember, Adam."

"Did he love you, your duc?" His tongue flicked out to begin a tortuous encirclement of her sensitive nipple.

Skye shivered as the warmth of his tongue and the cool air of the early evening worked together to bring her nipple to a hard point. "Fabron did not know how to love," she gasped as he bared her other breast and began to tease at it. "He was a sad man. Damn, Adam! You will drive me wild! Stop!"

"I adore you wild!" he chuckled indulgently.

Her answer was to fumble with the laces on his silk shirt, and successful at that, slip her hands inside to caress his broad back. She could feel the hard muscles beneath his skin tense as he restrained himself. Wickedly she ran her sharp nails lightly down the skin, and heard with total satisfaction his sharp intake of breath. She impishly caught at the lobe of his ear and gently bit it.

"Wench," he growled with mock fierceness, "you shall pay for that liberty!"

"Make me!" she taunted, and then squealed as he yanked the caftan apart, baring her to his fiery gaze.

His hands slid with delicious familiarity over her torso, and to his vast amusement she sighed with great delight. "Wanton!" he muttered at her.

"You don't understand, Adam," she said. "The last time a man made love to me it was not because he loved me. It was because I belonged to him, and he sought to relieve his lust. When you touch me it is with love. Oh, my darling Adam, I want you to touch me

with love! I want you to make love to me! I so very much need to
be loved again as a woman, and not as a possession!"

His smoky blue eyes gazed down into hers. "It is not a very hard
task you set me, Skye," he said softly.

"*Love me*," she repeated as softly, and his mouth again descended
upon hers to make her his warm and willing captive. Her arms
slipped up around his neck to draw him even closer, her round and
tender breasts pressed hard against his furred chest. He had never
kissed her with such deep passion, his sensuous mouth seemingly
welded to hers, sending alternate shivers and waves of heat
throughout her body. He demanded much, yet he gave as well, and
Skye felt herself soaring under the sweet pressure of his lips. She
yielded herself to him, to his care, and he kissed her hungrily, muttering fiercely against her mouth, "I love you! I love you, my sweet
Skye!"

Then they heard it, the insistent knocking at the bedchamber
door. With a smothered curse Adam broke away from her, roaring,
"What is it, dammit?!"

The door opened. "It is time that you begin to ready yourselves
for the evening meal, *mes enfants*," Mignon said calmly with all the
smug privilege of an upper servant of long standing.

"Go away, Mignon!"

"*Non*, M'sieur Adam! Your maman has had the cooks preparing
for days for your arrival. She would be most distressed if you did
not appear in the dining hall tonight." Her cherry-black eyes twinkled. "You had best eat, *mon chou!* I suspect you will need all your
strength for later." She chuckled. "Up with you now, and go to
Guillaume. He is waiting to dress you."

Grumbling about no privacy and being treated like a lad not yet
breeched, Adam de Marisco got up and, with a regretful look at
Skye, left the room.

With a pretty blush Skye drew the two edges of her caftan together and sat up. "Were you able to salvage one of my gowns?"
she asked in an attempt to change the subject and save her dignity.

"*Oui*, madame," came the cheerful reply, "and madame must not
be embarrassed. We French understand about love, and it is most
obvious that you and M'sieur Adam love each other. Then, too,
you are betrothed, and who is to gainsay you if you love a little
while you wait to wed." She smiled at Skye. "Come now, madame.
I have managed to ready a lovely silk gown for you the blue-green

color of the sea. Let me bring you your jewelry case so you may decide what you will wear with it."

"I have no jewelry case with my clothes," Skye said. "My jewels went back to England with my tiring woman."

"Perhaps she forgot, madame, for there is a small carved ivory box among your things," Mignon replied.

Skye shook her head. She did not remember an ivory box, and it was not like Daisy to forget her jewelry. "Bring it to me," she commanded.

Mignon disappeared into the garderobe a moment, returning quickly with a rectangular box carved of creamy ivory. "There you are, madame," she said, placing the box in Skye's lap.

As the maidservant turned away to finish her chores, Skye turned the little gold key that was in the lock, opened the box, and gasped with a mixture of shock and surprise as the lid raised to reveal the contents. Stuck within the lid was a folded parchment, and pulling it out, Skye opened it to read: *Doucette, I had these made for you when I thought you might return to me. Since I will not give my wife jewelry made for another woman, I beg that you take this small offering that was meant only for you. Nicolas.*

Skye gently put the parchment aside and concentrated on the jewelry before her. There was a marvelous assortment of pink-tinged pearls and a huge ring set in gold. And there was an absolutely stunning necklace of diamonds with matching earrings; a collection of hair ornaments of diamonds, pearls, and rubies set in gold; several more rings; bracelets, and additional earrings of sapphires, emeralds, and rubies set in gold. It was a small fortune, and for a moment she wasn't sure what she should do with it.

It had been wonderfully kind of Nicolas to send along the jewelry, but could she keep it? She was to marry another man. He was a married man. Then common sense took over. He had had the jewelry made for her before he married Madelaine, and before she agreed to marry Adam. He might have kept it, but he had chosen to give it to her, anyway. She would consider it a wedding gift, and tell Adam only what she had to.

"I think I shall wear the pearls," she said to Mignon. "I shall save the diamonds for Paris."

"Very good, madame," the tiring woman approved as she re-entered the room carrying the gown.

Skye stood up, and donned the silk undergarments that were

handed to her, but when she slipped on the bodice and the skirt of her gown both she and Mignon gasped with surprise, for they were too large. "I knew that I had lost weight," Skye exclaimed, "but I did not think I had lost so much that my gowns would not fit."

"Do not fret, madame," Mignon soothed her. "I shall pin the garments for tonight, and we shall have the seamstress come tomorrow to alter all of your gowns for Paris. The necklines must be lowered, for one thing, as it is now more fashionable."

"It is?" Skye was a trifle surprised, for she thought that the necklines were low enough.

Mignon worked quickly. All her movements were swift, and the little tiring woman seemed to waste neither energy nor time in anything she did. She firmly sat Skye down and brushed her hair out before fixing it in the lovely simple chignon that Skye favored. "When we go up to Paris, madame, and you visit the court," she said, "I am going to try doing your hair in the long curls that are the coming fashion. The style is most provocative, and M'sieur Adam will adore it." She fastened two white roses into her mistress's hair. "There, madame," she said, pleased. "Now, the gown."

When Mignon had finished with her Skye stood looking at herself in the pier glass. It was the first time in so long that she was dressed as the lady she really was. The bodice of her gown had a low, square neckline, and was embroidered in tiny crystal beads with gold thread. The sleeves were leg-of-mutton, padded and puffed, and the wristbands, held by many tiny gold ribbons, were embroidered in crystal beads and turned back to form a cuff. The silk overskirt of the gown was blue-green, separating in the front to show the skirt of the undergown which was striped in the same color and gold. Her stockings, which would only show if she danced, were pale-pink silk embroidered in climbing roses, and her shoes matched her gown.

"*Vous êtes très belle, madame,*" Mignon said quietly, as she daubed essence of damask rose on Skye's pulse points.

"Why is it you women take so damned long to dress, little girl?" Adam demanded from the connecting doorway.

She whirled prettily and curtseyed. "Is it not worth it, Adam?" she teased him, taking in his own appearance. She had rarely seen him dressed as magnificently as he was now in an elegantly fitted velvet doublet embroidered in gold thread and, she would swear, small diamonds! His jerkin was sleeveless and edged in ermine. He was dressed entirely in dark blue, which flattered his eyes.

Slowly he inspected her, and Skye found that she was blushing. Her heartbeat quickened, and she realized that she very much regretted Mignon's untimely intrusion. Raising her eyes to his, she could read in them that he felt the same way. He reached for her hand and slowly raised it to his lips. His mouth scorched her skin, but the warmth of his gaze filled her with rapture, and she could not tear her eyes away from him.

"How is it possible that you grow more beautiful with each year, little girl?" he asked wonderingly as he tucked her small hand into his.

"Adam . . ." she began, and then her voice died, for she was at a total loss for words. His deep and abiding love was so plain, and Skye was beginning to realize how different he was from the other men who had been in her life. Those whom she had loved had indeed loved her as well, but they had taken boldly of her, though giving something of themselves in return. Adam, she realized with some surprise, intended to take, but he was the first to truly consider her well-being and her own feelings along with his own.

Silently he escorted her downstairs to the family's dining room. It was a beautiful paneled room with an enormous red and white marble fireplace capable of holding whole logs. Above the mantel hung a large tapestry done in azure blue, green, red, silver, and gold, showing in intricate detail a castle under siege, a captive virgin, an embattled knight, and a rather ferocious dragon.

Antoine de Saville, noting Skye's admiration of the tapestry, came forward, saying, "It took three generations of women in my family almost four years to complete that tapestry. It is over two hundred years old."

"It's exquisite!" Skye exclaimed.

"No more so than you, my dear," was the gallant reply.

"*Beau-père*, I warn you," Adam said teasingly, "that I would fight a duel over this woman."

"I have no doubt, Adam, that she is more than worth it," the comte replied. "I am a most fortunate man, for I possess a beautiful wife, three beautiful daughters, a beautiful daughter-in-law, seven lovely granddaughters, and now you are to give us another beauty to add to the family. *Mon Dieu!* It is more than one man can bear!"

He peered at Skye through slightly nearsighted eyes. "You are going to join the family, *ma chérie*, aren't you?"

Suddenly the room, which was filled with the entire de Saville clan, grew quiet, and all eyes turned to Skye. "I suppose I must," she replied mischievously. "Adam refuses to give me any other choice, and I find that I love him. What else can I do but follow my conscience?"

The joyous noise that erupted about them as the whole family tried to offer their good wishes at the same time somewhat overwhelmed them. She found herself being kissed upon both cheeks first by Comte Antoine and then by Gaby. Next came Adam's sisters and their husbands and children, and his half-brothers and -sister and their families. Never in her entire life had Skye felt so cherished by a family. It was true that her own family loved her dearly, but they all depended upon her for everything, they expected that she would care for them all, no matter what. The de Savilles expected nothing of her. To them she was the woman who would marry Gaby's eldest son, another daughter-in-law to be treasured. At this moment in time Skye realized that that was more than enough for her. She was so tired of having total responsibility, and she wanted to be treated like a woman, just a woman for now.

His arm tightened about her shoulder, and she looked up at him. "You understand, don't you?" she said.

"Yes," was the simple reply. Nothing more. Just yes.

Suddenly Gaby de Saville cried out. "Adam, my son! The ring! Have you given Skye the ring?"

"No, maman, I have not," Adam replied. "I thought to do it when she accepted me, but she has surprised me by accepting *beau-père's* proposal in my name!" He reached into his doublet and drew forth a large round sapphire set in red gold. Upon the face of the sapphire was a small red-gold sea hawk with its wings outspread in flight. "This ring," he said quietly to her, "was given by Geoffroi de Sudbois to my ancestress, Matilde de Marisco, in token of their love. Ever since it has been the betrothal ring of the men in my family. My father gave it to my mother, and now I give it to you, Skye O'Malley. I need not tell you that with it goes my everlasting love, and my fidelity for all time." Gently Adam slipped the ring onto the appropriate finger of her left hand while, around them, the de Saville family once again proclaimed their delight at this turn of events.

Skye barely heard them. I am loved, she thought. Dear God, don't take Adam away from me as you have taken the others. I could not bear to hurt him! Please let us grow old together.

Again, as if she had uttered the words aloud, Adam de Marisco understood her feelings. Bending, he tenderly touched her mouth with his, then murmured softly, "I will always be here for you, little girl. Always!"

Looking up into his eyes, Skye had a sudden premonition that she was finally safe. This time there would be no parting or pain. She remembered that Osman had told her that her happiness would be assured by the influence of a strong Leo in her life. "What is your birthdate, Adam?" she asked him. "We are to be married and I realize that I do not know your birthday."

"His birthday is in two weeks, my dear," Gaby said. "It is the ninth of August. My oldest son is born beneath the sign of the Lion. Does it make a difference to you? Are you compatible?"

Skye looked again at Adam, and the relief in her eyes puzzled him. "Yes, Gaby," she answered the comtesse. "We are compatible, two fire signs, for I am born beneath the sign of the Archer."

"What is it?" he asked her in a low tone.

"Osman," she said. "But it is all right. My happiness, he said, would be assured with a man born beneath the sign of the Lion. For some reason I suddenly remembered that."

Adam smiled at her, half relieved himself, half amused. "You will always be safe with me, little girl," he promised. "Always!"

Chapter 13

Skye and Adam came together again as man and woman the night of their betrothal. The welcome-home dinner, a magnificent feast, began with thin slices of Loire salmon served on silver platters decorated with watercress and carved lemon halves. The fish was followed by a turkey stuffed with truffles from the Périgord, a Bayonne ham, Beef Rissoles, a small roe deer basted in Burgundy, rabbit pie with a marvelously flaky pastry crust, tiny whole partridges stuffed with rice and dried fruit, and small silver platters of Rhine perch. There were bowls of creamed onions, carrots glazed with honey, saffroned rice, cress and lettuce, scallions and radishes. The last course was made up of several cheeses; Brie, Angelot from Bray in Normandy, and a Caci Marzolini from Florence. There were baskets of black cherries and fat golden peaches; and a wonderful brandy-flavored gâteau with marzipan decorations. Throughout the meal the goblets were kept well filled with the fine red and white wines bottled on the estate from Archambault grapes.

The family ate heartily and with appreciation of the château's fine chef, but Skye and Adam picked at their food, casting long and languishing looks at each other throughout the meal. How strange, thought Skye. I feel like a young girl again instead of a woman who has seen a thirty-first birthday. Toast after toast was raised to the betrothed couple, and Skye's heart beat erratically as Adam took her right hand in his, and began to delicately kiss each fingertip with a slow, lingering kiss. His smoky eyes caught hers in a blazing blue gaze, and she was so fascinated with the passion she saw in their depths that she forgot to breathe and suddenly found herself gasping. She blushed, realizing that she could barely wait to be alone with him, and he chuckled softly.

"I, also," he said in a low voice, obviously reading her mind.

Her color deepened. "How can I feel this way, and Niall but newly buried?" she protested, her stern conscience demanding the answer.

"Niall was dead to you long ago," he replied softly. "A second death was but anticlimactic, sweetheart. You have had a bad time of it this last year in your attempts to rescue him, and now you need my soothing."

She thought a moment, and realized that it was true. "You were ever good at soothing me, Adam," she teased him, running a playful finger down his cheek.

Around them the de Saville family watched the lovers with tolerant amusement. They were French, and they understood better than any other race in the world the sparks that flew between Skye O'Malley and Adam de Marisco. Antoine feigned a yawn as the servants were clearing away the remnants of the meal from the long table. "*Mon Dieu*," he murmured. "I must be getting old, for I cannot seem to keep my eyes open." He turned to his wife. "Do you think, *mon amour,* that I should be considered a bad host if I called a halt to this day?"

"*Mais non, chéri*," the comtesse exclaimed brightly. "I am sure that both Adam and Skye are exhausted after their long journey, *n'est-ce pas, mes enfants?*"

"Yes, maman," Adam said solemnly. "We are quite fatigued."

Skye suppressed a giggle. *Fatigued!* Adam spoke with such delicacy. Was this the lord of Lundy, the very same fellow who upon their first meeting had so boldly demanded her presence in his bed in exchange for his aid? Her mirth but increased when he fiercely waggled his thick black eyebrows at her in mock warning as he rose from the table, pulling her up with him.

Taking her by the hand, Adam led her over to his mother and stepfather. "Good night, maman, *beau-père*," he said quietly, as if daring Skye to laugh.

"Good night, my son," Gaby murmured, and looking closely at her, Skye saw that Adam's mother was also close to total mirth. She obviously knew her big son well.

"*Bonne nuit*, Adam," the comte said. "*Bonne nuit, ma belle* Skye."

Skye bid him goodnight softly, and then taking her leave of

Gaby and all the others, she followed Adam from the dining room. Silently he led her up the main staircase of the château to the bedroom wing, then down the hall to their apartment. Inside both Mignon and old Guillaume awaited them, and they parted and went into their separate chambers.

Inside her bedroom Skye bore with Mignon's delighted chatter, for the tiring woman had already heard of the official betrothal. Indeed, the château's servants were all atwitter, and as pleased as could be that M'sieur Adam had at last found true happiness. Skye found herself smiling as Mignon asked, "Madame's children will like M'sieur Adam as their *beau-père?*"

"My children adore Adam. They will be very pleased, Mignon."

Mignon bridled with pleasure at her reply, as she silently admired Skye's ring. Adam was quite obviously a favorite of hers. "He is a good man," she declared, and then she lowered her voice. "I lit candles in thanksgiving when *that one* scorned him. She did not fool me for a minute with her virginal airs and her soft voice. She was ambitious for wealth and position, *that one!* She would have destroyed him the same way she destroyed the old duc she finally wed." Mignon handed Skye a silken nightgown, but Skye shook her head.

"I will not need it," she said. "Just this little knit shawl for my shoulders," and she climbed into bed.

"*Bon!*" Mignon said with a chuckle of approval. "Then I will let you *sleep*," she finished as she hurried out, leaving Skye alone, a little fire glowing in the fireplace and one small chamber stick lit by the bedside. She sat quietly enjoying the peace of the room, the smooth feel of the lavender-scented sheets beneath her, and the plump goose-down pillows behind her back. The fire cast playful shadows upon the ceiling as it sputtered and whistled softly in the grate. The door to Adam's room opened, and Skye looked up to see him silhouetted between the two rooms. She held out a hand to him, and he was quickly at her side.

Bending, he blew out the chamber stick, then climbed into the big bed. Pulling her into his arms, he held her gently. Skye's head was resting upon his shoulder, one palm flat against his chest. They lay together for some time in silence, and then as her fingers began to entwine themselves playfully in the dark mat upon his chest she asked mischievously, "How many hearts have you broken, my lord of Lundy, since we were last together?"

"I have never been a man for keeping count," he said seriously, "but know, my love, that I tried very hard to forget you. To forget the Kerry blue of your eyes, the sweetness of your kisses, the outrageous softness of your skin." His hand now began to stroke her as he might a cat, and Skye shivered with pleasure. Adam's voice deepened with his desire. "I could not forget you, my Celtic witch! You are in my blood, and now I shall never let you go, Skye! *Never!* I shall defend what is mine against all, including the Queen if need be, sweetheart!"

"I am not afraid anymore, Adam. I am not afraid, for I know that we are meant to be together, and what a pair we shall make, my darling! Elizabeth Tudor will be hard pressed to stand against us!"

"We may have to remain in France, Skye," he said quietly. "I intend to marry you with or without the Queen's permission, and before we return to England. If the marriage displeases her she will attempt to separate us, as she has done with others. Our only refuge then will be here in France."

"My children," she said softly.

"If we are forced to remain in France then your children must come here. Ewan is virtually a man grown with his own holding, and God willing, 'tis so small a holding that the English will leave him in peace. The others, however, must be with us. Murrough can study here in Paris, as did his father, and his little betrothed will live with us until the marriage. Robin cannot be left to Elizabeth Tudor, despite the fact that he is her favorite. His holdings will be safe in de Grenville's hands until he is ready to marry Alison de Grenville. Mistress Willow should be with us too. Your little Burkes have the most to lose I know, but the English will eventually snatch the Burke lands, as they will all of Ireland. Perhaps your O'Malleys can hold your son's lands until he comes of age, but until then it is not right that Deirdre and Padraic be separated from you, Skye." He turned his head and kissed her mouth quickly. "I want you to be happy, sweetheart."

"What of the responsibilities I owe to the O'Malleys, Adam? I cannot simply walk away from them. I promised my father! 'Twas a deathbed promise!"

"A promise made fourteen years ago, Skye, when your brothers were babes; but they are men grown now, and Brian already has children of his own. It is time they accepted their responsibility.

Brian O'Malley has run the O'Malley enterprises these last two years while you have been away. Your Uncle Seamus could not do it and defend Burke lands as well. He is growing very old, although he would knock me down if he heard me say it.

"I would take nothing from you, sweetheart, and neither would your brothers. We adore you, but if we must live in France, then you will have to allow your family to take care of themselves."

"I have always taken care of them," she worried.

His big hand reached out to cup one of her perfect little breasts. "You will have me to take care of now, Skye O'Malley, and I am a very big responsibility," he said as he rolled her in one smooth motion onto her back to take a nipple into his warm mouth.

"Ohhh," she gasped softly, his action catching her by surprise. His lips, clamped firmly around that sensitive little knob of flesh, seemed determined to draw her soul from her body. Gently he bit down upon the tingling peak, eliciting another "Ohhhh!" from her. She didn't need this torture to know that she wanted him desperately.

With a groan Adam raised his dark head, and she could see the hunger in his stormy eyes. "God forgive me, little girl," he whispered harshly, "but I cannot attend to any of the niceties this time. I must have you, Skye! I ache for you!"

"Oh, God, yes, Adam!" she answered, to his delight. "I cannot wait, either! I keep remembering how it was with us before I left England, and I shall die if you do not take me now!"

Assured he would neither harm her nor offend her, Adam covered her beautiful body with his own. Beneath him, her shapely thighs opened smoothly, and she eagerly reached for him to guide him home. With a low cry of pleasure he thrust deep, feeling her push up to ease his passage even more. Her arms wrapped themselves around him and their mouths met in a searing kiss. The kiss was seemingly endless, deepening and easing again and again as his strong hips drove her downward into the feather mattresses. He could not get enough of her, nor she of him. Skye reveled in his strong passion, urging him onward with soft little cries that were obvious in their delight. She felt the delicious tensing begin as his wonderful maleness filled her with his love and his warmth. The first rocket's burst came quickly thereafter, followed by several other starbursts in quick succession. Her sharp nails raked fiercely into his smooth back as he tore his head away from her, gasping for breath. "Sweet, hot little bitch!" he moaned. "Damn, but you have unmanned me too quickly!" Then she felt the warm rush of his love flooding her, and she wept with joy and murmured softly, *"Je t'adore, mon mari!* I love you, my husband!"

Adam de Marisco shuddered with the pleasure both her body and her words had given him. "Marry me when we return to Archambault after the royal wedding," he begged her.

"Will Michaelmas be soon enough?" she teased him.

"The end of September? 'Tis too far away," he grumbled.

"I need time for a trousseau," she pouted, "and perhaps we shall even be able to have the children here."

"I foresee problems in marrying an older woman," he said mischievously.

"Older woman!" With a little shriek of outrage she shoved him off her, catching him unawares in his relaxed and weakened condition.

"You'll be thirty-two in December," he countered, beginning to laugh.

"You are no gentleman, Adam de Marisco, to mention such a thing out loud!" she said with mock anger, and began to tickle him. "You are ten years my senior, a veritable graybeard! I might have a young man of twenty for a husband should I so desire," she mocked him from her perch atop his chest.

He laughed until the tears rolled down his cheeks. "Stop, witch!" he begged her as her nimble fingers found yet another sensitive spot upon his helpless flesh to tickle. God, how he loved her! It was a dream come true for him.

"Not until you apologize!"

"For marrying you, or for saying you will be thirty-two?" he teased.

"Ohh, beast!" She leaned forward and, grasping a handful of his thick black hair, yanked it hard in retaliation.

"Ouch!" he roared in pain. "Enough, you witch!" And reaching out, he grasped her about the waist and lifted her high off of him. For a brief moment he held her above him while she shrieked in mock terror, and then he lowered her gently onto the mattresses while his mouth swiftly found hers. "I love you, Skye O'Malley," he whispered against her trembling lips. "I love you, my little girl!"

They loved seemingly without ceasing that night and in the days that followed. The night before they left for Paris Skye drifted off to sleep, replete with his love and wondering how they would ever start off the next day. She was still tired when she was forced to crawl from her bed as the dawn was beginning to tint the edges of the horizon. Adam was gone, and Mignon was bustling busily about.

"I have already packed your things, madame, but you must hurry. The comtesse has arranged with Père Jean that the formal betrothal ceremony be said in the chapel before you leave for Paris! *Vite, vite* now, madame!"

Her bath was drawn, and she was not allowed to enjoy soaking in its perfumed warmth. The bath this day, Mignon declared, was for washing, not pleasurable daydreaming. Skye was washed, and dried, and powdered and perfumed quickly by her adept tiring woman. Her silk stockings with the climbing roses were rolled up her slender legs and fastened with rosette garters of silver ribbon. Her silk chemise, silk blouse, and silk petticoats were swiftly donned to rustle elegantly beneath her crimson silk gown with its pink satin undershirt. Creamy lace dripped from the sleeves and modestly garnished the neckline of the gown, which revealed more breast than Skye would have normally shown, but the château's dressmaker had sworn that it was the *latest* style and that Madame would be totally out of fashion if her necklines were any higher. While Mignon did her hair Skye slipped her feet into a pair of red leather shoes with tiny heels. The tiring woman dressed her hair in Nicolas's pearls, and she wore pearls about her neck and in her ears. When Mignon had finished with Skye's hair she signaled her mistress to stand, and then fastened about her waist a gold cordeliere to which she attached a small mirror and a pomander.

"If Madame will allow me I will escort her to the chapel," Mignon said as she picked up Skye's crimson silk cloak with its pink satin lining. "Père Jean is to say a late mass for the family, and then you and M'sieur Adam will repeat your vows before God."

Skye nodded to Mignon and followed her from the apartment. She caught her breath with delight as they entered the family's private chapel, for the octagon-shaped room was really a little jewel. Although she had seen it earlier, its beauty still astounded her. Situated in the oldest part of the small château it had floors and walls of stone; but on either side of the altar which faced the double doors entry doors were long Gothic windows of exquisite stained glass.

The rich reds and blues and golds of the windows cast dancing shadows on the gray stone. On either side of the room were dainty shrines, one to the Blessed Mother Mary, the other to her mother, Saint Anne. The delicately carved statues had been painted so that the two women resembled living creatures.

Mary had been portrayed as the young mother, and was gowned modestly in pale sky-blue robes, a white veil over her blond hair. Her coloring—pink cheeks, fair skin, and real sapphire eyes—was quite lovely. She was seated, and in her lap a laughing pink and white cherub of a baby boy sat waving his fat little hands. The statue of Saint Anne, opposite that of Saint Mary, represented her as a slender, standing woman. Her face was that of a warm and loving woman as she gazed with pride across the room to her beloved daughter and holy grandchild. Her skin was pale, her braids dark, her eyes genuine topaz, her robes a dark red.

There were only four pews on either side of the chapel, and they and the altar were beautifully carved with religious scenes. As Skye and Mignon entered the chapel a priest in green and gold vestments greeted them. Mignon stepped respectfully back and curtseyed. "*Bonjour, mon père.*"

"*Bonjour, ma fille,*" the priest replied softly, and then he gave his complete attention to Skye. "Madame la Comtesse has told me about you, Madame Burke. You are Irish, and I believe, a true daughter of Holy Mother Church?"

"*Oui, mon père.* My uncle is a bishop."

"And when was the last time you made your confession, *ma fille*?"

Skye reddened. "I have been in a Moslem country for over a year, *mon père*. It was not possible."

Père Jean smiled. "Of course," he murmured understandingly, "but you will, naturally, wish to confess to me now before the mass, and before you take your vows with M'sieur Adam."

"*Oui, mon père.*" Skye was mortified, but she knew that there would be no escaping her religious duties. She wondered almost hysterically what the priest was going to think of what she had to tell him. She would wager that he had never heard a confession such as she was going to give him now. Meekly she followed him to the confessional, where she knelt and said, "Forgive me, Father, for I have sinned."

Some twenty minutes later both she and Père Jean exited the

booth, the priest looking somewhat exhausted and bleary-eyed. "Never," the priest declared softly, "never have I listened to such a tale, *ma fille*. I am astounded that these things can occur in our poor world."

"Yet you gave me no penance, *mon père*."

The priest stopped, and looking into Skye's face, he took her hand in his. "What penance could I possibly give you, *ma fille*, that you have not already suffered? You have twice lost the same husband, a man for whom you truly cared. You have suffered a shameful and degrading captivity in your brave if foolish effort to free your husband from an equally shameful captivity. You have been bereft of your children, threatened wickedly by your sovereign Queen, and yet still you survive without bitterness. I may only be an unsophisticated country priest, *ma fille*, but I know anguish when I see it. God has already punished you. I can certainly do no more." He smiled at her and patted her hand. "You are a good daughter of the Church, *ma fille*. It has taken great courage to tell me your mountain of sins, but you were brave enough to do it. Now you are following the dictates of Holy Mother Church by marrying once more. I will pray that God bless this union between yourself and the Seigneur de Marisco with many children. Come now, the family is assembled and ready for the mass, *ma fille*." The priest gallantly escorted her to where Adam awaited her in the pew with his mother and stepfather.

As she knelt in prayer during the service Skye thought sadly that Père Jean's prayers would be wasted with regard to a child for her and Adam. She did not care for herself, but for Adam she was sad. He was a man who loved children, and should have sons of his own. She signed herself with the cross at the mass's end, and then with Adam she knelt before Père Jean and repeated her betrothal vows, as thrilled as a maiden to hear his deep voice speak back pledging himself to her till death.

Afterward they broke their fast in the family's dining room, and then the Comte and Comtesse de Cher and their family piled into several coaches with their servants and their baggage to begin the trek to Paris. There were twenty-one adults and children in the party, the six youngest children having been left behind. It would take them five days to reach Paris, traveling at a reasonable speed. As they crossed the river at Tours, suddenly the reality of the trip seemed to touch the family all at once. The marriage between

Henri de Navarre and Marguérite de Valois was the most exciting thing to happen in France in some time, especially considering the fact that the bride was most vocal in her opposition to the match.

Marguérite de Valois was as strong-willed as her Florentine mother, Queen Catherine de Medici, but being far more beautiful, young, and gay, she was more popular than the dowager queen. All Paris, devoutly Catholic, was in extreme sympathy with their lovely princess, who was being forced to wed with a Huguenot. Were not their fear of Catherine de Medici greater than their love of her daughter, the young prince of Navarre might have found himself in extreme danger. Even the princess's lover, Henri de Guise, dared not act against the bridegroom.

It was painfully obvious that the lovely young Queen of France, Elizabeth of Austria, would produce no more children than her little daughter; and King Charles IX's only son was a bastard by his official favorite, Marie Touchet. The king's heir was therefore his younger brother, the Comte d'Anjou, whose favorite pastime was dressing as a girl. The French, a practical race, realized there was not much hope there. The eventual king would be Henri of Navarre, who, it was hoped, would by then be converted to the true Church; and his queen would be their own beloved princess. Perhaps this union would bring an end to the religious wars that had been plaguing France the last few years.

The de Saville coaches raced onward toward Paris, the women of the family chattering excitedly about what they would wear to the ball that was to be held the night before the wedding at the Louvre. Skye could not but help feel some of their excitement in her own contentment and happiness. Outside the coach, the French countryside was lush with midsummer; the fields ripening, the vines heavy with their fruit. It was very different from both her beloved Ireland and beautiful England, but Skye thought it was just as lovely in its own way. She prayed that someday she might return home, but if she could not, it would not be so difficult to live in this fair France. At least here she had no fears that she would be disdained for her race or her religion.

Although there were many disreputable inns along the highway, the comte seemed to know the best places to stop; and despite the fact the roads were thick with other travelers on their way to Paris and the wedding, there always seemed to be places to sleep and a private dining room for them. Skye shared a chamber with Gaby, and her two older daughters, Isabeau and Clarice, while her youngest daughter, Musette, shared with Isabeau's sixteen-year-old, Matilde, and Alexandre's eight-year-old, known as petite Gaby, and Clarice's two daughters, Marie-Gabrielle and Catherine. The three youngest girls were in a positive frenzy of excitement, for it was their first trip to Paris. Their elder cousin, Matilde, a betrothed young lady, had been there twice, and was quite superior about it. Skye cheered the younger ones by telling them it was her first trip, too.

Suddenly they were there! Paris! Skye swiveled from one side of the coach to the other, looking, looking, looking. If anything, she was a bit disappointed, for it reminded her of London with its narrow, crowded streets. They would have to be ferried across the Seine, for the house they had rented from a wealthy Huguenot was next to that of the Duc de Guise in the Marais district on the Rive Droit. The Huguenot, unlike most of his persuasion, had been forced to remain in the country to mourn a recently deceased wife.

The de Savilles were not wealthy in the sense that Skye and Adam were wealthy. They had Archambault and its lands; successful vineyards; and a happy, productive peasantry. They had a small house in Paris, but as Adam gently pointed out to his stepfather, the small house in the Rue Soeur Celestine would simply not shelter them all, and no one had wanted to be excluded from the wedding of Henri of Navarre and Marguérite of Valois. The lord of Lundy suggested that the Paris house be rented to someone else coming up to Paris for the festivities, and it had been quickly and easily done. Then the larger house was rented for the Comte and Comtesse de Cher and their family. Adam discreetly insisted upon paying the lion's share of the rental.

"Our own mansion on the Rive Gauche was in a far better location," Gaby declared emphatically. "I don't care if the de Guises have made the Marais fashionable, this place was once a swamp, and the air is still bad if you ask me! I'm only sorry we couldn't all squeeze into our Paris house, but it only has six bedrooms, and we need a minimum of nine. Drat! I dislike renting other peoples' homes. They are never clean enough to suit me! You wait! The place will be thick with dust, mark my words!"

"Now, now, *ma cherie*," Antoine soothed. "Huguenot housewives are known for their cleanliness."

"But the lady is dead, and how long since she was last up to Paris? No, the servants will have to turn everything out!"

A little to the comtesse's chagrin and, Skye thought amused, even her disappointment, the rented mansion was fresh and welcoming to its guests. The owner, though bowed by grief, was nevertheless not so overcome that he forgot his wife's ways. He had sent orders to his caretaker to hire the necessary help to clean the house for its tenants. The windows sparkled, the draperies and the upholstery were cleaned and brushed. There were bowls of fresh flowers in every room.

"You see, *ma chérie*," the comte said to his wife, his brown eyes twinkling. "It is all quite in order. We have but to enjoy ourselves."

They had barely time to rest from their long journey. The royal ball was to be held the following evening, and the de Saville servants spent almost all the night and the following day pressing out ball gowns for all the ladies. Skye had chosen to wear a magnificent creation of peacock-blue silk, its shockingly low-cut bodice embroidered in tiny blue crystals and silver beads to match its embroidered cloth-of-silver underskirt. Skye lived in nervous apprehension that if she took a deep breath her entire bosom would be freed of its restraints. Adam chuckled with delight at the prospect as he fastened the diamond necklace about her throat.

"I do not remember this necklace," he remarked casually as he fussed with the clasp, "but then you have a great deal of jewelry."

"Nicolas presented me with it as a going-away gift when we left Beaumont," she said, deciding to hide nothing from him. "It was really quite thoughtful, and typical of his nature, for he knew that I had no jewelry, Daisy having returned to England with my own things." Skye stood very still wondering at Adam's reaction as he stood behind her, his hands yet on the clasp.

The hands moved slowly from her neck and smoothed over her shoulders. "Is it ducal jewelry?"

"No. He had it made especially for me when he believed that I might come back. It was before he was even contracted to his little duchesse. I would not have accepted it otherwise, Adam."

"I wonder that you accepted it at all." She heard the jealousy in his deep voice, though he strove hard to hide it. Funny, Adam thought, I have never been a jealous man before. Then he smiled to himself. I have never been betrothed to Skye O'Malley before, either.

"I cannot return the jewels without hurting Nicolas, but if it displeases you I will put them away for my daughters, and never wear them again," Skye said, and then she turned to face him. "I love you, my lord of Lundy!" Smiling, she stood on her tiptoes and kissed him sweetly. "The damned jewels mean nothing, and well you know it, Adam de Marisco!"

He grinned ruefully down at her. "You can hardly go to the most elegant court in Christendom without jewels," he admitted, and that was the end of it.

The carriages were at the door, and as they exited the house into the courtyard Skye could see that next door's inhabitants were also preparing to leave for the Louvre.

"The Duc de Guise!" hissed Adam's eldest sister, Isabeau de Rochouart, to Skye. "He is the Princess Marguérite's lover."

"Guard your tongue!" Gaby snapped at her daughter. "Like your late father, you do not know when to be quiet!"

"Well, everyone knows it," Clarice St. Justine declared, coming to her big sister's defense.

"What people know and what is said are two different things," Gaby replied, "and you two are more than old enough to comprehend that!"

The two sisters flushed under their mother's rebuke, and made a great pretense at smoothing down their ball gowns as they prepared to enter their coach. They would be sharing it with their husbands, Isabeau's daughter, Matilde, and Clarice's eldest daughter, Marie-Gabrielle. In the first coach Skye found herself wedged between Adam and his eldest half-brother, the widowed Alexandre, while across from them Comte Antoine sat between his wife and granddaughter, Catherine-Henriette St. Justine who was but eleven. It was her very first ball, and the child was almost sick with the excitement. In the third coach the rest of the party, Yves and Marie-Jeanne de Saville, Musette and Robert Sancerre, and their two nephews, Henri St. Justine, and his brother, Jean-Antoine, were crowded. The three younger children, who would be left behind, stood with their nurses watching sadly as the coaches pulled away.

Once out of the courtyard the coaches moved briskly through the streets of the Marais district, quickly gaining the Rue St. Honoré, which would take them directly to the Louvre Palace. Now, however, they were forced to join a long line of carriages that were also bound in the same direction, and their pace slowed considerably. Adam took Skye's hand in his and squeezed it lovingly.

"I am indeed blinded by the presence of so much beauty, maman," Alexandre remarked. "Both you and my *belle-soeur* are radiant tonight."

"Beware, little brother," Adam warned teasingly. "I have only this evening discovered how jealous a man I am."

"If I were betrothed to so glorious a creature as Skye I should also be jealous, Adam, but fear not. I don't believe I could steal her away from you. Now that my period of mourning for Hélène is over I shall have to find myself a nubile young heiress to wife. Little Adam, your godson, is a healthy fellow, but one son is not enough for Archambault."

Gaby, beautiful in midnight-blue silk, suddenly pointed. "Look! The Louvre! I have not seen it in over ten years. We were last at court during the brief reign of little François II and his lovely Queen, Marie of Scotland. I think Queen Catherine was almost glad to see her son die so she might be rid of the beautiful Marie. How they disliked each other, those two. I understand that it has not gone well for Marie since she returned to Scotland."

"The Scots are not an easy people, Gaby," Skye said. "Their rulers have ever had difficulty with them."

The de Saville coaches were now pulling into the grand courtyard of the Louvre Palace, which was magically lit up. Footmen in elegant livery were stationed everywhere and others ran back and forth with torches lighting the way for the guests who were disembarking from their vehicles. As they exited the coaches Comte Antoine said, "Let us all remain together, *mes enfants*. We will first present ourselves to the King, and then the evening is ours. Follow me, for I remember the way."

A court is a court, thought Skye as she hurried along clutching Adam's arm. She studied the faces of the other guests as they moved into the palace, distinguishing the ones who had just come into Paris for the wedding from the truly important who belonged with the court, from the hangers-on, and those hopeful of gaining entry into the fabled circle. One thing she did note was the magnificence of the clothing worn by almost everyone. She knew that only the most wealthy nobility did not have to make sacrifices to be decently clothed and coiffed tonight. On that score she had nothing to fear, for her gown was as elegant as any, and her jewels magnificent. Skye couldn't help the tiny smile that played at the corners of her mouth. Bless Nicolas for his marvelous French foresight!

At the wide double doors to the formal reception room their names were given to the majordomo who was presiding. Then, as their names were called, they advanced into the room toward the throne where France's royalty awaited their guests. Led by Comte Antoine and Gaby, Skye and Adam reached the King and his party.

Antoine de Saville bowed low. "Your Majesty, I am honored to have been included along with my family in this festive occasion."

"Merci, M'sieur le Comte," Charles IX replied in a bored voice. He had absolutely no idea who this provincial fellow was.

"You will remember the Comte de Cher, my son," crackled the dry voice of his mother, Catherine de Medici. "I have certainly never forgotten him, for he supported my marriage to your father from the moment it was proposed. Welcome back to Paris, Antoine de Saville. We are happy to see both you and your lovely Gabrielle."

Skye was fascinated. They could say what they would in England about Catherine de Medici, but by God she was politic. *Madame le Serpent*, she was called behind her back, and Skye could well imagine it was justified. She had no beauty, in fact she was rather plain—a small dumpy woman with olive skin and dark hair now streaked with iron gray, which showed beneath her cap. Her eyes, however, were incredible. Sharp and as black as raisins, they were the most alive thing about her. They were intelligent eyes; thoughtful eyes; secretive eyes. They saw all, and passed it on to her facile brain, which sorted and used every piece of information obtained. Here was a power to be reckoned with, Skye thought.

Antoine de Saville had introduced his large family to the King, young Queen Isabeau, and Queen Mother Catherine. Now Skye heard him say, "And this is my stepson, madame, Adam de Marisco, the Seigneur de Lundy; and his betrothed wife, Madame Burke." Adam bowed beautifully while Skye curtseyed low.

"You are English?" Catherine de Medici queried Adam.

"Yes, Majesty. I was born there. My father was an Englishman although my mother is French. My lands and title are, however, English."

"And your betrothed is English?"

"I am Irish, your Majesty," Skye replied.

"Irish. Ah, the Irish! Forever giving poor Elizabeth Tudor problems."

"No more problems than she gives us, Majesty."

Catherine de Medici stared hard at Skye, and then she cackled with laughter. "It is all in how one looks at it, eh madame?" Then her laughter died. "You are Catholic, madame?"

"Yes, Majesty."

"And you, M'sieur de Marisco? Are you a member of England's church, or the true Church?"

"I was raised in the holy Catholic faith, Majesty," Adam replied.

The Queen Mother nodded satisfied with his answer. "This is my daughter, the Princesse Marguérite," she said, "and her betrothed, our young King of Navarre."

Again Skye and Adam made obeisance to the royal couple. The princess had her mother's coloring, but fortunately, she looked like her Valois relations and was quite lovely. Henri of Navarre was a very tall, powerfully built young man with dark hair and merry amber eyes. Boldly he assessed Skye, his eyes dropping to her extreme décolletage. His eyes widened appreciatively, caressed lingeringly, and then shot up to meet hers in a daring challenge. Adam, being occupied with the princess, fortunately did not notice; but Skye grew warm with embarrassment.

"M'sieur!" she scolded the King of Navarre, gently determined that he should not even contemplate her encouragement.

"Madame cannot blame me," he replied. "I am a connoisseur of beauty, and you, madame, are the most beautiful creature it has ever been my incredible good fortune to meet. But tell me when and where we may meet! I must make love to you!"

"M'sieur! You are to be married tomorrow. What of your bride?"

Henri de Navarre smiled charmingly. "Margot? She won't mind."

"I am an affianced woman."

"Then we have something in common."

Skye was exasperated. She must discourage this impetuous man. Taking a deep breath, she said, "You are naught but a rude boy of nineteen, m'sieur. I am a woman past thirty."

"Ahh," he smiled warmly at her. "You are experienced then, and I adore women of experience."

While Skye tried to extricate herself from this very difficult situation, Catherine de Medici watched from beneath hooded lids. Deciding that her daughter's conversation with de Marisco was boring, she listened in on Skye and Henri de Navarre. So the Huguenot with the prodigious appetite for women was interested in the Irishwoman. Here was a situation that could perhaps be used to her advantage. Henri was going to need to be diverted soon, and the beautiful Irishwoman looked as though she could certainly divert him if only she were willing.

Skye wasn't willing, however, and Catherine knew enough about human nature to see that the lady was not playing coy. It was unfortunate, the Queen Mother thought, but then she had a number of lovely creatures in her *Flying Squadron* who could be ordered to distract the King of Navarre if the proper time came.

Henri de Navarre, however, was not discouraged by Skye's stern rebuffs. All women, he had discovered, could eventually be wooed and won. Some were just harder to win than others, but it had been his experience that those ladies were the sweetest conquests of all. Reluctantly he allowed Skye and Adam to pass on, but he was determined that sooner than later he would hold the Irish beauty in his arms, and she would swoon with delight as all the others did at his passionate kisses.

"You are angry," Adam said when they were out of earshot of the royals. "I must assume that the young King of Navarre made indecent suggestions to you, sweetheart." He took two goblets of chilled wine from the tray of a passing servant and handed her one. "I cannot imagine Henri of Navarre not being taken by your beauty."

"It is outrageous!" fumed Skye. "He is to be married tomorrow, and here he is propositioning women the night before!"

Adam chuckled. "Typical behavior of the young man, I am told."

"The poor princess!"

"God's bones, Skye, don't feel sorry for that hot-tempered little bitch, Marguérite de Valois. She is the Duc de Guise's mistress. In fact she wished to marry him, and he was quite agreeable. Unfortunately Catherine de Medici felt the match with Navarre more favorable to her, and de Guise had just hurriedly wed with the Princess de Porcienne to escape a possible royal assassination. The

Queen Mother wouldn't hesitate to inflict *la Morte Italienne* upon de Guise. In face I suspect she is quite sorry he escaped her. The de Guises are too ambitious, and Catherine considers them a threat to her sons. She has never forgiven them for the way they treated her when her eldest, François II, was married to their little niece, the Queen of Scots."

"What a family!" Skye exclaimed. "They are as bad as the Tudors!"

Adam chuckled. "Power," he said, "is a very heady draught, sweetheart."

From some hidden corner the musicians started to play, and the guests began to get into formation to dance. Skye moved gracefully in and out of the figure, smiling softly in her pleasure at Adam, who partnered her with the utmost grace for so big a man. Mischievously he stole a kiss, and she found herself laughing up at him with pure happiness. As far as she was concerned, they were the only two people on the face of the earth. How fortunate I am, she thought. Somehow it has all come out all right. In less than two months Adam and I will be married. Bess Tudor will be angry, but I know that eventually she'll forgive us, and we'll go home again. We'll rebuild Adam's castle on Lundy. It is the perfect place for us—an island between our two countries. We'll gather my children, and together we will grow old together. That didn't seem like such an awful idea to Skye.

He saw her smiling, and asked, "What makes you so happy, sweetheart?"

Gazing back up at him, she said, "I was thinking of our growing old together, Adam."

He chuckled. "Do you think we might be young for just a little while longer, Skye? With you for my wife, my life is but beginning."

"Oh, my darling!" she cried softly, and there were quick tears sparkling like diamonds in her sapphire eyes. "What a lovely thing to say to me!"

"*Adam!* Adam de Marisco, is it really you?" As the dance ended they heard an excited feminine voice.

They looked about for the owner of the voice and an incredibly beautifully woman whirled into their sight. Reed-slender with a magnificent high bosom and tiny waist, she was dressed in apple green and gold silk, which complimented her wonderful reddish-blond hair.

"*Merde!*" Adam swore under his breath, and Skye giggled at the oath.

The woman stopped before them, eyed Skye briefly, dismissed her insultingly, and then flung herself on Adam's chest. "A-dam, *ma chéri!* I cannot believe it is really you! *Mon Dieu!* You are a hundred times more handsome than when we last met!"

Detaching the woman from his doublet, Adam set her back from him, and said in an icy tone, "Skye, this is Athenais Boussac."

"*Non, non, chéri!*" The beauty was not a bit disturbed by Adam's unfriendly tone. "You will remember I married de Montoire. I am the Duchesse de Beuvron."

"And how is your husband, Madame la Duchesse?"

"Quite dead, *chéri*, and in Hell, I hope. He was the most wretched man, you know."

"But a *real* man, Madame la Duchesse, I have no doubt, knowing your opinion on that subject. Tell me, how many sons did he father on you?"

Now Skye knew who the woman was. This was the very same creature who had once scorned Adam's love when she found out he could not have children. Skye put a gentle hand on Adam's arm. "Come, my love," she said. "I see your mother signaling to us across the room."

"Who is this female, Adam? Tell her to go away! We have much to talk about, *chéri*."

"As always, Athenais, your manners are deplorable. This female is my betrothed wife, Madame Burke. Now if you will excuse us . . ."

"*A-dam!*" Athenais de Montoire caught at his sleeve. "Adam," she repeated pleadingly, "we must talk!"

"There is nothing to talk about, Madame la Duchesse," and taking Skye's arm, Adam moved across the floor to where his mother and stepfather were standing.

"*Sacre bleu!*" exclaimed Gaby, who had witnessed the entire exchange. "That creature is shameless! What did she want, my son?"

"To talk, she said."

"Hah!" was Adam's mother's angry reply. "Athenais de Montoire was never noted for her ability to converse. More than likely, she has decided she wants another husband, and now that she is rich and titled in her own right she is after you again! *Quelle chienne!*"

"You will remember, maman, that the reason Athenais broke our betrothal was that she learned I could not have children. I doubt she has changed so much over the last twenty years, and in any case I am not interested in the bitch."

"My son," Gaby de Saville said, "men can often be great fools. Athenais cares nothing for children. She said what she said to you twenty years ago because the Duc de Beuvron had made her father a rather handsome offer for her, and it was more to Baron Boussac's advantage to marry his daughter to a wealthy old duc than to a then penniless English lordling.

"It was a miracle that they received such a magnificent offer, but de Beuvron was elderly and childless. He lusted openly after Athenais, and she was a virgin. How she used that one honest jewel of hers to lure de Beuvron onward to his doom! It is said that the duc demanded to know from Baron Boussac what Athenais's dowry would be. Well, my dear, there was no dowry, as you well know, and so," here Gaby lowered her voice, "it is rumored that the baron brought Athenais into the room where he and the duc were ironing out the agreement, and when he removed her cloak she was stark naked beneath it! As I heard the story, de Beuvron looked at Athenais, who turned to show him all and the duc almost had an apoplectic fit then and there his lust was so hot. Then the baron said, 'There, monseigneur, is my daughter's dowry to you. A flawless face and form. No amount of gold that I could give you would equal such graces.' As he covered his daughter again with her cloak the duc practically fell over his feet to sign the marriage contract.

"Instead of Boussac *giving* de Beuvron gold, he received a fortune for Athenais's maidenhead! The duc did manage to get one son on her after five years of marriage. The birth almost killed her, it is said, for the baby came feet first. She was never able to have another, not that she minded. The old duc died two years ago, and his son is now fifteen. The boy is the image of his father, and it is said, a bit weak in the head. He dotes upon his mother, I am told."

"You have certainly kept up, Mother, haven't you?" Adam teased with a grin.

"Athenais de Montoire has always been the topic of gossip in the district, Adam. After her son was born any man who took her eye was quickly in her bed. Her lovers were legion. But since de Beuvron's death she has spent a great deal of time at court, and I have lost track."

"But only for a lack of any informant to gossip with," the comte chuckled.

"Antoine!" Gaby pouted, pretending to take offense.

"She is very beautiful," Skye said thoughtfully.

"*Oui*," Gaby replied, "but it is the same kind of beauty that a rotting lily has. To the eye, all is perfection, but beneath the surface one finds decadence and writhing maggots."

"You are far more beautiful," Adam soothed Skye.

"It is not her beauty that disturbs me," Skye said. "There is something about her, something wicked. I see it in her eyes." She looked across the room to where they had left the Duchesse de Beuvron.

Athenais de Montoire stared boldly back at her, but Skye was not one bit perturbed. Equally bold, she openly surveyed the woman. In defiance of fashion the duchesse wore her gorgeous reddish-blond hair long and loose. It fell in rippling waves down her back like a shining mantle. Her face was a little cat's face with a high, broad forehead, narrowing into a determined little pointed chin. Her amber yellow eyes were large and round, her mouth long and narrow and painted red. Only her nose might be considered less than flawless, for although long and elegant, it hooked under slightly at the end, spoiling the perfection. She was still a beautiful woman, though as she grew older she needed more of the artifice of paint to catch the eye.

Gaby put a hand on Skye's arm, drawing her attention away from the duchesse. "I have heard that Athenais is a member of the Queen Mother's *Escadrille Volantée*."

"Her Flying Squadron?" Skye cocked her head puzzled. "What on earth is that?"

"The Queen uses beautiful women here at court to seduce the men she wishes to use and to influence. The women who do her bidding are called the *Escadrille Volantée*, or, as you would say in your tongue, Flying Squadron. More than one hapless man has been lured to his doom in Catherine de Medici's quest for power."

Skye let her eyes wander back to where Athenais de Montoire had been standing, but the duchesse was gone now. The hidden musicians were playing another sprightly tune now, and Adam led her back onto the dance floor. Forgetting about the Duchesse de Beuvron, Skye began to have a wonderful time. She danced with Adam, and his charming half-brothers, and the husbands of his sisters, and his nephew. They all partook of the magnificent buffet that had been set out in the rooms surrounding the ballroom; a buffet so incredible that Skye thought never to be hungry again just looking at the bounty of France spread before her wondering eyes.

There were pâtés: foie gras from Toulouse, partridge pâtés from Nérac, fresh tunny pâtés from Toulon. There was seafood in profusion: raw oysters, opened cold and fresh by kitchen boys for the diners, mussels in Dijon mustard, sole in white wine, lamprey eel, platters with whole salmon on beds of cress, and with whole carp, both from the Loire River. There were dishes of salted white herring, smoked red herring, and a herring that had been bloated, salted, and smoked. There were silver platters of small game birds: partridge, woodcock from the Dombes, and skylarks from Pézenás. There was roast goose, and capons from Caux in ginger sauce, cooked tongue from Vierzon, Bayonne hams, boar, stag, roe deer, beef, and lamb. There were pies of sparrow and lark, rabbit and hare. There were plates of larded ducks and roasted teal, heron, and whole swans. The greens were few: artichokes in olive oil, bowls of new lettuce, scallions, and radishes. There was fresh bread and rolls, and tubs of butter both sweet and salted, as well as half a dozen varieties of cheese and platters of eggs both hard-boiled and deviled. An entire table was devoted to sweets, the centerpiece being a huge marzipan confection of the Cathedral of Notre Dame, its square complete with the bridal couple as they would appear tomorrow. There were gâteaux of every description, meringues, early apples, Anjou pears, sweet black cherries, large, round golden peaches, and small plump apricots. The wine flowed, both red and white, the entire evening. Catherine de Medici did not stint on the prenuptial feast of a Princess of France.

After they had eaten, and Skye swore that Adam sampled everything on all the tables, a point he vigorously denied, there was more dancing. When the young King of Navarre appeared before the startled de Saville family and claimed Skye for a dance he first made it a point to charm all the ladies. He was courteous and smiling to Gaby and her two eldest daughters. He flirted mischievously with Musette and two of his nieces, Matilde and Marie-Gabrielle. He was charmingly teasing to the youngest girl in the family attending the ball, and little Catherine-Henriette later swore to her mother she would never in her lifetime love anyone else but King Henri of Navarre. Then with a polite bow and a smile to the gentlemen, Henri of Navarre led Skye firmly to the dance floor.

"Have you missed me, *chérie*?" he laughed down into her face.

"How could I miss you, monseigneur? I do not even know you," was her cool reply.

His arm tightened about her waist. "We must remedy that oversight, madame, for you have enchanted me with your Celtic beauty."

"You would do better to contemplate the beauty of your bride, monseigneur."

Henri laughed at the severe tone of her rebuke, and bringing his face close to hers, he murmured, "You have a mouth that was meant for kisses, *chérie*. How can you be so cold to me when I burn for your touch, for a kind word?"

Skye turned her head to the left as the pattern of the dance dictated, and then she deliberately stamped upon her partner's foot. "Mind your manners, Monseigneur de Navarre!"

He winced as her little pointed heel dug into his foot, but he could still not resist a chuckle. "Your coldness inflames me, *chérie*," he said with disturbing intensity, "for I know that beneath the icy hauteur of your words is a passionate woman. The softness of your lips gives you away, as does the adorable little pulse in your beautiful white throat that is beating so frantically at this very moment."

Skye was momentarily disturbed. He was too young a man, this King of Navarre, to know so much about women; but gathering her wits, she replied calmly, "The pulse in my throat beats quickly because the pace of the dance is swift, monseigneur."

Henri smiled knowingly. "You have a quick mind, *cherie*. I like a woman who can offer a man more than just beauty."

"I have offered you nothing, monseigneur, nor do I intend to. I will be quite frank with you so that there is no further misunderstanding between us. My impending marriage is a love match. I would never betray Adam de Marisco in *any* way. Now that you understand this, Monseigneur de Navarre, I know you will cease this futile pursuit of me."

"The pursuit of love and beauty is never futile, *cherie*," was his answer.

Skye was becoming annoyed with this spoiled young king.

"Monseigneur, I do not doubt that this room is filled tonight with women who would kill for the honor of sleeping in your bed. I, however, am not one of them!" she said.

The dance had come to an end, and to her relief there was Adam at her side. Skye curtseyed low to the King of Navarre, and taking her betrothed husband's arm, she allowed him to lead her away. Adam was chortling softly beneath his breath. "From the look on the face of M'sieur de Navarre, sweetheart, you have just given him a severe setdown."

"What an impossible boy!" Skye fumed. "His attitude is that he is irresistible to women!"

"It is his reputation, Skye."

"He cannot understand the word *no*, Adam."

"It is not, I imagine, a word often tendered him, sweetheart."

She stopped and, looking up at him, said, "Aren't you even the tiniest bit jealous, Adam? The King of Navarre wishes to seduce me!"

"In truth, sweetheart, I am enraged, but I must think of our future. If Elizabeth Tudor refuses to recognize our marriage and we cannot return to England, France is our refuge. We cannot, however, remain safely in France if I have killed or wounded a royal prince of the blood in a duel. Therefore I must remain outwardly calm, Skye. But believe me, I am not calm. I stood and watched Henri of Navarre with his hands all over you, and his bold eyes mentally undressing you, assessing your finer points. I would have enjoyed putting my hands around the elegant throat of that puppy and squeezing the life from him!"

Skye smiled up at him, sweetly satisfied. "Do you think your mother would think badly of us if we went home now? We could send the coach back for them. It is not far."

"Now why, sweetheart, would we want to leave such a gay gathering?" he teased her.

"Because my mouth, which, the King of Navarre assures me, was made for kisses, longs to taste yours. Because, *mon mari*, I long to feel your hands on me. Because I am a totally shameless wench, Adam de Marisco, and I am hot for your loving!"

He felt a bolt of desire tear into his body at her provocative words, her smoldering look. Heedless of how it might look, he yanked her none too gently into an alcove of the ballroom, and his arm tightened about her as he looked with blazing eyes down into her face. "What sorcery is this you work on me, you Celtic witch?" His lips were dangerously close to hers, and Skye felt a weakness in her legs, which threatened to give way beneath her.

Love. She didn't say the word aloud, but rather mouthed it, and so tempting were her soft lips that, unable to resist, he kissed her passionately. Skye slipped her arms up around his neck, pressing her practically naked bosom against the soft velvet of his elegant doublet. Her pulse was pounding in her ears, and he groaned softly against her mouth, licking the corners of it suggestively. "Take me home, Adam," she whispered to him against his lips.

He drew a deep breath, and said, "You will have to give me a moment to collect myself, sweetheart, and it would be best if you untangled yourself from me and stood quietly."

Her blue eyes were twinkling as she stepped back, and folding her hands demurely, she waited for him to regain his composure. She said nothing, but her lips were twitching with her suppressed amusement. How she loved this big man! He reminded her of— Skye's eyes grew wide with the sudden realization—he reminded her of Geoffrey! In face and form they were nothing alike, yet there was similarity of spirit that could not be denied.

"What is it, sweetheart?" He had seen her face, heard her unconscious intake of breath.

"Geoffrey," she said. "For some reason, at this moment you remind me of Geoffrey Southwood."

"We were cousins," Adam reminded her.

"Yes," Skye said slowly. "I remember your telling me that the Southwoods were the legitimate branch of the family, and the de Mariscos the illegitimate branch."

"That's right," he said. "Geoffrey and I both descend from the original Geoffroi de Sudbois, who came with William of Normandy to England. He springs from Geoffroi's wife, Gwyneth of Lynmouth, and I from the line of Geoffroi's mistress, Matilde de Marisco. In fact his Southwood grandfather and my de Marisco grandmother were brother and sister, for over the years the family did intermarry. Whenever the Southwoods had a spare younger daughter and a little dowry they married the girl to the heir of Lundy, thus keeping the family ties strong." Adam sighed. "There will be no more heirs to Lundy," he said sadly, "and the de Marisco line dies with me."

She put a comforting hand on his arm. "Take me home, *mon*

mari. My greatest sorrow will always be that I cannot give you a child, but as the Blessed Mother is my witness, Adam, I will love you till death and even beyond as no one has ever loved you before!"

"Then I shall be the luckiest of all the de Mariscos in the last five centuries, Skye," he said gallantly; and taking her arm, he led her from the ballroom of the Louvre and to their waiting coach.

Chapter 14

The wedding of Marguérite de Valois, Princess of France, and her very distant cousin, Henri, King of Navarre, a Huguenot, was a most controversial match. It had been engineered by her mother, Catherine de Medici, over the protests of the Holy Catholic Church. The Pope had refused a dispensation, but that would not be known until after the marriage, for the Queen Mother knew that the Archbishop of Paris would not marry her daughter and Henri of Navarre if he learned of the Holy Father's refusal to cooperate.

Catherine de Medici had come to France as the bride of François I's second son, Henri. With the death of her brother-in-law four years later she found herself the future Queen of France. Her husband despised her, finding her physically unattractive. He was not intelligent enough himself to discover that behind the plain face was a highly developed mind. Catherine de Medici bided her time, ignoring the insults of the mocking court. Her husband's mistress was an astoundingly beautiful woman some twenty years his senior, and to Catherine the greatest offense of all was that Diane de Poitiers was in sympathy with her.

How the charming beauty strove to be kind to the dumpy little Florentine. How she defended her against baseless slanders! That, to Catherine, was the unkindest act of all, for she wanted to hate this woman who had stolen the heart of her husband before Henri even knew that Catherine de Medici, daughter of the Duke of Urbino, existed. It was six years before Diane could persuade her lover to consummate the marriage he had made for France, and afterward he only came to his wife's bed when forced. It was eleven years before Catherine bore her first child, the future François II. Two daughters followed.

One sickly boy was not enough, and Henri II, King of France, took to visiting his wife's bed on a more regular basis. These conjugal sojourns became embarrassing and emotionally painful for Catherine, for although she had never known any man intimately except her husband, she somehow sensed that there should be more to their coupling than there was. Each time it was the same. Henri would arrive announced in his wife's bedchamber. He would say but three things to her, and they were always the same. Arriving he said, "*Bon soir, madame.*" Beginning his legal assault upon her body, he would cry, "For France!"; and shortly afterward he would say in parting, "*Adieu, madame.*" Catherine was pregnant a total of eleven times, and bore seven live children, four of them sons.

When Henri II was killed as the result of an accident on the tilting field, his widow's first act was to send Diane de Poitiers from court; but Catherine was no longer Queen of France; a saucy and beautiful chit of a girl named Mary of Scotland was. Mary was guided in her every move by her mother's family, the powerful house of Guise-Lorraine, who, because Catherine's foolish son, François II, was so besotted by his little wife, also guided the king. Catherine gritted her teeth, and moved to block the dangerous and growing power of the de Guises. There could be no challenge to the house of Valois!

Fortunately, François II died within a year, and Mary of Scotland was quickly sent packing back to her own land where she had not lived since she was six. Charles IX, Catherine's second son, was but ten, and the Queen Mother ruled for him. This was what she had waited for all these years! Power! It was an incredible aphrodisiac. For twenty-seven years she had stood in the shadow of others, but now Catherine de Medici came into her own.

She was, surprisingly, a tolerant woman who strove hard to make peace between the two warring factions that threatened to tear France apart. During the reigns of both her late father-in-law and her husband, the Protestant movement had gained a strong foothold in France. Catherine had been born a Catholic, but she was too intelligent a woman to believe in only one possible path to salvation. When the de Guise family put itself at the head of the majority Catholic faction, Catherine subtly championed the opposing side. Religion meant nothing to her, although she followed the tenets of her faith enough to prevent Church censure. Her overriding concern was for France and its ruling family. They must survive, and she would do whatever she had to do to insure that.

Catherine de Medici had learned a great lesson from her husband's passion for Diane de Poitiers. A beautiful woman could gain much from a besotted man. Consequently, she began gathering together a small force of the most beautiful women at court, women who needed something from the Queen. Some needed money to maintain their extravagant life-styles. Others wanted favors for themselves or family members or even lovers. Catherine let it be known she was there to help, but once in the Queen Mother's debt you were expected to repay her by aiding her to manipulate the powerful men of the kingdom. Catherine de Medici's *Escadrille Volantée* became notorious, but not so notorious that those approached by its beautiful and sensual members did not give in to their demands.

Catherine was not one to fool herself, and she had seen the handwriting on the wall. François II had never even consummated his marriage to Mary of Scotland, being too ill to do so. The current King, her son Charles IX, had only a little daughter by his wife, Isabeau of Austria, and a bastard son by his mistress, Marie Touchet. Charles was sickly, and subject to fits, however, and there would be no more children, for his latest illness had rendered him impotent. Catherine's two other sons were not particularly promising. The Duc d'Anjou was disgracefully effeminate, wore an earring in his ear, and consorted with a band of similar young men. The youngest Valois son, Hercule, rechristened François after his elder brother's death, was also not physically strong.

The next in line for France's throne was therefore Henri, son of Anthony, Duc of Vendôme and Bourbon and his wife, Jeanne, Queen of Navarre. Henri de Bourbon, Prince of Navarre, was a big, healthy, ruddy boy who had been brought up to ride hard, run barefoot over the rocky hills of Navarre with the goats, fight, drink, and make love well. He was his grandfather's pride, and his mother's source of despair, for Jeanne of Navarre was a strict and militant Protestant. At fifteen, Henri proved, along with his younger cousin, the Prince of Condé, to be the Protestant forces' salvation. He was, it seemed, an excellent military leader.

Seeing this, Catherine de Medici decided there was only one course open to her. She had met Henri on several occasions. What had been clear to her was that he was no religious fanatic. This was a realist like herself, and when the time came Henri of Navarre would do what he had to do to gain the throne of France. She was betting that this would not involve trying to force the French to the Protestant faith. After her sons he was France's hope, and in her heart she knew he would be king, for the house of Valois would die with her sons. This had been told her by a great Parisian fortune-teller, and being a believer in such things, Catherine had decided to marry her youngest child to Henri of Navarre.

The King of Navarre was agreeable. He saw the obvious advantages in such a match. Marguérite of Valois was not so agreeable. She was in love with Henri de Guise, and had even allowed him to take her maidenhead in the childish belief that it would force her mother to consent to their marriage. Catherine laughed at her daughter's tactics, and hinted to the de Guise family that unless Duc Henri took himself a wife he might find himself in an early grave. To Marguérite's fury and frustration, Duc Henri quickly wed with the Princesse de Porcien, and now tomorrow, August 18th, 1572, she was to be married to that big boor, Henri de Navarre.

Staunchly Catholic Paris was outraged that their adorable Margot, who was so terribly in love with the handsome blond Duc de Guise, should be sacrificed this way; but Catherine de Medici wanted peace between Catholics and Protestants lest Spain and England involve themselves in France. Now, however, on the night before her so carefully arranged wedding, she was having second thoughts about the advisability of it all.

Paris was filled with wedding guests, many of them Huguenots. The Huguenots were in many cases being extremely offensive, boasting in the taverns of what they would do to the Catholics when their leader, the King of Navarre, became the King of France. Then, too, there was the very strong influence wielded by Admiral Coligny, the great Huguenot nobleman, on the weak-willed King. Twice today Charles had overridden Catherine's advice in favor of Coligny's, and it was not the first time this had happened. Catherine de Medici decided that Admiral Coligny had to be removed. She was convinced that once that was accomplished, the King would accept her advice again and the Protestants would calm down.

August 18th dawned fair and warm. Because the groom was not

a Catholic the marriage ceremony itself was to take place on the steps of Notre Dame Cathedral, and the bride would then enter the great church to hear mass while her new husband waited outside. The square outside the cathedral was crowded with the invited who ohhed and ahhed as the bride arrived clothed in azure-blue silk, the underskirt of her gown embroidered with the golden lilies of France. Several small children of the highest nobility held up the heavily trimmed ermine and cloth-of-gold cloak that fell from the bride's shoulders as she made her way to her place. All the agreements had been signed before the ball at the Louvre the night before, and now the actual marriage was to be quickly accomplished.

But Marguérite de Valois was defiant to the bitter end. When the elderly Bishop of Paris asked in his quavery voice if she would have Henri de Navarre for her husband, the princesse remained mutinously silent. A very long minute passed, and the bishop, now visibly nervous, repeated his question. A small, wicked smile played about Margot's mouth as she sensed victory. If she didn't answer, they couldn't force her to this marriage! It was all so simple. Why hadn't she thought of it sooner? Suddenly King Charles leaned forward, and hooking his fingers into his rebellious sister's hair nodded her head vigorously up and down. With a sigh of relief the bishop then demanded of Henri of Navarre if he would take Marguérite de Valois as his wife. Henri hesitated just a brief second, long enough to tease Margot into thinking that perhaps he wouldn't, after all. When he finally spoke up in a loud, sure voice she sent him a quelling look, but Henri was not intimidated and grinned back at his furious bride.

Along with the de Savilles, Skye and Adam had been invited to enter the cathedral for the mass. Afterward, as they rode back in the enormous royal procession toward the Louvre and the marriage feast, they heard people in the streets cheering the Duc de Guise, who pretended he did not notice. Skye raised an eyebrow, and said, "Well, that should take M'sieur de Navarre down a peg or two."

Adam laughed. Henri of Navarre had really annoyed his beautiful Skye with his persistent refusal to believe she was not interested in him. There had even been flowers this morning for Skye, brought by a dirty-faced street urchin who only said, "For Madame Burke from Navarre," before grinning impudently and running off. Skye had thrown the bouquet from the window with a shriek of outrage.

"De Guise deludes himself if he thinks he can overcome Navarre's claim to France," Adam said. "I suspect we have not yet seen the last of France's civil wars. How unfortunate!"

"How foolish of the French to fight over semantics," Skye replied. "I have never understood how sane men could argue about the way in which they worship."

"I have often thought," Adam said softly, "that if the Christ returned to earth today he would shed bitter tears over the cruelties men perpetrate in his name."

She nodded and slipped her hand into his. "Let us think on something more pleasant, my darling, like our own wedding."

"I have already sent a messenger to England for the children," Adam replied. "They all will be easy to gather, but for Robin. I have written to Robbie asking that he bring Robin from court on the pretext that his sister is ill and wishes to see him. I will not write to the Queen until after our marriage, for fear she forbid it. I do not want to have to go directly against Elizabeth Tudor."

"No," Skye said. "She will be angry enough when we present her with the fact of our marriage, but I, too, would prefer not to defy her openly."

For the next week Paris was a city of celebration in honor of the royal marriage. There were fairs with fortune-tellers, and dancing bears, and wonderful food distributed by the King in honor of his sister; and for the nobility the feasting and the dancing at the Louvre hardly stopped. Neither did the intrigue. The Huguenot Coligny's influence grew, and Catherine de Medici seethed.

"Well, madame, you see what your meddling has gotten you," the Duc de Guise sneered softly to Catherine one evening.

"It is not good, I will admit," the Queen Mother said. "I would be quit of Coligny. Navarre will come around eventually."

"Admiral Coligny must pass by the house of an old tutor of mine on his way home, madame. I would consider it an honor to aid you in your hour of need. We are both of us, after all, for France."

The Queen Mother's eyes gave no indication that she had even heard de Guise. "You will, M'sieur le Duc, of course do as your conscience dictates," she murmured as she moved away from him.

On the twenty-second of August Admiral Coligny was shot at and wounded as he walked the short distance from the Louvre Palace to his own Paris house. There had been witnesses, unfortunately, and it was ascertained that the shot had come from a house owned by the Duc de Guise. Who had fired the shot, however, was not known.

The Huguenots in Paris for the wedding were outraged, and it was all the King's men could do to keep order, for the city was seething with anger as the two factions met in various public places, trading insults, threats, and sometimes blows. The princes of Navarre and Condé as well as Admiral Coligny himself worked valiantly to keep their people under control. "A hothead," the admiral declared. "'Twas only a shot fired by a fanatic. Did God not spare me, my friends? Is that not a sign that I am meant to live on to carry out his work?" The Huguenots settled down to an uneasy truce with the Catholics.

In the Louvre Charles IX was outraged, furious, and fearful by turns. The lucid mood that had prevailed due to his sister's nuptials was fast dissolving into terrified paranoia, helped along by his mother and the Duc de Guise. Still rational, Charles demanded that the assassin and his accomplices be brought to justice.

"Coligny is my friend!" he shouted. "His first thoughts are for me, and for France. He would end this civil strife between his Huguenots and the Catholic League. Civil war is not good for the country! You have said so yourself, Mother! You have told me a hundred, nay, a thousand times that a king who cannot maintain order is doomed!" Charles paced nervously about his apartment. "A blow against Coligny is a blow against me, against France! I want the cowardly assassin found!"

Catherine de Medici sat very still in her chair. Her hands were folded in her lap, her black eyes flat and expressionless. "You are getting needlessly upset, Charles, and you are beginning to babble. No one has struck a blow against either you or France. Admiral Coligny has of late usurped your very authority, and it is obvious that someone who saw that attempted to correct the situation. That the means chosen were less than peaceful is regrettable. Still, we must examine why Coligny and his Huguenots have of late been less than cooperative."

"Come, sire," de Guise murmured, "you have been more than generous to these heretics, and now they attempt to stab you in the back."

"What do you mean?" The King was beginning to look terrified.

"Now, Charlot," the Duc of Anjou replied, the King's next brother, "is it not obvious?"

"Is not *what* obvious, Henri? I do not understand," Charles quavered.

Anjou put an arm about his elder brother, and spoke in a confidential tone. "Coligny is shot at, and his witnesses, all Huguenots, claim the shot was fired from a house owned by Coligny's archenemy, de Guise here. How do we know that Coligny did not plan the whole thing himself, and that the alleged assassin is a Huguenot."

"But why would he do that, Henri?"

"Most obvious, dearest Charlot, most obvious. If Coligny could rouse all his supporters to believe that you, our beloved King, and de Guise, your loyal servant, were responsible for the attempted murder, he could then incite them to rebellion right here in Paris. He could convince them to storm the Louvre itself, and the Louvre could scarce be defended against an armed mob, brother. They would kill all the Valois, and then put their Huguenot King of Navarre upon your throne. His claim, after we are all gone, is quite legitimate, and with our sister, Margot, as his Queen, who would gainsay him France? This is not a plot against Coligny, my brother. It is a plot against you! Against France!"

"Rubbish!"

Everyone, the frightened King included, turned to look to Charles's youngest sibling, the Duc d'Alençon.

"Really, Charles," the good-natured Alençon drawled, "you are allowing de Guise and Anjou to terrify you out of your wits. Whatever the truth of this matter, neither Coligny nor his Huguenots are plotting to destroy you. If I were looking for a villain I should certainly look closer to home, brother."

"And exactly what do you mean by that, Alençon?" the Duc de Guise demanded, his hand going to his sword.

"*Mon Dieu*, de Guise, you are bold, and quite sure of yourself," the youngest Valois prince taunted. "Will you dare to draw your weapon in the king's presence?"

"Messieurs, messieurs!" Catherine chided, seeing the situation begin to get out of hand. Damn Alençon, anyway! "We are getting away from the heart of the matter. Why are the two greatest houses in France, the Valois kings, and their premier noblemen, the house of de Guise—Lorraine, bound not only by blood but by religion, squabbling? May God have mercy on me for my shortsightedness in trying to make peace between the heretics and the Mother Church. I have been wrong, and it has caused needless suffering." Catherine de Medici rose from her chair, and walking over to her son, she knelt at his feet. "Forgive me, Charles! I have been wrong, and I have given you bad counsel! I shall retire to a convent and spend my days atoning for this terrible sin."

Both Anjou and de Guise cast their eyes heavenward in their attempt to appear pious, but the poor Duc d'Alençon was hard put not to burst into laughter at his mother's theatrical gesture. He knew, as did the others, that she had no intention of taking up the religious life. A less religious woman he had never known!

The King, however, was now totally shaken and confused. The one constant in his life had always been his mother. She had never, ever failed him. "No, Mother! No! Do not leave me! We will solve this problem together!" he cried, helping Catherine to her feet.

"There is only one way, Majesty," de Guise said ominously. "We must kill the Huguenots."

"But it is a sin to kill," the King whispered.

"No, brother," Anjou murmured soothingly, "the Church will not condemn us for destroying the heretics. They will sing our praises."

Charles looked to his mother. Catherine de Medici said nothing, but she did nod her head in the affirmative.

"I can't."

"*You must!*" de Guise pounded.

"There is no choice," Anjou said. "It is either you or them, dearest brother! We cannot lose you. You are France!"

"All of them?"

"*All!*" de Guise thundered, a fanatic's gleam in his eye.

"Not Navarre or Condé," the Queen Mother said with sudden determination in her voice. If Margot were freed of Navarre it would only be a matter of time before the Princesse de Porcien was put aside by her husband de Guise. Catherine knew that her sons would then be killed ruthlessly, and with Navarre gone, de Guise would press his slender claim to the throne with a Valois heiress as his wife. *Oh no, my clever friend*, Catherine thought. *I am smarter than that!*

"It must be all," de Guise insisted.

"Navarre and Condé will convert to Catholicism when faced

with no other choice. With their leaders gone the remaining Huguenots will also have no other choice but to return to Mother Church. We need these people, Charles. They are industrious and clever, and have much to offer us. Navarre and Condé must be spared."

"Yes, Mother, I understand, but as for the rest, kill them all! I want not one left alive to reproach me! Not one!" He began to shiver uncontrollably with fear. "Marie," he whimpered. "I want Marie!"

Catherine turned her all-seeing eyes to Alençon. "You," she snapped, pointing a fat accusatory finger at him, "Fetch Mademoiselle Touchet!"

With a mocking smile of congratulation and a sketchy bow, the Duc d'Alençon said, "Of course, maman. At once," and he left the King's chamber.

Mademoiselle Touchet, the King's mistress, was quickly brought to him from her nearby apartments. Seeing his distress, Marie Touchet ran to the King with a sympathetic little cry and began to soothe his fears with her gentle reassurances, from soft hands and voice. The Queen Mother nodded approvingly, and then signaled to the others to follow her out of the room. The frightened King never even saw them go.

Outside the King's rooms Catherine de Medici turned to her son, Anjou, and the Duc de Guise. "I mean what I say, gentlemen. If anything happens to Navarre or Condé, you will not survive them any longer than it takes me to find out; and you know that I do not speak idly, messieurs."

"When is it to be done?" Anjou demanded.

"Come with me to my apartments, and we will speak further on it," his mother said, moving swiftly away from the King's rooms. Entering her salon, she abruptly dismissed her women, and then, turning to de Guise and her son, said, "It must be done tonight."

"There is no time," replied de Guise, the soldier.

"You have no choice," Catherine said. "At this very moment Coligny lies wounded, but tomorrow or the next day he will be well enough to come to the King with his personal accusations. Then all is lost for us. It must be tonight! Now! Before Coligny has the opportunity to see Charles again."

"It is not yet evening," de Guise mused slowly. "Perhaps if we worked quickly, and spread the word to our people. Once it has begun, all Paris will join in to destroy the Huguenots. Yes, it can be done! When the tocsin sounds at two o'clock tomorrow morning, we will begin. Is that satisfactory, Majesty? Is that time enough?"

"Yes," was the reply. "It is a good time, for the pious Huguenots will be sleeping in their houses." She smiled. "All but my good *beau-frère*, who will be celebrating with the rest of the court at the last ball to be given in honor of his marriage to my daughter. Tomorrow Margot and Navarre will go down to Chenonceaux for their honeymoon trip away from all distractions of the court."

"I still say that Navarre should be killed, too," de Guise muttered.

"Why? So your adulterous union with my daughter might be made legal—after, of course, the removal of your wife? I think not, de Guise. Be grateful I did not have you removed forcibly these past three afternoons from my daughter's bed where you have lingered while Henri of Navarre played tennis with Alençon in the courts by the river."

"Madame!" The Duc de Guise made an attempt at denial, which Catherine waved aside.

"Do not bother to deny the truth, m'sieur. It is of no import in this matter. What is important is that we keep our dear Navarre and Condé amused tonight. I think for Condé it will be Mademoiselle de Grenier."

"You cannot lure Condé with a woman, Mother! He is newly married himself, and besides, he is an awful prude," Anjou said.

Catherine laughed. "You underestimate me, my son. Condé's passion, military strategist that he is, is chess. Mademoiselle de Grenier is the finest chess player at court. She will engage him in a tourney, and keep him thus occupied. As to his wife, I will see that Alençon keeps her amused, for she is quite fond of him in a sisterly way."

"And Navarre?" the Duc de Guise queried Catherine.

"For Navarre I have a special treat, messieurs. Since the night before his wedding he has been vigorously pursuing the Comte de Cher's soon-to-be *belle-fille*. She is an Irishwoman named Madame Burke, betrothed to marry the comtesse's son by her first marriage, a Seigneur de Marisco. The lady has been quite adamant in her refusal of Henri, which, of course, only makes him more ardent."

"What of the betrothed husband?" Anjou demanded. "Where does he stand in all of this?"

"He is amused," the Queen Mother said, "and does not consider Navarre a severe threat to his betrothed wife. Were it not for my aid, Navarre would not have a chance with the lady, but I shall give him that chance. The Duchesse de Beuvron was once to marry the Seigneur de Marisco. Now that she is widowed, she would like to regain his favor. I will see that she has a chance to plead her case tonight while you, Anjou, will lead Madame Burke to a secluded place to meet Navarre. She will not, of course, know she is meeting him. She will believe she is to see me, that I wish her to carry a personal message from me to Elizabeth Tudor when she returns to England."

"What if she plays on Navarre's sense of honor?" de Guise asked. "What then, madame?"

Catherine de Medici snorted. "Must I outline everything for you? Anjou, my secret study, you know it."

"The one with the bed in the alcove, Mother?"

"Yes! You will bring Madame Burke there. Drug her, or stun her with a light blow. Yes, perhaps that is better, for a drug might render her useless. Bind her hands, and see she is in a state of dishabille upon the bed. She has beautiful little breasts, and I note that Navarre is fascinated with them. One good look, and his gallantry will dissolve as his lust takes over." She chuckled richly. "Yes, one can depend upon Navarre's reactions when a beautiful woman is involved. Wait until after one o'clock before you lure Madame Burke away, Anjou. We want Navarre well occupied when the two o'clock tocsin sounds."

The final ball that night was a triumph that spilled out from the ballrooms of the Louvre Palace into its neat flower-filled gardens that bordered the River Seine. Except for Henri of Navarre's unwelcome and persistent attentions, Skye was enjoying her time in Paris immensely. Yet she decided that she preferred the Tudor court to this one. There was too much intrigue in the French court, whose inhabitants were a touch too chic and too wicked to suit her taste.

"I never thought," she said to Adam, "that I should say I preferred the English and their bluff, honest ways; but compared to the French, they are less complicated."

He chuckled down at her. "Do you think you damned impossible Irish will ever stop fighting us, sweetheart?"

She looked up at him, her sapphire eyes wide with innocence. "Why, Adam," she said sweetly. "'Tis not the Irish who are fighting the English, 'tis the English who are fighting the Irish."

"Not this Englishman," he murmured, bending low to brush her lips with his.

Skye's heart began to race wildly. He seemed to be having that effect on her these days. "Devil!" she whispered back at him. "If you don't stop your provocative behavior I shall certainly cause a scene."

"*Mes enfants*," Gaby said lightly. "I regret to intrude," and they broke apart laughing, "but the Queen has requested my son that you give audience to the Duchesse de Beuvron."

"*Never, maman!*" Adam's brows drew together in a frown.

"Adam, you cannot refuse Queen Catherine. Athenais is one of her favorites. I know that nothing the duchesse says can change how you feel, nor should it, but as the Queen has personally involved herself, you must give Athenais a fair hearing."

"Adam," Skye said softly, "how often have I wanted to refuse Elizabeth Tudor, and both you and Robbie have not let me. What is good for me must also be good for thee. Go and speak with the bitch. I do not mind."

"I suppose we cannot have Catherine de Medici angry at us, especially should we need her refuge from the Tudors. All right, sweetheart, I'll go and let Athenais prattle at me for a while, and I promise, maman, not to wring her deceiving little neck!" He stomped away across the ballroom to where the Duchesse of Beuvron waited by Queen Catherine's side, smiling smugly.

"You are so very good for him, my dear," Gaby said softly. "I have not really seen my son happy in many years. You are the cause of that happiness, and I shall ever be grateful to you for it."

"It is not hard to make Adam happy, Gaby. I love him," she said quietly. "Had he not been so concerned for my welfare, and I not so concerned about everything else, we might have wed long ago. Now I will let nothing stop us."

"Madame Burke?"

The two women turned, and recognizing the Duc of Anjou, they both curtseyed low. "Your Highness."

He acknowledged their obeisance, and then said, "Madame Burke, my mother would like to speak with you privately if you will follow me, please."

"Queen Catherine wishes to see me? Forgive me, M'sieur le Duc, but I do not understand."

"I believe, madame, that my mother wishes you to carry a personal message back to England when you go; a message to your Queen. They have become quite friendly due to the negotiations between our two families regarding the matter of a marriage between my brother Alençon and Elizabeth Tudor."

"Go, my dear," Gaby said. "You are being honored that Queen Catherine would speak to you herself." Gaby reached out to smooth Skye's hair and dress in a motherly fashion. "There, *ma belle*, you are quite ready. *Allez! Allez!*"

The Duc of Anjou smiled pleasantly and led Skye off. "I must say, madame," he said as they departed the ballroom, "that your gown is a triumph this evening. That particular shade of mauve pink highlights the creamy clarity of your skin, and I should have never thought to use silver with pink crystal beads for the panel of your underskirt. Your dressmaker is obviously French, and not English."

"You have found me out, M'sieur le Duc," Skye replied. "I must admit to having had this gown made at Archambault by the château's dressmaker."

"Did she choose the colors?"

"No, I always choose my own colors and fabrics."

"You have an eye, madame. Most women, I have found, are willing to be led in the matter of dress, which too often results in their looking ridiculous."

"Where are we going?" Skye asked Anjou as they seemed to be moving farther and farther away from the ballroom.

"My mother has a private study in a remote part of the palace. It insures that she not be disturbed. There are some who are very much against this proposed marriage between my brother, Alençon, and your Queen. You will therefore understand her desire for privacy, madame."

"Of course," Skye murmured, and followed the duc as he moved

464 · *All the Sweet Tomorrows*

through one corridor after another. She tried to keep track of where they were going, but she eventually gave it up as hopeless. The duc now led her up two flights of narrow stairs at the top of which was a small paneled door.

Flinging the door open, he stepped back, saying, "Please go in, Madame Burke. My mother will be with you in a few moments."

"*Merci*," she said politely as she moved past him, and then her brain exploded in a fiery burst of quick pain and the blackness rushed up to claim her.

Skye's instinct for survival aided her to climb back from the darkness, and she awoke with a small cry to find herself lying upon a curtained and canopied bed. Had she fallen? Had she suffered a fit that caused her head to ache so? Gingerly she attempted to sit up, and in doing so she discovered that her arms were bound behind her at the wrists. For a long moment confusion reigned as she tried to remember where she was. Slowly the memory became clear. The Duc of Anjou had told her that his mother wished to speak privately with her, and she had allowed him to lead her to Queen Catherine's private study. It was as she had been entering the study that she had . . . fainted? Why were her arms tied?

Skye now managed to sit up. The alcove in which the bed was situated had a curtain drawn across its entrance. "M'sieur le Duc," she called. "Are you there, M'sieur d'Anjou?" There was no answer. Only silence greeted her. She still felt too weak to rise from the bed, and Skye looked curiously about the alcove. To her total shock, she saw the bodice and skirt of her ballgown lying neatly upon a chair. Startled, she glanced down at herself and found that she wore only a single silk petticoat and her silk underblouse. The rest of her undergarments, including her stockings and garters, were with her gown. Beyond the drawn curtain Skye heard the door to the Queen's study open, and a man's firm footsteps crossed the floor of the room toward her.

The curtain was whisked aside with a jingling of brass rings, and Henri of Navarre stood there, a huge smile splitting his face as he said in a pleased voice, "Ah, *chérie*, you have come! All evening I have been sick with worry that you would change your mind."

In that instant Skye knew that she had been led to and prepared for a seduction, but by whom, and why? She was only a visitor to France's court. She had no part in its intrigues or its politics. Obviously the King of Navarre was not a party, or at least not a knowledgeable party, to the plot. He was being used, as she was.

"M'sieur de Navarre," she said in what she hoped passed for a calm and reassuring voice, "I do not know what you mean. Can you not see? My hands are bound most securely behind me. I am not here willingly."

Henri came into the alcove and, seating himself next to her on the bed, said, "But *chérie*, you have answered one of my love notes, suggesting that I meet you here in my *belle-mère's* secret study during the ball tonight at half after the hour of one o'clock."

"M'sieur, I am a stranger to the Louvre. How could I have known of this room? Please undo my bonds. I am most uncomfortable. Adam de Marisco and his family will be worrying and wondering where I have gotten to; and even I am not certain how to return to the ballroom. Will you aid me?"

"You did not answer my love note, *chérie*?" Henri of Navarre looked perplexed.

"I did not even receive it," Skye protested.

"Yet you are here," he persisted.

"The Duc of Anjou brought me here. He said that the Queen wished to speak privately with me. That she desired me to carry a private message to my own Queen in England."

Catherine de Medici knew her opponent well. She had predicted that the sight of Skye half dressed would divert Navarre, and in that she had been correct. He barely heard her words, for he was far more interested in her beautiful breasts, which swelled provocatively above the neckline of her silken underblouse, heaving temptingly in her agitation. The beautiful Irishwoman had inflamed his senses from the moment he had laid eyes on her, and now here she was quite conveniently at his mercy, her lovely body every bit if not more delicious than he had imagined it in his salacious daydreams of her.

"Still, madame," he said softly, "you are here, and I am here, and how foolish we would be not to avail ourselves of this golden opportunity." Reaching out, he undid the ribbons that held her underblouse together. The two halves parted easily, and when Henri had pushed them back over her rounded shoulders Skye was effectively bare to her waist. Navarre caught his breath in genuine admiration, for she had the most perfect little breasts he had ever seen.

"M'sieur de Navarre," she said pleadingly, "I beg of you do not do this thing. I am betrothed to a man I love. How can I go to him if I have been despoiled by another?"

Navarre reached out and reverently caressed the silken flesh of one creamy orb. "*Chérie*, I will wager that having seen these exquisite little fruits you possess, a saint could not be stopped in his intent toward you. Besides, you are not a virgin, madame. My knowledge of you is that you have outlived several husbands. You have no maidenhead to protect."

"I have my honor!" Skye cried.

"A woman's honor is easily mended, *chérie*," the King of Navarre said softly. "Give her a diamond necklace or a small château, and all is well again."

"You have acquired a great deal of knowledge in your nineteen years, m'sieur," Skye replied tartly.

He laughed, enjoying her show of spirit. "I had my first woman when I was thirteen, madame. I do not think that a night has passed since then that I have not had a woman to pleasure me." Henri of Navarre stood and began to divest himself of his clothing. "You have appealed to my finer self, madame, and you have scolded me, neither of which has deterred me from my intent. Perhaps, *chérie*, you did not come willingly to this bed, but you are here, and if I released you I should regret it all my days."

"I shall scream," she threatened him.

He laughed. "No one will hear you, *chérie*. Catherine de Medici put her private study in the most remote part of the Louvre for many reasons, not the least of which was that no one hear what transpired in this room should the Queen decide to interrogate a prisoner. If you scream not one soul will come to your aid, and you will give yourself a very sore throat." His forefinger reached out to smooth across her cheekbone. Then his hand slipped behind her head and loosened her hair, pulling the pins out and placing them on the small nightstand until her midnight-black locks fell about her naked shoulders like a satin mantle. "Don't be afraid, *chérie*," he soothed her in a low and now passionate voice. "You will like what we do together. I am an expert lover, I promise you, and I will only give you pleasure, *chérie*. I won't hurt you, I swear it!"

Skye looked into Henri of Navarre's amber-brown eyes, and knew that nothing she might say would divert the young King from his path of seduction. She was helpless before his lust, and the best that she could hope for was that he was telling the truth, and would not hurt her. He would, however, get nothing from her. She would lie quietly while he had his way with her, and she hoped he would be quick. They were leaving court and Paris tomorrow, and she would never see him again. Adam would never have to know. Skye was ashamed of her final thought, but she would not hurt the man she loved with this tale when there was no need.

"Will you untie my hands, monseigneur? My arms are numb and I am most uncomfortable. I promise not to fight you."

Reaching behind her, Henri undid the silken cord by which she had been held fast, and Skye rubbed her arms, which ached painfully as the blood began to flow back into them. In freeing her he had taken the opportunity to remove her blouse entirely, and now, to her surprise, he pushed her back onto the pillows, drew her arms above her head, and retied them quickly.

"I'm sorry, *chérie*," he said, genuine regret in his voice, "but despite your vow, I know that your natural morality will cause you to defend your virtue against me. I have far better uses for my hands at this time than fending off your blows." Standing up again, the King finished undressing.

Skye assessed him from beneath lowered eyelids. He was a tall man, almost as tall as Adam, and he was big-boned. If anything, he erred on the side of thinness, which gave him an awkward appearance, and she noted quickly as he climbed onto the bed with her he had huge feet. His hands, however, were big, slender, and very elegant, she saw as he drew her petticoat off her and caressed her hip.

He was gentle and soft in his leisurely exploration of her body. "How lovely you are," he said quietly. "You have skin like the finest silk, but I suspect I am not the first man to make that comparison. Still, I have never known a woman with such fine skin, *chérie*. It has an almost druglike effect upon me." He bent down and began to kiss her breasts, his lips scorching the tender nipples with their fiery touch. "*Mon Dieu, chérie*, but you are perfection!"

Damn him, Skye thought furiously as a tiny quiver rippled through her. He is an expert lover, and he is not going to devour me like a piece of cheese, but rather go slowly until I can no longer bear it, the bastard! The King's mouth closed fiercely over her left nipple, where it sucked hungrily, forcing a small cry from between her lips. Instantly he lifted his head.

"You like that, *chérie*? You must tell me what pleases you."

"I care not what you do," she replied coldly. "It matters not."

"What a little liar you are, *chérie*. Do you think that you can hold back your passion from me? You're too honest a woman," he laughed softly. "Soon, *ma belle*, soon," he whispered into her ear, "soon you will lie beneath me crying with your pleasure. You are one of those deliciously rare creatures born for loving, and I am a man who was born to love women! We will be incredible together!" Then his mouth left a trail of kisses down her straining throat before moving upward to capture her lips with his own.

He kissed her with an expertise born of much practice, forcing her own lips apart with the pressure of his. His tongue leapt forward to plunder within her mouth, tasting of her greedily, slid beneath her upper lip along her teeth leaving the scent of mint wherever he touched her. It swirled around her mouth to sweep downward, and Skye felt the first stirrings of desire awakening within her. She despised herself for her weakness. With an angry cry she tore her head away from him, hissing furiously, "You bastard! Have me and be done with it!"

He looked down at her, his amber eyes dancing devilishly, and then he laughed. "So, *chérie*, you begin to feel it, too."

"I feel nothing," she snarled back at him.

"I can feel you quivering, *ma belle*. Oh, it is very faint, and very deep down, but I am sensitive to such things."

"I am not sure, monseigneur, which is bigger, your imagination or your opinion of yourself!" she said scathingly.

Again he laughed. "Neither, *chérie*, as you will soon discover, for I possess an altogether larger part, and already it grows hungry for the taste of your wonderful body." Stradling her easily, he bent and again began to taunt her nipples with his tongue, nipping, licking, and sucking teasingly until she thought she would shriek with the pleasure that began to tug at her.

"I hate you! I hate you! I hate you!" Skye muttered the litany as she cursed her treacherous body, which was beginning to respond shamelessly to his ardent suit. Skye knew what she felt was lust, but she nonetheless was angry at herself that she could not prevent the delicious stirrings within herself.

What was worse was that he knew what she both felt and thought. The amber eyes looked mockingly down at her, daring her to deny the truth. With a sob Skye turned her head away from his gaze, hating him even more for his gentle tone as he soothed her distress. "No, *ma belle*, you mustn't hate yourself. Yield to me, *chérie*, and I will give us such pleasure."

"N-never!"

With a sigh of regret the young King moved from her lovely breasts and began caressing her long torso with his hungry lips. Slowly, tortuously, his mouth moved downward, firmly parting her resisting thighs, to stare admiringly at her hidden treasure, to kiss it softly. His curious tongue began to explore her, inhaling her haunting woman's fragrance, slipping along the folds of sensitive flesh, pushing gently into her to rouse her passions until she was no longer able to deny them.

Skye clenched her bound hands into fists, her rounded nails digging cruelly into her palms. She bit her lip so hard that it bled, but she could not prevent the sob that was torn from her reluctant throat. He lifted his head to stare at her, his eyes passion-drugged. Slowly he pulled himself up and atop her. Then with a quick thrust he was inside her warm body, moving smoothly, rhythmically. After what seemed like an eternity to Skye, the King demanded, "Does it please you, *chérie*? Will you admit now that I am the best lover you have ever known?"

"This is not love, monseigneur," Skye whispered. "This is rape! Do you not know the difference?"

"How stubborn you are, *ma belle*," he groaned, "but I will not give up. I have been known to stay hard and potent within a woman an entire night before spilling my seed."

From the city there was the faint sound of the two o'clock tocsin, and Henri of Navarre buried his face into the perfumed tangle of Skye's hair, inhaling the taunting fragrance of her damask rose scent. He had been modest, if anything, when he numbered the women he had possessed in his young life; but this woman! Never had he enjoyed a female as he was now enjoying Madame Burke. Had she been willing instead of reluctant, she would, he suspected, have unmanned him half a dozen times already.

Skye lay beneath him wondering if he would ever cease. She had been gone from the ballroom an hour now, and Adam might begin to seek her. How was she going to explain a longer absence? God only knew what Anjou would say to set Adam on the wrong track. The passion Navarre had managed to arouse in her died away with her concern. She had to force him to release his seed, and Skye knew just how to do it. Closing her eyes so he could not see she was deceiving him, Skye moaned convincingly, and began to move her body in time with his. Using the old trick she had learned in the harem she tightened her internal muscles about his manhood.

Navarre groaned with total pleasure. "Ah, *chérie*," he halfsobbed into her ear, "what delicious torture you abuse me with. Don't stop, I beg of you!"

He was not an easy man to break, she found, and she almost grew too tired to continue when, with a loud shout of triumph, he flooded her with his creamy tribute. Skye cried out herself, but it was with relief. Now perhaps he would be content, and she could go back to Adam before he learned of her shame. For several long moments the King lay on her breasts catching his breath. "*Mon Dieu, chérie*," he finally exclaimed, "you are magnificent, but then I will wager you have been told that, too."

Skye let a deep sigh escape her. "Now, monseigneur, now that you have satisfied yourself, may I please go?"

"*Chérie*, we have only just begun to love. I have no intention of releasing you until the dawn." Still lying atop her, he bent and kissed her softly. "Come, *ma belle*, did I not please you the tiniest bit? You most assuredly pleased me." He smiled winningly at her, and although Skye felt she should hate this arrogant young man, to her surprise she found that she did not.

"Monseigneur, if you hold me until the dawn what will I tell my betrothed husband? I will have to tell him the truth. That the Duc of Anjou kidnaped me from the ballroom under a false pretense, and prepared me for your rape. My husband's mother was with me when Anjou came to me. She will swear to my story. Think of the scandal, M'sieur de Navarre. You are married less than a week to a princess of the blood royal of France, and you are already philandering with another woman, and an unwilling woman at that. Release me now, and I can return to the ballroom with no one the wiser."

"You reason well, *ma belle*, but the fact I am already chasing other women will cause no scandal. It is my nature, and it is expected of me, bridegroom or no. My dear wife has already betrayed me with her lover, de Guise, allowing him into her bed in the afternoons when I have been with my brother-in-law Alençon. Now *that*, madame, is a scandal, but because I am a Huguenot and Margot a good Catholic, it is not considered a sin by the good people of France. Margot considers it her royal duty to cuckold me. Therefore my making love to you, madame, will be no scandal."

"M'sieur, be reasonable! Where is your pride? Do you truly find deep satisfaction and pleasure for your ego in forcing a bound woman who does not want you? For shame, M'sieur de Navarre!"

"You are really most adorable, *chérie*, when you are angry," he teased her, but before Skye could spit out her angry reply, the door to the study burst open, and the Prince of Condé rushed in frantically calling to his cousin.

"Henri! Thank God you are safe! Get up! Get dressed! We are about to be murdered, and we must escape!"

Navarre looked lazily at his cousin as he rolled off Skye. "Henri," he said, "your timing is deplorable as usual. What are you babbling about?"

"Paris is in civil disorder, cousin!" Condé cried. "Our people are being massacred in their beds by the members of the Catholic League led by de Guise! Already a mob looking for you and for me has tried to storm the Louvre. The King's soldiers held them back, but God only knows how long they can! I have already received word that Coligny is dead. Get up, Henri!"

But Navarre was already up, and pulling on his clothes. His smiling, boyish face of moments before had grown grim and old with his cousin's words. "I believe that we are safe, Henri," he told Condé. "I don't know *how* involved Madame le Serpent is, but she is involved." He turned to Skye. "Madame, I regret I ignored your words of caution earlier. My weakness has always been that my cock ruled my head; still, I regret nothing of our interlude but that it was not longer. Follow the stairs from this room down three flights. The door at the bottom opens into the gardens, and you will easily find your way back to the ballroom from there." Bending, he kissed her quickly, the regret clear in his eyes. "*Adieu, chérie!*" He turned to go.

"Monseigneur!" she cried after him.

Henri of Navarre turned. "Madame?"

"Monseigneur, you have not unbound my hands." The King leaned over and quickly undid the silken knots.

"Your pardon, *ma belle*," he said softly.

"God go with you, Navarre," she answered him quietly.

Suddenly he grinned rakishly at her, saying as he ran from the room, "I knew I had touched your heart, *chérie!*" Then both he and Condé were gone.

Skye had to laugh. That damned vain boy was within a hair's breadth of losing his life, and all he cared about was that he had been successful in his lovemaking. Suddenly she heard the sounds of battle and terrible cries of agony outside. Skye rose from the tumbled bed and dressed hurriedly, her fingers fumbling with the laces and ties of her gown. She had to find Adam, and she knew that he would be frantically searching for her. It was not easy getting into court gear without Mignon to help her, but Skye managed to attain some semblance of order with her clothes and her hair. Without a backward glance at the room, she fled down the staircase to the gardens.

Once outside, she could hear the frantic screams of the poor unfortunates being murdered in the various districts of the city. Stopping a moment to get her bearings, Skye saw the lighted windows of the ballroom across the garden from her, and she moved swiftly to gain its safety. The cacophony within the ballroom was tremendous as the court chattered frantically to dispel their nervous tension. Notably quiet were the few Huguenot noble families who felt like early Christians in the arena as they huddled in small groups about the room trying to look inconspicuous. On the raised royal dais Catherine de Medici sat quietly with her son, his wife, and her daughter, Margot. Navarre, Condé, and Condé's wife. Catherine's sharp eye noted Skye's entry into the room, and for a minute the two women's eyes met and Skye knew in that instant that the Queen Mother had planned everything, including her own seduction by Navarre. Shaking her head, Skye looked away, missing the look of triumph that flickered briefly across de Medici's fat face.

"Skye! My God, sweetheart, I have been frantic! Where have you been?" Adam, catching her shoulders, whirled her about and looked down into her face.

Suddenly seeing him, Skye realized the danger she had been in, and unable to control herself, she burst into tears. "Oh Adam! I was so frightened!"

"There, lamb," he murmured at her. "Come now, sweetheart, it's all right. Come with me. Maman was worried, too." His loving arm about her he walked her across the room to where Gaby and the entire de Saville family awaited.

"*Ma fille*, what is wrong?" Gaby was instantly anxious. "You were gone so long. I had begun to grow worried, especially considering the atrocities going on in the city now."

"Not here, Gaby," Skye pleaded. "Later, I will explain later."

"Now that we have Skye safe," the comte said, "we must get to the house, my sons. Are you ready?"

The men in the party nodded, and Adam, seating Skye next to his mother, explained, "Antoine is worried that because the house we are renting is owned by a Huguenot the mob is apt to attack it. He wants to go back to the Marais district and get the children and the servants lest they be hurt. We should not be long."

She nodded. "I'll be all right, my darling. Go with them. I'll be here with your maman."

The Comte de Cher, his sons, sons-in-law, and stepson moved quickly to the royal dais, where Antoine spoke urgently to Queen Catherine for a few moments. Finally the Queen nodded, and the party of men hurried from the ballroom. When they had gone Gaby turned to Skye.

She sighed. "It was a trick to keep Navarre occupied and safe from the mob, Gaby. The Duc d'Anjou took me to his mother's private closet, stunned me with a blow, disrobed me, and left me trussed up like a Christmas goose. Navarre thought I was meeting him for a love tryst."

"But when he found you had been duped, *ma fille*?"

"Alas, Gaby, chivalry did not prevail in Navarre's case. He raped me, and you mustn't tell Adam. Adam will lose his temper and kill him!"

"I would certainly hope so, *ma fille*," Gaby replied indignantly.

A small giggle escaped Skye. The whole situation was total madness. "No, Gaby. Adam cannot kill a prince of the blood, an heir to France's throne. He cannot even complain to the Queen, who is responsible for the whole situation. If Elizabeth Tudor refuses to recognize our marriage then we cannot go home to England, and France is our refuge. If we displease France, then where may we go, Gaby? Please promise me you will not tell Adam."

Gaby nodded. Skye was as practical as she herself was, and Adam's mother approved. There was no necessity to tell Adam. Skye was correct in that he would be monumentally angry, and of course would want his honor avenged. The disadvantages far outweighed the advantages. "You are right, *ma fille*," Gaby said, "but before we drop the matter there is one thing I must know. Is *he* as good a lover as they say?" Her lovely eyes sparkled with curiosity.

"He is young yet," Skye replied drily, "but his skill is growing, and the potential is there."

Gaby laughed softly, completely understanding Skye's point. "I imagine the King of Navarre would be most disappointed in your rather candid evaluation of him," she said low.

"Madame Burke."

Both Gaby and Skye started, and then rose quickly to their feet to curtsey to Catherine de Medici. The Queen Mother smiled warmly at Gaby, and then turned her eyes to Skye.

"I will not forget the favor you have done me this night, madame," she said. "Whatever may be said of me I do not forget those who give me their aid. You have a friend in Catherine de Medici."

"Why me?" Skye asked, quietly wondering why she felt no anger.

"Because, madame, you were his passion for the moment, and I needed you, for only you could keep him occupied long enough and safe from de Guise and his mob. You did not seek Navarre's attention, which in itself was a stronger attraction. My *beau-frère* is not used to being disdained and spurned by a beautiful woman. You are a member of the Tudor court, madame, and my information on you says that you are an intelligent woman. If you did not understand my position you would now be screaming and shrieking charges for all this court to hear."

"I would not hurt my betrothed, Majesty, with the dishonor that has been visited upon us both tonight; but know one thing, I do not like being used."

"Nonetheless," came the disconcerting reply, "it is the way of the powerful to use, and you well know it. When is your wedding?"

"At Michaelmas at Archambault."

Catherine de Medici turned to Gaby. "I shall come," she said calmly. "I will be staying at Ussé that week, but I shall stop a night at Archambault. I understand from Comte Antoine that you will be leaving Paris tonight, so I shall bid you *adieu* until Michaelmas." With a nod at Gaby the Queen Mother turned away and walked back to the royal dais.

"Mon Dieu!" Gaby gasped. "We have never entertained royalty at Archambault! I cannot believe it! Skye, *ma fille*, do you realize the honor being done us? The Queen is coming to your wedding!"

Skye had to laugh. Royalty! She would never really understand them. Royalty were the damnedest people in the world. Well, perhaps Catherine de Medici's appearance at their wedding would sit well with Elizabeth Tudor, and she would give her blessing to them despite the fact that they were marrying without her royal permission. "When I was married to Adam's cousin, Geoffrey Southwood, I was married in Elizabeth Tudor's presence at her palace at Greenwich," she told Gaby. "In fact Geoffrey and I spent our wedding night there."

Gaby was impressed. "Adam did not tell me that," she said. "It was a happy marriage with Southwood, was it not?"

"Very happy!"

"So the Queen's presence brought you luck. Now you will be married again in a queen's presence, and that will bring you luck once more, *chérie*."

"What a good thought, Gaby!" Skye leaned over and hugged the older woman. "Do you know," she said, "I have never had a mother-in-law, as my previous husbands' mamas were all dead. I am so glad you are going to be my *belle-mère*, Gaby!"

Gaby de Saville felt the tears pricking at her eyelids. She would have made the effort to love any wife of Adam's; but with Skye it was so easy. Not only that, they were friends, and Gaby considered that even better. "I shall light a hundred candles to the Blessed Mother that my son has you," she said feelingly.

"And I shall light a hundred more to her that I have him," Skye replied. "Oh, Gaby! This time I know that everything is going to be all right!"

Chapter 15

 he Comte de Cher and his
party reached the Marais district just in time. An angry mob was
preparing to storm the house that they had rented for their Paris
stay. All the mob knew was that the house was owned by a
Huguenot family. The comte and his sons clattered into the overrun courtyard of the house, while around them the mob bran-
dished pikes and homemade weapons, shouting, "Kill the heretics!"

"Stop!" Antoine de Saville shouted, but he could not make himself heard over the uproar.

Adam saw one of the Duc de Guise's men leading the crowd,
and riding over to him, he said, "M'sieur, though this house is
owned by a Huguenot, he is not in Paris. The house is being
rented by a good Catholic nobleman, the Comte de Cher. It is his
family and servants inside, not Huguenots."

"The house is to be burned," the duc's man replied. "Orders of
M'sieur de Guise."

"I understand," Adam replied, realizing that the duc, whose own
mansion was next door, was taking this opportunity to confiscate
the property for his own. "Nonetheless you will allow my stepfather to remove his people and his goods. The Comte de Cher is
in both the King's and Queen Catherine's favor."

The duc's man nodded. "We'll hold the mob, but tell your stepfather to hurry. The canaille grow madder with their blood lust
with each minute that passes by."

Adam turned his horse back to Antoine and, reaching him, said,
"We just have time to get our things, the children, and the servants,
beau-père. They're going to burn the house."

"Alexandre! Yves!" the comte shouted. "Go to the stables and have every coach in there made ready, even those we don't own! Louis, Henri, Robert! You will remain mounted before the front door. Adam, come inside with me!"

It did not take long to marshall the de Saville children, servants, and all their personal property. The servants had spent their evening packing for their master's departure the following day, and it was merely a matter of loading up the coaches in the rear of the house while the howling mob was held at bay out front. Within minutes the house was vacated, and Adam and the comte departed through the main door of the mansion, mounted their horses, and, thanking the duc's man, rode off. Behind them the Paris mob, freed of restraint, burst into their former abode, looting and destroying before putting the building to the torch.

When they reached the palace their women were eagerly waiting and anxious to leave Paris behind. In the confusion Skye found herself alone in a small carriage with Adam. She snuggled into his arms and, pressing her cheek against his hard shoulder, fell asleep. The whole evening had been a traumatic experience and, as always following a crisis, Skye was exhausted. When she awoke they were miles from the capital, but as they drove along there was evidence here and there of the same sort of violence and destruction and mayhem that they had left behind in Paris. In several places along their route gallows had been set up and both men and women as well as children dangled from them, swaying in the clear summer morning.

Skye wept at the sight. "I cannot believe that God condones such cruelty," she said sadly.

"The Huguenots are no better," he answered her. "Religious fanatics hear nothing but their own dogma. What matter how one finds God as long as we find him. Do not look, sweetheart. There is nothing you can do for those poor souls now."

They didn't bother to stop but for brief meals and to change the horses. Antoine de Saville was anxious to get back to Archambault. There was going to be another civil war, and in times of trouble it was best to be in one's own château. The trip to Paris had taken them five days, but the return only took three. They arrived at Archambault after dark, tired and emotionally exhausted by what they had seen and been involved in over the last two weeks. The Huguenots in the district around Archambault had for the most part been untouched, although their pastor had fled to La Rochelle with some of his flock. The majority waited, knowing that the comte would protect them, for they were his best vintagers, barrel-makers, and cultivators. It was fortunate that the village priest was a kindly old man with a good heart who abjured the Catholics not to imitate the excesses of Paris and the other cities that had followed its example.

Because they were far from Paris, the shock of the St. Bartholomew's Day massacre was not strongly felt among those who made Archambault their home. Life swiftly returned to normal with the return of the de Saville family, and the preparations began for the marriage of Adam de Marisco and Skye O'Malley. Originally it had been planned that the celebration be a small, intimate family one; but now with the Queen's promise to attend that was all changed. It would be a grand fête.

As August dissolved into September Skye counted the days eagerly until her marriage, and until her children were with her once again. The wedding was set for the twenty-ninth of September, the feast day of St. Michael, and Skye's children arrived on the twentieth, tumbling excitedly from the coach that had brought them from Nantes, where Skye's ship had docked. They were all there, even her eldest son, Ewan, who had left his holding in Ireland to be with his mother on her wedding day.

"Don't worry, Mother," he told her with a grin. "My uncles, Shamus and Conn O'Malley, are holding Ballyhennessey for me."

"Where is your wife?" she demanded.

"Gwyn and I decided to wait until you could be with us before getting married. She's still very young, Mother. Are you anxious to be a grandparent?" he teased.

"Are you so sure you can be a father, Ewan?" she countered.

He chuckled, and then blushed as his brother, Murrough, said, "He's spawned two bastards already, Mother!"

"*Ewan!*" Skye was mortified, but Adam and the de Saville men laughed heartily with obvious approval of Ewan's accomplishments.

"*Sacre bleu*," the comte said, wiping his eyes, "these are fine new grandsons you give me, Skye!" He peered at Ewan through kindly, nearsighted eyes. "So you like the ladies, eh lad? I, of course, am too old for such games, but my sons can, I am sure, tell you the nicest girls on the estate."

"*Beau-père*," Skye scolded, "you must not encourage him in this behavior."

"Why not, *chérie?* He is a man full grown! Be proud of him!"

Skye looked helplessly to Gaby, who raised her eyes heavenward in sympathy, but said nothing. Nonetheless the de Savilles welcomed all of Skye's children as if they were blood kin; and the children who had never had any real grandparents warmed to the French couple. The comte and comtesse loved children, and indeed their two sons and their daughter lived at Archambault along with their spouses and children. Isabeau and Clarice and their families were within just a few miles, and consequently the château was always filled with family. For Skye's children, who had had so little family life, the great change was wonderful. Ewan and Murrough quickly made friends with Henri and Jean St. Justine, who were close to them in age; and together the four young men spent their days riding and hunting and, Skye suspected from the occasional self-satisfied smirk on her sons' faces, wenching as well. Catherine-Henriette St. Justine was just a year younger than Willow, and the fact that the eleven-year-old had attended a ball at the Louvre made her an object of much admiration to Willow, who had still not been allowed up to the Tudor court. Robin's new friend was Charles Sancerre, and little Deirdre Burke, who was going to be five in January, was placed in the château nursery with five-year-old Antoinette de Saville. There was even a little boy his age for Padraic to play with, Michel Sancerre.

Skye marveled over her children. The older ones were, of course, happy to see their mother again, but the two Burke babies did not remember her and were cautious in their approach. Deirdre, however, remembered Adam, who had been with her a great deal of the time that Skye was away. She was quite determined that he was her "Papa," and Padraic Burke, who followed his older sister's lead in everything, therefore called him papa, too.

"Let them," Adam said quietly when she attempted to correct them. "In time they will understand about Niall, but for now they need a father."

To Skye's great surprise, her four older children took to calling Adam "Father" also. Robin had never called anyone but Geoffrey father before, and her O'Flaherty sons, who could not remember

Dom, had in their Irish pride not been able to call either Geoffrey or Niall by that title. Willow had called Niall "Papa," but even she succumbed to Adam de Marisco's charm.

"What magic is this you weave about my children?" she teased him.

"No magic, sweetheart, it is simply that we need each other."

"Oh, Adam!" she said feelingly. "I am so glad that you do!" and she kissed him with love upon his mouth.

Then, three days before the wedding, as the dressmaker worked on the final fitting of Skye's gown, the kneeling woman remarked, her mouth full of pins, "Madame, you have fattened again! You must be very happy indeed, for most brides lose weight before the wedding. I shall have to alter the waist again."

Skye stood very quietly as the woman did her job, but Gaby had seen how she had paled at the dressmaker's words. When the woman had made her adjustments and taken the gown away, Mignon helped her mistress into a comfortable chamber robe and departed on an errand. Gaby de Saville looked at Skye, and asked, "What is it, *ma fille*? Why are you so worried?"

Skye looked up at the lovely woman who was to be her mother-in-law, and said brokenly, "I am pregnant, Gaby. There is no mistake. I am pregnant. Dear God, what am I to do?!"

For a moment a stricken look crossed the Comtesse de Cher's face, and her hand moved instinctively to her mouth to stifle her cry of distress. Then seeing Skye's anguish, Gaby de Saville pulled herself together, and spoke firmly. "It is, of course, Navarre's child. Curse him! Why could he not leave you alone?"

"Once, Gaby," Skye said, her voice shaking. "He only took me once. How could this have happened!"

"Once, *ma fille*, is often quite enough," the comtesse remarked.

"How can I marry Adam now, Gaby? How can I marry the man I love while carrying another man's bastard? Dear Heaven, has not Adam suffered enough? I cannot make him accept someone else's child as his own. Oh, Gaby! What am I to do?!"

"You have no choice, *ma fille*. Adam must be told."

"*No!*"

"Yes! Listen to me, Skye. I know my son, and I believe that I know you, despite our short acquaintance. You and Adam love one another. You have traveled a rocky road to be together, and you, Skye, have made my son happier than I have ever seen him in his life. He was half a man, a shadow figure. It is you who have made him whole, and if you leave him I dread to think what he will do.

"We will tell Adam the truth of this matter. Surely you do not think that he will desert you, or blame you. If I know Adam his first thought will be of you, and what you have suffered at Navarre's hand. His second will be of revenge, and together we must keep him from that folly. I know an old witch woman in the forest who with potions can help you rid yourself of this unwanted child; or if you cannot do that, have the babe and we will find a peasant woman to raise it."

"I cannot destroy an unborn child, Gaby. It is not in my nature to do so. I know that Adam will forgive me, but it seems so unfair to ask him. If he decides to repudiate me I will understand," she said, and a large tear rolled down her cheek.

"Fetch M'sieur Adam," Gaby commanded Mignon as she re-entered the room.

The tiring woman turned around and hurried out while the two women sat in silence awaiting Adam de Marisco. Gaby noticed how terribly overwrought Skye was, twisting and shredding her cambric and lace handkerchief as they waited. "It is going to be all right, *ma fille*," she said. "I promise you that everything is going to be all right."

Entering the bedchamber, Adam heard his mother's words. He rushed to Skye's side and knelt, looking up into her face. "What is it, little girl?" he begged her. "What is the matter?"

Skye, however, could only look mutely at him as the tears began to trickle down her face. Before her son could go mad with worry Gaby de Saville quickly explained Skye's predicament to Adam.

"Dammit!" the lord of Lundy exploded at his mother. "You let her bear this cross all alone, and after what she has been through in Morocco? I thought you had better sense, maman!"

"Don't speak to your mother that way, Adam de Marisco!" Skye sobbed. "She has been wonderful to me!"

"I'll kill him!" Adam roared.

"Which is precisely why I did not share my knowledge with you, you great fool!" Gaby snapped. "A lot of good you would do us all, Skye included, killing the heir to France. Do you think that there is a place in this world where you might hide if you committed such a heinous crime? It is appalling that Skye is *enceinte*, but the chances of that happening were so slim that neither she nor

I even considered it after the attack on her. It is too late now to worry over it."

"I will understand if you do not wish to wed with me, Adam," Skye whispered.

"Woman," he shouted, "what damned-fool nonsense is that?! Of course I want to marry you! I have wanted to marry you for six long years! I've lain awake more nights than I care to remember aching for you, and cursing myself for my stupidity in letting you escape me! I could kill Henri of Navarre for raping you, but that child you are carrying is half yours, and I will raise it up as my own! We will have no foolishness about farming it out to some stupid peasant, Skye. Now stop your damned weeping, little girl, and come here and kiss me!" He stood up, pulling her with him, and his mouth tenderly took hers.

"Oh, Adam," she said against the warm pressure of his mouth, "I do love you so very much, but everyone in your family will know that the baby isn't yours. I cannot shame you like that."

"*Non, non!*" Gaby injected. "When Athenais broke her betrothal with Adam and spread her vicious lies, my de Saville children were too young to either understand or remember. Only Adam's sisters, his full sisters, know the truth, along with Antoine. I will tell them of your plight, *ma fille*, and they will understand and keep silent. They love you as much as I do for the happiness you have brought their brother."

"You see," he murmured down at her. "You cannot escape me this time, little girl. You are meant to be my wife."

Great happiness flooded her being, and she suddenly smiled up at him with a smile of pure radiance. "I had best watch my diet for the next few days," she said, "lest I grow out of my gown again."

The gown, however, was pure perfection when Skye wore it on her wedding day. The bride was a vision of loveliness in apple-green silk, the low bodice embroidered with gold thread and tiny pearls that matched the panel of her slightly darker velvet under-skirt. The leg-of-mutton sleeves were held by many tiny gold ribbons, the wristbands turned back to form a cuff with a gold lace ruff just above her slender hands. The bodice had a long wasp waist that ended in a pronounced downward peak. The bell-shaped skirt of the overgown separated in front to reveal the elegant skirt of the undergown; the shape of the entire dress being dictated by a cartwheel verdingale with a padded hip bolster. Beneath this all were silken undergarments, outrageous pale-green silk stockings embroidered with grape vines, and delicate silk slippers sewn with pearls.

Mignon had done her hair with pale-gold silk roses, and Skye wore with them tiny gold chains studded with small diamonds. About her neck she had chosen to wear creamy white pearls. With unusual foresight Willow had carried her mother's jewel cases from England, and Skye was able to put away the pieces that Nicolas had given her, knowing that Adam would be a lot happier if he saw she did not wear the duc's gift on their wedding day. The groom himself was attired in a magnificent bronze-colored velvet suit decorated with gold embroidery and creamy lace.

Because the ceremony had grown from a simple family celebration into a neighborhood fête by virtue of Catherine de Medici's appearance, it could not be held in the château's chapel. Instead, the village church was swept and cleaned and then decorated with roses and all manner of late flowers. The Queen had arrived the night before, and was housed in a suite of apartments that Gaby was sure would not be fine enough; but Catherine assured the comtesse otherwise.

The wedding party walked from the château upon its little hill above the Cher River to the church of Archambault down in the village. All the villagers had dressed in their finest, and even decorated their cottages in honor of the couple. Not knowing Adam's history, they nodded approvingly at the bride's six children, murmuring that the comte and comtesse were sure to have more grandchildren before it was all over.

As she knelt by Adam's side during their nuptial mass, Skye had the strangest feeling that behind her stood unseen guests—the ghosts of her former husbands—and in her mind's eye they were all smiling with their approval. Dom, of course, was not there, but she could see Khalid el Bey, and Geoffrey Southwood, the angel Earl of Lynmouth, and Niall Burke, and—yes!—even Fabron de Beaumont, that poor tortured soul whose wife she had been but briefly. Then as Adam placed the heavy gold ring on her finger, they were gone, and if Skye felt a moment of sadness for what had been, her heart was too quickly refilled with gladness for what was to be.

As they exited the church to the shouts of congratulations from the assembled guests and the peasants, she laughed with joy as, to the delight of all, Adam de Marisco swept his beautiful wife into a passionate embrace and kissed her soundly. Then, leading the procession, they returned to the château for the marriage feast. It was a beautiful day with a soft, warm wind and a cloudless blue sky. Never could Skye remember such a lovely wedding, and in her heart she believed that it portended a happy future for herself and for Adam.

"Are you as happy as I am, Lady de Marisco?" he asked her, and the smile she flashed him gave him his answer.

On the broad green lawns of the château tables had been placed, the bridal table upon a raised dais where all might see the happy couple, Catherine de Medici, and the Princesse Margot, who had arrived unannounced from Chenonceaux early that morning. Seeing Marguérite de Valois Skye's heart had leapt into her mouth for fear that Navarre had accompanied his wife; but she relaxed as the princesse scathingly and loudly told her mother, "Monseigneur de Navarre is occupied elsewhere." Then she had proceeded to attach herself to the Duc de Guise, who was also mysteriously there without his spouse.

The tables were quickly filled by the guests, neighboring nobility from the nearby châteaux. The lower tables were for the people of Archambault village, and its twin village of Saville, from which the family had taken its name. The cellars of the château had yielded up oak casks filled with rich and heady red wine put down three years before and saved for a special occasion. The silver goblets were filled with this brew while below the salt the villagers were delighted with earthenware cups of Archambault's *vin ordinaire*.

Comte Antoine rose and, lifting his goblet, said, "Adam de Marisco does not bear my name, nor will he inherit any part of my lands; but this son of my beloved wife is as dear to me as my own two boys. I rejoice with him this day! I rejoice that he has found himself a wife—but not simply a wife; rather a woman who has captured his heart. Long life to both you and your beautiful Skye, my son!"

"*Vive! Vive!*" shouted the guests, all raising their goblets enthusiastically.

The comte's toast was followed by many others, and Skye was forced to sit smiling as most of those good wishes called for the newlywed couple to have many children. At one point Adam reached over to take her hand in his, and squeezed it reassuringly. She turned her face to his for a moment, and the warm look in his eyes washed over her, leaving her feeling more loved than she had ever felt in her entire life.

The feast accompanying the toasts was bountiful. As a first course, there were several varieties of pâté and fish freshly caught in the Cher, along with a barrel of oysters brought from the nearby coast and packed in ice. There was goose, and small game birds, duck and capon, as well as beef and lamb. The estate huntsmen had been most active the last few days and on several open fires turned a wild boar, two red stags, and two roe deer. There were cheeses, and hardcooked eggs, and newly baked breads with tubs of butter, some bowls of cress and lettuce, all to be washed down with good Archambault wine. A last course consisted of newly picked apples and pears and grapes from the orchards and vineyards. A beautiful gâteau of several layers topped by a marzipan bride and groom, the sides of the top layer having alternating marzipan shields being the de Marisco and the O'Malley coats of arms, was the *pièce de résistance* of the feast.

Everyone ate until stuffed, and then the villagers danced for the entertainment of the nobility. To the peasants' delight, Skye and Adam joined the dancers at one point, encouraging the others at the high board to do so, too. Twilight fell, and then night. Torches were lit to brighten the scene and a fat full moon rose to gild the sky. No one wanted to go home, for it was a wonderful party. Finally it seemed that the only way they could get their guests to leave was for the bride and groom to go to bed. Skye was taken off with much ceremony by her mother-in-law and sisters-in-law, and Dame Cecily, who had come with the children.

It was at that moment that Skye missed her faithful Daisy most, but Daisy was back in England expecting a second child. She felt almost shy disrobing before all the other women, but neither Gaby nor her daughters seemed to notice. Dame Cecily, however, gave her an encouraging pat, saying, "I feel certain, dear Skye, that this marriage between you and Adam is one made in Heaven. I did not like it that Queen Elizabeth sent you so far from us the last time."

"The Queen knows nothing of this marriage yet, dear Dame Cecily," Skye replied. "Robbie must leave next week for court to bring her word of our nuptials."

"You'd best send some rich gift along with my brother, not that that's likely to placate the Queen." Here she lowered her voice, although of the de Saville women only Gaby could either speak or understand English. "'Tis said these marriage negotiations of hers make her fretful and irritable. She does not like to see happiness in others these days."

Before Skye might answer her old friend, there were cries of delight from the de Saville women as Mignon brought in and displayed Skye's nightgown for all to see; of pale pink silk, its low-scooped neckline was part of the molded bodice falling into a simple skirt that swirled about her ankles. The sleeves were long and flowing and deceptively modest. Skye's petticoats and blouse were quickly taken away and the gown dropped over her head. It slid down her body with a soft hiss of silk.

Gaby and Dame Cecily gasped at the open sensuousness of the gown, but Adam's sister Clarice spoke for them all, saying, *"Mon Dieu, ma soeur* Skye! Why have we bothered to clothe you? The gown fits you like a skin, and if I know my brother you will not wear it long. Try to see that he does not tear at it in his eagerness."

"The men are coming," Musette said from the door.

"Quickly then," Gaby cried as her wits returned, "into bed, *ma fille!* I do not believe that Adam would appreciate others seeing what is for him alone."

Skye climbed into the big bed, and with swift fingers drew the pins and silk flowers from her hair and handed them to Dame Cecily. Mignon was instantly there to brush the hair free of tangles. The door to the bedchamber burst open and Adam was pushed into the room by his half-brothers and the other male guests. He wore a silk nightshirt.

"He's as ready for you as he'll ever be, Madame de Marisco," Alexandre de Saville laughed.

"If I had something that lovely waiting for me," Yves chuckled, "I would not have been so long in getting to bed!"

"Out!" the lord of Lundy roared. "Get out, all of you!"

Gaby stopped to kiss her son, saying as she did so, "You are both so lucky, *mes enfants.*"

The bedchamber emptied slowly as the guests straggled out through the salon back into the hall of the château. When he was sure that the last of them was gone, Adam firmly closed the door to their bedchamber, walked back over to the bed, and sat down upon it.

For what seemed a long moment they sat in silence, and then

Skye said softly, "My God, it is really true! We are married, Adam!"

He grinned almost boyishly at her, and her heart contracted painfully. "I love you, Skye de Marisco," he said quietly. "I love you very much."

"You don't have to sleep with me if you don't want to," she said suddenly. "I will understand."

"Where else would I sleep, Skye?"

"You know what I mean, Adam!"

"Will it hurt the babe?"

"No."

"For how long, Skye? You have to tell me these things, for I've never been a father before."

You're not a father now! she wanted to cry at him in her pain. I can never give you, the man I adore, a child. This is a bastard I carry, and we both know it! Instead, she said, "It varies with each child, Adam. When I get too big and the baby is low, we dare not, but for now there is no harm."

"Good," he said, standing up and pulling off the silk garment that they had dressed him in. "For you see, Skye, I intend exercising my marital rights to the fullest."

Skye swung her own legs from beneath the coverlet and stood up also. Then she turned and, smiling at him, asked, "Do you like the gown, *mon mari?*"

His eyes raked slowly down her provocative length, and then he said pleasantly, "If you intend to keep that garment whole, madame, you had best remove it quickly before I rip it off you."

Slowly Skye slipped the gown from her shoulders, letting it fall to her waist. She hesitated a minute, allowing him a long look at her beautiful breasts before pushing the cloth over her hips and letting it slide to the floor. His mouth twitched appreciatively at her pretty performance as she stepped lightly from the puddle of silk at her feet. Then as boldly as he, she let her eyes sweep his long length.

"You like what you see, madame, I trust," he said, amused.

"I always have, *mon mari*," she returned. "Do you like what you see?"

"I always have," he chuckled. "Now get into bed, dammit, little girl. I need very much to feel your softness against me!"

Slipping back into the bed, she turned toward him to find that his arms were already reaching out to draw her to him. Skye wrapped her arms about her husband's neck, and sighed with delight. "Dearest Adam," she whispered to him, "I do love you! You are so wonderfully good to me." Then she boldly sought his mouth, and he groaned at the hungry touch of her lips, feeling the sparks ignite instantly between them as the kiss deepened and grew until they both drew away breathless.

Pressing her back into the pillows, he tangled his fingers in the night cloud of her hair and kissed her again until her lips ached with the sweetness with which he was filling her. Her breasts began to grow taut with her rising desire, her nipples thrusting up sharply and tingling with their longing. He felt the rounded push of her against his furred chest, and reaching down with one hand, he caressed the warm little globe of flesh, cupping it in his big hand, rubbing against the nipple with his thumb. Skye shuddered with the pleasure his touch gave her.

Adam laughed, a low and intimate sound of equal pleasure. "You are the most sensual creature I have ever known, *ma femme*. It pleases me that marriage has not turned you into a little prude." His shaggy dark head dropped so he might take the nipple in his mouth. Slowly he sucked on the tidbit of tender flesh while her fingers kneaded at his neck with increasing urgency. Leisurely he played with both of her beautiful breasts, kissing and touching and loving them with growing ardor. Skye could feel the hot, hard length of him against her leg, and she shuddered again with delighted thoughts of what was to come.

He made love to her that night as if he had never before known her. Slowly he explored her silken flesh as if he had never touched it. "*Ma femme*, my wife," he called her. "My beautiful bride. Sweet, sweet Skye!" His kisses burned across her body, leaving her shaken and yet yearning for more. Slipping his hand between her thighs, he stroked the softness of her sensitive skin until her legs fell open beneath his tender assault. Toying with her nether lips, he teased her with a single finger that rubbed at the very heart of her femininity until she was squirming and panting beneath his touch.

"Oh, my darling," she begged him, "let me touch you also!"

"Not yet, sweetheart, but soon," he promised, and then he turned her over onto her stomach. Slowly his big, warm hands smoothed over her legs and her back and her buttocks and her shoulders, fanning the flames of her burgeoning desire until she moaned low with her hunger. She felt his great weight on her as he placed his body atop hers, pressing her deep into the mattress. His throbbing maleness rubbed suggestively against the halves of her bottom, igniting her passion even further. She could scarcely breathe, but she cared not if only he would possess her.

"Adam! Adam! Please," she pleaded with him. "I am so hot for you tonight, *mon mari!*"

He rolled off her, returning her to her back as he did so, and swung himself around so that his dark head was pressed against her white thigh. Caressing her in leisurely fashion, he said softly, "Now, little girl, now is the time to touch me."

Skye's slender hand reached out to return her husband's gentle caresses, and the feel of him beneath her fingers roused her further. After a while she pushed herself into a half-sitting position, and turning, he cuddled against her breasts, kissing them lightly while she fondled the hard length of him. She suddenly realized the truth of what he had been telling her all these years. There was no need to rush; the passion that built slowly between them was far more exciting than any she had ever experienced. Finally, when she thought it could be no more wonderful than it was now, Adam pulled Skye beneath him, gently mounted her, and thrust into her warmth. She cried softly with the pleasure his entry gave her, molding him harder against her with the flat of her palms against his smooth back.

"It's like mulled wine," he groaned against her mouth. "Being inside of you tonight is like being in hot mulled wine," and for a moment he couldn't stir so delicious was the sensation; but then he began to move sensuously on her.

She barely heard him, for his tender possession of her had pushed her into a world of such uninhibited ecstasy that Skye was only aware of wave after wave of rapturous passion sweeping over her and surrounding her. It left her at last feeling totally satisfied and content. "Oh, Adam," she murmured, "how can it be so good between us?"

And he laughed softly, saying, "How can it not be, sweetheart, when we love each other so?"

Love. It was the unbreakable bond between them. A bond forged by the fires of experience, of pain and of passion. At Archambault love surrounded them, for the de Saville family was a close one whose members cared for and protected each other. As Adam's wife, she was now one of them. The comte had insisted that they remain with the family until after the baby was born. Antoine de Saville was a quiet man, but he was also a very wise one. He knew that the closer the bond between Skye and his family the easier this hard time would be upon her. He understood that her predicament, despite Adam's love and understanding, was a traumatic and harsh one. Yet he was a man who loved children, and he believed that not only the mother, but the coming infant must be protected in this situation.

Both Murrough and, surprisingly, Ewan, went happily off to the university in Paris. Ewan had decided that since he was here he would take advantage of a French education, as his father had. He was not the scholar that Murrough was, but he would do well enough, and given the situation in Ireland, it could not hurt him to have French connections.

Willow fretted about allowing her dearest Dame Cecily to return to Wren Court without her, but Robert Small's sister was adamant on the subject. "You've not seen yer mother in almost two years, miss, and she needs you now. Besides, with that silly Daisy having another babe by the New Year I'll have my hands full there. Daisy's ma has been too ill to help, and well you know it, Willow."

Secretly and guiltily, Willow was relieved. She loved Dame Cecily with all her heart, but she loved her mother more, and she had missed Skye so very much. This wonderful, voluble, loving new French family was very much to her liking. With a light heart she waved her surrogate grandmother off on the road to Nantes, where she would be embarking upon an O'Malley ship for Bideford. Then Willow attached herself to her recently acquired Grandmère Gaby, and began learning all the secrets of a good chatelaine. When she was not tagging after the comtesse she was with her new cousins, Matilde Rochouart, and Marie-Gabrielle and Catherine-Henriette St. Justine. It was the first time in her life that Willow could remember having friends of her own rank, and close to her own age.

Antoine de Saville, aged seven, and his cousin, Charles Sancerre, aged eight, became the close partners in crime of his lordship, Robin, the nine-year-old Earl of Lynmouth. Together the three boys roamed the estate of Archambault, riding, birding, and daydreaming, a troupe of shaggy dogs at their heels. The three scrapegraces became very adept at eluding their tutor, until finally Adam sternly threatened his stepson with a sound thrashing if he did not behave himself. Comparing notes in hushed tones, the three discovered that all had been promised the same punishment by their outraged elders, and so they finally settled down.

In the big nursery of Archambault little Deirdre Burke learned her first embroidery stitches with her very best friend, Antoinette de Saville, while wee Lord Padraic Burke played on the floor at wooden soldiers with his new cousins, Jean-Pierre, Claude, and Michel, the four watched over by their nurses, plump, rosy-cheeked country girls with broad laps and big pillowy bosoms who spoiled the little boys shamelessly.

It was an ideal situation, for Skye's pregnancy was not an easy one in the beginning. To her great amusement and equal annoyance, Adam reveled in her condition. He happily held the basin for her when she awoke in the mornings feeling wretched; her fussy appetite was an excuse for him to hover over her, offering any delicacies he thought might please her; he rubbed her ankles, which seemed to ache at the most inconvenient times. Sometimes it made her feel guilty as she remembered that this wasn't Adam's child, but the child of a royal rape. She tried for his sake to maintain a cheerful attitude, but occasionally a shadow of unhappiness would cross her face, and when it did there were four people who understood the reason for it. When they were together, Adam's sisters, Isabeau and Clarice, consoled their beautiful sister-in-law as best they could.

"You must not hate the child, Skye," said Isabeau, the elder. "Poor baby. 'Tis as much a victim as you were."

"I pray it not look like its father," Skye said. "If it does how can I help but detest it?"

"Think of Adam," Clarice said, her blue eyes filled with concern. "Oh, Skye, you don't know what it was like for him when that awful Athenais broke off their betrothal! He was so young then, and he believed himself in love with her. He needed her understanding at the most, and at the least he needed discretion. Instead she shamed him publicly, spreading terrible lies around the district concerning his manhood. With her quick match to the old Duc de Beuvron, nobody, of course, believed her. They thought she was attempting to make excuses for taking a better offer, but Adam, knowing the truth, was so shamed. He has always wanted a child. Let this be his child, I beg of you!"

Skye remembered how Adam had told her that several of the girls on Lundy claimed that he had fathered their babies; and he had not denied it, but rather acknowledged the paternity, and seen to it that neither mother nor child wanted for anything. She saw how good he was with her own children, slipping easily into his role of father. He wrote letters filled with news and advice to the O'Flaherty boys in Paris, and both Ewan and Murrough wrote back, respecting their stepfather and, Skye realized when they arrived for Christmas, even harboring affection for him.

Willow, Skye discovered, was trying out newly discovered feminine wiles on Adam, constantly soliciting his opinion on everything. When at New Year's he presented her with a strand of pale-gold pearls to complement her skin, which was darker than Skye's, Willow flung her arms about Adam, crying, "Oh, Papa! I do love you so, and I am so glad that you are my father!" Skye felt the quick tears pricking at her eyelids, and she turned away, her heart overflowing with happiness.

Robin quite openly idolized Adam de Marisco. He had been so little when his own father, Geoffrey Southwood, had died along with his baby brother, John. He had not been six when Niall Burke disappeared. Adam was the most stable male influence in his life, and had always, it seemed to him, been there. In Robin's mind, it was only natural that the lord of Lundy marry his mother. Adam, of course, reciprocated the young boy's feeling, loving the little golden lad, the child of his cousin, as he would love a child of his own had he one.

Each day the two would ride together early in the morning, Robin exchanging boyish confidences with his stepfather. Each afternoon Adam would invade the nurseries of the château to romp and play with Deirdre and Padraic; and the nursemaids nodded approvingly at the big bluff man when he tossed the little ones high, laughing with them as they shrieked their delight. Later, when the babies slept watched over by the undermaids, the nursemaids would gossip in the servants' hall about what a fine father the Seigneur de Marisco was to his wife's children, and smile that he was to become a real father himself soon. They knew that the babe would come *early*, but what did it matter that the Seigneur and his beautiful wife had celebrated their wedding night before the wedding? The child was fortunate to be born to two such lovers!

At New Year's the de Savilles held a fête to which the neighboring nobility were invited, including the Duchesse de Beuvron. It was not expected, however, that she would attend, as she far preferred living in Paris. To everyone's surprise, Athenais de Montoire arrived squired by her son, Renaud, a gangly youth with a pockmarked face, who danced attendance on his mother like a trained dog.

"Renaud is not yet betrothed," Athenais simpered coyly to Henri St. Justine. "Your Marie-Gabrielle is just a year younger than my son. Perhaps we might talk. It would be quite a feather in your cap to marry your daughter to a duc."

Inwardly Henri shuddered at the mere thought of turning his lovely daughter over to Renaud de Montoire. He knew the reason for Renaud's pitted skin. The boy had the pox. Left alone on his estate while his mother cavorted in Paris, he ran wild; and having Athenais's unquenchable appetite, he was hardly fastidious in his choice of partners. "Alas, Madame la Duchesse," Henri St. Justine said smoothly, "both my girls have previous contracts," and then with a bow he left her standing alone.

It was at that point that Skye and Adam entered the château's Great Hall, and to those who had been unaware of her condition it was quite evident that Madame de Marisco was *enceinte*. It was also quite evident that she and her husband were deeply in love. Athenais's green eyes narrowed maliciously. She had just received a hard setdown from Baron St. Justine, and she knew it. She felt a need to retaliate, and here was a perfect opportunity. Smilingly she approached the couple, and then as she reached them her eyes widened with apparent surprise as she gave a little shriek.

"Madame de Marisco, you are *enceinte!*" Athenais declared loud enough for everyone in the vicinity to hear. "I thought it was fat, but you really are with child. *Mon Dieu!* How can this be?"

About them the men snickered at what appeared to them to be obvious. Each had the same thought. If the beautiful Madame de Marisco was newly married to them she would indeed be *enceinte*. Adam, however, was aware of the hidden insult to his wife, but before he could defend her, Skye said sweetly, "*Mon Dieu*, Madame la Duchesse, has it been so long since you were able to lure a man to your bed that you have forgotten how these things are accomplished? I do not think it is something that we might discuss in mixed company, but if you would care to come with me I shall be happy to enlighten you privately."

About them everyone laughed at Skye's words, for although she did not know it, she had come very close to the truth. Athenais de Montoire, at forty, was finding it harder to get lovers, and it was said by the court gossips that she paid young men to service her desires.

The duchesse gritted her teeth angrily. "What I meant," she said cruelly, "but then perhaps, madame, you did not know it, was that my betrothal to your husband was broken off twenty years ago because of his inability to sire a child."

A soft hiss of shock escaped the assembled guests, and now the entire hall was listening avidly. "I do not understand, Madame la Duchesse," Skye replied, smoothing her hand across her distended belly, which was covered in claret-colored velvet, "how such a thing can be. On my husband's holding in England are several mothers who would, like me, disagree with such a statement. One might accuse a peasant of a less than accurate memory, but one could not accuse me of such a thing."

There was a dangerous silence while Skye's Kerry-blue eyes looked defiantly into the green ones of Athenais de Montoire. Then the duchesse said sullenly, "I only know what I was told back then, madame."

"Bah!" the Comtesse de Cher snapped, coming to her son's defense. "You rejected my son, for which I now thank God, because you were eager to marry the old Duc de Beuvron, Athenais! The entire district knows the story of how your late papa bartered your virginity in order to make you a duchesse! Do not put the onus on my son. You are just feeling spiteful because when you recently tried to regain his affections he spurned you, being in love with *ma belle* Skye! The entire court knows how you begged Queen Catherine to intercede for you; that Adam wouldn't even speak to you except Her Majesty requested it."

Athenais de Montoire gasped, and then grew pink with her outrage. "How dare you!" she cried. "How dare you insult me so! I shall complain to the Queen, Madame la Comtesse! She will see I am compensated for these insults! I will stay no longer at this stupid country gathering. My son and I but came to lend lustre to what would otherwise be a dull fête. Come, Renaud!" and with a swish of her gold-embroidered white velvet gown she stormed from the hall.

"Good riddance!" Gaby snapped, and then she signaled to the musicians in the gallery above. At once they began to play a sprightly tune and, unable to resist, the guests began to form the figures for the dance.

"I could kill that bitch!" Skye muttered.

Her mother-in-law replied, "You would have to stand in line, *chérie*, for Madame la Duchesse is a daughter of the Devil himself, and has made many enemies. You must not worry, however, for she cannot hurt you."

Skye's tart remarks to the duchesse earned her the instant respect and approval of the noblewomen of the district. For too long they had suffered under Athenais's superiority. The evening was declared a success by all.

The winter set in, and Skye grew larger with the child during Lent with its forty days of fasting. Because she was *enceinte* and also thirty-two, the château's priest absolved her from the strictest fast, allowing her meat on Sundays, Tuesdays, and Thursdays. On the other days she was expected to keep the fast with the others. She felt guilty about having the chef broil her meat while about her everyone was forced to eat fish. The de Savilles, however, were more fortunate than many, for they could catch fresh fish in the Cher rather than being limited to a diet of salted cod and herring.

To Skye's secret relief, Adam's devotion never wavered, even now as her time drew near. None of her other husbands had been so enchanted by her fertility as he was. It seemed to give him great pleasure to lie in their bed with her propped against his broad chest, her chamber robe open, while he stroked her swollen belly, and caressed and marveled over her suddenly heavy breasts. "God's bones," he muttered to her one morning, "how I long to see the baby suckling at your wonderful breasts!"

"I had thought to put the child out with a wet nurse," she replied casually.

"Perhaps later," he said. "But for a time I want you to nurse our child." Gently he lifted one of her breasts. "From the looks of it, sweetheart, you'll have plenty of milk for the baby. Why put the child with a peasant who must feed both her own and our baby when you are capable of nursing yourself.

"I am of a mind to stay in France for a while longer. We are happy here, and so are the children." His long face, however, belied the reasonableness of his words. What he had to tell her was something he'd been avoiding for several days in hopes of finding a good time. There was, it seemed, no good time.

"You have heard from Robbie?" She was instantly wary.

He nodded, knowing better than to conceal it from her. "Yes, I have heard from Robbie. The Queen, may God damn her sour and dried-up maiden soul, will not recognize our marriage. She says we have forfeited her goodwill by our deceit. What deceit, I should like to know? The witch is simply jealous of our happiness! She has never been woman enough to give up all for love, but she resents those who are brave enough to do what she secretly longs to."

"The Queen can go to Hell," Skye muttered irritably.

Adam laughed, but then grew serious again. "There is more, my love."

Skye smiled grimly. "I would expect that Elizabeth Tudor would not content herself with mere words. Tell me all, Adam, for it will get no better with the waiting."

"She's taken the Burke lands, Skye."

"The bitch! She swore to me Padraic's claim was safe if I wed with the Duc de Beaumont de Jaspre. I kept my part of the bargain, Adam. Damn these Tudors for the treacherous dogs they are! Damn her! Damn her! Damn her!" Then suddenly Skye remembered, and she asked of her husband, "Uncle Seamus? What has happened to my uncle?"

Here Adam chuckled. "He did not give in easily, Skye. First he tried diplomacy, reminding the Queen of her promise to you, and that you had indeed kept your bargain. When that did not work that wily old cleric secretly filled Burke Castle with gunpowder, and then blew it to smithereens the night before the new English owner was to take possession. Every tenant farmer on the property had been given notice of eviction by the new owner, and so, as Burke Castle went so did all the cottages and farmhouses on the estate. All that's left of the holding is the land itself and a number of piles of stones, the castle being the largest pile."

"But the people," Skye fretted. "What is to become of Burke people?"

"They've left the land, Skye. Some have gone to the O'Malleys, and others to Ballyhennessey, which so far has escaped the Queen's eye."

"Ballyhennessey is too small," Skye said. "It can barely support its own peasants let alone refugees from Burke lands. Where has my uncle gone?"

"To the O'Malleys, of course, with a large price on his head for wantonly destroying Crown property."

"My brothers will protect him, Adam, but he is such an old man now to have to face such a commotion. He's seventy-one, you know."

"Would you like me to bring him to France, Skye?"

"He'd not come, Adam, for he has his duty to his people as bishop of Connaught, especially now."

He could see that her eyes were sad with his revelations, and it pained him to fret her further, but he had no choice. "The Queen has also taken Lundy, Skye."

"Oh, Adam!" She looked up at him, stricken. "I am so sorry, my darling! All this is because of me!"

"Skye, I will not lie to you. I loved Lundy, and I even loved that damned tumbled-down tower which was all that was left of my castle. I will miss my rooms at the top of that tower, the rooms where we first met, first made love; but, little girl, if I had a thousand times the possessions I should gladly give them all up to have you for my wife. Besides, the Queen got nothing but the island. When I knew that I was going to come after you some instinct made me transfer all my wealth to my bankers in Paris. If we cannot persuade the Queen to relent then I shall obtain lands here in France, and we shall settle here.

"The Queen took nothing of Lynmouth, or Robert Small's possessions, which will one day come to Willow. It is only your Burke children she has acted against, and I suspect, Skye, that given the situation in Ireland now, the English would have eventually stolen those lands. I am sorry, but there is no help for it."

"What of the O'Malleys, Adam? What of Innisfana, my brothers, Anne, Geoffrey's two daughters?"

"For the moment they seem to be safe. I hope you will not be angry with me, Skye, but I instructed Robbie to take over the six ships that belong to you personally, and to separate them from the O'Malley holdings. Your brothers have joined forces with your kinswoman, Grace O'Malley, and she is the Queen's mortal enemy in Ireland. This way I have protected your own wealth."

Skye nodded her agreement. "My brothers are hotheaded fools," she said sadly. "They will tear down everything I have built up for the O'Malleys, and leave our people in poverty, but I can do nothing to help them. They are men now, and they will not listen to me, Adam. They see only the glory of rebellion against the English, and they see not the misery their actions will bring." A deep sigh of regret escaped her, and then she said, "Send for Geoffrey's two daughters, Gwyneth and Joan, and beg my stepmother, Anne, to come with them."

"I don't know if Anne O'Malley will leave her sons, Skye."

"Perhaps not, Adam, but I will ask her nonetheless. That much I can do in my father's memory."

"In time, Skye, the Queen will relent of her decision, I am sure."

"No," Skye said. "I am not so sure she will, Adam. Do you remember when Lady Catherine Grey married secretly with Edward Seymour, the Earl of Hertford? Like ours, it was a Catholic ceremony, but when the proof was needed the priest mysteriously could not be found. Both their sons were declared illegitimate by the Queen!"

"Catherine Grey was a claimant to the Tudor throne, Skye. The Queen was but protecting herself."

"No, Adam. Elizabeth Tudor likes to totally control the lives of her court. She is not capable of loving, or giving love. Once she told me, though she said she would deny it if I quoted her, that she would never wed, for if she did she would be neither a queen nor a woman in her own right, but rather a man's possession, and she feared it. She does fear it, Adam, but yet at the same time she longs for it. She tries to surround herself with women she deems like her, women of wit and beauty and intelligence. When these women fail her by falling in love she is merciless in her disapproval and her revenge. They have, she honestly believes, given in to their baser natures; but Elizabeth Tudor will never give in to her feelings. She will live and die a virgin queen."

"What will happen to England then?" he mused.

"Mary Stewart has a son," Skye said, "and it is this little boy, James, who, I believe, will one day rule England."

Adam listened to his wife, but in his heart he still hoped that one day Elizabeth Tudor would forgive them, so they might return to England. He liked France, but he was an Englishman in his heart. Eventually, although he did not tell Skye, he intended to win the Queen over.

Geoffrey Southwood's twin daughters, Gwyneth and Joan, arrived from Ireland in mid-April. They had stopped in Cornwall on their way to attend the wedding of their elder sister, Susan, to young Lord Trevenyan. Susan, at fifteen, had sent her stepmother a properly correct letter offering to accept responsibility for her two sisters now that she was to be a married woman. Gwyn and Joan, however, had fled happily from their strictly Protestant sister's household at the suggestion that they might marry her two young brothers-in-law.

"You should have seen them, *belle-mère*," Joan giggled. "Two pimple-faced boys with damp hands that were always seeking to get beneath our skirts when no one was looking; but oh, how pious they became when it was necessary."

Gwyn laughed with her sister. "Indeed, *belle-mère*, though Susan was shocked that we chose to honor our betrothals to your sons, we love Ewan and Murrough. When may we wed?"

"You are but fourteen," Skye said. "When you are sixteen we shall speak on it. This summer you shall stay with us here at Archambault, and then in the autumn perhaps I shall obtain places among the young French Queen's maids of honor for both of you and Willow. Do you think you would enjoy a few months at court?"

The answer was obvious, and shone in the delight upon the young girls' faces.

"I am sorry that Anne would not come with you," Skye remarked.

"She will not leave her boys, *belle-mère*," Joan said, "though they will surely be the ruin of the O'Malleys."

"That is why I sent for you," Skye replied. "I did not want you caught up in such an affair."

Joan and Gwyneth settled comfortably into the routine of the family, joining their stepsister, Willow, and her French compatriots in their studies and their games. On the twenty-ninth of April Skye went into labor with her child.

"A bit early," Gaby observed, "but I can see the child is large, and certainly ready to be born. Nature seldom makes a mistake in these matters."

"No, it does not," said Eibhlin O'Malley, the nursing nun who had accompanied her nieces from Ireland in order to be with her favorite sister in her travail.

The salon in the de Marisco apartments had been turned into a birthing room, and all the ladies of the household were available to help, though Eibhlin thought it unnecessary. This would be Skye's eighth child. It was not, however, to be an easy birth. The labor began, and then it stopped, began again, and stopped once more. Skye paced the room, feeling the nervous perspiration sliding down her back beneath her robe.

"Perhaps it is not a true labor," she said to Eibhlin. "This has not been like my other confinements."

"In what way, sister?" Eibhlin kept her voice level. She did not want Skye to know that she was nervous.

"I was very sick in the beginning this time, and the child has not been as wildly active as my others."

Eibhlin heaved a mental sigh of relief. "Each time is different to some degree, Skye. I just worry because this little one is so slow in coming. You have always borne your babes quickly."

Skye awoke on the morning of April 30th in severe labor. Before she might rise from her bed her waters broke, flooding everything. She was furious, and muttered, "Already this royal bastard causes me trouble. I wish to God it would never be born!"

"For shame, sister!" Eibhlin scolded. "The babe is innocent of its father's crime. Be grateful that your husband loves you so very much that he is willing to raise this child as his own."

Skye looked at her sister, her beautiful blue eyes ripe with raw pain. "I don't want him to raise this child, Eibhlin," she whispered. "I hate this babe that was forced upon me! The young King of Navarre used me like a whore, and I can never forget that as long as I must be a loving mother to his bastard! It is not fair, Eibhlin! It simply is not fair! Adam, who is the best man in this whole world, cannot sire a child due to a youthful fever, yet he is meant to be a father. It is his child I want! Not the bastard of France's future king!"

Eibhlin, who had always understood this beautiful and brilliant younger sister of hers, put an arm about Skye. "You can't change what has already been, sister," she said sadly. "You must face the truth of this matter. Henri of Navarre's child is soon to be born to you. Your husband, whom you profess to love above all, wants this child for his own. You do not have a choice in this, Skye. For Adam's sake, you must accept this little one with as good a grace as you can muster. It is the only thing he has ever asked of you, Skye, and Adam de Marisco has given you so much in return. For love of you he has lost Lundy. He has for love of you lost his country. Of all the men who have loved you, Skye, he has given you the most, for he has without shame or reserve given you his total heart. All he asks in return is this child which will put an end to any of the evil rumors that have been spread by the Duchesse de Beuvron. This babe will restore to him his own sense of manhood. You owe him that, sister."

Skye burst into tears at her sister's words, and sobbing, she flung herself against the nun's chest. "I know that all you say is true, Eibhlin, but I cannot in my heart resign myself to it. I know that I am being selfish, but I cannot! I cannot!"

"You will," Eibhlin said positively. "I have faith in your nature, Skye, which has always been a good and generous one." With a loving hand Eibhlin stroked her sister's head.

Skye sobbed her misery out against her sister's spare bosom for several long minutes. She wanted to be the woman that Eibhlin claimed she really was, and she wanted to make Adam happy, but every time she remembered *its* conception she rebelled with anger. She remembered Navarre's golden amber eyes filling with lust as he examined her bound and helpless body. She remembered the feel of his lips and his tongue upon her, and most of all she remembered that he had been totally aware that although she resisted him in her heart and mind, her body could not deny him. She remembered he had smugly voiced his knowledge, and had laughed at the futility of her rejection of him. All the love that Adam had to offer could not wipe out the terrible shame she felt, and having to face the result of Navarre's rape for the rest of her days was not going to help.

Then suddenly she was being pulled from her sister's embrace and enfolded in her husband's bearlike embrace. "Don't weep, little girl, please don't weep!" Adam begged her, his normally strong voice sounding somewhat distraught.

Tears of frustration poured down her face, scalding her, but looking up at this marvelous man whom she loved so dearly, Skye said in what she hoped passed for a reasonably normal voice, "Dammit, Adam, having a baby hurts, and all women cry! Would you want me to act any differently for *our* child than I did for the others?"

She saw his face sag with relief, and knew in that minute that he would give up his little dream for her if she asked. For a moment she was tempted to, but then she forced a small smile to her lips. Reaching up, she touched his cheek with her hand.

"It's truly all right, sweetheart?" he begged for her reassurance.

"It's all right, you big fool," she teased him wearily. "No wonder God gives the task of bearing children to women. You men go completely to pieces at the slightest little thing."

Adam nodded his head at her, saying, "I will admit that I should rather face an enemy in battle than go through what you are going through right now, little girl. Still, I will stay by your side if you want me."

"I would like that," Skye answered him, "but you must promise me that should you become distressed by my labor, you will feel free to go. I will understand."

Eibhlin sighed a secret sigh of relief. Part of the difficulty with Skye's erratic labor had been that she had not wanted to bear this baby, and her mind had been exercising a fierce grip on her entire body. Now that Skye had come to terms with herself, Eibhlin knew that the labor would progress, and indeed it did, but at a far slower pace than the nun had expected. Finally Eibhlin felt she must examine her sister more closely, and Adam and Gaby helped Skye up onto a table that had been prepared with a mattress and clean linens. Eibhlin washed her hands thoroughly, and then began a gentle examination of her patient. Skye was but half dilated as the nun slipped a hand within her sister's body. Scarcely breathing, Eibhlin reached out and found what she had been expecting. A soft Celtic curse escaped her as she withdrew her hand.

"What is it?" Skye was instantly alert.

Eibhlin washed her hands again. "The babe is turned the wrong way," she said. "'Tis breach."

"Will it right itself?"

"Perhaps. The situation is not yet acute, and so I think we can wait a bit."

Skye was helped from the table, and with grim concentration she began to pace back and forth, Adam walking with her. Knowing what was to come, Gaby and Eibhlin both took the opportunity to sit down and rest.

The pains began to come with greater regularity now, and finally after several hours Eibhlin felt she must examine her sister once more. This time Skye was fully dilated, but the baby had still not turned itself correctly. It was well past midnight, and now May 1st.

"I'll have to try and turn the child myself," Eibhlin told her sister.

"Can you do it?" Skye returned.

"I've done it successfully many times," was her answer. "Don't worry, Skye. It will be all right."

Skye tried to keep her mind off what her sister was doing while Adam sat by her head and sought to comfort her by talking. She had not wanted this bastard child, but suddenly, now that the babe was in danger, Skye's maternal instincts all rushed forward as she silently prayed all would be well.

"There!" Eibhlin said triumphantly. "Now, sister, bear down so we may get this child quickly into the world!"

"The infant is turned?" Gaby sounded anxious.

"Yes, Madame la Comtesse, the child is properly positioned now to be born. Look! You can even see its head."

A mighty pain tore through Skye, forcing a cry from between her lips. Instinct took over and she pushed hard to force the child from her body. Adam mopped her steaming brow with a cool cloth, and she saw that he was white about the lips. She was suddenly reminded of Geoffrey Southwood, who had helped her to birth their son in a barge on the Thames. If only Adam could stay by her as Geoffrey once had, she thought. She knew that, like Geoffrey, Adam was a man of great sensitivity who would treasure the memory of the birth.

Another pain cut into her, and she heard Gaby cry, "Ah, *ma fille*, the child is being born!"

"We've got the head and shoulders, sister," Eibhlin said. "Just a little more, dearest!"

Skye felt the proximity of victory, and it showed in her face, for

Adam said, "I want to see the baby coming from your body, sweetheart."

"Yes! Yes!" she said urgently through gritted teeth, and he stood up and went to stay by Eibhlin. She watched him with an almost pagan joy, for the look on his face was one of both wonder and amazement. Then he caught her gaze with his own for a quick minute, and the love and admiration that flowed from him gave her new and incredible strength. At the next pain she bore down as hard as she could, and she actually felt the baby sliding from her body. There was a tiny hiccough, and then a small cry of outrage as the infant was born and took its first breath.

"'Tis a little girl," Eibhlin said with a smile. "A perfect little girl!"

"Give her to me," Gaby said, holding out her hands for the baby. "I will clean her off so she may be properly presented to her mama and papa." She took the baby from Eibhlin, and Skye laughed with delight as Adam's eyes widened with pleasure at the sight of the baby. She was, she decided, going to love the child no matter the manner in which it was conceived, and more important, Adam loved it. Another pain knifed through her, and Skye worked to rid herself of the afterbirth.

Eibhlin worked swiftly and efficiently to finish with Skye the job of the birthing. As Mignon carried off the basin holding the afterbirth the nun cleaned away all traces of Skye's travail. "You've been torn a bit," she said, "by the size of the child. She is a big girl. Chew on this herb, sister, for I shall have to stitch you up." She handed Skye a piece of something green, and Skye obediently put the green herb in her mouth and grimaced, for it was bitter in taste.

Within Skye's sight, Gaby, watched by Adam, worked to make the baby fresh and pretty for its parents. Suddenly Adam's mother gave a startled little cry. "*Mon Dieu!* How can this be, but it is!" She turned to her big son, commanding, "Adam, fetch Isabeau and Clarice at once! *Vite! Vite!*"

"Maman, it is the middle of the night," he protested, "and as proud as I am of the child, it can wait until morning to tell them of it."

"*Do as I say!*" Gaby commanded again. "Please, Adam, do not argue with me! *Vite!*"

With a shake of his head Adam stumbled from his apartments to fetch his sisters, Isabeau and Clarice, who had come to stay at Archambault at the news that Skye was in labor. Walking through the chilly halls of the château he found their rooms and, banging upon each door, called to them. The doors were opened by sleepy tiring women, who eyed Adam balefully when he told them to fetch their mistresses.

"What is it, Adam?" Isabeau came to her door, pulling a quilted velvet gown about her.

"The child is born, and Maman insists that you and Clarice come immediately."

"Is Skye all right?" demanded Clarice, who had now come to her door.

"Both she and the child seem fine, but Maman has suddenly gone mad, I think."

The two sisters looked at one another, and then pushing past their brother, they hurried down the hallway. Adam quickly followed them, and they re-entered the apartments shared by the de Mariscos.

"Maman, what is it?" Isabeau cried.

"Maman, are you all right?" Clarice echoed.

"Yes, *mes filles*, I am fine, but I need you both here because there has been a miracle, and both of you can help me prove the existence of that miracle." Gaby picked up the newly born infant, which she had wrapped in a soft blanket. Carrying it over to Skye, she said, "*Ma chère* Skye, this is no child of Henri of Navarre. This child is of our blood, and I can prove it to you. *Ma soeur*," she said to Eibhlin, "take your niece a moment." She handed the baby to the nun and then Gaby bent down, lifted her skirts, and drew her undergarments down to bare her hip. "Do you see it?" she said. "Do you see the small mole in the shape of a heart, Skye?"

"Yes." Skye was puzzled.

Gaby dropped her skirts. "That birthmark is the mark of the St. Denis women. Only women of our own blood have that mark. Isabeau, Clarice, show Skye your birthmarks."

The two sisters undid their gowns and, raising their nightdresses, each revealed a tiny dark heart upon the left hip just atop the bone. The mark was identical to that of their mother's. "All our daughters bear the same mark, Skye," Isabeau said.

"Before I married I was Mademoiselle St. Denis," Gaby explained. "That particular birthmark has shown up on the women in my family for at least ten generations. Musette also bears the mark, as does her little daughter, Aimée. I did not call Musette, however, since she does not know her brother's difficulty. Nonetheless, *ma chère* Skye, this baby you have just borne is my own true granddaughter, the child of my son, Adam." She turned to Eibhlin. "Unwrap the infant, *ma soeur*," and when the nun had done so, she handed the baby to Gaby. "Look, Skye! On the little one's left hip just atop the bone! The birthmark of the St. Denis women! There has been a miracle, *ma fille! This is Adam's child, and no one else's!*"

Skye looked at her daughter, and then she looked to Ebbhlin, her voice confused. "Eibhlin, you are a physician. Can this be? Is it true? Is it even possible? Can this baby be Adam's daughter?"

Eibhlin looked closely at the newborn infant. The tiny dark heart atop the left hipbone was quite plain. There was no mistake about it. She took the baby, rewrapped her in the blanket, and handed her to her mother. Then, turning to Adam, she said, "Who told you that you could not have children, Adam?"

"'Twas an old herb woman," Adam said. "I had been ill with a very high fever, and she claimed that the fever had burnt all the life from my seed."

Eibhlin nodded. "An only half-accurate diagnosis, my lord. What I suspect is really the truth is that for a time your seed was lifeless, but nature sometimes has a way of reversing itself, and it is very possible that now, many years later, you have perhaps a small amount of life to your seed. I have heard of cases like yours." She looked down at the baby, and smiled. "She has your mama's nose. There is no doubt this child is of your flesh, my lord, but do not get your hopes high, for there is very little chance of your siring another child. You have been fortunate, and God has heard my sister's prayers, but, as your mother has said, this is a miracle!"

Adam de Marisco moved to Skye's side, and together they gazed wonderingly upon their daughter. "How do I thank you, sweetheart?" he said, and she heard the catch in his voice.

She shook her head, her eyes filling with happy tears, her own voice catching in her throat. "I . . . I can't believe it, Adam." Then she looked about the room and saw that both her sister and the others had tears in their eyes.

Finally Eibhlin managed to regain her equilibrium, and taking the baby from its parents, she said, "It is time that everyone went to bed. Is the cradle in the bedchamber?"

"Yes, *ma soeur*," Gaby said coming to herself. "Give me my newest granddaughter, and I shall put her in her cradle while you and Adam help Skye." She turned to her daughters. "Well, don't just stand there, you two! Go and open Skye's bed for her! Must I tell you everything?"

Isabeau and Clarice giggled, not one bit put out to be scolded by their maman. They felt giddy with happiness at the wonderful good fortune that had befallen their beloved brother and his beautiful wife. Hurrying into the bedchamber, they drew back the coverlet of the freshly made bed with its lavender-scented sheets.

Carefully Adam de Marisco lifted his wife up and carried her to their bed. Gently he set her in it and drew the covers over her. Skye's eyes were beginning to close as all the tension of the last months and the lengthy labor she had just endured caught up with her. She was asleep even as his lips softly brushed her mouth.

"Is she all right?" he asked Eibhlin.

"Yes," Eibhlin nodded with a kindly smile, "but she is very, very tired. Had this kind of a labor come when she was a girl I should be less concerned, but she is past thirty, Adam, and that is not a good time for a hard birth."

"Is there any danger, Eibhlin?"

"I don't believe so, for Skye has always been healthy. I am just cautious."

Eibhlin led them all from the bedroom, closing the door behind her as she went.

"Go back to your beds, *mes filles*," Gaby ordered her daughters. "I am certainly going to seek mine, and you, *ma soeur*, deserve a good rest also. I will see that the nurse is sent to watch the baby while we all sleep." Clarice and Isabeau hugged their brother and then departed the room, closely followed by Eibhlin and Gaby, who with tears in her eyes kissed her son, stating a final time, "*It is a miracle!*"

When they had left Adam de Marisco tiptoed back into Skye's bedchamber once more, and stood for several long minutes looking down at the sleeping form of the newborn child. *His daughter!* He had a daughter! Not some royal bastard that he would accept for Skye's sake, but his own child. *It was a miracle.* He wanted to pick the baby up and examine her carefully, but he was afraid to do so. They had all said she was a fine big girl, but to him she looked so tiny. Tomorrow. Tomorrow would be time enough to become acquainted with his new little girl. He walked over to the big bed where Skye lay sleeping, and his heart went out to his lovely wife. She looked so very tired after her long ordeal. He had loved her for so long, and now he owed her a debt that he could never repay, for she had given him a child. Somehow he was going to get them home to England. Ireland, he knew, was totally out of the question, and Skye knew it, too. If there had been troubles in Ireland before, they were going to double in the next few years. Bending down, he kissed her lightly once more, and then went through the connecting door between the two chambers and sought his bed.

In his sleep Adam heard the baby whimper, and he was instantly awake, stumbling across the room and through the door. To his surprise and his relief, the nurse was already there. She smiled at him, and curtseyed. "'Tis all right, monseigneur. Go back to sleep." He gratefully complied, and the sun was halfway across the skies above Archambault when he finally awoke again. He had fallen into bed without even removing his clothing, although he had remembered to take off his boots. Now Adam peeked into Skye's bedchamber, and seeing his wife sitting up in her bed eating an egg, he hurried to make himself presentable. Stripping off his clothes, he called for old Guillaume to bring him water for washing, and while he bathed and trimmed his beard and mustache, the old valet laid out fresh clothing for his master which Adam hastily donned.

Her blue eyes lit up as he came into the room, and she smilingly held out her arms to him. "*Bonjour, mon mari!*" she said gaily.

Sitting on the edge of the bed, he took her into his arms and kissed her passionately. "*Je t'aime*, I love you," he murmured softly at her. "You are the most marvelous woman in this world, Lady de Marisco!"

"Gracious," she teased him, "and what has made you so happy today, my lord?" But then Skye could not keep up the pretense, and she called to the nursemaid, "Ila, bring the baby for my lord to see. Oh, Adam, you should see her! She is so perfect!" Her own eyes were shining with joy and happiness, and he took her hand, raising it to his lips to kiss it.

"*Merci, ma femme,*" he said. "*Mille fois merci!*"

Ila brought the baby from its cradle. Laying her carefully upon the bed, she said, "I shall go and get the extra linen I need if Madame will permit it."

"Yes, yes," Skye encouraged the nurse, and then she turned to her husband. "Look at her, Adam. Isn't she just perfect?"

He looked down at the swaddled little bundle with only its small, heart-shaped face showing. "I really can't tell," he said honestly. "Can we undress her?"

Skye unwrapped the baby from her blanket, and carefully removed the little shirt and napkin. Then she looked up at her husband. "Well?"

Adam de Marisco gazed down with wonder at his daughter. She was indeed perfection. She had plump little arms and legs and a fat little tummy. She was rosy and creamy with a thick headful of dark curls, and now when she opened her eyes he saw that they were a beautiful blue. She stared at him boldly, and with a soft chuckle Adam touched the baby with a gentle finger. Her skin was softer than anything he had ever known, and he was enchanted by it. "She's roses and ebony, ivory and white velvet," he said quietly.

Skye smiled at his pride as she carefully redressed and rewrapped the baby. The infant whimpered, and quietly her mother opened her gown and put the baby to her breast. Skye's milk would not be in for another day, but her breasts already tingled with a clear liquid that preceded the milk, and it was this nourishment she offered her daughter. Adam sat watching her, and he felt more at peace now than he had ever felt in his life.

"What are we going to name her?" he asked his wife. A name for the child was something that Skye had not been able to discuss while she believed it to be Henri of Navarre's baby.

"Would you like to call her after your mother, and she might have Marie as a second name as May is the month of the Blessed Mother?" Skye looked to her husband.

"That is kind, sweetheart," he remarked, "but Clarice has a daughter who is Marie-Gabrielle, and Alexandre has a daughter who is Gabrielle-Marie. Our daughter might bear both those names, but she must also have her very own name, a name by which she can be distinguished from her cousins." He looked again at his daughter, who was busily and hungrily nursing upon her mother's breast. Once more he was overcome by the urge to touch her, and he did so gently, his pinky rubbing softly against her cheek. Again the word velvet came into his mind, and then Adam's eyes lit up. "Velvet," he said. "I want to call her Velvet!"

"It is perfect!" Skye said excitedly. "Velvet Gabrielle Marie. Velvet de Marisco!"

Velvet de Marisco chose that moment to get a bout of the hiccoughs, much to her parents' amusement; and then the baby, not the least bit impressed by the importance of the occasion that had elevated her from nameless infant to Velvet de Marisco, fell asleep. Over her daughter's head Skye looked lovingly at her husband, and Adam de Marisco smiled back. For the moment there was no longer any need for words.

Chapter 16

When she was three days old, Velvet de Marisco was baptized in the family chapel of Archambault by the château's priest. To everyone's surprise, Queen Catherine and her daughter, Marguérite, arrived from Chenonceaux, where they had celebrated May Day. The princesse insisted upon standing as godmother to the baby.

"She is not Navarre's child," Skye said boldly. "I would have no misunderstandings between us, Highness."

"She is too pretty to be Navarre's child, madame," the princesse laughed. "No, I choose to be this little girl's godmother because if I were a good wife I should now be giving birth myself. I am not a particularly good wife, but then Henri is not a good husband. Humor me, madame. I shall be good to the child."

Skye bowed her head politely. "You do my daughter great honor, Highness."

"Who is the other godmother-to-be?" Catherine de Medici asked.

"Elizabeth Tudor," Skye said softly.

"Ha ha!" the Queen laughed. "You play your cards well, Madame de Marisco. Well, it cannot hurt the little one to have both an English queen and a French princess on her side. Who knows where she may end up someday. Who is the godfather?"

"M'sieur le Comte," Skye replied, "and her half-brother, the Earl of Lynmouth."

"A good choice," the Queen approved. "Again you chose to straddle both sides of the channel."

The wars of religion were giving everyone a nervous summer. A nearby wealthy Huguenot merchant decided to relocate to the Protestant stronghold of La Rochelle, and was very grateful to find in Adam de Marisco a buyer for his small château, Belle Fleur. Belle Fleur was only four miles from Archambault, a fairy-tale gem of a house located upon a small lake and set in the middle of an enormous garden on the edge of a forest.

Skye was charmed by her new home, which had been built in the early fifteenth century by an ancestor of the previous owner's wife. Belle Fleur had an air of enchantment about it with its witch's cap roofs and its moat, which spread into a small lake on one side. The château appeared to hover on the smooth surface of the water, and seemed even more mysterious by virtue of the surrounding forest of Archambault. Built of flattened, rough-hewn blocks of reddish-gray schist, it had four polygonal towers crowned by dark slate roofs shaped like witch's hats which defended each corner of the building. Access to the *cour d'honneur* could only be gained through a tall, heavily fortified châtelet flanked by rounded and corbeled towers that rose high on either side of the entrance arch. Surrounded by water on three sides, the château was on its fourth side planted in an exquisite and colorful garden filled to overflowing with sweetly scented blooms. The creatures of the forest were kept from the garden by a low stone wall. It was this magnificent garden that had given the château its name.

It was not a large home, but it had a fine hall where the family might gather, and where they could entertain on a small scale; and there were enough bedchambers for all of the children, and room for a decent staff of servants. There were good-sized stables for the horses, a respectable kennel for the dogs, and a suitable place for the falcons. The former owner had sold the château furnished, and it was filled with pleasingly good furniture and hangings. Adam had a bed made to his own specifications for himself and Skye; she purchased both table and bed linens from a nearby convent; and they were ready to move into their new home. Mignon and Guillaume came with them from Archambault, along with a full staff of servants provided them by the comte.

They spent the rest of the summer settling in, surprisingly isolated from France's unpleasant religious wars. They were the contented parents of nine children, six of Skye's, her two stepdaughters, and their own baby daughter, Velvet. Skye could not remember a more content and domesticated period in her life. Ewan and Murrough were home from the university in Paris for several months, and along with their younger brother, Robin, and their stepfather, they spent long days on horseback hunting or sprawled lazily by the lakeside, fishing. Then, too, the older boys had suddenly become very aware of Gwyneth and Joan Southwood, to whom they had been betrothed since childhood.

Skye's stepdaughters, the children of Geoffrey Southwood's previous marriage, were pretty girls with long, dark-honey-blond hair and soft, gray eyes. They were now fourteen, and had been in Skye's care since they were five. The twins adored their stepmother, and Skye loved them back with all of her generous nature. She had placed them with Anne O'Malley when she had left for Beaumont, and under that sweet lady's tutelage the Southwood girls had learned all that needed be known by a good wife and mother. As little girls they had been rather plain, and their new prettiness delighted Skye and greatly pleased her sons.

In this happy summer Gwyn and Joan and their stepsister, Willow, were content to be with Skye, who took them riding and boating, and on wonderful picnics in the nearby forest. It was not long before Adam and the boys began to join them on their *al fresco* outings, and soon Deirdre and her little brother, Padraic, were clamoring to come also. It was a good time. In the evenings the family would gather in the Great Hall for the meal, and afterward Adam and Ewan would play chess while Murrough and Robin, both once pages at Elizabeth Tudor's court, would play upon their lutes while the ladies sang.

Skye watched her children with pride, and glowed herself in their reflected happiness. It had never been quite like this for any of them. In France they were far from the Anglo-Irish situation; they were far from the intrigues of Elizabeth Tudor's court. For the first time, Skye thought, we do not have to be wary. We do not have to be afraid.

In the autumn Willow, Gwyneth, and Joan went up to Paris accompanied by Ewan. Murrough had decided he had enough of education, and went off to sea with old Sean MacGuire. The girls were to take their places for a few months in the household of the young French Queen, Isabeau of Austria. Young Robin Southwood grew restless with his elder brothers gone and Adam concentrating on the running of the small estate.

"You want to return to England," Skye said understandingly.

Robin, now ten, looked sadly at his mother. "I am an Englishman, Mother," he said. "I am the Earl of Lynmouth. I know that I am but half grown, but I belong at the court where my father spent his youth, and I belong on my estates. My lord de Grenville cannot truly act for me."

"If you go," she said, "we may never see one another again. Neither Adam nor I dare set foot in England for fear of the Queen's wrath. She will not recognize our marriage, and she has branded wee Velvet illegitimate."

"She is not a happy woman," Robin replied wisely. "She longs for, yet she fears that which other women have. She is not so much angry at you, Mother, as she is at herself."

Skye was amazed at her young son's apt appraisal of Elizabeth Tudor, but then Robin had been the Queen's personal and favorite page, and he was not a stupid boy. "I will write to both Robbie and Dickon de Grenville to see if your return would be a welcome one," she said with tears in her eyes.

"Don't worry, Mother," he said in an effort to comfort her. "Bess Tudor cannot keep me from you if I desire to be with you. I am Southwood, the premier Earl of England!"

Skye looked hard at her son. He had grown taller over this summer, and she suddenly realized that the arrogant tilt of his head, the fierce pride in his voice, the very way that he stood made him his father's son. "Yes, Robin," she said softly, "you are indeed Southwood."

Skye kept her promise to Robin, and wrote that very day to both Robbie and de Grenville. For several weeks the correspondence flew back and forth between France and England. Skye insisted that she receive the Queen's word that Robin would be allowed to come to his mother and stepfather whenever either of them should desire it. The Queen wrote back that Robin might certainly come to visit his mother, Lady Burke, and Lord de Marisco, her lover, whenever he chose. Elizabeth Tudor wrote in her elegant hand, that she knew the pain of parental separation from her own personal experience, and she would certainly not visit it upon the child of her late, dear friend the Earl of Lynmouth. However, the Queen primly noted that she did not think the living arrangements chosen by Lady Burke, as well as the presence of her bastard daughter, were conducive to correct moral behavior; and young people were so easily influenced.

"Ohhhh, the jealous bitch!" Skye spit furiously. "If she could retain her maidenhead and still entertain a randy cock nightly, she would! The hypocrite! I'll not let Robin go!"

Adam roared with laughter, but then he grew serious. "You must not make him stay, Skye. I would go home too if I could, and if Robin desires it then he should go. He is lord of a vast estate, and his people need to see him. He has his place at court, Skye, even if we don't. It is his right."

Young Lord Southwood rode out from Belle Fleur on an early November day. He had bid his tearful mother a loving good-bye and, accompanied by his stepfather, made his way to Nantes, where he would embark for Plymouth on one of Skye's ships.

"I'll soften the Queen up so she'll recognize your marriage, Mother," he promised gallantly. "It is not right that she not do so, and I will not have my sister Velvet's honor compromised."

Skye hugged him, muttering motherly things about getting enough sleep and eating properly and not allowing himself to be seduced by anyone either male or female, for the pages were always prey to such debauchery, especially when they were as handsome as Robin.

His lordship flushed at his mother's words, and Adam swallowed a guffaw at Skye's concern, saying, "Enough now, sweetheart, else we miss the tide, and old MacGuire won't be happy with you then. Besides, you know how treacherous the Bay of Biscay can be at this time of year."

Skye understood her husband's silent message, and pulling herself together, she kissed Robin soundly on both cheeks, saying, "God go with you, my son. Remember I love you."

She watched them disappear down the forest road, and then Skye walked quietly through the château and upstairs to the bed-chamber she shared with Adam, where she had a good cry. After a while she began to giggle as she remembered Adam's remark about the tide, realizing that, as always, her tears would have rendered him helpless. The tide mattered not, for it was two days' ride to Nantes from Belle Fleur! Her sense of humor restored, and facing the fact that she really could not keep Robin from his heritage,

Skye put it all behind her and set to work to keep busy while Adam was away.

There were now only three children left at the château, her Burke son and daughter and little Velvet. Since they were all cared for by their nurses Skye could spend her time at other things. The previous winter had been a cold one, and neither had the spring and summer been successful growing seasons. The fourth French religious war raged on, but was thankfully confined to La Rochelle and Sancerre. Yet the coming winter would bring famine and shortages to all of France. Skye had already seen to the import of grain from the Barbary coast, which was brought into Nantes on her ships. This grain she shared with Archambault, and the miller there had seen to the grinding of the wheat into flour, which was then stored in a guarded stone granary hidden within the forest. Throughout the winter, the flour would be parceled out to the peasants so that they might survive.

In a burst of generosity, the Comte de Cher and his sons-in-law permitted hunting in the fields and forests of Archambault twice monthly on specific days. Poachers caught at any other time were subject to severe punishment. Both Skye and Adam knew the forest of Archambault abounded with rabbits, far more indeed than could ever be eaten. It was understood among the peasants of the neighborhood that the Seigneur de Marisco and his wife were known to look the other way when coming upon snares, and fishing discreetly in the Belle Fleur's lake was not discouraged.

"You are too kind to them," Gaby scolded Skye as she visited with her daughter-in-law while Adam was away.

"They have to eat," Skye argued. "By letting them snare rabbits without ceasing we make the rabbits wary enough to avoid the gardens, which means the vegetables have time to reach maturity. We will need the cabbages and carrots and the leeks and onions this winter. It is simply a matter of careful planning."

"You have managed an estate before?" Gaby was surprised.

"Did Adam not tell you of my estates, Gaby? It seemed to me that he told you everything else about me," Skye laughed.

"Oh, I know about the wealth you inherited from your husbands, but I was not aware you knew how to manage that wealth. It is not something a woman usually does."

"I have never been an ordinary woman, Gaby. When I was still a girl my father bypassed my five older sisters and their husbands to put his wealth and power in my hands. I am the O'Malley of Innisfana. I followed my father's teachings and increased the holdings and the wealth of the O'Malleys of Innisfana considerably. At the same time I managed my son, Ewan's, holdings, and later on the wealth left to me by my second husband for his daughter, Willow, and then all of Lynmouth's lands and goods, and finally the Burkes'. I was not so successful with the Burke lands, alas."

"The Irish!" Gaby threw up her hands. "Forgive me, *ma fille*, but they are an impossible people. Charming, but totally mad!"

Skye laughed. "Indeed we are," she admitted. "I regret that the Irish would rather destroy themselves than accept compromise and survive. Even I rebelled against the English in the end. Had I gone back to England instead of marrying Adam here in France, my son, Padraic, would still have his lands, and Adam would have Lundy."

"Lundy?! Good riddance!" Gaby snapped. "A pile of stones upon a rock, but ah, before Adam's father allowed his lust to control him so that he defied and insulted King Henry Tudor, ahh then, *ma belle*, Lundy and its castle was a most fantastic sight. I had my first glimpse of it when I arrived there as a bride over forty years ago. John de Marisco had come to Paris to wed me, and then brought me back to England. We stopped at Lynmouth to pay our respects to John's liege lord, your Robin's *grandpère*, and then we embarked from Lynmouth for Lundy across the water. It was early morning, and the fog was thick. Soon I could no longer see Lynmouth, and I could certainly not see Lundy. Then suddenly a light wind sprang up, and the dawn began to pour across the skies. Lundy appeared like a fairy-tale castle, seeming to float above the sea, streamers of mist swirling about its turrets. Ah, 'twas a glorious sight!" For a moment her face was soft with the memory, but then the practical Frenchwoman resurfaced. "Then that marvelous idiot I married managed to destroy my son's inheritance, and left us with barely enough for me to bring my children home to France! Lundy! Pah! You are better off here at Belle Fleur!"

"Excuse me, madame, but it is time for Mademoiselle Velvet's feeding," the nursemaid said, bringing the baby to her mother.

Skye took her little daughter, who was now six months old and growing more like her father every day. Her coal-black curls were already thick and tangled, her blue eyes were avid in their curiosity about everything.

"*Ah, ma petite bébé!*" Gaby crooned. "Have you a small smile for Grandmère?"

Velvet's eyes swept tolerantly over her grandmother, and then turning away, she grasped at her mother's breast, thrusting the nipple into her mouth. With a sigh she settled down to the business of food.

Skye chuckled. "Like her father and her mother, she will not be deterred from her desires."

"You are still nursing her? Why?" Gaby demanded. "Surely you can find a wet nurse. I could find you one, *ma fille.*"

"Adam prefers that I feed her myself," Skye said, "and frankly I am enjoying it, Gaby. This is the first time in my life I have been able to enjoy being a mother. There was always something to take me from motherhood. This time there is not!"

"Will you stay in France, Skye?"

"I do not know, Gaby. There is nothing for me in Ireland any longer, and I would far prefer not to have to live beneath Elizabeth Tudor's thumb. Still, Adam longs for England, and he says that it is Velvet's heritage. Perhaps one day the Queen will forgive us for marrying without her permission, and then I know that Adam will return. We are his family, and we will have to go with him, but we shall keep Belle Fleur even when that day comes, for I have been happier here than anywhere in my whole life."

Adam returned from Nantes, and shortly thereafter they received word that his lordship, the Earl of Lynmouth, had reached England safely. Christmas, New Year's, and Twelfth Night came and went, and the winter settled in around Archambault and Belle Fleur. Willow wrote from the French court that the King was not well, and it was expected he would die soon. As for court, she wrote, "It seems very much as Robin has described the English court to me. There is much intrigue both serious and silly. Most people are terribly impressed by one's title and/or pocketbook. The young men play a game as to who can seduce the greatest number of noble ladies. What they do not know is that these ladies are playing the same game. You need not worry, Mama," wrote Willow, "for my stepsisters and I are shocked by such disgraceful behavior. Gwyneth and Joan, of course, are relatively safe, for they are neither overly pretty nor wealthy enough. As for me, I have my share of admirers, but I will not permit them to be alone with me, thereby avoiding any idle gossip that should destroy my good name."

Skye smiled reading Willow's letter. She had no fears about Willow, who was a practical little miss with ambitions to wed an important title. *Little?* No, Willow could no longer be considered little. She would be fourteen in April, and it would soon be time, Skye realized, to seek a husband for her eldest daughter. Remembering Dom O'Flaherty, Skye prayed that her daughter would fall in love with a suitable young man and thus avoid the pain that she had suffered. She would not force her child to any marriage, as she had been forced by her well-meaning father.

The spring of the year 1574 was more promising, and Velvet de Marisco celebrated her first birthday. She was already walking, toddling about the château with so much zeal that Skye forbade the baby's nursemaid to leave her alone for a moment, for she feared her daughter would fall into the moat. Velvet was also talking, making her demands, which were many and constant, known in a mixture of both English and French.

Adam was an appallingly doting father, but then Skye had expected it. Yet she worried when her big husband took their tiny daughter up on his horse and rode out into the forest. Velvet, however, was no more fearful of that than Skye had been of the sea at her age. Skye could simply not bring herself to chide Adam, for his great love and delight in his daughter were so painfully obvious. She could not spoil his fun, and so it fell upon her shoulders the task of disciplining their child.

"Non, non, méchanceté!" Skye scolded her baby daughter one afternoon as Velvet attempted to stuff a sweetmeat into her mouth. She spanked the tiny hand gently, and wiped the stickiness from it.

Velvet's enormous eyes grew moist, and she ran on fat little legs to her father, clutched at his leg, threw her mother an angry glance, and distinctly said, "Papa loves!"

Adam longed to laugh and pick his precious child up in his arms for a kiss, but seeing Skye's warning look, he instead said, "Mama loves you too, Velvet, but you must always obey her."

Outraged at this unpleasant turn of events, Velvet stalked away to her nurse, who took her from the hall.

"What a minx she is," Skye said. "You realize that we are going to have our hands full with her? Could *le bon Dieu* not have given us a gentle and quiet child?"

He chuckled. "She is *our* daughter, sweetheart."

Skye smiled back at him. "You will not feel so indulgent when she is older, and the men begin to crowd about her," she teased.

"That's a long time away," Adam said smugly. "She's just a baby, barely a year old."

"The time goes quickly, Adam. Ewan is eighteen now, and I don't know where the years went."

"Madame, you are depressing me," he said. "Let us go to bed now before we are too old, although I have been told by authorities on the matter that one never grows too old. Based on the wisdom of your vast age, what do you have to say on the matter?"

"Come to our bedchamber, monseigneur, and I shall explain my thoughts to you in detail," Skye promised with a seductive glance at her husband as she went from the hall.

These were the times she loved the best; the times when they might retire to the delicious isolation of their apartment. In the big bed that he had had made specially for them—an enormous oak bed with its eight-foot-high headboard all done in linenfold paneling, its carved and turned posts, its natural-colored linen hangings with an embroidered design of grass green velvet—they could lie for hours in the nude, caressing each other leisurely, and making long, slow love until the fire burned down to nothing but glowing ashes and they were forced to retreat beneath the down coverlet.

For them the lovemaking grew better each time, particularly after Velvet was born. Adam could not love her enough, and Skye adored her giant of a husband when he lay his naked length against hers, pressing her deep into the mattress. She reveled in the firm flesh of his thighs against hers, the tickly feeling of his furred chest against her breasts, the hardness of his very maleness seeking to mate with her. There were times when she could not get enough of her handsome husband, and she would shamelessly awaken him with delicious kisses across his big, sleeping form. Several times Adam awoke to find she had roused him while he slept, and now sat astride him. Reaching up, he would caress her beautiful breasts until they thrust forward with taunting invitation. Yet with the incredible passion that blazed between them was also a profound sense of peace, as if both Skye and Adam understood that what was between them would be forever.

Charles IX died, and his next brother, Anjou, who had the previous
year been made King of Poland, fled his adopted country like a
thief in the night to return to his beloved France. Anjou, however,
stopped in both Vienna and Venice to be royally fêted before finally gaining his native borders, where his irritated mother awaited
him. Elizabeth of Austria retired from court, and because her retinue was smaller now, Skye's daughters came home to Belle Fleur
that summer. Ewan arrived from the university in Paris; Murrough
appeared bronzed and taller, home from his first voyage; and even
Robin appeared suddenly one day to surprise them all.

A great deal of fuss was made over the baby, although Skye
begged her older children not to spoil Velvet. "She is already quite
impossible, *mes enfants*," their mother said with an indulgent smile.

After several months back in England, Robin was once more the
perfect English courtier. "You should really let me take Padraic
back with me in the autumn, Mother," he said to Skye. "He will be
close to six then, and should begin his education at the Tudor
court. The Queen may have taken his lands, but my brother is still
Lord Burke."

"No!" Skye said. "As long as Adam and I are not welcome at the
Tudor court then none of my children except you, Robin, shall go.
A nobleman without lands is nothing, and until the Queen restores
the Burke lands to the Burkes I want nothing to do with either her
or England. Besides, Padraic is still a baby."

"I am not!" Padraic Burke, his father's image, glowered up at
her.

Skye looked down at Niall's son, and smiled at him. "In time, my
darling," she promised him. "Be patient for now." Then she looked
around the hall, and said, "I am so glad to have you all here again.
This is how I like it best, my children about me, Adam by my
side."

"I can only stay a month," Robin said. "I promised Her Majesty
that I would rejoin the court in its summer progress at Hardwick
Hall. I have given my word."

"I'll be returning to Ireland when Robin goes," Ewan said suddenly.

"*What?!*" Skye looked sharply at her eldest son. "This is rather
sudden, Ewan, isn't it?"

"I've been in correspondence with my Uncle Michael for over a
year, Mother. He's done the best he could, but he's a priest. My

other O'Malley uncles have not been interested in Ballyhennessey since they joined with Grace O'Malley to fight with the Queen. I have to go home, Mother. My lands need me," he finished, then he looked at his mother. "I want to take Gwyneth with me, Mother. It is time for us to marry."

"But she is just fifteen!" Skye protested. The twins had celebrated their birthday on June 4th.

"You were fifteen when you wed my father," Ewan said quietly.

"I was too young!"

"No, Mother, you were not too young. You were simply wed to the wrong man. That is not the case with Gwyneth and me."

"I cannot bear it if Ewan leaves me, madame," said the quiet Gwyneth. "I am past ready to be a wife."

"I, also," Joan said.

"But Murrough has just begun to learn seamanship. If he is to make it his life, he cannot stay home to husband you, Joan." Skye was beginning to feel besieged by her offspring.

"MacGuire is not sailing again for almost two months, Mother," Murrough said. "His ship needs repairs. Joan and I can be wed, and even have time together before I must leave. Whenever she weds me she still has to get used to having a sailor for a husband. I will buy us a home in Devon, near Lynmouth."

Robin coughed a bit, and looked a trifle uncomfortable. "All right, Robert Southwood," Skye snapped. "What else is there?"

"I bring an invitation from the Queen for Willow. She is invited to join the maids of honor."

"Ohhh," Willow shrieked esctatically, and then she turned on her mother. "You promised me that one day I might! *You promised, Mama!*"

"You've been to court!"

"A French court," Willow scoffed scornfully.

"No!"

"Please, Mama! Soon I shall be too old to go! Please!"

Skye looked at the children all ranged in a row, and seemingly allied against her. Ewan, Murrough, Gwyneth, Joan, Willow, Robin, and Padraic. They all wanted to leave. Her hand flew to her mouth, and she cried, "But I have had you such a short time!" Then turning from them, she ran from the hall.

Adam watched her go, his own eyes saddened, and then he said, "Of course you must follow your own destinies, *mes enfants*. You are all quite old enough now, but it is hard for your mother to understand this. Leave her to me, and I will make it all right for everyone."

Adam found her weeping piteously on their bed, and quietly gathered Skye into his arms. She sobbed for some minutes as he gently rocked her back and forth, and then gradually her sobs began to fade away. "It will be dull without them, I know," he said soothingly.

"I like dull," she said. "I have had enough adventure to last me three lifetimes, Adam! Why, when it is finally as I want it, does it have to change?"

"Because the years have flown, little girl, and they are grown, or half grown. They are their mother's offspring, for they wish to strike out on their own, and why shouldn't they? I know that it is hard for a mother to admit that her sons are grown, but your O'Flahertys have become men, my darling." He chuckled. "If you had eyes in your head, Skye, you'd see at least three of their bastards on this estate. High time that they were married, I say!"

"But Willow . . ."

"Skye, all of your children but Willow spring from the loins of noblemen. Willow may be a great heiress, but she hasn't a great name. She needs to go to court if she is to find a suitable husband."

"Willow's father was a Spanish nobleman," Skye said hotly.

"His family neither knows of her existence, nor would they recognize her as a legitimate offspring if they did. You and Khalid el Bey were married under Muslim law, and in the eyes of the Christian world that makes Willow a bastard. Your good name, your wealth, and your power, along with Robbie's generosity to Willow have, however, protected her from that stigma. Nonetheless she must make the proper contacts for a suitable marriage, and as the Earl of Lynmouth's sister, she will have the opportunity at court. Unless, of course, you propose a French marriage for her. My nephew, Jean-Antoine St. Justine, is seeking an heiress. He would be very good to her."

"And very French," Skye responded. "No, a Frenchman is not right for Willow. She is an Englishwoman to her toes, and she needs an English husband."

"Then let her go to the Tudor court, Skye."

"How strange this all is," she said. "We are not welcome there, but the Queen personally invites our children. I wonder at it, Adam."

"You are too suspicious, little girl."

"It never hurts to be too suspicious when dealing with the Tudors, *mon mari*," Skye warned him.

"Perhaps this is the Queen's way of making friendly overtures and eventually forgiving us."

"Why should she even be reminded of us?" Skye mused.

"Robin is with her," Adam reasoned, "and then, too, this business of a French marriage for her, and we are in France. It is logical."

"It is odd," she answered him. Then she sat up and pulled away from him. "Let us go tell the children that they may go before I am accused of breaking their hearts; or worse, before I change my mind."

Skye's two eldest sons, Ewan and Murrough O'Flaherty were married to Geoffrey Southwood's twin daughters on July 26th. Although the girls were not identical twins they chose to wear identical ice-blue satin gowns embroidered in silver thread and clear crystals. Their lovely hair was unbound and fell to their hips, and atop their heads they wore wreaths of white roses and fluffy baby's breath. The young Earl of Lynmouth proudly gave his half-sisters away in the church at Archambault, where the wedding was held. It was not a large wedding, the only guests being the family of the comte and comtesse along with Skye and Adam's family. Tables were spread out over the lawns for the feasting afterward, and following the dancing the young couples were put to bed with much teasing and hilarity. On the next morning two bloody sheets hung from the two nuptial chambers at the château, waving in the summer breeze as the two couples, accompanied by their brother, Robin, and their sister, Willow, rode off to Nantes to embark upon an O'Malley ship for Bideford, and Ireland.

Willow was torn between the wild excitement she felt over returning to England and joining the court, and leaving the security and love of her mother and stepfather. Skye hadn't stop lecturing her eldest daughter since the decision had been made to allow Willow to go.

"You must beware of the young men at court. Believe me, they will seek your virtue, and that virtue along with your fortune are the only assets you possess to obtain a titled husband."

"Yes, Mama."

"What you did in Paris last winter was very good, my darling. Never be alone with a young man lest you compromise your good name. Gossip can be such a vicious thing, Willow, and even if it is not true it raises an element of doubt."

"Yes, Mama."

"The Queen prefers her maidens to be virtuous, remember that."

"Yes, Mama."

"Do not lend money to anyone. People will quickly know that you are an heiress, and they will come begging. You cannot afford to lend to anyone lest you offend someone else. Say that you have a small allowance, and that barely enough to last until the next quarter. Dame Cecily will be in charge of your funds, Willow, and she will advance you nothing before you should have it, so be advised you must live within your income. I am sending you with more than enough clothes so what you will need monies for I know not. Still I would not have you penniless."

"Yes, Mama." Willow stifled a yawn. Her mother was being so tedious. She had said these things a hundred times over the last few weeks.

"You will listen to your brother."

"Robin? He's three years younger than I am!" Willow looked outraged.

"Nonetheless he has spent a good deal of his life at the Tudor court. He knows its ways, and he knows the gossip. Pay heed to him, Willow, for he would not have you shamed."

"Yes, Mama."

"A final word about men, Willow."

"Oh, Mama!"

"Do not *Oh, Mama!* me, miss! In this I have experience, and you would do well to listen to me. Men can be utterly charming creatures when they seek to gain their own way with a girl. When you are tempted to listen to some young gallant, Willow, ask yourself, If I give in to his pretty pleas will he still marry me? Is he in a position to marry me? If he is, why is he assaulting my virtue prior to our wedding night? Does he not respect the delicacies of my feelings enough to wait? You will find, Willow, that a decent young man will approach you through your brother, or Sir Robert, or the Queen. You do not have to settle for a relationship of stolen kisses in a dark corner."

"What makes you think that I would, Mama?" Willow demanded.

"You are ever a practical little puss, my darling," Skye said, "but you lack experience. I only seek to share my experience with you so you will not be hurt."

Willow flung herself at Skye, and hugged her hard. "Oh, Mama! I shall make you so proud of me, I promise you! I shall only have the most noble of husbands, and I shall make the Queen relent and allow you and Adam to come home."

Skye smiled through her tears, and kissed her daughter tenderly. "I am going to miss you," she said. "Oh, how I am going to miss you!"

"Let us be off!" the Earl of Lynmouth fussed impatiently. "She has either learned her lessons, Mother, or she has not. Willow has always been bright, and I do not expect her to be an embarrassment to us."

Skye next advised her eldest son to attempt to remain neutral in the continuing fight between the English and the Irish.

"It won't be easy," she said, "but try to consider the long run. You have a wife now, and soon there will be children, Ewan. All you have to offer them is Ballyhennessey, and it's been O'Flaherty land for over three hundred years. Don't be driven by the hotheads or the Church into losing your heritage, my son."

"It will come down to religion in the end, Mother."

"I know that, Ewan, but ask yourself this. What difference does it make *how* you worship God as long as you worship Him? Ask yourself why you should endanger your lands and your family because an Italian pope and an English monarch cannot decide, and argue over dogma?"

"Is that why you never took sides, Mother?"

"Your grandfather, Dubhdara O'Malley, of sainted memory, God assoil him, taught me that the family came first, Ewan. It has ever been thus with me. I have not had as much of a hand in raising you as I would have wanted, but you are my son. You will do what you believe best, and you will follow your conscience. I do not envy you, Ewan. Ireland is a torn and angry land." She held out her arms to him, and walking into them, he hugged her. "God speed, my eldest," Skye said.

The others came then for their hugs and kisses while his young and impatient lordship, the earl, stood tapping an elegantly shod foot. He had said his good-byes privately, as Robin believed befit his dignity. Finally the others were ready, and the three young women climbed into the coach. The men were to ride. Leaning from the windows of the vehicle as it pulled away, they waved happily to Skye and Adam. Behind them came a second, larger coach containing the tiring women, the valets, and the luggage. The household goods that the newly married young women would need had gone on to Nantes several days earlier.

When the travelers had disappeared from view around the bend in the drive Adam heaved a mighty sigh. "Let's go home, little girl!" he said, and he helped her into the smaller waiting carriage.

Skye climbed into the vehicle feeling terribly depressed. Her elder children were gone, and her three youngest would be staying at Archambault for several days visiting their cousins. She sighed deeply as the carriage moved down the drive and onto the forest road back to Belle Fleur. "I am old," she announced in a sad voice.

Adam looked at his wife's beautiful woebegone face, and began to chuckle. "Have I domesticated you so, sweetheart, that you are that lost without your brood of chicks?"

"Don't you understand?" she said. "My two eldest sons are married. After last night their wives could already be with child. My eldest daughter is off to court to seek a husband. I could be a grandmother in a year! I am old!"

He began to laugh, and pulling her into his arms, he slipped a hand into her dress to capture a plump breast. "Madame," he said as he began to tease at her nipple, "you are a woman of maturity, I will grant you, but you've not yet attained your thirty-fourth birthday, Skye." His fingers skillfully undid the laces on her bodice, successfully freeing both her breasts. "God, they're beautiful!" he groaned, burying his face in the valley separating them and covering her suddenly trembling flesh with hot kisses.

Skye felt herself begin to grow tingly with the pleasure he was arousing in her. Her slender hand entangled itself in his thick black hair, and began to slip softly down to the back of his neck to rub against the soft flesh. "If you think to turn my interest, monseigneur," she murmured with faint protest, and then as his other hand slipped beneath her skirts and moved upward, she cried out, "Adam! Oh, my darling!"

"What a shameless hussy you are, old woman," he teased her.

"I am not old!" she said suddenly, realizing how foolish she must have sounded, and also realizing that she didn't feel one bit older now than she had at twenty. Feeling better, she mischievously moved her hand to caress him, and felt her heart quicken at the hard, hungry length of him. "I shall never be old as long as I can do that to you, my darling," she whispered in his ear as she loosened his garments and released him.

Roughly Adam pulled her onto his lap, raising her skirts to position her on his mighty lance. With a gasp of delight she found he had taken the most complete possession of her. Her legs were over his thighs, her feet pushing into the velvet upholstery of the carriage seat. His arms were tightly about her as hers were about him, and he was suddenly kissing her ardently, his tongue fencing with hers while they rocked back and forth with the motion of the coach.

The sensation was one of complete rapture, and Skye cried out softly to her husband as the delicious warmth and excitement of his lovemaking began to fan a flame of incredible passion within her dazzled and stimulated body. "Ohhh, Aaadam," she breathed as the first small wave of pleasure swept over her, and then, "Oh! Oh! Oh!" as the full impact of the delight rendered her weak and satisfied, and she fell against his chest panting.

His breathing was ragged in her ear, but she was too weak to move for the minute. Finally, as the wild beating of their hearts calmed, he said softly, "Haven't you ever made love in a coach before, little girl?"

"No, though once Geoffrey mentioned it as we came down from London. In the end, however, he decided it was far more comfortable to do so in a bed," she laughed softly, remembering.

"Yes," Adam considered, "Geoff was always one for his comforts, as I recall. Tell me, madame, are you still feeling ancient and haggard?"

"I feel marvelous!" she enthused.

"How quickly do you think you can make yourself presentable?" he queried.

"Why?" She snuggled against him.

"Because, little girl, Belle Fleur is in sight, and I should hate to shock the footman who will open this coach door in a few moments."

With his amused aid she quickly scrambled off him, and began relacing her bodice, smoothing her skirts and her hair. "You had best see to your own dishabille, monseigneur," she teased him as his smoky eyes fastened upon her bosom.

"How long are the children gone for, little girl?"

"A fortnight," she answered.

"Good," he said. "I intend to spend all of that time with you, my love, and most of it in our bed. It has been a long time, it seems to me, since we were alone and free to be lovers."

"Can we not ride, and picnic in the forest?" she teased him.

"Only if you allow me to make love to you beneath the stately oaks."

Her face softened, and she whispered, "Yes, oh yes, *mon mari!*" just as their carriage clattered over the drawbridge and into the courtyard of the château.

Adam de Marisco was a man of his word, and so for the next two weeks he and Skye spent almost every waking and sleeping moment together. It seemed to them both that they were more deeply and powerfully in love than they had ever been. When the three youngest children returned Adam took it upon himself to begin to instruct young Padraic in the business of running an estate, while Deirdre began to follow after her mother, learning all that was necessary to the running of a household.

Of all her children, Skye noted, Deirdre was the quietest. She seemed to learn with ease whatever she was taught, be it the proper way to make soap and perfume, or her Latin. She was a pretty child who looked very much like her mother, but Skye could only assume Deirdre's shyness came from all the time she had spent away from her mother in her early years. Now Skye worked very hard to make up those years to her daughter. Still, it was to Adam that Deirdre always went with her successes and her problems.

"I don't think she likes me," Skye said to Adam one day.

"She is in awe of you," he said, "and she fears you a little, but I believe she loves you."

"She loves me because I am her mother," Skye replied with keen insight, "but she does not like me. I don't understand why. I have tried so hard with her."

"If you feel that way then why don't you ask her, sweetheart. Best to get it out in the open rather than let whatever is disturbing her fester until it is blown so out of proportion that it cannot be controlled."

"I will if you will be with me when I do."

"No. If we stand together while you attempt to interrogate Deirdre she will feel we are allied against her, and she will say nothing, and deny all. This must remain between you two."

It was not easy, but Skye finally screwed up her courage one afternoon in late summer as she and Deirdre sat on the lakeside making daisy chains. "Why is it you dislike me, Deirdre?" she asked bluntly.

For a moment Deirdre Burke looked startled, and she slowly flushed a beet-red. Then as bluntly as her mother had spoken, she replied, "Because you left Padraic and me when you went off to your new marriage. Because when you finally brought us to you, you sent us quickly away, again promising to bring our real father back to us. You never did, Mama. Before you married Adam we had not a happy life, and I cannot help but wonder how long it will be before you run off from us again with some excuse or another."

Skye was shocked by the venom in her small daughter's voice. "Does your brother feel this way, too?" she asked.

"Padraic says you love us. It seems to be enough for him."

"But not for you, my daughter, I can see. Your brother is right, you know. I do love you. It never, however, occurred to me to explain to a baby the difficulties of my life, Deirdre. If you had asked me when these things began to fret you, I would have told you anything I felt you needed to know."

Skye took her daughter's resisting and stiff little form into her arms. "Deirdre," she said, looking down into the child's cold and closed face, "I love you. You are a child born of love, the love that Niall Burke and I had for each other. I will try not to ever go from you again, although there will come a day when you go from me to marry."

"You say you will *try* not to go from me, but you must *promise* me you will not go!"

"Deirdre, I cannot," Skye said. "I have never lied to you, and I will not lie now, even to gain your approval. I will try!"

Suddenly Deirdre burst into tears, her whole small face crumbling with her distress. "Don't leave me, Mama! Don't leave me!" she begged her mother between sobs.

Wordlessly Skye took her daughter onto her lap and rocked her soothingly. All the others had survived her travels, but despite her stiff little spine, Deirdre was a creature easily bruised by life. In a way, Skye thought, she is much like Niall, despite the fact she looks like me. "I have no plans to go anywhere, Deirdre," she said quietly. "Do not weep, my baby. I'll not leave you, my precious one."

On Michaelmas the servants were paid for the year, but the nursemaid who had tended Velvet since her birth found herself with child by a footman, and was quickly married. A new girl, a plump, cheerful lass from Archambault village, was found to replace the first nursemaid, and Velvet seemed to take to the change well. But less than a week after the girl had been hired, both she and the baby disappeared, and could not be found.

Both Skye and Adam were frantic, afraid that the girl and her charge had fallen into the moat, but they quickly discarded that thought, for the château gatekeeper had seen Margerie and the baby walking across the drawbridge and down the forest road. A search was quickly made for fear that a wild animal had attacked the pair, but no trace of them was found. The search expanded to Archambault and its village in the hopes that Margerie had simply taken Velvet on a visit without requesting permission, but the girl's family had not seen her. Her best friend in the village, however, came forward timidly to say that Margerie had told her that she would soon have enough gold for a fine dowry, and it would not come from drudging at Belle Fleur.

Comte Antoine could see that his big stepson was close to the breaking point, and very desirous of shaking the informant until her teeth rattled. Taking the girl by the hand, he gently said, "Jeanne, *ma petite*, try and remember exactly what Margerie said to you. Did she mention where she would get the gold for her dowry?"

The peasant girl scrunched her brow in thought, and then suddenly she grinned. "But of course, M'sieur le Comte! Margerie said she met a man—though he spoke our language, she said she could tell he was a foreigner, for his accent was something terrible. He told her that he had heard that the petite Velvet was the most beautiful child in Christendom, and if Margerie would bring the baby to him to see with his own eyes he would give her six gold ecus!" Jeanne finished triumphantly.

"Where was Margerie to bring the baby?" the comte probed further.

"To some inn at Tours," was the reply.

"Did Margerie tell you the name of the inn, Jeanne?"

"No, M'sieur le Comte, but Gilleet the carter would know. 'Twas he who gave her a ride yesterday."

"Find the carter!" the comte ordered. "You're a good girl, Jeanne," he said, and then he dropped several pieces of silver down her bodice.

The carter, who had only just returned, was quickly brought before the comte, and readily admitted having given Margerie a ride from Archambault to the nearby city of Tours. Yes, she had a little girl with her, her sister's child for company, she said. He let her off at an inn, Le Coq D'Or on the west side of the town. Adam, the comte, and his two sons immediately rode for Tours. When they returned several hours later to Belle Fleur, Adam carried with him a heavy sealed parchment addressed to Skye. With grim face he handed it to her.

Skye broke the seal and tore the letter open. For a moment she could not breathe and her vision blurred at the sight of the familiar hand. The message was brief.

Madam, it began. *I have need of your services. Come immediately.* It was signed *Elizabeth R*.

"Where did you get this?" Skye demanded of her husband.

"It was awaiting me on my arrival at Le Coq D'Or in Tours. It had been left by two gentlemen who arrived alone, and departed with a nursemaid and a child. The innkeeper said they took the Nantes road, and they left the parchment for whoever came looking for a woman and a child."

"Do you know who has our child?" Skye handed Adam the parchment. "That damned Tudor bitch has Velvet! She has kidnaped our baby for God only knows what purpose, but you may rest assured, *mon mari*, that that purpose will be to Elizabeth Tudor's liking alone! Dear God, I had thought to be quit of the Tudors, and all their ilk!"

"I will go to England," Adam said.

"*We* will go to England," Skye amended. "She doesn't want you, my darling, she wants me; but this time, by God, I'll not be cowed by that bitch! She holds Velvet hostage in return for my aid, but before she's through we'll have lands for ourself, Adam de Marisco, and Lundy back, and my Burke son will be given back what belongs to him! The Queen will accept with good grace that we are truly and lawfully married, and there will be no more talk of Velvet not being legitimate!"

"Skye!" Adam's voice held a warning. "It is my daughter's life she holds in her hands. Do not trifle with Velvet's survival!"

"It is *our* daughter, Adam, and believe me, I would not allow any harm to come to Velvet. Listen, my darling, the Tudor Queen quite obviously desperately needs my help. Needs it enough to try to insure that I will be forced to give it. That is why she took Velvet. She knows that I will come after her; but Elizabeth Tudor is no murderer of innocents. She will not harm a hair on Velvet's head, Adam; but I shall bargain hard this time! We leave tonight!"

"I knew that you would leave me sooner or later!" Deirdre cried, entering the room and hearing only Skye's last words.

"Leave you? No, *ma fille*, you and your brother are coming with us! We will stand before England's Queen a family united, Deirdre!"

"I don't know if you are magnificent or a madwoman," Adam said as he put his arms about both his wife and his stepdaughter.

"Probably a little of both, my darling, for I don't even know what the Queen wants. Perhaps I go to do battle for naught."

"No, Skye, this time you will not do battle against the Queen alone. This time your lord will stand by your side. The Queen has never had to face that. Whenever you have been vulnerable you have been alone. This time you are not alone, little girl."

They left Belle Fleur that night, and it was with great sadness Skye left their home behind. The château would not, however, be closed, and the comte would watch over it for his stepson. While Deirdre and young Lord Burke dozed in the traveling coach their parents rode knee to knee through the early autumn night. A bright moon lit the coast road, silvering the villages and the vineyards and the small stands of oak forests. It took them two days of traveling at top speed to reach Nantes, where an O'Malley ship awaited them, for Skye had several of her vessels based in this French port to import wine to England and northern Europe from the Loire Valley's famous vineyards.

Even with a good wind it was several days' sail from Nantes to England. The weather was good as they edged around the Bay of Biscay, staying within sight of the French coast. Just past Brest they swung around into the English Channel to meet with a spanking sharp breeze from the south that pushed them across the water with greater rapidity than they had anticipated. Again they kept within sight of land, and Skye pointed out to her children the various landmarks as they went. They passed the Isle of Wight, and the great chalk cliffs of Dover, and at Margate Head moved into the Thames, sweeping up the river with the tide to the Pool of London. Skye stood silently with Adam at the rail of her ship as they anchored. On the shore beyond they saw a small party of the Queen's guards.

"My God," Adam said, "is she expecting us, then?"

"She's expecting us," Skye said with a smile of satisfaction.

"You have on your battle smile," he chuckled. "I haven't seen that look on your face since . . ." He thought. "I can't remember when, for it's been that long."

"The last time I smiled like this was probably the last time the Queen and I did battle. Once before I beat Elizabeth Tudor, Adam, and I will defeat her again. Pray God that this time will be the last time."

Part v

England
and Ireland

Chapter 17

"You play a dangerous game, madam," William Cecil warned.

"Nay, Cecil," Elizabeth Tudor replied, "'tis no game I play at all."

"You might simply have forgiven Lord and Lady de Marisco their marriage, and then asked for their help. Stealing their child is only bound to bring out the tigress in Lady de Marisco, and you do remember the last time you incurred that lady's ire, madam, don't you?"

"It was never proven to our satisfaction that Skye O'Malley was behind those piracies, Cecil!"

"Hah!" the Queen's advisor snorted, and then clamping his lips shut he said nothing more. There was no arguing with Elizabeth Tudor once she had her mind made up, and in this instance he wasn't sure she was not right. It was really very unlikely that Skye O'Malley would willingly help the English Crown against her own marauding family. They would need a strong hold over her, and what was stronger than the bond of mother love?

"The child is all right, Cecil. She is at Hampton Court with her nursemaid, and a proper little tartar she is, I am told." The Queen chuckled. "I saw her the night that she was brought from France. She is de Marisco's image, and I doubt not he loves her dearly. 'Tis another good card I have to play, Cecil! The child is doted upon by both her parents."

Cecil shook his head. "The *Seagull* was sighted off Margate Head this afternoon. I've dispatched some of your Gentlemen Pensioners to escort them here to Greenwich."

"You are too diligent, my old friend," the Queen chided him. "There is no need to bring them to me, for they will come of their own free will. We will say my gentlemen are a guard of honor." She laughed drily. "Skye O'Malley will appreciate that, Cecil! She has wit, that damned woman! She has great wit!"

While the Queen enjoyed her little joke Sir Christopher Hatton, captain of the Gentlemen Pensioners, found himself on shipboard facing a woman he knew by reputation alone. It was a confusing reputation, for Elizabeth Tudor admired this woman and spoke of her with great respect while at the same time Robert Dudley, Earl of Leicester, claimed that the lady in question was a passionate drab who could not get enough of his loving. Hatton was inclined to dismiss Leicester's boasting, for the Queen would hardly like any female or accept her at court if she was openly out to snare the earl.

"My lord?" Skye looked questioningly at Hatton.

"I am Sir Christopher Hatton, madam, the Queen's captain. I am here to escort you to Greenwich."

"And by what means, Sir Christopher, are you to escort me? I see no coach, nor do I see horses. Am I to walk, perhaps, behind your horse like a Roman captive?"

Hatton shifted uncomfortably, realizing he had forgotten to provide transport.

Skye laughed easily. "Do not fret, Sir Christopher. I have full intention of hieing myself to Greenwich as quickly as possible, but I have only just arrived after a hectic voyage. I am going to my house on the Strand to bathe and change my clothes before I see Her Majesty. I will not present myself before the Queen until then, unless, of course, you have orders to drag me before Her Majesty immediately."

He had no such orders, and Hatton was totally nonplussed by this beautiful woman who seemed so in command of the situation. "Of course, Lady Burke . . ."

"Lady de Marisco, my lord."

"I was given to understand that you were the widow of Lord Niall Burke, madam." Sir Christopher was further confused.

"Indeed, sir, and I am, but Lord Burke died some time back, and I remarried. Lord de Marisco is my husband, and has been for two and a half years now." Skye smiled sweetly. "Would you care to come with us to Greenwood, my lord? If the Queen has ordered you to bring us to her you had best not appear back before her without us. I will be happy to send a message to your men on shore."

The door to the main cabin opened, and Adam came in. "The barge is here, sweetheart."

"Well, Sir Christopher? Are you coming with us?"

"I can as easily ride, madame, if you will but tell me where Greenwood is located."

"It is on the river, next to the Earl of Lynmouth's house."

"I will meet you there," Sir Christopher said, and then he beat a hasty retreat.

Adam waited until he was sure the captain had gotten off the ship, and then he chuckled. "You've frightened him to death, Skye. Not an easy task under normal circumstances, I would imagine."

"I see that though the Queen still enjoys the virgin state her taste in handsome young men has not changed," Skye muttered.

"The rumor is that he dances divinely," Adam guffawed.

"Perhaps," Skye said, "but there is a good mind, I'll wager, behind those beautiful eyes of his. Bess Tudor does not suffer fools within her inner circle." With an impatient gesture she picked up her cloak. "Let us go, Adam. Even though I know that our Velvet is safe, I want to know what this is all about. Where are the children?"

"Gone on ahead in the first barge," he answered her, slipping the cape over her shoulders. Bending, he held her a moment against him, and kissed her gently on the cheek. "Don't worry, sweetheart. We'll soon have our little one back."

The Greenwood barge took them swiftly up the river to Skye's London town house. Mignon had been left behind in France with Guillaume, for they were too old to travel to England, and belonged at Archambault, where both had been born and spent their whole lives. I shall have to train a new tiring woman, Skye thought irritably as they arrived at the landing, but who was that coming down the lawn wildly waving?

"M'lady! M'lady! Oh, dear Mistress Skye, welcome home!"

Skye stopped, and her eyes teared briefly as Daisy came running up to her. For a moment the two women stared at each other, and then they were hugging frantically. "What on earth are you doing here, Daisy?" she exclaimed.

They broke apart, and Daisy explained, "When Dame Cecily told me that you were coming home I knew you would need me, m'lady. Old Mistress Kelly, Bran's mum, came to live with us over a year ago when her man died and the English landlord took her cottage. My babes have given her a new lease on life. 'Twas she who insisted I come up to London. The youngest baby's weaned, and don't need me anymore. Come along now, for you've been at sea several days and I know you'll want your bath." She turned her gap-toothed smile on Adam. "I've brought with me that pirate, Kipp, who always served you on Lundy, m'lord. They took everyone off the island, y'know."

"Good Lord," Adam exclaimed, "I didn't think they'd touch my people. What happened to them, Daisy?"

"The bailiff at Lynmouth made room, m'lord."

They had gained the house now, and as they climbed the stairs Skye said, "I'll have to hurry a bit, Daisy, for the Queen is expecting me even now."

"Ah," Daisy smiled, "I knew you'd be back in her favor quick enough."

Entering her apartments, Skye said grimly, "I'm not in the Queen's good graces at all, Daisy, and I'd not be in England except that she stole our daughter. Oh, Daisy, wait until you see Velvet de Marisco! She is the most perfect little girl!"

"But why would she steal your child, m'lady?" Daisy began to undress her mistress.

"She seems to want my help in some matter, Daisy, and felt I would not give it to her unless she had some sort of strong hold over me. She will not recognize my marriage to Lord de Marisco because we did not ask her permission, but it has mattered not to us. We have a beautiful home, Belle Fleur, in France. I did not think the Queen could touch us."

Daisy frowned. "I wonder," she mused aloud.

"What do you wonder?" Skye replied, climbing into the perfumed tub and settling down into the water.

"I'm wondering if it's about your brothers."

"Tell me what you know, Daisy."

"They're wild, m'lady, every one of them. I've heard Bran say it a dozen times a day. When you ran your family the O'Malleys prospered, and kept the peace; but your brothers have almost run through everything you built up for them, and they harry the English each chance they get. They deliberately bait them, m'lady, and taunt them something fierce, and you know the difficulties in Ireland are bad enough without that. Their mother, the lady Anne, has tried to control them, but she hasn't the strength. They laugh at her advice, and then gift her with things they've stolen from their raids and tell her not to worry, but she does fret and she'll not keep a thing they give her. Still, there is naught that she can do about them. They are too strong for her."

Skye nodded with understanding. Her brothers were proud and stubborn Irishmen with hot heads and no sense. She had left their raising to their mother, for it was indeed Anne's responsibility after Dubhdara O'Malley died, but Anne O'Malley was a gentle woman with a kind heart who had no real strength of her own.

"What have the O'Malleys been doing to irritate the Queen, Daisy? It can't simply be that my fool half-brothers have reverted to the piracies of my father."

"Bran says they've joined with your kinswoman, Grace O'Malley, to fight the English," came the reply.

"Fools!" Skye muttered.

"She's a fascinating woman, Bran says."

"She is indeed," Skye said. "She's from the nobler and more powerful branch of my family, the O'Malleys of Clare Island. She's even married to a Burke, as I was. Her husband is a distant cousin of Niall's. She's a dangerous woman, though, Daisy. She believes herself a patriot. She's fought the English since her youth, and I've no doubt she'll fight them right to the moment of her death. In one sense I admire her courage and her determination; but I have a cooler head than Grace, and she cannot win over England no matter the right of her cause. She does not see this, however, and if she were only responsible for her own life I should not argue how she live it; but she drags others into her schemes. If Elizabeth Tudor wants my aid in preventing my brothers from joining with Grace O'Malley then she shall have it, Daisy. I will not allow them to destroy everything I have worked and sacrificed for since our father, may God assoil him, left the responsibility of the O'Malleys of Innisfana to me!"

Daisy said nothing, but she saw the gleam of battle in her mistress's eyes. With a hidden smile she washed Skye's hair, thinking that it was good to be back here with her lady. She loved her bairns, but wiping their runny noses and wet bottoms was dull stuff compared to serving Skye O'Malley.

There was a knock at the door, and a housemaid appeared to say, "Sir Christopher Hatton awaits you, m'lady."

"Tell Sir Christopher that I am in my bath," Skye said mischievously, "and that I shall attend him eventually. Then see that he and his men have plenty of wine, beef, and bread."

"Yes, m'lady!" The housemaid bobbed a curtsey, and was gone.

"It will be at least two hours before you're ready," Daisy said.

"I make it closer to three," Skye said calmly, and the tiring woman giggled.

"You'll want to eat while your hair is drying."

"Aye, but sparingly. Enough to take the edge off my appetite so that my stomach doesn't grumble while I'm with the Queen, but not enough to spoil my appetite should we be asked to stay for the evening meal."

"Bread, cheese, and some good Devon cider, m'lady?"

"Aye, and a bit of ham too, Daisy. Bring enough for two, for my lord will be hungry also."

Daisy helped Skye from the tub, and carefully and thoroughly dried her mistress off before wrapping her in a long quilted velvet gown to ward off the chill of the autumn afternoon. Next she toweled all the water from Skye's hair, and settled her mistress by the fireplace to brush her own locks dry while she hurried downstairs to the kitchens to fetch the food. When Adam came through the connecting door between their rooms, Skye never even looked up as she continued brushing her hair by the fire.

"You're glad to be back in England, aren't you," she said, hearing his soft, happy humming.

"Aye, sweetheart," he admitted, coming to sit across from her. He loved watching her do simple feminine things.

"I've sent Daisy for food. Hatton and his men already wait below, but I'll not come down until I'm clean and fed. If I have to deal with the Queen I'd best do it from a position of strength. Daisy thinks it's my brothers. The four of them have managed to run through the wealth I spent years building up for the O'Malleys, and now they've joined forces with my hotheaded kinswoman, Grace O'Malley, to harry the English."

"They've not their older sister's wisdom," he said quietly.

"Ah, Adam," she answered, "I would have the English out of Ireland too, but I know that it will take more than the O'Malleys to do it. That is the problem with the Irish. They cannot unite, and as long as they can't, the English will hold Ireland whether the Irish desire it or not. It is our weakness, my love, for Ireland is a land where every man is a king. I am not the stuff of which martyrs or heroines are made, and I'll not sacrifice everything I've fought for and built up for that elusive will-o'-the-wisp called Irish independence. Even if they got it there's not one man they could all agree on to make king. Right now the Irish aren't even serious in what they do. 'Tis the fighting they enjoy. No matter the widows and orphans they make. No matter the misery they cause, the famine, the children dying from lack of decent shelter. All that counts for naught in the face of glorious battle with those who sporadically lead the rebellions. They switch sides with the regularity of a whore entertaining her customers; each of them always seeking a better position over his neighbor, and joining with his neighbor's enemies if he can't maintain his own superiority alone. 'Tis a wicked game, Adam, and I'll have none of it!"

"But if you openly join with the English, Skye, your own people will consider you a traitor. They are too simple to understand the complexities of the situation. Do you understand that, sweetheart?"

"I have no intention of joining the English, Adam. I am the O'Malley of Innisfana, no matter my half-brothers. They cannot take from me that which our father gave me. They must obey me or be outlawed among their own, and I do not believe that they have the stomach for being cast out by their own people. What I shall do will have nothing to do with politics, be they English or Irish. What I do I will do for the survival of my family, and that is all."

"Will you tell the Queen that?" he asked, amused.

Skye laughed softly. "Let Bess Tudor think what she will, for I shall not let her know that I intend to stop my brothers no matter what. If she thinks I do her a service, so much the better for us, Adam."

"You don't intend to be one bit repentant about us, do you?" Adam's dark eyebrows waggled with amusement.

"What difference should our marriage have made to her?" Skye demanded irritably. "Neither you nor I are of any importance to the English Crown dynastically. We have never been permanent members of the court. The only time I followed the court was when Geoffrey was alive. She may say whatever she will, but she has no excuse for denying our marriage or calling our daughter a bastard. We were married by a priest of the Holy Catholic Church, and though the Queen may deny the Church dominion in England before her own authority, she has never denied the right of the Mother Church in spiritual matters, no matter the Protestants and their clamor."

"What a pity," Adam said, "that you and Elizabeth Tudor cannot be friends. You have that sharpness of intellect that the Queen admires."

"She needs too much fawning upon, Adam, and I have not the patience. Neither have you, for that matter. Would you really enjoy spending your days dancing in constant attendance upon a very stubborn lady in her middle years? She would give us no time for ourselves, Adam, and I, for one, could not abide that." Skye gave her head a final touch, and putting the brush aside, she flung her hair back with a graceful motion. "There," she said, "'tis finished, and I hear Daisy coming. Open the door for her, my darling."

With pleased confusion and a rosy blush Daisy re-entered the bedchamber carrying a heavy tray of food. "Oh, m'lord! Thank you!"

"'Tis nothing, lass, and it is good to see your pretty face again," he answered the tiring woman gallantly.

Daisy flushed again with pleasure, and said, "I've brought cider for you, m'lady, but I knew his lordship would appreciate some good nut-brown English ale. 'Tis a while, I'll wager, since he's tasted it." She set the tray down on the table by the fireplace as they drew their chairs forward.

"Daisy, lass, you've the soul of an angel and the heart of a loyal Englishwoman!" Adam exclaimed. "My stepfather may bottle some of France's finest wines, but I far prefer honest English ale! Thank you, lass!" he said, and bending from his great height, he gave her a hearty buss on the cheek.

"Ohh, m'lord!" Daisy grew redder, and then she scolded, "Sit down, m'lord, and eat. The Queen will be in a fine, tearing temper as it is."

The tray that Daisy had brought them contained thick slices of bread upon which had been set slices of pink ham and wedges of good English Cheddar that had then been toasted. The cheese was yet soft and burning, and the meal delicious to their taste in its simplicity. When the last crumb had been eaten and the ale and cider all drunk, they sat back for a minute in their chairs, smiling across the small table at one another. Another knock at the door brought them the news that Sir Christopher and his men were growing restive.

"I suppose we must get dressed and attend the Queen," Skye said.

"I think so, little girl," Adam replied, rising from the table and walking across the room to the connecting door between their rooms. With a grin he blew her a kiss before re-entering his own quarters.

A delighted smile touched her lips, and then Skye rose with a lazy yawn. "Is the black sapphire gown still in fashion, Daisy?"

"Aye, m'lady. I'll fetch it immediately."

It took almost a full hour for Skye to dress completely, but when she had finished she was well pleased with the results. The blue velvet of the gown was so dark it seemed almost black in color. It had a low, squarish neckline trimmed with two loops of pearls that were sewn in such a fashion as to outline her bosom. From the sides of the neckline protruded a fan-shaped neckwisk of delicate gold lace, and the full gold beribboned sleeves had beautiful matching cuff ruffs of the same lace. The overgown was plain, the undergown of the same material and color, heavily decorated in pearls, gold beads, and golden threads that had been sewn in an intricate pattern of flowers, bees, and butterflies. The bodice was done more simply, being decorated only with pearls.

Skye's hair was gracefully fixed by Daisy into its elegant chignon, and dressed with loops of almost pinkish pearls. She wore a strand of matching pearls about her neck, from which bobbed one enormous sapphire teardrop that nestled between her full breasts. There were pearls in her ears, and even her dainty handkerchief was edged in the jewels. The buckles on her velvet shoes were carved from mother of pearl, and her heels had been covered in the iridescent shell.

With a smile Skye pirouetted for her husband as he entered the bedchamber. "What think you, m'lord? Am I formidable enough to discomfit the Queen?"

"Aye, little girl, and make her jealous as well." He struck a pose. "And what of me, madam? Do you approve my costume. Am I fit to be by your side?"

"Aye, m'lord!" she said with heartfelt admiration, taking in his black velvet costume, the doublet of which was outrageously and heavily decorated in diamonds and gold thread. About his neck Adam had chosen to wear the de Marisco pendant, a large, round golden medallion with a raised sea hawk, wings spread, done in enameled colors with a ruby eye. Between his great size, and the complete fashion of his costume he was really quite magnificent.

"Are you ready, madam?" he demanded, noting with some amusement that despite the richness of her jewels, she had chosen to wear upon her hands only his betrothal and wedding rings. Her subtlety delighted him, and he knew the Queen would notice, for Elizabeth Tudor rarely missed a thing.

As he watched them descend the staircase to the main floor of the house, Sir Christopher Hatton caught his breath. They were a simply stunning pair, and the Queen's captain could not help but wonder why they had never been to court in his time. He caught Skye's hand as she reached the bottom step, and raising it to his lips, he said with total honesty, "Madam, you are more than well worth the waiting for, if, my lord de Marisco, you will allow me the compliment to your wife."

"We accept the compliment in the spirit in which it was given, sir," Adam said softly.

The footmen hurried up with their capes, and Skye and Adam were enveloped in the fur-lined cloaks, Skye's with a fur-trimmed hood. Escorted by Hatton, they hurried outside into the crisp wind of the late afternoon and climbed into their waiting town coach. Immediately the door was shut upon them, they were off, their carriage surrounded and escorted on the road to Greenwich by the Queen's own Gentlemen Pensioners.

"Where in Hell is she?" Elizabeth Tudor swore for the hundredth time that afternoon. "Her damned ship anchored hours ago! Where is Hatton? This is intolerable, Cecil!"

"Patience, madam," counseled William Cecil, Lord Burghley. "She will be here shortly." He already knew that Skye O'Malley, that marvelous and impossible woman, had gone to her house on the Strand. He knew exactly what she was doing, but in this particular instance he had no intention of informing his mistress, for Elizabeth would only fly into a temper, and her anger could ruin everything. Lady de Marisco was as stubborn as the Queen. Cecil smiled to himself. He had thought of Skye O'Malley as Lady de

Marisco, and indeed, despite the Queen's petulance in the matter, she was. That, he knew, would be the first order of business between them. Cecil smiled to himself again, and a small chuckle escaped his lips. It was going to be an interesting evening.

"What do you find so amusing?" Elizabeth snapped, but before Lord Burghley was forced to answer there was a knock upon the door and a maid of honor popped through it to announce, "Lord and Lady de Marisco are here, madam."

Elizabeth whirled. "Surely, Mistress Ann, you mean Lady Burke and Lord de Marisco," the Queen snarled.

"Y-yes, madam, your pardon," the maid of honor quavered. She was going to be in a great deal of trouble if the Queen found out about her liaison with Lord Dudley, and Lettice Knollys, the bitch, had seen them and was threatening to tell.

"They may come in," Elizabeth said regally, and quickly sat down in a high-backed, thronelike chair. As quickly she stood again, remembering the height of her guests and not wanting to be at any disadvantage.

Cecil, knowing her thought, hid a smile behind his hand as Skye and Adam swept into the room. By God, Lord Burghley thought at his first sight of them, this time she has truly found her mate! We'll not beat her now.

Skye's gaze met that of Elizabeth Tudor, and neither of them wavered. Then Skye curtseyed low and prettily as, by her side, her husband bowed with incredibly elegant flair; a flair not missed by the Queen, who appreciated such graces and good manner.

"I have said more than once, Lord de Marisco, that you were wasted upon that island of yours. You are indeed a man fit for my court."

Adam smiled warmly. "Thank you, madam, but if I had my choice I should prefer my rock to your court. I am a simple man, and such radiance is too overpowering for me. I far prefer the quiet life."

"But your choice of companion, sir, is indeed not conducive to peace and a quiet life." The Queen looked defiantly at Skye.

"As I have said, madam, I am a simple man. Simple men follow their hearts, and I have followed mine, as I know you would follow yours were the burden of England not upon your frail shoulders. How fortunate your people are in their Queen."

"And are you, Lord de Marisco, fortunate in your Queen?"

"You have my loyalty, madam, until death."

"But not your heart?"

"No, madam, not my heart, for I cannot give what I no longer possess. I long ago gave my heart to Skye O'Malley."

"I could clap you in the Tower for that remark, Lord de Marisco. I could send you both there, but I suspect it would not make one bit of difference to either you or that Celtic jade you have married in France, in a Popish ceremony!"

A small grin teased at the corners of Adam's mouth, and he strove mightily to keep it from bursting into full bloom. "Madam, I must plead guilty, and I must beg your forgiveness and your indulgence for both my wife and myself; but in all honesty, neither Skye nor I would change anything we have done."

Elizabeth Tudor burst out laughing, and with surprising familiarity she gave Adam a friendly punch on the arm. "That, my lord, is what I like about you!" she exclaimed. "You are just what you seem, and there is no deceit in you! Very well, you are forgiven your marriage, for I am forced to admit that looking at the pair of you I can see you are meant to be together." She turned to Skye. "As for you, madam, we have other, more pressing business."

"First I want my daughter," Skye said bluntly.

"*What, madam?! You would bargain with me?*" Elizabeth looked outraged.

"Would you not bargain with me?" Skye demanded. "Why else have you taken my daughter?"

"The child is safe at Hampton Court, madam. She will be returned to you."

"When?"

The Queen looked at Skye closely, and then sighing, said, "I will send a messenger out tonight."

"Your word is not enough, madam," came the shocking reply.

Adam put a hand on his wife's arm in warning while Cecil thought for a moment his heart had stopped. It was a fierce insult, and Elizabeth Tudor's gray-black eyes narrowed in anger. At that moment she looked very much like her father.

"Madam, must I remind you that you are my subject, and I am your Queen?"

"You are the Queen of England, madam, but I am Irish. To protect my Burke son's lands I did you a favor, a great favor, madam. I left my homeland and my children to marry for England's sake. The husband you chose for me, madam, was a cruel and unhappy man, but I offered no complaint, for you promised me that you would protect Padraic Burke's lands and his rights. You have given those lands to an Englishman, madam. My son is bereft of his heritage despite your promise to me." Skye looked defiantly at Elizabeth Tudor. "I kept my word to you, madam. Would that you had done the same."

"You are a thorn in my flesh, Skye O'Malley," the Queen said, "and you have ever been thus; but I need your aid now, and I will have it!"

"Return what belongs to me and mine, madam, and you shall have that aid. I want my child, the Burke lands, and Lundy Island. In return I shall do your bidding."

"Your child I will send for this night. The Burke lands I cannot return for fear of offending a loyal Englishman who serves me well, but I will give your son lands here in England. As for Lundy, I return it with one stipulation. You may not live on it, either of you. I'll give you no island base from which to strike out at me again! I will, however, my lord de Marisco, give you lands and a manor house of equal value, for I suspect that in marrying this termagent you have actually done me a service."

"My son is an Irish Burke!" Skye cried, for despite the fact that she knew the Queen was being overly generous, she ached at the loss of Padraic's inheritance.

"Precisely, madam, and by resettling him here in England as a child I shall have one less rebel to contend with in my old age, for he will grow up to be a loyal Englishman I have no doubt!" Elizabeth Tudor laughed at the irony of her victory over Skye. "Now, madam, I have done much for you, you must in return do something for me."

"Give over, little girl," Adam said softly. "You'll not beat her in this. She's been generous where she might have been harsh." Skye looked up at him, and he saw the sadness in her eyes, which were wet with diamond tears she would not shed. "You cannot always win, Skye," he said, and she nodded. This time their battle was a draw.

"Very well, madam," she answered, but her very agreement was edged in defiance, "what can I do to help you?"

"Your brothers and the O'Malley fleet have joined with that great rebel, your kinswoman, Grace O'Malley, to wage war against me. They harry the shipping lanes, which hurts this nation's commerce, and they encourage rebellion in Ireland. It is impossible, madam, to stop them for they are, I am forced grudgingly to admit, marvelous sailors. I sent Drake to Ireland a year ago, and even he cannot catch them! You could. You could stop your brothers, madam, and if you do you will cripple Grace O'Malley. That woman is a menace to England, and I would have her stopped!"

Skye pretended to consider the Queen's request, and then she said, "If I can stop my brothers, madam, I will need pardons for them all. I will not betray my family even for England's Queen."

"Granted."

"Then I shall try, madam," Skye said with feigned innocence.

"You had best succeed, madam!" came the sharp warning.

"I can only do my best, madam."

"Then God help your brothers," the Queen cackled, her good humor suddenly restored. She peered closely at Skye. "You took your time in getting here, madam. I was told that your ship arrived at midmorning."

"I could not appear travel-worn before England's Majesty, madam. I went home and took a bath," came the calm reply.

"You kept me waiting while you frolicked in your bath?" Elizabeth was outraged.

"I should have done Your Majesty no honor had I not bathed and attired myself in my finest clothes, madam. I am not so ill bred as to arrive before you smelling of sweat and the sea."

"You claim to do me honor, madam, and yet I sense that you actually defy me," Elizabeth grumbled. "But enough! You will stay for the evening meal, and you will tell me about the Duc d'Alençon. He seeks to marry me, y'know."

"In France they speak of nothing else," Skye said demurely.

Elizabeth Tudor preened, and then with girlish enthusiasm asked, "What is he really like?"

"He is an amusing man, madam. I believe you would find him quite compatible."

"*Amusing?*"

"He has wit, Majesty, or at least as much wit as any son of Catherine de Medici could have."

"They say he is badly pock-marked."

"He grows a beard even now to disguise it, madam. He is an attractive man, and a great favorite with the ladies."

Cecil listened to Skye and marveled. One moment she gave to the Queen, and in the next instant she took away. The duke was charming, but he was his mother's son. He was pock-marked, but handsome. He longed to be with Elizabeth, but the ladies of the French court would be desolate when he left them. Cecil smiled. This woman was definitely the Queen's equal, but that was a thought he would keep to himself.

Leaving the Queen's closet, they adjourned to the dining hall where the court was awaiting the arrival of Elizabeth Tudor. The Queen had now transferred her attentions to Adam, and Skye was left to herself.

"As fair as ever," a displeasingly familiar voice murmured in her ear, and Robert Dudley, the Earl of Leicester, came around her into her view.

"As lecherous as ever, I've not a doubt," she returned, irritated as his eyes plunged boldly to fasten on her breasts. "You look as if you would eat me, my lord. Is there not meat enough at the Queen's board to satisfy you?"

"Only you could ever satisfy me, Skye."

"Only you, my lord, could ever revolt me so much with your want of delicacy."

"Ah, you Celtic bitch, as always your refusal of my passions ignites me with desire," he exclaimed, backing her against the wall. His arms pinioned her while his head dipped to press hot, wet kisses across the tops of her breasts.

Remembering a similar situation of several years earlier, Skye thought with a wicked little smile: *The fool never learns*, and then she brutally jammed her knee into the Earl of Leicester's groin. She was rewarded by instant release, and the silly, pained, surprised look upon his face. Calmly straightening her gown, Skye pushed past him, saying, "Dudley, I can't believe you don't remember our last encounter of this nature. I would also remind you that the last time you accosted me you were rather violently removed from my house by Lord de Marisco. He was only my friend then. Now he is my husband, and a most doting husband at that. I would that you think on it before you approach me again." Then with a polite mocking curtsey she moved from the shadows and up to the Queen's table, where a place had been made for her.

Robert Dudley swore, and then swore again as he heard low

laughter near his ear. "Hatton, say one word of what you saw, and I swear I shall run you through!" he hissed through gritted teeth.

Sir Christopher Hatton chuckled with pleased laughter. "I would not have believed it, my lord," he jibed at the earl. "Did you not tell me yourself that she was a passionate little drab, and quite hot for you? By God, Dudley, I should hate to see a woman who didn't like you!" Laughing merrily, he moved off, leaving the earl most discomfited.

After the meal there was dancing, and although Skye would have far preferred to leave Greenwich and return to her house, she could not depart until the Queen had left, and Elizabeth Tudor, it seemed, was full of energy, and as merry as May this night. She danced with verve, and more with Sir Christopher than any other man in the room. Remembering Adam's teasing remark about Hatton dancing divinely, Skye had to admit that he was the best dancer she had ever seen; and seeing Dudley sulking on the sidelines gave her great pleasure.

"Good even, Mama," Robin said, coming up to stand beside her.

Skye turned, and with a pleased smile gave her son a swift kiss. "You are not surprised to see me?" she asked.

"The Queen told us some weeks ago that you would be returning to court, Mama."

"Did she also tell you the manner of her invitation to us, Robin?"

The young earl looked puzzled. "I don't understand," he said.

"The Queen's agents kidnaped Velvet," Skye said quietly.

"God's nightshirt!"

"Do not use such language, Robin," the mother in Skye scolded.

"Your pardon, Mama, but I was so surprised by your disclosure I could not help myself. Is Velvet all right?"

"So the Queen assures me, although I have insisted that my baby be returned immediately. Velvet is at Hampton Court."

"Why?"

"Your uncles in Ireland are causing difficulties, and the Queen wants my aid in suppressing their high spirits."

Robin laughed. "The Irish are always causing trouble," he said matter-of-factly.

"This is serious," Skye said, "and I would remind you, my lord earl, that you are half Irish."

"By blood, yes, madam," Robin replied quietly, "but my heart and my loyalties are all English."

"Yes, Robin, they are. I have raised you to be your father's son. I might have done otherwise. I, however, am Irish, but I do not condone these useless rebellions in which your uncles have involved themselves, and I must stop them before they do any serious damage to the family."

The young earl nodded. He understood the difficulty of his mother's position. "I am sure that the Queen has not hurt Velvet," he said.

"No, she has not, but nonetheless it was a terrible thing to do to us. I have, however, exacted my price in return for my aid. The Queen has recognized our marriage, both Adam and your brother, Padraic, have been given estates, and Lundy has been returned to us."

"Padraic has his lands back?"

"Not in Ireland. The Queen would not give him back the Burke lands."

Robin saw the sadness in his mother's eyes, and he put a hand on hers, saying, "I am sorry, Mother, but at least we are now less a house divided, and for that I am glad."

"Where is Willow?" Skye asked her son, changing the subject, for she could no longer think of Padraic's loss without weeping.

"Look for the Earl of Alcester, Mama," Robin said. "Wherever he is, Willow will be."

"God's blood!" Skye swore. "Did I not warn her about involving herself with a man?!"

"'Tis not Willow who has involved herself with Alcester, but rather the other way around," Robin said with a smile. "He is quite smitten with her, and in a position to offer marriage, Mama."

"Tell me."

"James, Lord Edwardes, Earl of Alcester," Robin began. "Aged twenty-four, a widower with one child, a daughter. Educated, well mannered, neither drinks nor gambles to excess. He seems to enjoy the ladies, but is no lecher, I'm told. I rather like him, Mama, and Willow, for all her hoity-toity ways, likes him too, although she hasn't given the poor fellow the least encouragement." Robin chuckled, a sophisticated sound far beyond his years, Skye thought. "He's rather shy, I think."

"What of his family?" Skye demanded, for this young man surely had a family who would object to their son's marriage to a young woman not of the nobility.

"His parents are both dead, Mama. He has a paternal grandmother, I am told, but no one else of note."

"What of his finances? Surely there is some gossip about that."

"He's not rich, Mama, but neither is he a pauper. I have been told that his estate is small, but well kept." Here Robin made his voice even lower. "He doesn't know the extent of Willow's wealth, Mama. No one at court does, for she hasn't been here that long. Besides, Willow is rather closemouthed about her affairs, and spends very little of her allowance."

Skye smiled with satisfaction. Her daughter was being quite discreet, and that was all to the good. She looked about the room, and finally spotted Willow standing amid a group of laughing young people. How lovely she looked in her garnet-red velvet gown, and how delighted Khalid would have been with her, the doting mother couldn't help thinking. "Which one is Alcester?" she asked Robin.

"The young man by her right elbow."

Skye let her gaze assess her daughter's would-be suitor. He was a pleasant-looking young man of medium height with light brown hair. He was well built, and his young face had an intelligent and kindly look to it. "Introduce me," she commanded Robin.

Robin offered his mother his arm and led her across the floor to where his sister stood with her friends. Suddenly Willow saw them coming, and her eyes lit up joyfully. Breaking away from the group, she ran the few steps between them.

"Mama!"

Skye enfolded her daughter into her arms and hugged her tightly. "I have missed you these weeks," she said, "and how lovely you look tonight, my precious. I see you are wearing Nicolas's pearls, and how pretty they look on you."

"Mama."

Skye looked up, and then moving away from Willow, she saw Robin with the Earl of Alcester. "Yes, Robin?" she said, feigning surprise.

"Mama, I would present to you Lord James Edwardes, the Earl of Alcester. My lord, my mother, Lady de Marisco."

Alcester caught her hand and, raising it to his lips, kissed it.

"Lady de Marisco, it is my pleasure. Now I know where Mistress Willow gets her beauty."

"Really, Alcester," Willow said, flushing with pleasure though her voice was sharp with pretended annoyance, "I am said to look like my father."

"Both you and your mother have dark hair," poor Alcester protested.

"Quite true, my lord," Skye agreed. "How astute of you to notice it, and as for you, Willow, surely I have taught you better manners. His lordship offered you a compliment. Thank him, and accept it graciously." Skye smiled at her daughter, then at the earl. "Now," she said, "you will excuse me, for I must find my husband. Willow, we are at Greenwood for several days, and then we must go to Ireland. Please come to see us." Skye kissed her daughter, and then smiling again at Alcester, she bid him farewell.

Finding Adam, she remained with him until the Queen had left and they were free to depart for Greenwood. As they rode back to their house she told him of Willow's suitor. "I think we will be approached by his lordship before we leave for Ireland. Find out what you can about the young man. Robin's information is encouraging."

"What does Willow think of him?" Adam queried.

"I have not had the opportunity to find out, but I suspect from what I have seen she is not averse to his suit. We shall see. I will never force her to a husband, as my father forced me to Dom O'Flaherty."

Adam put his arm around his wife. "All that was long ago, sweetheart. We will be certain it is what Willow wants."

Neither Skye nor Adam had the opportunity to check further on the Earl of Alcester, however, for the following afternoon he arrived unannounced at Greenwood. "I hope you will forgive what must seem a lack of manners on my part," he apologized, "but I understand that you will not be staying in London long, and I wished to speak with you about Willow."

"Indeed, sir, be seated," Adam invited the earl, who sat down on the edge of a chair. "What is it you wish?"

"I want to marry your daughter, sir," the earl said.

"Willow is my stepdaughter, my lord. She is my wife's child by her second marriage to a Spanish nobleman."

"Why is it you wish to wed with my daughter, my lord?" Skye asked quietly.

Alcester flushed, and then said as quietly, "Because I love her, madam."

"I do not see how you can love her, my lord, though I doubt not your good intentions. You have known Willow but a short time. My daughter and I are very close, and she has not written me of you, nor has she said anything about her affections being engaged."

"Madam, Willow is the most discreet of maidens. From the moment she arrived at court I could see she was different from the others. She is chaste where many are not. She is kind, and devout, and intelligent. I worship the very ground she walks upon, and I would make her my wife."

"If, my lord," Adam said, "we were to consider your suit—and mind you, we will do so only should Willow approve—what dowry would you ask?"

"I am not a wealthy man, my lord," the earl replied, "but I am not poverty-stricken. I can provide comfortably for a wife. Whatever dowry you wish to offer I will accept."

"You are not aware then that my daughter is an heiress, my lord?" Skye looked closely at James Edwardes.

"*An heiress?*" The Earl of Alcester looked dumbfounded. "I d-did not know, madam."

Studying the young man's face, Skye decided that he was telling the truth. "Willow's father was a wealthy man, my lord, and she is also the heiress to her godfather, Sir Robert Small. Should she agree to entertain your suit a generous dowry will be set aside for you, but the bulk of my daughter's wealth must remain in her hands. If you are willing to agree to that then we shall speak with Willow."

"Do you control your own wealth, madam? I had heard the rumor that it was so."

"I do, my lord, and it has always been thus since my first marriage. A man is entitled to his dowry, but a woman is also entitled to have her own monies so she may not be beholden to anyone. You have noted that Willow is an intelligent girl, and so she is. Intelligent enough to know how to invest her capital, for I have taught her and so has Sir Robert. If you will trust her she will increase her wealth."

"Unusual as it is, madam, I will agree to your terms, for I truly do love Willow. There are others, madam, like the Countess of Shrewsbury, Bess of Hardwick, who control their own wealth. If Shrewsbury can live with it then surely I can." He smiled mischievously, and seeing his smile for the first time, Skye thought that the earl was a most handsome young man. "Besides, madam, Willow is far prettier than Bess of Hardwick."

"I should certainly hope so!" Willow exclaimed, coming through the door of the morning room. "Good day, Mama, Papa. Alcester, what are you doing here?"

"He has come to ask for your hand in marriage, Willow," Skye answered, thinking that her daughter was perhaps a trifle too pert. "I am not sure you are old enough, however."

"Mama!" Willow shrieked, and blushing, she turned to James Edwardes. "Mama is not teasing? You really want to marry me?"

The earl looked down at Willow with a tender expression in his brown eyes. "My dear, I have wanted to marry you from the moment I first set eyes on you. Will you have me, Willow? I will do my best to make you happy." Boldly he drew her close to him, and gazed into her face.

Looking up at him, Willow whispered, "Oh, James, I did not dare to hope. Yes! Oh, yes! I shall be so proud to be your wife!"

The earl bent to kiss Willow, and Skye felt Adam reach for her hand. She looked at him, and he saw the tears in her eyes. He knew her thoughts in that moment. She was thinking of Willow's father, Khalid el Bey. "He would be proud of her," Adam said softly.

"Yes," she answered him, "he would be proud of her." And then Skye thought of how she had kept Willow safe all these years, safe to reach adulthood, to marry a fine young man like James Edwards. Yes, Khalid would be content.

Willow looked positively radiant, all rosy with blushes, and the earl was suddenly very sure of himself and totally masculine. Skye and Adam both smiled at the young couple, and then Skye spoke.

"You cannot be married until next spring after Willow's fifteenth birthday," she said, "and you must have the Queen's permission. She becomes, I have found, most irritable when not kept informed with regard to the lives of her courtiers."

The earl nodded, and then turned to Adam. "When would you like to sign the betrothal agreements, my lord?"

"Not until after the Queen has given her permission, Alcester. We will not give Elizabeth Tudor the chance to spoil your happiness by claiming that she was not informed from the very beginning."

The Queen was told that evening that the widowed Earl of Alcester wished to marry Mistress Willow Small, a maid of honor. Looking at the pair, Elizabeth Tudor was strangely touched. Usually the defection of one of her maids was cause for a temper tantrum; and in the short time Willow had been at court the Queen had grown fond of the young girl. Still, Willow's innocence was unquestionable, and Alcester was known to be an honorable man. "If I give my permission," the Queen said, "when would the marriage be celebrated, madam?" and she looked at Skye.

"Not until after Willow's birthday next April, Majesty," came the calm reply.

The Queen nodded. It was a respectable amount of time for a proper betrothal period. "I am happy to give my permission for your daughter to wed with the Earl of Alcester, Lady de Marisco. I shall expect to be invited to the wedding provided that you have settled things in Ireland by then."

"I shall do my best, madam," Skye said demurely. Not for the world would she spoil Willow's good fortune.

There was a knock at the door of the Queen's closet where they had been gathered, and Elizabeth called out her permission to enter. The door opened to reveal Sir Christopher Hatton, who was carrying something in his arms.

"You sent for this, Majesty."

"Give it to Lady de Marisco," the Queen commanded.

Hatton handed his bundle to Skye, and with pounding heart she took it as the woolen cloak fell away to reveal the sleeping Velvet. "Oh, my baby," she whispered as Adam leapt to her side with a soft oath to gaze down at their daughter. With a gentle finger he touched Velvet's pink cheek, and the baby opened her blue eyes to sleepily murmur, "Papa," at him.

"Now, madam," Elizabeth said, "you have your daughter back. When do you leave for Ireland?"

"As soon as I have settled my children, Majesty."

The Queen, who knew that little Velvet was her godchild, chucked the baby under the chin, and said, "Court is no place for my goddaughter. I assume that you will send her to Devon, but what of young Mistress Burke and her brother? Would you allow them to remain here at court? Lord Burke may join my pages, and his sister would be safe in the Countess of Lincoln's household."

Skye knew that Elizabeth Tudor was demanding her children as hostages for her success in Ireland. "Lord Burke," she said, "I know would be thrilled to take his place among your pages, madam, and with his brother, the earl, to watch over him I know he would be safe. My daughter, Deirdre, however, is another matter. Although I feel she would be better off with the countess, she carries a fear of being separated from me again. Might we leave that decision up to her?"

The Queen's face softened with sympathy. She understood the fears of a lonely child well, having been motherless since age three. "Of course," she agreed. "If mistress Deirdre wishes to go with you I will understand."

Much to Skye's surprise, Deirdre wanted to stay with Geraldine FitzGerald, the lovely Countess of Lincoln. Like her sister and her brothers, the little girl was fascinated by the Tudor court. It was one thing to be left with an elderly uncle or aunt, but to be left at court was quite another matter! Skye felt almost betrayed, and grumbled indignantly. Adam, however, found the whole thing amusing on one hand, and very fortuitous on the other.

"Your mission is a serious one, sweetheart," he said. "It is better we not be encumbered by the children. I fear not the Queen's captivity, but in Ireland it could be dangerous for them to be used as pawns."

She knew that he was right, and so they drove down to Devon where Velvet was left safely at Wren Court with Dame Cecily. Told of Willow's betrothal, Dame Cecily burst into tears, sobbing that she was so very, very happy for her baby.

"I can't believe she's old enough to wed," the good woman wept joyously. "'Twas only yesterday I was changing her nappies."

Skye smiled to herself as she patted her old friend comfortingly. Willow, she thought, amused, would be simply mortified to be reminded of such a thing. She reassured Dame Cecily that James Edwardes was a wonderful man, and the perfect husband for Willow.

Then Skye took the opportunity to see Daisy's two small sons. Both looked like their father but for their gap-toothed smiles, which were their inheritance from their mother. The de Mariscos did not stay long in Devon though, departing the day after their arrival for Innisfana Island, on the west coast of Ireland, the ancestral home of Skye O'Malley.

Skye had taken the precaution to send a message on ahead calling her brothers into a family council. She knew that were they not on Innisfana they would be easy to reach for Grace O'Malley's sailors never ventured far from Ireland. It had been a long while since she had seen them, over five years, and in that time they had squandered everything she had built up for the O'Malleys since her father's death. She knew that her gentle and soft-spoken stepmother had exercised no control over her four sons; but why had she allowed them to take up with Grace O'Malley? She knew her brothers well enough to know that they were not patriots. She could only conclude that they had joined with Grace simply for the fun of a little hell-raising.

It was not harmless fun, however, Skye thought, and had her own family not been so intimately involved, she would have let her half-brothers pursue their own destructive course. She had no future in Ireland, and neither now did any of her children. She agreed with Elizabeth Tudor, who had said: "There is only one Christ Jesus, and one faith; the rest is a dispute about trifles." She and the Queen would never be friends, but Skye's loyalty was never seriously questioned, for her views were Erastian enough to protect her.

They sailed south into St. George's Channel, around Cape Clear, and north to Innisfana. It was November now, and the northerlies were sweeping down the Atlantic from the Arctic. Still the sky was clear, and although cold, it was pleasant sailing. Only once did they see another sail on the horizon, but that was from a ship inward bound to England from the New World, and they did not pass within hailing distance of each other.

Skye owned eight ships, and they were all with her, having by fortunate coincidence been in England at this time when she needed them. Like all the O'Malley ships, they were sleek and built for speed as well as cargo. Each one was well armed in order to defend itself, and as a fleet they were a powerful weapon, particularly since they had added more cannon as they were carrying no cargo this time.

Several days before they sailed Skye had assembled all her crews, and spoken quite frankly to them about why she was going home, and the fact that they might find themselves in a fight. About half her men were Irish, and she offered them the opportunity to remain in port and take passage on other vessels rather than fight their own people.

Bran Kelly spoke for the Irish. "We're your men, and our loyalty is to you, the O'Malley. We've all got family in Ireland, most of our people on Innisfana or O'Flaherty lands. If yer brothers cause more trouble with the English it's our women and children who'll bear the brunt of their vengeance."

There came a chorus of ayes as the Irish nodded and whispered among themselves.

"We'd just as soon stick by you, m'lady," Bran continued, and the rest of the men again nodded their agreement.

There was little to do on the voyage, and Skye spent a good deal of time pacing restlessly about the decks, or leaning over the bow rail staring hard ahead into the endless horizon. She disliked dissension, and because she must reassert her clan authority upon her brothers she was going to cause much dissension within her family. She wondered how Anne would react. Would she agree with her stepdaughter, or would she side blindly with her beloved sons?

"Dammit," Skye said aloud, "it was not up to me to raise them! Why could Anne have not been strong?"

Adam stood behind his wife, his strong arms wrapped about her lithe form. "You judge people by your own yardstick, Skye," he said softly. "Most women are not strong like you. They are meek, gentle creatures who rely upon their men for everything, including their very thoughts. Anne O'Malley has been widowed for sixteen years now. Her whole life has been the memory of your father, and her boys."

"My dear brothers, who have all been spoiled rotten and obviously have no sense of responsibility," Skye fussed. "I sent them to the sea to learn its ways, and I saw that they were taught to read and to write, and to do their numbers. Yet they waste everything I have built up for them, and they play at rebellion without a care for their families or their people. In Da's time a man might be a freebooter without incurring the royal wrath, but times have changed."

"Yes, little girl, you see that, for you are out in the world, but your brothers have never left Ireland, and have no desire to do so. Change is slow in coming to your green and misty land, Skye.

Your people are a hundred years behind England, and you know it."

Skye pressed her lips tightly in a narrow line of disapproval. There was no use talking, for talk would change nothing. Adam was right, Ireland was behind the times. She sighed deeply with regret, and wondered if she could really prevent her four half-brothers from destroying themselves, from destroying Innisfana and their people.

"Is this a fool's chase?" she asked Adam, turning her face up to his.

"I don't know, sweetheart. You can only try."

"Damn Grace O'Malley," Skye said vehemently. "She plays the power game, as does the Queen. But I'll not let her destroy us. I'll not!"

Chapter 18

Grace O'Malley, the pirate queen of Connaught, looked directly at Anne O'Malley, her kinswoman, and then said to her first in command: "Signal my ship to fire on anyone attempting to enter Innisfana's harbor without my permission."

"Aye," the man grunted, and went off to do his mistress's bidding.

"You can't do that!" Anne protested. "My stepdaughter, the O'Malley, will be arriving any day now. 'Tis her domain, and you've no authority over it."

"She forfeited her authority when she married an Englishman," Grace spat.

"Aye," Brian O'Malley agreed. "I'm the O'Malley now, Mother."

"Unless Skye passes on her responsibility to you, Brian, as your father passed it on to her, you're not," Anne snapped, "and none of our people will recognize you as such."

"Shut yer mouth, woman," Grace ordered rudely, and with an outraged look Anne fell silent.

There was going to be some difficulty when Skye finally came, Anne knew. Skye and Grace would detest each other on sight, but she prayed that her stepdaughter could right things. Most of it was her own fault, Anne realized. She had been so lost after Dubhdara had died, and she had clung to her sons, indulging and spoiling them so they would love her and she wouldn't be alone. They had grown into four big mirror images of their father, but they had not Dubhdara O'Malley's strength of character.

They were, Anne was ashamed to admit, weak but well meaning men who drank too much, and wenched too much, and were given to foolishness, such as pirating with their distant cousin, Grace, and her men. Eventually the English were going to descend on Innisfana and wreak their vengeance. Thank God that Skye was coming home! She would set everything to rights, even this matter of Grace O'Malley.

There was a dull boom, followed by several more, and running to the window, they saw a fleet of eight ships entering the harbor under full sail. Behind them, Grace O'Malley's vessel keeled slowly over and sank into the bay. Even at this distance they could see men in the water, clinging to the rigging.

"Sweet Jesu, my ship's been sunk!" Then Grace O'Malley swore a violent string of vulgar Gaelic oaths that caused even Brian to redden.

Anne put a hand over her mouth to stifle her laughter as her eldest son said with pompous understatement, "My sister is come home at last. Now we'll settle this matter between us."

"Aye," Anne said softly, "Skye will settle it, I've not a doubt, Brian, but I think mayhap 'twill not be to yer liking."

"Mother, you must uphold my right!"

"Brian, I've warned ye that you've no rights in this matter. Yer father of sainted memory, may God assoil his dear soul, passed on his authority to your sister, Skye. It is her right to hold that authority, or pass it on to whomever she deems fit."

"It's not right that she hold the title if she's not here to physically hold the authority," Grace O'Malley said slyly.

"Skye has always taken care of Innisfana and its people, even from a distant shore," Anne defended her stepdaughter. "She's done a fine job building our wealth, which my sons have squandered. Perhaps if one of them had shown any maturity, she would have passed on her badge of office."

"The woman is in England's hire," Grace said scornfully. "She's no better than an English landlord!"

"That's right!" Brian agreed.

"I wonder if you have the courage to say that to your sister, my son," Anne murmured.

"I'm not afraid of Skye," Brian blustered.

"Well, you damned well ought to be if you're the one responsible for trying to prevent me entry into *my* own harbor," Skye snapped, striding into the hall of the O'Malley tower house, her husband and her captains at her back. She glanced about the room. "Good day, Anne," she said, and then her glance flicked to the other woman who was sprawled insolently in a chair.

"You sunk my ship," Grace drawled.

"It got in my way," came the reply.

"Could you not have asked it to move then?" Grace said with some humor as she stood up.

Skye looked at this woman who was her relative. She had to be at least six feet tall. She was big-boned like a man, but handsome in appearance with sparkling deep-blue eyes, and short, dark curls. Skye knew that Grace was a good ten years older than she was, but the woman didn't show it. "Anyone sending a warning shot across my bow is looking for a fight," Skye said. "No one bars *me* entry to *my* own harbor, *my* own holding. Do you think to add Innisfana to your own lands, *cousin?*"

Adam watched, amused. Here were two well-matched hellcats, although he felt that Skye and her eight ships held the advantage.

Grace O'Malley caught his assessing look, and gave him a slow smile as she calmly took him in from head to toes. "Innisfana's too small for me to be bothered with, *cousin,*" came her reply, and then she said, "Who is this big handsome stud? If he's one of yer captains I've a mind to hire him away from ye." Grace O'Malley's appetite for attractive men was well known, and her lovers were legion.

"That's something else you can't have, *cousin.* This is my husband, Lord de Marisco."

"'Tis the second Englishman ye've married, Skye O'Malley," came the faintly insulting reply. "The first, I'm told, was a golden-haired fop, but as for this one . . ." Again she raked him with a bold look, her eyes deliberately lingering where they should not. "Well, dearie, 'tis enough to make me curious to perhaps sample one."

"*Not this one,*" Skye said in a cold, even voice.

"Are ye Englishmen then ruled by yer women, Lord de Marisco?"

"Only when they're beautiful and hot-blooded Irish wenches.

madam," Adam said with an amused grin. "One O'Malley is more than enough for me."

Grace laughed, appreciating his humor and seeing with her shrewd eye that the man was in love. Her younger cousin had always had the Divil's own luck when it came to men, she thought enviously.

"I'll have someone sail you up to Clare, *cousin*," Skye said, "and any of your pirates we've managed to fish out of the sea." She turned. "MacGuire! Take her home, man!"

"Aye, m'lady," came the reply. Then the old captain turned to Grace O'Malley. "Follow me," he said shortly, and departed the room.

Grace picked up her fur cloak from where she had carelessly thrown it and, with a wink at Adam, said, "Farewell, *cousin*, de Marisco. We'll meet again, I've not a doubt." Then without any pretense at hurry she sauntered after MacGuire.

Skye turned on Brian. "Where are your brothers?" she demanded.

"They're about," he answered sullenly. "We just didn't expect ye so quickly."

"I'll wager you didn't! Fetch them, Brian. I want them here within the hour! Get out now!" Brian O'Malley almost ran from the room. When he had gone Skye turned to her stepmother. "Anne, I'm sorry, but I'm going to take their hides off. 'Tis bad enough what they've wasted, but you realize they're within a hair's breadth of losing everything else."

"I couldn't handle them, Skye. I needed yer father, for they're his lads right enough. Michael, bless him, never gave me a moment's grief, but my own four needed a man's influence. Yer Uncle Seamus couldn't be around all the time, and there was no one else."

"I know, Anne. 'Tis just the way things turned out," Skye soothed her stepmother, although she secretly thought that had Anne been a stronger woman, there would have been no problem. She looked about the hall, and was surprised at what she saw. "This place is filthy," she noted. "I've never known you to keep a dirty house, Anne."

"'Tis not my house any longer, Skye. Ever since Brian married my niece, Maggie O'Brian, she's been mistress here, and she'll accept neither help, nor advice from me."

Skye felt a bolt of irritation shoot through her. She remembered how lovely the hall had been when it had been Anne's responsibility. The tables had gleamed with beeswax and rubbing, reflecting back the huge porcelain bowls of flowers, either fresh or dried depending on the season, that Anne always filled the house with. Looking around, she saw that the tabletops were smeared and dull; the chair cushions dusty, frayed, and worn. The giant andirons were black from lack of polish and the fireplace walls thick with greasy, black soot. There were dust balls in all the corners, and rushes filled with bones covered the floors. The corners of the ceilings were cobwebbed, and the place stank to high heaven.

"I'll not have it!" Skye roared furiously. "Where in hell are the servants! Dammit, Anne, get the servants in here at once!" She turned to her captains. "Secure the harbor," she commanded. "I'll expect you all for dinner tomorrow. I don't dare ask you tonight for fear there is no dinner in this badly run establishment!"

Skye's captains hurried from the room, glad to be free of what promised to be a battle royal with their mistress taking on not only her half-brothers, but a sister-in-law as well. Anne O'Malley had already fled the hall seeking the servants. Alone with her husband, Skye said, "It's impossible, Adam! The whole damn thing is impossible! Anne is a sweet woman, but she is so easily overridden by not only my brothers, but obviously Brian's wife also! What am I to do? I cannot stay here and control their lives always. We have our own life to live, and dammit, I want that life!"

He took her in his arms and held her tightly. Skye pressed herself against his velvet doublet while the familiar, clean smell of the spicy clove-scented soap he used soothed her turbulent emotions. He knew how Skye loved a calm and orderly house, and to find that her childhood home, which she had left well tended, had become a slovenly disgrace was disturbing to her, especially coupled with the fact she must regain control of her brothers. "It will be all right, little girl. Lady Anne knows what must be done. Delegate the authority back to her, and with your support she will be able to function once more."

"Ummm," Skye murmured, hearing him, but suddenly wishing she were anyplace else with Adam but the middle of the hall of O'Malley House. She snuggled against him for a brief moment, and feeling his own desire awakening, Adam scolded her gently.

"Dammit, little girl, this is neither the place nor the time!"

"Don't you want me?" She rubbed teasingly against him, suddenly feeling mischievous.

"*Skye!*" He tried to put her away from him, but she clung tighter, and to both his horror and his delight her questing hand slipped beneath his doublet and around to caress his buttock. "Skye, you vixen, cease your torture or I swear I'll take you right here and now, no matter the consequences!"

"Do you want me, Adam?" she repeated.

"Yes!" he groaned through gritted teeth, and she released him to stand demurely back, laughing softly at his discomfort.

"I want you too," she said. "For the life of me I don't know why we didn't take Velvet back to Belle Fleur and leave the O'Malleys to Hell!"

"Because, sweetheart, you are your father's daughter. You accepted the responsibility for your family from him, and you are not a woman to go back on your word."

"I could pass the mantle on to Brian," she said.

"Knowing that he's not fit for it, Skye? You've too much conscience, I'm thinking."

"Aye, worse luck!" she agreed.

Adam chuckled. "You'll feel better after you've knocked a few stubborn O'Malley heads around," he promised her as into the hall straggled a group of shabby-looking women and several men led by Anne and another, younger woman.

"This is my daughter-in-law, Maggie," Anne introduced the girl.

"How old are you?" Skye demanded, too angry to even greet her unknown sister-in-law civilly. The girl was a little bit of a thing with sharp features and carrot-red hair.

"Seventeen," came the mumbled reply.

"Didn't your mother teach you how to manage a household?" Skye demanded.

"Me mother died when I was four or five. I was the eighth child, m'lady."

"Then what in the name of God gave you the idea you could run this house, lass? Why did you remove Lady Anne from her position as chatelaine?"

"I'm the O'Malley's wife," came the reply. "I couldn't allow another in me place. My older sisters all said if I didn't make clear from the beginning that I was the lady of the house, I wouldn't ever be."

"I think we'd best get several things straight," Skye said patiently, although she was longing to smack this rather stupid girl. "My brother, Brian, is *not* the O'Malley, *I am*. This is *my* house in which you live, and you've turned it into a pigsty! Rushes on the floors! Sweet Jesu, this house hasn't seen rushes on the floors since my father was a boy! Where are the fine carpets we had? Now listen to me, Maggie O'Malley, the Lady Anne will resume her duties as chatelaine of this house until she no longer desires that position. You will learn from her so that when the day comes she believes you competent you may take over from her. From the looks of this place 'twill take at least ten years for you to learn! How many children do you have?"

"Four."

"Any girls?"

"One."

"When she's old enough then she'll learn too, and her sisters, should she have any!" Skye turned and looked with a hard eye at the servants. "Diligence will be rewarded in this house, and laziness will be punished. I'm not averse to beating my servants when they don't perform." She glared fiercely at them, and the little group visibly quailed while Adam sought to not laugh, for Skye had never been known to hit a servant. "I am the O'Malley. D'you understand? 'Tis my orders that will be obeyed here, and you're to obey as well Lady Anne unless I tell you not to. Is that understood?"

Wide-eyed, the group nodded.

"The hall first, Anne, please."

Anne O'Malley, her confidence suddenly restored, began issuing quick orders. "You, Maeve, get those rushes up! Mab, bring the beeswax, and let's get started on those tables! Paddy, you and Tam clean the fireplaces and the andirons! The rest of you, use yer eyes and yer brooms! I want this hall shining by nightfall!" With a quick smile she turned to Skye. "Use my apartments until this place is clean. I'll send the boys to you as soon as they arrive."

Skye kissed Anne lightly on the cheek. "My thanks," she said, and with Adam following her she led the way to her stepmother's rooms. They had barely settled themselves when Skye's brothers arrived, banging noisily into the room without knocking and causing their elder sister to shriek outraged at them as they tracked mud across Anne's beautiful Turkey carpet. Sheepishly they backed out again, removing their footwear at her command before re-entering the chamber. Anne's rooms were the only haven of cleanliness right now in the entire house, and Skye had no intention of allowing her brothers to ruin it.

Grinning, they stood before her, all big men as their father had been. Three had his startlingly bright blue eyes, each sported a bushy black beard, and all had black, black hair, which they wore longer than was currently fashionable.

"Well," Skye said quietly, "you all look like Da, but you're not one whit like him, for our father wasn't stupid and the four of you certainly are! Between you you've not the brain of a chicken!"

"Ye're not being fair, Skye," Brian whined.

"*Fair!*" She looked scornfully at them. "I spent my youth building up the wealth of this family, for wealth, my dear brothers, is power! I was forced into making a foreign marriage, and so I left you, Brian, in charge of the O'Malley wealth. And what have you done with it? You've squandered it!"

"Money is to be spent!" Brian reasoned.

"Spent intelligently, not squandered, you dolt! What have you done to increase our wealth? Where did you think additional monies were going to come from?"

"Da had monies."

"Da had little," she replied. "He scavenged wrecks, some of which, I am certain, he caused. He preyed upon an occasional fat merchant vessel caught without protection. He was more pirate than I care to admit! He wanted better for you when he died."

"Died and left his authority to you, Skye," Brian said bitterly as his brothers, Shane, Shamus, and Conn, nodded in agreement.

"Ah, that's what rankles you, isn't it, Brian? Da left the authority to me. How you would love to be the O'Malley! Well, my little brother, you were barely six when Da died, and our brother Michael, only eight. There was no one else that Da chose to trust. He knew that I would not fail him. Authority, Brian, comes only to those who are willing to accept responsibility, and so far I have seen nothing on the part of any of you to indicate to me that you are willing to grow up! When I see maturity in any one of you, Brian, I promise you that I will pass on my authority. Until then I will continue to keep my faith with our father, may God assoil him."

Adam sat back quietly in the shadows of a window seat to watch and listen as Skye spoke with her four half-brothers. He understood the frustration the younger men must be feeling, but he was forced to agree with his wife in her judgments. The O'Malley brothers were not capable of handling responsibility.

"Dammit, Skye," Shamus O'Malley exclaimed, "it's embarrassing having to answer to a woman! 'Tis all right for children, but we're grown men!"

"Strange," Skye murmured. "You chafe under my very light authority over you, but you're quick to throw in with Grace O'Malley and her cutthroats. Don't tell me that our kinswoman doesn't issue orders to you, for I know if you sail with her you answer to her, Shamus." She looked piercingly at her four brothers, who shuffled their feet nervously, and then she sat down, waving the men to chairs also. "Tell me, Brian," she said, looking hard at him, "tell me what you would do if you were the O'Malley of Innisfana?"

A huge grin split his face, and it was obvious that Brian had thought often about being the head of his family. "Why, I'd go apirating with Grace, and I'd fight the damned English right back across the sea to their own puny island! God's bones, what fun we'd have, eh brothers?!"

Shane and Shamus O'Malley nodded at their elder sibling, and each sported an identical foolish grin upon his broad face. Skye had the incredible urge to hit them, for despite their ages, they were terribly childish.

"How would you feed your peoples while you were gone?" she demanded. "Who would protect Innisfana from our marauding friends and neighbors, not to mention the vengeful English? Having nothing of your own, Brian, what provisions could you make for your family, and all the others for whom you would be responsible? I've seen the results of giving you even small authority."

"What in Hell is that supposed to mean?" Brian shouted.

"It means you wasted all you had, and now you have nothing! You delivered the management of this house into the hands of your wife, a nice enough girl I've not a doubt, but a slattern when it comes to household matters! You've no judgment, Brian! You don't look at the long run. You'd run off with Grace O'Malley, leaving Innisfana and its peoples unprotected and poverty-stricken. While you fought the English your neighbors would be making up to them, aiding them and taking your holding in payment for their treacherous service!

"The first rule of survival is to stay out of politics! The second is to avoid a situation in which you cannot win. The English are just that, Brian. Ireland will never be free of them until they can unite beneath the banner of one leader, and I see no hope of that. Therefore your first duty is to survive, and to aid this family in its survival! If you want to be the O'Malley then show me the qualities that make a good leader, Brian. God knows I'll be glad to pass on my authority! I'm tired of being responsible for you all! I'm tired of having to answer to an English Queen for your behavior, and I want to live my own life free of such encumbrances! I cannot be quit of you, however, until I am satisfied that you can really be a leader! Until then you'll obey me, for I am the O'Malley!" She looked directly at them, daring any of them to argue with her, but they avoided her gaze. She knew they resented her, but she also knew that she was right about them.

Suddenly Shane asked, "What do we do then, Skye? If we don't go pirating with Grace O'Malley, and fight the English, what do we do?"

For the first time that afternoon Skye smiled. Her brother's plaintive question was what she had been waiting for. She didn't want to have to order them about. She wanted them to *want* her aid. "Well, Shane, I think that you and your brothers should do what you do best, and obviously that is pirating. However, don't pirate the English, for they're not rich enough. The Spanish are."

"The Spanish?"

"Aye! You want adventure? Then get yourselves letters of marque from the Queen, and harry the dons along the Spanish Main. You'll rebuild your wealth, and therefore your power base in no time."

"We need no letters of marque from the English," Brian boasted. "We can go on our own."

"That's up to you, Brian, but go on your own and you're prey to anyone and *everyone*. Get caught, and you'll be hung for a common pirate. Carry letters of marque, and you're protected by a powerful queen, and you've powerful allies in every other ship sailing with

Bess Tudor's blessing. Should you get caught by the French or the Dutch, you're more apt to be ransomed than hung." She smiled lazily at her eldest brother. "'Tis your decision, of course, Brian. Now get out! I've said all I am going to for now. I will see you later, for I've not come home to go away quickly, little brothers."

The four men shuffled to their feet and clumped from the room, pausing at the door to pull their boots back on before departing. When the door had closed on them at last, Skye moved across the room to settle herself in Adam's lap. "Kiss me," she demanded, and he was happy to comply, covering her mouth with his in a fiery possession that left her breathless. "Hmmmmm," she purred at him, slipping a hand around to caress the back of his neck.

"Do you really want to be quit of them?" he asked her as she sent wonderful little shivers down his spine and he moved a hand around to slip into her silk shirt.

"Yes," she said, and nuzzled him just below his ear.

His hand cupped her breast, the thumb stretching up to tease at the nipple. "What if they don't take your suggestion?"

Skye gently bit on the lobe of Adam's ear, and then blew softly into it. "They will," she said with certainty, loving the warmth of his hand as he cupped her.

"And then what, little girl?" Adam could feel himself beginning to stir with desire as she nestled provocatively against him, kissing his face and neck with wonderful little kisses.

"Then, my lord, we will be finished with the Tudor Queen—*and* her court! We shall go home, wherever that may be, and I shall spend my days being a dutiful chatelaine, and my nights being your own personal wanton!" She turned his head with her fingers and kissed him passionately.

The beast within him leapt forth, crushing her within the iron of his arms, meeting her flaming challenge with a fire of his own that burned hot and fierce. He turned her so that she lay helpless within the enchantment of his embrace, her fair breasts half exposed, their little nipples pushing arrogantly forth to taunt him. With a groan of surrender he buried his face in the perfumed softness of her. "Dammit, Skye, I want you! I cannot get enough of you, and 'tis unkind of you to tempt me so now."

Skye laughed, and wiggled from his arms. Walking across the room, she turned the key in the lock of the door, and with an almost impish grin she sauntered back across the room to stand before him. Slowly she drew her silk shirt off and slipped from the half-chemise she wore beneath it, letting them fall to the floor. Adam expelled his breath in a slow hiss of delight at the wonders she displayed to him so proudly. She slid her legged skirt over her hips, and removed the remaining undergarments and stockings, rolling the latter down shapely legs that he had viewed a thousand times before and still found beautiful.

Boldly she moved forward to face him, and began undoing his silk shirt while with eager hands he yanked and pulled at the rest of his clothing, anxious to join her in this natural state. Seating him, Skye removed his boots and pulled off his hose. He was quickly as nude as she, and made no resistance when she led him across the room to lie with her on a sheepskin rug before the warm fire.

They clung together, their bodies touching the length of one another while they kissed, their lips moving softly against each other. He stroked her satiny flesh gently, feeling the desire rise in him as it had the very first time he had touched her, as it always did when they made love. She hovered over him, her breasts brushing his chest as she twined her fingers in and out of the dark mat upon his torso. Her touch incited his passion, and he pulled her against him only to turn her so that now she lay underneath. His lips traveled a tender pathway over her face, pausing at her closed eyelids, her nose, her rose mouth. He kissed a trail down her neck to the throbbing hollow in her throat, and paused there to feel the very blood coursing wildly beneath his lips.

"Sweet Skye, how I love you!" he whispered against her fragrant skin.

"And I love you, my darling husband," came back the breathless reply. "Oh, Adam! I love you so!"

There had never been a moment in time like this, she thought. Oh yes, there had been others to whom she had given her heart and genuinely loved in their time, but none had been like Adam de Marisco. The others had loved her, but there had always been a pride of possession of her in their love. Niall had been her first love; and Khalid the only safe harbor in a frightening and unremembered world. Geoffrey! Ah, for Geoffrey Southwood, the Angel Earl, with his pride and his arrogance, she had been the only woman he had ever really loved. She had loved him too, she thought with a touch of sadness in her heart. Nicolas St. Adrian, her charming Frenchman, had caught her heart when she most needed him. They had all been marvelous, but Adam was different.

Adam de Marisco had always treated her like his equal, and perhaps that was why he was her friend as well as her husband and her lover. He adored her with a mixture of love and amusement and wonder; but he had always respected her intelligence as well. It made him different from the others. He was proud that she was his wife, but his pride stemmed from the fact that he had been fortunate enough to win her. To all the others she had been a possession to be proud of and to be envied. To Adam she was simply sweet Skye, his beloved wife.

As he slowly filled her with his pulsing manhood she opened her sapphire eyes and took his head in her two hands. Turning him so that their eyes met, she held his gaze as he entered her, her eyes growing ever more full of the love she felt for this wonderful man. There were no words spoken between them, for their beating hearts spoke silently for them. With tender passion he moved upon her until finally she could bear the sweetness no longer, and her eyes closed again as a soft cry welled up and burst from her throat.

Adam's own heart was so filled with love for Skye at that moment that he could barely contain his own passions. With wonder he watched her, seeing all the turbulent emotions that played across her beautiful face. Gently he bent his leonine head to kiss her, and tasted the salty tears on her cheeks. That she wept from sheer happiness he understood, yet it moved him just the same.

When moments later she opened her beautiful sapphire eyes again he smiled softly at her, and she smiled back dazzling him with her love for him which shone so clearly in her face.

"How very much I need you, little girl," he whispered to her.

"How very much I need *you*, my husband," she returned, and then as he moved them so that they lay on their sides she touched his mouth with a delicate kiss. They were still joined in conjugal embrace, but he had wanted to spare her his weight while they loved, for he was not yet ready to spend. In this half-facing position Skye had one leg between his, and one of Adam's legs was between hers. It was an intimate position that allowed them to stroke and caress each other freely. Adam enjoyed taking her sensitive little nipples in his mouth from this posture, and sucking long and lovingly upon them.

She began to feel the flames flickering throughout her body once more as he did this, and she ran her hand down his long back to fondle a taut buttock with teasing fingers. "Witch!" he growled at her, nipping playfully on her sentient flesh and beginning to feel his own hunger rising once more. She bit at his earlobe, and then ran her tongue about the shell of his ear, whispering shamelessly to him how he made her feel at this moment. "Oh, my darling, you're so very big! Why is it I cannot get enough of you, Adam? I love it when you fuck me. Oh darling, don't stop! Please don't stop, my love! Ahh! I could go on forever!"

She was his wife, and yet her bold words roused his lust to a furious pitch. He shuddered with passion and ached with the pleasure possessing her gave him. Once more he towered over her, his great manhood thrusting again and again and again into her excited flesh. He vaguely felt her nails raking down his back; heard her excited panting hot in his ear; felt her body writhing beneath him.

Beginning to slip from reality into the golden world of sensual rapture, Skye had a brief, startling thought. It was with Adam as it had been with Geoffrey! Each time it was better. Each time it was more passionate than the last time. If this was her reward for all she had borne then it had been worth it, for to be loved by such a man was worth anything! Then she was caught up in the whirlwind of passion and, flying high, was lost to everything except their love.

"Ah, sweet Skye, you've unmanned me!" she heard him cry, and collasped upon her breasts. Her arms tightened about him as he whimpered with his own pleasure, and she could not help but kiss his tousled dark head.

They lay together for some minutes, attempting to regain their composure. He finally managed to roll off her, and catching her hand in his, they lay silently side by side. Beneath them the thick sheepskin was soft, and the warm fire crackled merrily, the only witness to their passion. Outside they could hear the soft roar of the rising wind about the stone tower house. Everything else was silence.

He spoke first. "I wish we could stay like this all winter."

She laughed softly. "So do I, but I suspect that Anne will want her rooms back this night. I feel almost guilty thinking on how we have spent this afternoon while Anne has overseen the servants at their cleaning chores."

"If this sheepskin could talk . . ." he teased her.

"Poor Anne would be shocked. I imagine my father was not a particularly inventive lover. Stamina and vigor were his traits, I have been told. He was a simple man."

"Why didn't she remarry? She was yet a girl when your father died."

"Aye, she was twenty-two to his fifty-eight. She says she didn't remarry because she had the boys to raise, and no dowry. I would have given her a dowry, though; and a good man seeking sons would have been happy to have her to wife, for she was certainly a proven breeder. No, I think she chose not to remarry. She had borne my father four sons in four years, and I think she had no wish to place herself in another man's care. It was far more convenient to deify my father and his memory. Not all women like the marriage bed. I suspect Anne is one of those women. To my knowledge, she has had no lovers since Da died." Skye propped herself up on an elbow and, lowering her head, kissed her husband lingeringly. "I can't imagine not loving you," she said.

He smiled back at her. "I don't ever intend you stop loving me, little girl. It would break my heart if you did," and then his arm came up to draw her down against him.

When they finally heard the knocking on the door both felt silly and foolish. They were behaving like young lovers instead of the adults that they were.

"Skye dear, the hall is cleaned and sweetened, and if you and Adam would care to come forth the servants are waiting for your approval," Anne O'Malley called.

"We'll be there in a moment, Anne," Skye said, her voice quavering with amusement. "Help me to dress, you buffoon!" she hissed at Adam who lay on his back waggling his black, bushy eyebrows at her while she attempted to maintain her composure. They both heard Anne's retreating footsteps.

"Gracious, m'lady, yer gown is all rumbled, and bless me, is this a tear in yer bodice?!" Standing up to his full six feet six inches, Adam successfully mimicked Daisy.

Skye burst out laughing. "You devil!" she scolded him. "Stop teasing me."

His warm laughter rumbled about the room. "Very well, little girl, I'll behave if you'll tell me where we're going to sleep tonight in this ancient pile of stones you call your ancestral home." He picked up her undergarments from the floor, and began handing them to her.

"My old room is at the top of the tower," Skye told him. "I imagine Anne will have it prepared. This is actually the only decent-sized apartment in the whole place, and it was my father's. I am pleased to see Anne did not give it to Brian and his wife."

Adam and Skye redressed as quickly as they could and, leaving Anne O'Malley's rooms, returned to the hall. Skye was delighted, for the room once more looked like the one she remembered. A smile split her face, and seeing it, the servants visibly relaxed. "Anne, you've worked a miracle!"

"No miracle, only proper cleaning, and the return of the pretties with which I once decorated this hall."

Coming in for the evening meal, Skye's brothers were equally pleased, and even Maggie shyly admitted carpets upon the stone floors were nicer than rushes. The meal was a simple one, for Anne did not set an elaborate table. There were mussels boiled in white wine, baby lamb roasted with rosemary, and a bowl of cress. There was fresh bread and a tub of sweet butter, a hard cheese and a dish of apples. The men ate heartily, washing it all down with brown ale. Eibhlin O'Malley had come from her convent on Innishturk to see her sister, and after the meal the four women sat companionably talking about the fire while the men remained at the table drinking and, from the sound of the ribald laughter, telling stories a lady should not hear. Skye could not help but notice how well her brothers got on with Adam, and it gave her great pleasure. The O'Malley brothers might not realize it, but they were taking their first step along the road to tolerance. They had accepted an Englishman into their midst without any trouble at all.

Skye was surprised when Brian came to her amid the chatter of the women, and drew her aside. "My brothers and I have been talking this afternoon about what you said. Do you really think the English Queen would give us letters of marque?"

"Yes, but make no mistake, Brian, 'tis for her good as well as yours."

"Ye mean she'll be getting a share of the booty we capture?"

"Aye, but she'll also be getting the O'Malleys of Innisfana off of her royal neck. If there is one thing Elizabeth Tudor believes in, little brother, it is peace. She wants no wars, for she knows that wars destroy a country's economy.

"There is one other thing about the Queen, Brian," Skye continued. "You'll have to come with me to England if you're to get your letters of marque."

"Never!" Brian shouted, and everyone in the hall turned to look at him. "I'll not leave blessed Ireland to set foot in that accursed land!"

"Don't be an ignorant and superstitious fool, Brian!" Skye retorted as quickly. "You'll come with me to England, and present yourself before the Queen. You can't ask Elizabeth Tudor for a favor from afar."

"I'd rather not ask her for anything," Brian grumbled.

"You'll be a rich man in no time, Brian," Skye wheedled him. "You can then afford to build a whole new wing onto the house just for yourself and Maggie and the children. Wouldn't you like that, Maggie?" Skye appealed to her young sister-in-law.

"Aye, I would!" Maggie said bluntly.

"You'd all be rich," Skye promised her half-brothers, "and then you could each build a wing onto the house and marry the lass of your choice, for with gold in your pockets you'd have a choice and be a desirable match to any father's eye. Isn't that better than the cheap chances you take with Grace O'Malley?"

"I'll not go to England," Brian said firmly.

"The Queen won't give you the letters of marque sight unseen," Skye argued.

"I'll go."

They all turned to look at Skye's youngest brother, Conn. "You'll go?" she said.

"Aye," Conn replied. "I've a mind to see England, and the red-haired virgin vixen who rules it. Will I do, Skye?" He grinned engagingly at his sister.

Skye looked him over critically. Conn was the youngest, but he was the biggest, standing almost as tall as Adam. Cleaned up, his beard barbered decently, elegant clothes upon his back, and a quick course in manners, he might very well do. Elizabeth did like clever and attractive young men, and Skye had to admit that Conn was both. "Aye," she said. "You'll do quite well." She looked at Brian and the others. "Do you have any objections to Conn going?"

"Nay," they replied with one voice, all obviously relieved not to have to go themselves.

"It's settled then," Skye said.

"When will you leave?" Brian asked.

"Not for several days," Skye answered him. "I want to see Ewan and Gwyneth and our uncle, the bishop. I'll send a message off tomorrow, however, to tell Bess Tudor that we're coming to pay her a call."

The next morning Skye arose early to write to the Queen.

> *Madame, My brothers beg your indulgence for the*
> *overabundance of high spirits that caused them to foolishly*
> *join with our distant cousin, Grace O'Malley. I have*
> *suggested that a proper channel for my brothers' exuberance*
> *would be to carry letters of marque from Your Gracious*
> *Majesty that would allow them to exercise their energies in*
> *foreign waters to both their own and Your Majesty's great*
> *advantage. I will shortly be arriving in England with my*
> *youngest brother, Conn O'Malley, who will tender a request*
> *for Your Majesty's favor on behalf of his brothers and*
> *himself. I remain as always Your Majesty's friend. Skye,*
> *Lady de Marisco*

Skye watched dispassionately as the thick green sealing wax dripped onto the folded letter, and she pressed the O'Malley ring of office into the hot puddle before it hardened. The letter was dispatched immediately aboard one of her ships, captained by Bran Kelly. She was relieved to have the letter off, and the matter settled. She walked back into the bedchamber, crawled back beneath the down coverlet, and sighed.

Adam reached out and pulled her into his embrace, his arm cradling her, settling her head against his shoulder. "What is it, little girl?" he asked, kissing the top of her head.

"I find I'm losing my taste for adventure," she said.

He understood her completely. "You've borne a heavy burden all alone, and for a very long time, Skye. 'Tis no wonder you're weary, sweetheart, but will you not rely on me now? Let me shoulder some of the load, or at least help you with it."

"Oh, Adam, how can I involve you in this? You're English."

"English, Irish," he replied. "It matters not, Skye. You are a woman; I, a man. We love each other, and because we do one's problems become the other's. It's really that simple. Your brothers' nationality has nothing to do with their being pigheaded. I've known Frenchmen, and Devonmen, and other Englishmen just as stubborn. It's simply their nature, and together you and I will overcome that nature. I am encouraged that Conn desires to see the Tudor court."

"Let's take him back to Lynmouth first," she said. "We'll have to clean him up, and get him outfitted, and teach him how to behave, for I'll not have the court laughing at him. Like as not, Conn would kill half a dozen men should he feel insulted. I'm not introducing him into Elizabeth Tudor's world to cause havoc and be sneered at as a typical Irisher. I want those letters of marque for the O'Malleys."

"You'll get them, Skye."

"I wish I was as sure as you are, Adam."

Adam chuckled. "If Conn is half the charmer I suspect he is, the Queen will melt. Besides, being a practical woman, she will be relieved to have the O'Malleys of Innisfana off harrying the Spanish instead of the English."

Skye smiled to herself, realizing the simple truth of Adam's words, and she snuggled harder against him. "Then I'll not worry, my husband, and instead I shall concentrate on indulging my baser appetites," she murmured, sliding her hand beneath his nightshirt. With teasing hands she fondled him, caressing and cupping him, and feeling him grow hard beneath her touch.

Adam lay very still, only the sudden quickening of his breath indication at first of her success. He loved the way she touched him with her hot and gentle little hands. In his lifetime he could not remember any woman rousing him as completely and as quickly as Skye could. When she moved herself down to take him in her mouth he groaned with unashamed pleasure at her actions, and fought to maintain his control, for now he desperately desired to possess and be possessed. "Ahh, my Celtic witch, ride me!" he finally begged her, and Skye willingly obeyed her husband's request, lifting her head from his manhood, kissing its throbbing scarlet head, and then mounting him to plunge downward so that he was enclosed by her eager sheath. Reaching up, Adam played gently with her beautiful breasts, tormenting the little nipples so that they thrust and quivered with his touch. Watching her through half-closed eyes, he was amused to find her own eyes closed.

Drawing her closer, he raised his head up and took one of those little peaks into his mouth. Balanced on one elbow, he cupped her breast in his other hand, loving it thoroughly as he did so. His tongue encircled the tautness, warm and so, so soft against her hardness. He sucked and nibbled on her flesh, and Skye gasped with pleasure as small darts of liquid fire raced through her veins, leaving her weak. With a smile of triumph Adam rolled her onto her back, and began thrusting into her honeyed warmth. Skye's nails dug fiercely into his muscled shoulders, but her rounded hips began to thrust back at him. He pushed deeper and deeper into her until she thought he could go no further, but the next thrust penetrated deeper still as she threw her legs up and wrapped them around him. Now her nails raked down his back, scoring the smooth skin with fine crimson lines. Skye felt she was soaring; soaring higher than she had ever gone before. She felt helpless beneath his strength, and yet she felt stronger than she ever had.

The first wave of passion washed wildly over her, and Adam slowed his movement despite her whimpered protest. He laughed softly, a deep and sensuous sound. "Oh no, little girl, not quite yet. You're a hungry wench, I can see, but I'm of a mind to play with you a bit longer. What you started, sweetheart, I shall finish." All the while he spoke he moved slowly upon her. Again he increased the tempo of his erotic rhythm until she was sobbing with pleasure.

The whirling world was filled with a golden light that pulsed and throbbed all about her. His possession filled her with unbelievable peace amidst the turbulence of their passion. He gave so much, and Skye wanted to give back, but the second wave overtook her, and then in quick bursts the third and forth waves overcame her, rendering her almost unconscious, and she cried out. To her surprise, he cried out also, and then she felt his seed filling her full, and his head dropped to her breasts. She could barely catch her breath, but she kissed his head and caressed the back of his neck soothingly.

He rolled away from her, and they lay side by side until at last the storm had passed and they drifted into a contented sleep.

When they awoke the morning was well along, and Skye scrambled guiltily from the warmth of their bed. "God's nightshirt!" she swore. "My family will think me a slugabed. 'Tis past nine, I'm certain, and I had planned to visit my Uncle Seamus today. Where in Hell is Daisy with my bath water?" She flung open the bedchamber door and peered into the dayroom.

"So, ye're up!" Daisy looked somewhat askance at her mistress, and Skye realized she was nude.

"Where's my bath?" she demanded with an effort at nonchalance.

"If I'd fetched it earlier," Daisy replied tartly, "'twould be ice cold at this moment. I'll see to it now, m'lady," and she bustled out of the room.

"You've the prettiest bottom I've ever seen," Adam teased her.

Skye whirled about, laughing. "Oh, 'tis a bold one you are, my lord husband! It's a good hour's ride to my uncle's house, and I did promise him I'd come whenever I arrived back on Innisfana. 'Tis certain he knows I'm here, and has, I've not a doubt, been waiting for me since dawn. He's an old man, Adam, and frail. I would not disappoint him."

"We'll not disappoint him, little girl, and I intend to ride with you, for I've not met the good bishop. Does he hate the English, too?"

"I'm not sure it's all the English, Adam. Just the ones who happen to gain his disfavor by not agreeing with him," she chuckled, and Adam laughed.

"In other words," he said, "a typical O'Malley."

She launched herself at him, grabbing a large handful of his dark hair and yanking. "Beast! I can see I must teach you to be more respectful of the O'Malleys of Innisfana!"

He wrestled her to the mattress, and then across the bed as they playfully fought and struggled until both collapsed in a fit of laughter. Mischievously he spanked her bottom, eliciting a shriek of outrage from her. "'Twill teach you better manners toward your lord, wench!" he scolded with mock ferocity.

"My lord is a lop-eared ass," she threw back, rubbing her injured flesh.

Adam grabbed Skye and drew her down into a passionate embrace. "My lady is a hot-blooded little bitch who arouses me beyond mortal comprehension," he murmured softly as he began to nibble at her lips.

"Is *this* bath to get cold too, or will you wash?" came the scathing demand from Daisy.

Skye squirmed from her husband's arms, but their eyes met in total understanding and love. "I'm coming," she said to her tiring woman.

"So am I," Adam said, beginning to rise from the bed. "Get thee hence, Daisy lass, unless you're interested in my bottom and . . ." He waggled his eyebrows at her threateningly.

"Who's to wash my lady?" Daisy demanded, outraged.

"I will," came Adam's reply.

"More than likely ye'll end up back in that tumbled bed," Daisy grumbled, "but who am I to say. Very well then, I'll give you both fifteen minutes, and as fer being interested, m'lord, there's nothing ye've got I ain't seen before." Then with her nose in the air Daisy flounced out.

Skye giggled at Adam's look of outrage as much as Daisy's tart comment. "Aye, Adam," she further teased her husband, "Daisy's a married woman now, and I've heard it said that Bran Kelly can hold his own with the best of them." Then sticking out her tongue at her husband, Skye scampered from their bedchamber to the dayroom, where the tall oak tub had been placed before the fire. Wrinkling her nose with pleasure, she breathed in the rose bath oil already perfuming the room in the tendrils of steam that came from the hot water. Quickly she pinned her hair atop her head. Adam caught up with her as she was about to climb up the three wooden steps that led to the tub, and twirling her about, he kissed her.

"We're never going to get bathed and off to my uncle's," she protested faintly against his mouth, thinking how good it felt to be enclosed in his arms.

"Yes, we will," he said, and lifted her into the tub before climbing in to join her. "Good God! I'm going to smell like a damned garden, madam!"

"'Twas your idea to bathe with me," she pointed out.

"Aye," he grumbled, "but I can imagine what your brothers will think if they get a whiff of me."

"Our delay in getting up, plus Daisy's gossiping should reassure them on all counts," Skye laughed. "Come now, m'lord, you promised to maid me." She handed him her soap. "Wash my back!"

"Only if I can wash your front as well," he countered.

"*Adam!*"

He turned her around and began soaping her long back. "You were more fun when you were my sometime mistress," he teased, chuckling at her gasp of outrage. "Aye," he murmured, kissing the tempting back of her neck, "being a wife has sobered you greatly, little girl." He turned her around, kissed her on the nose, and, handing her the soap, said, "Now you wash my back, madam."

"Only if I can wash the front, too," she mocked him.

"If you dare, little girl," he said.

"What will my uncle think of you, Adam de Marisco?" she lamented.

The old bishop of Mid-Connaught thought very well of his favorite niece's new husband. They had never met face to face, but Seamus O'Malley felt he knew Adam de Marisco from all the things that Skye had said of him over the years; from his reputation as the lord of Lundy Isle; and from the letters they had exchanged, letters that usually had to do with Skye and her well-being. Seamus O'Malley knew that Adam loved his niece, and the old man understood that love was what she needed most of all. The love of a strong and good man; a man who would stand tall and prevent Skye from pursuing any future reckless course.

Seamus O'Malley was in his middle seventies, and he had not been a well man for two years now. Because of his destruction of Burke Castle there was a price on his head; a price no one had dared to collect yet. Still, the fact of it filled his life with a tension that had not been there before. In the last six months his health had deteriorated greatly, and he had not left Innisfana Island to care for the spiritual well-being of his people. He lived in a big stone house on the cliffs overlooking the sea, but despite his illnesses, he yet said the early mass in the nearby village church each morning.

It was midday when Skye and Adam arrived to see him. The door to the house was opened by Maeve, the wife of Connor FitzBurke, Niall Burke's bastard brother. When they had been driven from Burke lands, the FitzBurkes had come with the elderly bishop, to care for him. The two women embraced warmly, and

Maeve FitzBurke stepped back to hold Skye at arm's length. She was a small, pretty woman with warm, brown eyes and reddish hair.

"How is it possible?" she said. "You're as beautiful as ever! D'ye never age, Skye O'Malley?"

"Look closely, Maeve, and you'll see the lines," Skye laughed. Then she drew Adam forward. "This is my husband, Lord de Marisco, Maeve."

Maeve smiled warmly. "I'd heard ye were a big man," she said. "Come in then for he's been waiting impatiently for ye to arrive since after mass."

"Where is Connor?" Skye asked as they entered the house.

"Off seeing to the sheep and cattle that His Grace keeps these days," was the reply as Maeve led them up a staircase. "Don't be too shocked, Skye. Yer uncle is an old man, and it broke his heart when the English Queen took Burke Castle from little Lord Burke. He's failed over the last few months, and he's not strong. He feels the cold greatly this autumn, and I doubt he'll live to see the spring."

Skye felt unbidden tears pricking at her eyes, and she stopped a moment to regain her control. Maeve seemed to know, and paused before the paneled oak door, her hand upon the latch. "I'm all right now," Skye said softly, and Adam reached for her hand and squeezed it reassuringly.

Maeve swung the door wide, saying as she entered the room, "Well, my lord Bishop, and here she is at last!"

The old gentleman in the plaid woolen shawl by the fireplace looked up, and Skye ran toward him to kneel at his side and kiss his gnarled hand with its heavy gold ring of office. "So, lass!" His body might be frail, but Seamus O'Malley's voice was as strong as ever. "Get up, Skye, and let me look at ye! At least my eyes are still sharp. Ye're as fair as ever, lass. I remember when ye were born, and Dubhdara was so disappointed ye weren't a lad, but ye were a beauty even then and immediately stole his heart." He paused a moment, "Even as ye stole mine, too."

Skye bent and kissed him on the forehead. "Dearest Uncle," she murmured.

"Now dammit, lass, don't be going sentimental on me," he grumbled. "Introduce me to this giant I suspect is yer husband." He thrust his hand forward for Adam to kiss.

"Indeed, Uncle, this is Adam de Marisco, my husband," Skye said.

As Adam made his obeisance to the bishop, Seamus O'Malley grinned, and said, "Aye, he's just right for ye, Skye. Worships the ground ye walk on, I can see, and spoils ye shamelessly. Still I see enough strength in him that ye'd best beware of driving him too far lest he beat ye, as ye no doubt deserve on occasion. Sit down, nephew! Ye're as tall as a tree, and I prefer to speak to ye face to face, not face to codpiece!" He cackled at his own wit, then commanded, "Maeve! Bring some whiskey, for I'm fair chilled. 'Tis a bitter day, a bitter day."

They drew up chairs, and sat facing the old man. Almost at once he engaged Adam in a lively conversation. Skye was content to sit back watching the men she loved, and swirling the amber fire called whiskey around in her goblet. Her eyes devoured her uncle lovingly. He had grown old in the several years since she had seen him. His hair was now snow white, though once it had been as black as hers. His eyes, however, were still bright blue, and lively with interest in the world about him. He was thin, and his bony hands trembled with the effort of holding his glass. How he conducted the daily mass she did not understand, except that he obviously put all his strength into it and then spent the rest of his time resting from the effort.

"Skye?" His voice penetrated her thoughts.

"Aye, Uncle?"

"I'm sorry about Burke Castle. Will the Queen return Padraic's lands?"

"Nay, Uncle. She gave him lands in England. She said he'd be raised as a good Englishman, and 'twould be one less Irish rebel for her to worry about."

Seamus O'Malley nodded and smiled slightly. Although he saw the humor in it he also saw the wisdom in it. "Ye've few ties left in Ireland, lass."

"I'm still the O'Malley, Uncle."

"For how long, lass? 'Tis not fair ye retain the office now that Dubhdara's sons are grown."

"Grown into selfish fools, Uncle!" Skye snapped. "I'd be doing Da a disservice to make Brian the O'Malley right now. All he wants to do is pirate with our cousin Grace. He cares nothing about building our wealth. All he wants to do is waste it!"

"What will ye do then, lass?"

"I've suggested if he wants to go pirating with his brothers that they obtain letters of marque from the Queen, and pirate the Spanish Main rather than English shipping. That way, they can keep on the good side of the Queen without really serving her, and fill their own coffers with good gold at the same time. Brian agreed, and Conn is to come to England with me to speak with the Queen. If Brian and the others will keep out of trouble in the next year, I'll turn over my badge of office to him, and consider my duty to the O'Malleys done."

"'Tis fair," the bishop agreed.

"I don't want the power any longer, Uncle," Skye said. "I've had it all my life, it seems, and I'm tired. My children have grown up barely knowing me, but I'll not let my youngest, Velvet, be without me after this. I've a home in France, and the Queen has promised us estates to make up for Lundy."

"The restlessness is gone then, lass?"

"Aye," she said. "I seek peace now, Uncle, and I know that it lies with Adam and our daughter, and my other children."

Seamus O'Malley nodded. "Yer father, God assoil him, was like that when he married Anne. He never wanted to go far after that. Ye've already found yer peace, Skye lass, and I'll not tell ye to be a good and faithful wife to Adam, for I can see that ye already are. It makes me happy to see it, for if things are right with ye, then I can rest easy and face my brother with a clear conscience."

Skye rose from her chair and, bending down, kissed her aged uncle, hugging him hard. "Seamus O'Malley, I love you!" she said.

The old man smiled over her shoulder at Adam, and hugged her back. "Whist, lass! Next ye'll be weeping all over me!" he scolded her lovingly, but his expression was one of pleased delight at her open show of affection.

They stayed the entire day, and overnight as well. It was a happy time for them all. In the morning when they were ready to leave Skye hurried to her uncle's rooms to bid him farewell, Adam following. Seamus O'Malley sat by the fire once more, his head upon his narrow chest, his hands resting quietly in his lap. The fire crackled noisily, but it seemed not to disturb him. Skye smiled down on him, and called softly, "Uncle, I must go now." There was no answer. "Uncle?" She reached out to gently shake him, and he was cold to her touch. Skye's hand flew to her mouth. "*Adam!*"

Adam de Marisco knelt to inspect the old man. When he rose there were tears in his eyes. "He's dead, Skye," the lord of Lundy told his wife, and then gathered her into his arms while she wept stormily.

The Bishop of Mid-Connaught, Seamus O'Malley, was buried on his favorite niece's thirty-fourth birthday. He had been waked for five long days, for it had taken that long to gather all of Skye's brothers and sisters and their families on Innisfana. Looking around at Skye's sisters, Moire, Peigi, Bride, and Sine, Adam was startled by their plainness in comparison with his wife's beauty. He had never noticed that plainness in Eibhlin, for the nun was so full of life and her work. The others, however, were prim women who openly disapproved of their youngest sister's liaison with an Englishman. Only the fact that Adam de Marisco shared their faith made him barely tolerable to them. Hearing their tales of their struggles with the English, he could understand their bitterness. They were old before their time with childbearing and the harshness of the land in which they lived. None had attained either the wealth or the fine matches that their youngest sister had. They had come with their husbands, bluff, red-faced men, none of whom could speak the English tongue. Adam, fortunately, knew enough Gaelic to converse briefly with them; and it was decided among Skye's brothers-in-law that if her English husband could speak the Gaelic, he mightn't be too bad a fellow. It was also noted with approval that he could hold his whiskey, and seemed to have firm control of his wife, who was thought to be too forward for a woman.

Michael O'Malley said the mass for his uncle, and afterward the coffin was carried to the family burial ground by the bishop's four younger nephews, his great-nephew, Ewan O'Flaherty, and Connor Fitzburke. In the hall afterward, Moire said what they were all thinking.

"'Twas our last link with the past and Da. Now 'tis gone."

"We'll always have the memories," Sine said hopefully.

"Pah!" Peigi said sharply. "The age has ended, and that's all there is to it!"

"Uncle Seamus was the one thing that kept this family close, and together," Bride volunteered. "Now, I suppose we'll all go our own ways."

"We've been doing that for years," Moire replied.

"'Tis the way of it," Eibhlin said quietly. "All families scatter at one point in time. Especially the daughters, and God knows Da had his share of daughters."

"We've made Da proud," Moire said, "at least some of us have. I've borne eighteen children, thirteen of whom lived. Peigi has twelve living, Bride nine, and Sine eleven. Even you, barren stock though you chose to be, would have made him proud with yer medicines and piety." Moire looked around at her siblings. "Aye, Da would be proud of some of us."

"Da would be proud of me also, Moire," Skye said quietly. "You've been most obvious in leaving me out, but let me tell you that I've done just what he would have wanted me to over the years, and I've borne eight children as well. I've overseen three estates for my children as well as great wealth, and I've done well, Moire, by the O'Malleys!"

"Ye lost the Burke lands with yer carryings on!" Moire snapped.

"I lost the Burke lands because I was married in France without the Queen's blessing," Skye retorted angrily. "The Queen broke her word to me, for we made a bargain and I kept my part of that bargain. Had I returned to England without a husband Elizabeth Tudor would have used me again, and I will never be used again by anyone, Moire! What in Hell could you possibly know about it, living in a backwater manor house in an out-of-the-way village in Ireland?"

"Brian tells me that ye've advised him and our brothers to go into service with the English Queen."

"Nay! I've advised them to obtain letters of marque from her and to go plundering along the Spanish Main. 'Twill keep them out of trouble here in Ireland, and fill our coffers as well, Moire. Should they keep on the way they're going, they'll lose everything, and Da wouldn't want that."

"The Spanish are our friends," Moire protested. "We share the same faith!"

"Spare me your religious qualms, Moire," Skye replied impatiently. "The Spanish use us the same way the French use the Scots. 'Tis to their own advantage. Religion plays no part in it. If the Spanish occasionally give the Irish arms 'tis only so they'll harry the English, which is to Spain's interest and certainly not Ireland's. Do the English punish the Spanish? Nay! Rather they come with a vengeance to us, and 'tis Irish blood that flows in the streets, and Irish women who weep tears of pain and shame, and Irish children who starve for lack of their fathers to feed and defend them. Our *friends* never suffer; rather we, the Irish, do, and 'tis our own fault! We will not unite beneath one banner, and until we do there will be no peace or real freedom in Ireland!"

"Ye were always different," Moire countered, and then she spoke no more on it.

The next morning Skye's sisters and their families departed for their own homes, bidding their youngest sister farewell with little warmth. The years had treated them quite differently, and sadly, Skye was as much a stranger to them as a woman taken in from the streets would have been. She understood them all too well, for her life experience had been broad. They understood her not at all, for their experience had been narrow. Still she kissed them and bid them God speed.

"Good riddance!" Eibhlin muttered as the last of them rode off down the road, and Skye laughed, tucking her hand through her favorite sister's arm as they walked back into the hall.

"Why is it that you understand and they don't?" she asked.

"Because they are more cloistered in their lives than I, despite my religious calling, have ever been. My medicine has allowed me to see more of the human condition and the world than they have. Besides they have always been jealous of your beauty, Skye, as well as your husbands. Think on it, sister. For thirty-one years Moire has been humped by but one man, and from her sour face I wager he scarce comes near her anymore. And I've always suspected that she says the rosary while he is atop her. I'll wager you don't say yer rosary while Adam makes love to you!"

"*Eibhlin!*" Skye blushed rosily, and Adam, overhearing his sister-in-law's wry remarks, roared with laughter.

"Nay, Eibhlin, she says not her rosary, for I keep her far too busy saying other things!"

"You're shameless!" Skye cried, "and 'tis worse with you, Eibhlin, for you're a nun!"

"True," her older sister agreed, "but I'm also a woman." Then she changed the subject. "What think ye of Mistress Gwenyth?"

"That I'm overyoung to be a grandmother," Skye laughed. "Isn't it wonderful, Eibhlin! You'll be with her when her time comes, won't you?"

"Aye, Skye, I will, and believe me, Ballyhennessey is a far better place today in which to have a child than it was when you birthed Ewan and Murrough. I'll not forget the snow drifting across the floor while I tried to keep you and the baby warm."

"Ewan is nothing like his father," Skye replied. "Neither, thank God, is Murrough! They're *my* sons, and they are good boys."

"Tell me of my newest niece?" Eibhlin said.

Skye looked at Adam, and they smiled. "Velvet's an impossible baggage, Eibhlin, but we love her dearly!"

"In other words," Eibhlin chuckled, "she is her parents' child."

"Aye!" they both replied with one voice, and then laughed.

"When will you return to England, for I imagine you are anxious to be with your child."

"We sail tomorrow, Eibhlin. Brian has promised me he will immediately disassociate himself and the O'Malleys of Innisfana from Grace O'Malley and her pirates. 'Tis easily done right now, for the winter is upon us and they'll be no more ships to chase until spring. By then I hope to have the letters of marque for the O'Malleys, and they can sail west to play havoc with the Spanish in the New World."

Eibhlin nodded with approval. "Ye've saved those four dolts, though they know it not. If they'd continued on their merry course, they'd have ended up on the gallows for sure, and then ye'd never be free of the O'Malleys. Give Brian the office as soon as you reasonably can, Skye. 'Tis past time ye had yer own life."

Adam silently agreed with Eibhlin O'Malley, and he was not sorry the following day to bid farewell to Brian, Shane, and Shamus O'Malley, and their mother. Anne, of course, was worried for her youngest, Conn, who was to sail with them, but Adam saw that the young man was anxious to free himself of both his mother and his three older brothers. Secretly Adam wondered if his youngest brother-in-law would ever go privateering in the New World. From Conn O'Malley's questions about Skye's trading business, Adam suspected he'd not.

They reached Devon several days later, anchoring in the harbor of Lynmouth Castle, and then rowing ashore. Daisy hurried to her cottage to see her small sons, while Skye sent out messengers to

Dame Cecily at Wren Court and to the Queen saying that she had returned and would be keeping Christmas at Greenwich with her Majesty. Then she put her mind to the task of turning her brother into a gentleman worthy of the Tudor court.

Conn roared like a lion as his shaggy hair was shorn from his head, and his thick bushy beard cropped neatly. He howled like a banshee to find himself in a steaming tub that smelt of lavender while his own sister, her sleeves rolled above her elbow, plied the scrubbing brush herself.

"Ye're killing me!" he yelled in Gaelic as she scrubbed his newly barbered hair.

"Speak English, you clod!" she roared back at him. "You'll be laughed right out of the damned English court unless you do!"

"To Hell with the English!"

"My sentiments, too," Skye laughed, "but you need the bastards, Conn! Besides, the court is filled with pretty girls just dying to meet a big, handsome man like yourself. If you don't speak their language, how will you communicate with them?"

"I've not done so bad to date, sister," he replied.

"With the serving girls?" she mocked him. "Haven't you ever learned the difference between a lady and a wench, little brother? You'd best if you're to be a success at court, and you'd better be a success at court, Conn. Your brothers need those letters of marque."

Conn O'Malley put his mind to becoming a gentleman. He was nineteen years old, and stood several inches over six feet in height. Like his sister, he was fair with midnight-black hair. A recalcitrant lock tumbled over his brow, giving him a look both innocent and rakish. Of all the O'Malleys he was the only one whose eyes were neither gray nor bright blue. His, instead, were a grayish green. He was an enormously handsome man with a straight nose, high forehead, and square, chiseled jaw.

He looked marvelous in decently tailored clothing, having long, elegant legs, narrow hips, slim waist, and a broad chest and shoulders. Seeing him suitably garbed a week after they had arrived, Adam swore softly, saying, "By God, the women will be throwing themselves at his feet. We'll have to fight every father and husband at court, Skye." Conn grinned back engagingly with a flash of white, white teeth. "I promise not to be too hard a man on all the little darlin's, Adam," he said.

"God help us," Adam muttered.

Conn was quick, and he easily learned all that Skye and Adam could teach him. Dame Cecily worked with him too, drilling him in his speech so that by the time they were ready to depart for Greenwich, Conn spoke English fluently, albeit with a soft trace of a brogue. It only added to his charm.

They departed for London several days before Christmas, and riding within the coach with Skye and Adam, Conn O'Malley could scarce be pulled away from the windows. His young eyes devoured the passing countryside with its neat farms and orchards and houses. The same eyes widened as they passed through the towns with their bustling shops and open markets and four-story houses. He had never in his young life seen the like of it, and he was fascinated by it all. He asked questions unceasingly, and Skye suddenly realized how different this last child of her father's was from his siblings. He was, she decided, more like herself and Eibhlin than any of the others. She could just imagine Brian seated in Conn's place, a dour face on him, grumbling the entire way. Skye was rather happy to get to know Conn better, and she found that she liked him.

"Look, Conn!" Leaning out the coach window, Skye pointed. "London!"

Conn O'Malley's jaw dropped in honest surprise as the city came into his view. The churches were enormous with spires that soared skyward as high as the mountains in his homeland. The houses were all jammed in together along with the shops, and there were more people than he'd ever seen in one place at one time. The noise was ferocious, but it was the stink of the streets that surprised him more than anything else.

"'Tis worse than an unshoveled cow byre," he said.

Adam laughed. "In a sense that's exactly what it is, Conn. The sanitation isn't the best in London. You'd best be careful when walking the streets lest you get the contents of a slop jar poured over you. Should you hear the cry of ''*Ware!*' get out of the way, lad!"

"Where are we going?" Conn asked his sister. Not realizing the size of London, he hadn't thought of where they might stay, assuming it would be another of the comfortable inns they had stopped at along the way. Now he wasn't quite so sure.

"I have a house in a small village just bordering the city, called Chiswick on the Strand. The house is on the river, and within easy barge ride of Greenwich. Your nephew, the Earl of Lynmouth, has a house next door to mine. His is very grand, but mine is quite simple. You'll be comfortable there, brother."

Conn O'Malley's eyes widened again as the coach trotted smartly through the gates at Greenwood. A small man holding the gates open doffed his cap respectfully, and an equally small lady with a smiling face curtseyed from the gatehouse door. Skye waved gaily at both of them. "'Tis Bates and his wife," she said to her brother. Conn sat still and silently. The coach made its way through the beautifully landscaped park and up the curving drive to the house. Skye's brother took in the lovely house of mellowed pink brick, partly covered in shiny green ivy.

Before the house now stood several men in green-and-white livery, who hurried to open the carriage door, take down the steps, and help the occupants forth. As they entered the house a slightly more elegant liveried man hurried forward, saying, "Welcome home, m'lady!"

"Thank you, Walters," Skye replied. "This is my youngest brother, Master Conn O'Malley. He's come to court."

"Welcome, sir," was Walters's reply. Then he turned back to Skye and Adam. "A message came for you from Greenwich with Lord Burghley's man. It was verbal, and I was asked to repeat it to you. You are to let Lord Burghley know as soon as you arrive in London. He will inform Her Majesty, and a date will be set for you to be received at Greenwich."

"Send someone at once," Adam instructed. "I've not a doubt the Queen is anxious to see us."

"Very good, m'lord."

Skye moved up the main staircase of her house to the library, her husband and her brother following. Behind them the baggage was being brought in, and Daisy busily directed the footmen with each piece. Velvet, in the arms of her nurse, Nora, a younger cousin of Daisy's, was carried up to her nursery to be put to bed. As Nora hurried past Conn, he stopped her long enough to place a soft kiss upon his niece's head.

"Good night, kitten," he said softly. "Have happy dreams."

"You spoil her," Skye noted, but she was pleased that Conn had developed such a deep affection for her little daughter, an affection that was quite mutual, for Velvet adored her handsome uncle. Velvet, her mother thought, liked all the gentlemen, and Lord knew the men were easily enamored of her child.

"You're smiling," Adam said as he poured them each a goblet of red wine.

"I'm thinking that Velvet already knows her powers with regard to the gentlemen," Skye replied.

"Aye," Conn grinned. "She's a proper minx, Velvet is. She's but nineteen months old, but I've no doubt ye'd best find her a husband early. With luck ye might turn her into a well-brought-up little lady, but I doubt it!" he chuckled, and then he sat down by the fire opposite his sister.

"We have more important things to think on now," Skye said. "I've turned you into the perfect courtier, Conn, provided you don't lose your fine Irish temper and spoil it. There are plenty of Irish at court who are civilized, despite what some of the greater snobs will say. Don't let those idiots make you ruin your reputation, brother. The worst of them are the least among the English, and they only naggle at us in order to bolster their own puny egos. If you don't let them get to you, they will soon grow tired of their silly game and devour each other."

"Don't they know that while their ancestors were still painting themselves blue for battle, and living in tree shelters, we Irish had universities and great poets?" Conn demanded irritably.

"No, Conn darlin', they don't know. They believe that the sun rises and sets on England, and nothing you can say will alter their ignorance. Don't even try, Conn. You need only have faith in yourself to succeed. If you do, none of the stupid insults thrown at you will matter. Remember what Da always taught me. The survival of the family is paramount, Conn. Nothing else matters."

"Do you think the Queen will see us fairly soon?"

"Oh, yes! Elizabeth Tudor will be curious to meet you. Oh, Conn, you've such an advantage! You're young, handsome, clever, well mannered, and fairly well educated. In short, just the kind of young man the Queen adores. Use that advantage. Pay her court. Flirt with her. Remember, though, that 'tis only a game with the

Queen. You will be a success, I promise you, and then you will get the letters of marque that the O'Malleys need."

"Is she attractive? I mean, *really*? I know that all the gossips praise her, but what is she really like, Skye?"

"She'll be forty this year, Conn. She's old enough to be your mother, but she's a handsome woman. She has marvelous white, white skin, and golden red hair. Her eyes are a gray-black and they see everything. She is very educated, and enjoys quick repartee. She's a brilliant and clever woman. She likes to dance, so there you'll shine. You'll like her, but beware, little brother. She can be stronger and harsher than any man I've ever met if the occasion warrants it."

"You intrigue me, sister," Conn replied. "I am more anxious than ever now to meet this paragon of womanhood."

Conn O'Malley arrived at court two days before Christmas of 1574. He wore dark green velvet, and his trunk hose was striped in green velvet and gold silk. His doublet was embroidered with gold threads, pearls, turquoises, and small diamonds in a seascape pattern. The buttons on the doublet were gold, and at the wrists and neck of the garment the finest lace showed. He wore a short Spanish cape lined in beaver with a half-erect collar lined in cloth of gold. On his feet he wore tight-fitting leather boots with cuffs that turned upward, and about his neck was a heavy gold chain and a red-gold medallion with the O'Malley sea dragon carved upon it, its ruby eyes most real.

At the last moment Skye had convinced her brother to shave his beard and mustache off entirely, and, as she had suspected, beneath the black hair there was an outrageously handsome face.

"God's blood," Adam swore, looking at the younger man. "You could be your sister's twin!"

"Considering I'm fifteen years older than he is that's quite a compliment, my darling," Skye laughed, "but I knew there was a handsome devil lurking beneath all that growth. Dear Lord, Conn, the women will be throwing themselves at you. You'll have your pick of the entire court!"

"Poor lasses," Conn mourned with a long face. "'Tis only Bess Tudor I'll court."

Both Skye and Adam laughed, and then leading the way, they left the house. Embarking upon their barge, they moved downriver to Greenwich. Adam sat silent watching the landscape go by as Skye instructed her brother in last-minute details. God, how beautiful she was, Adam thought as he watched her. She was dressed in crimson velvet, her cloak lined and edged in ermine, her jewels—rubies and diamonds—sparkling in the torchlight. She carried an ermine muff embroidered with diamonds and pearls, and framed within the hood of the cloak, her face was radiant. She scented victory, he thought, and he was glad. Once this matter of the O'Malleys was settled, he intended to take her away and never again share her with anyone but their large and loving family.

The towers of Greenwich Palace came into view, and Adam reached out to take his wife's small hand in his own big one. She never turned her head, but she squeezed him, and he squeezed back. The barge took its place in the line of barges heading for the royal landing.

"Skye! Oh, Skye!" A lovely red-haired woman in the barge ahead of them waved her lace handkerchief frantically.

Skye nodded an acknowledgment as Conn noted, "A prime piece of goods, sister. You will introduce me?"

"To Lettice Knollys? She's the Countess of Essex, Conn, and much too rich for your blood. Besides, I suspect she is involved with Lord Dudley, though if the Queen knew it she'd have her cousin Lettice's pretty head."

"Behind us," Conn said. "Who is that overly fashionable gentleman?"

"Edward de Vere, the Earl of Oxford. He's Burghley's son-in-law, though he's a bad one, I'm told."

Their barge bumped the landing, and the Queen's footmen made it fast so its occupants might disembark. They stood a moment upon the quai landing, Skye shaking her skirts to be sure all the wrinkles were out when Lettice Knollys approached them.

"Skye darling! You're back! Who are these two handsome gentlemen escorting you?" she demanded playfully.

"Lettice, my husband, Adam, Lord de Marisco." Adam smiled, and kissed the Countess of Essex's beringed hand while she assessed him with frankly admiring eyes. "And my youngest brother, Conn O'Malley. Conn, this is the Countess of Essex."

Conn slowly lifted Lettice's hand up to his lips while his gray-green eyes caught her amber ones in a passionate gaze. With equal slowness he pressed a long, warm kiss upon the milk-white back of her hand. "Madam," he said, his eyes never leaving hers, "I have been told you are but a pale imitation of your cousin, the Queen, but the beauty I see before me blinds me."

The Countess of Essex was stunned by this incredible compliment, and for a moment she could not draw her breath. She felt nearer to fainting than she had ever been in her entire life.

A slow smile lit Conn O'Malley's face, turning up the corners of his sensuous mouth and crinkling the corners of his eyes. Firmly he tucked Lettice Knollys's hand into his arm. "Allow me to escort you into the palace, madam," he said smoothly, and then moved off at a sedate pace, taking the still stunned countess with him.

Skye bit her lip to keep back the laughter, and didn't even dare to look at her husband whom, she guessed, was in the same state of amusement as she. Quietly she took Adam's arm and allowed him to lead her away. When she believed she had regained her control she said softly, "Conn has made an important first conquest. I only pray that Dudley doesn't see him hovering over Lettice like a bee over a particularly fragrant flower."

"Dudley doesn't dare to publicly lust after Lettice," Adam replied. "He'll find himself in the Tower again if he does. No, I think if Conn manages to be discreet it will be all right."

They had no sooner entered the palace when Lord Burghley's secretary was at their side, begging them to please follow him. Skye detached her brother from Lettice Knollys and drew him off with them.

"So, madam, you have returned," Cecil greeted them as they entered his cabinet. "I hope the news you bring Her Majesty is good news."

"It may be, Lord Burghley," Skye replied.

"*May be?* Come, madam, I will accept nothing but success!"

"You may have it, my lord, but only in exchange for something of equal value."

"*What, madam?!* We have already given you lands for your son, Lord Burke, recognized your marriage to Lord de Marisco, returned Lundy Isle to him, and presented him with lands in Worcestershire with a fine manor house. The Queen has graciously consented to the marriage of your daughter, Willow Small, with the Earl of Alcester. What more could you possibly want?"

"Everything you have said is true, my lord Burghley, but please to note that all that the Queen has given has been for others; for my husband and my children, but there is nothing for me. What I want is very little, but it is for the O'Malleys. My lord, allow me to present to you my youngest brother, Conn O'Malley. Conn, this is William Cecil, Lord Burghley, the Queen's Secretary of State."

Conn made a respectful bow to Cecil, instinctively understanding that this was a man he could not play with but must be totally honest toward. The Queen's secretary looked the young man over carefully, and then said, "He looks like an O'Malley, that is for certain." Then he smiled a small, sour smile. "Well, young Master O'Malley, what is it the O'Malleys desire from the Queen?"

"Letters of marque, my lord. We are the finest sailors alive, we O'Malleys, and 'tis only natural that we harass our natural enemies, the English. My sister, Lady de Marisco, however, has assured me of our demise should we not cease our boyish activities, and so she suggested we channel our energies into a little privateering in the New World. We might simply go, but we feel we'll be safer sailing under the Queen's flag. And," here he grinned broadly, "a great deal more successful, too!"

William Cecil's eyes never betrayed his thoughts, but once more he was admiring of Skye. He had wondered how she would stop her now grown brothers from their rebellious activities against England. Once again she had been extremely clever. If only she were a man, he thought. He could have used that intelligence of hers for England's good. Of course, they would give the O'Malley brothers the letters of marque, but 'twas best to keep them on tenterhooks for a bit.

"I shall have to speak to the Queen about this, Master O'Malley," he said. "You are asking for something of great value from England."

"I offer England something of equal value," Conn replied pleasantly, but Burghley saw the hard look that had come into his eyes. The boy might be young, but he was his sister's brother, Lord Burghley had not a doubt.

"We shall see, we shall see," he murmured, and then turned back to Adam and Skye. "Lord de Marisco, I have here from the Queen the papers that will make you the new resident of Queen's Malvern, a royal estate outside of Worcester. Her Majesty understands that it will not make up for your beloved Lundy, but she knows you understand her reasons for forbidding you residence on your island."

Adam nodded. "I understand, but please tell Her Majesty that anyplace Skye and I are together is home for me. I will thank Her Majesty myself this evening for her generosity."

"Ah, yes, the Christmas revels," Burghley said. "Go and enjoy yourselves. I am happy to tell you that your children do quite well here at court. The Queen is most pleased with Mistress Willow, whom she is constantly holding up as a model of all the feminine virtues."

"Poor Willow!" Skye said without thinking. "How hard that must be on her."

"On the contrary, madam. She is much envied by her peers, yet at the same time both admired and loved by them. A fine young woman, madam! A fine young woman!"

"Meaning, my lord, that you wonder how I could have ever raised such a dutiful daughter," Skye gently teased Cecil.

The Secretary of State was not beyond humor, and he chuckled with dry mirth. "Quite so, madam. Quite so!"

"Be patient, my lord, I have two others. One should hopefully prove to be more like her mother."

"We can but wait, madam," he replied.

Skye swept Cecil a generous curtsey, dipping low enough to offer him a fine view of her bosom which, she noted, he was not loath to admire, for all his talk of virtue. Men, she thought, were ever thus. "I shall save a dance for you, m'lord," she said mischievously, and then taking her husband's arm, Skye, Adam, and Conn exited the room.

The Queen was sitting down to dinner in the banqueting hall, and though it was crowded, they quickly found places with Lettice Knollys, who couldn't wait to make room for Conn O'Malley.

"D'you think she'll devour him whole?" Skye whispered to Adam.

"Nay, Lettice may be greedy, but she's wise. She'll eat Conn up in little bites," he chuckled.

The hall was decorated with garlands of greenery, the fireplaces banked above with masses of pine and holly that gave the room an unusually fragrant scent. The tables were laid with white damask linen cloths, and by each place was that rarity invented in Florence only a few years before, the fork. It was gold as were the spoons and graceful knives with their sheffield blades. The plates used to set Her Majesty's table were silver, as were the goblets, each one engraved with Elizabeth Tudor's own crest. Conn never batted an eye. His sister had taught him to use forks, explaining that the high nobility, and royalty in particular, no longer liked to see daggers at their tables. There was always the chance that the dagger could be turned on one's own self or one's guests instead of the meat.

A servant hurried up to fill his goblet with a heady red wine. Conn raised the goblet, sniffed appreciatively, and took a healthy draught. Skye had warned him not to swill his wine lest his manners be considered boorish, for the Queen prized exquisite manners. The food was bounteous, including shellfish and every other kind of fish he'd ever heard of; poultry and game birds; beef, lamb, boar, ham, venison, pies with flaky crusts containing lark, sparrow, and rabbit, bowls of carrots and cabbage, artichokes in wine, cress, breads and tubs of butter. He was unable to resist such delights, but although he ate heartily, he ate with delicacy.

"I like a man who enjoys his food," Lettice murmured, and her hand strayed beneath the cloth to squeeze his thigh.

"One healthy appetite is merely indication of another," he grinned lazily at her.

"Meet me after the banquet," Lettice suggested eagerly.

"Madam, you tempt me sorely," Conn replied with honest regret in both his gray-green eyes and on his handsome face, "but you must remember that I need your royal cousin's favor. Were we caught, my fortunes would be destroyed. Surely you wouldn't want that?"

Lettice pouted. "You men newly come to court are all so serious in your intent to please Bess."

"She is the sun which rises and sets upon our world, my beauty."

"My God," Lettice said drily, "with a silver tongue like yours, Conn O'Malley, you'll have Bess behaving like a schoolgirl!"

"I can only hope," Conn murmured softly, and Lettice Knollys laughed in genuine amusement.

"Tell me, Conn O'Malley," she asked, "do you make love as well as you talk?"

"Better!" he grinned, "for it takes me less effort and thought."

Lettice Knollys's amber eyes narrowed in contemplation. "Methinks you know well the ways of a man and woman, Conn O'Malley, but I suspect that you need some schooling in the refinements. Come and see me when you've gotten what you want from my cousin, the Queen. It would be my pleasure to instruct you thoroughly in *les arts d'amour*."

"M'lady will never have a more willing pupil, I can assure you," Conn proclaimed, and then he let his eyes drop to her bosom. Slowly he feasted himself upon the lush display of ripe flesh, and then taking her hand, he kissed the palm and the pulse.

Lettice shivered with delight. "Devil!" she hissed.

"*Conn!*" Skye pulled her brother away from his amorous dalliance. "The Queen has finished eating, and 'tis time for us to present ourselves."

Elizabeth Tudor had indeed finished her meal, and left the table to sit in a comfortable chair that gave her a full view of the room. In the minstrels' gallery above, the musicians were beginning to tune their instruments, and many of the guests had also left the tables to stroll about the floor greeting each other while the servants cleared the tables and moved them away.

Lord and Lady de Marisco, Conn O'Malley safely in tow, moved across the floor and stood before Elizabeth Tudor, awaiting her acknowledgment. The Queen did not keep them standing long. With a quick word to the courtier to whom she had been speaking, she turned and smiled brilliantly at Skye and Adam. Her sharp gaze flicked to Conn, and obviously liking what she saw, she favored him with a smile also.

"Majesty," Adam said, "may I present to you my wife's brother, Master Conn O'Malley."

Elizabeth nodded to Conn pleasantly. "You are most welcome at our court, Master O'Malley," she said.

Conn's look was one of intense admiration. Kneeling, he caught at the hem of the Queen's skirt and kissed it. "In Ireland," he said in his soft, lilting voice, "they say ye are the Divil's own daughter, madam, but having seen yer Majesty I must disagree. Thou art Gloriana herself, and I worship willingly at yer feet."

Elizabeth's mouth twitched at the corners with suppressed mirth. She was not so foolish as to believe his outrageous compliment was totally sincere and from the heart, but nonetheless she was flattered. "Rise, Conn O'Malley," she said. "I want a better look at you." He rose gracefully, and the Queen assessed him frankly. A very handsome lad, she thought, pleased, and quite eager to be in her good graces. A sharp Irish wit and tongue, she had not a doubt. Ah, how she loved such rogues! "Do you dance, Conn O'Malley?"

"Aye, Gloriana," he answered her boldly.

"Then you'll open the ball with me this night, Conn O'Malley," Elizabeth Tudor said, standing up and taking his quickly offered arm as at once the musicians began to play.

Sir Christopher Hatton looked crestfallen, for he had fully expected to dance the first dance with the Queen. The lad was no clod on his feet either, he observed, although he was not worried about losing his place to this young Irish upstart.

"They come and they go, the dancing masters," murmured a satisfied voice in his ear. "I wonder how long the bog trotter will last."

"It's been a while since she's confined all her attention to you also, Dudley," Sir Christopher returned. "The Queen, being a woman of intellect and refinement, likes choice and variety in those about her. You bored her to death long ago."

"They're worse than jealous women," Adam said low to Skye.

"She plays them off against each other so none will ever gain ascendancy over her," Skye said softly.

"An astute judgment, madam," said William Cecil, who without their knowing it had come up behind them.

"Dammit, m'lord, you walk like a cat!" Skye said irritably.

Lord Burghley gave a dry chuckle. "A talent that has stood me in good stead on many an occasion. You need have no fear, madam, as long as your intentions toward England are honorable." He gently took her arm. "Will you both come with me?" he asked. "I have something to say to you that requires privacy."

They walked with him from the room where the revels were being held, and out into the deserted corridor. "What is it you have to tell us, my lord?" Skye said.

William Cecil stopped, and looking around to ascertain that they would not be overheard, he spoke. "The Queen wishes you to know that should she find your brother worthy of her trust, Lady de Marisco, then the patents that he desires for your family will be forthcoming in a few months. For now, her Majesty wishes Conn O'Malley to remain with the court so she may judge his worth.

After Twelfth Night, however, you and Lord de Marisco are to be excused from court to go to your new home at Queen's Malvern. You are forbidden for the next few months from traveling to France. Is that understood?"

Skye nodded. "May I tell my brother, my lord?"

"No. It is better he not know for now."

Adam agreed. "Aye, my love. If Conn feels his goal is not yet attained he will continue to be on his best behavior. It would not do," he finished with meaning, "for Conn to feel free of all restraints."

"Yes," Lord Burghley replied. "Her Majesty should be most displeased should the young O'Malley divert his attentions from her to say, ah, the Countess of Essex."

"Is there anything you don't see, my lord?" Skye said, amused.

Again the dry chuckle. "Very little, madam, very little indeed." He took her hand and raised it to his lips. "I would be pleased, madam, if when we return to the revels you would honor me with your first dance."

"Honor you, my lord? I think it is you who honor me," Skye said.

Lord Burghley smiled his sour smile. "You O'Malleys have charm, madam. I am frankly relieved to find you safely within the keeping of a loyal Englishman again. We shall have to see what we can do to win over your young brother. I tremble to think of any of you loose upon England again."

"There was a day not long ago, my lord, when you had cause to tremble," Skye rejoined. "I shall keep the peace if England does. The treachery has never been on my part, and well you know it."

"Come, madam," William Cecil said, pretending to ignore her words. "Both the night and I grow older by the minute."

Then the Queen's Secretary of State led Skye back into the paneled chamber where the musicians were playing a sprightly tune. The Queen was still favoring young Conn, and he partnered her with grace and charming devotion; but everyone's attention was diverted from Elizabeth Tudor and her latest swain by the sight of William Cecil dancing gaily with the beautiful Lady de Marisco. It was very rare that the Queen's loyal and dour servant was seen to dance, and no one in the room that night could remember him ever dancing with anyone other than his wife or the Queen.

"I think you have made me the envy of all in the room, my lord Burghley," Skye laughed.

"Nonsense," Cecil chuckled. "It is I who am to be envied, madam."

"You have caused an outrageous amount of gossip by your behavior, my lord," Skye teased him. "They will spend days trying to decide why you have danced with me when everyone knows your habit is not to dance."

"Yes," Lord Burghley murmured, "they will wonder, won't they?"

"Why, you have done it on purpose," Skye said, delighted by his unlikely attitude.

"Yes, madam, I have. It is better that none, even yourself, madam, be too sure of William Cecil."

"You have one constant, my lord, that all may be sure of."

"Indeed, madam, and what is that?" He cocked an eyebrow at her.

"Your loyalty to the Queen, my lord. That will never change."

Cecil nodded. "You are right, Skye O'Malley. My loyalty to Elizabeth Tudor will never change, nor will it cease, and now, madam, I will return you to your devoted lord. I thank you for the dance. It has been a long time since I allowed myself such a frivolity."

With a gallant bow he handed her over to her husband, and Skye watched as he moved off back to the Queen's side. Adam smiled down on her from his great height. "You will be both envied and feared by almost everyone in this room for the rest of your stay at court," he noted.

She smiled back at him. "There are few here I should care to call friends."

"Then I know it will not displease you that we are not to follow the court now that we are back in England."

"No, it does not displease me. I would like at least one of my children to have a secure home with both parents." She sighed. "Home. I wonder what it will be like, Adam. Is the midsection of England beautiful, or is the Queen punishing us?"

"I have only been in the Midlands once, Skye, but it is a fair green land of well-watered valleys and rolling hills. It is, I think, probably the most peaceful place in England. I suspect the Queen has been kind in her way."

Skye remembered his words some three weeks later as they sat astride their horses looking down upon their new home. It was a cold, clear day in the middle of January. The sky was smooth and bright blue, the sun sharp and yellow. The land lay brown and quiet in the sparse and frugal warmth of midday. Above them a small flock of pigeons whirled softly.

Queen's Malvern was set like a small, perfect jewel in a little valley that nestled in the Malvern Hills between the Severn and the Wye rivers. The house, built in the shape of an E, had been constructed a hundred years earlier, during the reign of Edward IV, and his wife, Elizabeth Woodville. It had been Edward's gift to his wife, hence its name, Queen's Malvern. Throughout all its years, it had remained a royal property. Now it belonged temporarily to the de Marisco family, a gift from Elizabeth Tudor.

Built of mellowed pink brick, some of its walls ivy covered, it sat silently awaiting its new owners. As they rode down the hill to the house Skye felt that the building had an almost expectant air about it, and she thought to herself: We are alike this house and I. We both need each other. It suddenly came to her that no family had ever really inhabited the place. It had always been a royal residence, to be visited during a progress if its owners happened to be in the neighborhood. Still, as they approached it she could see with her critical eye that the house appeared to be in good repair. The diamond-paned windows were dirty, but unbroken.

As they reached the main entrance of the building it opened and a small man emerged. "Be ye Lord de Marisco?" he asked politely.

"I am Adam de Marisco," came the reply.

"I'm Peter, the bailiff, m'lord. Welcome to Queen's Malvern. Ye'll find the house in good condition, but there ain't much in the way of furnishings, being the royalty always carried their things with them. There's a good cabinetmaker in the village, should ye need him."

Their horses had come to a halt, and Adam said, "We left our family and things in Worcester while we came on to see the house, Peter. Though we have much, I am sure my wife will make use of the cabinetmaker."

Peter bobbed his head in acknowledgment of Adam's words. "Then I'll be on my way home, m'lord. The wife and I occupy a little house on the edge of the property. If you need anything we'll be there."

"We will need servants," Skye spoke. "Tell the village that anyone wishing to enter service should come tomorrow morning."

"Aye, m'lady! There's many that'll be happy to hear that news." He bobbed his head again, and then shuffled off out of sight around the side of the house.

Adam dismounted his horse and tied it to a nearby bush. He then helped Skye to dismount and secured her mount, too. For several long minutes they stood looking at the house, and about them, each caught up in their private thoughts. As much as he had loved Lundy, Adam had to admit to himself that this beautiful estate was a better and more fitting place for his wife and child. He felt a great contentment as he looked about him.

Skye gazed at the house and thought: This is the first home that belongs to Adam and me. Lundy and Belle Fleur are his, Greenwood mine, Lynmouth Robin's; but this is ours, and I am at last free of all my responsibilities to the O'Malleys. She smiled thinking about how the Queen had made a decision for her that Skye hadn't thought she would be able to make herself. Before they had left London Elizabeth Tudor had suggested to Skye that she appoint her full brother, Michael O'Malley, to the office of the O'Malley, head of the clan.

"But he's a priest," Skye had protested. "I often think that one of the reasons he became a priest was to avoid being the O'Malley."

"That was when he was a boy," the Queen replied. "I understand from the Spanish ambassador that the Pope intends to appoint your brother to the bishopric held by that old reprobate, your late uncle. The Church doesn't appoint men who avoid responsibility to high places, madam. If the Pope thinks highly of your brother you can think no less. None of your other brothers will ever be fit to hold the office, I suspect from what Master Conn has told me. Let the priest run the family, and pass on the office to one of his nephews eventually. He'll not necessarily pick the eldest, and they'll all have to scramble to gain his approval."

"I had thought that perhaps Conn would suit," Skye mused.

"Hah!" The Queen's bright eyes snapped with amusement. "Conn O'Malley is an ambitious man, madam. He seeks to make his fortune here in England. I will shortly appoint him to my Gentlemen Pensioners. There is always room for another handsome young man."

Skye was astounded. "*Conn?*" she gasped. "A member of your personal guard?"

"Aye," Elizabeth replied. "He's a rogue, 'tis true, madam, but he has a good heart, I've found. Be sensible, my dear. Your brother is. What is there for Conn O'Malley in Ireland? Not only is he the youngest son, he is the youngest child of your father. He has neither lands nor wealth to recommend him. He must make his own fortune, and what better place to make it than here in my service?"

She had known that the Queen was right with regard to her brother, and after she had spoken with him Skye decided to do as the Queen suggested and make Michael O'Malley the head of the family. The Queen had made it very clear that she would no longer tolerate Skye in such a position of potential power; power that could be used against her.

"I do not mind your dabbling in trade, madam, but I will not give you shelter and then have you use your O'Malley ships against me."

There was a time when Skye would have rebelled against such an edict, but not now. She was wonderfully content with Adam and all her children, and she wanted peace in her life at last. She wrote to her brothers in Ireland telling them of her decision to appoint Michael the O'Malley. To Michael and to Anne, she wrote the reasons for her decision. To her three younger brothers, she explained her decision simply by saying that they had too much to do rebuilding their wealth to be bothered with the care of their people. With her letters went the Queen's patents for privateering that the O'Malley brothers had desired.

Several days after Twelfth Night Skye and Adam had left London with Deirdre and Velvet to travel to their new home. Bran Kelly intended to sail in convoy with Robbie to the Far East, a voyage that would keep them out of England for two to three years. Daisy, therefore, decided to stay with Skye, and packing up her two sons and her elderly mother-in-law, she came along. Dame Cecily, also getting along in years though she vigorously denied it, was persuaded to close up Wren Court and come to live with the de Mariscos.

029   "Haven't you always been mother to me and grandmother to my

children since I arrived in England?" Skye had demanded. "I would worry myself to death if you stayed alone down in Devon."

"I have stayed alone most of my life, dearest Skye," the old woman protested weakly.

"But I need you, Dame Cecily," Skye replied, and she smiled coaxingly.

"Well, if you are sure you need me . . ."

"Oh, I do!"

"We both do," Adam had said, putting an arm about Dame Cecily.

Skye now smiled to herself as she remembered how the tears had filled Dame Cecily's eyes. They were all so fortunate to have each other! She stood before Queen's Malvern, and she knew with certainty that she had at last come home.

"You're happy," Adam said quietly.

"Yes," she answered, taking his hand. "I'm happy, Adam, my darling. Do you realize that this is our first *real* home? We are home at long, long last, my Adam!"

"Yes," he replied. "*Our home!* Our home for now, and for all the sweet tomorrows!" Adam de Marisco bent and kissed Skye with a deep and passionate kiss. Then sweeping his wife up into his arms, he carried her through the open door of Queen's Malvern and into their home. Their home for now and all the sweet tomorrows.

O wind-drifted Branch, lift your head to the sun,
For the sap of new life in your veins hath begun,
And a little young bud of the tenderest green
Mine eyes through the snow and the sorrow have seen!

O little green bud, break and blow into flower,
Break and blow through the welcome of sunshine and shower;
'Twas a long night and dreary you hid there forlorn,
But now the cold hills wear the radiance of morn!

—Ethna Carbery

ABOUT THE AUTHOR

Bertrice Small is the best-selling author of *The Kadin, Love Wild and Fair, Adora, Skye O'Malley, Unconquered,* and *Beloved.* She lives in the oldest English settlement in the state of New York, a small village on the eastern end of Long Island. She is called "Sunny" by her friends, and "Lust's Leading Lady" by her fans; but her son insists that to him, she's just plain "Mom."

Mrs. Small works at an antique desk in a light-filled pink, green, and white studio overlooking her old-fashioned rose and flower garden. It is furnished in what she describes as a mixture of office modern and Turkish harem. Mrs. Small's only companions as she writes creating her handsome rogues, dashing renegades, and beautiful vixens are her typewriter, Rebecca, and Checquers, a black and white kitten with big pink ears, who has recently joined the family and is trying very hard to fill the large niche left by the departure of Ditto, who died after 15½ happy years. As Ditto so often said:

> *Man can live without pandas, gorillas, or frogs;*
> *He can live without chickens and live without hogs.*
> *He can live without sparrows and live without bats,*
> *But civilized man cannot live without CATS.*
> —*Hiram and Other Cats,* by Lawrence Dwight Smith,
>   Grosset and Dunlap, Inc., New York, 1941

A Note from the Author

When *Skye O'Malley* was published in October of 1980 the overwhelming response to its heroine was nothing short of incredible. No one was more surprised than I was, for although I had created Skye, I had never expected her to assume such larger-than-life proportions. The one question asked of me over and over again was: "Will there be a sequel?" Quite honestly, at the time I did not think so. Four husbands, five living children, and all those passionate adventures seemed quite a feat for a sixteenth-century Irish lady who wasn't even thirty when the novel ended.

What I had not reckoned on was that although I was through with Skye, Skye was most assuredly not through with me! My characters do have a way of taking me over. I hope you have enjoyed this sequel to *Skye O'Malley*, and I am pleased to tell you that a third book in this series, the story of Skye and Adam's beloved daughter, Velvet, will be coming out eventually. Do write to me at P.O. Box 765, Southold, NY 11971, and tell me if you have enjoyed *All the Sweet Tomorrows*. As busy as I am, I always find time to answer my mail. I'll be waiting to hear from you.